P9-DMI-334

PATRIOTS

PATRIOTS

A NOVEL OF SURVIVAL
IN THE COMING COLLAPSE

JAMES WESLEY, RAWLES

Ulysses Press

Copyright © 1990–2009 by James Wesley, Rawles. Fourth Edition (Expanded). All Rights Reserved. Any unauthorized duplication in whole or in part or dissemination of this edition by any means (including but not limited to photocopying, electronic bulletin boards, and the Internet) will be prosecuted to the fullest extent of the law.

Published by ULYSSES PRESS
        P.O. Box 3440
        Berkeley, CA 94703
        www.ulyssespress.com

An earlier version of this book, entitled *Patriots: Surviving the Coming Collapse*, was published by The Clearwater Press

ISBN: 978-1-56975-599-0
Library of Congress Catalog Number 2008911760

Printed in the United States by Bang Printing

10 9 8 7

Acquisitions Editor: Nick Denton-Brown
Managing Editor: Claire Chun
Cover design: what!design @ whatweb.com
Cover photos: istockphoto.com
Editor: Jennifer Privateer
Indexer: Sayre Van Young
Production: Judith Metzener

Distributed by Publishers Group West

IMPORTANT NOTE TO THE READER

This is a work of fiction. All of the characters (other than public figures), events and settings described in this novel are imaginary, and all character names and descriptions are fictional. In all cases, any resemblance between the characters in this novel and real people is purely coincidental.

Real public figures, products, places, businesses, government agencies or other entities are depicted fictitiously in this novel for purposes of entertainment and comment only. No affiliation, sponsorship or endorsement is claimed or suggested.

This novel is only for the entertainment of the reader and is not intended to be used as a source of information or instruction. All activities of the fictional characters in the novel are depicted for storytelling purposes only. The author and the publisher do not intend the reader to make any use of the contents of this novel and strongly caution the reader against doing so.

For purposes of a realistic narrative, the author has described various survival techniques and the fabrication of various devices in detail. However, this book is not meant to take the place of a survival manual and is not meant to instruct the reader on the fabrication of devices that may be dangerous, illegal or both.

For example, the making and/or possession of the some of the devices and ingredients depicted in this novel may be illegal in some jurisdictions. Mere possession of the uncombined components and/or ingredients might be construed as a violation of criminal law. Consult your state and local laws!

The case citations contained within this novel do not constitute legal advice. Consult a lawyer if you have legal questions or need legal advice.

The medical details contained within this novel do not constitute medical advice. Consult a doctor or other appropriate health professional if you have medical questions or if you need medical or nutritional advice.

The author and publisher shall have neither liability nor responsibility to any person or entity with respect to any injury, loss or damage caused, or alleged to be caused, directly or indirectly, by the contents of this novel and/or the use of the contents by any person.

to my excellent wife,
"The Memsahib"

Acknowledgments

Above all else, it takes faith and friends to survive. I've been blessed with a lot of friends, and they have helped to strengthen my faith in Almighty God.

This novel is dedicated to the not-so-fictional Group: Conor, Dave, Hugh, Jeff, Ken, Linda, Mary, Meg, P.K., Roland, and Scott. *Keep your powder dry!*

My thanks to the readers of SurvivalBlog.com and the many other folks who encouraged me, who contributed technical details, who were used for character sketches, and who helped in the editing process: Arne, Barbara, the Bee Man, Bill L. (with the French Resistance, 1943–1944), Bob "The Soap Maker," sharp-eyed Dr. Boris K., "R.F. Burns," the HAM wizard, Carolyn, The Chartist Gnome, Cheryl the Economatrix, Chris the Rocky Mountain Diver, Commander Zero and his new bride, Dr. Craig in New Zealand, Col. "CRM Discriminator," David in Israel, the late Jonathan Davis, Debbie, Pastor Dennis, 1/2 M.O.A. Dick in Orofino, Quiet Donny, Dr. Eric, Fred the Valmet-Meister, Frank in "Nah-lens," Gayle, "The Glock pro" in Connecticut, Pastor Hale, the anachronistic H-man, Huff the dynamite shooter, "Joe Clutch," "John Jones" in the desert, Kirk and Karen in Montana, "All-Grace-No-Slack-Really-Reformed" Kris in Oregon, Lance in Moscow, "LVZ" in Ohio, "Froggy" Mark, Marshall the Cyberpunk, Marvin "The Wordmonger," "The Millwright," Nadir, Nick in Australia, Patton, Peter in Switzerland, PPPP- the Pioche Professional Polymer Pistolero, Preston, Ranier, Roland in Germany, Rolf and Sandy (both in Washington), Sara the Reenactor, Sherron, Stefan in Sweden, Tina "The S.C. Clone" in Kooskia, Wes in Boise, and MRE Woody.

Thanks also to those who have provided web space, outlets, publicity, motivation, and/or prominent links for my novel: Howard Albertson, Patrick Alessandra, Joseph Ames Jr., Jeff Baker, Billy Beck, Ed Bertsch, BOHICA Concepts, Bill Brumbaugh, John Bryant, Ammon Campbell, The Christian Survival Intelligence Network, the late Jeff Cooper, Jim Crews, Captain Dave's Survival Page, Richard DeCastro, the late Carla Emery, First Virtual Bank, Detra Fitch, "The Frugal Squirrel," The Fraud Information Center, The Gospel Plow, Bob Grenert and the Sacred Covenant Resource Center, Bob Griswold and the staff of Ready Made Resources, Mikael Häggström, Ken Hamblin, Michael Heinze, Fred Heiser, Richard Horton, Peter Huss, The Staff of the *Idaho Observer*, Dean Ing, Devvy Kidd, Mark Koernke, John Leveron,

Live Oak Farms, Dr. Lawrence Martin and Lakeside Press, Henry McDaniel, Mike McNulty, Mike Medintz, The Mental Militia Forums, Patty Neill, Dr. Gary North, Nick Norwood, Mark Nowell, Michael Panzner, Dr. Ignatius Piazza, Maj. John Plaster, Jerry Pournelle, Larry Pratt, Project Epsilon, Steve Quayle, Dr. Norm Resnick, John Ross, "Rourke," Kurt Saxon, John Stadt-miller, David Stott, Gabe Suarez, Kurt and Angie Wilson of Survival Enter-prises, Nancy Tappan, Truth Radio in Delano, Two Toes Consulting and Design, Ed Wolfe, Weapons Safety, Inc., Tom Woolman, and Aaron Zelman of Jews for the Preservation of Firearms Ownership.

Thanks to Paul B. and Randy K. for their sharp eyes in editing the previous edition.

Most importantly, this novel is dedicated to my excellent wife ("The Memsahib"). She has patiently put up with the heaps of supplies in the barn and garage for twenty-plus years. She suffered through nine months of voluntary separation while I moved to Idaho alone to pound nails and write the first draft of the novel. She cheerfully joined me for the following eighteen months with no running water, living amidst Sheetrock dust in a half-finished house. She helped fill the chest freezer with her livestock, garden produce, and wild game. She "wrote the book" (or at least the chapter) on home birth. Most of all, I praise her for displaying the patience to live in loving Christian submission with a husband who spends far too much time clicking away at a keyboard. I am truly blessed!

James Wesley, Rawles
The Rawles Ranch
March 2009

CHAPTER 1

The Crunch

"... nuclear warfare is not necessary to cause a breakdown of our society.
You take a large city like Los Angeles, New York, Chicago—their water supply
comes from hundreds of miles away and any interruption of that, or food, or power
for any period of time you're going to have riots in the streets. Our society is so fragile,
so dependent on the interworking of things to provide us with goods and services,
that you don't need nuclear warfare to fragment us anymore than the Romans
needed it to cause their eventual downfall."

—*Gene Roddenberry*

When the landing gear came down, Todd Gray gave an audible sigh of relief. He was almost home. The seventy-seat Horizon Airlines Bombardier CRJ-700 commuter jet started its downwind leg, with its engines throttled back to low thrust. Todd looked out his window at the familiar rolling Palouse Hills, a neat patchwork of wheat fields. This time of year they were shorn to a short golden stubble. By early October even the straw had been hauled out. Just after the plane touched down, the air brakes flipped up, and the engines reversed with a roar. The plane wheeled to a stop at the tiny Pullman-Moscow air terminal, just west of the state line dividing Washington and Idaho. When the plane switched to external power, Todd unbuckled his seat belt, but didn't get up. He hated standing in the aisle, waiting for everyone to pull out their carry-on bags, and waiting for what always seemed like an eternity for the cabin door to open and for the passengers to shuffle out. So he sat and waited for the aisle to clear. He closed his eyes, said a prayer, and considered what had gone on in the last seventy-two hours.

• • •

The meeting had been called on short notice, and attendance was mandatory. Everyone from mid-level account executives on up were there—even the field office managers from as far away as Baltimore. Todd Gray and the firm's two other telecommuters were also corralled into the meeting by the management. It was *important*, they said. So Todd dutifully packed his best suit. He drove from Bovill to the Pullman-Moscow airport, took a commuter flight to Seattle, and then a United flight to O'Hare. He rented a car and checked into the Marriott, where he usually stayed on his quarterly trips to Chicago. That blew the entire first day. With the two-hour time difference from Idaho, it was 7 p.m. by the time he got to the Marriott and clicked on Fox News. There was lots of bad news on the television. He watched the news for a half hour and then started making phone calls and sending e-mails to his friends in Chicago. He spoke in urgent terms. After a fitful night's sleep, he sat through a full day of meetings that started with a 7:30 a.m. working breakfast. This early start time for a major meeting was unprecedented at Bolton, Meyer, and Sloan.

The firm had brought in two consultants for the daylong meeting, a Russian from Florida, and an Argentinean from New York City. Both were considered subject matter experts on high inflation. Both were well-seasoned accountants, and both had lived through it in their home countries. *Triple-digit* inflation. Todd heard from one of the mid-level managers that the consultants were each paid twenty thousand dollars for the day.

He also mentioned that a third expert, from Zimbabwe, could not attend due to a foul-up with his visa application. Todd regretted this, knowing that with the recent 15,000 percent annual inflation rate and where ten zeroes were knocked off the currency, the Zimbabwean would have had the most recent subject matter expertise.

The Argentinean was on loan from Peat Marwick. His name was Phillipe y Bordero, and he was far more informative than the Russian. He talked about his experience in Argentina in the 1980s, when inflation ran as high as 100 percent *per month* as well as the economic crisis of 2002. He went on to describe how president Raoul Alfonsin had instituted a thousand-for-one currency exchange. He mentioned that his firm had to run daily calculations to compensate for the inflation. Sometimes twice a day for the bigger accounts. He went on at great length about how the firm would park money in "day accounts" and shuttle money quickly into dollars to protect the money from *"El Inferno"*—the inflation that was burning up the Argentine peso.

The Russian arrived an hour late, with loud apologies, claiming that his flight had been delayed. Todd mumbled to himself, "Great. He could have flown in last night, all expenses paid. We pay this guy twenty grand, and he doesn't even get here on time."

The account executive sitting next to Todd snickered in agreement.

The Argentinean was cool and deliberate. In contrast, the Russian was a manic speaker. He chattered about what things had been like for Russian accountants in the 1990s. His discussion soon degenerated into a rambling discourse on bribes: bribing the Moscow police, bribing the tax officials, bribing the *Federalnaya Sluzhba Bezopasnosti* (FSB)—the main successor of the KGB, bribing the Russian mob.

On some topics, the Russian was succinct. He said forthrightly, "You've got to figure out which is the most stable currency, and exchange into that currency as quickly as possible, before your local currency melts away. At one point in time in Russia we had 1,800 percent inflation. It was madness to leave it in rubles for more than a few days. For us then—at the time—the safe haven was greenback dollars. For us now, I dunno. Euros maybe. Swiss Francs maybe, but it's got to be something more stable than these cruddy dollars. Latest figure is 115 percent and *climbing*. To be fair to your clients, and to be fair to your firm, you've got to get all incoming receivables out of dollars very, very quickly."

Todd never caught the Russian's name. It was something multisyllabic and unpronounceable, ending in "ski." One thing that the Russian asked soon after he arrived made Todd sit up and take notice: "Where are the security men? No guards in the lobby? You've got to increase security! You handle just account ledgers and thumb drives and data disks now, but pretty soon you are gonna be carrying around a lot of cash. So you need a couple of big guys with guns. Get the biggest, meanest looking guys you can find. And mean looking guns. One guard for the parking garage, and one or two for the lobby. Trust me. You *won't* regret it."

After the catered lunch, there was a convoluted question from the far end of the long conference table. It was about how they should go about calculating daily depreciation of a currency and precisely how aggregates should be derived. Phillipe y Bordero was about to answer, but the Russian spoke first. He said something that astounded Todd and everyone else in the room. He said, "Just make something up that sounds reasonable. You're talking about a fast-moving target. Who gives a sheet? Make something up."

At that point old man Meyer cleared his throat. He was obviously perturbed. He retorted, "We aren't going to 'make up' anything. We are going to develop a set of accounting practices that will compensate for the inflation. We will use elaborate computer modeling and projections if need be." The Russian was nearly silent for the rest of the day. It was clear that Mr. Meyer did not get his twenty thousand dollars' worth from the Russian. The day ended with nearly as many unanswered questions as it had started.

Todd took a 5:30 a.m. flight back to Seattle the next morning.

• • •

Todd was shaken from his reverie by the stewardess, who was walking up the aisle, making sure that none of the passengers had left anything behind. Todd stood up and carefully extracted his one and only bag from the overhead bin.

He never checked luggage on his trips to Chicago. Todd was the last passenger off the plane.

Since he didn't have any checked baggage, Todd was in his Dodge pickup within five minutes after getting off the plane. Parking was right out in front of the little Pullman–Moscow air terminal. It was quite convenient, compared to O'Hare with its lineal miles of glittering concourses, dozens of baggage carousels, and several square miles of parking lots that charged twenty dollars a day. Fifty minutes later, Todd pulled in the gate of his property. Shona ran alongside the pickup, yipping and wagging her tail. It felt very good to be safe at home.

Mary ran out the front door and gave him a long hug. They talked while he unpacked.

• • •

When the Crunch came, it did not arrive without warning. By the turn of the century, Federal spending was out of control, and the debt and deficit problems were insurmountable. By 2008, with the global credit market in freefall, bank runs and huge Federal bailouts were becoming more frequent. Collectively, the bailouts were a massive, unstoppable hemorrhage of red ink. The debt and deficit numbers compounded at frightening rates. But it was too agonizing to confront them, so they were ignored. A report by the Congressional Budget Office was alarming. It said that just to pay the *interest* on the national debt for the year, it would take 100 percent of the year's individual income tax revenue, 100 percent of corporate and excise taxes, and 41 percent of Social Security payroll taxes. Just before the Crunch, *interest* on the national debt was consuming 96 percent of government revenue.

The debt piled up at the rate of nine billion a day, or fifteen thousand a second. The official national debt was over six trillion dollars. The unofficial debt, which included "out year" unfunded obligations such as entitlements, long-term bonds, and military pensions, topped fifty-three trillion dollars. Even the official national debt had ballooned to 120 percent of the gross domestic product and was compounding at the rate of 18 percent per year. The Federal government was borrowing 193 percent of revenue for the year. The president was nearing the end of his term in office. The stagnant economy, rising interest rates, and creeping inflation troubled the president. Publicly, he beamed about having "beat the deficit." Privately, he admitted that the low deficit figures came from moving increasingly large portions of Federal funding "off budget." Behind the accounting smoke and mirrors game, the real deficit was growing. Government spending at all levels equated to 45 percent of the Gross Domestic Product. In July, the recently appointed chairman of the Federal Reserve Board had a private meeting with the president. The chairman pointed out the fact that even if Congress could balance the budget, the national debt would still grow inexorably, due to compounding interest.

The president didn't let trifles like ledger sheets and statistics get in his way. The economy was on a roll. The stock market was at an all-time high. It was business as usual for his administration. Instead of reducing the growth in government spending, he launched an immoderate bank lending stimulus package, corporate bailouts, mortgage-backed securities bailouts, and another extravagant round of his pet "infrastructure building" programs in inner city areas as well as in Iraq and Afghanistan.

In Europe, international bankers began to vocally express their doubts that the U.S. government could continue to make its interest payments on the burgeoning debt. In mid-August, the chairman of the Deutsche Bundesbank made some "off the record" comments to a reporter from *The Economist* magazine. Within hours, his words flashed around the world via the Internet: "A full-scale default on U.S. Treasuries appears imminent." He had spoken the dreaded "D" word. His choice of the word *imminent* in conjunction with the word *default* caused the value of the dollar to plummet on the international currency exchanges the next day. T-bill sales crashed simultaneously. Starting with the Japanese, foreign central banks and international monetary authorities began to dump their trillions of dollars in U.S. Treasuries. None of them wanted the now risky T-Bills or U.S. bonds. Within days, long-term U.S. Treasury paper was selling at twenty cents on the dollar.

In short order, foreign investors at all levels began liquidating their U.S. paper assets—stocks, bonds, T-bills—virtually anything denominated in U.S. dollars. After some halfhearted attempts at propping up the dollar, most of the European Union nations and Japan announced that they would no longer employ the U.S. dollar as a reserve currency.

To help finance the ever-growing debt, the Federal Reserve decided to make a tactical move. It began monetizing larger and larger portions of the debt. The Fed already owned $682 billion in Treasury debt, which was considered an "asset" for the purposes of expanding the money supply. In just a few days, Federal Reserve holdings in Treasury debt more than doubled. The printing presses were running around the clock printing currency. The official domestic inflation rate jumped to 16 percent in the third week of August. To the dismay of the Fed, the economy refused to bounce back. The balance of trade figures grew steadily worse. Leading economic indicators declined to a standstill.

In reaction to the crisis, the lawmakers in Washington, D.C. belatedly wanted to slash Federal spending, but were frustrated that they couldn't touch most of it. The majority of the budget consisted of interest payments and various entitlement programs. Previous legislation had locked in these payments. Many of these spending programs even had automatic inflation escalators. So the Federal budget continued to expand, primarily because of the interest burden on the Federal debt. The interest payments grew tremendously as interest rates started to soar. It took 85 percent interest rates to lure investors to six-month T-bills. The Treasury Department stopped auctioning longer-term paper entirely in late August. With inflation roaring, nobody wanted to lend Uncle Sam money for the long term. Jittery American investors increasingly distrusted the government, the stock market, and even the dollar itself. In September, new factory orders and new housing starts dropped off to levels that could not be properly measured. Corporations, large and small, started massive layoffs. The unemployment rate jumped from 12 percent to 20 percent in less than a month.

The catalyst for the real panic, however, was the stock market crash that started in early October. The bull stock market had gone on years longer than expected, defying the traditional business cycle. Nearly everyone thought that they were riding an unstoppable bull. From fifteen to twenty billion in new mutual fund money had been pouring into the stock market every month. The mutuals had become so popular that there were more mutual funds listed than individual stocks. By 2009, there were 240,000 stockbrokers in the country. It was the 1920s, in *déjà vu*. Just before the Crunch, the Dow Jones Industrial Average was selling at a phenomenal sixty-five times dividends—right back where it had been just before the 2000 dot-com bubble explosion. The market climbed to unrealistic heights, driven by unmitigated greed.

Soon after the dollar's collapse, however, the stock market was driven by fear. Unlike the previous crashes, this time the U.S. markets slumped gradually. This was due to circuit breaker regulations on program trading, implemented after the 1987 Wall Street slump. Instead of dropping precipitously in the course of one day as it had in '87, this time it took nineteen days to drop 7,550 points. This made the dot-com "bubble burst" in 2000 look insignificant. Nobody could believe it. None of the "market experts" thought that the market could go down that far, but it did. Only a few contrarian analysts predicted it. Finally, the government suspended all trading, since there was almost no one buying any of the issues that came up for sale.

Because all of the world's equities markets were tied inextricably together, they crashed simultaneously. The London and Tokyo markets were hit worse than the U.S. stock exchanges. The London market closed five days after the slump started. The Tokyo market, which was even more volatile, closed after only three days of record declines. Late in the second week of the stock market collapse, the domestic runs on U.S. banks began. The quiet international run on U.S. banks and the dollar had begun a month earlier. It took the GDP—the "generally dumb public"—in America that long to realize that the party was over.

The only investors that made profits in the Crunch were those that had invested in precious metals. Gold soared to $5,100 an ounce, with the other precious metals rising correspondingly. Even for these investors, their gains were only illusory paper profits. Anyone who was foolish enough to cash out of gold and into dollars after the run up in prices would have soon lost everything. This was because the domestic value of the dollar collapsed completely just a few weeks later.

The dollar collapsed because of the long-standing promises of the FDIC. "All deposits insured to $200,000," they had promised. When the domestic bank runs began, the government had to make good on the promises. The only way that they could do this was to print money—lots and lots of it. Many Americans were already leery of Federal Reserve Notes due to successive waves of changes in the large portrait currency that began in 1996.

Strange new money tints caused a subtle change in the American psyche. The paper money didn't *look right*. It looked phony. And, in essence, it was. Since 1964, the currency had no backing with precious metals. All that was backing it was empty promises. Rumors suggested, and then news stories confirmed, that the government mints were converting some of their intaglio printing presses. Presses originally designed to print one-dollar bills were converted to print fifty and one-hundred dollar bills. This made the public even more suspicious.

With the printing presses running day and night turning out fiat currency, hyperinflation was inevitable. Inflation jumped from 16 percent to 35 percent in three days. From there on, it climbed in spurts during the next few days: 62 percent, 110 percent, 315 percent, and then to an incredible 2,100 percent. The currency collapse was reminiscent of Zimbabwe, just a few years earlier. Thereafter, the value of the dollar was pegged hourly. It was the main topic of conversation. As the dollar withered in the blistering heat of hyperinflation, people rushed out to put their money into cars, furniture, appliances, tools, rare coins—anything tangible. This superheated the economy, creating a situation not unlike that in Germany's Weimar Republic in the 1920s. More and more paper was chasing less and less product.

With a superheated economy, there was no way for the government to check the soaring inflation, aside from stopping the presses. This they could not do, however, because depositors were still flocking to the banks to withdraw all of their savings. One radio talk show host described this situation as "watching a snake eat its own tail." All that the bureaucrats in Washington, D.C. could do was watch it happen. They had sown the seeds decades before when they started deficit spending. Now they were reaping the whirlwind. The workers who still had jobs quickly caught on to the full implications of the mass inflation. They insisted on daily inflation indexing of their salaries, and in some cases even insisted on being paid daily.

Citizens on fixed incomes were wiped out financially by the hyperinflation within two weeks. These included pensioners, those on unemployment insurance, and welfare recipients. Few could afford to buy a can of beans when it cost $150 dollars. The riots started soon after inflation bolted past the 1,000 percent mark. Detroit, New York, and Los Angeles were the first cities to see full-scale rioting and looting. Soon, the riots engulfed most other large cities.

• • •

When the Dow Jones average had slumped its first 1,900 points, Todd Gray made his "mobilization" calls to the six members of his retreat group still living in the Chicago area. He followed up with a multiple-addressee e-mail message. There was no need to call Kevin Lendel. He had been coming over for dinner and extended conversations for the past three evenings. Most of the group members agreed to attempt to make their way to the Grays' home in Idaho as soon as possible.

The only voices of doubt came from the Laytons and Dan Fong. When Todd first called Dan—before his trip back for the accounting firm meeting— Dan listened to his full spiel, and then remarked, "Yeah, Todd, remember what you did right after the 9/11 terrorist attacks? You went positively ape. You were Chicken Little, and the sky didn't fall, now did it? I remember the 'emergency meeting' that we had at T.K.'s. You were really panicky. You even had Mary loading magazines from stripper clips during the meeting, as I recall. Now how do you know this isn't just *another* false alarm?"

Dan's doubts disappeared a few days later when he was on his way to work. He slowed down when he saw a queue of people stretching a full block. It ended at the doors of the First Chicago Bank on Columbus Avenue. "Oh maaaan," he commented aloud to himself, "It's six o'clock in the morning, and they're already lined up. This looks way serious." He remembered that bank lines were one of Todd's touted "warning signs."

Turning the corner, Dan had to stop and gawk, along with several other drivers. A man was smashing an ATM machine with a tire iron. The machine was obviously either out of cash or had been shut down by the bank. The man was still in the process of venting his rage with the tire iron when Dan drove away. The food rush started that same day. Supermarket shelves were completely emptied in a coast-to-coast three-day panic.

• • •

On the last day of October, the Grays found that their phone was still working, but only for local calls. When they tried making long-distance calls, they got an "All circuits are busy now" recording, at all hours of the day or night. The next day, there was message advising, "All circuits will be restored shortly." Two days later, there was no dial tone.

By early November, there was almost continuous rioting and looting in every major city in the U.S. Due to the financial panic and rioting, the November election was "postponed" to January, but it never took place. Rioting grew so commonplace that riot locations were read off in a list—much like traffic reports—by news broadcasters. The police could not even begin to handle the situation. The National Guard was called out in most states, but less than half of the Guardsmen reported for duty. With law and order breaking down, most of them were too busy protecting their own families to respond to the call-up. An emergency call-up of the Army Reserve three days later had an even smaller response. All over America, entire inner-city areas burned to the ground, block after block. No one and nothing could stop it. On the few occasions that the National Guard was able to respond to the riots, there were some massacres that made Kent State seem insignificant.

Many factories in proximity to the riots closed "temporarily" in concern for the safety of their workers, but never reopened. Most others carried on with their normal operation for several more days, only to be idled due to lack of transport. Shipping goods in the United States of the early twenty-first century in most cases meant one thing: eighteen-wheel diesel trucks traveling on the interstate highway system. The trucks stopped rolling for several reasons. First was a fuel shortage. Then came the flood of refugees from the cities that jammed the highways. Then cars that ran out of gas disrupted traffic.

As cars ran out of gas, they blocked many critical junctions, bridges, and overpasses. Some highway corridors in urban areas turned into gridlocked parking lots. Traffic came to a stop, motionless cars began to run out of gas, and the forward movement of traffic was never resumed. In some places, cars were able to back up and turn around. In most others, people were not so lucky. There, the traffic was so densely packed that drivers were forced to just get out of their cars and walk away.

Every major city in the United States was soon gripped in a continual orgy of robbery, murder, looting, rape, and arson. Older inner-city areas were among the hardest hit. Unfortunately, the design of the interstate freeway system put most freeways in close proximity to inner-city areas. The men who had planned the interstate highway system in the 1940s and 1950s could not be blamed. At that time, downtown areas were still flourishing. They were the heart of industry, population, commerce, and wealth. Thus, it was only logical that the highways should be routed as close to them as possible, and preferably through them. These planners could not then have predicted that in fifty years the term "inner city" would become synonymous with poverty, squalor, welfare, drugs, disease, and rampant crime.

America's once proud and efficient railroad system, long the victim of government ineptitude, was unable to make any appreciable difference in the transportation crisis. Most of the factories that had been built in the past thirty years had been positioned near highways, not railroad tracks. Also, like the highways, most rail lines passed through urbanized areas, placing trains at the same risk as trucks. Gangs of looters found that it did not take large obstructions to cause train derailments. Within a few hours of each derailment they stripped the trains of anything of value.

A few factories managed to stay in operation until early November. Most had already closed, however, due to failing markets, failing transportation, failing communications, or the failing dollar. In some instances, workers were paid through barter, rather than cash. They were paid with the company's product. Chevron Oil paid its workers in gasoline. Winchester-Olin paid its workers in ammunition.

The last straw was the power grid. When the current stopped flowing, the few factories and businesses still in operation closed their doors. Virtually every industry in America was dependent on electric power. The power outages forced even the oil refineries to shut down. Up until then, the refineries had been operating around the clock trying to meet the increased demand for liquid fuels. Ironically, even though refineries processed fuel containing billions of BTUs of energy, most of them did not have the ability to produce enough electric power to supply all of their needs. Like so many other industries, oil refiners had made the mistaken assumption that they could always depend on the grid. They needed a stable supply of electricity from the power grid for their computers and to operate the solenoids for their valves.

The power outages caused a few dramatic effects. At a Kaiser aluminum plant near Spokane, Washington, the power went out during the middle of a production shift. With the plant's electric heating elements inactive, the molten aluminum running through the hot process end of the plant began to cool. Workers scrambled to clear as much of the system as possible, but the metal hardened in many places, effectively ruining the factory. If the plant were ever to be reopened, the hardened aluminum would have to be removed with cutting torches or jackhammers.

Electricity also proved to be the undoing of prisons all over America. For a while, officials maintained order in the prisons. Then the fuel for the backup generators ran out. Prison officials had never anticipated a power outage that would last more than two weeks. Without power, security cameras did not function, lights did not operate, and electrically operated doors jammed. As the power went out, prison riots soon followed.

Prison officials hastened to secure their institutions. Under "lock down" conditions, most inmates were confined to their cells, with only a few let out to cook and deliver meals in the cell blocks. At many prisons the guard forces could not gain control of the prison population, and there were mass escapes. At several others, guards realized that the overall situation was not going to improve, and they took the initiative to do something about it. They walked from cell to cell, shooting convicts. Scores of other prisoners died at the hands of fellow convicts. Many more died in their cells due to other causes; mainly dehydration, starvation, and smoke inhalation.

Despite the best efforts of prison officials, 80 percent of the country's more than one-and-a-half-million state and federal prisoners escaped. A small fraction of the escaped prisoners were shot on sight by civilians. Those that survived quickly shed their prison garb and found their way into the vicious wolf packs that soon roamed the countryside.

The economic depression and resultant chaos that gripped America also occurred around the world. Each evening, Todd and Mary Gray turned on the Drake R8-A shortwave receiver that Mary had mail-ordered from Ham Radio Outlet the previous year. They listened to the civilized world disintegrate. It was a sort of macabre form of entertainment. In many cases, radio stations went off the air altogether. The first to go was Radio South Africa, followed by the BBC, Radio Netherlands, and Radio Deutsche Welle.

On one notable evening of listening, Todd and Mary were listening to HCJB in Ecuador, and were surprised to hear gunfire in the background as the news announcer spoke. Then, even more incredibly, the radio station was taken over by revolutionaries while they listened. The Grays turned off their receiver after the microphone was taken over by a "Commandante Cruz" who was shouting in rapid-fire Spanish.

With the same radio, Todd and Mary were also able to monitor amateur radio broadcasters throughout the western United States. For a brief time after most other U.S. stations had vanished, WWCR in Nashville, Tennessee, remained on the air at 3.215, 5.070, 5.935, 9.985, 12.160, and 15.825 megahertz. Todd had the most success with the amateur band centered on 7.2 megahertz. The news that they heard from these ham operators was almost universally bad. They reported civil unrest in nearly every city with a population over forty thousand. Most of the hams were operating on standby power, as there were only a few isolated areas that still had regular utility grid power.

In Bovill, Idaho, the town nearest the Grays' farm, there were not many noticeable effects of the Crunch during its early stages. The sawmill in nearby Troy, which had cut back to one shift per day two months earlier, shut down completely. The nearby Shell gas station sold out of gas in a two-day period. Most Americans had a hard time dealing with the galloping inflation. This phenomenon had an only limited effect in Bovill. The local grocery store was sold completely out of stock by the time inflation reached triple-digit figures. When there was little or nothing available to buy, the value of the dollar was inconsequential.

As in other small towns across America, most people around Bovill just stayed at home, glued to their radios and televisions. In rural Idaho, the riots that were breaking out in the major cities seemed a million miles away. The catchphrase of the day was, "Isn't it terrible what's happening in New York?" To Todd, the phrase had a tone that he had heard before. It was the same tone used when people talked about famines and floods overseas. It seemed that the local residents were trying to deny that what was going on had any impact on them. The Grays' neighbors expressed concern for their personal safety only when there were disturbances reported in Seattle. That was six and a half hours away by car. Things were getting steadily worse all over the country, but in remote regions like the Palouse Hills, there was a time delay.

During this pause, Todd started making some final preparations. First, he closed and latched all of the steel shutters over the windows of their house. Mary commented that it made the house seem dark and gloomy. Todd just shrugged his shoulders and said, "Well, I guess we'll just have to get used to it." Next, Todd mandated that they lock—and keep locked—both the gate at the county road and the gate on the chain-link fence around the house, and the doors to the house. Mary suggested that they also keep their Power Wagon pickup and her Volkswagen Beetle locked up in the garage with their distributor rotors removed.

Mary also suggested that she and Todd have a meeting with the Latah County civil defense coordinator in Moscow. By this time, however, the phone line—and with it their Internet connection—was dead. They finally decided that the benefits of such a meeting were outweighed by the expenditure of now precious gasoline that they would have to use. It was a sixty-five-mile round trip to Moscow. Further, Todd did not rule out the risk of social unrest in Moscow—even if the city did have only thirty thousand residents.

The Grays also started using up the contents of their electric refrigerator and chest freezer. With extended power failures expected, they did not want food to spoil unnecessarily. Todd methodically sliced, marinated, and jerked nearly all of the elk, venison, and salmon in the chest freezer. The exhausting process took five days. With the same thought in mind, Mary took the initiative of recharging all of the nickel metal hydride batteries for their flashlights and various electronic gear. As they only had two small chargers, this took nearly as long as the jerky making.

They didn't know how rough things might get, or whether or not any of the other group members would show up to help secure the retreat. So Todd completely refilled the firewood storage area in the basement. He told Mary, "It would be ironic to make all these preparations and then get blown away doing something so mundane as walking back and forth to the woodshed."

As further insurance, Todd and Mary also began carrying their Colt .45 automatics at all times. They also loaded half of the magazines for each of their guns. Todd's plan was to alternately unload these magazines and load the other half of their magazines twice a year. This would prevent the magazine springs from "taking a set." On the few trips that he took into town or down the road to Kevin Lendel's house, Todd carried both his .45 and his short-barreled Remington 870 shotgun. There was no worry of being arrested, as there was no prohibition on carrying a loaded gun in public. In fact, Idaho was one of the few states where citizens could carry a loaded gun in a car. The only prohibition was on carrying a concealed weapon without a state permit. In Idaho, concealed carry permits were easy to obtain.

Surprisingly, the U.S. Postal Service still made regular deliveries until early November. Local mail got through promptly, but longer distance deliveries were sporadic at best. The Grays took advantage of this in several ways. First, they sent letters to their family members, letting them know that they were safe and well. Next they wrote all of the group members still in the Chicago area, once again urging them to "Get out of Dodge." They hoped that if and when their letters arrived, that the group members would have already departed.

After a long talk, Todd and Mary decided to make an $800 prepayment on their electric power bill. They also sent a check covering the next three years' property taxes on their farm. Although it appeared that the local government would likely evaporate in the next few weeks, they felt more secure knowing that they wouldn't lose their farm to taxes as some of their relatives had in the depression of the 1930s. The check to the tax assessor office was relatively small, as their annual tax assessment was only $780 for their house and forty acres.

Writing these two checks brought the balance of their checking account down to $220. Their savings account had long since been cleaned out when they bought the house and upgraded it. One of the reasons they wrote these checks was that the dollars that they represented were rapidly becoming worthless. They agreed that it was better to spend their money on something useful than to see it lost to hyperinflation.

Todd and Mary walked down the hill to their mailbox in silence. Todd had his Remington riot shotgun tucked under his arm. As they got to the box, Todd blurted out, "This seems so absurd. Here we are, mailing checks drawn on a bank that has closed its doors—probably forever, denominated in a currency that is basically worthless, to a couple of organizations that will probably be nonexistent soon after the checks arrive!" He had meant the comment to be funny, but Mary didn't laugh. She tossed the envelopes in the box, closed the lid, flipped up the flag, and turned back toward their house. There were tears welling up in her eyes.

Four days after the riots started, Paul and Paula Andersen, the Grays' neighbors to the south, dropped by the house to explain that they were going to go "double up" at their son's place. He had a large cattle ranch near Kendrick, about twenty-five miles south of Bovill. The Andersens offered the Grays the use of their house, barn, water supply, firewood, stored hay, and pasture in their absence. Todd told Paul, "Thanks for the offer, but I probably won't need to take you up on it. I'll be happy to keep an eye on your place while you're gone, though."

Paul Andersen thanked Todd and handed him a slip of paper, saying, "Here's my son's address and phone number in Kendrick. When the phones are working again, give us a call." They never saw the Andersens again.

The other two neighbors with property contiguous to the Grays' parcel left under similar circumstances. Most of these neighbors didn't bother to stop by and make their goodbyes. By the haste of their activity when packing up, Todd presumed that they were in too much of a hurry for formal goodbyes. The neighbors across the county road, the Crabbes, waved to Mary as they pulled their heavily laden flatbed Ford pickup and trailer out their front gate with their last load. Mary later mentioned to Todd that it seemed like a scene out of *The Grapes of Wrath*. They never saw the Crabbes again, either.

Todd and Mary began hearing the term "doubling up" with great regularity as they tuned from channel to channel on Mary's CB radio. It was the local parlance that developed for two or more families relocating and setting up mini-strongholds. The residents of Latah County were plain country folks, but they weren't stupid. When times got tough, most realized that a single family on a remote farm would be no match for a band of looters. It was a natural and logical reaction to cluster into small defensive groups.

Both Todd and Mary had trouble sleeping during the interval between the onset of the riots and when the other members of their retreat group started to arrive. Adrenaline wouldn't let them sleep. Todd found himself lying awake in bed, listening anxiously for anything that sounded out of place. Every time their dog Shona let out a loud growl or bark, both of them would immediately be on their feet. Todd would look out the back shutters while Mary checked the front.

Once the rest of the group members arrived, they would be able to set up a regular guard schedule at the listening post/observation post (LP/OP) that Todd had prepared. Until then, however, they would have to be light sleepers. The stress of getting only snatches of sleep began to show after only a few days.

The first of the members of the Group to arrive at the retreat were Mike and Lisa Nelson. They came roaring up in their Bronco and their Mustang, late in the evening of October fifteenth. They reported that they had not run into trouble on their trip, aside from having to pay sixty-five dollars a gallon for gas at one stop. They commented that there were a lot of people on the road, even late at night, and that a lot of the cars they saw were "full to the gunnels and towing U-Haul trailers."

Mike said that they had both called in sick the day before they left, and that neither he nor Lisa had bothered calling back again. When Todd asked if this was wise, Mike replied, "Todd, if you had seen the panic that we saw, you'd have done the same thing. We're not going back. Ever. We split the whole program. Besides, at this point, I probably couldn't get my job back even if I wanted to, so there is no turning back."

The conversation didn't go on much longer because they were exhausted and wanted to get some sleep. They had driven straight through from Chicago.

The next to arrive, seventeen hours later, were Dan Fong and Tom Kennedy. By prior arrangement, they had convoyed out west together. Dan was driving his Toyota pickup. Tom's flat brown-painted Bronco, riding down on its overload springs, followed close behind. After they stopped, Todd noticed that the Toyota's windshield, passenger side window, and rear window on the camper shell were missing. What clearly looked like bullet holes peppered the passenger side of the camper shell. Their "debriefing" went on much longer than that given by the Nelsons.

CHAPTER 2
Old Friends

"A few honest men are better than numbers."

—*Oliver Cromwell*

The morning following the arrival of Dan and T.K., there was still no sign of Ken and Terry Layton, the last of the group members still in Illinois. Dan said that he was beginning to wonder if they would ever arrive. When Mary voiced the same concern to Todd, he smiled and declared, "Don't worry, if I know them, they'll get here even if they have to cover the whole distance in three-to-five second rushes."

After his conversation with Mary, Todd went to see Mike, who was inventorying his equipment in his wall lockers in the Grays' basement. As he reached the bottom of the stairs, Todd told Mike, "It would be wise to start a round-the-clock guard mount, starting this morning. I'd like you to work up a duty schedule. We'll use that sked until Ken and Terry arrive, then we'll set a permanent watch."

Mike raised an eyebrow and asked, "So you really think that they'll make it here? You know, if they had a chance to make it out in a car, they'd be here by now. They could be on foot by now, or worse. You saw how Dan's rig got shot up. That's pretty strong evidence that we're in a world of hurt."

Todd gave Mike Nelson a glum look. "I know Mike, I know. At this point, though, all we can do is hope and pray. Care to join me?" They kneeled and bowed their heads. They prayed aloud, each beseeching protection and travel mercies for the Laytons.

Later that morning, Todd called for a formal debriefing of the Nelsons, Dan, and T.K. Everyone got together in the living room of the house, with the exception of Mary, who was up at the hillside listening post/observation post (LP/OP).

"The drive itself was a piece of cake, really," Mike began. "Like I told Todd before, the hardest part was loading up all of our gear. We spent half a day putting everything into three heaps: 'Essentials,' 'Second Priority,' and 'Nice to Have.'"

16

"We thought that we had pre-positioned most of our gear here at the retreat, but once we started setting out everything that we still had at our house, we realized that we had seriously underestimated the weight and volume."

Lisa interjected, "I suppose that we should have done a practice load-up a long time ago. It would have made our underestimation immediately apparent, and prevented having to consciously think through what we absolutely needed to take. Anyway, after prioritizing, we started loading. The guns got packed first. Then all of our ammo. Then our ALICE packs. Then twelve five-gallon gas cans. Those went on the rack on the tailgate and just inside it, so we could refuel without having to unload anything to get to the cans.

"Next we loaded our 'tactical' food supplies—you know—the MREs and various freeze-dried and retort packaged stuff. We are thankful that we brought most of our MREs here last year. Otherwise, we would have had to leave them behind. This got us through the 'Essentials' pile. The real headaches came with the 'Second Priority' pile: clothing, bulk foods, field gear, most of our medical supplies, the hand crank generator, and so on. We just didn't have room to fit it all in, even with both the Bronco and the Mustang. I considered trying to get a rental trailer, but I figured that by then they'd all be long gone.

"The end result was that we had to leave behind half of our wheat, our generator, our kerosene lamps, all of our cans of kerosene, and half of our survival reference books. Before we took off, I left the extra gear along with a goodbye note on our next door neighbor's back porch. I figured that there was no use in having them go to waste. Besides, I knew that we wouldn't have the opportunity to come back for another load. The only thing that we took from the 'Nice to Have' pile was my old family Geneva Bible. It has been through floods, tornadoes, you name it. I'm glad it's with us."

"By the time we got everything packed, it was three a.m. We were going to coordinate, but the phone was dead. As it turned out, leaving in the middle of the night worked out for the best. There was not much traffic. Even still, we saw quite a few cars and pickups towing trailers. Mike drove ahead of me. We talked to each other on the CB. We didn't chatter. It was just the occasional 'slow down!' or 'watch out for this truck that's coming up to pass!' We had the CBs set to channel 27, upper sideband—the Get Out Of Dodge (G.O.O.D.) frequency—so Mike occasionally tried to reach the Laytons, or Dan or T.K., in case they were monitoring, but they either weren't listening or were out of range. I was really nervous the whole way. I had the doors locked and kept my Colt Gold Cup tucked under my thigh on the seat of the car."

Mike continued, "We didn't want to use up any more of the gas in cans than we had to, so we stopped several times to fill up. One station was charging sixty-five dollars per gallon for all grades of fuel."

Lisa interjected, "That was the station where we met this guy and his family stranded in their minivan. Because the gas station had started to refuse checks and credit cards the day before, they wouldn't even accept their own franchise card. This guy had every credit card in the world—American Express, VISA, you name it—but only eighteen dollars in cash. Just as the guy was taking off his fancy gold wristwatch to offer the station manager in exchange for a tank of gas, Mike walks up to him and hands him nine one-hundred-dollar bills. He thanked him and offered to send the money back later. Mike said to him 'No prob, keep it fella. Besides, by the time you'd get a chance to mail me the money, people will be kindling their fires with fifties, and wiping their behinds with hundreds.'"

Mike concluded, "Anyway, the long and the short of it is that we got here, and saw no serious disorder along the way. But, as Lisa told you, there were a lot of determined-looking people with very heavily loaded vehicles on the road."

Dan and T.K.'s debriefing was next. T.K. began, "I was listening to my Cobra CB base station, set to the primary G.O.O.D. frequency, as I was packing up. All of a sudden, I heard this voice saying: 'Dude, are we getting out of here or what?' It was the Fong-man. Boy, I was glad to hear him. I 'rogered' back, and he told me that he was all packed up and ready to go. I said, 'Great, come on over and help me load up.' He showed up in about ten minutes. As it turned out, he was on 'security' while I packed. I made sure that I had a gun handy throughout the process as well. I had my Colt Commander cocked and locked in the inside pocket of that flyer's jacket I bought last year.

"Basically, I packed while Dan sat in the cab of his Toyota, holding his old Model '97 trench gun. I asked him why he wasn't carrying his Remington 870. He says, 'This gun is much more ominous....' Then he whips out this bayonet about a mile long and snaps it on. 'This oughta make any hungry neighbors think twice,' he says. By the time I was done loading up, it was nearly midnight. I brought all I could think of, and got the old Bronco pretty well loaded down. Luckily, I just made a caching trip out here last summer, so I didn't have to leave much behind that I would have wanted aside for some books and bed linens. When we took off, Dan was in the lead."

Dan stood up and continued, "I started packing up a day before Tom. I couldn't figure which of my guns to bring along, so I said to myself, 'Aw shucks, I'll just take *all* of them.' Most of the guns are still wrapped up in blankets at the bottom of everything else in the back end of the Fong-mobile—all twenty-nine of them.

"Because I had my doubts, I worked the next three days after I got Todd's 'The sky is falling!, the sky is falling!' call. My last afternoon at the cannery, the general manager gave me a list of fifteen employees that I was supposed to hand pink slips to at four o'clock. I told him, 'Sorry boss, can't do that. These people depend on their jobs, and we depend on them. We can't put out a safe-to-eat product without a minimum level of staffing on each shift.' Then he says to me, 'If you refuse, I'll have no choice but to let you go as well.' Then I said, 'You can't fire me, because I just quit,' and walked away. I didn't even bother to clean out my desk. I just grabbed a few of my engineering reference books, and the Sykes-Fairbairn 'letter opener' that I kept in the top drawer. On my way out, I stopped by the employee's thrift shop and bought sixteen cases of various late-date-of-pack canned fruit and vegetables. They were still tagged at the old employee price which is like two cents on the dollar from current prices."

Fong scanned the room and then went on. "Soooo, that same evening I started packing up. By then the phones had been out for a couple of days. It took a lot longer than I thought to pack up. As T.K. told you, I spent the next few hours keeping a look out while he got his gear loaded. We left late, eleven o'clock—no, I guess it was after midnight."

T.K. nodded in agreement.

Dan shrugged his shoulders and went on. "It didn't seem that late. Any-hooo, we got ourselves on the road. On our way out of town we saw one house totally in flames, but not a single fire truck was in sight. We also saw two cars that had been gutted. The traffic on the freeway was nearly bumper-to-bumper, even at midnight. All of the gas stations were either closed or had big signs, mainly sheets of plywood spray painted with the words 'NO GAS.'

"By the time we were an hour and a half out of Chicago, we started seeing cars that had run out of gas alongside the road. A couple of times I had to swerve around people trying to flag us down. They were really desperate. By that time, I figured that stopping to help anybody out would be far more dangerous than it was worth. By the time we crossed the state line there were cars out of gas on the shoulder every half a mile. It was at that point that I got on the radio to T.K. and suggested that we cut over to the older two-lane highway that parallels the interstate. Things were really starting to look hostile on the interstate, so we cut over as soon as we got the chance. By that time, T.K. and I were both low on fuel.

"My gauge read a quarter full, and T.K. radioed to say that he'd switched over to his reserve tank, so I started looking for a good place to refuel. I picked a side road that went out by a bunch of farms. There were no cars on it at all. We stopped about a mile down this side road at a straight stretch where we could see both ways for quite a distance. I got out with my Model 97, and had my Beretta nine mil in a shoulder rig. T.K. got out with his CAR-15, and slung it across his back. I played security for him while he refueled, and then he did the same for me.

"Just as I was putting the last of a third jerry can into my rig, T.K. gave a whistle, and I saw a car's headlights. Both of us got down on the far side of our rigs, trying to put as much engine block as we could between us and them. When the lights got within about 150 yards, I could see it was a patrol car.

"At that point, both T.K. and I played it cool, and we slipped our long guns under my pickup, lengthwise, so they were out of sight. Turned out it was a sheriff's deputy. When he stopped his patrol car behind our rigs, T.K. walked back to talk with him. Needless to say, he was very curious about us, and wasn't taking any chances. He had a big Glock 21, and it was *out* of the holster.

"T.K. explained to him that we were on our way to stay with friends in Idaho and had just stopped to refuel. He had already figured that out, and pointed his flashlight at the jerry can sitting by my rig. At first, he thought we'd both been riding in my Toyota, and that we had stopped to siphon somebody's Bronco. It wasn't until we showed him our driver's licenses and the registration for both vehicles that he started to relax.

"Boy, was I scared. The last thing that we needed was to get locked up in some county jail in Iowa just as the shit was hitting the fan. As it turned out, the dude was pretty cool after all. We shot the breeze for a bit while I finished gassing up, and cramming the cans back in the rigs. Just before he left, he said, 'Well, I hope you make it to your hidey-hole in Ide-ho in one piece.' He sure had us pegged. Anyway, we waited 'til he was well out of sight before we picked up our guns. He never spotted them. Jeez, that would have taken even more explaining."

After a brief pause, T.K. spoke. "I was scared to death, too. After the deputy left, we praised God for his protection, and got turned around and headed back for the highway. We tooled along just fine. In fact, Dan kept picking up speed. Sometimes he got up to about seventy-five. I had to get on the CB and yell at him to slow down. We made another refueling stop using the same method just before dawn in eastern South Dakota, and then again about ten in the morning. After that stop, I took the lead. By then, there were virtually no cars on the road at all.

"Not long after we crossed into Montana we had to slow down because there was a pair of wrecked cars almost blocking both lanes. At first, it looked like just another accident, two cars smashed together, typical fender bender. Then I realized, hey, there aren't any intersecting roads there, so how could they have been in a fender bender unless one car had rear-ended the other? I knew that couldn't be the case, because one of the cars was practically perpendicular to the road. By the time I had figured that out, we were practically on top of them. Luckily, the shoulder was pretty wide. I didn't have time to call Dan on the CB to warn him. I just hit the gas and swerved around onto the shoulder around the wreck. All I could do was hope that Dan would catch on and do just the same thing. Luckily, he did."

Dan picked up the thread of the story, "I saw the munched cars up ahead, and then I saw a puff from T.K.'s tailpipe when he hit the gas. A second later, I did likewise. I followed right behind. As we went around the two wrecked cars, I saw two guys with shotguns stand up behind the car on the right-hand side. They weren't riotguns either, just regular old pump action birdguns. When that happened, I just ducked, and kept on going. They got about three or four shots off at me.

"The first shot took out my windshield and passenger's side window. The second and third pretty well peppered my camper shell. Needless to say, it took out the back window of the camper, as well. Nothing inside got wasted except my sleeping bag. It's leaking goose down like crazy now. Some pellets also hit two of my gas cans, but luckily they were empties. Otherwise, the back end would have been swimming in gas.

"Judging by the holes, they must have been using shells loaded with good-sized buckshot. Probably number four buck, possibly a bit larger. It went through my camper shell and just kept on going. Anyway, after we got about ten more miles down the road, we pulled off along a straight stretch. T.K. pulled security while I assessed the damage. The windshield was shattered. I could hardly see through it. The passenger's side window had disintegrated into chunks.

"I spent the next ten minutes kicking out the windshield and sweeping out the majority of the broken glass. It was pretty cold, and I didn't want to freeze my tail off driving without a windshield, so had to spend another five minutes pulling gear out of the back of my rig until I found the box with all my cold weather clothes. I bundled up in my field pants with the cold weather liners, a woolly pully, my down jacket, and then my DPM camouflage smock. I also put on my army gloves with liners and one of those navy watch caps that we got at Ruvel's Surplus. Even with all that, I felt cold, but at least I didn't freeze. That was the only exciting thing that happened on the way here. The last part of the trip was rather anticlimactic. Saw some nice looking deer and elk, though."

With the formal debriefing over, the newcomers continued their tales over lunch. To everyone's surprise, it was a hearty spread, with fresh meat, cheese, and vegetables. T.K. asked Todd, "Hey, what's with wasting all this fresh food? I thought you'd be starting on the storage food by now."

"Savor it while you can, T.K. We're just in the process of using up all the food from the refrigerator and freezer. We don't know how much longer we'll have power."

T.K. looked glum. He moaned, "We'll be eating wheat berries for breakfast tomorrow, I suppose." They all laughed.

• • •

After concerted study, Todd and Mary Gray had chosen the Palouse Hills region of north central Idaho as a place to look for their retreat. It fit all of their criteria. It had a low population density. It was more than six hours' drive from the nearest major metropolitan area, Seattle. The entire region had deep, rich topsoil and diverse agriculture. Most importantly, it had precipitation through most of the year, eliminating the one weak link in most modern agriculture in America—water. The region did not need electrically pumped irrigation water to grow crops.

A "vacation" trip in the summer of 2001 proved out their hopes about the region. Everyone they met was friendly, there was no traffic, and most of the pickups had gun racks and N.R.A. stickers. Aside from the occasional double-wide mobile home or satellite TV dish, it looked more like the 1960s than the "Aughts." To Todd and Mary, who had both grown up in the suburbs of Chicago, the price of land and houses seemed absurdly low. The price of a three-bedroom house on twenty acres ranged from $140,000 to $300,000.

After three subsequent trips looking at real estate, they finally found a forty-acre farm that they wanted to buy. It was a mile out of Bovill, a small town thirty miles east of Moscow, Idaho. Bovill was situated at the eastern fringe of the Palouse Hills farming region. The town was a bit colder than much of the surrounding area, but that also meant that the price of land was lower. Further, the economy of the area had a mix of both agriculture and timber to support it. Todd also liked the prospect of being close to the Clearwater National Forest. As he put it, the 1.9 million acre forest would make "a big backyard." The brick farmhouse was built in 1930. It needed some work, but it met all of their needs. It had a full basement, three small but adequate bedrooms, a wood cook stove that also looked 1930s vintage, and a metal roof. There was also a garage/shop, a barn, a woodshed, a meat house, a large orchard of fruit and nut trees, and a spring house a hundred yards up the hill behind the house. Unlike most of their neighbors, who were on well water, they had a five-gallon-per-minute spring gravity fed to the house. Because the current owners were retiring and moving to Arizona, a seven-year-old John Deere tractor also went with the house. The owners had asked $178,000 for the place. The Grays offered $125,000. After two counteroffers, they finally settled on $155,500. They paid cash.

• • •

The path that led Todd and Mary Gray to the Palouse Hills began one evening in October, 2006, as Todd and his college roommate Tom "T.K." Kennedy walked back to their dorm. They had just watched a DVD of the Australian film *The Road Warrior* at a mutual friend's apartment. Todd commented, "Pretty good movie, T.K., but not too believable. Personally, I think that in a situation like that, the gasoline would be gone long before the ammunition, not the other way around."

"Yeah, I was thinking the same thing myself," T.K. said. "Also, the best way to survive something like that wouldn't be to zoom around from place to place. That just increases contact with other people. Consequently, that increases the chance of trouble. Mel Gibson's character should have set up some sort of retreat or stronghold." After a few moments of silence he asked, "Do you think a scenario like that—total collapse of society—could ever really happen?

"I think all this talk about 'The Y2K Bug' is overblown. But given the complexity of society, and the interdependence of systems on other systems, it probably could. In fact, all it might take would be economic trouble of the same magnitude as the Great Depression of the 1930s to set something like that off. That could be all it would take, and the whole house of cards would collapse. Our economy, our transportation system, communications systems— everything, really—is so much more complex and vulnerable than back in the 1930s. And our society is not nearly so well-behaved."

T.K. suddenly stopped on the sidewalk and cocked his head. He looked Todd in the eyes and proclaimed, "If something like that is truly possible, even on an outside chance, then I think it might be prudent to make some preparations."

Back at their dorm room, their conversation on the subject went on with great intensity until three a.m. Without knowing it at the time, Todd and T.K. had formed the nucleus of an organization that eventually would have more than twenty members, regular meetings, logistics standards, a set of tactical standard operating procedures (SOPs), and a chain of command. Oddly, despite its formal organization, their survival group was not given a name for many years. It was simply referred to as "the Group."

When they recruited new members, Todd and T.K. described "the Group" as a "mutual aid" organization. Members could depend on help from each other, both in good times and in bad. If a member had their car break down, or got into a financial bind, for example, the other group members were sworn to give immediate aid to the best of their ability—no excuses, and no questions asked. The group's major benefit was that in truly hard times it would provide strength in numbers and a solid logistics base, allowing the members a greater chance of pulling through a crisis unscathed.

Within a few months Todd and T.K. had gathered a number of friends into the Group. Most of them were fellow students at the University of Chicago. Since nearly all of them were short on cash, they didn't get far beyond a lot of talk until most of the members had graduated from college, and started making decent salaries.

For the first few years following its inception, Todd and his fellow group members talked, argued, and reasoned their way into a formal organization.

Todd held the overall leadership and guiding role. He was simply called either "boss" or jokingly, "head honcho."

T.K. became the group's personnel specialist. He counseled group members and ironed out wrinkles in interpersonal relations. In addition, T.K. emerged as the organization's main recruiter. He carefully sized up each prospective group member, weighed their strengths and weaknesses, and did his best to judge how each would react to a prolonged period of high stress.

CHAPTER 3
Ready and Able

"... it would be appropriate ... to have organized groups charged
to conserve certain data and certain civilized forms,
and to foster a new beginning when the right time for it comes."

—*Roberto Vacca,* The Coming Dark Age

Less than an hour after the second debriefing ended, the TA-1 field telephone at the "Charge of Quarters" ("C.Q.") desk clacked three times in succession. Mike snatched it up. "Mary says that a pickup truck just stopped at the front gate."

Mike asked, "Pickup? ... but Ken and Terry own a ... Bronco!" Anxious looks spread around the table, then in a blur everyone was snatching up their weapons and heading for the windows. If it weren't serious business, it might have looked comical, with everyone bumping into each other. Todd was shouting, "Hold on! hold on! We can't all man the front windows! Kevin, watch the back! Dan, west side!" Meanwhile, Mike was still at the C.Q. desk with the field telephone held to his ear. Mike yelled, "Mary says whoever it is, is out of the truck and is waving his arms."

By now, Todd was scanning the road with his rubber-armored binoculars. "I don't believe it," he muttered, adjusting the focus wheel. "Well, I'll be! The old super-warrior came for a visit. You can relax, everyone. It's Jeff Trasel."

Todd and T.K. jogged down the hill to the gate, their rifles carried at "high port." As they approached Jeff's Power Wagon, they could see that Jeff was agitated.

"Got any room for an ex-member with a big problem?" Trasel asked.

Todd answered, "Could be. What's the matter, Jeff?"

Trasel blurted, "It's my girlfriend. She's been shot!"

They got Jeff's truck through the gate and up the hill as quickly as possible. Todd clicked his radio from the off to the VOX position. "Mike, call Mary on the landline ASAP. Tell her we have a medical emergency at the house. Send Dan to relieve her at the O-P."

Jeff's girlfriend, Rose, was in bad shape. Jeff and Todd carried her into the house. Rose was unconscious. They temporarily laid her on a blanket on the floor near the wood-heating stove. Mary quickly but thoroughly examined her, briefly removing three blood-soaked pressure dressings. She had been shot in the left side of her upper chest. The bullet had entered just below her collarbone. It then traveled at an upward angle, shattering the upper portion of her left shoulder blade before exiting the top of her shoulder. The entrance wound was scarcely larger than the diameter of the bullet. The exit wound, in contrast, looked like a patch of red raw meat two inches in diameter.

"What happened?" Mary asked, as she was digging through a large box of sterilized medical instruments that were individually wrapped in Ziploc bags.

"We were on our way up here. We stopped because Rose said that she had to pee. She couldn't wait. So I stopped by the side of the road, and Rose scampered off into the bushes. Just as she was walking back to my truck, a Corsica with Wisconsin plates pulled up behind me and stopped. Two guys jumped out, and one of them intercepted Rose before she could get back in her door. He had a big revolver pointed right at her head. She just froze there. The other guy walked up to my door, and leveled a Mossberg riotgun at me. What was I supposed to do? I was thinking we were history.

"The next thing I knew, the guy with the shotgun ordered me out of the cab. Then, he had me open my flight jacket and he pulled my .45 out of its shoulder holster. He put that in their car. Then, like a fool, he turns his back and starts rummaging around under the seat without finishing searching me. I figured that this was my one and only chance. I pulled my little AMT Backup .45 out of the inside pocket of my flight jacket, and shoved the barrel right up against the back of his head. Now, I had the drop on *him*. I told him to verrrry slowly put the shotgun on the seat of the truck and back out, again, real slowly. At this point, his partner started getting panicky. He didn't know whether to take a shot at me, run, or what.

"Next thing, I ordered the guy on my side of the truck face down on the pavement, keeping one eye on his fidgety partner. I gave the guy a quick frisk. All that I came up with was a Bucklite pocketknife. The other guy just stood there kind of shaking. Finally, he says, 'Drop the gun and let him go, or I'll shoot the girl.' Real original line, huh? Then I told him, 'No, you drop your gun, you half-wit, or I'll shoot both you *and* your partner. Unlike you, I know how to use a gun.' At this point, he goes into a real panic. He points his gun at me, then back at Rose, then back at me. He was shaking like he had spent too much time in a meat locker. This guy obviously had a room temperature IQ, and no nerve whatsoever. Throughout all this, I had my pistol pointed at the back of the head of the guy on the ground. It was the old Mexican standoff.

"The next time he switched to pointing his gun at Rose, I leaned my fore-arms across the hood of my rig and lined up the sight rail on his chest. Then, when he looked back at me, his eyes got as big as saucers and he started back-pedaling. As soon as the muzzle of his gun swung away from Rose and toward me, I gave him the 'double tap.' I hit him once in the chest, and the second shot grazed the top of his head.

"When he heard my shots, the guy on the ground tried to get heroic, and jumped up at me. I emptied the four rounds left in the magazine into him. The last shot was right into his face. The whole back end of his head exploded. I guess I was on autopilot at that point.

"Then, I realized that the other guy—the one with the revolver—wasn't yet one-hundred-percent dead. He was sitting on the ground gurgling and waving his gun around. He started pulling the trigger. By pure chance, one of the rounds hit Rose. Before I could put in a fresh magazine and line up the sight rail on him, his revolver was empty. He kept clicking on fired chambers, with the muzzle pointing sorta randomly. After another few seconds, he collapsed.

"I grabbed my medic's bag and got to Rose as soon as I could. I saw that it was a through and through wound, saw it wasn't a major hit, and applied direct pressure. I got sterile bandages on both sides of the wound as soon as I could, and then got her into the truck. I picked up both of their guns and threw them on the floor of the passenger side of the truck. Then I went and got the full-sized Colt .45 they had stolen from me and put it back in my shoulder rig. I just left their bodies and their car where they were.

"Because we were only about an hour away, I figured my best bet was to beat feet up here. It was hard to believe, but Rose didn't go into complete shock. She was coherent until just before we went through Bovill. Then she passed out. Up until then though, she was able to monitor the amount of bleeding, and put pressure on the top of the exit wound dressing with her right hand. Luckily, Dan had once described how to find your place to me, so I didn't waste a lot of time looking for it."

By now, Mary had pulled the instruments she thought that she'd need out of their sterile wrappers. "What's her blood type?"

Jeff replied, "I don't know, but she keeps a donor card in her wallet—in her purse out in the truck." Trasel sprinted away to look for it. Mary estimated that Rose had lost at least two or three pints of blood. She then checked Rose's pulse, respiration, blood pressure, and pupils. Speaking to those gathering in the room like a group of surgical interns, she pronounced, "She's pretty well out. Her pulse is rapid at 115, but her BP is a bit on the weak side—110 over 40. That may sound strange, but I've heard that that isn't unusual in cases where someone has lost a lot of blood."

An impromptu surgery room was set up in the kitchen. The kitchen table was used as the operating table. Lisa washed the table down with half the contents of a bottle of denatured alcohol, while T.K. put on a five-quart stockpot of water to boil. Jeff returned, reporting that Rose had indeed been carrying a blood donor's card. As it turned out, the only other person at the retreat with Rose's blood type, A negative, was Dan Fong.

Mary prepped Rose's arm. Jeff helped her hang a colloid IV bottle from the light fixture above the dining room table. She left the roller clamp on the IV tube in the wide-open position, providing a rapid drip.

• • •

Fortunately, Mary had learned how to give transfusions from a surgeon at the hospital where she formerly worked in Chicago. The surgeon was curious to know why she wanted to master an obsolete technique. She explained that she thought it might come in handy if there was a major disaster and the hospital's supply of whole blood ran out. He winked and said, "Oh, so you're one of those *survivor* types." The surgeon was very precise in his instructions. He also gave her a complete description of the equipment needed. "None of the large companies make traditional person-to-person transfusion sets anymore," he explained. "Everything is geared to working from bladder-packed units of whole blood, plasma, or solutions like Ringer's lactate like the paramedics use. However, all the tubing connectors are modular, they use the same fitting as a Luer lock. You can even set up a piece of tubing with needles at both ends for a direct transfusion if absolutely necessary." He instructed that it was generally better to collect blood for transfusion, rather than making a direct transfusion. "There is too much risk of losing track of how much is coming out of the donor if you don't take out measured units. Donors have gone into shock and died from giving too much blood in direct transfusions. It happens a lot in Third World countries where they do direct transfusions."

Soon after her conversation with the surgeon, Mary added six disposable sets of transfusion rigs to her mini-surgical kit. Although she had long hence memorized blood type compatabilities, for everyone else's benefit, she typed up "cheat cards." The rules were generally accepted for packed red blood cells from blood banks, but could be used for freshly donated blood in an emergency. She photocopied and laminated them, and put them in each transfusion kit. They read:

O+ can receive [O+ and O-] and can give to (O+, A+, B+, AB+)
O- can receive [O-] and can give to (all blood types ... universal donor)
A+ can receive [A+, A-, O+, O-] and can give to (A+, AB+)
A- can receive [A-, O-] and can give to (A+, A-, AB+, AB-)

B+ can receive [B+, B-, O+, O-] and can give to (B+, AB+)

B- can receive [B-, O-] and can give to (B+, B-, AB+, AB-)

AB+ can receive (all blood types ... universal recipient) and can give to (AB+)

AB- can receive [AB-, A-, B-, O-] and can give to (AB+, AB-)

Mary taught a class to the group members on basic transfusion techniques. In the class, she stopped just short of starting an actual transfusion, but she showed how to position both the donor and the recipient, how to set up and monitor the flow of blood, and demonstrated how to "prep" an arm or leg artery on two group members.

• • •

Both Dan and T.K. had their arms prepped to give transfusions. T.K. was the group's only type-O negative universal donor. Dan was positioned on the couch. Mary then loosened the catheter cap and inserted the end of the tubing to start the flow of blood down to an empty bladder pack on the floor. By that time, the IV that was connected to Rose was nearly empty, so Mary replaced it. She said tersely, "I'm going to put another unit into her, again at a rapid drip, while we are drawing Dan's blood." Mary continued to check on Rose's vital signs in the next few minutes while Dan was giving his first unit. She noticed that Rose was drifting in and out of consciousness. Soon, Dan's first donor bag was full. She waited until the second bag of colloids was nearly empty, and replaced it with the unit from Dan.

Then she dashed across to Dan and started to fill a second bladder pack. "Let me know if you start to feel dizzy at all, Dan. We'll be drawing you down this second unit." Next, Mary prepared a heavy dose of Ketalar, a disassociative general anesthetic. The dosage was based on a table included with each bottle. She adjusted the dose based on Rose's body weight of 120 pounds, and her already semiconscious state. She judged that with this dose Rose would be fully unconscious for four hours. Mary introduced the Ketalar into the flow of transfused blood coming from Dan, using a small bladder of saline linked to the T-connector positioned just below the unit of Dan's blood.

After about fifteen minutes, Mary cut off the supply of blood from Dan, and had T.K. take Dan's place on the couch. She slowed the rate of flow from the unit of Dan's blood to Rose, using the roller clamp, explaining, "We don't have an unlimited supply of blood, so we'll hold off on the transfusion until after I get started with the exploratory."

Washing her hands once again, Mary donned a surgical mask and a pair of sterile gloves. The mask wasn't necessary, but since she had them handy, she used one. "Ninety-nine percent of the risk of infection comes from my hands and the instruments. But it doesn't hurt to add a bit of insurance with a mask."

She then gingerly removed Rose's bandages, sodden with half-clotted blood. "I'm going to probe the entrance end of the wound first." Thirty seconds later, she declared, "It looks clean. The bullet didn't hit anything major on this end." Mary then shifted to the top of her shoulder. "There's a lot of blood-shot here," she mumbled. To T.K., Mary's last sentence sounded more like something someone quartering a deer would say.

"I'm going to have to debride quite a bit of this muscle tissue. If the wound channel is this large after collapsing inward, the temporary channel must have been enormous when the bullet went through. There are also some bone fragments from her scapula. It's really trashed. What did she get shot with, anyhow?"

"A .357 magnum. And boy, am I pissed," Jeff replied.

Mary set down the dull probe she had been holding, and picked up a number four curved scalpel. After resuming the transfusion from Kennedy, she began slowly and carefully cutting away some of the most badly damaged tissue.

A few minutes later, Mary spoke again. "Ah haaaah. I see our culprit now. An artery less than two millimeters across, but just a bit too big to clot closed by itself. I'm not skillful enough to rejoin it, so I'll just have to suture it off, and hope that nothing goes necrotic. Supposedly a fairly safe bet with arteries this small. The Good Lord was prescient and provided a dual supply to most areas of our bodies. Some of the smaller veins and arteries can be sacrificed and there is still a supply. You can't do that with anything major like the femoral or subclavian arteries, but it is allowable with the smaller ones."

As she spoke, Mary picked up a "derf" suture needle holder and clamped a pre-threaded 3-0 absorbable suture into it. The suturing took an unnerving twenty minutes. "This is a real pain," Mary groaned. "It would be a lot easier if this little artery would stay in place and if it weren't spurting blood."

When the suturing was completed, Mary asked T.K. to remove the clamp from the transfusion tubing, resuming the flow of blood. By now, Lisa had replaced the second bladder of blood from Dan with the first one from Kevin, tapping on the tube with her fingers repeatedly to force some air bubbles in the tube up to the expansion chamber. After a couple of more minutes of probing around, Mary asked, "Okay, now I'm going to have to do something with what's left of her scapula. The only thing is, I don't know what to do. I've removed the loose bone fragments, but that still leaves a really rough edge. Any suggestions?"

There was silence for a few moments, then Dan spoke up, "Couldn't we just file the edge of it smooth?"

"Yes, I suppose so," Mary replied, "but I don't have anything like a file in my bag of tricks. The only thing that comes close is my bone saw, and that's way too big for this job. What I need is a miniature version of a machinist's flat file."

Dan then offered with his characteristic smile, "I've got a set of Swiss pattern files in my gunsmithing box. You can take your pick from all sorts of profiles. I'll go get them." While Dan was gone, Mary again checked Rose's vital signs.

Less than ten minutes later, Dan pulled the chosen Swiss pattern file out of the boiling water, using a huge pair of obstetrics forceps to reach down to the bottom of the stainless steel stockpot. Dan handed her the file using the forceps. Mary nodded and enunciated, "This should do the trick." She shook the file in the air to help cool it. After five minutes of judicious filing, more probing, a second look at the sutured artery, some irrigation with saline solution, and some swabbing, Mary was almost done.

Meanwhile, Lisa finished taking the second unit of blood from Kevin, and capped his catheter, taping it securely in place.

Seeing this, Mary half-shouted, "Both T.K. and Dan should go lie down and start drinking fluids, pronto. I think that there are still a few bottles of Gatorade in the pantry. Let's leave them prepped, in case they have to donate again. If absolutely necessary, they could each probably give another half unit tomorrow, if they take it easy. Let's pray that Rose doesn't start bleeding again."

Next, Mary opened a bottle of saline and soaked several small rolls of gauze. She looked up at Lisa, who was standing by her side, and declared, "I'm going to leave this wound open for the next few days. I'll just pack it with this damp gauze. It would be a mistake to stitch her up prematurely. At this point drainage is much more important. We'll watch her wound closely the next few days. I expect in a few days we'll close the entrance side and a day later, the exit side, but even then I'll probably want to leave a drainage tube in. Final closure won't be done for about a week."

Only when Mary glanced up at the clock did she realize that nearly three hours had gone by since she had started scrubbing up. After checking Rose's vital signs once again, she said resolutely, "Well, that's all I can do. She should make it though. The damage wasn't too great, and I didn't have to try anything fancy. Thank God for Colonel Fackler."

"Who is he?" asked Jeff.

"He's the surgeon who wrote the chapter on gunshot wounds in the NATO Emergency War Surgery manual. I wouldn't have had a clue how to perform that operation if it weren't for him." With that, Mary pulled off her gloves and went to take a nap. She was completely spent.

• • •

The first addition to the group after it was started by Todd and T.K. was Ken Layton, a lanky, red-haired man with an infectious smile. He was an acquaintance of Tom's. T.K. first met Layton through a Catholic "young adults" group. Ken was of interest because he was an automobile mechanic. Although he had the necessary acumen, Ken had shown no interest in pursuing college when he graduated from high school. Instead, he immediately started working full time as an automobile mechanic. Turning wrenches was Ken's idea of fun, and he certainly was good at it. By the time he joined the group, Ken had changed jobs twice, and was making $58,000 a year. By 2009, Ken was earning $98,000 a year as the assistant manager of a shop specializing in off-road vehicle repairs and modifications.

The next recruits into the group were Mike Nelson, a botany major at the University of Chicago, and his girlfriend, Lisa. Mike had met Lisa by chance at the university's Regenstein Library. As Mike was walking through the stacks, he noticed an attractive young woman who was sitting at a study carrel reading Musashi's *A Book of Five Rings.* He soon struck up a conversation with her about martial arts. For Mike, it was love at first sight.

Lisa was a graphic design major with interests that ranged from backpacking to tae kwon do, to sport parachuting. Lisa was of average height, with dark brown hair and unusually heavy eyebrows. She joined the group a few months after she and Mike began dating. Lisa was a talented airbrush artist. Over several years, she painted camouflage patterns on most of the group members' long guns, to match their camouflage uniforms. She put three coats of clear flat lacquer over the camouflage paint, to keep it from chipping or wearing off. Initially, Lisa approached the group as just another one of her many hobbies. Later, it became an all-consuming passion that overwhelmed most of her other interests.

Upon getting his Bachelor of Science and Master of Science degrees, Mike Nelson was unsuccessful at finding any position relating to botany. The only positions that he found available were low-paying GS-5 pay grade jobs as forest survey assistants. Out of desperation, he ended up taking a job as a Chicago police officer. He graduated second in his class at the police academy. Curiously, Mike found that he genuinely enjoyed police work. Like most newly hired officers, Mike was assigned night patrol duty. However, unlike the majority of his contemporaries, Mike enjoyed the assignment. He later volunteered to continue night shifts, and even asked for assignments in Chicago's rougher neighborhoods.

Mike told the other group members that his attraction to police work was the adrenaline rush of stressful situations. He said that the "fun" part of his job was getting into "a worst case do-or-die survival situation every other night." Meanwhile, Lisa found a job as an artist with a large architectural design firm. She mainly did renderings of what a completed building would look like, complete with parking areas and landscaping. Eventually, she got the chance to take on other projects such as design and layout of a promotional brochure for the company, as well as work with the firm's computer system that generated blueprint designs. Although it was not exactly the type of job she would have chosen, she enjoyed most of the aspects of her work, and it paid very well.

Mike and Lisa dated for two years before getting married. Although their schedules were not entirely compatible, they had a happy relationship. They both enjoyed the same activities, and both had the survival bent long before they joined the Group. Mike's grandparents had built a bomb shelter in the early 1960s, and both they and his parents had encouraged Mike to be independent and self-reliant. Above all, they had told him: "Be Prepared." Lisa received similar nurturing. She grew up in a large Mormon family where food storage was a way of life. Her strenuous and often dangerous hobbies had also built confidence, self-reliance, and an abiding love for the outdoors.

When she was a freshman in college, a fellow dorm resident loaned Lisa a copy of *How to Prosper During the Coming Bad Years* by Howard J. Ruff. Reading Ruff's book had already adjusted her to a "survival mind-set" as it was termed by the Group. Mike first mentioned the existence of the group to Lisa soon after they first began casually dating, just to see if she would give a positive or negative reaction. When he mentioned the Group's plans to "head for the hills if the world falls apart," the first words out of her mouth were, "Will you take me with you?" As their relationship blossomed, Mike and Lisa began spending nearly every weekend together. Most of these weekends were devoted to hiking, rock climbing, hunting, or fishing—anything to get out of the city.

It was Mike who first told Todd and T.K. about northern Idaho. During his graduate study, Mike had spent nine months living in Moscow, Idaho. There, he had studied "microclimate growth patterns of the Ponderosa Pine in eastern Washington and northern Idaho." His graduate adviser had loved his paper, but that didn't help him get a job as a working botanist.

Mike spoke in glowing terms about northern Idaho. He reported, "Idaho is big-time survival country. Half the population is composed of survivalists that don't even realize that they *are* survivalists. Self-sufficiency is just their native way of life up there. They definitely have the survival mind-set. Almost everybody hunts. A lot of people use woodstoves and they cut their own wood. Most people do home canning, and a lot of families are set up with their own reloading presses. Lots of them homeschool their kids. Home birth with midwives is popular, and a lot of families do what they call 'home churching'—small congregations of one to four families, meeting at home. All in all, they are just a lot closer to the land than your average city dweller, and they are about ten thousand times more self-sufficient."

The next person brought into the group was Kevin Lendel, a shy, bookish electrical engineering major. His only claim to fame, and virtually his only form of exercise aside from bicycling, was foil and saber fencing. His constant fencing practice gave him a wiry build, tremendous flexibility, and lightning-fast reflexes. Kevin was a member of the University of Chicago fencing team for three years. He was never a phenomenal fencer, but he was good enough to help the team win several tournaments.

Kevin was not like most of the other members of the Group. He wore glasses with thick lenses, and had a mop of black hair that he constantly brushed out of his eyes. When he fenced, he wore a green bandanna to keep the hair out of his eyes. Kevin was Jewish. All of the other Group members were devout Christians. He was not particularly interested in the outdoors, and until he joined the Group, he had never fired a gun. However, Lendel did see the wisdom of preparedness, and changed his lifestyle and spending habits accordingly.

Lendel influenced the Group in a number of subtle ways. Most importantly, his cautious, well-considered approach to conversations and life in general tended to "ground" the group. He often said things like, "Hold on, let's not be hasty" at group meetings, and even in the field during training exercises, and in planning patrols. Another influence he had was on the importance of quality knives and sharpening stones. His saber fencing experience made him "edged weapons conscious." With his guidance, each of the group members eventually bought two or three skinning knives each, as well as a defensive knife.

Kevin taught several classes on knife fighting, and one on saber fencing. The latter was more or less for fun. Kevin also individually taught each member the art of putting a fine edge on a knife with a soft Arkansas stone. For skinning knives, most of the members bought standard mass-produced Case and Buck knives, but a few opted for custom knives made by Andy Sarcinella, TrinitY Knives, and Ruana. Most of them also bought a Leatherman tool and a CRKT folding knife. For fighting knives, most purchased standard factory produced knives made by Benchmade or Cold Steel. Kevin bought an expensive New Lile Gray Ghost with Micarta grip panels.

Against Kevin's advice, Dan Fong bought a double-edged Sykes-Fairbairn British commando knife. Kevin warned him that it was an inferior design. He preferred knives that could be used for both utility purposes and for combat. He observed that the Fairbairn's grip was too small, and that the knife's slowly tapering tip was too likely to break, particularly in utility use. Dan eventually wrapped the knife's handle with green parachute cord to give it a more proper diameter. Because the Fairbairn did indeed have a brittle tip, Dan did most of his utility knife work with a CRKT folder with a tanto-type point.

Kevin Lendel was very quiet at most of the group meetings. Typically, he had his nose in a book during most of the meetings that were dominated by discussion. This unnerved the others until they realized that Kevin was not missing a word being uttered. He could actually maintain two points of concentration simultaneously. On the few occasions that Kevin did speak up during meetings, it was either because he had been asked a question, or to make a point that everyone else had missed.

One of Kevin's favorite phrases to use at meetings was, "I've just had a blinding flash of the obvious." Many of his suggestions later ended up in written form as SOPs. For example, it was Kevin who first suggested that during times of crisis, every trip outside the perimeter be treated as a patrol, and that as such, the "two-man rule" be used. Kevin was also the initiator of group regulations on sanitation and the oft quoted, "Every injury or illness, no matter how slight, will be reported to the group medic as soon as possible." Kevin's motivation as a survivalist was never fully understood by most of the group members. Todd, in awe of Kevin's intelligence, but with doubts about what made him tick, referred to him as "a riddle wrapped in an enigma."

After graduating, Kevin put his degree to use as a software engineer for Y-Dyne Propulsion Systems in Chicago. He started out in 2007 as a junior programmer with a salary of $85,500. By 2009, he was the senior systems analyst, and made $122,000.

In 2002, Kevin launched a second career as a freelance software writer. He offered his services in Pascal, Fortran, C, and Ada, the specialized programming language used in many projects by defense contractors. When he started doing freelance software, he was not sure if he could make enough money for his sole source of income, so he stayed on half-time with Y-Dyne. After six months of doing work for a variety of companies, he found that he actually had more work than he could handle. At this point, he resigned from his position with Y-Dyne, and he started working entirely at home, using a Sun Microsystems Sparc-20 workstation—which was loaned to him by Y-Dyne—and two computers of his own: a Macintosh tower, and a hybrid IBM clone later upgraded with a 2-GHz processor.

Many of Lendel's contracts came from outside of the Chicago area. He generally sent his software using a modem, since Bovill was not in a DSL service area, and it was just beyond range for the local wireless broadband service. Occasionally, he would send the programs on Zip disks via Federal Express. FedEx came right to his doorstep, since his house was just off the county road. To his surprise, nearly a third of Kevin's contract dollars came from his former employer, Y-Dyne. They couldn't get along without him. Although he did not make quite as much money as he had with Y-Dyne, Kevin enjoyed the escape from the mindless process of daily commuting and working 9-to-5. He told the other members of the group that it felt good to get back to working the "hacker's hours" that he had enjoyed in college. He often worked as late as two or three a.m., and slept in until noon.

Most of Kevin's contracts were to write software for industrial applications. Few of the group members could relate to or even understand the complexity of Kevin's work. It was not until he showed off a dazzling fractal graphics program that he had recently written, that the other group members got a full appreciation of his skills.

When Kevin saw Todd and Mary's house in Idaho for the first time, his eyes lit up. He quickly realized that he was looking at his future, as well. Because he worked almost entirely from home, it did not matter if he lived in the suburbs of Chicago, or Outer Mongolia. All that he needed to work on his software writing contracts was power, a telephone line, and an Internet service provider. He started looking for a place near the Grays' farm almost immediately.

Kevin soon found a place that he wanted to buy. Ideally, Kevin would have liked to have bought a parcel contiguous to Todd and Mary's. Unfortunately, all of these farms were 120 acres or more, and none were likely to be on the market anytime soon. In fact, on three of the four sides, adjoining farms had been owned by the same families for two or more generations. The fourth adjoining parcel, to the east, was a full section of land belonging to the Bureau of Land Management, part of the federal government. Beyond that was National Forest. Gray was told that B.L.M. lands were sometimes put up for auction, but that this piece probably never would be because it had historic significance. It was a traditional site for digging camas bulbs, a staple food of the native Nez Perce tribe. In fact, the camas plants still grew there, competing with the non-native grasses that had all but taken over the area.

The house that Kevin eventually bought was less than a mile away from Todd and Mary's. It was on the same county road, but farther out of Bovill. His house was an earth-bermed passive solar design. It was situated on twenty-six acres. About half of the acreage was open, and suitable for hay cutting or pasture. The other half of the land was in second growth pines that averaged forty feet in height. Kevin would have preferred more land, since he eventually planned to pasture cattle, but he went ahead and bought it. The house was well built, and the price was right, at only $92,000. He paid cash.

Todd Gray was twenty-two years old when he and T.K. first formed the group. He was six-foot-two with sandy brown hair and blue eyes. He stayed slim, never letting his weight get over 185 pounds. By the time Todd entered college, his father was ready to retire. The owner of three hardware stores in the Chicago area, Phil Gray had amassed the magical million-dollar figure, and decided that he should slow down and take life easy. Just a year later, when Todd was a sophomore, his father died of a heart attack. Todd's mother Elise was the classic TV mom. Dinner on the table at six o'clock. Laundry on Thursdays. Canning in the summer. Homemade candies for Christmas gifts in the winter. Years later, she still talked about Phil as if he were still alive. She died of cancer just after the turn of the century.

Todd graduated with a Bachelor's degree in economics. Soon after graduation, he landed a position with Bolton, Meyer, and Sloan, a major accounting firm with branches in metro areas throughout the country. It was at about the same time that Todd married Mary Krause, an Occupational Therapy major that he had met during his senior year at the University of Chicago. Mary appealed to Todd for many reasons. First, she was quite attractive. She had waist-length naturally blond hair, a cute smile, and a trim, compact body. Todd also liked the idea of dating a woman with a strong background in medicine. As he explained to T.K., "She might be a good prospect for a medical specialist for the group."

T.K. replied, "Naaaw, admit it. You like her 'cause she's a total babe."

• • •

Tom Kennedy was Todd's roommate for all four years of college. As with so many college freshmen, Todd and T.K were assigned to the same dormitory room at random. They had never met before the day that they helped each other move in. They immediately became good friends. Tom, or "T.K." as everyone (including his parents) called him, was reserved, polite, and soft-spoken. He was getting his Master's degree in business administration. Kennedy was the youngest son of a retired Air Force pilot. Upon retiring as a full colonel after thirty-two years of service, T.K.'s father took up calligraphy as a retirement hobby. This eventually developed into a second career, occupying at least twenty hours a week. He even taught calligraphy classes at a local junior college. His mother was a Spanish woman that T.K.'s father had met while stationed in Spain. His father died in 2008 of a heart attack. His mother died a year later, of leukemia.

His half-Spanish ancestry gave Tom black hair, a medium complexion, and piercing dark brown eyes. Because T.K. had been born prematurely, he only reached a height of five-feet-four. Even at his heaviest, when he was in training for wrestling in high school, T.K. weighed 140 pounds. Because of his small stature, when he was in college he was often mistaken for a high school student. He was "carded" when entering bars well into his thirties. To combat being mistaken for a child, T.K. grew a mustache during the summer between his freshman and sophomore years of college.

After graduating, T.K. got a position as a management trainee with a Sears & Roebuck store in Glen Ellyn, Illinois. He soon rose through the ranks, and in 2002, after a stint at the Sears corporate headquarters in Hoffmann Estates, he was made the general manager of the Sears store in Wheaton, Illinois.

T.K. was always shy around women. He never dated when he was in college, and he never married. Tom remained active in the Catholic Church.

When he was young, he served as an altar boy. After college, he became a lay minister. He helped with communion and training altar boys.

When T.K. was in high school, his father introduced him to target shooting. He found that he greatly enjoyed engaging in a sport where his small stature was not a handicap. T.K. eventually became an active high power competitive shooter and achieved an expert classification. Although he practiced regularly and went to every match that he could, T.K. never got scores high enough to qualify him for a position on the state High Power team. His dream of shooting at the National Matches at Camp Perry, Ohio, was never fulfilled.

T.K. was the oldest of the group members. He was also the first to get out of college and start making a good salary. This gave him the opportunity to become the first group member to get completely squared-away logistically. Like any other dedicated survivalist, T.K. did not rest on his laurels after he had bought his "group standard" equipment. He continued with a well organized purchasing plan, putting away a large stock of storage food, ammunition, medical supplies, and a comprehensive personal library on survival and practical skills.

T.K.'s only unusual purchase was a crossbow. He bought a Benedict S.K. 1 with a 150-pound draw weight. He also bought several dozen aluminum broad head bolts, a fishing reel modification kit, fifteen spare strings, and a spare bow limb. At a group meeting in early 2008, T.K. mentioned casually that he had bought the bow. Dan Fong instantly pounced on him, asking him why he wanted a "medieval" weapon like a crossbow. Kennedy replied, "The crossbow isn't any more impractical than your black powder guns, Dan. In fact, it has several advantages. First, it will give us the capability to hunt game silently. That could be a real advantage if we are out in the boonies and want to avoid detection. Second, crossbows are much more effective at killing game than traditional bows. That's the reason that they are illegal for hunting in most states. Third, I'll never have to worry about running out of ammunition. Once I start to run low on bolts, I can start making my own. The last advantage is that it takes some 'oomph' to cock the darned thing. Practicing with it is more than just target practice, it is also good exercise."

Mary Krause became a de facto member of the group when she became Mary Gray. At the time that they married, Mary knew that Todd was a member of a survival group, but had no idea how deeply involved he was, or the full ramifications of his membership. Mainly, she was surprised at the amount of money that Todd had "invested" in his survival preparations. In six years, he had spent more than $5,000 on guns and ammunition, $3,000 on storage food, $4,800 on buying and restoring a 1969 Dodge Power Wagon pickup, and $1,800 on various web gear, backpacks, sleeping bags, tents, et cetera.

To her dismay, Mary discovered a thickly padded clipboard that listed hundreds of additional items that Todd intended to buy. With his accountant's mentality, Todd had itemized the purchases, compared prices from several suppliers, set priorities, and noted the sequence in which he planned to buy them. It was then that Mary realized that her plans for long vacations overseas would probably never come to fruition.

Just before marrying Todd, Mary landed a job as a sports medicine therapist at Cook County Hospital in Chicago. She truly enjoyed the healing arts. Naturally, she became the group's medic. In jest, she was sometimes referred to as the "Medical Honcho."

In 2008, Todd was able to work out an arrangement with his manager to begin working half-time from home. In requesting the arrangement, Todd was very direct with his boss. He told him that his "forty-minute, each way, each day commute" was driving him crazy, and that it was "contributing to premature burnout." His boss was upset when he heard Todd use the term "burnout," as it had precipitated the loss of several good accountants in recent years. Even though Bolton, Meyer, and Sloan was an "old school" accounting firm, Todd's boss was able to push through an arrangement whereby Todd could begin to work from home three days of each week.

To start working from home, Todd bought himself a 1.8 GHz IBM clone with a twenty-gigabyte hard disk and dial-up modem. All of the accounting software that he needed was supplied free of charge by his firm. After he began working from home, Todd's boss noticed an increase in his productivity almost immediately. When he mentioned it to Todd, Gray replied, "Well, it only stands to reason that if I'm spending four hours less each week on the road, I'm sitting at my computer that much more, right?"

A year later, when Todd was offered a raise in salary, he asked to start working entirely from home, instead. When the senior partners in the firm heard about this and were told about his increased productivity, they gave him both the raise and the go-ahead to start working from home full-time. He was Bolton, Meyer, and Sloan's first full-time employee with a "work from home" arrangement. Todd joked that the firm had finally emerged from the Dark Ages.

When Mary heard about Todd's raise and new working arrangements, she was ecstatic. They talked until late in the evening about the possibilities of moving to Idaho. When Todd mentioned how late it was getting, Mary asked, "What are you worried about? You're commuting down the hall in your slippers tomorrow."

The next person to join the group was Dan Fong, an Industrial Design major who eventually landed a job as the engineering manager for a large canning company. Dan, a second-generation Chinese-American, had a passion for guns. Fong was frequently criticized by the other group members for being a "gun nut." Specifically, they chided him for continually adding to his large gun collection, which mainly consisted of exotic guns in oddball calibers. While Dan kept buying guns, his cache of food, ammunition, and medical supplies remained pitifully small.

Dan was always a bit chubby, but ate remarkably little. He prided himself on his frugality. His only extravagance at dinnertime was premium beer. He had a taste for Anchor Steam, Samuel Adams, and ales from various Midwest microbreweries. He once told T.K., "I save major bucks by eating cheap." Typically he ate a light breakfast, skipped lunch, and after returning from work, made a dinner that was invariably dominated by rice. He only cooked meat or fish twice a week. From these few high-protein meals, he saved his meat drippings to make a sauce to flavor his rice later in the week. He attributed his rounded belly to beer rather than overeating.

Fong's gun collection changed drastically after he joined the group. It never numbered less than twenty guns, however. When he first joined the group, his collection consisted primarily of target rifles, big game hunting rifles, and black powder muzzleloaders. Later, the composition of his collection had shifted more toward the paramilitary, but was still exotic.

Among others, Dan owned a Belgian FN/FAL assault rifle, an early 1960s Portuguese contract version of the Armalite AR-10 (predecessor of the AR-15, but chambered in 7.62 mm NATO), a SSG "Scharf Shuetzen Gewehr" sniper rifle made in Austria, a Beretta Model 92SB 9 mm pistol, two Browning Hi-Power 9 mm pistols, including one with a tangent rear sight and shoulder stock, a stainless steel Smith and Wesson .357 magnum revolver, a Winchester Model 1897 twelve-gauge riotgun, a McMillan counter-sniper rifle chambered in the .50 caliber machinegun cartridge, a scoped Thompson-Center Contender single shot pistol chambered in .223 Remington, and several World War II vintage guns including a Walther P.38 pistol, an M1A1 folding stock carbine, and an M1 Garand. Eventually, with much prodding from the group, he also bought a full set of the group standard guns and spare magazines.

Jeff Trasel joined the group at roughly the same time as Dan Fong. At twenty-five, Jeff was lingering in junior college for the fourth year. He still lived at home with his parents, in a small bedroom crammed with bookshelves. Shortly after high school, Jeff did a hitch with the Marine Corps. In the Corps, Jeff was assigned to a Force Reconnaissance Team. An excellent athlete and a bright student, Jeff spent most of his time attending special service schools. No one ever figured out how he wangled it, but in rapid succession, Jeff attended the Marine Corps Force Recon School, the Army Airborne School, the Army Air Assault School, the Marine Corps Sniper School, the Navy SCUBA School, the Navy Underwater Demolitions School, the Army Ranger School, the Army Pathfinder School, and the Navy SEAL course. In all, Jeff logged more time at special schools than with his actual unit of assignment.

When Jeff left active duty in 2002, he had a hard time readjusting himself to civilian life. Despite his academic talents, he could not bring himself to enroll in a regular university. Instead, he loafed around the house, worked out, and attended a few junior college courses. At one point, he considered working overseas as a mercenary with Blackwater or one of the other "contractors." But the choice jobs in Iraq went to soldiers who had served two or more tours in "The Big Sandbox." A quirk of fate had kept Jeff out of the Middle East. Thus, there were no prospects for "merk work" for him aside from the *Légion Etrangère*—the French Foreign Legion. Jeff scoffed at the idea of fighting for the government of France. Even though he admired the fighting record of the Legion, he said that he wanted nothing to do with the French Army. The French, he said, "could screw up a two-car funeral procession."

Trasel contented himself by keeping his military skills current in the Marine Corps Reserve. Because he was not employed, and only a half-time student, it gave Jeff the time to take several extra short tours of active duty each year. He typically did two, two-week annual training tours each year instead of just the one tour required. He also put in extra drill days at his unit, doing administrative tasks and keeping the unit's intelligence briefing book up to date. He eventually attained the rank of Staff Sergeant.

Jeff added a distinct paramilitary flavor to the organization. During his tenure as the group's tactical coordinator, Jeff insisted that all of the group members get physical exercise regularly, and that the group hold bimonthly field training exercises similar to those conducted by small military units. Starting with "tactical hikes," Jeff taught the group the essentials of traveling quietly through the bush, hand and arm signals, keeping a proper interval space between members of foot patrols, and so on. Under Trasel's tutelage, the group eventually graduated to night patrols, defensive fields of fire, immediate action drills, standing listening post/observation post (LP/OP), picket shifts, raids, and ambushes. On these "field trip" days, the group members ate military surplus Meal, Ready to Eat (MRE) rations. Jeff often joked, "MRE: That's three lies for the price of one."

Most of the group members, including the females, enjoyed the field training exercises. Curiously, one of the most enthusiastic participants was Kevin Lendel. Kevin frequently volunteered to be the point man on patrols. Typically, Kevin was armed with his riot shotgun equipped with a strip of white bandage tape running down the top of the barrel to provide better sighting in low light-conditions. Kevin proved to be an excellent point man. He had acute hearing, outstanding night vision, a fencer's fast reactions, and a curious "sixth sense" about potential ambushes. He liked the position of point man, and quickly earned the respect of all the group members—even the super warrior, Trasel. Previously, Trasel had his doubts about how Kevin might react to a "terminal situation." After seeing him in field training, however, Jeff felt as confident as everyone else about Kevin's skills and calm nerve.

Because most of the training was done in civilian clothing and without carrying their weapons, it never attracted the attention of law enforcement. When questioned as to their particulars, they were simply "a hiking club." Mike Nelson, as a Chicago police officer, had developed the cover story of "training aggressors for my department's SWAT team," but he never had cause to use it, or even to flash his badge. The group was careful to conduct their armed training patrols (using blanks and blank-firing devices) in only civilian clothing, and only in remote areas of the northern Michigan peninsula. The standing rule was, "If we are carrying guns, no camouflage clothing, but if we are unarmed, camo uniforms are okay."

Jeff had a few habits that annoyed most of the other group members. Their biggest complaint was that he was notoriously late for group meetings. He also occasionally missed group meetings and other appointments. When confronted about these incidents, he would shrug his shoulders and say, "Sorry about that." With a large circle of drinking buddies and several lady friends, Jeff often found too little time available for group meetings. Jeff's other annoyances were his booming voice and his tendency to verbally chastise other group members for relatively minor faults.

Jeff Trasel was a member of the group for only three years. At his last group meeting in 2006, he announced that he was quitting the group because he was "bored," and because the group wasn't "going anywhere." When pressed, he wouldn't be any more specific about his complaints. He just got up and left the Nelsons' apartment.

With the exception of Trasel, the original group was still intact when the Grays activated their retreat in Idaho during the stock market crash. After so many years, the group seemed almost like an extended family. All of the group members felt that they could trust each other with their lives. With the gloomy scenarios they envisioned, they knew that they might have to do just that.

CHAPTER 4
Gearing Up

"Oh how great is the interval between the conception
of a great enterprise and its execution. What vain terrors!
What irresolution! Life is at stake—much more is at stake: honor!"

— *Johann Christoph Friedrich von Schiller*

Throughout its first five years, the Group "geared up" and trained with varying intensity. The 9/11 terrorist attacks first inspired the formation of the group, but their interest was redoubled with the advent of Hurricane Katrina in 2005.

There was no such thing as a "typical" training session for the group. Training was a loose term with eclectic boundaries. It ranged from anything from an evening learning how to can fruit, to a night of target shooting using tritium sights, to a practice session suturing induced wounds on a dead piglet. One memorable three-day weekend training session was "The Bucket Weekend." The weekend was designed to teach the importance of prioritizing. Everyone was limited to packing all of their food and camping supplies for the weekend in one five-gallon plastic bucket. After 9/11, meetings were held twice a month in the winter and once a month in the summer. At least one of the two meetings was dedicated to training. With the greater resources derived from holding full-time jobs, the group members embarked on a well-calculated buying spree.

Purchasing for each member began with a battle rifle, a riot shotgun with a spare "birdgun" long barrel and screw-in choke tubes, a .45 automatic pistol, and a .22 rifle for target practice and small game hunting. Next came all of the paraphernalia to support these guns: ammunition, dozens of magazines, cleaning kits, spare parts, holsters, and an Army LC-1 "web gear" harness with canteen and gun magazine pouches. Next, each member was expected to buy a good quality cold weather sleeping bag, and a good quality "four season" backpacking tent. All of these purchases had to conform to specific standards set by the group.

The first major point of disagreement in standardizing the group's purchases came when they selected their field uniform. Some of the group's members thought that wearing a camouflage uniform might attract more attention than it was worth. Eventually, however, it was decided that camos were a must when Jeff pointed out that they would assure positive identification of group members at a distance. He explained that this would make it difficult for a non-group member to slip into the perimeter of their retreat without being noticed. By the time that the Group was standardizing their uniform, the U.S. Army had long since issued the woodland camouflage battle dress uniform (BDU), which replaced the old olive drab fatigues. The issue of digital pattern Army Combat Uniform (ACU) camouflage to the U.S. Army starting in 2005 did not alter the situation significantly, since woodland pattern BDUs were so ubiquitous.

Rather than buy woodland BDUs or ACUs, which were widely available on the surplus market, Todd's group decided to standardize with the British DPM (disruptive pattern, marine) camouflage fatigues and jackets, which were then available as surplus at a reasonable price. The reasoning behind the DPMs was that because the BDU pattern was so widely available as military surplus, it had become ubiquitous. It was Kevin Lendel that made the cogent observation that if the Group were to standardize with the BDU pattern, then outsiders might still be able to slip into their perimeter without being noticed. It was better, he said, to be in camouflage, but in a different pattern than that normally seen in the States. The only serious drawback to the decision to standardize with DPMs was that the dollar lost value on foreign exchange markets in the early "Aughts." Just before the Crunch, the price of DPMs had risen to ninety dollars a set. In retrospect, Todd wished that that they had standardized with a civilian camouflage pattern like Real Tree or Advantage. And at the time there was yet another option available—the plethora of surplus uniforms from former Soviet Bloc countries that flooded the market. Any of these would have been less expensive options than continuing to pay high prices for the increasingly scarce DPMs.

The second point of disagreement over standards, which was never fully settled, was about the group's standard rifle. Most of the group's members realized the potential of the powerful 7.62mm NATO cartridge (also known as the .308 Winchester), and wanted to standardize with either the Springfield Armory M1A (a civilian version of the Army's M14) or the West German HK91 battle rifle. Others, mainly the women and those of small stature such as T.K., wanted to standardize with the less powerful 5.56 mm NATO cartridge, (also known as .223 Remington). A number of good defensive rifles were available chambered in this cartridge, including the Colt AR-15 (a semiautomatic version of the Army's M16) and its collapsing stock and short-barreled sibling, the Colt CAR-15, later called the M4. Two other well-made alternatives were the Ruger Mini-14 and the Armalite AR-180. One of the main lines of reasoning for .223 was that more cartridges per pound could be carried than with .308. This weight would make a difference on long-range patrols.

The argument over a group standard semiauto rifle raged for three meetings. Dan Fong voiced the key question: "Why do we need a standard rifle anyway? All we need is a standard cartridge. Everyone can just stock their own spare parts."

Jeff Trasel rebuked: "When we are out on a patrol, and get into a firefight, some of us will undoubtedly run out of ammunition so darn quick that they won't believe it. At a time like that, when they are shouting to other patrol members for spare ammo, they certainly won't want to be worrying about whether one magazine will fit in another weapon. That's why we absolutely need to have a standard rifle. Interchangeability of magazines is the key factor, but interchangeability of spare parts is also a plus."

When the issue could not be resolved, Todd finally put his foot down and set a "dual standard." Group members preferring the .223 cartridge could go ahead, but they had to be either an AR-15 or CAR-15, because they used the same magazines, and had compatibility for critical spare parts. Those preferring .308—mainly large-statured members—would buy a Heckler and Koch Model 91. Period. Anyone who already owned a nonstandard rifle could keep it, or those desiring to do so could buy one, but they also had to buy one of the group standard rifles and at least ten spare magazines. Further, every standard semiauto rifle also had to be equipped with radioactive tritium night sights.

Luckily, the arguments over standardizing a shotgun, pistol, and .22 caliber rifle for the group were neither as lengthy nor intense. The group eventually decided to standardize with the Remington Model 870 in twelve-gauge, the Colt .45 automatic pistol, and the Ruger Model 10/22 rifle for target practice and small game shooting.

When the issue of exactly what model of the .45 auto to standardize on was raised, it was decided that "any model of the .45 (such as the Government Model, Gold Cup, or Commander), as long as it is Colt or Kimber made" was sufficient, because they all used the same type magazines and had largely interchangeable parts. Eventually, most of the group members bought the Gold Cup model with adjustable sights. Typically, they bought the factory standard Gold Cup and added extended slide releases, extended safeties, and Trijicon tritium sights. After a failure of one of their Gold Cup's fragile rear sights, those members who owned Gold Cups also had them drilled out for a larger solid cross pin to replace the thin roll pin that came from the factory.

The trend toward stainless steel guns was in full swing when the group was gearing up. Most of the group members either bought stainless steel handguns from the outset, or later upgraded to them. In some cases, they sold their old blue steel .45s when they upgraded to stainless steel. Others decided to keep their older blue steel Colts as spares, or for barter. Kevin Lendel spent more than the other group members when he upgraded to stainless steel. He used an annual Y-Dyne bonus check to buy a "factory custom" stainless steel model that the Colt Custom Shop called the "Special Combat Government." It came from the factory with Bo-Mar sights, an extended thumb safety, and a beaver-tail grip safety. Kevin added Pachmayr rubber grips and an extended slide release. In all, he invested more than a thousand dollars in the pistol.

Dan Fong got the group members to sell off all of their old seven-round magazines, and buy supplies of the new eight-round magazines for their guns chambered in .45 ACP (Automatic Colt Pistol). The newer magazines held an extra round. At twenty-eight dollars each, the new magazines did not come cheap, especially when most of the group members had eight or more magazines for each of their .45s.

Although each group member was expected to acquire basic skills, specialization was encouraged. The theory was that each group member would develop a specialized skill, and then, as time permitted, cross-train other members. Todd chose logistics as his specialty. T.K. chose personnel. Mary became medical officer, Mike Nelson chose explosives and demolitions, and his wife Lisa chose martial arts. With expertise on nearly every firearm, Dan Fong became the "unit armorer."

Kevin Lendel held two specialties. The first was communications. The second was food storage and preparation. He chose the latter specialty because he had always loved cooking. Ken Layton was transportation coordinator, while his wife Terry volunteered to coordinate purchasing. During his brief membership, the already overtrained Jeff Trasel declared himself "tactical coordinator" and group librarian. After he quit the group, Mike Nelson replaced Trasel as tactical coordinator, while Kevin took over Jeff's responsibilities as librarian.

To supplement the tactical training given by Jeff and Mike during their respective tenures, Todd, Mary, and T.K. took pistol and rifle training courses. They attended the Front Sight firearms training school, near Las Vegas, Nevada. They each took the "Four Day Defensive Handgun" and "Four Day Practical Rifle" courses. These intensive courses greatly increased their confidence with firearms. On their return, the Grays and T.K. cross-trained the other group members in much of what they had learned at Front Sight. At $1,600 each, the courses were relatively expensive, but as Todd repeatedly told the other group members, "They're worth every penny."

Aside from guns and storage food, the group's other major investment was in vehicles. Before the Grays and Kevin Lendel moved to the Palouse Hills, all of the group's members lived either in Chicago or the outlying suburbs. As most of their survival scenarios envisioned the need to "Get Out of Dodge" in a hurry, there was correspondingly strong emphasis placed on transportation. On this issue, the group members deferred their judgment to Ken Layton.

Layton convinced the group members to buy older American-made cars and trucks and then fully restore and modify them. To Ken's way of thinking, new model cars and trucks were far too complex, broke down too easily, required specialized tools to work on, and were just too expensive. He also pointed out that late-model cars are a conspicuous sign of wealth, and might serve as a target during periods of social unrest. He convinced the group members to buy either late 1960s or early 1970s Ford cars and trucks or Dodge Power Wagon pickups. His only stipulation was that they had "straight" bodies (never involved in a collision) and were free of rust. That meant that most of the members bought their cars and trucks from "rust-free states" like California, Arizona, and New Mexico. They found them through the Internet or *Hemming's Auto News*.

Eventually, most of the group members complied with Ken's suggestion. The Grays bought a 1969 Power Wagon, but never got around to replacing Mary's 1979 VW Super Beetle. The Nelsons bought a 1968 Ford Bronco and a 1968 Ford Mustang, both of which used the same type of 289 engine. T.K. bought a 1969 Bronco, but kept his Plymouth Horizon for commuting. Kevin Lendel bought a 1971 Ford F 250 four-wheel-drive pickup. While a member, Trasel bought a Power Wagon; his was a 1970. Dan Fong, ever the nonconformist, replaced his 1989 Camaro with a 2003 Toyota four-by-four pickup. Ken and Terry Layton followed suit with the Nelsons' approach and bought a 1968 Bronco and a 1967 Mustang, both with 302-cubic-inch engines.

One advantage of having Ken as a member of the group was the fact that he had access to a fully equipped automotive garage after normal working hours. Although he volunteered to do most of the restoration work himself, he insisted that each group member be there and assist him during the most important phases of the work. This way, Ken reasoned, every group member would know how their vehicles were put together, how they worked, and hopefully, how to handle most minor repairs.

The vehicle restoration process that Ken insisted on turned out to be relatively expensive and time consuming. He started by pulling the engine and transmission from each vehicle, and then farming them out to other shops to be completely rebuilt. Next he would make minor body repairs, sand out the bodies, and put on a flat paint finish, usually in an earth tone. They used standard glossy car paint with a special flattener added. This gave much better rust protection than regular flat paint. At roughly the same time, he would either rebuild or replace the carburetor. Next, when the engine and transmission came back, he would reinstall them, at the same time replacing all of their auxiliary equipment, aside from carburetors, with brand new components. This included radiators, starters, alternators, fuel pumps, water pumps, batteries, voltage regulators, starter solenoids, hoses, and belts.

Next, Ken would rework the vehicle's suspension, usually modifying it for tougher off-road use, and do an alignment and brake job, sometimes involving replacing the master cylinder. In most cases, the vehicle's existing wiring harnesses did not need to be replaced. By the time he was done, Ken had in effect built a whole new vehicle that would be good for at least ten years of strenuous use.

After getting their vehicles back from Ken and recovering financially, most of the group members went on to further modify their vehicles to their own liking. Most of the four-wheel drives were equipped with extra fuel tanks, beefier bumpers, and roll cages. Typically, most of the group members also added Bearcat police/weather scanners and Cobra 148GTL single-sideband forty-channel citizens' band radios. It was Kevin that convinced the group to standardize with a more expensive single sideband (SSB) model. With the SSB feature, their CBs could be set to the full band, the upper sideband, or the lower sideband. This effectively made them eighty-channel radios. SSB transmission was also more efficient, so it provided longer-range transmissions. Since SSB broadcasts are unintelligible when heard on the much more common standard AM CBs, it added a modest level of security.

All of the group's communications equipment was standardized soon after the debate on standardizing weapons was settled. The primary communications system was in the form of the TRC-500 headset type 500-milliwatt walkie-talkie. The "Trick Five Hundreds," as they were soon dubbed by the group members, turned out to be an ideal choice. They were inexpensive, reliable, and because they had a hands-free, voice activated (VOX) switch mode, they proved to be ideal for use on patrols.

The only drawbacks to the TRC-500s were their limited range and that they were only available in one of two frequencies. Both of these frequencies were well known and subject to interception. This problem was solved by the electronic wizardry of Kevin Lendel. Through ads in the back of a ham radio magazine, Kevin was able to find a supplier who cut custom crystals. Kevin selected a frequency just below the 49.830-megahertz frequency of the group's TRC-500s. Realizing that what he was doing was not exactly legal, Kevin placed an order using an assumed name. He had them delivered to a commercial post office box company in downtown Chicago that didn't ask a lot of questions when one rented a box.

When soldering in the custom crystals into all of the group members' TRC-500s, Kevin also took the time to seal all of the seams in the radio cases with RTV silicone sealant. This made them much more waterproof, and hence even more suitable to rough field use.

On the advice of Jeff Trasel, the group also decided to buy several military field telephones. As Trasel so pointedly put it, "If you haven't got comm, you haven't got jaaack." The field telephones, connected by WD-1 two-conductor wire, would reduce the group's reliance on their radios in the immediate area of the retreat. The two models considered were the TA-312 and TA-1. Both were available as military surplus. The audio quality of the TA-312 was better than that of the TA-1, but it was more expensive. The TA-1 was wholly sound-powered, and thus did not require batteries. The TA-312 could also be used in a sound-powered mode, but it was normally operated with a pair of D-cell batteries installed to give it better range. Because the group only anticipated needing short-range field telephone communications, they settled on the TA-1 model.

Eventually, four TA-1 field phones and over a mile of surplus WD-1 were bought as a "group purchase." Unlike most preparedness purchasing, which was done individually, a few items such as the field phones were bought for the benefit of the entire group. The cost of most of these group purchases was shared equally, while some were "gifts to the group" on the part of individual members, and a few were paid for with unequal shares, based on the varying financial resources of the individual members.

One optional but encouraged item of equipment for group members was body armor. Mike Nelson recommended that each group member buy an extra heavy-duty bullet resistant vest of the variety worn by police SWAT teams. Mike recommended the Second Chance brand Hardcorps 3 model with extra ballistic inserts. Unlike the relatively thin vest that Mike wore on a day-to-day basis while on police duty, these extra heavy vests would stop virtually every type of pistol or shotgun projectile. With luck, they could even stop some rifle bullets. The vests were not a panacea. They could only stop a high-power rifle bullet only if it stuck directly in the small trauma plate over the chest area. And they could do nothing, of course, to stop a head shot, groin shot, or disabling shot to a limb. However, the vests were better than nothing. Eventually five of these relatively expensive vests were bought by the Grays, the Nelsons, and Tom Kennedy. Most of the other group members promised to buy vests, but never got around to it.

Another piece of ballistic protection that was recommended was a helmet. In the mid-1980s, the U.S. Army started issuing a helmet for its ground troops that was molded out of woven Kevlar, the same material used in modern bulletproof vests. The new helmets were immediately nicknamed "Fritz helmets" by soldiers, because they had a lip that extended below the wearer's ears, reminiscent of the steel helmets worn by German soldiers in both of the world wars in the twentieth century. Like the vests, Kevlar helmets were expensive, so not all of the group members bought them. When they first came on the surplus market in the late eighties, they cost three-hundred-and-fifty dollars apiece. By 2002, the supply of surplus Kevlar helmets had increased to the point where their price on the civilian market dropped to roughly a hundred. Occasionally, they were found at gun shows or flea markets for even less.

Very early on in the development of the Group, the issue of exactly what scenario they were preparing for was raised. Most members were thinking in terms of banks runs and an economic collapse, followed by a general breakdown in law and order. Others leaned more toward nuclear, biological, or chemical warfare.

Dan Fong insisted that the main emphasis should be on preparedness for resistance following a takeover of the government by socialists, fascists, or communists. In the end it was decided that the group had best prepare for all conceivable scenarios, rather than just one. As Todd put it, "It would be kind of embarrassing to get ourselves all prepared for some big socioeconomic collapse, and then get nuked."

• • •

The only preparation that Todd's group made that they decided to keep an absolute secret was their purchase of blasting supplies and equipment. When Mike was doing research for his graduate work, it brought him into contact with a broad spectrum of loggers, farmers, and ranchers. One rancher that Mike met was Spence Loughran. Spence and his wife had a 640-acre spread twenty-five miles north of Moscow. Spence's ranch was used to both run cattle and harvest timber. When he first met him, Mike discovered that Spence was in the middle of a project blasting some stumps on his ranch, clearing a logged-over area for hay cutting.

Mike mentioned to Spence that he had an interest in explosives, and offered to help out. They had a great time, as they both liked to "see things blow up." By the end of the day, they were great friends. When Mike bemoaned the fact that there was an "ocean of paperwork to wade through" in getting set up with an explosives permit in Illinois, Spence offered to add Mike to his blaster's permit, listing him as an "employee." Five weeks later Mike got a copy of the updated permit in the mail, along with a copy of The Blaster's Handbook, which was crammed with safety information and useful tables. Loughran had inscribed its flyleaf, "Big City Boy: Move slow and use your noggin. God Bless, Spence."

During subsequent visits to northern Idaho before the Crunch, first on hunting trips with Lisa, and later to help out Todd and Mary with upgrading the retreat, Mike stopped by and visited with Spence and his wife. He also regularly went to do business with an explosives distributor in Spokane, Washington. With the permit supplied by Loughran, he was able to get everything that he needed. The first time at the distributor's shop, the owner was skeptical of Mike, as he had never met him before.

Just to be sure, the owner called Loughran to check on his identity. Loughran told him, "Heck yeah, Bob, I sent him over there! Now just give him everything that I had him put on the list of what to buy."

After hanging up the phone, the distributor cocked his head and said, "Well, you check out all right. What can I get you?" Mike breathed a silent sigh of relief.

On his first trip back to Idaho, Mike picked up a case of 75 percent dynamite and a reel of PETN detonating cord, often called primacord or simply "det. cord," and a pair of cap crimping pliers. On subsequent trips, Mike purchased electric and fuse type blasting caps, a small hand crank "blasting machine" generator for setting off electric blasting caps, thirty pounds of Composition 4 (C-4) plastic explosive, two additional cases of dynamite, and a twenty-pound roll of Dupont Detasheet C sheet explosive.

Eventually, all of these supplies were carefully transported from Mike and Lisa's to the retreat in Idaho. Mike gave the Grays specific instructions on storing the materials. The most important thing, he told them, was to store the caps and the bulk explosives at opposite ends of the basement. As long as the basement stayed cool and dry, and the dynamite was up off the floor, there would be no problem with deterioration.

One task that had to be done regularly was rotating the boxes of dynamite. Because Mike's dynamite was of the variety that had nitroglycerin suspended in diatomaceous earth, it was much more stable than the older variety that had nitroglycerin suspended in sawdust. However, there was still a slight risk that the nitroglycerin could settle and seep out of the casings of the individual sticks. To prevent this, it was simple enough to inspect a few of the sticks, and turn the cases upside down once every three months. So that they wouldn't lose track of this responsibility, Mary marked a circled red "R" for rotation day in her desk calendar at quarterly intervals.

CHAPTER 5
Squared Away

"Man's mind is his basic tool of survival."

—*Ayn Rand*

Dan and Mike helped Mary set up a bed for Rose next to the C.Q. desk. It seemed to be the logical location, since someone would be there to watch her condition around the clock. The only detractor was that everyone had to be especially quiet when they were in the front end of the house. Rose slept almost continuously for two days. Every four hours, whomever was on C.Q. duty woke her to give her dose of ampicillin and offer her something to eat or drink. She refused anything but water for the first eighteen hours, then she started drinking some juice. At four a.m. on the third morning, Rose sat up in bed and asked for some pancakes. T.K., who had C.Q. duty at the time, stepped over to the kitchen and filled her request. She was working on her fourth pancake and gulping down her second glass of orange juice when she asked, "Who are you?"

"My name's Kennedy, Tom Kennedy. Everybody calls me 'T.K.' I'm the personnel honcho around here."

"Oh, so *you're* T.K. I've heard Jeff talk about you. He said that you study ancient languages and that you're a Catholic minister."

He gave a half smile, and retorted, "That's not quite right, I'm only a lay minister. I helped give communion at mass. I'll be leading the daily Bible studies here."

"He also said that you're an awesome shot with a rifle."

"Well, gosh, 'awesome' is a superlative term I don't deserve, at least not among the serious shooting fraternity. By most people's standards, I guess I am an excellent shooter. I practice with an Anshutz .22 match rifle, my AR-15, and my M1 Garand at the range quite a bit. I also like to shoot in the quarterly competitive High Power matches."

Rose frowned. "You should start using the *past tense* when you're talking about things like that. From what we saw getting out of Illinois, there's total anarchy everywhere. Houses on fire or burned down. We went through some neighborhoods where there had been frame houses, and all that was left standing were the chimneys. Lots of bodies just littering the street. People looting stores. It looked like footage from Iraq."

After a pause she asked, "Are you going to let Jeff and me stay here? I mean, from what he told me, Jeff hasn't been a member of your group for a couple of years, and you've just *met* me."

T.K. stroked his chin. "I don't know. With an issue this big, it'll be up to a vote of the entire group."

As soon as Rose had eaten her fill of scrambled eggs and pancakes, T.K. went to wake up Jeff, who was asleep on the hide-a-bed sofa. "Hey, Trasel," he said, "There's a cute-looking gal with a tremendous appetite in the next room that I think would like to see you."

Later the same morning, the power went off. Everyone in the house immediately met in the dim gloom of the shuttered living room. None of them held out much hope of it being a temporary power failure. With an air of finality, Todd pronounced, "Well, that's it. I suppose that our clocks will be reading 10:17 for who knows how long. Months? Years? Maybe decades. From now on, we'll have to conserve power considerably. We do have a lot of power sources to charge the batteries though. We've got the solar panels, the Winco when it's windy, and our hand crank generator. Starting now, no one will use any more power than is absolutely necessary."

Todd went to the circuit breaker box in the utility room and toggled off most of the breakers. The only ones that he left on were the breakers for the inside power outlets. He then turned off the main breaker, disconnecting the house's circuits from the power main. He explained that if the power were to come back on unexpectedly with the inverter set up, it could cause some real fireworks. Then he switched on the Xantrex inverter—a device that turned 12 volts D.C. into 120 volts A.C.

Next, Todd went around the house unplugging the "nonessentials." This included the computer equipment in his office, and nearly all of the lamps. As he was unplugging his now-silent PC, Todd said, "Well now I'm glad that I didn't sink any money into that mega gighertz machine I was planning to buy."

The only lamps that he didn't unplug were five low-wattage bulbs located in the kitchen, in the bedrooms, and on the C.Q. desk in the living room. All five of these used Panasonic fifteen-watt compact fluorescent bulbs. Once their small supply of fluorescent bulbs ran out, Todd planned to rely on a set of light-bulb adapters that he had purchased from Real Goods in Hopland, California. These adapters screwed into a standard lamp socket. Within each was a "bayonet socket" that held twelve VDC automotive tail lamps. Todd predicted that there would soon be a lot of abandoned vehicles from which to procure spare tail lamps.

The only other electronic items that still had power were the shortwave radio, the police scanner, the CB base station, an alarm system, and the charger for small batteries. All four of these ran directly on twelve-volt power, rather than through the inverter. When he had unplugged the last of the unneeded items, Todd announced: "That should do it. If it turns out that the battery bank stays up at a reasonable level, then we'll reconnect things, one at a time. In the meantime, however, we'll just take the conservative approach. We'll be using the kerosene lamps to supplement the compact fluorescents from this point forward."

"Now I know why they called the last one of these little setbacks 'the Dark Ages,'" Mary offered, with a wry smile.

Todd called for a meeting during lunch. He posted Jeff on LP/OP duty during the meeting. Just before Jeff left to walk up the hill and relieve Lisa, Todd remarked: "I guess that you have already figured out why I want you away during the meeting. I just want you to know that you'll be getting my vote. Don't get your hopes up, however. The process for voting in new members hasn't changed. It's still just like at a fraternity. One black-ball, and that's all she wrote."

Jeff nodded stiffly. "I assure you that I'll pull my own weight around here. I'm sure that Rose will, too. She's a good little worker." With that, Jeff turned and left.

Kevin fried elk-burgers for everyone, using the last of the meat from the freezer, and some of the last of the store-bought bread. He seasoned the burgers with onion salt and teriyaki sauce. Todd began the formal part of the session with the words: "There are two purposes for calling this meeting. The first is to decide if Jeff and Rose, assuming that she recovers, can stay. The second is to get squared away with the operations of the retreat. On the first order of business, I want to let you all know that Jeff has promised me that if they are voted in, he and Rose will pull their share of the weight. To my way of thinking, the key questions are: First, do we really need their help? Second, can they be trusted to perform well, especially under stress? Third, can we afford the extra mouths to feed?"

The debate on Jeff and Rose went on for half an hour. In the course of the debate, Dan Fong, the only member who had kept in contact with Jeff regularly after he had left the group, was asked to bring everyone up to date with what had been happening with him during the interim. He recounted: "Jeff is still in the Marine Corps Reserve, and was still running and doing calisthenics three times a week to stay in shape. Right after he left the group, he got a job as a quality control inspector with Radian Corporation, working in their microwave tube division. He worked full-time for a year, then switched to part-time to go back to school. The last I heard, he had transferred from junior college to the University of Illinois. God knows how many credits he's accumulated by now. As most of you have heard, at last report, Jeff was still living at his parent's home."

Without pausing, Dan went on to brief the group on Rose's particulars: "Her last name is Creveling. She's young, only nineteen, maybe twenty. She was just starting her sophomore year at the University of Illinois—the Chicago Circle campus—when the Schumer hit the fan. She was majoring in advertising, but she hadn't started her upper-division courses yet. Jeff just met her last spring. They've been dating steadily ever since. Jeff told me that he was attracted to Rose because she seemed intelligent and was real outdoorsy. Skiing, backpacking, kayaking, that sort of thing. Trasel started teaching her how to shoot last summer. She's a Christian. Reformed Lutheran, I think. She's also a vegetarian. She doesn't eat meat or fish, but she does eat eggs, milk, and cheese. I really can't say that I know much more than that about her, except that Trasel told me that she came from a 'La-Ti-Dah' family in Aurora."

As the debate progressed, it became apparent that with the LP/OP, C.Q., and work schedule that they had planned, they would be shorthanded even with the help of Jeff and Rose, especially during the summer months. It was also clear that there would be plenty of food. The only remaining issues were their willingness to work, their loyalty, and their ability to handle stress. On the latter issue, all present were confident about Jeff, but Rose was an unknown. The issue of her vegetarianism was raised by T.K., who asked, "Does anyone feel that it will be a liability?" Mary piped up strongly in reply: "On the contrary, I think that she'll be better metabolically adjusted than we are, given the fact that our diet will be heavy on grains and legumes." Kennedy simply nodded in agreement.

The last major issue raised was by Lisa Nelson. She asked, "What about Rose's health? What if she doesn't fully recover from her wound?" Again, Mary spoke up on her behalf. "I'd like to say something on that. From what I've read, it's very unlikely that this kind of wound will leave her an invalid. I've been checking her wound three times a day. It is healing nicely. I've given her lots of antibiotics, and there is no sign of infection. Once she makes it past the stage she's in now, where there's risk of infection, her chances are pretty darned good, especially considering that she is young and has kept in good health. Past that, the biggest risk in the next few weeks is of a hemorrhage, and presumably we can keep her on very light duty while her tissues heal. In the long term, she'll probably feel some aches and pains, and at worst she may have a limited range of motion in her shoulder, but probably nothing that would make her a burden on the rest of the group."

When the discussion started winding down, T.K. suggested a paper ballot vote. When all of the votes were tallied a few minutes later, the vote was unanimous to bring both Jeff and Rose into the group. Following T.K.'s reading of the ballots, Todd again took the floor. He ran down his view of how things should be operated on a day-to-day basis at the retreat. There were few surprises in what he had to say. Most of what he said had been discussed at meetings before the Crunch, and much of it was already in written form in SOPs.

He began: "I've got to remind you of some ground rules. The LP/OP and the Charge-of-Quarters desk are to be manned continuously. No one quits their post unless properly relieved. We'll find some pretty disgusting chores— or worse—for anybody that we catch asleep on duty. One new item: to generate power to supplement the solar panels and wind generator, whomever is on C.Q. duty will turn the hand crank generator at least one hour out of each shift." With this comment, there were groans all around the table. Todd bit his lip and then added, "Just think of the great exercise we'll be getting. By next spring, we'll all look like Fiddler crabs."

Todd waited for the group to settle down, and then went on. "Next, we don't ever, ever walk out of the house unless we're armed. That means a .45 as a *minimum*, preferably a rifle or a riotgun. When you are working on something outside, you always keep your long gun within arm's reach.

"Nobody fires any weapon for target practice, test firing, pest shooting— any shooting at all—without the permission of the tac coordinator. The same goes for firing up a chain saw, the two-kilowatt generator, or anything else that has a noisy signature. Any trips outside the perimeter are to be treated as patrols, with a full combat load, an op. order, inspections and rehearsals, assigned rally points, the whole works.

"Next item of business: starting now, especially because the utility power is out, we have to keep full light, noise, and litter discipline. We don't want to be sticking out like a 'come loot me' beacon in the countryside at night. That means that the blackout blankets have to be in place before sunset every night. It will be the responsibility of whoever is on C.Q. duty to walk around the outside of the house to check for light leaks and make the necessary corrections. The same thing goes for up at the LP/OP. No flashlights without two thicknesses of red filters, and even then, you can only turn on a flashlight to consult a map or whatever with the flaps down over the gun ports. If you are outside and need to use a flashlight to examine a map or something, you do it under a poncho to block the light. Also, starting this afternoon, I want everybody in uniform whenever they go outdoors. No exceptions."

Todd had only a few more words before he opened the floor for discussion. "So much for all the macho stuff. Now down to some more mundane issues, such as, how are we going to handle the eating and sleeping arrangements?"

The discussion on these subjects went on for another half hour. It was decided that aside from meals eaten on picket duty, everyone would eat communally, albeit at different hours. Nominally, the food for any given day was to come out of the stored food of one individual, on a rotating basis. This worked out well, because most of the group members had stored similar, or in many cases, identical, foodstuffs.

Sleeping arrangements also worked out well, although things were as Mike described it, "A bit cozy." The group's three bachelors, T.K., Kevin, and Dan, were to share one of the bedrooms. The room had only two twin long size beds, but because of round-the-clock security shifts, they could "hot rack" them, as the Navy did on its submarines. The Grays would have a bedroom to themselves, while the Nelsons would have the other bedroom. Jeff and Rose, being low couple on the totem pole, got the basement. The hide-a-bed from the living room would be moved down for their use. The Laytons were the only missing part of the equation. It was decided that sleeping arrangements would be reorganized if and when they arrived.

Also in reference to the Laytons, Todd declared, "Last item of business: Assuming that they won't be arriving for a while, I'd like to temporarily assign Lisa with Terry's responsibilities as logistics coordinator. Does that sound agreeable?" There were nods all around the room.

"Very well then, Lisa is now the authority and final arbiter when it comes to 'beans, bullets, and Band-Aids.'"

After looking down at his boots for a moment, Gray added, "Oh yeah, I almost forgot to mention it, but for Rose's reference, and as a reminder to you all, we're now living a strict 'Conserver' lifestyle. We've got to make virtually everything we own last as long as possible. Just use common sense. For example, don't waste a drop of anything, use both sides of each sheet of paper, and then when it is completely filled, save it for kindling. All vegetable matter goes to the compost heap, and all meat scraps and bones not used in soups or stews go to Shona. All metals, including aluminum foil, will be washed if necessary, sorted, and stored in scrap bins. Basically this means that we are going to have virtually no 'trash.' We have to live as if each item we use is our last, because with no means of resupply on the horizon, the day will come when we really are out of some things. And under the present circumstances, that may be more serious than a little discomfort."

The next day, traveling in an armed convoy of four trucks, half of the group went to move out anything that might prove useful from Kevin's house. With six people working and one posted on security, the moving process lasted just under five hours. The bulkiest item was Kevin's set of photovoltaic panels. The entire solar tracker assembly, minus its support pole, was carried back sandwiched between a mattress and box spring in the bed of Todd's pickup. It was the only Power Wagon in the group that was not equipped with a camper shell. Todd would have liked to put the tracker back in action at the retreat, but he did not have any of the extra heavy Schedule 40 four-inch diameter galvanized steel pipe that was needed for a new support pole. Moving Kevin's support pole was out of the question. The lower three feet of the tracker pole was encased in a thirty-six-inch diameter cylinder of reinforced concrete.

When they got the array back to the retreat, they were able to get it hooked up in a series-parallel arrangement with the retreat's existing eight-panel array. Unfortunately, without a tracker pole, they had to make do and bolt the array up against the south side of the house at a forty-five-degree angle in a space between two windows. This at least provided 75 percent of the array's potential power, and Kevin's panels were safe from theft or vandalism during what looked like was going to be a prolonged absence from his home.

When Kevin's stocks of storage food were added to the rest stored in the basement, it made a considerable difference. In fact, there was scarcely enough room to walk around. After the gear from Kevin's was moved in, Todd asked Lisa to coordinate an inventory of all the expendable items that the group members had brought with them, including food, ammunition, and fuel. Lisa was told not to bother doing another inventory on their pre-positioned stocks, as Todd had been keeping up running inventories of these all along. Lisa asked for everyone to give her their inventories by 8 p.m.

In order to meet this deadline, Mike, who was on picket duty, had to dictate his inventory to the C.Q. over the field telephone. That evening, Todd and Lisa sat down with the inventory sheets and made some rough calculations. They were surprised at the results. Todd called for yet another meeting early the next day.

The meeting was held in the living room so that Rose could listen in without having to get out of bed. Todd began by reading from a written report that he and Lisa had prepared the evening before. "Assuming that Ken and Terry make it here safely, and nobody's granny decides to show up, we'll have a total of eleven people to support at the retreat. Also, assuming a normal diet, our combined stored food will last about 1,140 days." On hearing that point, Jeff Trasel let out a loud whistle of descending pitch.

After the interruption, Todd went on. "If put on a more stringent diet with fewer calories, the supply could be stretched to last more than 1,700 days. Furthermore, this figure does not take into account any food that could be grown in our garden, or Camas bulbs or Bitterroot bulbs that we go out and dig, or game that we shoot or trap. And further still, there's plenty of water available to expand our garden's present capacity. The only constraint on expanding the garden would be fencing materials to keep the local deer population from wiping out our garden."

At this juncture, Kevin spoke up. "I've noticed that the locals around here all fence their gardens, but they don't bother fencing their corn patches. Couldn't we do the same thing? All we have to do is cultivate another plot the size of the garden and we could have a great stand of corn."

Todd gave a thumbs-up sign and replied, "Your point is well taken. Thanks, Kevin." After stopping to look around the room, Todd explained, "We planned our food needs pretty well. We even socked away four hundred pounds of kibble for Shona. Once that is gone, she'll have to make do on meat scraps. As for ammunition, we are in excellent shape—in all nearly 300,000 rounds, almost half of which is .22-rimfire. I won't give a detailed list. Suffice it to say that we have plenty of ammunition. Assuming that ammunition will become the first recognizable form of currency when society starts to rebuild, consider yourselves filthy rich. Joe Schmo on the street probably only has a couple of hundred rounds on hand, on average."

Lisa cut in. "Most of our calculations last night concerned fuel. There are currently a little over fourteen cords of firewood on hand. What can I say— Todd really likes cutting and splitting wood. Each summer, he cut twice as much as he needed. Given winters with normal temperatures, this supply could be enough to last at least three years. Of course, more wood can always be cut next summer and the summers thereafter. When the gasoline for the chain saws is either used up or has broken down too far to be usable, we can always use the hand two-man saws. That reminds me. We'll have to find one of the old-timers around Bovill to teach how to set and sharpen those saws. It's an almost lost art.

"The category of fuel that I am most concerned about is liquid fuels. Our diesel storage tank is presently almost full—about nine hundred gallons. It has been stabilized, and it has been treated with an antibacterial. You've all heard this before, but for Rose's benefit, I'll repeat it. The basic rule for fuel storage is: the more highly refined the fuel, the shorter its storage life. That means that kerosene will store for fifteen years or more, diesel stores for eight to ten years, and gasoline normally has only about a two-year storage life. Beyond that, it builds up gums and peroxides, and suffers decomposition of anti-knock compounds to the point that fuel filters clog up and engines won't run. Also, the butane that is added to gasoline tends to evaporate. Once the butane burns off, starting an engine can be hard. You usually have to use a squirt of ether down the carb.

"In general, high temperatures and exposure to oxygen encourage the decomposition process. Stored fuel also tends to attract moisture, and that causes a whole 'nother set of problems. The storage life of all liquid fuels can be extended by the use of a special additive called Sta-Bil that delays the decomposition process, and we have plenty of that on hand. Overall, the best way to store fuel is in a completely full, sealed underground container."

Todd picked up a beat later, "For our tractor, which is the only vehicle with a diesel engine, let's assume that we have about a ten-year supply of fuel. I was planning to buy a diesel-powered pickup, but I never found one at a reasonable price. In retrospect, I should have made that a much higher priority. We'll only be using the tractor for tilling and towing the trailer we use for hay and firewood. So for all intents and purposes, let's assume we have plenty of diesel, unless this turns out to be one of those major whammy multigenerational scenarios that we've talked about.

"Gasoline, however, is probably going to be more of a problem. Our tank filled with premium unleaded is just under half full—about four hundred to four-hundred-and-twenty gallons. There's another eighty-two gallons of various grades of gas in cans, and roughly sixty gallons in the fuel tanks of the various vehicles. All of the fuel in the underground storage tank has a stabilizer added to it, and is pretty well sealed against moisture, so I'm issuing a directive right here and now that the fuel in cans will be used first. We'll probably be doing very little driving around the retreat, aside from wood and compost hauling. Therefore, most of the gasoline can be saved for use in chain saws or the Weed-Eater, or the occasional times that we have to fire up the gas-powered generator to provide power for larger electric tools such as drills, the Skilsaw, or the table saw. With gasoline, our problem is going to be storage life, not the total quantity we have stored. Even with stabilizer, we cannot depend on having reliable gasoline beyond five or six years. Hopefully, by then things will be back to normal.

"By far, our biggest headache is kerosene. Even though it stores quite well, there's not enough of it. Mary and I only had four gallons of kerosene of our own stored here. Of the rest of the group, only T.K. thought to pre-position any, and that was only three one-gallon cans. Only two additional gallons were brought by those of you who recently arrived and we found about half of a one-gallon can at Kevin's yesterday. Mary and I had planned to buy several twenty-gallon drums of kerosene, but we never got around to it, with so much else going on in fixing up the retreat. Oh well, like they say, 'hindsight is 20-20.' The bottom line is that we are going to have to be very, very conservative in using kerosene lamps, and we cannot run Mike and Lisa's Kerosun space heater at all, unless there's an emergency or some special occasion."

Lisa raised her hand and chimed in, "Well, Todd, that makes kerosene our highest priority for bartering, assuming that we find someone to barter with. Perhaps we can either trade some gasoline or some ammunition for kerosene. Otherwise, even with minimal use, we'll probably be out of kerosene within at most three years."

Todd nodded his head to the affirmative. "Very well. Unless there are any questions, that pretty well covers it for critical logistics. We are in good shape on all of the other categories, like medical supplies, batteries, toilet paper, clothing, camouflage face paint sticks, distilled water for the storage batteries, insect repellent, ladies' supplies, and condoms."

Rose giggled after hearing Todd's last comment.

Lisa eyed Rose and offered, "I think that as time goes on, aside from the odd glitch like the kerosene, you'll find that we thought out what we would need very carefully and thoroughly right down to the last diaper pin."

Just then, Todd felt a cold, wet nose touch his elbow. He shouted, "Now who let Shona in?"

Lisa said weakly, "I'm afraid I did."

Todd gave Lisa a scowl and said, "One more point of clarification. Shona has a job to do just like the rest of us. Her job is to secure the area inside the chain-link fence, and give warning of anything she detects is amiss within range of her eyes, ears, or nose. Basically, she operates as a backup for the LP/OP, and as such, she's part of our life insurance. Please resist the urge to spoil her. She is not to be let into the house again. Period. Don't worry if it's cold outside. Shona is used to it. She has a nice snug and warm insulated doghouse that I built for her. It's okay if you give her the occasional pet or pat her on the head, but please remember that she's a working bitch."

After letting Shona back outside and giving her a scratch under her collar and a pat on the head, Todd walked back in and carried on with his agenda. "The next item of business is our duty schedule. I think that Mike is much better qualified to brief this subject."

With that, Todd sat down, and Mike stood up and cleared his throat. "Okay, here's the rundown on the duty sked. Both picket and C.Q. shifts are six hours long and are on a semi-rotating basis. That means that once you get assigned a block of time, say 0700 to 1300, you can always depend on having the same shift. Because there are nine of us here, everybody should have either C.Q. or LP/OP duty once a day. Security is always the priority, so work schedules will be made around the picket and C.Q. sked, rather than vice versa. I tried to set the shifts based on my past experience with you during field exercises. Kevin and I, for example, are night owls by nature, so we will almost always have the swing or graveyard shift. So will you, Jeff. Not so much because you are a late sleeper, but because your night vision is only one notch below Kevin's, and, as everybody here except Rose already knows, Kevin's night eyes are pretty phenomenal.

"Okay. I'll be posting copies of the sked at both the LP/OP, and at the C.Q. desk. That way, nobody can plead ignorance as an excuse for not showing up to relieve somebody on time. I'm going to have to insist that we stick to the rule in the SOP that only the tac coordinator has the authority to make changes to the sked. If two of you mutually agree to occasionally swap a shift, okay. But let's not make a habit of it, and once again, every change has to be specifically approved by me, and well in advance. That's the only way we can keep the sked from disintegrating into chaos. Also, I cannot overemphasize that when you are on either LP/OP or C.Q. duty, your main job is to keep your counterpart awake and alert. Call each other on the field phone at least once each half hour. That's all I have to say. Any questions? Okay, I'm done."

Mike sat down abruptly and Todd again took his feet and said, "The last item of business that I had planned also has to do with security, in a way. That item is our vehicles. In case you haven't noticed, our gravel turn-around circle out there looks like a used car lot. To my way of thinking, the only vehicles that we will be likely to use right here at the retreat are the pickups and the tractor, primarily for hauling hay and firewood. We have room to store three vehicles in a row in the garage, so I'd like to put T.K.'s Bronco up on blocks or jack stands in the back, Mike's Power Wagon in the middle—also on blocks, to make the tires last longer—and my Power Wagon in the front. Because it doesn't have a camper shell, it seems to be the handiest vehicle for hauling things. We should keep all three of these vehicles topped off with stabilized fuel at all times. As for the tractor, we'll park it in the end of the woodshed for the time being. When we cut more wood and fill that overgrown woodshed, probably late next spring, we'll make other parking arrangements.

"As for the other vehicles, I think that we should drive them all out under the cover of the trees in the wood lot. The ground is frozen solid in the mornings this time of year, and it's relatively level so we won't have any problems getting even the two-wheel-drive rigs back there. I'd like to get them as far back into the woods as possible. We'll cover the shot-out windows on Dan's Toyota with sheet plastic to keep the rain out. The windshield area will also have to be covered with plywood or whatnot, otherwise snow will just pile up and push in the Visqueen.

"I also want you to cover all the exposed glass on your vehicles with burlap sacks to stop reflections. We have a large supply of burlap sacks, so we can cover all the glass. We also have a lot of olive drab duct tape, so go ahead and tape over all of your reflectors and turn signal plastic. You can either take off or tape over your license plates since they reflect too. I also have several cans of flat black spray paint and rolls of masking tape that you can use for blacking out any residual chrome plated pieces. For any vehicle that might have its outline show from the road, we'll cover it with a camouflage net held up by spreaders or hung from tree limbs. Once we have these vehicles parked, we'll drain their gas tanks into cans, disconnect their batteries, drain their radiators, and put them up on blocks." There were a few sour looks at Todd's last suggestion. "I knew that this wouldn't be a popular decision, but we just don't have the storage space, and it's a security risk having all those cars out in plain view."

All around the room, heads nodded in agreement.

"Is there any other new or old business?" Todd asked.

Lisa raised her hand. "I just want to remind everyone about the importance of brushing and flossing our teeth after every meal. Mary bought two of those Navy surplus monster rolls of floss. And we have a considerable supply of salt and baking soda for once the toothpaste runs out. We have absolutely got to be conscientious about this. Without a dentist here, the best we can do is to replace a filling that falls out, and we only have the weaker temporary-type filling compound for that. The only other option is pulling teeth. Enough said."

After seeing that she was done, Dan Fong raised his hand and remarked, "Boss, I have an item, too. I'd like to see everyone that owns an AR-15 or CAR-15 in the back bedroom after lunch."

After the meeting, Jeff lingered by Rose's bed. "Is that the way the meetings usually go?" Rose asked.

"Yep, Todd pretty well calls the shots except for tactical things, where he used to depend on me, and now defers to Mike. Luckily, Todd has a good head on his shoulders, and has sound judgment. Also, I've never known him to hold a grudge."

"How did the group get set up like this? Isn't it a bit autocratic?"

"Well, I'll tell you, Rose, ten years or more ago, when they first set up the Group, they tried running it with votes on every issue. They realized that that was fine in peacetime. The only detractor was that it slowed some meetings down to a snail's pace. But in times like these, what we need are firm, prompt orders, and no messing around. One-man-one-vote and endless debate just doesn't cut it in a survival situation."

Meanwhile, T.K., Mary, and Lisa showed up to meet with Dan, just as he had asked. "Go ahead, take a seat there," Dan said, pointing to the rumpled bed. They all had curious expressions. Dan held up a milled block of metal just over an inch long and articulated, "This is a drop-in auto-sear. I'm sure that at least one or two of you have heard of these. They're illegal as all get out, but under the current circumstances, I don't think that the Bureau of Alcohol, Tobacco, and Firearms is likely to send anyone out to investigate if somebody hears a gun get a bit hyperactive here at the retreat."

A smile widened across T.K.'s face. Mary and Lisa still looked puzzled. Dan carried on with his lecture. "There was a neat loophole in the law. Machineguns were of course tightly restricted in the Federal United States, subject to a two-hundred-dollar transfer tax. They have been taxed this way ever since the National Firearms Act got passed in 1934. There are also some separate laws in some states that require registration of full autos, and in some cases an absolute ban.

"After about 1981, some full auto conversion parts like auto-sears themselves also became illegal. However, a loophole existed for a few years that allowed people to sell auto-sear component parts 'for repair or replacement purposes only.' In fact, there was at least one outfit that sold 'repair' auto-sear bases, and another that sold 'repair' auto-sear springs, cams, and pins. Just by 'coincidence,' these two businesses were located only a few miles apart. For a couple of years, these guys did a brisk business. I actually bought these a few years after that loophole closed. These were manufactured before the McClure-Volkmer law was signed, so they were grandfathered under a different loophole.

"I got mine the same way that Kevin got the bastard crystals for our Trick five hundreds. I used a drop box using a false ID that I worked up, just so I wouldn't get caught. Because I knew that the loophole would eventually be closed, I took the opportunity to buy six of them. They cost me one-hundred-seventy-five dollars each." Now, all three of Dan's guests were grinning.

"An auto-sear is a key part in converting an AR-15 or CAR-15 to selective fire. It means that instead of having a two-position selector switch—SAFE and FIRE—you have a three-position switch—SAFE, SEMI, and AUTO. The D.I.A.S. can't do this all by itself, though. You also need an M16 bolt carrier and a set of M16 lower-receiver internal parts. Now all of you already have early model hard-chromed M16 carriers in your ARs. That was part of the group standard set of upgrades. As you recall, I once insisted that we standardize with the chrome carriers, tritium front sights, and the five-slot closed cage M16A2 flash hiders.

"Just after I got the auto-sears, I also bought six sets of M16 lower-receiver parts at a gun show. At that time these parts were only about one hundred dollars for the full set. In recent years, BATFE agents have even been hassling people who they've caught with just a few of the lower-receiver parts. Those 'F Troop' guys don't cut any slack.

"I never told anybody about the M16 lower-receiver parts sets or about the auto-sears.

"I didn't want to get into any big arguments about legalities, or whether it's right to obey a law that is contrary to the Constitution—you know, the Marbury versus Madison decision, and all that. Also, I didn't want to put Mikey into one of those 'police officer's moral dilemma' tizzies. Soooo, I just tucked them away in a wall cache, saving them for a rainy day. Needless to say, we got our rainy day. In case you haven't noticed, there's a freakin' Wagnerian thunderstorm out there, at least in the big cities.

"Soooo, here you go. I've got an auto-sear and a set of lower-receiver parts to give to each of you. I've already put one in my AR-15. After you install yours, that leaves two more sets. I'll be saving one for when Terry Layton gets up here. As for the sixth and last set—well, I guess it will make one *fine* barter item.

"Now, I'm also giving you some advice along with these marvels of innovative machining. Number one: don't think that just because you have the potential to rock-'n-roll that you're an instant Rambo. That's a mistake that could be fatal. Remember that the best practical use of full auto is at very close range, versus multiple opponents. Even then, don't use it like a garden hose. If you do, you'll just be wasting precious ammo, and probably missing more than you are hitting. Stick with short, controlled bursts. Three to five rounds at the most."

After a brief pause for his last statement to sink in, Dan continued, "Number two: Don't even think about switching to the 'group therapy' mode unless your targets are at thirty yards or less. Beyond that range, well aimed semi-auto shots will be much more effective. One more thing: If you are in a large-scale firefight and start shooting full auto, guess who the bad guys are going to concentrate their fire on?" Dan tilted his head and raised an eyebrow for emphasis. Then he concluded, "Well, that's basically it. I'll get together with each of you individually on how to swap out the lower-receiver parts and install the auto-sears."

After they had cracked a few jokes, Lisa, Mary, and T.K. walked out of the back bedroom, Ziploc bags in hand, wearing conspiratorial grins.

• • •

Aside from the term "group standard," the other term used most often at group meetings was "case lot." Before the Crunch, the group bought as many items as it could in bulk, and in many cases directly from their packagers and manufacturers. This included not just storage food but also many others, including ammunition, bandages, and nickel cadmium ("ni-cad") rechargeable batteries. In the long run, buying items in case lots instead of in "onesies and twosies" saved the group thousands of dollars. Gun and ammunition purchases were handled by Dan Fong, who had obtained a Federal Firearms License (FFL) as soon as he turned twenty-one. The FFL allowed Dan to order guns through the mail from distributors at dealer's cost. This too saved the group a lot of money, as it eliminated the 30 to 60 percent markup normally charged by gun dealers with storefront operations.

Most large quantity purchases were coordinated by Terry Layton. Often, the Laytons' garage looked more like a warehouse than a place to park their cars. At one point, nearly half the garage was stacked from floor to ceiling with cases of military MRE field rations. Terry wondered what the neighbors thought of all of these goings-on, but she was never questioned by them.

Like many survivalist groups, Todd's group was faced with a seemingly insolvable quandary. Nearly all of the group members wanted to move to a safe haven, but there were virtually no prospects of finding work in their chosen professions in a remote, agrarian area like north central Idaho. Eventually, only the Grays and Kevin Lendel were able to make the move. In their cases, this was only possible because they were able to work at home with an out-of-state income. The rest of the group members kept their G.O.O.D. backpacks packed, and their jerry cans of gasoline full and frequently rotated. They also took advantage of the Grays' offer to "pre-position" most of their survival supplies at the retreat. Todd and Mary had left most of the basement of their farmhouse largely empty for just this purpose.

During the course of the first two years after they bought their home near Bovill, the basement was gradually filled. Aside from the bulkier items such as five-gallon plastic buckets filled with grain, rice, beans, and powdered milk, most of the group members' supplies were stored in G.I. surplus wall lockers that Mike Nelson found on sale at Ruvel's Surplus on West Belmont Avenue in Chicago. Todd gave all of the group members the option of putting padlocks on their lockers if they preferred. By the turn of the century, all of the outer walls of the basement were lined with wall lockers. Much of the center of the basement was tiled with wooden pallets and heaped with the more bulky supplies such as five-gallon grain buckets, camouflage nets, and tan plastic five-gallon G.I. water cans. Each container was marked with an Avery label with the owner's name, date of purchase, and the anticipated expiration.

Having to traverse nearly sixteen hundred miles to get to their retreat was a less than ideal situation for the members of the Group. Under the circumstances, however, it was the best that they could do. All that they could do was hope for the best, and watch the newspapers very carefully.

CHAPTER 6
Lawyers, Guns, and Money

"The evils of tyranny are rarely seen but by him who resists it."

—*John Hay, Castilian Days II, 1872*

Matt and Chase Keane made their way back to eastern Washington shortly after the dollar collapsed. Unlike most other Americans, the Crunch was a relief to them. The anarchy spreading across the nation was their chance to go home with little fear of arrest. Four years earlier, the Keanes had a shoot-out with a North Carolina state trooper and a Randolph County sheriff's deputy, and only minutes after, another one with an Asheboro police officer. Those events would irreparably change their lives.

• • •

Before the shoot-outs, the Keanes had made their living as traveling gun show dealers and day laborers. They were both intelligent and hard-working young men. They could have made good salaries in Spokane Valley industry, but they refused to apply for Social Security numbers. This limited them to self-employment or occasional short-term jobs where they could work for cash. Between gun shows they built stock fences, cut and hauled firewood, worked at a brickyard, ran combines at harvest time, and bucked hay.

Matt and Chase were dyed-in-the-wool conservatives. Like many other conservatives, they felt that the Waco and Ruby Ridge incidents were nothing short of government massacres of law-abiding Christians who just wanted to be left alone. They thought that the Brady Law requiring a waiting period on handguns was a farce. They considered the Omnibus Crime Bill of 1994—which banned the manufacture of so-called "assault rifles" and magazines over ten-round capacity—absolutely unconstitutional. They were relieved when the law "sunsetted" in 2004, but were then horrified by the election of Barack Obama, and the threat of the onerous law being reinstated.

The Keanes derided the unconstitutional policies and legislation that came out of Washington, D.C. They referred to D.C. as "the District of Criminals" or "the District of Chaldeans." The Keanes hated Washington, D.C. career politicians. They also hated the BATFE and the FBI. They had grown up admiring the FBI, but eventually despised it. The agency had been totally politicized, corrupted, and purged of any agents not loyal to the D.C. careerists. Even its world-famous crime lab was caught fabricating evidence, as in the Lockerbie bombing case. They were convinced that the Oklahoma City bombing was a government setup. There was too much evidence pointing to *two* bomb blasts in rapid succession, one of which must have been *inside* the Alfred P. Murrah Federal Building. There was also strong evidence that the ATF had prior knowledge that the explosions were going to occur.

The Keanes concluded that the OKC bombing was a government sting operation, much like the previous World Trade Center bombing. In that incident, an undercover agent gave the terrorists detailed instructions on how to construct the bomb, helped supply materials, and even gave driving lessons to the recently immigrated terrorists, so that they could get the truck to its target.

The Keanes were convinced that in the Oklahoma City case, FBI under-cover agents were again co-conspirators. For some reason, just as in the World Trade Center case, they did not make their arrests until *after* the bombing. The Keanes concluded that the FBI had become so politicized and so ruthless that it was willing to sacrifice the lives of hundreds of citizens for the political "big score." They considered Timothy McVeigh and Terry Nichols "little fish" and patsies. They knew that the Federal government had intentionally avoided tracking down and convicting "John Does" number two through seven, and had quickly ordered the demolition of what was left of the Murrah building to destroy evidence of bomb blasts inside the building. At least one of those John Does, they concluded, was on the Federal payroll.

The brothers had a number of minor scrapes with the law, mainly over traffic citations. Matt rarely carried a driver's license, and more often than not, he owned cars that had not been re-registered with the state of Washington into his name. As far as he was concerned, a valid bill of sale was all that he needed to prove that the car was his property under common law. He once told his friend Dave, "If you read the state vehicle code, it doesn't say a word about privately owned automobiles. It only pertains to commercial *vehicles*, operating in *commerce*. People are tricked by the authorities into thinking that all these laws pertain to them, but they don't. A 'motor vehicle' is used for commerce, using the privilege to *drive* on the highway. That means carrying commercial goods under a bill of lading, or paying passengers. If it is just you and your *guests*—not 'passengers' mind you—*traveling*, then you are exercising your right of locomotion on the right of way rather than using the privilege to drive. That's an important distinction that most people don't grasp, and that these statutory jurisdiction kangaroo courts rarely recognize."

Both of the Keanes and their younger sister had been homeschooled. Once they had mastered the "three Rs," their parents let them do independent study. The youngest, Eileen, wanted to be a veterinarian. She worked part-time as an assistant at a local vet clinic. Chase was interested in music. He took guitar, violin, and piano classes. Matt was fascinated by the legal system, so he spent nearly two full years commuting with his father to downtown Spokane. Each day his father dropped him off with a sack lunch at the county law library, and picked him up each evening. This began when he was sixteen years old. Seeing that Matt was genuinely interested, one of the librarians immediately took Matt under her wing. She started him off with a copy of *Legal Research* by Stephen Elias, and *Black's Law Dictionary*. Most of the lawyers that saw Matt using the library assumed that he was a law clerk or a paralegal researcher. Matt dug into his law research with gusto. He was gifted with a photographic memory. Within a few weeks he was reciting the names and key points of cases verbatim. He had been doing the same with Bible verses since he was a child.

Matt and Chase were accused of selling firearms without a Federal Firearms License (FFL) three different times: twice by other dealers, and once by a gun show promoter. It was true that neither of them had a license, but they didn't see the need for one. Matt had researched the Federal gun laws in detail. In 2007, the promoter of an Oregon show came by the Keanes' tables and asked Matt casually, "Are you selling a private collection, or do you have an FFL?" The term "private collection" was the standard gun show euphemism for a table rented by someone who sold modern guns without a license. Matt replied frankly, "Sir, I am indeed a full-time gun seller, but I don't have an FFL."

The promoter replied huffily, "Well, if you're 'engaged in the business,' then you are required by law to get an FFL." When the promoter quoted the "engaged in the business" phrase from the Federal law, it was enough to get Matt going. For the next five minutes, the promoter sat in stunned silence as the young man lectured him about the inapplicability of Federal gun laws to state Citizens. Matt began, "Now sir, I'm going to explain some terms and applicability of laws, as I understand them, and please hear me out.

"Now this is what I've learned: Both the National Firearms Act of 1934—the NFA—and the Gun Control Act of 1968—the GCA—are deliberately deceptive, making millions of Sovereign Citizens unwittingly and needlessly subject to a false jurisdiction. Both laws indicate that they are applicable 'within the United States,' for 'interstate or foreign commerce' unless otherwise excluded by law. Further, these laws define the 'United States' to *include* the District of Columbia, the Commonwealth of Puerto Rico, and possessions of the United States. This corresponds to the 'exclusive jurisdiction' as defined in Article 1, Section 8, clauses 17 and 18 of the Constitution.

"If you refer to Public Law 99-308, Chapter 44, section 921(a) (2) which reads: 'The term *interstate or foreign commerce* includes commerce between any place in a State and any place outside of that State, or within any possession of the United States (not including the Canal Zone) or the District of Columbia, but such term does not include commerce between places within that same State but through any place outside that State. The term *State includes* the District of Columbia, the Commonwealth of Puerto Rico, and the possessions of the United States (not including the Canal Zone.)'"

A small crowd of curious onlookers began to gradually gather around Matt's tables when they heard him rattle off the legal citations in a loud voice.

"Based upon my research, it is my understanding that the term *includes* restricts rather than expands a definition. This was clearly established in a large body of State and Federal cases, such as *Montello Salt Co. v. Utah*, 221 U.S., 452 at 466, and in Treasury Decision Number 3980 Volume 29, of 1927. That one said that 'includes' means to 'comprise as a member,' 'to confine,' and 'to comprise as the whole part.' If 'includes' meant an incomplete list of examples, such as in the common vernacular use of the term, then Congress would have certainly used the phrase 'including *but not limited to...*' or something similar.

"In the strict Federal legal definition—the so-called 'black letter law'—of the word, as opposed to common interpretation, if something is not 'included,' then it is *excluded*!

"Since the term *includes* is one of strict definition, when lawmakers wish to temporarily supersede that definition for the purposes of an individual section or paragraph, they often use the word *means*. To illustrate this, I quote Internal Revenue Code section 6103(b)(5)(a) in which Congress temporally expanded (*'for the purposes of this section'*) the term *State* to encompass the fifty States: 'The term 'State' *means* any of the 50 States, the District of Columbia, the Commonwealth of Puerto Rico, the [U.S.] Virgin Islands, the Canal Zone, Guam, American Samoa....'

"Now by 'possessions' I assume that NFA and GCA both refer to the U.S. Virgin Islands, Guam, and American Samoa, as well as certain Federal enclaves *within* the fifty Sovereign States, such as Federal military forts, dockyards, et cetera. Clearly, the fifty Sovereign States are not 'possessions' of the Federal United States. The nature of the possessions of the Federal United States is described in Art. 1, Sect. 8, clauses 17 and 18 of the Constitution. So the bottom line is that Federal jurisdiction in no way extends to individual Citizens of the fifty Sovereign States and Commonwealths!

"Now sir, I fully understand that the definitions included in a number of Federal regulations concerning firearms (such as Title 27) amplify the terms *includes* and *including* to 'not exclude other things not enumerated which are in the same general class or are otherwise within the scope thereof.' However, the fifty Sovereign Union States are not by any stretch of the imagination in the same *class* as Federal 'States' such as the Commonwealth of Puerto Rico or other federal possessions. They are not the possessions of the U.S. Federal government, but rather have their own distinct sovereignty, and their respective systems of laws and legal jurisdictions."

The promoter scratched his head and opened his mouth, but Matt went on before the man had a chance to comment. Keane added, "Now if you have any doubt about my reasoning, I should point out that the Territories of Hawaii and Alaska were both originally listed as territories included in the Federal United States, but they were removed in the new versions of the U.S. Code that were published after they became Sovereign Union States."

The crowd around the table was growing larger. Matt paused, waiting for his words to sink in. The promoter said nothing, so he went on. "Anyone who is not a citizen or legal resident of the Federal United States should be exempt from any requirement to obtain a Federal Firearms License to conduct intrastate commerce or commerce between any other of the fifty Sovereign States. The only exception would be if someone were to do business with, say, for example, an individual or Federally licensed dealer in Puerto Rico or the District of Columbia or some other Federal 'State' as defined in the NFA and GCA.

"Now here's the kicker. It's not *just* the Federal *gun laws* that are written this way. Nearly all the Federal laws apply only in the 'District of Criminals' and the Federal Territories. Only a few laws regarding the Postal Service, the Patent Office, and espionage apply in the fifty states. Except for those few laws, the Federal laws don't apply to state Citizens or carry true force of law within the states. So when you see these ninja-suited Federal alphabet soup agency boys running around the fifty states, collecting taxes, arresting people, levying fines, burning down churches, and shooting nursing mothers in the head; guess what? *They're outside their jurisdiction.*

"Now here are some other cases you might want to ponder: 'It is a well established principle of law that all federal legislation applies only within the territorial jurisdiction of the United States unless a contrary intent appears.' That's from *Foley Brothers Inc. v. Filardo,* 336 U.S. 281.

"'The laws of Congress in respect to those matters'—*that is those outside of those Constitutionally delegated powers*—'do not extend into the territorial limits of the states, but have force only in the District of Columbia, and other places that are within the exclusive jurisdiction of the national government.' That's from *Caha v. U.S.,* 152 U.S. 211.

"'Since in common usage, the term *person* does not include the sovereign, statutes not employing the phrase are ordinarily construed to exclude it.' That's from *U.S. v. Fox*, 94 U.S. 315."

The show promoter began nodding his head repeatedly. Matt carried on. "'Because of what appears to be a lawful command on the surface, many Citizens, because of respect for the law, are cunningly coerced into waiving their rights, due to ignorance.' That's from *U.S. v. Minker*, 350 U.S. 179 187."

"'Waivers of Constitutional rights not only must be voluntary, they must be knowingly intelligent acts, done with sufficient awareness of the relevant circumstances and consequences.' That's from *Brady v. U.S.,* 397 U.S. 742 at 748."

"'The words 'People of the United States' and 'citizens' are synonymous terms, and mean the same thing. They both describe the political body who, according to our republican institutions, form the sovereignty... They are what we familiarly call the 'sovereign people,' and every citizen is one of this people, and a constituent member of the sovereignty.' That's from Wong Kim Ark, quoting the *Dred Scott v. Sanford* decision.

"'Under our form of government, the legislature is not supreme. It is only one of the organs of that absolute sovereignty which resides in the whole body of the People; like other bodies of the government, it can only exercise such powers as have been delegated to it, and when it steps beyond that boundary, its acts are utterly void.' That's from *Billings v. Hall.*

"And last but not least: 'All laws which are repugnant to the Constitution are null and void.' That's from *Marbury v. Madison,* 5 U.S. 137, 176." With that, Matt sat down on the edge of one of his rented tables and folded his hands. The crowd that had gathered applauded. The promoter walked away speechless and red-faced.

One of the men from the crowd stepped up to shake Matt's hand and said, "I wish I had that one on tape. What are you, an attorney?"

"No sir. I'm just a private Citizen that spends far too much time in law libraries."

• • •

Four years before the Crunch, Matt was twenty-four years old. His brother had just turned twenty. On a chilly February evening, Matt and Chase were on their way back from the Charlotte, North Carolina, gun show in Matt's light blue 1987 Ford van. The Keanes had had a good show. They had sold seven guns, and bought two. They also nearly sold out of their small remaining inventory of magazines, knowing that magazine prices would collapse following the sunset of the 1994 Federal law. So instead of selling magazines to supplement their gun sales, the Keanes switched to selling web gear, gas masks, first-aid gear, bulletproof vests, police and military memorabilia, and ammunition. They had the majority of their gun show inventory in the back of the van. The rest of it was in Chase's aging Dodge Executive motor home.

They had left the gun show promptly at five on Saturday, as was their habit. Unlike most dealers, they did not operate their tables on Sunday. The Keanes refused to buy or sell on the Lord's Day. This often angered the gun show organizers, who didn't like seeing bare tables on Sunday. But they stood firm. They just quoted the scripture, "Remember the Sabbath day, to keep it holy. Exodus 20, verse 8."

On Friday morning, they had left Chase's motor home at the campground where Chase was working temporarily, near Greensboro. Chase had worked out a barter deal where he could have a free space for his motor home and free laundry room privileges in exchange for picking up trash, cleaning the laundry room, spreading sand on icy mornings, and helping travelers use the septic dump station. The latter was the campground owner's least favorite job. He was happy to find someone willing to do it and not ask for wages in return.

On their way back from the gun show, Matt was driving. He was wearing his trademark black BDU cap—the one that Chase jokingly referred to as "that Sarah Conner cap." Just before they reached the city of Asheboro, sixty miles southeast of Greensboro, Matt noticed that they were being followed by a North Carolina state trooper. The car paced them for several minutes. This made Matt nervous. "They probably don't like the look of our Washington plates."

Chase muttered, "We should have registered the van and brought the tags up to date before we left on this trip. They've got no sense of humor about expired tags here in these 'miscellaneous eastern states.'"

Matt replied with his oft-quoted catchphrase, "But we're not *driving*, little brother. We're locomoting on a right-of-way. I'm not a driver. I'm a traveler. Traveling is a right, but driving is a privilege. Why should I register this van for commerce, when...." Just then, the trooper turned on the cruiser's light bar. Matt declared, "Oh mercy's sake. Another ticket. Swell. There goes a good chunk of today's profit. Time to render unto Caesar." He waited until there was a wide spot in the road, and pulled off onto the shoulder. The cruiser stopped five yards behind the van.

The trooper didn't approach immediately, which made Matt even more nervous. In the rearview mirror, he could see the trooper using his radio handset. He asked Chase, "Is North Carolina on that NRVC you researched?" He was referring to the Non-Resident Violator Compact, an agreement signed by more than thirty states. The NRVC shared records of motor vehicle registrations and driving privilege suspensions in a computer database that was available to law enforcement agencies in each of the signatory states. Under the NRVC, any violation in any compact state was treated as a violation in any other NRVC state. Cars and trucks were often impounded until fines and late penalties were paid and records were cleared in distant states. This process often took more than a week, leaving motorists stranded.

"I don't recall," Chase answered tersely.

As they were waiting, Matt flipped down his visor and pulled out the expired registration form and the notarized bill of sale signed by the man in Spokane from whom he had bought the van.

With his citation book in his left hand and his right on the butt of his holstered Glock Model 17, the trooper walked up to the van. He paused to examine the plate's registration sticker, and then to peer in the back and side windows at the pile of cardboard boxes and plastic storage bins in the back. Then he walked up passenger side window, which Chase had already rolled down.

A Randolph county sheriff's deputy approached from the south. As soon as the deputy saw the sharp angle at which the trooper had turned his car's front wheels, he applied his brakes and pulled his car in behind the state patrol car. He had recognized a secret signal used by law enforcement officers in the area. Sharply turned wheels meant: "I need back up on this traffic stop—from an officer of any jurisdiction." The deputy dutifully but regretfully stepped out to assist. He disliked the typically arrogant attitude of the state police, and their weekly ticket quotas. He mumbled to himself, "Gotta keep up that revenue...."

The trooper, who was six-feet-two and weighed two hundred and ten pounds, leaned over and gazed down at Matt. Matt was just five-feet-seven and weighed one hundred and thirty five. "Your registration sticker expired three months ago. That's going to cost you." With practice and precision he intoned, "Driver's license and registration, please."

The sheriff's deputy stepped out of his car and walked to the front bumper of his patrol car, so he could assist, if necessary. He edged forward so that he could hear what the trooper was saying. He didn't want to intrude on the state police's business, but to provide an effective backup, he had to hear what was going on.

Fumbling with the papers in his hands, Matt said, "Here's the registration, but as for the driver's license, I haven't got it on me now, sir."

"Just where is your driver's license then, in your luggage?"

"No, it's at home in Washington. I only carry it for when I'm *driving*."

"Then you weren't driving? So the other young man there was? I didn't see you switch places."

"No. He wasn't driving either."

"Don't play friggin' games with me, son. One of you was driving! Now which one of you was it?"

"Neither of us was. We're *traveling*. Driving is a privilege, and requires a license. Traveling as a free *de jure* Sovereign Citizen doesn't. If you refer to *Sha-*

piro v. Thompson and U.S. v. Meulner, the case law is well established on the unconditional right to travel."

The trooper put on a stern expression. "You know, about ten years ago some uppity militia-Sovereignty-Citizen type like you with custom plates that said 'Militia Chaplain' tried to smart mouth the Ohio state patrol. He was saying the same sorta things you are, and he was packing a pistol. And they settled his hash, *but good*. The Federal Task Force boys showed us a training video on that incident. Did you hear about that one?"

"Yeah."

The trooper tightened his grip on the Glock and thumbed off the retention strap with a loud pop. "Do you want the same thing to happen to *you*?"

Now Matt wasn't just nervous. He was scared.

The trooper intoned with a practiced voice, "Your passenger can stay where he is. Will you please step out of the vehicle?"

"It's not a 'vehicle,' and he's not a 'passenger.' He's my guest. I'm not getting out. You don't have probable cause or even reasonable suspicion. You just want an excuse...."

"Get out, *now*!"

Matt obeyed the order. He was shaking. They walked in unison on either side of the van and met at the double rear doors. Matt asked, "Don't you want to see these papers?"

"No. I want you to step back to my car. I'm going to search you for weapons first!"

Hearing the urgency in the trooper's voice, the deputy jogged forward.

Matt replied, "I don't want to be violated like this!" and took a step backward.

"You friggin' sovereign-militia types are like peas in a pod. You quote two-hundred-year-old laws, and refuse to be ruled by those in authority over you. You've got no respect for legal statutory jurisdiction. The guys on the task force told me how to deal with you and your uppity attitudes. So you 'don't want to be violated.' All right, son. Then I'll just arrest you for not having a driver's license, and then I'll search you, and I'll put you in jail, and I'll im-pound your vehicle and its contents. How do you want to play it? You tell me."

Matt stood his ground. The trooper snorted, and said in a demanding voice, "We have three options.... Option one is I'm going to search your person to make sure you have no dangerous or deadly weapons. Odds are I'll find some-thing on you or in your van that could be construed as deadly. Then I'll put you in jail. Option two is I can arrest you for not having a driver's license. Then I can search you, and I'll put you in jail.... Option three is if you continue to resist being searched, claiming your mythical 'rights' I'm going to *ventilate* you. Those are the options you have, son. Which would you like to exercise?" The trooper tucked his citation book under his left arm and pulled the Glock from its holster.

The sheriff's deputy now stood immediately to the trooper's right. Seeing the trooper draw his pistol, he instinctively drew his, too. He asked quizzically, "What's going on here? Are there warrants on these guys?"

Matt asked, "How long will it take for you to call the state of Washington and have them confirm that I have a valid driver's license?" He looked down at the muzzles of the two guns pointing toward him at "low ready."

The trooper's mouth contorted into a crooked grin. "Timezup! You just picked 'option three,' scumbag."

Matt turned and ran back toward the front of the van, yelling to Chase, "Go!"

The trooper jerked the trigger of the Glock and it roared, even before the sights came in line with Matt's body. The bullet barely grazed Matt's leg, tearing a neat hole through his black denim jeans, just below the knee. The bullet bounced harmlessly off the pavement.

As he scrambled for cover into the van, Matt yelled "Don't shoot!" The trooper fired again, a wild shot that went over the van. The trooper's hands were shaking.

Chase jumped out of the other side of the van, and was firing his Glock 19 in the direction of the cruisers. He aimed for the light bar on the lead car, attempting to protect his brother by diverting their fire. The trooper and the sheriff's deputy crouched to the left and right, respectively.

The Randolph County sheriff's deputy instinctively shot back at Chase, rapidly. All of his shots were high, even though Chase was only fifteen feet away. One of his shots hit the van. Now both the trooper and the deputy fired at Chase, very rapidly. All of their shots missed. Chase fired two more shots, and then jumped back into the van. The deputy ran up to the passenger-side door.

The deputy shouted "Halt!"

The state trooper fired again. This shot shattered the van's rearview mirror, just inches from Matt's shoulder.

Matt pulled his door shut and again shouted, "Don't shoot, don't shoot!"

The trooper thought that his gun had jammed. He was taking careful aim at the driver's head and pulling the trigger repeatedly, but nothing was happening. He looked down to see the slide locked to the rear. The gun's nineteen-round "+2" magazine was empty.

The deputy ran up to the open passenger-side door. Thinking that the officer meant to kill them, Matt shoved the column shifter down into drive, and stomped on the gas. The deputy held onto the swinging door's window frame briefly, and was dragged ten feet before letting go. His S&W Model 915 pistol fell to the ground.

The van was more than one hundred and fifty yards away and accelerating rapidly by the time the state trooper had reloaded his Glock with a fresh seventeen-round magazine from the horizontal double magazine pouch on his belt. Knowing that the driver was out of range, the trooper super-elevated the front sight and fired five more times anyway, in anger. Watching the van speed away, he shouted, "Son of a...!"

The deputy retrieved his pistol from the ground where he had dropped it. He examined it, and reloaded it. He only had one round left in the fifteen-round magazine, and one in the chamber. Between them, the trooper and the deputy had fired thirty-eight rounds. Not one of them hit flesh. As the deputy reloaded, the trooper ran up to him and asked, "You hit?"

"No. I just pissed my pants, is all. How 'bout you?"

The trooper replied, "I'm okay, I think. You know I think I hit the driver a couple of times. Okay! You call this in, while I pursue that blue streak." He started toward the door of his cruiser.

"No! No! No! What do you say *you* just shut up, and sit down, hot shot!"

The trooper stopped and glared at the deputy.

The deputy questioned him. "Why were you trying to shoot that kid in the back? He wasn't a threat! I don't know about *your* department's policy, but under ours what I just witnessed was excessive force, *big time.* And I was stupid enough to go along with it. Now that the shooting has stopped, I realize that what I *should* have done was ... holstered my piece and *tackled* you."

The North Carolina trooper was speechless. He started looking for blood-stains on the ground. Meanwhile, the deputy reported shots fired and requested backup. Finally, the trooper offered, "I really do think I hit that one guy a couple of times."

The deputy answered sharply, "You didn't hit *jack*, Jack. And I don't think I did, either. Did you find any blood?"

The trooper answered sullenly, "No." He stared at the more than three-dozen pieces of brass that lay scattered on the pavement, and shook his head slowly from side to side. They could hear the first of many sirens approaching in the distance.

The trooper looked anxiously at the deputy and said, "Here comes the cavalry. I guess, we'd better get our story straight."

Quoting an old Lone Ranger joke, the deputy replied, "'What do you mean *we*, white man?'"

• • •

Matt Keane turned right at the first intersection he came to, and then started making semi-random turns at each subsequent intersection.

After taking a few deep breaths, Chase exclaimed. "Those bastards were trying to kill us!" He reloaded his Glock with a magazine from his duffel bag. He handed it to Matt, who tucked the gun under his thigh.

"Where do they get off, trying to back-shoot an unarmed man?" Matt asked.

"Beats me. They are some kinda 'mo-bile and hos-tile' around here. That guy was *definitely* trying to kill you! I generally don't have any beef with local and state law enforcement, but that guy had a serious BATF-jack-booted-thug attitude! I always thought that if we were ever going to have any confrontation, it was going to be with *Federal* law enforcement."

Matt cocked his head and retorted, "Guess who is developing all the training curriculum for the state and local departments? Guess who is running the multi-jurisdictional task forces? But I just can't believe these local guys are falling for the Federal brainwashing."

Chase snaked into the rear of the van. He pulled out a Colt Sporter HBAR from their show inventory, new in the factory box. The box's large red-orange price tag declared: "SALE! Colt after-ban: $1,100." He tossed aside the Colt factory five-round magazine that came with the rifle in disgust, and started digging through inventory bins until he found a bin partly full of contract M16 magazines. He grabbed five, all still new in government contractor's wrappers. He peeled the clear plastic wrappers off quickly and laid them down.

After finding the magazines, Chase picked through a group of .50 caliber ammo cans until he found the one with a price tag marked "Canadian 5.56 SS-109 (62 Grain) Ball. $28.00 per bandoleer." He unclipped the stripper clip guide from one of the bandoleers, and started loading the magazines rapidly, emptying three stripper clips into each of the magazines with a ratcheting sound. Once all five magazines were loaded, he set them and the rifle between the front seats, and slid forward to take his seat. He exclaimed, "Little-big brother, we gotta ditch this rig, fast, or we're dead meat!"

"No kidding."

Chase popped one of the loaded magazines into the Colt, cycled the charging handle, checked the safety, and tapped the forward assist with the butt of his right hand. He looked up and asked, "Where are we?"

"I don't know exactly. I've been on the side roads. We must be coming into Asheboro, proper. I just set the cruise control to thirty-five. Without it, I think I'd be up to sixty without even noticing it."

"Good idea."

"So do we go rent a car, or what?" Chase asked.

"No way. They'd ask for ID, and even if we made it out of a rental agency lot, they'd have an All-Points-Bulletin on the rental car within an hour or two."

"We should have built ourselves false IDs a long time ago, like we talked about. Too late for that now. How about the bus, or hitchhiking?"

"Goshamighty! Then we'd have to leave most of our inventory, Chase. We've got a good chunk of our life savings tied up in the inventory, not to mention the thirty-five hundred that I paid for this rig. We're going to have to steal a car or a truck."

"Are you kidding? *Steal*? We've never stolen so much as a candy bar, and you want to try grand theft auto! No. No way. 'Thou shalt not steal.' That's the law. That's the covenant. We can't go stealing a car. It's a sin. It's a crime."

"So is 'attempted murder of police officers,' so is 'carrying a concealed weapon,' so is 'flight to avoid arrest.' That's what they're going to charge us with, little bro. No doubt about it."

"But *they* started shooting first, not *me*, Matt. I can rightfully claim self-defense—or more precisely, that I was defending you."

"Try proving that to a jury. It'll be our word against theirs. They'll be the upstanding Dudley Do-Rights. We'll get tarred with a broad brush. They'll make us out to be 'scruffy-red-neck-trailer-trash-anti-government-survivalist-militia-whackos.' The district attorney will have a field day. He'll have the jury convinced that we were Osama Bin Laden's pen pals, and that we took corre-spondence courses on bad check writing from the Montana Freemen. You know how these admiralty jurisdiction perverts operate. They'll nail us for twenty years, minimum."

"Then we're totally hosed."

"Not if we can find a car with keys in it, ditch the van, and get back to the campground. The best place to find a car with keys in it is in a parking lot of one of those oil change places, or a mechanic's shop."

Chase shook his head and complained, "It's still stealing."

"Yes, you're 100 percent right. It is stealing. But I'd say under the circum-stances, that it's justifiable, and a pardonable sin."

Matt didn't see any mechanic shops, so he started cruising through shopping center parking lots, looking for an appropriate size vehicle.

Just after Matt turned down a steep drive into a strip mall parking lot, an officer in a passing Asheboro police cruiser spotted the van. The officer slammed on his brakes. Matt turned his head when he heard the screech of the cruiser's skidding tires. He yanked the wheel, trying to maneuver the van back out of the parking lot.

The officer was immediately on the radio: "All units! This is Alpha Six. I've got him coming out of Randolph Electric!"

The officer leaned over and unlatched the vertical shotgun rack. Once he had the gun out, he turned the car's wheel and goosed the gas pedal. He stomped on the brakes again. Now the cruiser was perpendicular to the entrance of the shopping center. He said to himself gleefully, "Now I *gotcha*!"

Chase looked at the steep landscaping berms that surrounded the parking lot, and warned, "Matt ... There's only one way out of this lot, and he's *blocking* it."

"I know, I know. If we try any of those berms, we'll go high-center, sure as anything. We're going to have to go out of here on foot. Hand me my briefcase and my AUG duffel bag. And get your range bag ready." Chase quickly did what he was told. He tucked the loaded Glock into the range bag.

The officer stepped out of his cruiser and pointed the Remington riotgun across the hood. He fidgeted with the safety and the slide release. Then he pumped the action. A live shell skittered across the hood of the car. "Aaaaagh!" the officer growled at his own incompetence with the gun.

Matt picked up the Colt Sporter and said quietly, "Okay, I'm going to lay down some suppressive fire, and you skee-daddle. Meet me on the back side of these stores."

Matt and Chase jumped out of the van simultaneously. Chase ran directly for the end of the strip mall, carrying his black nylon range bag. Consciously avoiding shooting directly at the officer, Matt took cover behind the open door and began to pepper the back of the Asheboro cruiser. He shot out the rear windows and both of the rear tires. He fired twenty-eight cartridges, at roughly one-second intervals.

The Asheboro police officer ducked behind the cruiser as soon as he saw Matt emerge with the rifle. As the shooting started, he scampered back to the passenger compartment and grabbed the handset. "Shots fired at Randolph Electric! This is Alpha Six. Shots fired at me by an AR-15 rifle!" The officer was not hit by any of the bullets or flying glass. He didn't get up from his crouched position until other units began to arrive.

Matt set the rifle down, picked up his duffel bag and briefcase, and ran in the same direction that his brother had gone. Chase was waiting, as ordered. They could hear sirens wailing in the distance. They ran across the street into a residential neighborhood. They covered three blocks in a zigzag, checking parked cars for keys as they ran. They found none. Chase pointed to an apartment complex on their right. "This way!"

They walked briskly through the apartment complex, again looking for cars with keys. An Asheboro PD car roared down the street that they had left just moments before, with its red lights flashing. When they got to the back of the complex, Chase peered at a concrete drainage ditch through a chain-link fence. The brothers nodded to each other. Chase handed Matt his range bag, and scrambled over. Once he was over the fence, Matt lifted over all three of their bags. Then he climbed the fence. It was nearly fully dark now.

They spent forty minutes in the drainage ditch, making their way through ankle-deep cold water. Matt stumbled once and got wet up to his thighs. They emerged from the ditch fourteen blocks east. They started looking for a car with keys again, slowly working their way east. They saw just two more police cars flash by, traveling together at high speed, three blocks distant.

It took nearly an hour to find a car. By then, they were twenty-five blocks from the strip mall where they had left the van. It was a 1985 Olds Cutlass, parked in an open garage. The car had belonged to a man who had died of cancer just two weeks before. The man's son-in-law had been at the car earlier that same day. In anticipation of placing a newspaper ad to sell the Cutlass, he had been there to check if the battery had enough current to start the engine. Distracted by the registration, owner's manual, and the stack of service receipts he had gathered from the glove box, he accidentally left the keys in the ignition when he departed.

Matt drove toward Greensboro on minor roads. Chase lay in the backseat of the Cutlass, clutching his Glock. Chase tried to stay out of sight, knowing that any police would be on the lookout for *two* men traveling together. They listened to the car radio as they drove. Matt scanned through the dial, trying to catch any news about the shooting incidents. They caught just one brief blurb: "State police are still on the lookout for a pair of heavily armed men that fled on foot, eluding arrest, following two gun battles in Asheboro late yesterday afternoon. They are described as armed and extremely dangerous." There was nothing more, so Matt scanned on, hoping to catch another news report.

Matt laughed when he heard Warren Zevon's "Send Lawyers, Guns, and Money." He proclaimed, "Hey Chase, they're playing our song!" He tapped the scan button again to hold the station. He sang along:

... I was gambling in Havana,
I took a little risk
Send lawyers, guns, and money
Dad, get me out of this

I'm the innocent bystander
Somehow I got stuck
Between the rock and the hard place
And I'm down on my luck
And I'm down on my luck
And I'm down on my luck

Now I'm hiding in Honduras
I'm a desperate man
Send lawyers, guns, and money
The s**t has hit the fan....

They parked on a side road at 2 a.m. to assess their situation. In the briefcase they had just over one thousand and one hundred in cash—the gross from the day's sales, Matt's address book, his customized ParaOrdnance .45 "race gun," four loaded thirteen-round magazines, and a Galco shoulder holster. Between their two wallets, they had another hundred and eighty in cash. In the range bag, they had Chase's Glock and his Auto-Ordnance .45, three pairs of earplugs, five spare loaded magazines for each, and two extra boxes of ammunition—one of .45 ball, and one of 9 millimeter ball.

The duffel bag held Matt's prized Steyr AUG rifle, stowed with its barrel removed, a M65 field jacket, a set of web gear, five bandoleers of .223, and nine magazines—one forty-two round and the rest thirty-rounders. Only one thirty-round magazine was loaded, so Matt took the time to load three more. His father had bought the AUG for him just before the 1994 ban. When the ban passed, its value suddenly doubled. He had originally considered the gun "inventory" but once its value shot up, he realized that it would be a very expensive gun to replace, so he added it to his personal collection.

Once they had finished their inventory, Matt turned off the car's interior lights. They each said prayers aloud. After sitting for a few moments in silence, Matt asked, "Well, the big question is, do we risk going back to the motor home? You know we could just take off straight from here. I don't think that we left anything in the van that would point the lawmen to the campground, did we?"

"No. Not that I remember. But you know, if they act fast, the cops could check on other 'motor vehicles' registered in our family name. The motor home is registered in dad's name."

Matt pondered for a moment and then said matter-of-factly, "Okay then. Let's set a limit of twenty-four hours to get out of North Carolina, and another twenty-four hours to ditch the motor home. Anything beyond that, and we've got to expect that they'll be circulating the license plate number, and a description of it."

"Fair enough."

"So then we're agreed that we've got to go back to the campground. We can't just abandon everything there. If we're going to be on the run, we'll need the rest of our money, our coins, our guns, and our survival gear. We've already lost the van and most of our inventory. We absolutely can't afford to lose any more!"

Chase nodded gravely, and said, "Agreed."

They got back to the campground at 3:30 a.m. They stopped two hundred yards short of the entrance and walked the rest of the way to the motor home. After carrying in their bags and the briefcase, Matt emerged from the trailer, carrying a can of WD-40 and a roll of paper towels. Alone now, he drove the Cutlass a mile away and parked it behind a tavern. He sprayed every surface that they might have touched with the lubricant, and rubbed them thoroughly with paper towels, leaving behind a light coating of the WD-40. "Forensics will have fun trying to lift any prints off of this one," he whispered to himself. He left the keys in the ignition and the driver's side window rolled halfway down, hoping the car would be stolen again.

Matt tucked the used paper towels under a trash bag in a dumpster that was halfway back to the campground. He was back in Chase's motor home just before 5 a.m. He found Chase sound asleep. Matt lay in his bed fitfully for an hour, working out their getaway strategy. Finally exhaustion let him sleep.

Chase awoke at 7 a.m. and made breakfast. Matt awoke to the smell of coffee. They spent the next hour sorting their things into piles, talking escape and evasion possibilities as they worked. Everything that was nonessential but that might be somehow incriminating or otherwise point to any of their friends went into black plastic trash bags that they intended to either dump or burn. Nearly everything else except a few clothes, linens, books, cookware, dishes, and perishable food items went into the rapidly growing pile that lined the motor home's center aisle. This included their remaining gun show inventory—mostly duplicate items that they hadn't brought with them to the show. These were: three laminate-stocked Russian SKS rifles, eighteen ammo cans, three sets of web gear, two sleeping bags, duffel bags full of clothes and BDU uniforms, five cases of MREs, an Army shelter half-tent set, and their Army CFP-90 backpacks.

Using a Phillips screwdriver, Matt extracted the rest of their "non-inventory" guns from their hiding places behind the motor home's fiberboard paneling. These included an M1 Garand, an HK-93, a pre-ban Olympic Arms AR-15 clone, a glass-bedded .30-06 bolt action with a 4-12x scope, and two Smith and Wesson .357 Magnums. After sorting through ammo cans for appropriate ammunition, clips, and magazines, Matt loaded all the guns. He also loaded forty extra Garand clips with AP ammo, and thirty-two assorted spare magazines, mainly for the AR-15.

Meanwhile, Chase retrieved a slim metal box that was attached with magnets in the back of the motor home's LP tank compartment. This box contained cash, four Canadian Maple Leaf one-ounce gold coins, and twenty-eight one-ounce silver ingots and trade dollars. He counted out $3,850 in cash. He divided all of the assets equally into two canvas moneybags, and put one into Matt's backpack, and one into his range bag.

The sorting went on until 10 a.m., when Chase glanced up at the clock and declared, "Hey, we're going to be late for church!"

After showering, shaving, and changing clothes, they walked the six hundred yards to the Baptist church that they had been attending for the last three Sundays. They sat down at a pew just as the pastor was about to begin the sermon. Some of the regular congregation members were later quoted by reporters as stating that the pair seemed deep in prayer for most of the service. One commented, "They were very pious looking."

They got back to Chase's motor home just before 1 p.m., and again started sorting. It seemed like a monumental project. Just reprioritizing and repacking their backpacks took two hours. When they were done, each of the packs weighed nearly eighty pounds. In deciding how to set the ratio between food and ammo, they both opted to go "heavy on ammo, light on food."

They finished their organizing at just after 8 p.m. Matt and Chase shared a pan of soup and studied their road maps. They picked out intended primary route, a secondary route, and decided on two different rendezvous points in case they got separated.

Chase was melancholy. He declared, "I don't think it is either fair or wise to go stay at any of our friends' places. The cops will probably start checking them and maybe even phone tapping and keeping them under surveillance. It's just a matter of time. And we sure can't go back to Spokane. They'll trace the van to there very quickly."

They tried to get some more sleep, but couldn't. Finally, at 1 a.m., Matt stepped outside, disconnected the power ponytail and septic hose, and wiped the power receptacle box vigorously with an oily rag. Then he yanked the wheel blocks and stowed them in their bin near the rear wheels. They left the campground an hour and a half after midnight.

CHAPTER 7
Low Profile

"I tell ye true, liberty is the best of all things;
never live beneath the noose of a servile halter."

—*William Wallace, Address to the Scots, circa 1300*

After leaving the campground, Chase did most of the driving. Matt rode in the back of the motor home, out of sight. They stopped first for fuel, filling the motor home's sixty-five-gallon tank in Roanoke, Virginia. An hour later they dumped the black plastic trash bags in a large commercial dumpster behind an office building that looked like it had just been constructed, but was not yet leased. They drove as far as Baltimore that day, and parked behind a Flying J truck stop an hour after dark. Matt went into the truck stop and bought a Sunday newspaper and a few groceries.

There was nothing in the Baltimore newspaper about the shooting incidents, but they surmised that the events were top news stories in North Carolina. They went through the want ads and discussed the various possibilities that they saw. They picked out five likely candidates. Chase complained that he couldn't sleep because of the noise of the idling big rigs. They started making phone calls at 8 o'clock Monday morning.

It being a weekday, there weren't many people home to answer their calls. When Matt called the number in the fourth ad that they'd circled, he got an answer. He was promptly given street directions. Chase waited in the motor home three blocks from the proffered address for what seemed like an eternity.

Matt looked the truck over carefully—smelling the transmission dipstick, looking for oil leaks, watching for telltale smoke from the tailpipe when the owner started it up cold, and listening carefully under the hood as it was idled. It had some defects. The passenger-side rearview mirror was broken, the rear quarter panels were starting to rust out, and the upholstery was torn up on the driver's side of the bench seat. Otherwise it was a good, serviceable truck. He dickered with the old man for a few minutes, quizzing him about the leaf springs, the air shocks, and how "dry and tight" the camper shell was, and finally settled on a price of fourteen hundred dollars. The man had advertised it at sixteen hundred. Matt counted out the fourteen hundred in cash, and was handed the signed title and two sets of keys. Just before he drove the truck away, the old man told Matt, "She don't burn much oil." It wasn't until ten minutes after Matt had left that the man realized that he should have got the young man's name and address. He said to himself, "Makes no never mind. I'll get word back from the DMV, soon as he's re-titled it."

Matt pulled the Chevy pickup behind the motor home and tapped his horn. Without pausing to get out and examine their new purchase, Chase started up the motor home's engine and headed out. They were well out of the Baltimore metro area into the farm country of Frederick County before they stopped. There, they pulled into a deserted county park. Playground equipment near the front of the park sat idle, since the weather was cold and drizzly. There were several corrugated metal buildings there that looked like they were used to house exhibits during the summer county fair. Chase pulled in behind the biggest of the buildings. Matt backed up the pickup to the motor home's side door. They rapidly transferred their load, putting the heaviest items at the front of the truck's bed.

Their gear completely filled the pickup bed, all the way to the roof of the camper shell. Matt stowed his backpack, briefcase, and AUG duffel bag in the cab. Chase kept only his range bag and his rucksack in the motor home. He realized that he was going to need something to read during his upcoming journey, so he tucked a copy of Ayn Rand's *Atlas Shrugged* into his rucksack. Before Matt stepped out of the motor home, Chase hugged his brother and vowed, "Okay. I'll see you in four days, maybe five. God Bless."

As they drove the motor home and the pickup out of the fairgrounds gate, Matt turned left and Chase turned right.

Chase drove west to Fargo, North Dakota, driving twelve hours a day. He left the motor home at an informal campground a mile north of town. Following Matt's advice, he left it unlocked, with the keys in the ignition. He made no attempt to remove any fingerprints. Their prints were so numerous, and on so many items in the motor home that he would have certainly missed many, even if he had worked a full day. He further reasoned that the authorities probably already had several samples of their fingerprints from the van and merchandise that they left behind in Asheboro.

Shouldering his rucksack and heavy range bag, Chase walked back to town. He bought a bus ticket for Grand Forks, but instead boarded a bus bound for Fergus Falls, Minnesota. Both buses left the station about the same time. He apologized to the driver for boarding so late, and paid cash for the ride to Fergus Falls. Chase immediately stuck his nose into his book, to avoid eye contact that might encourage conversation. After having dinner and waiting four hours in

Fergus Falls, he took a bus to Minneapolis. He slept most of the way there. In Minneapolis he shaved in the restroom at the McDonald's across the street from the bus depot. Then he walked five blocks and had breakfast at a diner. From there he walked another five blocks in the same direction, toward the financial district, and hailed a cab, and asked to be taken to the Amtrak station.

Two hours later, he was on an Amtrak train headed for Chicago. The next day, he left Chicago on a bus to St. Louis. In St. Louis, he took another Amtrak train. This one was bound for Dallas. Eighteen hours and thirty-three chapters of *Atlas Shrugged* later, he got off in Hot Springs, Arkansas, even though he had bought a ticket that was paid all the way to Dallas. In Hot Springs, he thumbed a ride to Texarkana. In Texarkana, he bought a bus ticket to Baton Rouge. From a Baton Rogue bus station he hitchhiked to De La Croix State Park, five miles west of town. He arrived at the campground totally exhausted. It had been one hundred and seventeen hours since the brothers had said their goodbyes in Maryland. He found Matt sitting in a lawn chair, sipping a root beer. Matt exclaimed, "Hey little brother, I've been waiting here a day and a half. What took you so long?"

• • •

The day before, Matt had stored most of their gear in a commercial storage space. He chose a small "mom and pop" storage company, because they were less likely to have a lot of paperwork to fill out. Matt made up a story about inadvertently leaving his wallet on the counter at a truck stop two days before. "Hey, give me a break," Matt pleaded. "I just moved down here from Maryland, my wallet was ripped off, I haven't found a house to rent yet, and I'm scared to death that all my clothes and TV and stereo are going to get stolen out of my truck!" The owner was reluctant to rent him a space without ID, but was finally persuaded when Matt offered to pay a full year's storage fee in advance, in cash. Matt rented the storage space in the name of Marcellus Thompson.

When he arrived at the campsite, Chase immediately noticed that the Chevy pickup was now adorned with Louisiana license plates with current registration stickers. He asked, "Now where did those come from?"

"I bought them at a wrecking yard—well, sort of. I paid for them at least. Let me explain. The same day I got into the state, I went and found myself two cardboard boxes about eighteen inches square, back behind a restaurant. I cut one of the boxes up. I made a panel of cardboard the same size as the bottom of the box and laid it inside—basically a false bottom. Then I selected a few tools from my tool kit and threw them in the box. I found a wrecking yard on the interstate. I walked into their office carrying the box, and told them that I was looking for an exterior mirror for a '79 Chevy pickup, and a few odds and ends. It was one of those 'pick and pull' places. I paid my five-dollar fee to get into the yard, and went to work. I found a new mirror all right, from about the same year Chevy. I also got replacements for the missing radio knob and door lock button. And ... a set of license plates off a recent wreck that still had a few months to go on the registration sticker. I put the plates under the false bottom. They deducted the five-dollar yard fee off the price of the stuff, so everything only cost a total of nine-fifty."

They spent that night in the back of the camper. They were surprised at how warm the weather was, compared to the Carolinas, even in February.

The Keanes got busy building their "legends" the next day. Their first stops were graveyards. They spent hours walking row after row of headstones, looking for males of about the same birth year, who had died before the age of three. Matt picked "Jason Lomax." Jason was born a year later than Matt was and had died at the age of six months. Chase picked out a "Travis Hardy" who would have been a year older than him, had he lived. That afternoon, they rented drop boxes using their new names from two different UPS Store franchises in Baton Rogue. Both franchises told them that they could use "Apt. number" in place of "Box number" if they wished. A quick phone call yielded the address of the parish recorder's office, and the fee required to obtain a duplicate notarized birth certificate. "Jason" bought his money order at the post office. "Travis" got his at a Circle-K.

Matt's letter explained that he needed a spare notarized birth certificate because he was getting married. His envelope went in the mail to the recorder late that afternoon. Chase's letter explained that he had lost his original birth certificate. His letter and money order went in the mail the following day. Both of their birth certificates arrived at their respective drop boxes two days later.

Not wanting to linger too long and attract suspicion, they moved their camp to St. Pierre State Park, on the other side of Baton Rogue. They also each bought fishing licenses in their assumed names. They bought spin cast fishing outfits, a Coleman camp stove, a cast iron frypan, and a small inexpensive barbecue. They spent a lot of time bank fishing at the park, and caught a surprising number of fish.

Soon after their birth certificates arrived, they got library cards at two different library branches. Then they sent in SS-5 forms to apply for Social Security numbers. Their cards took an agonizing two weeks to arrive. During the interval, the Keanes started looking for work. Chase got a job with the local power company, working on a pole replacing crew. Since Chase was young, the fact that he didn't have a Social Security number didn't arouse any suspicion. He explained that he had been in junior college and hadn't previously worked jobs that required a SSN. His Social Security card, he explained, was "on the way." The card in fact arrived just two days before his first payday.

They carried their fishing licenses, library cards, and folded birth certificates inside their shoes, to quickly give them a "used" look.

Chase was assured steady work in the pole yard, due to the ongoing infestation of Formosan termites in New Orleans. Not only were they destroying many historic buildings and eating the cores out of living trees, the termites also had an appetite for power poles. Most termites wouldn't eat treated wood, but the Formosan termites were ravenous. In three years' time, his crew had to replace more than half of the power poles in the Venetian Isles area, one of the most extensively infested regions in the parish. The work accelerated following the 2005 hurricanes, which left thousands of poles downed or waterlogged.

After another week, they moved their camp back to De La Croix State Park. Chase used the pickup to commute to work, while Matt fished and casually guarded their tent. Immediately after their Social Security cards arrived, Matt and Chase got drivers' licenses in Baton Rogue suburbs, using their drop box "apartment numbers" as mailing addresses. Chase's birth certificate and SS card was considered sufficient identification. Only Matt was asked to show additional ID. He flashed his fishing license and library card.

Two days after getting his driver's license, Matt bought another pickup with a shell in his new name, again from a private party. This one was a 1990 Ford, rust free, and had four-wheel drive. It cost $2,200. This wiped out the last of their cash. Chase sold one of his gold Maple Leafs at a pawnshop to provide them enough cash to live on until they started bringing home paychecks. Chase was disgusted that the pawnshop owner paid him twenty-five dollars under the spot price of gold for the coin. He considered that highway robbery. At least the man at the pawnshop didn't ask for any ID.

Wearing gloves, Matt vigorously rubbed both sides of the title to the Chevy pickup with a gum eraser, to remove fingerprints, and then put it in the truck's glove box. The following day, he drove the pickup to Beaumont, Texas. He spent hours laboriously wiping it clean of fingerprints with a bottle of Break Free CLP lubricant and two rolls of paper towels. Then, wearing gloves, he drove it to the worst looking neighborhood he could find. He parked it in front of a liquor and check-cashing store that had bars on the windows. As with the stolen Cutlass, he left it unlocked, with the keys in it. The signed title was still in the glove box. He took a Greyhound bus back to New Orleans, arriving late at night.

Matt rented a single-wide trailer in New Orleans East for $275 a month. There was a shopping center with a Laundromat and a grocery store within walking distance, and a city bus stop just two hundred yards from the trailer park. It was an ideal location. The New Orleans East neighborhood was appealing because it had an independent streak and was decidedly blue collar. Nobody asked a lot of questions. Matt read a newspaper editorial that derided the residents of New Orleans East for shooting rabbits with .22s even though the district was within city limits.

The Keanes rented drop boxes at separate firms in downtown New Orleans. Now that they had driver's licenses, it was a breeze. Then they each opened checking accounts at different nearby banks. It took a month of looking, but Matt found a job as a warehouseman with an oil distributor outside of New Orleans. It paid nine-twenty-five an hour. He ran a forklift, wrote up orders, and kept inventory. Compared to previous jobs he had held digging postholes and stringing barbed wire, he considered it easy.

A month after Matt started his job, he picked up a crumpled March first issue of a national news magazine that was on a desk in the company office. He was shocked to see an article titled "Radical Right Gone Wrong" and subtitled "Carolina Shootouts Part of Growing Militia Resistance to Traffic Stops." He brought the magazine home for Chase to see that evening. There was a large but blurry photograph of the shootout. The photo was digitally captured from a "much aired" video that was shot through the front windshield of the trooper's car.

The article explained that the trooper's cruiser was one of a group of North Carolina patrol cars that was equipped with dash-mounted automated video cameras to film traffic stops. The intended goal was to get footage of motorists who were pulled over for suspected driving-while-intoxicated, to gather court evidence. It was coincidentally one of those camera-equipped cars that ended up behind the Keanes' van. Matt studied the photo carefully, and decided that their faces were not recognizable.

Matt turned the page to see a muddy picture of Chase and a disturbingly clear photo of himself. By the background and the way he was dressed in the photo, he immediately recognized it as one taken the previous June, when he was a groomsman at a friend's wedding in Coeur d'Alene. Below these shots was a color photo of Chase's Dodge executive motor home, captioned "Abandoned getaway vehicle." The article had a rough chronology of the two shooting incidents, and a surprising number of biographical details about Matt and his brother.

Matt was disgusted by the blatant statist bias of the magazine article. In describing the first incident, it incorrectly stated that Chase had fired first, and that the trooper and deputy had "fired back in self-defense." The article went on to describe the later "rapid fire sniper attack" at the strip mall. It described the officer "bravely radioing in reports...while at the same time Keane allegedly concentrated his deadly fusillade of full metal jacket armor piercing bullets on the officer, trying for a head shot."

The article went on to gleefully describe the items that the Keanes had left behind in the van. It described the six "paramilitary" guns—"two of which were described by a sheriff's deputy as easily convertible to full automatic fire," four thousand rounds of ammunition "most of which could easily pierce bulletproof vests," a stretcher, body bags, FBI logo hats, FBI raid jackets, U.S. Marshall's badges, latex gloves, and a roll of duct tape. The lists were set in the context of describing the gear as an "arms cache" and "crime tools." Whoever wrote the article failed to mention the fact that the guns, ammunition cans, and law enforcement items all had price tags on them, because they were part of the Keanes' gun show inventory. The stretcher and body bags were also both gun show merchandise, and were similarly marked with price labels. Nor did the writer mention that the duct tape was inside the van's tool kit, and that the latex gloves were inside Chase's medic's bag, along with various first aid supplies, bandages, and minor surgery instruments.

The lengthy article was full of innuendoes and references to the Keane brothers as "gun nuts" (somewhat true), "survivalists" (true), "militia cell members" (a lie), "white separatists" (a lie), "with ties to the KKK" (a lie), "unlicensed gun dealers" (a half-truth), "organizers of a jural society" (true), "adherents of racist 'Identity' Christianity" (a lie), "reputed members of the Aryan Nations neo-Nazi group" (a lie), and "having extensive contacts with the Elohim City neo-Nazi compound" (a lie).

The most blatant piece of innuendo was a reference to the roll of duct tape. It was described by an ATF spokesman as "the same type of tape that is often used to bind the hands and feet of victims in home invasion robberies." These comments infuriated Chase. He quipped, "You know, they ought to rename it the BATFE&DT: 'The Bureau of Alcohol, Tobacco, Firearms, Explosives, & Duct Tape.'" Putting on a mocking falsetto, he added, "If they just put all the sickos in this country who own any of that evil 'assault duct tape' in prison, we'd live in a much safer society. There is no legitimate purpose for private citizens to own duct tape. Mere possession should be viewed as *criminal* intent."

Matt added, "Yes, and only properly trained law enforcement officers should be allowed to own duct tape, or high capacity duct tape dispensers."

In the following weeks, Matt often joked about the magazine article and others like it that they saw later. "I sure am glad to live in a country with a fair and unbiased media!"

In early June, Matt bought a copy of *The Gun List* at a New Orleans newsstand. He was still hoping to find some additional high capacity magazines for their guns. There were none advertised. Leafing through the magazine, he was stunned when he saw a prominent half-page reward ad, placed by the BATFE. The agency was offering a fifty-thousand-dollar reward, and North Carolina authorities offered another ten thousand. The ad had blurred second-generation photos of Matt and Chase.

It read:

WANTED BY THE FBI; ATF; NORTH CAROLINA STATE HIGHWAY PATROL,
RANDOLPH COUNTY OHIO SHERIFF'S OFFICE, ASHEBORO, NORTH CAROLINA
POLICE DEPARTMENT; FOR THE ATTEMPTED MURDER OF THREE LAW
ENFORCEMENT OFFICERS...

$60,000 REWARD

CAUTION: SUBJECTS ARE CONSIDERED TO BE ARMED AND EXTREMELY
DANGEROUS. ANYONE WITH INFORMATION, CONTACT THE ATF 24 HOUR
ENFORCEMENT OPERATIONS CENTER AT 1-888 ATF-GUNS OR YOUR LOCAL
FBI OFFICE.

After seeing the article and reward advertisement, the Keanes were glad that they'd gone completely underground, changed their identities, and made no attempt to contact their family or friends. They were on the BATFE's "10 Most Wanted" List. After seeing the pictures of himself with and without a beard, Matt decided to grow a mustache. He wore his dark Ray-Ban shooting glasses almost constantly. Chase began growing a full beard. He let it grow for the four years that they were in hiding. It eventually extended three inches below his chin.

Each workday, in what became a relentless grind, Chase took the bus to the pole yard, and Matt drove the pickup to the warehouse. They didn't use any of their accrued vacation, and consciously avoided developing more than a "wave and say hi" relationship with anyone at the trailer park or at work. Because of their reclusive habits, some of their neighbors at the trailer park concluded that they were gay. They rarely ate out, and saved as much money as possible. For relaxation, they mainly went fishing on weekends. They developed tastes for Cajun music and Creole cooking. With a conscious effort, they soon slipped into a slower pattern of speech and a soft southern accent.

They realized that since they knew so many people from their gun show days that it would be a risk being recognized at a gun show. So they avoided going to any gun shows. They began attending a nearby Baptist church. There, too, they kept a low profile. It was frustrating, but they avoided all contact with their family or any of their old friends. It was the only way to make a clean break. They knew that the vast majority of wanted criminals were captured because they returned to their old haunts and renewed contacts with their former associates. The Keanes weren't stupid, and they wouldn't make those mistakes.

In June, Matt emptied out their storage space in Baton Rogue, and rented another one near New Orleans, as Jason Lomax. In August, Chase found a large box trailer for sale. It was a sturdy homemade trailer, made out of a pickup bed. He bought a used camper shell that fit it the following weekend. After getting the trailer registered to Jason Lomax, rewiring the trailer lights, and fitting overload springs, they left it in their new ten-by-twelve-feet storage space. They stored it with all their tactical gear packed inside it, ready to go at a moment's notice. The humid Louisiana climate could quickly destroy guns that weren't kept clean and well oiled, so four times a year, they brought the trailer home from the storage space to oil their guns and rotate the packets of silica gel dessicant. The day before each of their gun maintenance trips, Chase would put a batch of silica gel packets in the oven on low heat to drive out any moisture that they had gathered. Chase had a ready supply of free silica gel from a New Orleans piano shop. The shop had large packets of silica gel that came in each of their pianos received from overseas shipment. Until Chase started asking for them "for his tools," the shop had thrown most of the packets away.

The following January, using his company discount, Matt bought four twenty-gallon drums of gasoline and a pint can of gas stabilizer. He waited until January to buy the gas. From his experience at work, he knew that gasoline made in the winter months had more butane added to it to provide better cold weather starting. This also greatly increased its shelf life. The drums of gasoline soon went into storage with the trailer. Starting the following January, and in the subsequent winters, Matt replaced the drums with fresh ones. Since he had just a short commute, burning up the old fuel took several months.

Not content with just one false ID apiece, the Keanes gradually developed two more false IDs each during the next eighteen months. They had gone through the experience of living in campgrounds while waiting for their documentation to arrive, and they feared being so vulnerable again. With their later false IDs, they decided to "go all out." They even got passports.

In May, unexpected transmission and differential repairs on the pickup used up most of their savings. They slowly began to build up their savings again, becoming even more frugal.

Once their budget had restabilized, Matt and Chase worked on increasing their food storage program, and made themselves ghillie camouflage suits. Ghillie suits were first developed in the nineteenth century by British game wardens. The wardens used them to camouflage themselves as they lay in wait for poachers. A ghillie suit is covered with strips of random length rag material, in earth tones. It is designed to thoroughly break up the outline of its wearer. When still and sitting or prone, someone in a ghillie suit looks like a clump of brush.

To make his ghillie, Matt started with a large piece of shrimp netting that he found at a surplus store. It was from a nearly new brown nylon shrimp net that had been caught on a snag and ruined. The undamaged portion was perfect for Matt's purposes. He cut the netting material to the shape of a rectangular poncho that reached his knees. He reinforced the hole for his head by stitching it with a four-inch-wide ring of forest green denim material. This kept the netting from tearing at the point where it would take the most stress.

After he had bought the net, Matt mail ordered ten rolls of two-inch-wide military surplus camouflage material from The Gun Parts Company in West Hurley, New York. The company advertised them as "Cama Rolls." Half of the rolls were forest green, and the others were brown. The burlap made perfect ghillie suit making material. The Keanes supplemented the green and brown strips with a few strips of tan burlap that they cut from potato sacks. Sewing the random length strips of burlap to the net poncho took countless hours. With their evenings and weekends free, however, the ghillie construction work went quickly. They laboriously shredded the edges of each of the strips, to give them a frazzled, uneven appearance. After the poncho was done, Matt used more of the burlap to cover one of his boonie hats. The burlap hung down to his shoulders in the back. The full coverage ghillie effect was completed when a camouflage face veil was worn beneath the hat. When the entire ensemble was completed, he soaked it in Flamecheck FC-1055 fabric flame retardant.

Chase decided to make an even more elaborate ghillie. His was similar to those he had seen commercially made by Custom Concealment. He started with a set of Army surplus mechanics' coveralls that was one size larger than he would normally wear. He did this because he had heard from a man at a gun show that the material in the overalls would gather together as each successive band of camouflaging material was sewn on. The man was right. By the time he was done sewing on twelve pounds of garnish, the overalls fit Chase nicely. Since the ghillie material came down over the top of his boots, the effect of the suit was astounding. Even when standing up, Chase looked like a bush. When he tried on the full suit, hat, and face veil, he proclaimed: "Look at me, I'm the incredible shambling mound!" Before it went into storage in its duffel bag, his ghillie suit was also treated with Flamecheck flame retardant.

When they were done making the ghillie overalls and cape, the Keanes had a lot of shrimp net and burlap material left over. They eventually used most of it to make ghillie covers for each of their CFP-90 backpacks, and covers for each of their long guns. The backpack covers were attached with sewn-in rings of elastic material they bought from a fabric shop. The long gun covers were specially designed to not interfere with the operation of the gun's actions. It took several tries to get them just right.

• • •

When the dollar started its dive and the riots began in the north, "Jason" and "Travis" gave two days' notice at their jobs. They spent nearly all of their saved cash on canned foods. With the galloping inflation, their money didn't buy much. At the end of his last day at the warehouse, Matt got another twenty-gallon drum of unleaded premium gas. His boss gave it to him in lieu of his last week's paycheck. That evening, Chase dropped off the key to their rental trailer with the manager, and told him that they were moving out immediately. It didn't take long to pack up the back of the pickup, drive to the storage space, load the other drums of gasoline, and hitch up the trailer. They were on the highway by 8 p.m. They drove in shifts to West Yellowstone, stopping only to refuel. They camped near West Yellowstone for one night. Then they did another marathon drive to Spokane. Most of their drive had been uneventful, but they arrived to find a city in flames. There were more than twenty fires burning out of control in the downtown Spokane area.

Except for the prolonged power failure, things were fairly normal in their parents' neighborhood. There was no answer when they rang the doorbell, and the front door was locked. They got through the back door by reaching in the dog door to unlock the back door lock; a trick that Matt had used on the door for many years. It was clear that their parents, sister, and dogs had made a rapid departure. Coat hangers were scattered in their sister's room. Some dog food was spilled on the garage floor. The pantry was empty. The hand tools and chain saws were gone. Most of the dishes, pans, cutlery, and clothes were missing. All of the camping gear, fishing equipment, archery gear, and guns were also gone. The family's car, Suburban, and utility trailer were absent. None of the furniture except a futon had been taken. After surveying the house, Matt and Chase met in the living room. Chase said, "It definitely doesn't look like burglars did this—much too systematic. Looks like they just decided to take a philter. If I know Dad, he went up to the cabin."

Matt and Chase left immediately for the Kaniksu National Forest, in Pend Oreille County. Their father had a cabin there on a deeded mining claim, fourteen miles east of Chewelah, Washington. As they wound their way up Flowery Trail Road, Chase wondered out loud, "Are they going to be up here, or over in Montana with Uncle Joe?"

When they arrived at the cabin there were shouts of joy, dogs barking, and a torrent of conversation. Everyone tried to talk simultaneously, both about the current situation and about where Matt and Chase had been for the previous four years. Their mother and father looked noticeably older. Eileen was by then twenty-one years old. One of the family's dogs had been hit by a car during Matt and Chase's long absence. It had been replaced by a pair of golden retrievers to keep their aging dachshund company. Their father said that the dogs were "city bred" and "worse than useless." He complained, "They don't watch for intruders worth a darn, and they bark at the game and scare it away."

While their mother started a stew for dinner, the rest of the family spent some time going through Eileen's "Fugitive Scrap Book." It contained dozens of newspaper clippings, the "Radical Right Gone Wrong" article, fourteen letters to the editor that had run in the *Spokesman* newspaper, one of the *Gun*

List reward ads, and a FBI wanted poster that Eileen had taken from the local post office.

One article that Chase found considerably alarming was a piece from *USA Today* that had a color picture of Chase's motor home. The article had run the very same day that he had left the motor home in North Dakota. Another *USA Today* article that ran the following week described where the motor home was abandoned, and was titled, "Keanes in Canada? The Hunt Continues."

As they leafed through the scrapbook, Eileen kept up a running monologue, describing the media hoopla, "You probably saw this one...and, of course, you saw the video...."

Matt answered, "No, we never saw the video of the shootout, just a still shot from it. We didn't have a TV at the trailer."

"You didn't see it? You've got to be kidding! Nearly everyone in the country saw that video! It's ironic that you two are in the tiny minority that didn't see it. It was on the network news two days in a row, and on CNN about a bazillion times—you know how they keep repeating things. Mom taped it and sent a copy to Uncle Joe and Aunt Ruth. Then a while later it was on *America's Most Wanted*. I saw it again last year. They put it in a PBS documentary on the militia movement."

That evening over dinner, Eileen teased her brothers about their acquired southern accents. She said, "I'll bet you spent all your time sipping mint juleps and taking those southern belles to cotillions."

Mrs. Keane was beaming. She was happy to have the family together. Mr. Keane voiced his concerns to Matt just after dinner. He breathed, "You don't know what kind of stress you boys have put your mother through, Matthew. From seeing that video and from what I read in the papers, I'd say you showed very poor judgment. You should've just let them arrest you, and argued it all in court."

"You weren't there, Dad. They were about to splatter us all over the pavement. That trooper had made up his mind, I could tell. That's why I ran. And *they* shot first."

His father sighed. "Well, there's nothing to be done about it now. It's history. It's time we got back to more pressing local concerns. I just thank the Lord that you boys made it here to help us out."

The small cabin was crowded. To save on floor space, Mrs. Keane made three hammocks out of spare blankets for Matt and Chase.

That winter they ate the dogs.

CHAPTER 8
M-C-Ls

"A stone's throw out on either hand from that well ordered road we tread,
And all the world is wild and strange: Churel and ghoul and djinn and sprite
Shall bear us company to night, For we have reached the Oldest Land
Wherein the Powers of Darkness range."

—Rudyard Kipling

Most of the coffee—all except for a small "emergency" reserve—ran out in January. Lisa Nelson was the one most vocal about it. As she was making one of her last cups of coffee with a miniature packet of Taster's Choice that she'd scrounged out of an MRE, she quipped, "I was mentally prepared for a world without electricity, or refrigeration, or gasoline. I was ready for the rioting, the worthless greenbacks, and the umpteen uncertainties. But life without French Roast? Now *that's* a tragedy of epic proportions."

The monotony of winter, with its interminably boring and chilly shifts of LP/OP duty, was broken on the afternoon of February twelfth. Dan Fong was on duty on the LP/OP. He called in a terse message on the TA-1: "Deliberate, front. Two men. Armed. Pushing a cart. From the east. Five-hundred meters, moving slowly."

All of the members of the group knew the drill. They had practiced both hasty and deliberate ambushes dozens of times in the last three months. Todd, T.K., Mary, Mike, Lisa, and Jeff sprinted down the draw to their positions. Kevin and Rose stayed behind to "hold the fort." Meanwhile, Dan held his position at the LP/OP, which served the double duty of overlooking the ambush site. His job was to take out anyone who tried to maneuver behind and outflank the ambusher's positions. They had been in their freezing spider holes for what seemed an eternity but was in fact only five minutes when they heard Mike blow his whistle. In unison, they popped their heads and shoulders out of their holes, and pointed their weapons at the road. Still a cop at heart, Mike yelled: "Freeze, or you're dead men!"

Ten minutes earlier, two young men, one tall and angular, the other short and overweight, were trudging along the county road at a snail's pace. Both carried heavy packs, and it was the short man's turn to push the cart. He whined, "David, my pack's too heavy and my shoulders are killing me. I've just got to get rid of some of this weight."

"Just shut up and deal with it, Larry," the tall man replied. "You're always complaining. Do you hear me complain? My pack's just as heavy as yours."

They continued down the road. The only sounds were the crunch of the frozen gravel beneath their feet, and the steady rhythm of their breathing.

Approaching a side road that looked like dozens of others they had passed before, they heard a shrill whistle. A moment later, four men and two women armed with riot shotguns and assault rifles sprang as if by magic from underneath the "junk" by the side of the road.

When ordered to freeze, they did exactly as they were told. "Don't shoot! Please don't shoot!" Larry exclaimed, as he dropped the handle of the cart.

"Drop the rifles!" Mike Nelson ordered. Without hesitating, Larry and David shrugged their slung rifles off of their shoulders, sending them clattering to the frozen ground. "Now the packs," Nelson commanded. They complied just as quickly. With a flick of the muzzle of his rifle, Mike gestured and said, "Now you—the gun belt." It too hit the ground with an unceremonious thud. "Put your hands on top of your heads and step back five paces, then kneel upright." They followed Nelson's command. Once they were on their knees, Mike added, "Now cross one leg over the other."

"We're just refugees, we don't mean any harm. We're just passing through," David cried feebly.

"That remains to be seen." Without turning his head, Nelson ordered, "Jeff! Frisk them."

With that, Trasel set down his Remington riotgun, and jumped out of his spider hole at the far west end of the kill zone. He then circled behind the two "refugees."

Trasel methodically searched the two men. He even had them take off their boots. All that he discovered in his search were some empty candy wrappers, one pack of cigarettes, a twenty-round Mini-14 magazine loaded with hollow point ammunition, a disposable lighter, two pocket knives, and two spoons. Neither man carried a wallet. Jeff threw the contents of their pockets into a pile a good distance away from the two men. "They're clean now," Jeff reported, as he stepped aside.

By a prearranged SOP, Mike and T.K. got out of their positions shortly after Jeff got back into his. T.K. questioned the two strangers while Mike began to search their gear. "Where are you from, guys?" T.K. asked with a friendly voice.

"Denver!" blurted out Larry.

"Denver, huh? That's a long way off. You didn't walk all that way, did you?"

"No, we drove until we couldn't find gas, and ran out. We've been on foot for more than a month. Look, we're not looking for any hassles. If it's money you're after, David and I can give you some. Just let us go!"

"We're not interested in your money, or your possessions—we don't steal from anyone—we're just interested in fully knowing your intentions," T.K. retorted. He breathed deeply and went on, "Now then, we are going to find out just what you are up to...."

David broke in, "That's not your job. You don't—you don't—have any right to take the law into your own hands."

"The only law left, at least around here, is in the chamber of this little persuader," T.K. mused, patting the top handguard of his CAR-15.

Mike looked at their guns first. One rifle was a Remington Model 700 bolt-action chambered in .270 Winchester. It was equipped with a three-to-nine power adjustable Leupold scope. The other rifle was a Ruger Mini-14, loaded with what appeared to be a forty-round magazine. Mike had never seen a magazine for a Mini-14 of such prodigious capacity before. He shrugged his shoulders and mumbled to himself, "I suppose it would work, but how would you get into a good prone position using it? How useless."

The handgun, which was still strapped into a fancy tooled western style holster, appeared at first to be a Colt .45 "Peacemaker." On closer inspection, it was in fact an original Colt single action, but chambered in .357 magnum. It had a seven-and-a-half-inch barrel. Mike had once read that some "third generation" Colt single actions were made in .357, but he had heretofore not yet encountered one. All three of the guns were fully loaded. Next, Mike shifted his attention to the packs.

For a few uncomfortable moments, T.K. stood exchanging nervous glances with the two strangers. Their gaze was broken when Mike exclaimed, "Holy crud, look at this." He held up two baseball shaped grenades that he had found in the outer pockets of one of the packs. He closely examined the yellow markings on the green painted grenades. "These are live frags all right. There's six of them here. Four of them are still in cardboard shipping tubes with the paper tape seals intact."

"What are we going to do, Mikey, call the BAT-Fags on them?" T.K. asked with a chuckle. After a few moments, he added, "I suppose if they didn't rob or kill anybody to get them, there's no law left to say that they can't have a half a dozen 'lil old M26 frags. What else do they have in those packs?"

Mike let out a slow whistle as he poured out a large jumble of coins, wristwatches, gold chains, rings, and bracelets from a heavy sack. He gave a brief, matter-of-fact inventory. "They've got the whole gamut here. Silver dollars, Krugerrands, Pandas, Maple Leafs, a couple of Platinum Isle of Man Nobles, and a Platinum Koala. The watches look like they are mainly Rolexes and Tag Heuers. A lot of 'em still have price tags hanging on them."

With an odd lilt to his voice, T.K. asked, "I suppose that you're going to tell me that you owned all that stuff before the Schumer hit the fan? Let me guess ... you were in the jewelry business."

"Look, look, we can explain, we *found* all that...." Larry said, peevishly.

T.K. frowned.

"Shut *up*, Larry," David muttered under his breath.

In a sharper voice, Kennedy mocked, "Oh no, let's let Larry tell us where you 'found' all those valuables."

Silence.

"Where were you two heading?"

More silence.

"All right, step back from the road toward me five paces and sit down. Leave your hands on your heads. We're going to have us a little talk," T.K. said.

The two strangers did as they were told. T.K. backed up at the same time, so that the strangers would not close the distance that divided them. After the two men had sat down on the ground, T.K lowered himself into a squat, with his CAR-15 resting across his knees. Watching these proceedings, Mary leaned over to Todd in the hole next to hers, and commented, "There's nothing lower than looters."

Todd replied with a nod.

Mike, still digging through the two strangers' packs, started reeling off an inventory of ammunition that he had found: "Two and a half boxes of .270, a bandoleer of 5.56 mm ball, about forty rounds of .357 magnum, ten rounds of .38 special bird shot, and six loaded twenty-round mags for the Mini-14. Three of them are loaded with ball, the other three are loaded with hollow points." Next, he held up and waved six English copies of Chairman Mao's *Little Red Book*. Nelson commented dryly, "Looks like these two are a little leftward leaning."

"Are you communists?" T.K. asked.

Larry nodded yes, while David nodded no.

T.K. spat out, "Let's get our act together, shall we? If you can't give me straight answers, we might just have to trade off and question you in continuous shifts. It might get a bit cold out here tonight."

"We're both party members," Larry announced. "We joined in college...."

"Shut *up*, Larry," David cursed again, louder this time.

"Oh no, let Larry talk. If you can explain yourselves satisfactorily, we'll let you go on your merry way, or on your Long March, or whatever it is you want to call it. We aren't interested in your politics. That is your own business and none of ours. It has no bearing on the determination that we are trying to make," T.K said.

Both David and Larry got perceptibly more nervous when Mike shifted his attention away from the backpacks to the cart. It was a typical two-wheeled garden cart, much like the Grays', equipped with bicycle tires. It was covered by a small blue plastic tarp held down with bungee cords.

Looking at the cart, David said anxiously, "That's just our food. You don't have to search that."

Undaunted, Mike continued his task, taking off the bungee cords one at a time. "They've got a lot of canned food." Mike stacked the cans into a growing pile on the ground. He described: "Beef stew, chili, peas, pork and beans, string beans, and some dog food."

Todd joked with Mary, "I wonder if it's Dinki Dee?"

Mary gave him a puzzled look.

"Don't you remember, Max and his dog from *The Road Warrior*?"

Mary flashed a grin of recognition, and then giggled, "Oh yeah, now I remember. All that he had to eat was cases of dog food."

Mike spoke again, "What, did you sweet guys shoot a poor little Bambi?" he queried, holding up a plastic bag of raw meat. "Or did you just pick out some farmer's fat little calf to shoot?"

Larry started to cry.

Nelson continued unloading the cart, pulling out a large sack of potatoes. "It's a good thing that it's so cold, otherwise all your fresh meat would have spoiled in a heartbeat." Mike stopped talking abruptly, and doubled-over, vomiting uncontrollably.

"What the...?" T.K. exclaimed. He got up from his crouch, and walked toward Mike and the cart. Mike could not talk while retching. T.K. looked puzzled, and then glanced into the bottom of the cart. There, he saw that Mike had just uncovered a clear plastic bag containing three small human legs and four small human arms. He turned back toward the two strangers with an iron look on his face and walked toward them. T.K. flipped the selector switch of his CAR-15 past the semiautomatic position and around to the full-auto position. Still walking toward them, he fired two long bursts, emptying the magazine in his weapon. Both men toppled to the ground, stitched with bullets.

With a glazed look in his eyes, T.K. punched the magazine release on his carbine, dropping the duplexed pair of magazines from the magazine well into his waiting hand. Shifting the magazines to the left, he inserted the still-loaded magazine of the pair, and slapped the bolt carrier release with the base of his left palm. He took two steps forward, and again fired another entire magazine on full auto in long bursts, the muzzle pointed almost straight downward.

"Save your ammo, Tom, they're already *very* dead!" yelled Mike.

Kennedy replied with his lower lip quivering, "They'll never be dead enough, damned murdering cannibal looters." With that, he turned and began walking unsteadily back up the hill to the house, leaving the others in stunned silence. Instinctively, T.K. reloaded his now smoking carbine from one of the thirty-round magazine pouches on his web gear as he walked. Mary was the most startled of them all. Even with all of her experience in the medical field, she had never actually watched anyone die, much less blasted into oblivion only a few yards away. It was also the first time that she had ever heard T.K. curse.

The members of the group drew lots to determine who was going to clean up the mess. The unlucky pair of short dowels were drawn by Jeff Trasel and Kevin Lendel. They spent most of the afternoon hauling the dead strangers' gear up the hill, inventorying it, and cleaning and oiling the captured weapons. The looters' equipment, with the exception of the garden cart, fit into one wall locker that Todd and Mary emptied out.

Kevin volunteered to dig a hole and bury the looters' cargo of "meat." He felt queasy when handling it, but managed not to vomit. With Todd's okay, Jeff and Kevin went ahead with their idea of displaying the bodies. With considerable effort, they used a come-along to hoist the bodies onto two adjacent power poles, securing them with wraps of WD-1 commo wire. They wore surgical gloves when handling the bodies and the "meat." Mary painted signs on scraps of plywood to hang around their necks. The signs read, "Murdering Cannibal Looter." They left the frozen bodies up for five weeks before cutting them down and burying them beneath the garden plot.

In a meeting that evening, the Group first said prayers for the victims of the cannibals. Then they were confronted with the dilemma of what to do with the dead men's equipment. Lisa Nelson pointed out the fact that much or nearly all of it was probably stolen. The options suggested were: one, keep the gear and divide it equally among the group; two, wait until order was restored and donate it to a charity, preferably one dedicated to refugees; and three, distribute it as charity to refugees as they passed through the area, based on legitimate need. Todd called for a vote. T.K made an objection to a voice vote or a show of hands. He called for an "Australian ballot," the term typically used by the Group when referring to a secret, written ballot.

When the vote was tallied, it came in overwhelmingly for donating the gear and booty to charity after some order was restored. A second vote, this one with a show of hands, was taken to make an exception of the Mini-14 carbine, its ammo, and accessories. Dan Fong had made the motion, suggesting that it would make a good weapon for Rose.

The motion was voted down after Lisa mentioned that she felt that to take something from a looter for one's own use was only one notch above the act of looting itself. Dan was visibly upset. "It's a perfectly good weapon. Do you think that it's somehow been jinxed? It's an inanimate piece of steel. It's incapable of being good or evil. It's just like any other tool. Any good or bad intentions are up to its owner. You can use a hammer to build a house—or to bash in someone's skull. The hammer doesn't decide that. The man who owns the hammer does."

T.K. settled the issue by offering to give Rose his CAR-15. He would instead begin carrying his other .223, an AR-15 that he had "parted up" himself for rifle matches. This weapon was by far the most expensive AR-15 in the group. T.K. built it using a commercial Eagle Arms lower-receiver, a Colt flat-top M16A2 upper receiver with a A.R.M.S. "Swan Sleeve" rear sight, and a heavy air-gauged Krieger match barrel. He also had two scope bases for the rifle. One mounted a Zeiss 4-12x scope. The other was equipped with an Armson O.E.G. reflex sight.

After the meeting, Dan apologized to T.K. for losing his temper. Before he left, he handed Kennedy a Ziploc bag containing his spare set of M16 lower-receiver parts and auto-sear. He put in with a smile, "In the future, try to keep it to nice controlled, short three-to-five-round bursts. It sounded like a rerun of *The Untouchables* down there this morning."

• • •

On March twentieth, Jeff announced that he and Rose wanted to get married. He said forthrightly, "We've been living in sin, and we've repented." Later that same day, the entire Group gathered in the living room. Tom Kennedy led the service. He began with a long opening prayer. He asked for God's guidance for Jeff and Rose, for God as the Great Physician to restore Rose's strength, and as usual, for God's protection of everyone at the retreat. Then Rose and Jeff joined hands. Addressing them by their Christian names, he asked them to exchange their vows. Jeff promised to "love, honor, cherish, provide for, and protect" Rose, and she in turn promised to "love, honor, cherish, and obey" Jeff.

Tom then mentioned the lack of a marriage license, but explained, "I don't know how the states ever got involved in the marriage business to begin with. A piece of paper doesn't make you married. It doesn't truly grant rights or privileges. The covenant that we have all just witnessed is what matters. That's the marriage. Marriage is a holy covenant between a man and a woman, in obedience to God's law. You are now, in the sight of God and those gathered here, and under the Common Law, man and wife."

• • •

Soon after Todd and Mary bought their house in Idaho, they started making some changes. First, they installed a metal firewood chute that fed into the basement. It put the wood supply in close proximity to the stove.

The next upgrade was the construction of a new wood storage house. It was big enough to store three full cords of wood. Todd opted for an open-sided wood house of pole frame construction with a corrugated metal shed type roof. When combined with the wood storage capacity of the basement, the Grays would have enough wood for at least three winters.

At Mary's insistence, the Grays got a dog soon after moving in. Mary had always wanted a dog, but with their former house lot measured in square feet rather than acres, they didn't think it would be a humane way to treat a dog.

After long deliberation, they decided to get a Rhodesian Ridgeback. Their decision-making process on selecting a dog breed first narrowed the field to the hound family. From Mary's research, they learned that nearly all the members of the hound family make good watchdogs. Most of them also have good noses for scent trailing. Based on individual breed's attributes, the selection was narrowed to either a Black and Tan coonhound, Redbone coonhound, or Rhodesian Ridgeback. Todd and Mary finally selected the Ridgeback because it was more aggressive than the other breeds. Rhodesian Ridgebacks, first bred in Africa for lion hunting, have a few odd features. First, and most noticeably, they have a crest of fur along their backbones that lays down in the opposite direction than the rest of their fur, "against the grain," as Todd put it. This was how the breed got the name Ridgeback. Secondly, Ridgebacks have an odd habit of climbing trees. Lastly, and as Todd and Mary were to find out after they bought their puppy, Ridgebacks tend to be strong willed, if not downright stubborn. Luckily, with both Todd and Mary around the farm at all times, they could give their puppy constant supervision until it was fully grown and had gained emotional maturity.

Their puppy, a bitch, came from a breeder near Boise. The pup was a reddish-brown color, with a small white patch on her chest, and one white paw. The white paw constituted a flaw that put the pup in the "pet" category, rather than the "show" category. It also meant that the pup cost three hundred dollars rather than the normal thousand dollars or more. Mary picked the name "Shona" for the pup. Shona was a reference to the language of the Mashona tribe in Zimbabwe, formerly Rhodesia.

Although Shona was strictly an "outdoor" bitch, she was affectionate and very much a part of the family. She was also a vigilant watchdog. To the Grays' dismay, Shona's concept of protecting the farm included running off any wild game that ventured onto the property. This included deer, elk, pheasants, grouse, quail, chuckars, and occasionally, bears. Eventually, Shona's bad habit was broken. An exception was made for bears. Todd and Mary praised Shona liberally when she scared off her first bear. Luckily, Shona was bright enough to distinguish between wanted and unwanted creatures.

To make Shona comfortable during Bovill's cold winters, Todd spent a day and a half building a doghouse. The doghouse had an unusual design. Todd made it with double walls, with two thicknesses of foam insulation between the inner and outer plywood walls. This insulation went in all four walls, the floor, and the ceiling. The doghouse was built on foot-long cedar stilts to keep it up off the ground. This prevented rotting and kept it warm. For a door, Todd made a flap from a scrap of carpet. An old blanket was folded up inside for Shona to sleep on. Shona appeared to like her house, but she seemed to spend more time on top of the house's gently sloping roof than she did inside it. As expected, this phenomenon changed radically when the first cold snap arrived.

Todd and Mary continued their "upgrades" throughout their first summer at the house. The next improvements, which were both expensive and time consuming, all involved security. When Dan was visiting, he pointed out the fact that the existing doors on the house were both very well weathered, and although of solid core construction, not particularly stout. He suggested, "You should build doors that match the ballistic resistance of your house, otherwise they will turn out to be your proverbial weak link. The house itself will stop repeated hits from a .460 Weatherby, but your doors probably wouldn't stop a .22 magnum. You should build some totally mondo doors. While you are at it, you should build shutters for your windows to match." Although it turned out to be far more work and a lot more money than he had expected, Todd took Dan's advice, and went ahead with the project the next summer.

First, they removed the old doors and doorframes. They replaced the original doorframes with metal frames. The frames were mounted using six-inch-long, half-inch diameter anchor bolts installed at eight-inch intervals into the surrounding brick. To do this, Todd had to rent a heavy-duty three-quarter-horsepower hammer action drill and buy special masonry bits. Even with the hammer action drill, the job took several hours. Next, Todd had a local cabinetmaker build him custom doors out of three-and-one-half-inch thick maple wood. The doors were hung on not three, but five extra-heavy hinges. Before he left, the cabinetmaker commented, "No one will ever kick these doors in." Little did he know that the Grays weren't even halfway done building their doors.

With prior coordination, Todd and Mary had the help of Dan Fong, the Nelsons, and the Laytons for the next phase of the project. As it turned out, they needed all of them to complete the job. They started by drilling a row of half-inch diameter holes around the perimeter of the doors. Next, with the oxyacetylene torch welding expertise of "The Fong Man," they cut corresponding holes in the steel plates that he had special ordered from Haskins Steel

Company in Spokane. At the same time, Dan cut holes for the positions of the doorknob lock set and the dead bolt lock set.

Originally, Dan had suggested either one-inch thick mild plate steel, or half-inch thick hardened steel to go over the windows and doors. That was before he realized how much they would weigh. When he got back to Chicago, he consulted one of his books of engineering tables and found the formula for figuring the weight of plate steel:

Length (in inches) x width (inches) x thickness (inches) x .2560 = weight (pounds)

To cover the larger of the two varieties of windows on the house, they would need plate steel measuring thirty inches by fifty inches. If they were to be made out of one-inch plate steel, these pieces would each weigh 384 pounds. Clearly, such plates could not be put in place with anything but a crew with a special hoist. To Todd, this was unacceptable, because he wanted to keep the "Harder Homes and Gardens" portion of his preparations very low profile. The last thing that he needed was to be labeled as the local paranoid survivalist.

The solution to the weight problem also came from Fong: stacking thinner steel plates to build up the same thickness. Hardened plate steel was both more expensive than mild steel and very hard to drill. It was also hard to find hardened steel in the dimensions required. So Todd opted for thicker mild steel. Although four quarter-inch plates stacked together would not provide quite the same protection as a single homogeneous plate, it would still be a formidable barrier. To go a step better, Mary suggested that they mount five thicknesses of quarter-inch steel plates, rather than just four. This would provide a comparable or even slightly better level of ballistic protection than a one-inch homogeneous plate.

The stacks of five plates for each door were bolted together with half-inch diameter carriage bolts six inches long. To provide even greater security, the ends of the bolts were welded in place, so they could not be unbolted. Next, the outermost steel plates and the exposed edges and hardware were given two coats of Rust-Oleum paint. Finally, a quarter-inch veneer of walnut was glued over the top of the steel plating. This was stained and then received three coats of Varathane marine-grade varnish.

Todd had a difficult time finding a supplier for locksets and dead bolts that would fit doors this thick, but he finally found one in Seattle. They shipped the locks out via UPS "second day air" service. Inside, Dan Fong again put his welding rig to use, and fabricated four sets of massive bars—two for each of the doors. The brackets for these bars were made from three-inch wide, half-inch thick stock. The bars themselves were two-inch wide I beams. In a nifty arrangement again designed by Dan, the bars pivoted on a bolt at one end, and then could be locked in place with a three-eighths-inch bolt that slid through the bracket as a cross pin.

To the casual observer, the doors appeared to be typical residential doors, thanks to the wood veneer. Only when they were swung open did it become obvious how heavily they were constructed.

All of the house's window openings got a similar treatment. First, each of the metal plates to be mounted was slotted in a cross pattern. The cross slots had openings two inches wide, and were eight inches high and ten inches wide. These slots would make it possible to aim and fire guns from behind the protection of the plating. While Dan was busy at work with his cutting torch, Mike Nelson approached him and asked if he had gotten the idea for the cross slots out of one of his collection of Kurt Saxon books. Dan turned off his torch with loud pop and pulled up his face mask. Sweat was rolling down his face. He replied with a broad grin, "Oops! Oxy first. My bad. No, Mikey, the idea for the plates themselves came from Kurt Saxon's *The Survivor* compendium, all right, but the cross slotting idea came from the Clint Eastwood movie, *The Outlaw Josey Wales*." Nelson just shook his head and walked away.

Throughout the shutter-making process, Dan took the time to teach the others present the basics of cutting and welding. Ken Layton had used a torch many times before, but did pick up a few new tricks from Dan. To the others, it was a new experience. Lisa Nelson seemed to develop the knack of welding a smooth bead faster than any of the others, so along with Ken Layton, she became a "relief welder" to help out Dan. She was very proud of her newfound skill, and this became immediately apparent to Mike. "When we get home, I'm calling your office and telling them that you are quitting your job as an arteeest to become a precision welder." She replied with a smile, "You're just jealous, you dumb, uncoordinated flatfoot."

The next phase of the job was even more time consuming than laying out and cutting the cross slots in the dozens of steel plates. They began by mounting extra heavy-duty hinges on anchor bolts installed in holes drilled in the brickwork at eight-inch intervals. Next, the first of five steel plates was welded directly onto the free hanging half of each hinge. Rather than cutting holes in each plate as they had for the carriage bolts for the doors, it was decided to simply weld each successive plate to the one beneath it.

The last of the gas in Dan's cylinders was used up fabricating what would eventually be called "mini" shutters. These inner shutters consisted of three stacked quarter-inch plate thicknesses welded to a hinge. These covers were designed to cover the cross slots when they were not being used. As a finishing touch, standard sliding bolts were fitted to both the main shutters and the mini shutters, so that they could be locked in either the closed or open position. A similar shutter, minus cross slots, was built for the Grays' new wood chute.

After three days of almost continuous cutting and welding, Dan Fong was dog-tired and blistered. When asked by Terry Layton what he thought of the end result of their labors, Dan replied in a drawl, "They'll suffice. But I think that if I ever build a place of my own, I'll make mine a bit more sturdy than these here lightweight jobs." He was promptly greeted by a chorus of raspberries.

The "window treatment" was completed much like the doors, with a coat of Rust-Oleum, gluing on a wood veneer, and then stain and Varathane. Covering up the cross slots took a little ingenuity. It was Mary that came up with the idea of making friction fit wooden inserts to go in each cross slot. "They'll just look like decorative trim," Mary posited. When Mike Nelson stood behind one of the completed shutters with his HK for the first time to test them out, it worked beautifully. All that he had to do was open up the glass portion of the window, swing back the plate covering the cross slot, and pop out the wooden insert with the muzzle of his rifle. "Oh yeah!" he declared. "Come and get it, you stinking looters. Today's special is on hot lead!"

After Kevin bought his house in Idaho, he decided to do some upgrading, as well. Although his new house was wood heated and had double pane windows throughout, it did not have true "retreat potential" for any serious confrontation. There were several detractors. First, it was of wood frame construction, with decorative cedar siding, and a shake roof. A few Molotov cocktails, and it'd be history.

The house was served by a two-hundred-feet deep well, which produced twelve gallons per minute. He decided to upgrade the survival potential of the house by installing a Solarjack Type G pump to replace the existing submersible pump that ran off regular line current. In most scenarios, the power grid would be one of the first things to go. Outwardly, the pump looked like a miniature version of an oil field "cricket." The Solarjack pump ran directly off of photovoltaic solar panels, with no batteries involved in the system at all. When the sun shined, the ninety-volt D.C. motor ran the pump. When the sun stopped shining, the pump stopped pumping. Kevin bought the Solarjack pump from Sam Watson, the owner of Northern Solar Electric Systems near Sandpoint, Idaho.

On several successive weekends the Grays helped Kevin pour the pad for the pump, install the draw pipe, pump cylinder, and fiberglass "sucker rods," the pump, and the pole for the solar panel tracker. Even more than the jack pump, the tracker assembly appealed to his engineer's sense of a good design. The tracker, built by Zomeworks Corporation of Albuquerque, New Mexico, used a metal frame charged with Freon to turn the panel rack to match the angle of the sun. It worked on the simple principle of heat expansion. Because two sides of the frame were mounted with aluminum sunshades, part of it would be exposed to the sun, while the rest was not. As one side of the frame heated up, the Freon expanded as sunlight heated it up. This changed the balance of the frame, and hence the tilt of the tracker, roughly matching the angle of the sun. According to Watson, the tracker would provide a 25 percent increase in the output of his panels. Although he did not anticipate the need, Kevin went ahead and bought a tracker that could hold up to six solar panels, even though his system would only be using three Kyocera forty-eight-watt solar panel modules. The ability to increase his pumping capacity by simply strapping on more panels appealed to Kevin.

The installation of the solar powered pump also necessitated changing the house's water storage system. As it was configured when he bought it, the house used a thirty-gallon pressure tank connected to the submersible pump. Kevin decided to go whole hog with the water storage side of the equation. He requested bids from several makers of cisterns in the area, as well as distributors of poly and fiberglass tanks. He soon selected Adam Holton of Lenore, Idaho, some fifty miles away, to build him a concrete storage cistern. Holton put in an incredibly low bid of "$2,050 complete" to build a thirty-five-hundred-gallon cistern. This was about one-half the cost of putting in a pair of fifteen-hundred-gallon fiberglass tanks. It would also last much, much longer.

The cistern was situated on a hillside, four-hundred-and-fifty linear feet and seventy vertical feet, above the house. This provided a large, stable water supply with gravity feed. Because the solar pump ran almost continuously during daylight hours, it would keep the cistern constantly full. Rather than install a float switch to turn off the pump when the cistern was full, Kevin decided to have a pond excavated at the base of the hill below the cistern. The overflow from the cistern ran down a pipe to keep the pond full. Even at peak usage when watering his garden and small orchard, the pond remained constantly full.

While he was installing the solar pump and cistern, Kevin decided to install first-class water lines as well. He contracted with Underwood Pump Supply of Lewiston to provide the pipe and to do the trenching. Because Bovill was at fairly high elevation, Kevin opted to have the water lines buried at a four-foot depth to rule out the risk of frozen pipes. Despite a couple of unexpected breakdowns of the "Ditch Witch" trenching machine that caused delays, Chuck Underwood did an admirable job of digging clean, deep, trenches. With the incredibly deep topsoil of the Palouse, they encountered only a few rocks.

Again with system longevity in mind, Kevin selected Schedule 40 PVC pipe to use throughout. He opted for two-inch pipe for the service line, and three-quarter-inch pipe for the overflow line. Underwood also sold Kevin a dozen Merrill frost-proof spigots. In all, Kevin had to buy over eight hundred feet of pipe and have over seven hundred feet of trenching done. This was because he wanted to position several spigots around the house, several at his garden site, and two at his orchard site. To install the spigots and glue together the pipe, Kevin did not need the assistance of a contractor. He did most of it himself, with a bit of assistance from Todd in the more difficult steep section of the system just below the cistern.

The other upgrade that Kevin made to his house the first summer he was there also involved water. He installed a row of sprinklers on the peak of his roof, as well as an array of sprinklers around the house. When turned on full blast, the ground sprinklers thoroughly soaked most of the walls of the house, while the roof sprinklers did a good job of soaking the cedar shakes. Although not fully proof against his envisioned bands of arson-prone looters, Kevin felt a little better about the fire safety of his house. "Besides," he suggested, "if things get really bad, I can go down the road to stay at the home of the little piggy that built his house of brick."

Todd and Mary were so impressed with Kevin's water system that they upgraded their own water system along the same lines. First, they had Underwood dig up their existing water lines. Once they saw the pipe that came up, they were glad that they decided to go ahead with the job. The pipe appeared to be about the same vintage as the house. It was rusty, had several small leaks, and at half-inch diameter, it was woefully undersized. They replaced the pipe with two-inch diameter Schedule 40 PVC. At the same time, they extended their water lines to accommodate a larger garden and their plans for a bigger orchard. Again following Kevin's lead, they also replaced all of the old water spigots with Merrill "frost frees."

Because Todd and Mary's system was served by a spring, rather than a well, there was no need to install a fancy solar pump. Mary was particularly impressed with the photovoltaic array, however, and convinced Todd to take the plunge and install a photovoltaic twelve-volt DC power system for the retreat house.

With the help of Sam Watson, the Grays installed an eight-panel Zomeworks tracker, and a full complement of Kyocera forty-eight-watt panels. The tracker was mounted eight feet away from the south side of the house, between two sets of windows. Because of the tremendous line loss of DC power, on the advice of Watson, the Grays decided to wire only the living room with twelve-volt DC. This circuit charged a bank of nickel cadmium batteries, which Todd installed in the bottom of an old armoire. The batteries in turn powered the Grays' numerous twelve-volt DC radios and gadgets, as well as an inverter. The inverter built by Xantrex of Arlington, Washington, converted twelve volts DC to hundred and seventeen volts AC. Because it used a modern sine wave inversion design, the Xantrex was very efficient.

Later, Todd added a Winco twelve-volt wind generator to the system. Mary saw it advertised in the for-sale ads in the *Idahonian,* a Moscow newspaper. Including the fifteen-foot tower, the used five-hundred-watt generator cost only two hundred and fifty dollars. It even came with two extra sets of bearings and brushes for the generator.

Because the retreat was not in a particularly good location for wind exposure, the fifteen-foot tower was insufficient. Rather than buy a larger steel tower, the expense of which would have dwarfed the cost of buying the wind generator, Todd decided to build his own tower.

After studying several options for building their own guy-wired tower out of steel, it was Kevin who came up with the idea of building a wooden tower. He said, "What you can do is build a three-legged wooden pole tower, and put a platform on top of it. Then, you can just bolt your fifteen-foot tower on top." As it turned out, it was a good, inexpensive, albeit time-consuming idea. Again through the newspaper, Mary found a source for used telephone poles. They bought three forty-footers. They cost a total of forty dollars, delivered. They used Todd's McCullough Pro-Mac 610 chain saw to cut the poles off to equal lengths. It took some sweat and ingenuity, but Todd and Kevin were able to dig the holes for the posts, and raise them using a "gin pole" arrangement. Next, using a set of tree climbing spikes, Todd climbed the poles and built a platform out of two-by-tens. With foresight, they had already drilled holes through the poles for the bolts to attach the cross-members. All of the lumber for the platform was raised using a pulley arrangement.

After the wooden tower was in place, it took even more sweat and ingenuity to disassemble, raise, and reassemble the fifteen-foot "stub" tower for the Wincharger. Next, even more precariously, came the generator and, finally, its propeller. Even though Todd used heavy number-six cable to run the power from the generator to the twelve-volt system junction box, there was still considerable line loss in the fifty-seven feet of cable.

In retrospect, Todd was disappointed by the contribution of the Wincharger to the system. Even with a twenty-five-m.p.h. wind, the generator did not put out as much current as the eight PV panels on a sunny day. At least Todd had the satisfaction of knowing that in the winter, when their PV panels were putting out their least amount of power, the Wincharger would be cranking away, however inefficiently. Later, Todd admitted that the Wincharger was not worth the investment in dollars, time, and sweat that went into its installation. It was, however, as Todd put it, "good practical experience, and a chance to apply some brain power to something other than crunching numbers."

The next upgrade for the retreat was the construction of "spider holes" for ambush positions by the side of the county road. There were a total of seven one-man foxholes, dug at roughly twelve-foot intervals. Todd then lined the foxholes with pressure treated plywood. To provide drainage, Todd dug the holes an extra fifteen inches deep and laid down a base of gravel beneath the floorboards. A dozen half-inch diameter holes were drilled in each set of floorboards.

Gray also took the time to dig a pair of "grenade sumps" for each spider hole. This design trick, which was taught to the group by Jeff Trasel, consisted of an eight-inch diameter hole, four feet long dug downward at a forty-five-degree angle, starting at each of the two front corners of each spider hole. As Jeff explained, the idea behind the sumps was that if anyone were to toss a grenade into a spider hole, whoever was occupying it could kick it into either of the sumps where it would explode harmlessly. This, of course, assumed that they could get the grenade into the sump before it exploded. Although it was considered a last ditch defense against grenades, it was better than nothing.

Todd and Mary found some interesting ways to camouflage the lids to the spider holes. Most were covered by old pieces of scrap plywood or odd-shaped pieces of corrugated sheet metal roofing material. One used a Volkswagen car door. The one that Todd was particularly proud of used an abandoned refrigerator laying on its back for a door. Because the sides of the refrigerator were above ground level, Todd reinforced them from inside with six sheet thicknesses of the quarter-inch plate steel left over from the door and window shutter project.

As the spider holes were positioned at twelve-foot intervals, Todd thought that their positioning might attract suspicion, so he scattered additional pieces of junk around the area. When completed, the set of spider holes was undetectable. It just made the area between their fence line and the county road resemble a junk pile.

The last major physical security upgrade for the retreat was a chain-link fence around the house. Its gate got one of the last of the set of keyed-alike locks. As it turned out, the lowest price available on chain-link fences came from Sears. When the installation crew inquired why they wanted the fence, Mary just pointed to Shona and answered, "I don't want our Ridgeback wandering off and getting shot by some farmer. I hear that it happens quite a bit around here."

The fence was to serve two purposes. First, it would slow down anyone trying to gain entrance to the house. Second, it would pre-detonate the warheads of rocket propelled grenades (RPGs). Todd didn't mention this second aspect to Mary. The thought of anyone using a LAW rocket or a Soviet RPG against their house seemed far-fetched. He didn't want Mary laughing at him. She had already told him that she thought that the spider holes were "a bit much."

Late in the summer Todd set about getting his supply of wood ready for winter. Although he didn't have to, he decided to split all five cords of wood before stacking it. "We won't have to stack it twice this way," he declared. Todd had never split large quantities of wood before, so he ended up regretting the fact that he had committed himself to splitting the wood all at once. As it turned out, it took him two weeks to do the job, because he also had six hours of accounting work to do every day.

As his experience at wood splitting grew, Todd became a better judge of where to strike with the splitting maul, and with the larger rounds of wood, where to place his wedges. Consequently, Todd got quite a bit faster at the job. Mary, who was doing all the stacking while Todd did the splitting, noticed the quickening of his pace. She complained, "Slow down, Arnie, I'm starting to have trouble keeping up with you."

"Who's Arnie?" Todd asked.

"You know, Arnold Schwarzenegger. I figured with all those bulging muscles that you've been building, you'll look like Arnie in no time at all."

Todd grinned and joked in his best pseudo-German, "Yah, das ist true, mein Leib-churn. I vill be zee Arrnee of your treams."

After a long pause and a shared smile, Mary wiped her brow, and said, "I've got to take a break and get some water. I'll finish up stacking the rest of this wood later in the afternoon when it starts to cool off." She then turned and walked back to the house, her hips swinging enough to make Todd whistle.

Todd was seldom so intensely happy. Married life suited him well.

CHAPTER 9
Shank's Mare

"The sun went down an hour ago,
I wonder if I face toward home.
If I lost my way in the light of day
How shall I find it now night is come?"

—*Old Song*

In late May, following two months of boredom, Rose Trasel spotted a stranger approaching the perimeter of the retreat. It was just after dawn. At first she thought her eyes were playing tricks on her. She thought she saw movement, but then could see nothing. Rose picked up the binoculars and scanned the area where she thought she had seen the movement. Still she saw nothing. Finally, she saw more movement. It was a single figure, well camouflaged, carrying a long gun, moving a few paces at a time, and pausing. From the LP/OP, she called in an agitated message on the TA-1: "Hasty-rear. A probable solo. Armed. Approaching slowly from the east, cross-country. Estimate four hundred and fifty meters."

Because it was during daylight hours and most of the group members were up and about, there was time to set a hasty ambush before the stranger came into view of the house.

In low prone positions within the concealment of the wooded area north of the house, Todd, Mary, Kevin, and Dan waited for the stranger to approach. The man walked toward the waiting ambush cautiously.

The man stopped occasionally to scan his surroundings. When he saw smoke coming from the chimney of the Grays' house, he cautiously moved inside the tree line of the wood lot. He was carrying a Springfield Armory M1A with a padded black nylon M60 sling. The rifle was slung across his chest, ready to fire quickly. He was wearing BDUs and carried a forest green Kelty backpack. As he got closer it became apparent that the stranger was also wearing camouflage face paint.

Since he had veered to enter the tree line to avoid observation from the house, the stranger passed only ten feet in front of Kevin Lendel, who lay prone, his face covered by a camouflage sniper's veil. Just after he had passed Kevin without noticing him, approaching Mary's position, Todd yelled, "Halt!" Normally, Todd would have waited until a stranger was in the middle of the kill zone of the ambush, but because he had unexpectedly entered the tree line, the ambushers were in great danger of being spotted.

In a booming, no-nonsense voice, Todd warned, "There are four rifles trained on you. Just lay your rifle down, very slowly." After a pause to look around him and confirm the number of ambushers, the stranger did as he was told. "Take three steps backward. Put your hands on top of your head. Now, drop to your knees and cross your legs." Again, the stranger obeyed.

Todd motioned forward in a jabbing motion of his index finger to Dan Fong. From his spot at the far end of the kill zone, Dan set down his HK and rose to his feet. He quietly padded around their unexpected visitor, positioning himself on the far side of the kill zone. He then drew his .45, leveled it at the man, clicked off its safety, and said, "Okaaay, I want you to very slowly unstrap your belly band and then toss your backpack toward my friends over there."

With a grunt, the stranger tossed the pack toward Mary. It landed only a few feet in front of her. "Okaaay. Now the same for your web gear." With that the stranger unsnapped his belt and pulled off his LC-1 harness. It fell next to the Kelty pack. Dan thumbed up the safety of his Colt, reholstered it, and approached the intruder. He frisked him thoroughly. In the pockets of his M65 BDU field jacket he found a pair of D3A gloves and wool liners. In his shirt and pants pockets, he found a German army pocketknife, and a U.S. Army issue lensatic compass with tritium markings. Wrapped in Ziploc bags were AAA Idaho/Montana and Western States and Provinces road maps. In other pockets, he found a foil wrapped maple nut cake from an MRE, and a camouflage face paint stick. He also discovered a custom T.H. Rinaldi Sharkstooth fighting knife strapped to his left calf, under his BDU trousers. Dan commented, "Wow, a Rinaldi! You've got nice taste in knives...Always good to have a little backup."

After gently tossing the Kydex-sheathed knife and the contents of the stranger's pockets into a pile near the pack, Dan declared, "He's clean now, Boss." Dan walked back to his position, snapped his Bianchi holster's retention strap closed, flopped down prone, and reshouldered his rifle.

As soon as Dan was back in position, Todd stood up. Holding his HK91 at waist level, pointing at the stranger, he proclaimed, "We're not bandits. We are sovereign Idaho citizens. I own the land you are standing on, free and clear. We just want to ask you some questions, and then you can go." Todd lowered the muzzle of his rifle, and then continued, "Who are you?"

"My name's Doug Carlton."

"Where are you headed?"

"West."

"Where'd you come from?"

"Missoula. I went there to see if my parents were still alive. They weren't. Half the town was burned out, including my parents' place. I buried them in the backyard, and moved on. Not many people left there."

"And where before Missoula?"

"Pueblo, Colorado. I'm, or *was* rather, a senior at the University of Southern Colorado. I was studying mechanical engineering."

Todd clicked the push-to-talk button on his TRC-500. He spoke into the black foam-padded microphone, "Any signs of anyone else, Rose?"

From the LP/OP, Rose replied, "Nope, looks like he's a solo rather than somebody's point man."

Todd replied, "Thanks. Just keep your eyes open, out."

After adjusting the thin wire antenna of the TRC-500, Todd resumed his questioning. "You look pretty military, Doug. Are you a National Guardsman or reservist?"

"Neither. I'm an Army ROTC cadet—an MS 4—that's a fourth-year cadet. I went to ROTC Advanced Camp last summer and Basic Camp at Fort Knox the summer before that."

"If you're really a cadet, then you'll know a few things ... such as: What does 'PMS' stand for, in the context of a ROTC department?"

"Professor of Military Science. Usually a Colonel, sometimes a Lieutenant Colonel."

Todd nodded affirmatively, then asked, "What are the four Army staff functions?"

Carlton quickly recited, "At brigade level and lower, the S-1 shop is for personnel. S-2 is intelligence. S-3 is for training in peacetime, and operations in wartime. S-4 is logistics. The functions are the same at higher echelons, except they have G prefixes: G-1, G-2, G-3, and G4."

"Correct. What is the maximum effective range of an excuse?"

Carlton snapped back: "Zero meters!"

Todd nodded again and grinned. "You're a kay-dette all right. Sit down Indian-style there, and let's talk." Carlton sat down as ordered. Todd also sat cross-legged, fifteen feet away, the HK91 now resting crossways on his knees. He looked the stranger in the eye, and asked, "Now where exactly were you headed?"

In a more relaxed voice, Carlton replied, "Just west into the Palouse country. Nowhere in particular. I thought I'd try to find some little town that wasn't wiped out, and hire on as a security man. You know, sort of a *Yojimbo*."

Todd cocked his head. "I'm not sure how many towns are still intact, Doug. Besides, you'd be lucky if you were able to approach one without being shot on sight. From what I've heard on the CB and the shortwave, there are itchy trigger fingers all over America." Todd paused and asked, "Why weren't you down on the county road?"

"Roads are for people who like to get ambushed! If you've *got* to travel, you live longer traveling cross-country. I've learned that it's best not to follow trails that look like they've been used by anything but deer."

Todd vigorously nodded his head in agreement. He eyed the heap of Carlton's gear on the ground. Looking back toward Doug, he pronounced, "To save us some time, give us a complete rundown on the contents of your pack, your clothing, and web gear. Be honest. We'll check for ourselves later."

Doug Carlton began a matter-of-fact inventory. "In the web gear I've got six spare magazines for the M1A: one loaded with match, one with hundred-and-fifty-grain soft nose, and the rest with ball. A Gerber multi-plier tool. Two canteens. On the outside of the pack is clipped a parachutists' first aid kit. Inside the pack I've got a cleaning kit and a few spare parts for the M1A. A Wiggy's sleeping bag. A poncho. Several sets of socks and underwear. An extra set of BDUs. What's left of a tube tent. Five MREs. Four cans of chili and beans. A bag of venison jerky. Some miner's lettuce. A half dozen smoked trout. A small fishing kit. Some snares. A gill net. A toothbrush. A hank of olive drab 550 parachute cord. A little Tupperware container of salt. Some Ziploc bags and three plastic trash bags. Signal mirror. One of those Navy signal strobe lights with a spare battery. A small sewing kit. A little over twelve dollars face value in pre-1965 silver dimes and quarters. A Case skinning knife and small sharpening stone."

He hesitated briefly, and then went on, "Let's see, what else? Some pieces of tanned deer hide. A pocket address book. Three bandoleers of seven-sixty-two ball. Forty-seven rounds of .308 soft-points. Some granola bars. A bar of soap. A couple of camo sticks. A cable saw. Matches in a waterproof container. About seven or eight packs of damp-proof matches out of MREs. A 'Metal Match' fire starter. About ten trioxane ration heating bars. In the bottom of the pack I've got a Survival Arms AR-7 .22 rifle, stowed in its stock. Three spare magazines, and 462 rounds of .22 long rifle—a mixture of soft nose and hollow points. I may have forgotten a few odds and ends, but that's about it."

"No handgun?" Todd asked.

"Negative. That was going to be my next purchase, but then the economy went ballistic."

"Sounds like you had the survival bent well before the Crunch hit, Doug."

"Yeah, I'm a 'prepper.'"

"How old are you?"

"Twenty-two."

"Are you a member of a survival group?"

"No. Last spring semester some of the cadets in our ROTC department and I *talked about* forming a group, but nothing ever came of it. So you have a group retreat here?"

With a frown, Todd rebuked, "For now, let me ask the questions, Cadet Carlton. If we decide it's appropriate, you might get some of your questions answered later. It sounds as if you have some information on what is going on outside our immediate vicinity that would be of interest to us. I also need to discuss some things with my friends. Now...what I want you to do is to get up and walk slowly toward the house. You are now our *guest*. Once again, you don't have to fear for your life or property. You can collect your gear later and go in peace. We'll just leave it exactly where it is for the time being."

They slowly walked to the house, with Carlton leading the way, five paces ahead. When they got to the house, Todd asked Mary to wait outside and watch Carlton. She stood twenty-five feet away, with the muzzle of her CAR-15 pointed toward him. Gesturing to the gun, Carlton said, "That really isn't necessary, ma'am."

"Let me be the judge of that," Mary replied, with her exhaled breath making a miniature cloud of fog.

After twenty-five chilly minutes, Todd poked his head out of the door. "You can come inside now."

Doug Carlton sat in an easy chair at the end of the living room near the stove, warming his hands and sipping a cup of instant coffee. After waiting a few minutes, Todd inquired, "Very well then, Doug, let's hear your life's story, beginning with 'I was born...'."

"My full name is Douglas John Carlton. My father was a telephone lineman and later a phone company office manager. Before that, he did two tours in Vietnam with the 101st Airborne Division. He was awarded the Bronze Star and the Purple Heart. He got out as an E-6. My mother was a legal secretary. They wrote letters back and forth the whole time he was overseas. I guess you could say that they fell in love via correspondence. They got married just a month after he ETSed, and I was born exactly one year from the day that they were married. Every year we celebrated my birthday and their anniversary together. I was an only child. Something about a complication from when I was born prevented my mom from ever having any more kids...."

Carlton sighed and went on. "I was born and raised in Missoula. I had a pretty typical childhood, at least by Montana standards. My dad liked hunting and fishing, so I got to do a lot of both. I've always been mechanically inclined. I guess I took my Erector Set and Legos too seriously as a boy.

"When I was five or six years old I was building little forts in the backyard. By the time I was ten, I had free rein at the junkyard that was a quarter-mile away from our house. The old guy who ran the place humored me by selling me scrap box-bar stock, sprockets, pulleys, and wheels and whatnot for nickels and dimes. I built pushcarts at first, and later chain drive pedal carts. By the time I was a freshman in high school, I built my first motorized go-cart. It was powered by a five-horse Briggs and Stratton engine. It's a wonder that I didn't get myself killed, driving those go-carts around.

"It was only natural that I wanted to study engineering. I started out at the junior college in Missoula. I tried getting into the engineering program at the University of Montana there in Missoula, but it was 'impacted.' So I started applying all over the place for scholarships. I got a two-year scholarship from the University of Southern Colorado. That was more than enough to make up for the higher cost of out-of-state tuition. I only paid the out-of-state fees for the first two years. After that, I had my Colorado residency, so I paid the lower resident tuition.

"The University of Southern Colorado is in Pueblo. Everyone calls it USC, which of course leads to some confusion. When I told my friends in Montana that I was enrolled at USC, they immediately thought that I was talking about the University of Southern California. Personally, I thought that *our* USC was the better school. I really liked the people there. On campus everybody got along, whether you were Mexican, Indian, Anglo, or anything in between. The engineering program there at USC was excellent. We called it the University of Solid Concrete, because of all the concrete architecture.

"Pueblo is essentially a blue-collar town. So the campus and town are two different worlds. Off campus, there were already some interracial problems, so I knew it wouldn't be a good town to stick around in, during an upheaval.

"Two years ago, one of the guys in my dorm asked me if I wanted to go with him to Army ROTC Basic Camp at Fort Knox, Kentucky. Since I had grown up hearing my dad's stories about his Army days, I was naturally interested. My dad had talked about shooting M60 machineguns and Browning .50s, and here was my chance to get trained on all that stuff, with no ROTC contract obligation. I thought 'wow, I'm going to get *paid* to go shoot up Uncle Sam's ammo and get tactical training?' I went to go talk to the PMS, Colonel Galt, and he signed me up. It didn't pay much for the six-week camp, but they let us keep the two pairs of combat boots that they issued us. The weather was really hot and humid, but other than that, I had a blast and I learned a *lot*. When I got back, I signed up for a Guaranteed Reserve Forces Duty contract with ROTC. That pays four hundred dollars a month for an MS-4. Last summer I went to Advanced Camp. That's another six-week camp that cadets usually take between their junior and senior years.

"I liked the idea of the GRFD contract, because I knew that I wanted to work in civilian industry, rather than spending four years in the active Army. My only active duty commitment was a five-month officer's basic course, and then six years in the Army Reserve, with two weeks of active duty training each year. I had applied for branch assignment to the Ordnance Corps with the Engineers as my second choice. But then everything collapsed and I had to bug out before my branch assignment ever came down from the Army Personnel Headquarters.

"When the dollar took its swan dive, things in the dorms at USC got *strange*. More than half of the dormies had bugged out by the time I left. Some of them that didn't have cars had family members come and pick them up. Nearly everybody who bailed out left things behind, but it was amazing seeing some of the useless stuff they took with them, like computers, and stereos, and desk lamps. They just weren't thinking the scenario through to its logical conclusion. I probably should have bailed early on too, while there might have been gas still available. But I made the mistake of sticking around an extra day, waiting to see if things were going to get back to normal. Big mistake. I should have gone *didi mau* and not worried about missing any classes.

"I was able to buy some gas before the stations in Pueblo ran out. I had to wait two hours in line. They were limiting everyone to six gallons, positively no filling of cans, and strictly greenback cash. It was thirty dollars a gallon for premium and twenty-eight for regular. I always kept a few hundred dollars or so in cash on hand for contingencies, and the gas wiped out most of that. I had to try three instant teller machines before I found one that had any money left. I took out six hundred of the six-hundred-and-two dollars that I had left in checking, and I got a cash advance on my VISA card. The maximum I could take was nine hundred, so I took the max.

"It started getting weird in a hurry. At this point the power was still on, the water was running, the phones were working, and the central heating co-generation plant for the campus was still running. Most of the classes were still meeting on schedule. But each successive night it got a little stranger in the dorms. One gal on the third floor of our dorm had a gallon jar full of coins, and she used it to empty out all the candy machines. Most of the people who were left in the dorms were starting into some stage of mental breakdown.

"My roommate, Javier, packed a few things and went to stay at his girl-friend's apartment. When he was packing up he kept chanting to himself, 'What am I gonna do? What am I gonna do? What am I gonna do?' There were some students from Taiwan on our floor that were crying and practically screaming: 'We go home now! We go home now!' What a lousy situation for them. Here they were in a foreign country, they could hardly speak the language, and suddenly things got terminal. It made me count my blessings. At least I had a clear destination with some way of getting there, a couple of practical rifles, and a pretty well-stocked bug-out bag.

"The night before I left, a few of the football players started cleaning the food out of the dorm Dining Commons and the Joe O. Center, and stockpiling it all, plus a bunch of water, up on the fourth floor. They thought they were pretty smart. They disabled the elevators and had the fire escape doors barricaded with couches and desks. Those dumb bunnies mainly had baseball bats for self-defense. Talk about having no clue about eventualities. It was just a matter of time before somebody with guns came and cleaned *them* out. And even *if* they had the necessary coercive force to hold their position, what were they going to do for heat that winter? Once the co-gen plant was down and the electricity was kaput, they'd be S-O-L.

"With all this going on, I could see the handwriting on the wall. It was going to get very ugly once people started getting hungry, and that was going to be real soon. I figured that it was definitely strength-in-numbers time, so I started going through the ROTC department phone roster, starting with the MS-4s and working my way down. The cell phone system was down, and nobody answered their land line phones. They had all bugged out. All that I got was either continuous rings or answering machines. I remember Cadet Pickering had a funny message. It just said, 'Will the last student leaving Escalante Hall please turn out the lights?'

"Finally, I got hold of somebody, but it wasn't a cadet. It was Ross, I guy that I knew who lived on the first floor of the dorm. Ross was in my Wednesday evening Bible study class. One time he happened to mention to me that he kept a Model 12 shotgun in his room, that he used it to shoot skeet. I made a little mental note of that. So he was the first guy I called after I went through the cadet roster. He answered on the first ring. Our deal was that I would guard him while he hauled his stuff to his car, and then he'd guard me.

"It worked out just fine. Ross had his Model 12 all right. The night before, he'd used a tubing cutter to cut the barrel off at about nineteen inches. A shame to butcher a collectible gun like that, but 'desperate times call for desperate measures.' Nobody messed with us. By that time there was no campus security left around, and the Pueblo police and County Sheriff's departments had bigger fish to fry. You could hear lots of sirens, any hour of the day. The night before I left, I heard shooting off in the distance toward old Pueblo, every half hour or so.

"Parenthetically, I should mention that I had previously carried my M1A in a guitar case whenever I took it in or out of the dorm, because they had a 'no guns on campus' rule at USC. It was one of those rules that didn't make any sense and was rarely enforced. I was hardly the only one who kept a gun in my dorm room. For example, USC had an official pistol team that practiced at an on-campus indoor range, and most of those guys used their own guns rather than ones issued by the ROTC department. So they didn't fall under the exception in the rule for school-owned guns and ROTC department guns. The team members just didn't bother mentioning to anyone that those guns were their own property. And they didn't keep them in the ROTC arms room, either. They were just very low key about it. My roommate Javier wasn't bothered by the fact that I kept my M1A and AR-7 in our dorm room. He even went out to the range with me a couple of times.

"Well, so much for obsolete legalities. Let's see, I was telling you about packing up...The power was still on when I was packing up my '95 Jetta and Ross was packing up his old Chevy minivan. We could hear somebody up on the fourth floor with their stereo cranked up full blast. They were playing that old REM song, 'It's The End of the World as We Know It, and I Feel Fine.' I thought it was kind of apropos.

"It would've been much better to have our cars travel together for mutual security, but I was headed north to Montana, and Ross was headed south to his uncle's ranch outside El Paso. So after we'd both packed up, we just said prayers for each other, shook hands, and hopped in our cars.

"I anticipated that the whole I-25 corridor up though Colorado Springs and Boulder was going to be impassable, so I immediately headed west on I-50 toward Grand Junction.

"I decided it would be best to take US 50 only as far as Salida, then US 285 north to Leadville, basically following the Arkansas River. From 50 I'd then take US 24 over to I-70 into Grand Junction. I knew there'd be less people and less social stress, along that route.

"My goal was to travel the Basin and Range route north, where there's hardly any population. I didn't see any traffic to speak of; just a few people who were obviously refugees, with trailers piled way up high, and a few truckers. I saw several diesel prime movers without trailers. I guess they'd abandoned their loads and were just trying to get home.

"I usually kept my car's tank three-fourths full, and I always carried a spare five-gallon can, treated with Sta-Bil. Wouldn't you know it, but I had a lot less than my usual average when things hit the fan. With what I had in the tank, even after buying the extra six gallons in Pueblo, I calculated I had only about a two-hundred-and-forty-mile range. If I had really planned ahead, I would have found someplace there in Pueblo to store more cans of gas.

"I checked every station that I came to on the highway, and took some exits to cruise through some of the smaller towns, but they were all out of gas. A few of them still had diesel, but there was no gas left. Man! If I'd only bought one of the later *diesel* Volkswagen Jettas instead of a gas model, I could have found plenty of fuel and driven all the way to Missoula. You can even run a diesel on home heating oil, since it is basically the same stuff. It's just dyed differently so that people don't try to cheat on the road taxes. For that matter, you can even stretch diesel with used vegetable oil if you filter it. Before the Crash you could get used vegetable oil for *free* at most restaurants ...As it was, I had over six hundred miles to go when I ran out if gas.

"If I had to do it over again, I would have bought a car or truck that burned diesel. It stores better, it's safer to carry in bulk, and it was available for sale a while longer than gasoline. Diesel will store for a decade or more if you put an antibacterial in it, and don't let water seep in. I had a friend in Montana who worked for a road contractor. He had a full-size diesel pickup with a big extra tank in the bed, right behind the cab. They used it mainly to carry extra number-two diesel fuel for the graders and dozers. The tank was L-shaped so that most of it went underneath a cross-bed toolbox, so effectively it only took up ten linear inches of bed space beyond the toolbox. He said that it held ninety-eight gallons. You can go a loooong way with an extra ninety-eight gallons.

"The night my car ran out of gas, I was about twelve miles short of Grand Junction, near Orchard Mesa. When the engine started to stutter, I pushed in the clutch, took it out of gear, and coasted downhill for the last two miles. As I was coasting, I starting whistling the tune to 'It's The End of the World as We Know It.' It *was* the end of the world as *I* knew it, all right. No more soft life. No more car. It was time for a long ride on 'Shank's Mare.'

"There wasn't much left worth salvaging from the car that was light enough to carry. All that I took was a few road maps, a fifteen-minute road flare, some plastic bags, a space blanket, and two two-liter pop bottles full of slightly chlorinated water that I had kept in my car for emergencies. My first goal was to get off the highway so I didn't get robbed. I left my car out on the shoulder, locked. I suppose that it's still sitting there. It was pitch dark, and I had quite a time struggling to get my pack on, and getting moving. I had a lot of food crammed in my pack, plus those extra pop bottles, so my pack weighed nearly seventy pounds. My rifle and web gear were an extra sixteen pounds. It seemed unbearable at first, and I wasn't able to travel very fast. After a few days, my back muscles got used to the weight, and since I was eating up some of the food, my pack gradually got lighter, but not much. Right now, for example, it's probably still well over fifty pounds.

"I only covered a mile or so that first night. I thought that I'd follow the Gunnison River. I hiked the first quarter-mile, stumbling around in the dark, when I came up to a railroad bed. I figured that it was safer than traveling on the road, and easier than tripping over sagebrush. Since it ran north-south, it was even going in the right direction. When it started to get light, I set up cold camp a couple of hundred meters off the track, in a thick clump of brush. As I was laying there that first night, trying to get sleep, I made a mental checklist for my walkabout. I decided that since I was on my own, it was best to travel stealthily, to avoid detection. I had to treat everyone I met as a potential adversary. Traveling alone is a very vulnerable situation. I realized that it would be best to travel with no detectable actions like noticeable cooking fire smoke or any firearm discharges unless absolutely necessary, because evasion is always easier than escape or—God forbid—a firefight.

"I was awakened by the sound of a northbound Denver Rio Grande Western freight train coming, a couple of hours after sunrise. I thought to myself, 'Great! The trains are still running. Maybe I can catch a ride.' That train was going at least forty, so I didn't bother chasing it, but just seeing it cheered me up quite a bit. Now I at least I had a vague plan. I slept off and on until just before full dark, ate a can of beef stew, and started out again.

"I made it all the way to Grand Junction that night. I was lucky that the ballast was packed nice and level with the ties most of the way, so aside from the weight I was carrying, it was easy walking. I stopped short of town, and got way back into some pinon pines to sleep. I was pretty tuckered out. That day two trains went by—one southbound and one northbound; and that was encouraging. All that I did that day was refill my water bottle from a creek and dose it with a purification tablet. I slept off and on. A couple of those big gray Clark's Nutcrackers kept waking me up. I thought about shooting one with my .22 to eat, but I was too close to town and I didn't want to attract attention. As close as they were, a wrist rocket would have worked perfectly.

"I waited until full dark, and picked my way back down to the tracks. It was strange and scary walking through Grand Junction. The tracks skirted the east side of town, so I just stayed on them. I figured that those big rails would at least offer some ballistic protection if I got into a firefight. The power was out there, but I could see candles and kerosene lamps in a lot of houses. There were no cars moving on the streets. There was a marshaling yard on the north end of town, where they put together trains. I thought that it would be a good place to catch a ride.

"Just as I got close to the marshaling yard, a freight train throttled up one of its power units and started heading north. I quick-timed it toward the train, but I couldn't move very fast with the weight I was carrying. The train picked up speed before I could get to it, so I had to stop and just watch it go.

"I heard someone up on a knoll at the edge of the yard shouting at me, 'Hey soldier boy! Did you miss your train?' That scared the dickens out of me. I dropped down to one knee, swung around in that direction, and clicked off the safety on my M1A.

"The guy up on the hill stood up, laughing. He said, 'Hold your fire there, pilgrim!' There was plenty of moonlight, so I ascertained that he was alone, and—at least from a distance—looked unarmed. He walked toward me. He was a crusty-looking old hobo, who introduced himself as 'Petaluma Bob.' He said, 'Don't worry, son. They'll be coupling together another northbound tomorrow.' He invited me to his camp, which was two hundred and fifty yards away, back in a stand of mesquite. He was camped out by himself.

"He carried all of his gear in an old blue Air Force duffel bag. For protection, he had an old .38 Smith and Wesson top-break revolver with most of the nickel finish worn off. The thing looked ancient, but functional. This guy Bob looked to be around sixty years old, and smelled like he hadn't had a bath in a long time. He didn't have any front teeth—top or bottom, so it made for a hilarious smile.

"Petaluma Bob spent half an hour describing the train schedules to me. He had a greasy old railroad map that he kept in a plastic bread bag, along with some passenger train schedules, some road maps, and some handwritten notes on freight train schedules and routes. We used his little stub candle to read the maps and schedules.

"Bob told me that he was waiting for a train headed southwest. He said that he was going to Ajo, Arizona, where he had a bunch of his things including a couple of other guns and extra ammo in a plastic olive shipping barrel that he buried as a 'cach-ay.' Hearing that kind of surprised me. I'd heard the term 'cache' used by survivalists and Special Forces NCOs before, but never by anyone else. From what he said, he knew lots of hobos that buried extra food and clothes along the routes that they frequented. He mispronounced it 'cach-ay' but from the way he described it, he sure knew how to dig one and camouflage it.

"We waited there that night and all the next day, sharing stories. It may have been foolhardy, but I trusted him and I slept for a while, and I shared some of my food. Bob said that he'd never had anyone point a gun at him his whole life, but that in the past three days, he'd had guns pointed at him three different times. He said, 'And you just now, Soldier Boy, was the third!' I had to laugh at that. I pumped him for information on 'hoboing'— like where and how to catch trains, what cars it was safe to ride on or in, and even where it was safe to ride if you couldn't get inside a car.

"Petaluma Bob was right about the next train heading my intended direction. We could see them using a small DRGW switcher engine to hook up the cars for a couple of hours in the evening. The train was scheduled to leave at 11:10 p.m. I wanted to get down there and pick out a car early, but Bob advised me to wait until the brakeman did his rounds checking brake lines and 'bulling' the cars. He made his final check, carrying some kind of big lantern, around 10:30. Finally, Bob said, 'You can go hop onboard now, Pilgrim. Pick out a boxcar marked Northern Pacific, and you won't go wrong. Good luck.' I wished him God's speed. His southbound was due to leave the next morning. I prayed that he made it. He was a nice old guy.

"I found a Northern Pacific boxcar near the middle of the train with an open door. I got in as quietly as I could. All that was in the car was fifteen or twenty flattened cardboard boxes, great big ones for appliances. I positioned two of them at one end of the car and set my gear down. Then I gathered four more and draped them over the top of me, and my gear. I wanted to be as inconspicuous as possible, in case someone made another 'bull' run. The train pulled out right on schedule. I was absolutely thrilled. I was making progress north at a great rate. We went over the Douglas Pass around midnight. Then I fell asleep for several hours. I woke up at civil twilight, and watched the miles go by, praising God.

"The train's route took it north though the Salt Lake City area, and that had me nervous, that being a metropolitan area. I couldn't see any signs of trouble in the Salt Lake area aside for the power being out. There was a stop to switch out some cars in Ogden, late in the afternoon. That was a nervous time. Luckily, my car ended up with the train that continued north. I stayed hunkered beneath my boxes the whole time we were in the yard. The train pulled out again around sunset. We had another brief stop at what I suppose would have been Logan, based on the timing. When the train was stopped there, I heard a couple of men's voices. One guy said, 'Hey let's try this one—this one's empty!' I yelled in my best command voice, 'This car is *not* empty! Move along!' One of the guys answered all meek-like: 'Okay, okay, we were just leaving! Sorry to bother you.'

"I got off when the train stopped in Pocatello, because it was going to continue west to Boise, and I, of course, needed to go north. So I was back to Shank's Mare. After the train, it was quite a letdown. It was full daylight by the time I was all the way out of Pocatello proper. A paperboy on his rounds stopped his bike and put both of his feet flat on the ground and watched me walk by. I waved at him and said 'Hi.' He must have thought I was from another planet. I often wondered how many more days he was delivering papers. That might have been his last day.

"I paralleled I-15 up past Idaho Falls. It was pretty slow going, since I had a heavy load, and again, I was trying to avoid contact with anyone. I averaged around ten miles a day. I traveled mainly at night. I could hear shooting and fire engines sirens, and police sirens in even some of the smaller towns, so it was clear that the situation was deteriorating.

"I cut off to the west, following Highway 28, since it went through less population than if I'd continued on I-15. That route would have taken me through Butte. Highway 28 follows the Lemhi River and the Salmon River, up through the town of Salmon. That's Elmer Keith's old stomping grounds. I nearly froze up in the Lemhi National Forest, way up in the Lemhi mountain range. A storm front came through and dumped about five inches of early snow. Here it was the second week of November, and it was already starting to snow at the higher elevations, and I still had over two hundred miles to go!

"When that snow hit, I had to build a shelter quick, or freeze to death. I found a ponderosa pine that had blown over, and still had a big root ball of soil on it. I cut a bunch of limbs off of some fir trees with my cable saw, and piled them around the base of that tree, weaving them together into a wickiup with a vent at the top, snugging them down with parachute cord. I put my tube tent, a space blanket, and a couple of trash bags between the layers. I got a fire going, hunkered down, and did my best to dry out my clothes. The wickiup worked pretty well, but I don't know what was worse, the cold or the smoke from that fire.

"The snow stopped the next day, and it took another day and a half to all melt. During that time, I got busy with my AR-7, and shot a marmot. By the way, I'm glad I have a .22 rifle. The .308 is a *lot* louder, and doesn't leave much usable meat on small game. The marmot was pretty tough, but nutritious. I cooked it all in strips skewered on sticks over the open fire. I ate the whole marmot in a day and a half.

"Also during that time, I melted a bunch of snow in my canteen cup to refill my water bottles with boiled water. You have to melt an outrageous quantity of snow just to fill one two-liter bottle. Of course I could have used water from a creek, but then I would have wasted purification tablets. Besides, I had a fire going all the time, and nothing but time on my hands. Like my dad used to say, 'What's tiiiime to a hawwwg?'"

Kevin Lendel interrupted, asking, "Pardon me, did you say *hog*?"

"Yeah, *hog*. It was one of my dad's favorite jokes: 'A traveling salesman is driving through Arkansas. He sees a farmer struggling under the weight of a hundred-pound pig, carrying it from tree to tree, so that it can nibble on the apples that are hanging. The salesman is dumbfounded by what he sees. Finally, he can't stand it any longer, and he goes and asks, 'What are you doing?' And the farmer answers, 'I'm just a-feedin' my hawwwg.' Then the salesman asks, 'Why don't you just knock down a bunch of apples?' 'I jus prefer to do it this a-way,' the farmer says. Then the salesman asks, 'Isn't it a waste of time, doing it that way?' And the farmer asks, 'Well, what's tiiiime to a hawwwg?'"

Kevin and the others laughed. Carlton took a sip of coffee and resumed his tale. "I slowly worked my way north. The days were getting shorter and progressively colder. It took me fifteen days to make it from Pocatello to Salmon.

"As I got farther north, water wasn't nearly as much of a problem as it had been down in the Pocatello and Idaho Falls area. That's dry country. A couple of times down there I had to purify water that I got out of cattle tanks.

"I foraged as I went. I shot a couple of rabbits and another marmot. I had some snares and a gill net, but I didn't get a chance to use them, because I was never in one place long enough. I got pretty good at fire starting, even when things were damp. First you...."

The TA-1 on the C.Q. desk made its distinctive cricket-like chirp, interrupting Doug's story. It was Rose. She inquired, "Mike was supposed to have relieved me fifteen minutes ago. Where is he?" When he was relayed the message, Mike apologized profusely for losing track of the time, and then dashed out the door.

"Where's he headed?" Doug asked.

Dan replied casually, "LP/OP."

Doug nodded his head. "Sounds like you have a squared-away tactical operation here. Now where was I? Oh yeah, fire starting. The trick is to always start with a tiny fire and work it bigger gradually. I always carry a little dry tinder. Dried moss works the best. And, if you have nothing but damp kindling to light, nothing beats using half a trioxane fuel bar or a full hexamine tablet. That'll start just about anything."

"The boots that I had been wearing all this time started to fall apart at the seams. I had them all wrapped up in duct tape. They looked pretty comical, and worse than that, they leaked. I had to wear plastic bags between my inner and outer socks to keep my feet from getting soaked.

"I crossed the Bitterroots the last week of November. I'll tell you, at seven thousand feet of elevation, it was plenty cold that time of year. I got close to Darby, which is seventy miles south of Missoula, when the winter really set in, in early December. It was frustrating being so close to home, but unable to go any farther. 'So close and yet so far.' The snow was really starting to pile up. I knew that I had to find some decent shelter or I was going to end up a human popsicle for some bear.

"Out of desperation, I broke into an unoccupied hunting cabin in the Bitterroot National Forest that was off the beaten track. It was a small seasonal cabin without much insulation, but it served my purposes well enough. It had a good supply of firewood under the porch. There was a Franklin stove, bedding, a big year-round spring for water, a couple of good axes, and a bucksaw. There were some canned goods there too. It took a monumental force of will, but I didn't use anything I found there in the cabin except a bit of salt, soap, and some medical supplies to keep me regular. Those cans of soup, chili, and vegetables were practically singing to me like the sirens of lore. But I resisted the urge. It was bad enough that I was an uninvited lodger, but I wasn't going to stoop so low as to steal another man's food.

"Between snowstorms I gathered as much firewood as I could, and I knocked down two fat does. There was a set of gambrels, two meat saws, and several gutbuckets there at the cabin. I used a pulley and ropes to hang up the skinned-out deer-quarters way up in the fir trees near the house to keep them away from bears. Luckily I didn't have any bear problems that winter. The meat froze so hard that I had to use an ax to cut it. I left the deer hanging outside and just took each quarter down on an as-needed basis. I used everything from those deer: the brains, the meat, the fat, the heart, and liver. I even sawed the bones open for the marrow." He added with a snort, "It's an *acquired* taste."

"I spent most of the winter in my sleeping bag—just hibernating like a bear. It's a real warm bag—a Wiggy's Ultima Thule. They make 'em in Colorado. With the heavy bag, I only had to burn a low fire to take the chill off the cabin. I used bedsheets from the cabin as bag liners to protect the sleeping bag from sweat and grime. I piled up another sleeping bag and some blankets from the cabin on top for extra warmth. Tending the fire, cooking one meal a day, and reading is about all that I did for three months. Oh yeah, I also stitched together three pairs of deer hide moccasins. The first pair turned out pretty crummy, but the other two pairs fit me fairly well.

"I didn't want to burn any of the candles or kerosene there, for two reasons. First, they didn't belong to me. Second, burning lights might attract unwelcome attention. I didn't hear any evidence of anyone living in the area except for a chain saw way off in the distance a few times, and a couple of shots, even further off. I wasn't taking any chances. I adjusted my sleeping hours to match the sun cycle, so I did all of my reading and cooking during daylight. During the shortest days of the year, I must have been sleeping fourteen hours a day.

"By about when I estimated it was the middle of February, I was sick and tired of venison and had a bad case of cabin fever. I shot two more deer—both yearlings—in the late winter. I never want to spend a winter by myself like that again. Thankfully, there was a Bible there in the cabin, so I kept sanity by digging into God's word. It was a Catholic Douay-Rheims version, so I got a chance to read the apocryphal books for the first time. I'm a Methodist and I don't consider those apocryphal books to be the inspired word of God, but they were fascinating, nonetheless. Aside from the Bible, there was *not* a full winter's worth of reading material in the cabin. There were a few hunting and fishing books, and about thirty magazines. I read them all cover to cover—some of them several times.

"The snow got three feet deep. When it got close to the spring solstice, the snow started receding, and finally it stopped sticking. Since I had burned up the two cords of wood that were stored there at the cabin, I felt it was my responsibility to replace it. I spent most of the mud season cutting down small tamaracks, cutting the wood to stove length, hauling it back to the cabin in a wheelbarrow, splitting it in halves, and stacking it. Without a chain saw it was exhausting work, but it was good to get my muscles back in shape. I wore out a pair of work gloves in the process. I piled the wood box inside right up to the ceiling, and I left more wood under the cabin than I had found originally, so I figured that I was square with whoever owned the cabin.

"Once I got the firewood in, I started spring cleaning. Before I left, I felt honor bound to clean the cabin. I started out by cleaning the chimney, which had so much creosote in it; it was a wonder that I didn't have a chimney fire that winter. I swept and scrubbed the floors, washed all the towels and bed linens, and hauled out the buckets of ashes and creosote. All in all, the place looked much better than when I found it. Finally, I washed all my clothes, washed my sleeping bag, gave my web gear a good brushing, trimmed my beard, and gave myself a long hot bath. It was the first bath that I'd had in months. It felt reeeeally good.

"Before I left, I wrote a long and apologetic thank you letter to the cabin owner and left it on the kitchen table, along with two dollars in the old 90 percent silver coins and all the rest of my paper currency—not that *it* was worth much. I also left behind two of the four deer hides that I had brain tanned. I rolled them up together around a five-foot length of pine sapling. I hung it from two pieces of wire in the center of the cabin so the mice and rats wouldn't get to the hides.

"I got an early start, not long after the snow stopped sticking. I really wanted to get home to my folks' place. I covered the distance to Missoula in just over a week, up through Hamilton and Stevensville. Most of the towns going up the valley looked downright fortified. In most of the towns they had huge abatis roadblocks made out of big logs on all the roads leading in.

"I took a few risks in covering those last seventy miles. For example, I traveled some in daylight, which I don't normally do, near population. I guess I was rushing a bit, but again, I couldn't wait to get home.

"Past Stevensville, which was fortified, things were pretty well wiped out. Florence and Lolo were burned completely down. There wasn't a soul around. From a distance, I could see that more than half of the houses and nearly all the stores in Missoula were burned down. My parents lived on the outskirts of the east side. Not knowing who controlled the town, I came into town from the east in the middle of the night. When I saw the ruins of my folks' house, my heart just sank. All that was left standing was the chimney. The garage was still intact, so I spent the rest of the night in it. I just cried and cried. There was just one neighbor living down the block, named Mack. He was an old widower. Everyone else was either dead, moved out, or burned out.

"When I left for college last fall, Mack probably weighed two-hundred-and-forty pounds. This spring, he weighed maybe one-hundred-and-sixty pounds. I didn't hardly recognize him at first. He was practically skin and bones. Mack told me about what'd happened. The brigands came through in a convoy of more than sixty pickups, Suburbans, Hummers, and Blazers, stripping all the food and fuel they could find. They stayed several weeks, raping, getting drunk, and burning a few more houses just to be mean. Anyone who resisted them in the least was shot or burned out.

"The evening after I buried what was left of my mom and dad's bodies, I dug up my cache in my folks' backyard. In the cache I had a spare pair of combat boots, four pairs of boot socks, half of my silver coins, some .22 and .308 ammo, some Duracell batteries, a few camouflage face paint sticks, two bars of soap, multivitamins, some canned food, salt, cocoa powder, trioxane fuel bars, and eleven MREs. I had it all cached in three of those tall steel ammo cans—the kind they make for the 60-mike mortar rounds. The outside of the cans had gotten pretty rusty, and that scared me when I first dug them up. I thought that they might have leaked. I suppose that I should have painted them with asphalt emulsion to make them last longer. But luckily they kept their seals and everything inside was just the way I left it."

Looking down at the pair of sturdy Army combat boots that he was wearing, Doug declared, "Like I said before, the boots that I had been wearing the last year were falling apart at the seams. I wore my moccasins part of the time, but they were a poor substitute, particularly on rocky ground. It was kind of odd, you know. I had put these boots in the cache as sort of an afterthought, because I still had room in one of the cans. I was going to put in more canned food—my mom always bought tuna by the case—but then the idea of the extra boots popped into my head. Ironic, but a year later, of everything in the cache, it was these boots I needed the most. It must have been Divine providence. I'm sure that it was the good Lord that put that thought into my head.

"I spent another full day there, mainly just praying and thinking. I talked and prayed with Mack quite a bit. Since by that time my hair was so long that I was looking like an angora goat, he gave me a short haircut and beard trim. Then I did the same for him. I'm afraid that I wasn't very good at it. We used some scissors and a pair of hand clippers that had belonged to his wife. I gave him some venison and canned food. He gave me a big bottle of mild laxative, which was something I needed, given the fact that my diet was mostly venison.

"I didn't find anything of value in my parents' garage except for a bottle of Rem-Oil. Practically everything else including all the tools, the camping gear, and even the scrap lumber had been stolen. There wasn't much in the garage at all except my folks' car—which was minus its battery and had no fuel in its tank—and a couple of old tire rims. It was like locusts had come through. All that I got out of their car was an Idaho/Montana map. It was identical to the one that I had been carrying all along, but it was in better shape. I had folded the first one so many times that it was coming apart into a bunch of long strips.

"Neither of my folks had any family west of the Mississippi, so I didn't have a clear destination. I knew that there was a much less severe climate in the Clearwater River valley, just over the pass, so that seemed like a reasonable first area to look for a place to settle. I'd been across there, fishing steelhead with my dad lots of times, so I knew the Clearwater country fairly well.

"I spent the first three weeks in the canyons west of Missoula, waiting for the snow to clear in the high country. I shot a young buck, and that fed me for the whole time I was there. It took nearly a week to turn it into jerky. I found some Camas plants and a big patch of miner's lettuce, and I pigged out. Between the venison, the bulbs, and the miner's lettuce, I started to put some weight on.

"I transited the Lolo Pass three weeks ago. By then, the snow was shallow on the northern facing slopes and in the heavy timber, and patchy most every-where else. Since I wasn't in any great hurry, I traveled even more slowly than before. I only averaged about four miles a day. I like to move with some stealth, and take lots of listening halts. I gradually worked my way down the Lochsa River, and then the Clearwater. There's no sign of any organized commerce or travel at all down there. Everybody is just hunkered down, big time. I tried approaching the town of Kamiah, but I got shot at by a guy with what looked like an SKS. I was two-hundred-and-fifty yards away, so I didn't even have a chance to explain myself. I just got myself out of there, double-time.

"That same day, I started getting a horrible toothache. It was one of my lower molars. By two days after that, the pain was so bad that I knew the tooth was rotten and had to come out. I couldn't bring myself to pry it out with my Gerber multi-pliers. So I managed to tie a piece of monofilament around the tooth. I tried pulling it by hand, but I chickened out. It just hurt so badly. I didn't have anybody to help me. Finally, I ended up tying the fishing line to a big sapling that I had bent over. I sat down, pulled my lips out of the way, opened wide, and let it fly. The tooth came out all right. I screamed for a second. The void bled a couple of days. I did my best not to spit, because I'd heard that that creates suction and causes additional bleeding. It was painful, but luckily I had some Tylenol left in my first aid kit. The gum has healed fine, now.

"I did some fishing along the Clearwater before I headed up onto the Palouse. There are a lot of fish in that river. Even with just a hand line, I was able to catch a Dolly Varden and a good-sized salmon. That was enough food for three days eating, in less than an hour of fishing. It would have been nice to have one of those collapsing fishing poles, though. A few days later, I did some gill netting on some of the little tributaries going into the Clearwater. I caught a mess of trout. I cooked some, and smoked some.

"My trip up here toward the Palouse was relatively uneventful. I saw a lot of wild turkeys, several elk, and deer beyond counting. This is good country for foraging."

Todd interrupted: "Is there anything else you wish that you'd had in your pack or cache, or things you would have done differently, in retrospect?"

"Let me think." Doug paused to ponder. "Several things come to mind immediately. First and foremost, I should have found somebody to travel with. Going solo cross-country is a dicey proposition. You never know when you might get ambushed. If somebody gets the jump on you, you're history. Also, there is no simple way to provide security while you're sleeping. Just twisting an ankle badly or one bad swing with an ax could be fatal. You need a partner. Preferably two or more partners.

"And needless to say, traveling at all in anything less than an APC these days is foolhardy. There are too many chances of running into brigands; too many uncertainties. Staying put at a well-stocked and defensible ranch or farmhouse is the best approach. Traveling is only for the foolish or the desperate.

"Secondly, if I had cached some MREs and a few essentials in a few places along my route from Colorado, things would have been a lot more comfortable. I had some hungry days. For that matter, I could have cached some gas too, and just zoomed home.

"Third, I would have really benefited from a pocket-sized Bible. A few memorized verses aren't enough. You need the Word to keep you going and to maintain your balance.

"Fourth, this may sound pretty minor, but it isn't. I should have bought a pair of gaiters. I can't count the number of times that I've had to start a fire at midday to dry out my pants from the knees down.

"Fifth, I should have taken better care of my teeth. Brushing with just salt works fine in a pinch, although a mix of three-quarters baking soda to one-quarter salt is preferred. I should have carried a toothbrush, floss, and a tin of powder. They would have added hardly any weight at all to my pack, and in the long run, they could have saved me some grief.

"Sixth, I should have invested in an expedition-quality four-season tent. Tube tents—or even three-season tents for that matter—don't cut the mustard. Every time it rained, part of my gear would get wet and I'd spend hours drying it out."

Kevin chimed in, "As we often say around here, 'hindsight is twenty-twenty.' We planned ahead for what we could foresee and bought all that we could afford, but there's a lot of gear that we now *wish* that we'd bought."

Todd declared, "Speaking of gear, Kevin ... Go gather up Doug's gear out at the wood lot, bring it back to the barn and inventory it." Lendel nodded his head, picked up his 870 from the ready rack, and headed out the door.

Watching Kevin go, Doug said, "You certainly have a very well-organized retreat here."

Mary chimed in. "Yes, Cadet Carlton, you stumbled into the perimeter of a real-live survival retreat. You're looking at the culmination of about nine years of active preparation. Nobody wanted things to fall apart, but our group was part of the minority that was ready for it."

"*Nine* years?" Carlton asked.

"Yeah. Nine years ago most of us were in college, and not anywhere near the same stage of preparedness as you. We just have the advantage of having been at this a lot longer, methodically getting ourselves trained and storing up all the necessities, *in quantity*," she said smugly. With her last comment, Carlton's eyebrows raised and then a smile spread across his face.

Mike Nelson made a large batch of popcorn for everyone to share. Mike was the only one at the retreat that had yet learned the knack of making popcorn on the woodstove without burning it. As they were finishing the popcorn, Kevin returned. His report was terse: "Everything was just the way he described it, although he didn't mention that the socks and underwear were dirty. Whew! They're very frausty."

Todd called for another meeting late that evening. Everyone was present, with the exception of Kevin, who was by then on picket duty. Mike listened in over the TRC-500. As the conversation developed, it became apparent that there were two avenues that could be taken. The first option was that if he was interested, Doug could be nominated for consideration for a position in the group. If he accepted, it would be with the understanding that he would be treated as a full and equal member. However, he would have to give up any ideas that he might have of being a paid employee. If anything, he would owe the group redoubled efforts, as he would be using up part of their precious food supply. The second option was that Carlton could be resupplied with food and sent on his way, with the group's best wishes.

After being given the options, Carlton replied, "I don't think I'm likely to encounter a better survival setup anywhere in the country. Yeah, I'd certainly like to be a member of your group!"

The next morning, Doug Carlton was voted in as a member. He was temporarily housed in the hayloft of the barn. For his first two weeks he would only be assigned C.Q. duty. Thereafter, he would be allowed and expected to pull both C.Q. and LP/OP duty. He was warned that his position was probationary. Any foul-ups, and he would be banished.

After a week at the retreat, Doug already fit in and felt like an old hand. With his military background, he became a fast friend of Jeff Trasel. His interest in guns also brought him close to Dan Fong in short order.

In an orgy of generosity, Jeff gave Doug his spare blue steel Colt Commander .45, five magazines, a UM-84 holster, a cleaning kit, and more than two hundred rounds of assorted ammunition. Dan Fong gave Doug his beloved Winchester Model 1897 riot shotgun, its bayonet, and a surplus engineer's satchel filled with Remington number-four buckshot, twelve-gauge shells, and twenty rounds of Brenneke rifled slugs. Mike Nelson donated his spare "Trick Five Hundred" and a pair of nine-volt nickel hydride batteries to power it. Todd, who was roughly Carlton's size, gave him a set of DPM camouflage fatigues and his spare Moss Stardome II tent.

Doug commented several times that it seemed like Christmas.

CHAPTER 10
Curriculum Vitae

"A prudent man forseeth the evil and hideth himself;
but the simple pass on, and are punished."

—Proverbs 27:12, KJV

A call that was beginning to sound familiar came over the TA-1 late one after-noon in June. "Deliberate Front. Large group on foot—maybe ten of them. Some armed. Coming from the west. Four-hundred-and-fifty meters." In now typical fashion, seven group members popped out of spider holes when the party on the county road was in the middle of the kill zone. Once again, the ambush was a complete surprise. There were eleven people in the party: five men, four women, and two children. All carried backpacks. One pushed a large-wheeled baby carriage filled with supplies. When ordered to lay down their guns and packs, they did as they were told.

"Who are you, and where did you come from?" asked Mike Nelson.

A man with long hair and a beard replied. "My name's Rasmussen. We're from Spokane. We're heading to Helena, Montana. I have a brother who lives near there."

"Why did you leave Spokane?"

"Spokane is history, man. Most of it burned to a crisp last fall. Then, over the winter, the damnable convicts came, hundreds of 'em. They call themselves *La Nuestra Familia*. And they *didn't leave*. The few people left there started run-ning out of food this spring. We got out of town in the middle of the night while we still had the chance."

"How much food do you have with you?"

The bearded man replied, "Only enough for another day or two."

After quick consultation between the spider holes, the party of refugees was ordered to step back from the road and sit down with their hands on their heads. A quick search by T.K. showed that the refugees were not lying about the scarcity of their food supplies. Their packs mainly contained clothing, pots and pans, and a few mementos.

"We can give you some food, but we can't let you stay," Todd declared. "If you come back again, we won't give you anything the second time. Do you understand?" Across the road, heads nodded in agreement. Mary and T.K. were sent to the house to gather food for the refugees. They came back with a sack of onions and potatoes, a five-gallon plastic bucket of hard red winter wheat, ten pounds of rice, a bottle of multivitamins, and two cans of dehydrated peanut butter powder. These foodstuffs were set down in the road next to the refugees' packs.

"Is there anything else that you desperately need?" Todd asked.

"Yes. We have four guns but only seventeen cartridges between us. Can you spare any ammunition?"

"Which calibers?" Todd asked.

"We have two .22s, a .25-35 Winchester, and a .30-06."

After more consultation between foxholes, Todd jogged up to the retreat house, and returned with a twenty-round box of .30-06 one-hundred-and-seventy-grain soft points, and a plastic box of one hundred CCI .22 long rifle cartridges. These, too, he set down on the road.

"Well folks, we wish you luck," Todd said, after he had returned to his position. "We only wish that we could do more for you, but this is all that we can spare. As I said before, don't come back. You'll get nothing. Don't try and come back and take anything by force, either. We are well armed and have tight security. We'd cut you down like sheep. You can now get up and very slowly pick up your packs and the supplies that we left you, and be on your way. Keep the muzzles of your guns pointed away from us. Wait until you are out of sight before you stop and open your packs to redistribute your load."

The longhaired leader of the refugee band proclaimed, "Mister, I can't thank you enough."

"Don't mention it. It's the Christian thing to do. Goodbye and good luck. May God bless you and grant you safe travel." Todd and the others waited until the band of refugees was well out of sight before they got out of their spider holes and re-covered them.

"It seems that the summer refugee season has begun," Mary mused.

"Yep, it sure has," Todd replied. "I'm just glad that we're off the beaten path, rather than on a highway. If we were on a main drag, we'd be up to our elbows in refugees. Under those circumstances we wouldn't be in any position to dole out charity."

T.K. chimed in as they made their way up the hill, "It's not so much the refugees that would worry me. It's the escaped convicts that they talked about."

Yet another ambush on the county road was called in over the field telephone a week later. As she snatched up her Remington 870, Lisa Nelson exclaimed, "Not again!" The three strangers that approached were unusual. All three were riding Giant brand mountain bikes. Two of the bicycles were towing small two-wheeled trailers. When the ambush was sprung, the bicyclists skidded to halt, completely surprised.

"Keep your hands on the handlebars!" Mike Nelson ordered. After a moment, he added, "We are not looters! We mean you no harm. Okay. Now I want you to get off the bikes one at a time, real slowly. You first, mister." A balding, slightly chubby man dismounted. He engaged the bike's kickstand, and raised his hands. Nelson gestured with his HK91. "Now you, ma'am." The woman, who Mike judged to be in her fifties, dressed in blue jeans and a khaki shirt, also did as she was told. Like her husband, she raised her hands without being asked to do so. "Okay, now you, miss." A young woman with red hair who appeared to be in her late teens joined her parents. Unlike her parents, she let her bike drop to the ground. She looked very frightened.

"Who are you, and where are you from?" Mike asked.

"My name's Porter, Lon Porter. This is my wife Marguerite and my daughter Della. We're from Seattle."

"You came here directly from Seattle?"

"No. Last fall we drove our Volvo station wagon until we ran out of gas down on the Columbia River gorge, just east of Biggs Junction. We had to abandon the car and a lot of our clothes and things there. We were on our way to La Grande, Oregon, to stay with my brother's family. We made it the rest of the way there on our bikes.

"My brother Tom has a little ranchette on the outskirts of La Grande. We stayed with his family at his house. It was a small house, so they didn't have a spare bedroom. We slept in the living room. Everything was fine there, once Tom and I got over our nicotine fits. Neither of us was ready to quit smoking, but circumstances dictated that we went 100 percent cold turkey. Tom's neighbors raise cattle and were generous, but it was obvious that the food was going to start running low, so we offered to move on. We didn't want to be a burden."

"Where are you headed?"

"Montana. I've heard that things are less torn up there."

"Do you have family in Montana?"

Porter replied hesitantly, "Nn-no. Assuming that things are closer to normal there, I thought that I'd look for work. I'm a machinist."

After a pause, Mike offered, "Again, we don't mean you any harm, but we have to make sure that you aren't looters. There have been some passing through the area. Cannibals, some of them. We are going to have to search you and your belongings. Once we are convinced that you are indeed whom you say you are, and that you have no hostile intentions, you'll be free to go. Okay?"

"Okey-dokey," said Porter.

Sounding more like a police officer now, Mike said, "Now step away from your bikes, turn your backs toward us, and put your hands on the back of your heads, fingers interlocked."

The Porters did as they were told.

Mike spoke again. "Jeff, frisk Mr. Porter, and make it thorough." Jeff set down his HK and approached the stranger from behind and searched him methodically. He found no weapons.

"Okay, Jeff, get back in your hole. Mary, search the women," Nelson ordered. As soon as Trasel was back in position and had reshouldered his HK91, Mary popped out of her refrigerator hole, and frisked Mrs. Porter and her daughter.

When she began to search Della, Mary noticed that the girl was trembling. She said in a soothing voice, "Relax, kiddo. We're the good guys." In searching the two women, Mary found that they were both carrying stainless steel Leatherman multipurpose pocket tools. Otherwise, she found no weapons.

Mike told the Porters that they could lower their hands, but warned them not to make any sudden movements.

Next, Mary searched the panniers on the bicycles and their trailers. The process took fifteen minutes. During the search, she called out a running inventory: "Rain gear. It's Gore-Tex. Good quality, but awfully bright colors; a tool kit. Gosh, it's heavy! In it we've got ... a socket set, a big drill register ... a set of taps and dies ... a couple of micrometers, all kinds of stuff. I don't even know what some of these tools are. A lot of them look custom made." She then began delving deeper into the first trailer. "Here's an AR-7 .22 rifle like Doug's. But this one has a kind of brownish camouflaged stock instead of black. That's different." She pulled the plastic cap off the butt and extracted the gun's receiver from its compartment. "No wonder! It's an original *Costa Mesa*-marked Armalite! Dan told me that these things are pretty scarce."

After restowing the AR-7, she continued her search. "About fifteen boxes of .22 shells. A half a box of .380 ACP Federal HydraShok hollow points. An over and under shotgun, broken down in this leather case. It's a Ruger Red Label, twelve-gauge, a real beaut! Three boxes of twelve-gauge shells. Number seven bird shot, low base. A whole bunch of canned food. Some Mountain House freeze-dried stuff."

She examined the bikes themselves. All three were made by the Giant company, and were in good repair. Della's had a slightly smaller frame than the other two. There was a glaring difference between the two adult-sized bikes. They were both the Sedona model, but Mrs. Porter's was equipped with a large spring-loaded motor casing. It was connected by a pair of wires to a large black rectangular nylon case, which was cradled in a piece of black sheet metal. The sheet metal was bolted to the bottom tube of the frame. Mary eyed the system curiously. Looking toward Marguerite, she asked, "What is this thing, some sort of generator?"

More relaxed now, Mrs. Porter answered, "An E.R.O.S. motor unit, actually. They're made by a company called Omni Instruments, down in California. The motor is powered by a pair of gel cells there in that black case. The batteries are almost dead right now, though. When you swing the lever on the handlebar shaft, it drops the motor into contact with the rear wheel of the bike. Then, when you push the little switch on the right handlebar, it engages the motor. When it is fully charged, it will motor you along at twelve miles an hour on level ground. It has about an eight-mile range. I mainly use it to help climb hills. It also does what is called regenerative braking. When you go downhill, you can drop the motor down and it acts as a generator and partly recharges the batteries. It also helps keep the bike from picking up too much speed on the down grades."

Mary unzipped the battery case and examined the tops of the sealed gel cells. "Wow, this is a pretty neat set-up." She then shifted her attention to the large handlebar bag on Lon's bike. "Several road maps. A two cell Kel Lite. And ... aha!, an automatic pistol. I've never seen this type. Has anyone here ever heard of an 'Ortgies?'" Removing the gun's magazine, she announced, "It looks like a Three-Eighty." After slapping the magazine back into the pistol's grip and stowing it back in the bag, Mary continued with her inventory. "Two spare magazines for the pistol. Both are loaded with hollow points. A hot patch tire repair kit; a coil of wire; a bike chain-link tool; some duct tape; and a pair of pliers. That's all for this bag."

After a few more minutes of searching in silence she declared, "Not much worth mentioning in the other trailer and the saddle bags. Mostly clothes. There's a 117-volt power cube here, and a power cord with a cigarette lighter type plug. They must be for charging up the batteries for the motor unit." Mrs. Porter nodded in agreement. "There's also a photo album, a King James Bible, and a pretty well-stocked first aid kit. Nothing else worth mentioning."

With that, Mary returned to her position. After a pause, Lon Porter asked expectantly, "Well?" Drumming his fingers on the redwood lip of his spider hole, Mike asked, "Where did you work in Seattle, and for how long?"

"I worked at Boeing for seventeen years. I'm a master machinist." There was another pause.

"Do you know how to weld?" Mike asked.

Porter replied, "Of course. T.I.G., M.I.G., oxyacetylene, you name it. Boeing even sent me all-expenses-paid to take a special two-month course with Escher Wyss over in Zurich, Switzerland. That was in '93. Welding isn't my specialty now, though. I specialize in prototype machining."

"How about sheet metal fabricating?"

"Of course."

"Are you familiar with automobile mechanics?" Mike asked.

"Yes, indeedy. I've rebuilt I don't know how many car and truck engines in my spare time. Kind of a hobby of mine. About the only thing that I'm not well versed on is the newer cars with electronic ignitions or the other computerized doodads."

"And tool making? Lathes, milling machines?"

"Sure. I've worked with all the major brands—both traditional machines and the later computer-controlled ones."

After yet another pause, Mike said, "Okay Mister Porter, I'd like you and your wife and daughter to sit down on the far side of the road there for a while. Please be patient, but there is something that I have to discuss with my boss up the hill at the house." Turning to his side, he commanded, "Mary, you're in charge while I'm gone."

As Mike got out of his hole, the Porters sat down in the grass by the side of the road. They now wore expressions that were more curious than anxious. A few minutes later, Mike trotted back down the hill, with Todd following five yards behind.

"Mister Porter, is it? My name is Todd Gray. I'm in charge of this operation. My friend Mister Nelson tells me that you are a master machinist with no certain destination, who is 'seeking after employment,' as they say. If you'd care to join me up at the house, I'd like to explain our situation here, interview the three of you, and possibly make you an offer."

The debate on whether or not to take in the Porters was brief. With summer approaching, it was clear that the retreat would be shorthanded, especially with all of the gardening tasks that needed to be done. Mary summed up "the bottom line": Without additional help, they could either have a secure retreat, and quietly starve, or plant a large garden, and have less than full round-the-clock security.

The other key factors were Lon's skills. Because it now appeared highly unlikely that Ken and Terry Layton would show up, there was a perceived need for someone who knew the intricacies of cars and trucks. In addition, Marguerite, or Margie as she was commonly called, had grown up on a farm in Woodburn, Oregon. This gave her a wealth of practical farming and cooking skills. The Porters were voted in unanimously.

After rearranging the basement, one end was partitioned off with wall lockers and hanging blankets to form a bedroom for the Porters. Unfortunately, the only beds available were three Army surplus folding cots. The Porters didn't object. Soon after their sleeping arrangements were taken care of, Mike was given the task of getting the Porters set up logistically. Uniforms were not a major problem. Jeff Trasel gave up a set of DPMs for Lon, and Mike gave Margie a set. Because Margie was "big boned" but not overweight, they turned out to fit well. Mary gave two of her five sets of DPMs to Della. They too were about the same size.

The next, and more difficult, task was getting the Porters properly armed. Dan Fong's large gun collection saved the day. Although they were not group standard guns, Dan agreed to "indefinitely loan" his FN/FAL and his Portuguese contract Armalite AR-10 to the Porters. Both guns were chambered in 7.62mm NATO. Lon would use the FN, while Margie would use the much lighter AR-10. Dan had eleven magazines for the FN, but only two for the AR-10. This presented a problem, as two twenty-round magazines would not suffice for a firefight of any duration.

Lon went to work in Todd's shop the next day. First, after disassembling it, he used a dial micrometer to take a complete set of dimensions from one of the AR-10 magazines. He compared the AR-10 magazine with the magazines of other assault rifles chambered for the same cartridge, and came to the conclusion that their dimensional differences were too great to attempt to adapt any other type of .308 magazine to fit the AR-10. Next, he looked through Todd's collection of sheet metal for stock that would have the equivalent strength of the aluminum used in the original magazines.

The process of making the magazines took two days. The magazine bodies were bent from sheet steel. Their springs came from extra HK magazines. Their followers were cast from scrap aluminum, using the lost wax method. Once they were fully assembled, the magazines all functioned flawlessly. With the permission of Mike Nelson, the AR-10 was test fired and re-zeroed to suit Margie's preference. Using the new magazines, the rifle functioned without a stutter.

Jeff, who had been serving picket duty, came down the hill after he was relieved. He asked Dan, "What was all the shooting about?"

Fong replied, "We were testing the new AR-10 mags. They work great."

Jeff had missed seeing most of the magazine manufacturing process because he had LP/OP duty for two successive days. He asked, "Were they hard to make?"

"Nope," Dan answered. "If I had been doing the work, I probably would have made several prototypes before I got one that would finally fit and function properly. Old man Porter just whipped out all five at once. He went straight from concept to finished product. The guy is incredible. I can see that I'll be learning a lot from him. He's a far cry from Ian Doyle."

Jeff stroked his mustache and asked, "Doyle? Hey, wasn't he that Air Force cadet that you and Todd used to hang out with in college?"

Dan smiled. "Ah, so you do remember Ian. Yep, that's the guy. Todd and I kept up with him after college, mainly by e-mail. In fact, I had a chat with him on the phone just a couple of months before the Crunch. At the time he was flying F-16s down at Luke Air Force Base in Arizona. Hard to believe, but he was a Major-Select when we talked. He was married and had a daughter, too. She must be close to ten years old now. Seems like yesterday that we were in college. When we were living in the dorms, I helped him weld up and part together an Ingram M10 and a Sten gun in his parents' garage. He had Sionics type suppressers for both of them. The dude was very low key, but he had a secret life as a major gun nut. His motto was 'Cut to size, file to fit, and paint to match.' I wonder whatever happened to him, once the Schumer hit the fan."

"He probably has his own private little empire set up somewhere by now," Trasel said with a chuckle.

The diminutive Della, or "Little Dell" as Lon called her, also needed to be armed. After Rose was given T.K.'s CAR-15, there were no more spare .223 rifles or carbines available. A special meeting was held on the subject. After much arguing, the group finally voted to give Della the Ruger Mini-14 and accessories that was captured from the looters. For a handgun she was given Mary's spare blue steel Gold Cup. At roughly the same time, Lon "traded" his Ortgies .380 for Dan's long barreled Model 686 .357 magnum revolver. Although it was hardly an equal trade, Dan went ahead with it, knowing that the gun would be more useful in the hands of Lon than sitting in the back of Dan's wall locker. Margie traded most of the Porters' small cache of U.S. and Canadian silver coins for Dan's Beretta nine-millimeter pistol. This too was a lopsided trade, but the same logic applied, so Dan consented.

Because she had never done much shooting before, Della was given extensive target and combat shooting training over the course of the next few weeks. Doing this much shooting was judged an acceptable risk by Mike Nelson. As he explained his logic, the advantage of having another trained shooter outweighed the risks associated with making a lot of noise. Della had several instructors, starting with Rose, who spent several days teaching her the basics of marksmanship and shooting positions, using a Ruger 10/22. Next, she learned the functioning of her Mini-14 and how to field strip it, by Dan Fong. Then she was taught how to shoot the weapon accurately by T.K., using the techniques he had learned at the Front Sight Firearms Training Institute, and drawing on his many years of high-power competition experience.

Tom Kennedy, as "the marksmanship guru," insisted that she memorize the tables for bullet drop at different distances, and for bullet drift with varying crosswinds, and uphill/downhill compensation. After a few weeks practicing with different shooting stances and firing deliberately, Della developed into an accurate shooter. Eventually, she was hitting man-sized targets with regularity at ranges out to four hundred yards. Considering that she was shooting a .223 Remington, which was never known as a good long-range cartridge, her performance was commendable.

Her next phase of instruction, which she shared with Rose, Lon, and Margie, involved pistol shooting. They had two instructors: Mike and Todd. This training took eight days. On the first four days, the four students used bull barreled Ruger Mark II .22 target pistols that belonged to the Grays and Nelsons. Together, they fired nearly two thousand rounds of .22 ammunition. During the last four days of their training, they graduated to their full-power "carry" pistols. Through these, they fired almost eight hundred rounds of .45 ACP, .38 Special, .357 magnum, and nine-millimeter Parabellum.

In addition to deliberate target practice, they also practiced speed draws, combat stances, barricade shooting, tactical and emergency reloading, and low light shooting. Their "final exam" was a combat course on the run over a distance of five hundred yards, shooting at targets as close as five feet, and as far as one hundred yards. It was a demanding course, but all four did fairly well.

Following their pistol training, the four inductees were given instruction in tactics, patrolling, and combat rifle shooting. Mike Nelson, Jeff Trasel, and Doug Carlton served as the instructors.

Lon's mechanical ingenuity soon made itself evident. After his first shift of C.Q. duty, Lon suggested to Todd that he modify the hand crank generator to increase its efficiency. Mary had already expressed her worries of "repetitive stress" injuries. After Todd heard Porter's idea, he agreed enthusiastically. Lon started out by fabricating a metal stand to support Mary's old bicycle. Because it had large "outriggers" that extended outward for three feet, the stand firmly held the bicycle in position without fear of it tipping over.

With the rear wheel removed, and the bike mounted firmly in the stand, Lon made a mounting bracket for the hand crank generator. After taking some dimensions and doing rough calculations on gear ratios and crank speeds, Lon cut a piece of square bar stock to fit one of the two slots for the hand cranks. He then centered and welded a gear onto the end of the bar stock. Next, Porter bolted the generator onto the stand and connected the bicycle's chain and adjusted the tension. The new bicycle generator worked perfectly. With the increased efficiency of the generator, group members assigned C.Q. duty only had to operate it for forty-five minutes of each shift to generate the same amount of power that had previously taken three hours. This made everyone at the retreat happy. Cranking the generator was still not a fun job, but at least it was no longer an onerous task.

The Porters quickly integrated themselves into the day-to-day working of the retreat. All three pulled C.Q. and LP/OP duty. This provided the man-hours necessary for many of the more labor-intensive tasks, including garden-ing. Margie soon corrected one glaring defect that she had noticed. All of the men at the retreat had shabby looking haircuts. As there had been no one trained in how to give a proper haircut, the standard practice had been to wait until hair began to interfere with proper vision, and then proceed to hack it off unevenly. Some of the results were less than flattering. Margie, who had been giving haircuts as a hobby for two decades, soon set up shop. After giving all of the men fresh haircuts, she started working on the coiffures of the ladies.

Three weeks after the Porters arrived, Todd noticed that Della Porter was deeply engaged in conversation with Doug as he sat at the C.Q. desk. They were looking directly into each other's eyes. Della was smiling—a lot. Todd brought up his suspicions with Mary. She asked with disbelief, "What, didn't you notice before? Those two gravitated together more than a week ago."

A look of amazement spread across Todd's face. "But Della is only seventeen, isn't she?"

"Yes, hon, she won't turn eighteen until a few weeks from now. However, under the current state of affairs, I don't think that Doug is liable to be prosecuted. Besides, I don't think that anything has happened. Doug and Della are good Christians. They'll wait until they're married."

Todd scratched his chin. "Well, I don't want any fornicating or even 'bundling' going on under my roof. I guess that T.K. ought to have a talk with Doug, and determine his intentions. Then, I suppose it'll probably be time for Doug to ask Lon for permission to marry his daughter."

Mary smiled. "Yes, that's the thing a young man traditionally does, isn't it? Don't you remember your conversation with grouchy old Mr. Krause?"

"Are you kidding? That conversation with your dad is permanently etched in my memory." In a gravely voice, Todd quoted Mary's father: "'What exactly are your prospects, Todd?'"

• • •

One morning early in August, as they were dressing, Mary told Todd, "Honey, I've got something to tell you. I missed my last period, and I've been feeling really nauseated the last few days."

"You mean…you mean…." Todd stammered.

"Yes, you big oversexed stud, you got me pregnant."

Grinning from ear to ear, Todd asked, "You didn't intentionally…?"

Mary scowled. "No, of course not. But, like I briefed everyone in the group years ago, condoms are not the most efficient form of birth control. I should have insisted that all the ladies got fitted for cervical caps, since they're the best."

Todd put on a crooked grin and joked, "Personally, I think that you covertly put some pinholes in our supply of rubbers."

Mary slugged Todd in the shoulder and shouted, "Todd Gray! How could you say a thing like that? I swear, you have the biggest ego on the planet. I'll bet that you think that I just couldn't wait to become the mother of your first child, 'oh great tribal chieftain.'"

"No, darling. I just think that you are the most wonderful woman that any man could ever ask for. You have made me very, very proud. I love you very much."

• • •

Following the installation of the water and power systems, soon after they bought their Bovill property, Todd selected a site and built the listening post/observation post (LP/OP) for the retreat. The site that Todd selected was fifty yards above the spring. It had a commanding view of the entire property, and a good view of the county road in both directions. He resisted the urge to put the LP/OP at the very peak of the hill. Using knowledge gleaned years before from Jeff Trasel, Todd instead put the LP/OP five yards below the hill's crest at the hill's "military crest." By positioning the LP/OP on the military crest, it eliminated the risk of LP/OP sentries "sky-lining" themselves when they walked to and from their posts. This would eventually make it much easier to keep the location and existence of the LP/OP a secret.

The design for the LP/OP itself came straight out of one the Army field manuals in Todd's collection. The foxhole was dug armpit deep and eight feet long. It was lined with pressure-treated plywood to prevent the walls from crumbling. A stairway leading into the position was dug immediately to the rear.

The floor was "stair-cased" to three different heights to accommodate sentries of differing heights. At five-feet-two-inches, Mary was used as the model for the shorter LP/OP pickets. Next, the floor of the foxhole was covered with the same type of plywood used on the wall, and then industrial open weave rubber floor mats were added to provide a quiet, non-slip surface. After the experience of the first winter, Todd eventually built wooden steps to replace the earthen steps, and cut up floor mat material to nail on each step.

Another later addition was a roof for the LP/OP, something that Jeff Trasel would have referred to as "overhead cover." After building up banks on both ends of the LP/OP trench, Todd laid down a row of six-by-eight-inch treated timbers, parallel to the trench. On top of the timbers, he glued and nailed two-by-six-inch tongue and groove boards cross-wise to the support timbers. Next, Todd laid down four thicknesses of ten-mil black sheet plastic. This sheet plastic extended well beyond just the roof, so it would provide better drainage for rainwater. Finally, he covered the whole works with six inches of earth and then the squares of sod that he had originally dug up and set aside when he first started the hole for the trench. Within a few months, this sod grew back in a healthy coat of grass, all but obscuring the LP/OP. From the front, sides, or down the hill, it was practically invisible. Its vision slots were detectable only if someone knew where to look.

There were then just a few finishing touches on the LP/OP. First, Todd and Mary buried two strands of WD-1 field telephone wire that ran between the house and the LP/OP. Todd also made a few modifications to make the LP/OP more livable. First, he cut a few slots in the walls, and inset-mounted ammunition cans to act as shelves. The way they were arranged, the cans could be pulled out and their lids replaced. In this way, the rubber gasket lids would protect the contents of the boxes when they were not in use. Next, Todd bought a comfortable wooden desk chair at a secondhand store in St. Maries. He modified the chair by fitting a foam cushion, and then bolting on wooden extensions for its legs. With the extensions in place, the eye level of whoever was sitting in it would be virtually the same as if they were standing.

In addition to a TA-1 sound powered field telephone, Todd selected a variety of gear with which to equip the LP/OP. This gear included two angle head flashlights each with two thicknesses of red lens filters, a pair of rubber-armored Bushnell binoculars, a large spiral-bound note pad and pen to use for a duty log, a compressed-air powered boat horn for use as a backup alarm signal, four surplus white star parachute flares, and Todd's spare Remington 870 riot shotgun and a satchel of number-four buckshot rounds.

Unlike his other riotgun, this particular shotgun was customized for close-in night fighting. It had an eight-round extension magazine installed, as well as a Pachmayr rubber pistol grip. Using a special fore end mount built by Sure-Fire, there was a flashlight mounted below the barrel. A momentary on/off switch was built into the SureFire mount. Todd figured that it would make a good weapon to have handy if whoever was manning the LP/OP got jumped at close range. All of the gear for the LP/OP was packed in an olive drab foot-locker. Mary later used a hot glue gun to install thick foam padding inside the footlocker to protect its contents. To put the LP/OP in operation, everything was in one handy "strack box" that could be carried up the hill.

Next, again based on his training by Jeff Trasel, Todd made a range card and sector sketch for the LP/OP. Using a hundred-foot measuring tape, he and Mary took measurements from the LP/OP to each significant landmark on the retreat. Then Todd drew a sketch, with the distances written beside them. Thus, LP/OP pickets would be able to know the exact distances to various points, something that might come in very handy in the future. With her artistic talent, Mary later improved on the sector sketches with a diagram that she hand-painted on a piece of scrap plywood. This was later mounted on the wall of the LP/OP with wood screws. Todd liked her creation so much that he asked her to make similar "range paintings" for each of the windows of the house. If the house eventually had to be defended with their rifles, Todd didn't want anyone guessing at the range to any particular target.

The last of the stored toilet paper was exhausted the month after the Porter family arrived. The small packets of toilet paper that members of the group had saved from MREs was henceforth set aside for patrolling. At the retreat, the group switched to using paper from phone books. Mary had secured a tall stack of Chicago phone books years before, for just this purpose. Everyone realized that even this paper would be expended eventually, so it was used sparingly. The prospect of someday using leaves was not appealing.

CHAPTER 11

Dawn

"The sun's rim dips; the stars rush out:
At one stride comes the dark."

—*Samuel Taylor Coleridge*

Once the cold weather began to set in, during the first fall after the Crunch, the members of the group at the retreat settled into a routine. The main activity was standing picket and C.Q. shifts. As the weather began to get wetter and colder, the members began to dread LP/OP duty. In contrast, C.Q. duty was referred to as "soft duty." When not standing guard shifts, the other members worked on projects around the house, did laundry by hand in a large tub, and helped with the cooking. With few gardening tasks, there was even some spare time to read, talk, or play board games. Formal meetings were held only as circumstances made them necessary.

With Lon's permission, Doug and Della were married on the first of November. It was a ceremony much like the one that had been held for Jeff and Rose. The only difference was that there was more warning, so everyone took the time to dress better. All of the men wore ties from Todd's closet. Margie made a wedding cake. She was adept at getting the temperature of the woodstove oven just right.

The most popular games at the retreat were chess, Risk, and the card game Hearts. The radios yielded little more than static. On most evenings they would listen to the news on Swiss Radio International at 9.910 megahertz, the only commercial shortwave station on the air. It was all bad news.

Bible study and prayer meetings were held each evening after dinner. Either Lon, who was an agnostic, or Kevin, who was Jewish, took a short stint of LP/OP duty during these meetings. Kevin attended only the Bible studies when they were on Old Testament scriptures. Almost every evening, Todd, who had a melodic speaking voice, would read aloud for half an hour in the living room. Everyone would sit and watch the fire and listen to Todd read out loud. He started out reading short stories like Joseph Conrad's "The Secret

Sharer" and Carl Stephenson's "Leinengen Versus the Ants." Later, he began reading novels, a few chapters at a time. These included *The Fountainhead* by Ayn Rand and *Unintended Consequences* by John Ross. Todd skipped over the lewd passages from the latter, which he thought detracted from an otherwise top-notch novel. Todd often wore his TRC-500 headset during the readings so that whoever was standing LP/OP duty could listen in. For a generation reared on television, Todd was the next best thing.

Each Thursday was movie night. Using Kevin's wide-screen Mac laptop, they clustered chairs in the living room and watched one of the eighty-three DVDs in the combined collection at the retreat—most of them came from the Grays or Kevin Lendel. Saturday night was "movie rerun night," for the benefit of those who missed the Thursday movie because of LP/OP or C.Q. duty. The Saturday nights were nearly as well attended as the Thursday first showings.

One of the regular chores at the retreat was grinding wheat and corn, roughly every other day. For this, the group members took turns using Mary's Country Living grain mill. It was a well-made and reliable unit that verged on being overengineered. The mill's body was die-cast. Mary said that she would have preferred a cast iron body, "But of course it would weigh as much as an anvil," she said with a laugh. The mill was adjustable from very coarse (for simply cracking grain), to very fine, for making bread flour. The internal parts could be removed for service or repair. It had ball bearings on the shaft, which was a nice feature that most other small mills didn't have. In addition to the hand crank, the unit had a steel v-belt pulley wheel. Soon after they arrived, Lon fabricated a mount for the mill on the bicycle/generator with an adjustable travel to provide proper belt tension. Pedaling was far easier than turning the crank by hand. Mary bought the mill in 2002. It cost three hundred and forty dollars, and Mary soon spent an extra seventy dollars on spare parts, "just in case."

Once every two weeks, Mike had each member take turns at leading a practice patrol or ambush. Their performance was critiqued after each training session. Within a few weeks, the group's patrols took on a heretofore unknown level of precision. Noise was minimal or nonexistent, hand and arm signals were relayed expertly, and operations orders were given professionally, using the Army's standard five paragraph "op order" format.

The only problem that arose in the weeks after the new members were added to the group came when the septic tank backed up. From the day that the Nelsons arrived, Mary had insisted that everyone collect their used toilet paper in paper bags rather than flushing it. The contents of these bags were burned daily. The bags were euphemistically called "clothespin bags," in reference to the clothespins that were used to keep them shut to control odors. Even though there was no toilet paper going through the septic system,

Margie surmised that the large number of people at the Grays' house was over-taxing it. The first sign of this problem came when the kitchen sink drain started gurgling ominously. Margie recognized this symptom and alerted Todd. Resolving the problem took several days. First, the lid to the septic tank had to be found. This involved nearly a full day of probing with a pointed steel rod to determine where the outer edges of the concrete septic tank were located, and then digging down to the pumping cover.

A quick inspection showed that the tank's sanitary tee was clogged, and there was a fairly heavy layer of "cake" or "scum" in the upper potion of the center section of the three-section tank. The color of the liquid in the tank was almost black, which Margie said was a good sign that the friendly bacteria were doing their job. The blockage was soon cleared with a length of one-inch galvanized pipe. So that not as much digging would be required the next time the septic tank had to be inspected or worked on, Todd and Lon cut a fifty-five-gallon drum to the proper length to use as an inspection hatch. A piece of quarter-inch plate steel was laid on top, with the realization that the thin sheet metal drum would eventually rust out. With the new hatch in place, only a six-inch layer of soil had to be removed rather than twenty-five inches.

The inspection of the septic tank confirmed Margie's suspicion that the increased number of people living at the house had exceeded its carrying capacity. Todd consulted with the rest of the group members about their options. Two suggestions were made: frequently pumping the tank or con-structing an outhouse to supplement the septic tank system. The first option was out of the question because they did not have the pumping apparatus available to empty the tank. So they built an outhouse.

The outhouse was constructed a hundred feet from the house, far downhill from the spring, and away from the natural course of rainwater runoff. Mike mentioned that he had once seen an easy way to build a privy, at a hunting camp. His design suggestion was the one that was eventually used. All that had to be done was to bury two-thirds of the length of a fifty-five-gallon drum into the ground. An oval-shape hole was then cut in its top with a cutting torch. Then the entire bottom of the barrel was also cut out. After the jagged edges were filed off, a used toilet seat was mounted with its bolts through the top of the drum. To make it a private privy, a movable wooden shed was built over the top of it.

The new outhouse had several advantages. First, it took the burden off of the house's flush toilet septic system. Second, it would provide a valuable source of fertilizer for the flower garden that had previously been wasted. Todd soon instituted a rule that the group members would use the outhouse exclu-sively—except in cases of illness or when there was a certifiable blizzard blowing. This was not a popular rule, but it was heeded.

With the exception of Rose, all the group members maintained good health during the first winter at the retreat. A few of the members caught colds in the first weeks, but there were no cases of the flu or other illnesses that winter. Mary surmised that their isolation from other people was keeping them away from the infectious diseases transmitted by personal contact. All the original group members had received pneumonia vaccinations, in anticipation of eventually having a large group living in cramped quarters.

The group kept busy, even in the winter months. Since the house had an electric hot water heater—now defunct—they heated water on the wood-stoves for washing dishes, laundering clothes, or bathing as a daily chore. Water for baths was hauled in kettles from the kitchen to the bathroom. Luckily, it was only a few steps away. Laundry was done twice a week in a James hand washer and wrung with a hand wringer. Mary had had the foresight to order the James washer from the Lehman's Amish mail-order catalog. Kevin Lendel picked up the wringer at a farm auction in Clarkia, the summer before the Crunch. On the "non-laundry days," it was a couple's turn to have bathwater. Saturdays were bath days for the bachelors. All of this water heating and haul-ing made Todd wish that he had installed hot water coils in the heating stove.

Most of the group members kept in good spirits as the winter set in. Unlike millions of their fellow Americans, they weren't wet, cold, or hungry. Each evening before dinner, group members took turns saying a blessing. For anyone who was forgetful, it was there that they enumerated their many bless-ings. Only two members had any significant difficulties adjusting. One was Rose, who frequently got depressed worrying about her family, or thinking about the situation in general.

The other was Lisa, who roughly once a month would get into a verbal fight with someone or throw a temper tantrum over something that annoyed her. In most cases, she stormed off to her room and pouted. The next morning she would emerge, make her apologies, and then act as if nothing had happened.

T.K. counseled anyone who was showing signs of irritability or depression. Both most commonly occurred during the winter months, when everyone was by necessity living in close quarters. His counseling sessions usually consisted of a half an hour of prayer, questions and answers, some advice, and occasionally a good cry. T.K.'s never-flagging positive attitude and sense of humor did a lot to keep everyone else in good spirits. It was infectious.

One evening, when everyone around the dinner table was quiet and glum, absorbed in their own thoughts, T.K. yelled "Food fight!" He started throwing dehydrated peas at anyone and everyone. It turned into a major conflagration, with peas and instant mashed potatoes flung with abandon for at least a full minute. When the combat and the laughter died down, T.K. did most of the cleaning up of the food and putting it in Shona's scrap bowl. The clean up job took nearly half an hour. As he later explained to Todd, it was worth it just to hear everyone laughing.

LP/OP duty was a tremendously boring experience. Aside from being able to watch the sun rise and set, and refamiliarizing themselves with the constellations, there was not a lot to do. Reading while on guard duty was forbidden, lest a picket lose track of time and let an intruder slip in. There were a few false alarms at first, mostly caused by visiting deer, porcupines, and bears. Eventually, though, everyone became familiar with the normal activity patterns, sights, and sounds of the game.

At night, guards listened for sounds of movement or vehicle engines. They also watched for any of the twenty trip flares that were set up around the perimeter. These military surplus M49A1 trip flares were strapped to the sides of trees and poles. They were mechanically activated when anyone stumbled into their trip wires. At first, a few were inadvertently set off by group members forgetting where they were located. A few more were tripped by deer or by Shona. This latter phenomenon ended when all of the trip flares were repositioned to a greater height. During daylight and twilight hours, pickets glassed the hillsides and the county road in both directions with binoculars. For countless days, nothing happened. No one was seen on the county road. Kevin Lendel aptly described LP/OP duty as "tedium *ad nauseam*."

• • •

It was Lisa's turn at picket duty when something finally interrupted the monotony. She stood in the LP/OP, snuggled in a surplus N-3B Extreme Cold Weather parka, occasionally stamping her feet, watching the gathering gray gloom of dawn. As she was looking at the tree line at the back of the property, Lisa heard Shona barking. She turned to see four pickup trucks in a tight column, coming down the gravel county road, running with only parking lights on.

As soon as she saw the trucks, Lisa picked up the TA-1 field telephone and pulsed the clacker on its side. Mary, who was on C.Q. duty, answered. "There are four rigs in a row coming in from the west. Just a minute ... They are slowing down. They are stopping at the front gate. Get everybody up, now. Now, now, now!" Mary hit the panic switch. Mallory Sonalerts throughout the house began emitting a piercing, high-pitched tone.

Everything started happening very quickly when a man carrying a pair of thirty-six-inch bolt cutters hopped out the passenger side of the lead truck and ran up to the gate. Lisa rotated the selector switch on her CAR-15 and popped open the carbine's scope covers. "Crud! Hardly enough light," she cursed to herself. At about the same time, the gate swung open and the lead pickup gunned its engine. The truck didn't stop to pick up the man at the gate, who had dropped prone and out of sight in the high grass and teasels.

Lisa sighted on the passenger side window of the second pickup, which was slowing down to negotiate the turn a hundred yards down the hill from her foxhole. She fired two rounds, and missed, her shots passing well over the cab of the pickup. The words "Slow down, Breathe, Relax, Aim, Slack, and Squeeeeze, or you won't hit anything" echoed in her mind. With her next two shots, the passenger window of the third pickup crumpled satisfactorily. By now the first of the trucks was less than seventy-five yards from the house. Lisa continued to fire, much more rapidly, primarily at the backs of the pickups.

Inside the house, it was pandemonium. "From the front, four trucks!" Mary yelled.

Todd was the first in the house to start shooting, his HK91 bucking steadily against his shoulder. Just as most of the others got to their prearranged positions behind the slotted steel plates over the windows, three of the four trucks disappeared from view, wheeling quickly behind the barn. The fourth sped on, heading for the chain-link fence that surrounded the house.

No driver was visible behind the truck's smashed windshield as it hit the fence. The fence gave way with seeming effortlessness. The pickup then skidded sideways and nearly rolled over as it came to a stop only twenty-five feet from the house. A crescendo of fire that sounded more like tearing canvas than individual shots peppered the side of the truck. Its driver and anyone who might have been lying in the truck's bed were undoubtedly well ventilated.

Thirty seconds later, the firing stopped. Not out of self control, but rather because every one of the guns on the south side of the house were empty. All except Todd's. After firing most of a twenty-round magazine, he replaced it with his one and only thirty-round magazine, scanning for targets. "Reload, and fire only at definite targets!" Todd shouted. He then heard the clatter of numerous rifles being reloaded.

"What on Earth's happening up there?" asked Della from the back bedroom.

"Shut up and watch your sector of fire!" Todd shouted in reply.

A man briefly emerged from around the corner of the barn and fired three rounds from a SKS carbine at the house. All three rounds bounced harmlessly off the steel plates covering the windows. His shots were returned by several volleys from the house, which sent the man scurrying back behind the cover of the barn. The man popped the SKS around the corner and emptied it blindly. Only two rounds hit the house. Another volley of return fire from the house shredded the corner of the metal barn.

Todd quietly asked himself, "Now what?" He could not see any movement behind the barn, far off to his right. All that he could do was wait.

The only one with a view of the attackers, and a partial view at that, was Lisa, one-hundred-and-fifty yards away at the LP/OP. She could see two of them, both armed with riot shotguns, and the back end of one of the pickups. Fighting to control her breathing, she said quietly to herself, "Now let's do this right." She reached down into her ALICE pack and pulled out the bipod for her CAR-15. She clamped on the bipod and tried to center the four-power scope's crosshairs on one of the attackers. This took some time because she was shooting downhill and the bipod's legs were the wrong length. Only after she had shifted her position so that she rested on her knees on the chair was she able to acquire her target.

She fired twice, hitting the first man cleanly between the shoulder blades on the first shot. She couldn't be sure about the second shot. Lisa quickly changed her point of aim to the second man, who at that time was dropping to the ground to take cover. She felt no recoil and heard nothing when she pulled the trigger. At first Lisa thought that her CAR-15 had jammed, but soon realized that its bolt carrier was locked to the rear—the magazine was empty.

Disgusted with herself, she dropped to the bottom of her hole and swapped the magazine for one of the stack of loaded thirty-round magazines from the .50 caliber ammo can dug into the side of the foxhole that served as a shelf. "How could I have fired thirty rounds that fast?" she asked herself out loud. When she popped up to try again, the other man was gone. Although he was not moving, she fired three more times at the now motionless man she had shot in the back, just to be sure. She then flattened both of the truck's back tires, put a dozen rounds into the pickup's camper shell, and used up the rest of the magazine puncturing the truck's gas tank. Lisa again slithered down to the bottom of the foxhole, wondering what to do next. The answer came when she saw a Dymo label on the bottom of one of the magazines, as she reached up to the shelf to again reload her weapon. The label read, "Tracer."

Hearing a steady popping from up the ridge, Mary stated, "Sounds like Lisa has them in sight from the LP/OP." There was a long pause, then another two shots followed immediately by a loud explosion. A ball of fire welled up from behind the barn. To Mary, it looked like a miniature version of her imaginings of a nuclear ground burst.

It was relatively quiet for the next two minutes. No shots were fired, and the defenders sat anxiously at their positions, waiting for targets to present themselves. All that they could see were clouds of black smoke rising behind the barn. Then, as quickly as they came, the two remaining trucks roared out from behind the far side of the barn and back down the road to the gate. Todd, Mary, Dan, and Rose, all positioned at the front of the house, had the opportunity to fire several dozen rounds at the retreating pickups. They were disappointed to score only a few hits.

Lisa, still firing the magazine loaded with all tracers, got a few more hits as the two trucks sped away. To her surprise, the man who had used the bolt cutters, and who was now carrying only an automatic pistol, ran after the trucks waving his arms. Lisa took a steady aim with the bipod resting on the edge of the foxhole. It was eerie, almost seeming like slow motion, watching the red glow of the tracer arc out the two hundred and fifty yards to hit the man in the small of his back. He fell to the ground and began writhing violently. Lisa fired twice more. From the traces, she could see that both shots hit their mark. The man stopped moving.

Mike ordered everyone to reload their weapons and sit tight. A call to Lisa up at the LP/OP confirmed that she was all right. Mike asked, "Did you reload?"

She replied tersely, "Roger that."

Next, Mike asked her if she saw any movement or anything unusual behind the barn. She replied, "No, just the pickup truck that they left behind. The tires are still burning like crazy." Dan asked Mike, "Can I go out and check out the two trucks?"

Mike answered firmly, "No way! They could have left wounded or a 'stay-behind' out there. If there are any wounded, let's give them time to hemorrhage. We've got allllll day."

It was almost an hour later that Mike dispatched a squad to clear the area. By then the pickup truck at the corner of the barn had stopped burning. The squad moved in rushes as two separate fire teams, with one supporting the other on each bound. They didn't find anyone living. In addition to the dead man down at the county road, they found one dead man in the truck that had crashed through the fence, and two bodies on the ground behind the barn. The two men's weapons were missing. There was also a body burned beyond recognition in the back of the pickup that Lisa had set on fire.

When they examined the pickup nearest the house, they found that the driver was very, very dead. He had been hit by at least ten bullets. In the cab of the pickup, they found a Smith and Wesson Model 66 .357 magnum revolver with a four-inch barrel. Luckily, it had not been hit in the fusillade, and it was still serviceable. In the glove compartment of the pickup, they found a variety of road maps. These were later closely examined because they bore a variety of marking and marginal notations.

In the bed of the pickup they found four empty five-gallon plastic hydraulic fluid containers, which had apparently been used to carry gasoline. All four containers had been punctured by bullets, but had been empty at the time they were hit. They also found a sleeping bag, several cans of beer (some punctured by bullets), a spare tire, three pornographic magazines, and half a case of canned tuna.

Not much was recognizable, and even less was usable, in the burned truck. It had mainly carried food, much of it in cans. The only salvageable item that was found was an eighteen-inch pipe wrench. Down at the county road, they found the abandoned pair of bolt cutters. Twenty yards down the road, next to the body of the man Lisa had shot in the back, they found a badly pitted Ruger P-85 nine-millimeter pistol. In the man's pants pockets, they found a Case pocketknife, a set of lock picks in a leather case, and two loaded magazines for the pistol. On his belt, there was a crude handmade leather holster for the Ruger.

In case the group of looters turned out to be the vengeful type, Mike ordered that a second LP/OP be set up and manned continuously for the next twenty days. This put an extra burden on the group, but both he and Todd thought it prudent. The second LP/OP was set up on a low hill near the west property line. Because it was temporary, it was not dug in. It consisted of a diamond-shaped camouflage net supported in the center to a height of eighteen inches. This gave the observer just enough room to lie down comfortably. A length of WD-1 was run from the new LP/OP to the house. A TA-1 was set up at the LP/OP, and a second TA-1 was added to the C.Q.'s desk.

After setting up the new LP/OP, Todd called for another group meeting. There, he asked everyone to reorganize their backpacks as "bug out kits" to use in case the retreat was completely overrun. For this purpose, most of the group members' packs carried a selection of contents similar to Doug Carlton's pack when he first arrived at the retreat. At the same meeting the group discussed various options for additional security enhancements.

All of the usable items salvaged from the looters were locked up by Todd in the same locker that held the items seized from the pair of cannibal looters the previous year. The two wrecked pickups presented a problem. Neither of them could be easily towed because their tires no longer had integrity. Rather than fabricate a towing dolly, spare wheels from the group's vehicles were temporarily mounted on the two trucks until they could be towed away. After they were towed to the grove of trees behind Kevin Lendel's house, the trucks were put up on blocks so that the borrowed wheels could be taken back off.

Fixing the chain-link fence took four people an entire day. First, the sections of the fence that were damaged were cut away from the rest of the fence. Next, two fence poles were straightened, and another replaced entirely, with scrap pipe. Then, using two cable-ratchet hoist "come-alongs," the mangled section of fence was straightened out. The bumper of the shot-up pickup and the bumper of Todd's Power Wagon provided the anchoring points for the process. Finally, this section of fence was put back into place and lashed back into the mesh, using three strands of baling wire that was twisted together to provide the necessary strength. The finished job was far from aesthetically pleasing, but it was functional. Jeff Trasel declared the repair, "Crude, but effective."

Mike Nelson also replaced the cut lock at the gate on the county road with the last of Todd's spare Master locks. Soon after, with two other Group members posted as security, Lon welded a special sleeve to the galvanized steel gatepost. It was made from a three-inch diameter pipe for the lock to fit into, so that it would be immune from attack by bolt cutters. The chain itself was a special rubber-coated type, normally used to secure motorcycles, which Todd had bought before the Crunch. It was guaranteed as virtually "un-cuttable" by its manufacturer. After they had done all this, Mike went to talk with Todd. "Do you suppose that they'll come back?" Mike asked.

"I really can't say, Mike. If they do though, it won't be nearly as easy to stop them. They'll either try for a stealth blitz or come back with something so well-armored that they can just bull right in here with our bullets bouncing off of them."

"There's only one way we could stop something like that, and that's some dynamite."

"Well, Mikey, why don't you put your thinking cap on and develop a plan to use some of your goodies in the basement."

The next day, Nelson began the construction of his first fougasse, a sort of homemade cannon. He used some six-inch diameter pipe he found in the scrap heap behind the garage. All the material had been left behind by the farm's former owners. It was heavy-gauge pipe. It looked like the same variety that he had seen used for water well casings. With Lon's help, Dan cut off a six-foot length of pipe. Then, using some of the scrap left over from the window-plating project, they welded a one-half-inch thick cap on one end of the pipe.

With the help of several "stray bodies," Mike moved the pipe down the hill to the front gate. Just inside the front gate there was a gently sloping grass-covered mound of earth six feet high and about fifteen feet in diameter. It sat about ten feet back from the road. It appeared to be soil left behind many years ago when a bulldozer was used to first cut the grade for the road up to the house. Using a pick and two shovels, Mike and his assistants cut away a strip of sod, and then dug a seven-foot-long trench across the top of the mound. They made the trench just wide enough to accept the six-inch pipe. Next, the pipe was laid down in the trench, with the open end facing the road. Mike ensured that the pipe pointed slightly downhill.

The next stage of the fougasse construction was the dangerous part. Mike went down to the basement and dug out the oldest of his three cases of Dupont 75 percent dynamite sticks. He found the dynamite to be in excellent condition. Mike pulled nine sticks of dynamite out of the case, and after thoroughly examining each of them, laid them in a cardboard box that was half filled with Styrofoam pellets. He handed this box to Rose, who with very wide eyes—it was her first time handling explosives—slowly and carefully carried them down to the front gate. "Get out of the way, I'm a suicide jockey!" she shouted, as she walked up the stairs from the basement.

Todd, who was standing at the top of the stairs, gave a hearty laugh. He quipped, "You can relax, Rose. There aren't any blasting caps in those sticks." From the other end of the basement, Mike gingerly opened his box of blasting caps. He had a total of eighty-five caps. Fifty were of the electric variety. The rest were fuse type caps. As he examined them, he said to himself, "My little babies! How are you today?" He selected two of his Ensign-Bickford electric caps for the fougasse. Holding the caps by their wires at arm's length, Mike carefully walked up the stairs, out the front door, and down the hill to the gate. He then gently set the caps down, well away from the box containing the dynamite.

Mike went back up the hill to gather the materials he would need to finish the job. He collected ten pounds of scrap metal—mainly bent nails, rusty hardware, and the like; two pounds of broken glass; half a paper shopping bag of old rags; a reel of WD-1 commo wire; a pair of wire strippers; a roll of black electrical tape; a caulking gun loaded with a tube of clear silicone sealant; a box of plastic trash bags; a long push-broom handle; and a large plastic coffee can lid.

When he got back to the base of the hill, Mike began preparing his charge. First, he bundled the sticks of dynamite together with the electrical tape. He formed a circular bundle just over five inches in diameter. Next, he whittled a point on a wooden stick and used it to poke holes into the ends of two of the sticks of dynamite. Rose asked, "Why go to all the trouble of whittling a stick? You could use a screwdriver or a penknife."

Mike replied, "I always try to avoid using metal. That rules out the risk of a spark of static electricity." Rose frowned, and then nodded in agreement.

Next, with his hands trembling slightly, Mike inserted one blasting cap into each of the holes he had made. The caps were then securely fastened with several wraps of the black tape. He explained, "The second cap is just for redundancy. This could be buried for a long time before we ever have to touch it off."

By now everyone except Rose and Doug were already back up the hill, hoping that they didn't hear a big bang. They stayed to watch and get further instruction on the fine art of blasting from Mike.

Mike next cut off a fifteen-foot-length of commo wire, and stripped the ends of the pair of wires. In a few minutes, he deftly spliced the two sets of wire from the blasting caps to the commo wire, and covered the splices with electrical tape. He explained, "Again, I used two caps for extra insurance, just in case one is bad. It doesn't happen very often, but for an application like this, it would be more than just embarrassing if it didn't go off." He then ran several loops of the commo wire around the bundle of dynamite and secured the loops with electrical tape. "This is so if there is any tension on the wire, it won't pull the caps apart or out of position," Mike explained. Next, he wrapped two thicknesses of plastic from one of the trash bags around the bundle, and sealed it with tape.

Then, with his breath held, but trying to appear calm, Nelson slid the bundle of dynamite down the metal tube of the fougasse. Once it was at the end of his arm's reach, he completed pushing the bundle to the back-plate using the broomstick handle. "As you can see, I just left the commo wire dangling out the front of the pipe. I'll deal with it later."

Next, Mike began stuffing the rags down the pipe.

"What are those for?" Rose asked.

Still looking down at his work, Mike replied, "They act just like the wad in a shotgun shell."

After he had lightly tamped in the rags with the broomstick, Nelson began tossing the rusty scrap metal and broken glass into the mouth of the pipe. These, too, he tamped with the broomstick. An odd look came across Mike's face, and he let out a chuckle. Turning to face Rose and Doug, he pressed the ends of his eyebrows upward with his fingertips. He quoted, "If propelled with sufficient force, they would make formidable projectiles."

Doug began laughing uproariously. Rose didn't get the joke.

Doug said, "What's the matter, Rose, didn't you ever watch *Star Trek*? Remember the episode where Captain Kirk has to duel with the captain of the Gorn spaceship, the giant lizard man?"

"Oh yeah, now I remember," Rose said with a smile. "Is that where you got the idea for building this 'foo-gas?'"

Mike shook his head. "No, the basic concept is the same, but the design for this is straight out of one of my Army Engineer field manuals. This sucker isn't portable, like Captain Kirk's. However, it's also about ten thousand times safer to use."

Mike was nearly finished with the job. Using his pocketknife, he poked a hole near the edge of the plastic coffee can lid. He then threaded the ends of the length of WD-1 through the hole. Mike then slid the lid down the wires until it fit over the end of the six-inch pipe. "An almost perfect fit," he declared. Next a bead of silicone caulking was run around the lip of the pipe, and another dab was squirted through the hole through which the commo wire passed. He then shoved the lid onto the pipe. "Doug, can you hold this in place while I secure it with some tape?" Mike asked.

Carlton stepped forward with a loud, "Yes, Sir!"

After a few wraps of tape were in place over the lid, Mike placed two thicknesses of the plastic trash bag over the cap. Then, it too was secured with several wraps of tape. Brushing his hands together, Mike offered, "Okay, that oughta keep it watertight."

During the next half hour, Mike, Doug, and Rose back-filled the trench and relaid the sod over the top of it. Less than an inch of sod covered the muzzle of the fougasse. Unless someone knew what to look for, the existence of the fougasse was not detectable.

Later that afternoon, with the aid of several more shovels and shovelers, a shallow trench was dug from the fougasse up to the house. After another splice was made and wrapped with electrical tape, the WD-1 was reeled out in the trench. At the house, the WD-1 was fed into the house via an air vent in the brickwork. The far end of the commo wire was positioned at a front window with a good view of the gate. The ends of the two-conductor wire were then connected to a Claymore mine firing device, commonly called a "clacker."

The clacker belonged to Dan Fong. It had been given to him several years before by a coworker at his cannery who was an Iraq War veteran. After testing the circuit with a volt/ohm meter, the clacker, with its heavy wire "safety bale" in place, was then put in a cigar box that was marked with a hand-painted red warning sign. It read, "Hands Off. This means you. By order of the Tac. Coord."

Todd liked the fougasse so much that he had Mike and his understudies build five more over the next seven days. This used up most of the rest of the scrap six-inch pipe. The second fougasse was lined up with a large downed tree some fifty yards away from the house. Todd picked this spot because the tree would be a tempting piece of cover for anyone attacking the house. Todd said, "If we spot anyone laying behind the log and shooting at us, Ka-Boooom! End of story."

The third fougasse protected a blind spot beneath the LP/OP. The fourth was aimed at a trail junction at the edge of the wood lot. As a cue to trigger this fougasse during hours of darkness, a trip flare was strung at chest height. The fifth was aimed at the area behind the barn—the blind spot that the last group of looters had used to their advantage. The sixth and last fougasse was planted in a hole in the middle of the county road, in the center of the ambush zone covered by the spider holes. This fougasse, designed to fire vertically, was specially designed to defeat vehicles. It was loaded with a single pointed three-inch diameter hardened steel penetrator backed with a small coffee can filled with two pounds of scrap metal shrapnel and all the powder from a thirty-minute road flare. This coffee can had slits running its full length, cut at one-inch intervals. This was designed to delay the spread of the shrapnel until it entered a vehicle.

The clacker in the cigar box was soon replaced by a control panel, built by Kevin. It had enough indicator lights and switches to control up to ten devices—be they fougasses or Claymores or anti-vehicular explosive charges. The first five fougasses were wired into the panel soon after it was tested. Using her artistic talent, Mary added numbers and diagrams of the expected fans of effect for the fougasses to the sector painting next to the window where the "Mr. Destructo" control panel was placed. All the operator had to do was spot a target, consult the sector painting, and hit the correspondingly numbered button. A child could handle it. So a child *couldn't* handle it, Kevin had included an electrical key switch to the panel. This key acted as a master cutoff for the motorcycle battery that powered the panel. The battery was constantly trickle-charged by the house's twelve-volt DC power system.

Still concerned about the threat of vehicles crashing through the chain-link fence surrounding the house, Todd asked Mike to coordinate the construction of a trench completely surrounding the fence. This upgrade was suggested to Todd by Kevin Lendel. The trench, which was affectionately referred to as "the moat" by most of the group members, took the entire work force of the group a week of hard labor to dig.

Consulting one of his "five series" Army Engineer manuals, Mike specified that in order to be effective, the trench should be in a sloping L-shape. The short end of the L was a vertical wall on the side closest to the fence, while the gradual upward sloping part of the trench faced outward. The trench was sixty inches deep at its deepest point. The total width was nine feet. A narrow wooden footbridge covered with some half-inch plywood was positioned over the trench in front of the gate.

In a private conference with Mike, Todd expressed his continuing concerns about another attack by the band of looters. He told Mike, "I guess that we've done all that we can, under the circumstances. I'd feel better if we were able to put up some antipersonnel barbed wire, but there's just none available. If I'd only thought to buy some surplus concertina wire, or maybe some civilian razor wire. The surplus stuff was real *cheap*, too. I could have bought it for practically scrap metal prices. It must be worth a fortune, now."

He and Mike then shared a now familiar facial expression with their jaws gaping. In unison they chanted, "Oh well, hindsight is twenty-twenty." After some consideration of numerous alternatives including pungi stakes, Todd and Mike decided to install "tangle foot" wire.

Mike gave a quick briefing to his assembled crew of workers. "Okay, the idea behind tangle foot is to slow down anybody trying to rush your position. In this case, it's the house. What we'll be doing is driving metal fence T-posts into the ground all over the yard inside the fence in a semi-random pattern, but no more than ten feet apart. Next, we'll be stringing baling wire at random heights between six inches and forty inches off the ground between all of the fence posts. It forms a sort of giant spiderweb. This way, anyone who manages to get over the fence won't be able to just dash up to the side of the house. The tangle foot will slow them down considerably, forcing them to cut it, or step over it, or crawl under each strand. During this interval, we'll have more of an opportunity to spot them and take them out." With all available hands at work, the construction of the tangle foot array took only three hours.

With the new security measures in place, the Group waited anxiously for several weeks for another attack by the same band of brigands that had come before. Eventually, they were not quite as nervous, but the attitude at the retreat would never be the same as before the attack.

CHAPTER 12
The Templars

"Third Fisherman: 'Master, I marvel how the fishes live in the sea.'
First Fisherman: 'Why, as men do a land; the great ones eat up the little ones.'"

—*Pericles,* Prince of Tyre

Todd Gray's group began to patrol outside the perimeter of the forty-acre retreat later the same winter that the looters attacked. They had decided to delay leaving the retreat because they were well supplied and becoming increasingly self-sufficient. They reasoned that the longer they waited, the more likely that the bands of looters would have been thinned out through attrition. They also wanted to avoid getting shot by nervous neighbors. Typically, the patrols consisted of seven group members. They were broken into two three-member fire teams, plus a patrol leader. The first few foot patrols were relatively short. They started by making contact with surrounding farms. All of the contiguous farms had been abandoned, due to farmers relocating to "double up." The nearest occupied farm was just over a half-mile away. It was held by the farm's original owners, plus two other families.

The group soon set a SOP for making initial contact with farms. First, they would approach until they were just in sight of a farmhouse. Then, waving a large white flag made out of half a bedsheet, one of the patrol members would approach the house with their rifle or riotgun slung across their back. It was risky business, but with no electronic communications available, it was the only way to avoid a firefight. Generally, the contacts with the farm-strongholds went well.

The group member first making contact would inquire if any assistance was needed by the farmers. In most cases, the answer was no. In a few instances, there were requests for items like antibiotics or matches. The Group did their best to fill these requests. Todd's general guidance on charity was to "give until it hurts." He wanted to make it clear that the Group was there to help their neighbors, and absolutely not to bully them. Without providing a lot of details, the farmers were briefed on the existence of the Group. It was made clear that if any farm in the area came under siege by looters, the Group would do their best to respond and drive them off.

Next, the patrol got any information that the farmers could provide on the activity of looter bands in the area. Before leaving, they left word that the Group constantly monitored channel seven on the CB. The CB base station recovered from Kevin's house was set up on the C.Q. desk for just this purpose.

As the group's patrols made probes to the west, they began to hear farmers making references to "The Templars," representatives of an apparently well-organized stronghold located near the town of Troy, nineteen miles west of Bovill. When pressed for additional information on these "Templars," the farmers reported that some of their neighbors had been contacted by men dressed in camouflage uniforms and carrying "Army rifles" and riot shotguns. Like "the Group," they had inquired if the farmers were in need of any assistance.

Only when the Group's patrols traveled west of the hamlet of Deary did they contact a farmer who had actually come face-to-face with the Templars. In fact, when the patrol was first spotted by the farmer, he hailed them with the words, "Hello there, Templars! Come on down the hill!" It was not until the patrol entered the man's barnyard that he realized that they were not members of the Templar group.

When questioned, the farmer told Mike, who was leading the patrol, that the full name of the organization was the Troy Templars. They did indeed wear camouflage uniforms, and carried paramilitary weapons. The farmer said that the Templars had worn a different camouflage pattern than the patrol was wearing. When pressed, he could only describe the pattern as "not the new digital things. It's the old style—green, brown, and black, and kinda curvy." To add to the confusion, he said that the Templars often referred to their own organization as "the Group."

The farmer, who had only been visited by the Templars once, could give no further details on the undefined organization. Mike then told the farmer, "If you are contacted by these Templars again, please ask them to call us up during the evening hours on CB channel seven so we can discuss some things."

"Are you two groups in competition?" the farmer asked.

"We don't know yet. Just ask them to give us a call."

The farmer then asked, "Who should I say that they are calling?"

Mike was momentarily dumbfounded. He finally blurted out, "The Northwest Militia."

That evening, as soon as Mike's patrol had gone through the formalities of a challenge and password and had passed back into the retreat's perimeter, he strode up the hill to consult with Todd and T.K. In a few minutes, Mike reported what he had seen and heard during the patrol. When he got to the point in his story where he had identified their group as "The Northwest Militia," Todd asked incredulously, "The *what*?"

Mike shrugged his shoulders and replied, "It just popped into my head. I couldn't think of anything else to say. I knew for sure, though, that I couldn't just say 'the Group.' That's not a proper name to use with outsiders, and we have to be identifiable somehow."

After cracking a wry smile, Todd mused, "Well, with a name like that, we'll certainly have them guessing at our strength. Makes us sound like a small army. By current standards, I guess we probably *are* a small army. Did this farmer give any indication as to the size of this Templar outfit?"

Mike shook his head. "No, the guy just said that they had come to his farm in a five-man patrol, and that when he asked how many men they had at their stronghold, that they changed the subject."

"Hmmm," Todd remarked, "these Troy Templars sound cagey. They definitely sound like they were prepared before things fell apart. Most likely survivalists or militia members, although there is a chance they could be some sort of radical kooks."

T.K. interjected, "Just what sort of name is 'the Troy Templars,' anyhow? It sounds like a bit of a mixed historical metaphor to me."

"What do you mean by that?" Mike asked.

T.K. bit his lip and then queried, "Well, if they are from Troy, then properly they should be Trojans, right? But they call themselves Templars. The Knights Templar was a clerical order that first got started during the Crusades. They were in roughly the same category as the Hospitalers. The Templars' job was to guard pilgrimagers as they traveled through the Holy Lands. They were real stud monks—you know, a cross in one hand, a sword in the other. I suppose that these new Templars chose the name in reference to the fact that they see themselves as protectors of the area. Interesting."

After considering T.K.'s words, Todd pronounced, "As I see it, the key questions are: one, what are their intentions? Two, are they moral, ethical, and law abiding? Three, what is their manpower? Four, what, if any, are their politics? And five, assuming that they are on the side of 'truth, justice, and the American way,' are they going to be friendly toward us?"

Todd's questions went unanswered for nine days. Then, at exactly 6 p.m. on the evening of January twenty-second, a call came over the CB on channel seven: "Com 1 of the Troy Templars calling the Northwest Militia, over."

As most of the group had just finished eating dinner, Todd was there to pick up the CB's handset. "This is Todd Gray of the Northwest Militia, go ahead."

"Mister Gray, this is Roger Dunlap, Com 1 of the Templars. Are you the head of your group, over?"

"I am indeed, over."

"I understand that our patrols have started coming into contact with some of the same farms and ranches, over."

"Yes, that appears to be the case, over," Todd replied.

"We have heard that you are from the Bovill area, is that correct? Over."

"Roger that. And you are from the Troy area? Over."

"Affirmative, over."

Todd then asked, "I hadn't heard of your retreat's existence before things fell apart, over."

"Nor had we of yours. It seems we both kept a low profile, over."

"Well, I would like to parlay with you further, but this is hardly the proper venue, if you gather my meaning, over."

"I agree; this is hardly a *secure* form of comms. When and where do you want to meet?"

A meeting of two representatives from each group was scheduled for noon the next day, weather permitting. They were to meet at the cemetery on the west side of Deary, a town roughly equidistant between Bovill and Troy.

Todd and T.K. drove to the meeting in Jeff's pickup truck. Todd decided to drive the truck for both psychological effect, and to give the ability to get out of an ambush in a hurry. Todd and T.K. were ten minutes early. They wore clean sets of their best-looking DPMs. The Templars, on horseback, arrived at two minutes before noon.

As the two Templars approached, Todd could see that they were wearing BDU uniforms and woodland pattern pile caps. Their clothing, too, was clean. The two men both carried M1A rifles, and wore standard Army issue LC-1 harnesses. Both also carried Beretta Model 92 pistols in Army issue olive drab nylon Bianchi hip holsters.

The older of the two men, about forty-five, with thin features and balding gray hair, greeted Todd and T.K. with the words, "Hello, my name's Dunlap, which one of you is Mister Gray?"

"I am," Todd answered. "A pleasure meeting you, sir."

"And you. This is Ted Wallach. He's our Com 2—the security coordinator."

Not knowing what to say next, Todd said, "Nice horse."

Dunlap crossed his arms and replied, "Nice truck."

They stared at each other for a few moments. It was Todd who spoke next. "It seems that we have a lot in common. Tell me, just what sort of survivalist *are* you?"

Dunlap considered his question, and replied, "I'm basically of the Mel Tappan school, with a little Bruce Clayton and Kurt Saxon mixed in." Todd nodded his head and echoed, "Tappan was my main influence too, with an admixture of Dean Ing, Rick Fines, Jeff Cooper, Mike Carney, Bill Cooper, and a dash of Ayn Rand."

Dunlap gave a chuckle. "Your friends are my friends. I guess that puts us on the same team."

"Perhaps," Todd intoned, trying to sound ambiguous. He added, "Are you Christians?"

"Of course we are. We have all repented and committed ourselves to Christ. There has been quite a revival at our retreat since the collapse." Dunlap folded his hands and looked Todd in the eye. He asked, "Now what are the intentions of your 'Northwest Militia?'"

"Oh, I would assume something very much like the Troy Templars."

"What do you mean, exactly?" Dunlap asked.

Todd now knew that the ball was placed firmly in his court. He answered resoundingly, "To restore order and the primacy of constitutional law, and to protect free trade and travel."

"Now we're talking! We used very similar words when we wrote the bylaws of the Templars." Both men smiled.

"Just how large is your group, Mr. Dunlap?"

"We have twenty-six members. They range in age from five to seventy-three. We had twenty-seven, but one of our men died of appendicitis. And yours?"

"We have twelve members. No children—not yet at least. All of the militia members are trained in weapons and tactics, and our oldest member just turned fifty-two. They are all trained and able-bodied."

"Meaning...?" Dunlap asked.

"Meaning that we can field all twelve members for combat, if need be."

After pausing and staring at the ground, Dunlap looked up. "I think it might be possible for your group to be integrated into the Templar organization."

Todd slowly shook his head from side to side. "That isn't what I came here for. I had assumed that we would be talking as equals. I had cooperation, not consolidation in mind."

"But our group is more than twice the size of yours. We undoubtedly have a larger pool of useful skills available. We are also on excellent footing, logistically. You see, I was independently wealthy before things fell apart. This gave us the wherewithal to put away a *substantial* stock of food, weapons, tools, and medical supplies. It only stands to reason that you should come under the wing of a larger, better supplied group."

Todd frowned. "In the first place, the total size of your group may be larger, but in terms of your actual ability to police a given area, it is probably no greater than ours. As I mentioned before, we can field all twelve of our members. In terms of fit and trained combatants, I would expect that your strength is essentially comparable or perhaps only slightly greater. Also, keep in mind that we're pretty well squared away logistically, ourselves. We didn't have the benefit of a 'Sugar Daddy,' but we spent every dime we could spare for nearly ten years, preparing."

Roger Dunlap looked as if he did not like what he had heard. "Look, I've made a reasonable proposal, and you haven't even taken the time to fully consider it."

"I didn't consider it because it is totally out the question, Mister Dunlap. Our militia has its own bylaws, and its own leadership. Granted, our two groups have similar philosophies and goals, but there's no way that we are going to just 'come under your wing.'"

"But you'd be part of our organization, with full voting rights."

"No matter how you cut it, we'd still be relinquishing an independent organization to yours. Furthermore, we'd constitute a minority when votes were taken. I find your proposal unacceptable. I'd rather propose another arrangement."

"Which is?"

"That our groups retain their independence, but that we form an alliance."

"I came prepared today only to offer you a part in our organization, Mister Gray. Our group would have to take another vote before we entered into any alliance."

"Well then, I guess that marks the end of our conversation," Todd retorted.

Dunlap sighed and said, "What do you say that we meet three hundred yards west of here at noon on the day after tomorrow, under the same conditions?"

"Very well. Please come prepared to discuss the parameters of an alliance."

"I can't promise you anything until I consult with the rest of the Templars."

Todd looked Dunlap squarely in the eye, and enunciated, "When you brief your group about our conversation, please pass on the following message: 'You will find that the Northwest Militia will be either the most valuable, loyal, God-fearing, and trustworthy of allies, or ... if you try to coerce us—the worst of enemies. The choice is yours.'"

"I'll pass along your message. Goodbye, Mister Gray."

"Goodbye, Mister Dunlap."

The two then shook hands, but neither of them managed more than half a smile. With that, they turned and walked away from each other.

As T.K. shut the door on the passenger side of the truck, he asked, "What do you make of them, Todd?"

Todd didn't answer Kennedy's question until after he had started the engine of the pickup, and turned it around to get back on the road to Bovill. After this interval, he replied, "That's hard to say, T.K. That Dunlap character is hard to read. He has a real poker face. At least we found out how large their group is."

T.K. cocked his head and asserted, "That is *if* he was telling us the truth."

"On that particular point, I think that he was. If he wasn't, I don't think that he would have mentioned the age composition of his group in the same breath," Todd said.

After driving for a few minutes in silence, T.K. asked, "So, do you think that they'll agree to an alliance?"

With a grave voice, Todd replied, "I hope so. If they don't, things could get real nasty. I tried to make it clear where we stood without sounding too brash, but I wanted to be firm. Like that line from the second *Buckaroo Banzai* movie: 'Treat us good and we'll treat you better. Treat us bad and we'll treat you worse.'"

After they got back to the retreat, Todd called for a meeting after dinner. There, he and T.K. briefed everyone on what had transpired. Although all of the group members agreed with Todd's refusal of the Templars' offer, there was some criticism. Mary, now eight months pregnant and looking very plump, said forthrightly, "You should have found more in common and established a better rapport before you talked turkey."

Mike agreed with Mary's assessment. He commented, "If Terry Layton were here, she'd probably say that it was a case of two warriors having a discussion that should have been handled by people with a different personality type. Someone more diplomatic."

Todd flushed. He implored, "What are you saying, that I blew it?"

Mike shook his head. "No, what I'm saying is.... What I'm saying is that 'a beginning is a very delicate time.' I don't differ one iota in the substance of what you told Dunlap, but I think that you could have acted friendlier."

"You weren't there, Mike. If you had been, I think that you would have said the same things, and used the same tone of voice. I wasn't about to play the weak sister. I was trying to negotiate from a position of strength. As near as I can tell, these Templars aren't quite as altruistically motivated as we are. They seem to want to exert some power at the same time they do good works like doling out charity."

"Do you think they've been corrupted?" Mike asked.

"Corrupted in the sense of Lord Acton? As in, 'Power tends to corrupt and absolute power corrupts absolutely?' Probably not yet, to any great extent, but there is definitely the potential there. You know we've discussed that at so many group meetings. Everyone in our situation has to be on guard for that. It's not just the Templars. Neither group is immune. We're *all* sinners. The building blocks for tyranny are right here in this house. Look at our situation compared to most of our neighbors. We've got real organization, superior arms, above average tactical skills, and plenty of beans and bullets. In today's economy, a deep larder and a big pile of ammunition is the equivalent of a millionaire's bank account. We can't let all that go to our heads. It would be all too easy for us to declare ourselves petty dictators over the region."

Todd interlaced his fingers and clicked his thumbnails together. "We've got to show restraint, heed our conscience, and always remember that we are Christians. Instead of playing 'lifeboat captain' and just plain taking or 'requisitioning' what we want or need, we have always got to engage in fair barter. When those in need don't have anything that they can spare to barter, we've got to do our very best to dispense copious charity. To quote Matthew Chapter 8: 'Therefore all things whatsoever ye would that men should do to you, do ye even so to them: for this is the law and the prophets.' I believe in salvation solely by Grace, but I don't believe in faith without good works. It's our duty as Christians...." Todd glanced at Kevin Lendel, and quipped, "Sorry, no offense intended with that New Testament stuff, Kevin."

Lendel replied, "No offense taken. My God is the same God of Abraham, Isaac, and Jacob. I subscribe to the same code of ethics. I just don't eat pork." Everyone laughed.

Todd waited for the laughter to die down, and thrust his hands into the pockets of his DPM trousers. He said, "Enough of my lecturing. Now, getting back to the issue of image we want to put forward. What do you folks think we should do next?"

Mary spoke up. "I'd suggest that the next time you go back to talk to Dunlap one of the women goes with you to soften our image. We can't come across as being entirely militant. We've got to show that we are human, and that we've got compassion and balance."

Todd's shoulders slumped. "I think that you're right." When a series of votes were taken later in the evening, it was decided that Lisa should go with Todd to the next meeting, and that she should attempt to intervene if Todd and Roger Dunlap started to show any friction. There was general agreement among the group members that it was important to have the militia patrol a large territory. In the short term, it would be a burden to patrol the area and give critical aid to the territory's inhabitants. In the long term, however, as a more stable situation developed, a large territory would mean a larger base of population with more resources available to barter, and most importantly, a large pool of manpower to form a network of militias to defend against well-organized hostiles. T.K. predicted a situation "somewhat akin to the city states of Italy during the Middle Ages and into the Renaissance."

Mike brought out a large map that had been assembled from nine USGS topographical maps and mounted on a piece of plywood. The map was covered with heavy clear "combat" acetate so that it could be marked with water-based fine point felt tip markers. The acetate was already extensively marked with property lines and the surnames of landowners. Mike often used the map board when briefing and debriefing patrols. Following the discussion of how much territory they could handle, it was decided that a north–south line near Deary should mark the dividing point for the two groups' areas of responsibility for providing aid and security.

At the end of the meeting, T.K. led the group in a Bible study in 1st Kings, studying Solomon's alliances with Hiram and Egypt, and Asa and Ahab's alliances with Ben-Hadad. Then they prayed that God would give them wisdom and strength. They also prayed that God would allow the two groups to reach an understanding and form a lasting, equitable alliance.

Just before noon on the twenty-fifth, with a light snow falling, Todd and Lisa arrived at the Deary cemetery, again driving Jeff's Power Wagon. As Todd pulled the pickup to a halt, they could see Dunlap and a woman standing next to two horses that were tied up to the fence that surrounded the graveyard. Lisa observed quietly, "Looks like the Templars decided to soften their image as well."

Todd let out a faint chuckle in reply. When they stepped out of the cab, they felt a cold blast. The weather had deteriorated considerably since their last meeting. Carrying only their holstered .45s, Todd and Lisa approached Dunlap and the woman.

"Hello!" Dunlap half-shouted.

"Hail and well met," Gray replied.

As they approached to within a few steps of each other, Todd said, "Roger, I'd like you to meet Lisa Nelson. She's our logistician, and the wife of our tactical coordinator."

Dunlap smiled and replied, "Pleased to meet you, ma'am. This is my wife Teresa, she's our group counselor."

Todd tipped the brim of his boonie hat, and let out a quiet "Ma'am." After a pause, Todd suggested, "It's pretty cold today. If you'd like, we can talk in the back end of our rig. We've got a kerosene heater and a thermos full of hot tea."

Roger Dunlap and his wife exchanged glances, then nods. "Sure, that sounds great," Roger said.

Carrying their rifles with them, the Dunlaps crunched through the snow, following Todd and Lisa. Once they were inside the camper shell, Todd shut the tailgate and the back window, propping it open a crack with a scrap block of two-by-four for ventilation. Nobody spoke as Lisa lit the Kerosun kerosene heater-cooker. The four sat cross-legged on the carpet that covered the bed of the pickup, staring at the light of the heater that sat between them. The Dunlaps took off their gloves and wool glove liners and warmed their hands. Again without speaking, Lisa poured tea into four heavy porcelain coffee mugs.

Finally, after taking a sip of tea, Roger spoke. "Earl Grey—my favorite." Next, everyone tried to speak at once, then laughed.

After a few pleasantries and talk about the weather, they proceeded to talk business. Roger reported, "We took several votes in the course of two meetings of the Templars. We are prepared to talk terms of an alliance."

Todd beamed. "Excellent. What scope for the alliance did you have in mind?"

After a pause, Roger answered, "We want to set up a mutual aid and security pact. We would each be assigned a geographical area to patrol and secure."

Todd beamed. "That's exactly what we had in mind. However, we also wanted to clearly set our priorities for providing charity—with no strings attached—both to local residents and bands of legitimate refugees."

"Agreed," Dunlap said.

"Also, one important point: If a lawless band should threaten the region, and if it is too big for either group to handle on their own, then our treaty would commit both groups to provide assistance, even if it means the risk of loss of life."

Roger turned up one corner of his mouth and said, "I guess that's the bottom line, isn't it?"

"Yes, indeed. That's the bottom line," Todd echoed.

Dunlap and his wife again exchanged glances. Roger stated, "We agree. We're willing to covenant on that."

For the next fifteen minutes, the two hammered out their differences in terminology and concepts. Lisa and Teresa occasionally made comments and suggestions, but it was mainly Todd and Roger who did the talking. In all, their conversation was much friendlier. The only time that there was any hint of hostility came when the two men discussed where the dividing line between the two groups' "Areas of Operations" or "A.O.s" should be drawn. Dunlap wanted the line three miles east of Deary. Gray wanted it one mile west of Deary. They eventually reached an agreement after Lisa spoke up and suggested that the residents of Deary would have the benefit of being able to call on the aid of either group if the line was drawn right through the center of town.

Pulling out an Idaho road map, Dunlap traced a line for the Templars' A.O. "Very well then. Our common boundary will be this line running north-south through Deary. Our line will then run back west to Kendrick. Then it will run north just to the east side of Moscow, and then back east along a line centering on Potlatch. There's no need for us to cover Moscow itself. As I'm sure you heard, most of it went up in flames early last year. The residents that were left soon afterward set up a 'committee of vigilance' as they call it, complete with roadblocks. We've already made a treaty with them, and everything's copacetic."

Todd spoke next. "Those boundaries are perfectly agreeable to us. I'd like the boundaries of the Northwest Militia to run as follows: From this 'Mason-Dixon' line north to where it meets the Palouse River, east to Hemlock Butte, due south on a line passing just east of Elk City, and then west to a point four miles south of Deary. Agreed?"

Roger nodded. "I have no problem with those boundaries." After the boundaries had been sketched onto a copy of the map for each group, the two men shook hands.

The next item of business was coordination between the groups. "Do you have access to a single sideband CB?" Todd asked.

Roger nodded, saying, "Yes, one of our base stations is a forty-channel S.S.B. rig."

"Okay then, what I'd like to do is set channel one, upper side band, as our main line of communications for coordination between the two groups. We won't publicize the fact that we use that freq. I'd also suggest that channel seven, full band, be our regional frequency, on which any of the locals can get in touch with either retreat. Normally I'd say channel nine, the old civilian emergency channel, would be the most logical choice, but it still has a lot of garbage traffic. So channel seven it will be. We'll both monitor it around the clock. When we need to talk privately, we'll come up on channel seven, make contact, and then use the code phrase 'Okay, I'll meet you in Coeur D'Alene, goodbye,' as the cue to switch to channel one, USB."

Dunlap considered Todd's words, and commented, "That all sounds great. However, there's just one problem. We both have plenty of power, but only a few of the locals still have power sources for their CBs. As people started running out of gasoline, they couldn't maintain the charges in their car and truck batteries."

Lisa chimed in, "I've got an idea. We've got those small Sovonics photovoltaic panels for each of our vehicles. We normally leave them on the dashboards to keep the batteries maxed up. They put out about a hundred mil-amps in full sunlight. We aren't using all of our vehicles now, so we could distribute most of these little panels to the locals who have CBs. They could use them to trickle-charge twelve-volt car batteries. That would give them enough power for occasional emergency use of their CBs."

Roger raised his eyebrows. "That's an outstanding idea. We have about five or six of those little 'Car Pal' PV panels too, and we're only using one of them. We have a big Jacobs wind generator and racks of Arco Solar panels for both of our stronghold houses, so we really don't need the small panels. Since our two groups only have a limited number, we'll just have to be very selective about whom we give the panels to. Logically, those on the main roads, and at the farthest reach of our territory, should get the highest priority. That way we can get early warning of any looters coming into the area."

Todd said, "Okay then, that's agreed. Now for short-range tactical communications, our militia uses Radio Shack TRC-500 headset radios. There's no way that we could have interoperable communications, though, because we use specially made crystals cut to an odd frequency. If we need to communicate between patrols for a joint operation, we'll have to use portable CBs set to the same channel. Normally, we'll use channel seven. For individual operations we'll agree on another channel and an alternate freq."

"That sounds fine, we have two handheld CBs and a boatload of ni-cad and nickel metal hydride batteries. Let's both put out orders to our groups that at least one CB walkie-talkie will be carried by each of our security patrols."

Next, Lisa asked Dunlap if his group had any critical logistic needs. He answered no, then asked the same question of her. She also replied to the negative.

"Then I suppose that anything we can spare will continue go to refugees and/or the local farmers," Dunlap said. After this exchange, the conversation once again degenerated into small talk.

After more tea and nearly an hour of exchanging stories about their recent experiences, Teresa said, "Well, I guess we had better be on our way if we are going to get back to Bovill before dark." The four then exchanged smiles and handshakes. After brushing the snow off of their saddles, the Dunlaps mounted their horses, waved, and rode into the timber. Todd was glad to see that they didn't use the road. He mentioned, "We're going to have to get ourselves some horses." Then, as he got into the cab of the pickup, he quoted Doug Carlton's words: "Roads are for people who like to get ambushed."

As they drove back to the retreat, Lisa said, "When you two were talking over the map, I couldn't help but be reminded of something I read about the conference that was held in Yalta at the end of World War II. As the story goes, Roosevelt, who was quite ill at the time, and Stalin sat down with a map that was torn out of an issue of *National Geographic*. Over the objections of Churchill, they decided right then and there how they would carve up eastern Europe after the war. Incredible. Two men with a pen and a map decided the fate of millions of people and more than a dozen sovereign states. It boggles the mind when you think of the significance of that one event: the cold war, the Berlin airlift, the Berlin wall, the absorption of Balkan states. I don't know why historians have glossed over the Yalta conference. I think that if more people paid attention to it, Roosevelt wouldn't have such a positive reputation. That bastard gave away half of Europe to Uncle Joe Stalin."

A sad expression spread across Todd's face, and then he breathed, "Well ... our little treaty that we made today will affect the fate of only a few hundred people, not millions, and hopefully all for the better. One thing is for sure; I feel a lot more comfortable having a big security buffer on our west side. That's undoubtedly the main approach route for trouble coming into our A.O. The bad guys will probably have to get past the Templars first."

CHAPTER 13
Spring

"Let us never forget that the cultivation of the earth
is the most important labor of man. When tillage begins, other arts follow.
The farmers, therefore, are the founders of civilization."

—*Daniel Webster*

For the three months before the birth, Mary had read and read again everything in their library about pregnancy and childbirth. The book she read the most was the midwife's training book called *Heart and Hands* by Elizabeth Davis. She made Todd read all the books at least twice, too. She had a fairly easy pregnancy. Mary weighed herself and checked her blood pressure twice a week. From her reading, she knew her best chance for a healthy baby was exemplary diet and plenty of exercise. Using the test strips provided in one of the birthing kits that were stocked at the retreat, she tested her urine for sugar which would indicate gestational diabetes. She also tested it for protein which would indicate toxemia. However, she never had much swelling of her hands and feet, so she was not really concerned about the possibility of toxemia.

She wished she wasn't the first woman to give birth at the retreat, since no one else had ever been involved in a birth except herself during her obstetrics rotation in her nurse's training. Margie had given birth to Della but it was a hospital birth and Margie said that she was "pretty well knocked out" at the time. She had also seen and assisted farm animals give birth. But she had had a pretty difficult time giving birth to Della, and increasingly radiated nervousness about the upcoming home birth. Finally, Mary decided she didn't want Margie there at all for the birth, even though she was the only one to have gone through it.

Lisa Nelson, who was about Mary's age, told Mary she would really like to be there for the birth. She said, "Mary, you might not be able to help at every birth here. I really think I ought to learn as much as I can from you. Someday Mike and I would like to have a family and I want to know what I'm getting myself into." Lisa was a disciplined and dedicated pupil. Mary was happy she would have her help at the birth. Mary wasn't too worried about the baby needing any special medical attention since most floppy babies are caused by anesthesia. But Mary was concerned about tearing her perineum when birthing the head and shoulders. The last thing she wanted was Todd or Lisa sewing up her most delicate parts. She wished she could reach to sew herself up if necessary—but that was impossible.

On the evening of March twenty-fourth of the second year, Mary had a "bloody show." This was the mucous plug being dislodged as the cervix began to dilate. Mary, Todd, and Lisa were very excited, because they knew that this meant that labor would be beginning soon. She had about three hours of irregular contractions that night, but then they stopped. The next afternoon, irregular contractions began again.

By dinnertime the contractions were eleven minutes apart. Mary had very loose stools during the day, which was another encouraging sign of early labor. About 7 p.m. she became nauseated and vomited, but she knew that this too was nothing to worry about. During this early labor phase, Mary went about her usual daily tasks to keep her mind off the discomfort of the contractions, but she was careful not to tire herself.

At 8 p.m. Mary felt like she was tensing up more than she wanted to, mainly because her contractions were so strong. Lisa and Todd were invaluable at this time. They reassured her, and started her on breathing exercises to help her get through the intensity of the contractions, and to distract her attention. Suddenly she felt a tremendous pressure, and her bag of water broke. There was amniotic water everywhere. Todd and Lisa were aghast both to see so much fluid, and to see Mary crouched down over the bedsheets, carefully examining them. "What a relief! Great!" Todd and Lisa were still quizzical. "Don't you get it?" Mary asked. "The fluid is clear! There's no sign of merconium in the fluid. That would have darkened it. That means that the baby probably isn't in fetal distress." All three were grinning now.

Lisa asked, "What does it feel like, Mary?" She replied, "I wouldn't say my contractions are painful. But they are incredibly intense. It is r-really hard to stay relaxed and not tense up." The contractions began coming closer together. Todd massaged her entire back and put counter-pressure on her lower back. She remarked that it really helped. She started feeling an urge to push. After scrubbing up with Betadine solution, Todd and Lisa both checked her dilation. Todd estimated ten centimeters. Lisa agreed that she felt like she was fully dilated. They couldn't see any more cervix holding back the head. Mary squatted to get gravity working on her side—getting the baby down more quickly. She pushed with each contraction for thirty-five minutes. Gradually, they could see the crown of the baby's head.

Mary moved to a semi-sitting position on the bed so Lisa and Todd could control the emergence of the head and prevent tearing. If she were to remain squatting, the baby would come too quickly. Lisa checked the presentation and declared with a whoop, "The baby is looking backwards and is well flexed." Lisa and Todd urged Mary to pant to ease the baby out as slowly as possible and avoid tearing. They asked her to refrain from pushing hard on the next few contractions. The baby's head was eased out slowly, with a liberal application of mineral oil. As soon as the baby's head had emerged, Todd reached down and ran his finger around the baby's neck, checking to make sure that that none of the umbilical cord was wrapped around it. He let out a sigh of relief, both from feeling the absence of any cord, and seeing the healthy pink color of the baby's head. Lisa bent down and quickly suctioned the baby's mouth, throat and nose with a bulb syringe. She knew that this was an important step, so that any mucous would be cleared before the baby took its first breath.

With the next contraction, Todd eased out the baby's shoulders one at a time, again to prevent tearing. Once the shoulders were clear, the baby practically fell into Todd's hands, all slippery and gurgly. "It's a boy!" he exclaimed. They wiped him and dried him quickly and covered him with sterilized blankets. Lisa waited until the umbilical cord stopped pulsing and then clamped it in two places with a sterilized retractor and a special plastic umbilical clamp from the birthing kit. Todd then cut the cord about two inches from the navel. Lisa and Mary examined the baby. They agreed that his breathing was rapid but strong, and that his color was exceptionally good. Lisa nudged Mary and said, "High Apgar, right?" Mary was too overwhelmed to reply. Todd said, "Thank you for bringing me a son, darling," and leaned over to kiss Mary. Then he picked up his son's impossibly small hand in his own in wonder. "He's so small, he's so small!" Mary put the baby to her breast, and he suckled instinctively, but not skillfully. "Don't worry, he'll learn," Todd said.

The third stage of the birth felt like it took longer than the twenty minutes that Todd and Lisa anticipated. Mary was so entranced with looking at her baby's face, she hardly paid any attention to the passage of time. Lisa noticed the telltale lengthening of the umbilical cord dangling from Mary. She knew that this meant that the placenta was separating from the uterus. Lisa urged, "Come on Mary, you need to stand up so we can deliver the afterbirth." With Todd's help, Mary did as she was told. Mary's knees were shaking from exhaustion. The placenta came out on its own into a large bowl with one easy push from Mary.

Todd and Lisa carefully examined it to make sure that it was complete. Although it was torn, all of the pieces were there, and they felt relieved, knowing now that there was little chance of a uterine infection or a postpartum hemorrhage.

Lisa then checked Mary's perineum for any tears, and was happy to report that there were none large enough to require stitches. She chuckled and said, "There's just a few little skid marks on your taint, Mary. No stitches for you!" Mary laughed and said, "That's good, because I wasn't sure that I was going to trust you to stitch me up anyway. I remember you always used to tie your practice stitch knots backwards!"

Todd took care of cleaning up both Mary and the bed. The bedsheet was soaked, and the rubber sheet beneath it saved the rest of the linens and the mattress from sure ruin. Looking at the soaked linens, he exclaimed, "I'm not sure we'll ever get these stains out!" He wrapped up all of the sodden linens and towels and threw them in a bucket of cold soapy water to soak. Mary looked up and said, "Well, since it's a boy, I guess we'll call him Jacob, like we discussed. Is that okay with you, Todd?" Todd walked over to the bed and picked up the baby in his arms, and said, "Yep, he's definitely a little Jacob. He comes to us as a gift from God, and our God is the God of Abraham, Isaac, and Jacob, so it is only fitting that we call him Jacob." Jacob weighed nearly nine pounds at birth. The next day, when the rest of them got their first peek, Mary pronounced him "very healthy."

The boy's full name was Jacob Edward Samuel Gray. It was Todd who suggested the name. He said, "I wasn't even given a middle name by my folks, so I didn't have any choice as to what I'd be called. It was always just Todd. I wanted to give our son some more leeway. Little Jacob here will be able to choose from Jacob, or Jake, or Edward, or Ed, or Eddie, or Samuel, or Sam. How's that for options?"

• • •

The first summer after the retreat was activated, the group made only a half-hearted attempt at gardening. Security was the main concern. With a large quantity of stored food available, a big garden was not a necessity. Only a quarter of the garden plot was put under cultivation that summer. By the spring of the second year, however, all of the group members were tired of eating storage food. As Kevin so aptly put it, "There's only so much you can do with wheat, rice, and beans."

Most breakfasts consisted of heated wheat berries (whole wheat soaked overnight in water), and fresh baked wheat bread slices dabbed with a bit of reconstituted butter, peanut butter, or occasionally some jam. On alternate days they made pancakes, oatmeal, or cornmeal mush. Lunches were typically either peanut butter sandwiches (using dehydrated peanut butter) and soup, or simply a large kettle of steamed rice. Dinners were more varied. There were stews, elk and venison steaks, casseroles, rice pilafs, dehydrated vegetables, canned fruits, canned vegetables, and canned meats. In the summer there were fresh vegetables available, including lettuce, cabbage, and tomatoes.

For the first half of each winter there were crocks of slaw that Mary kept out on the north porch. After the slaw ran out each year (usually just after the New Year—a sad day), Mary sprouted alfalfa or beans to provide fresh greens until spring. Kevin, who emerged as the head cook, did an admirable job of making an otherwise bland diet more palatable by coming up with interesting dishes. There was often fresh game served. This included venison, elk meat (jokingly called "elkison" by Todd), pheasant, and quail. Any game that was shot outside of the coldest months of winter were either eaten immediately, canned in mason jars, or dried into jerky.

Kevin got most of his recipes from two books, *Making the Best of Basics* and Carla Emery's *Encyclopedia of Country Living*. Both were invaluable references. Kevin was generally in charge of making dinner. His most frequent assistants were Margie, Mary, Dan, and Dell. These four also did most of the breakfast and lunch cooking. Margie did most of the bread baking. She was soon renowned as the group's "baking wizard." In addition to bread, she baked most of the cookies, pies, and cobblers. Dell, who had a sweet tooth, made most of the candy. Her favorite was molasses taffy. Dan cooked many of the meat dishes including venison steaks, roasts, and meat pasties. He also did many of the rice dishes including Mexican style rice and rice pilaf. Mary did most of the canning and cooked up most of the gravies and sauces. Doug Carlton, who professed to be a "fumble fingers" cook, helped out by being in charge of big game butchering and making jerky and pemmican.

Although their diet was at times monotonous, it was nutritious. Dan Fong, Lon, and Margie, the only three members of the militia who were chubby, slimmed down considerably. Rose, who was thin even before she arrived at the retreat, lost ten pounds while recovering from her gunshot wound. She soon regained the weight, however. A few months later, Jeff noticed that Rose wasn't eating well and had started to lose weight again. With the combined efforts of T.K., who counseled her regularly, and Jeff, who insisted that she take second helpings at most meals, Rose gradually got back to her normal weight. Most of the other members maintained their "pre-Crunch" weight. Some of them, including Todd and Mike, noticed that they had to take in their belts a couple of notches, but they did not lose weight overall. They attributed this to the greater amounts of exercise that they had been getting. Fat was being replaced by muscle.

Late in the second spring after the Crunch, Mary headed up the effort to plant a large-scale garden. Everyone pitched in for the effort. They started by cultivating the entire garden plot by breaking up the soil with the cultivating attachment for the tractor. Next, with a heavy gardening fork, they finished breaking up clods and cultivated the areas near the fences and in the corners of the garden that the tractor's cultivator did not reach. They then went back through the garden with the hand fork, further breaking up the soil. Most of the contents of their now large compost heap were worked into the soil. Mary, with the help of Dan, Doug, and Della, then began planting the "early" crops. These included potatoes (lots of them), turnips, beets, radishes, onions, and corn.

At the same time, they started the more delicate crops in cold frames. These protective frames were made from the old windowpanes from the house that Todd had saved after they had been replaced with double-pane glass. The more delicate crops included melons, squash, tomatoes, and cucumbers. After the twentieth of May, these seedlings were transplanted from the cold frames to the garden proper. Many of the crops were planted at two-week intervals, to provide a steady supply of vegetables throughout the late summer. The first two crops of corn were planted inside the garden fence, while the three later crops were planted in a patch outside the garden. Only a few ears of corn were lost to the local deer, thanks to the watchful eyes of the LP/OP pickets and Shona.

• • •

At one end of the garden, Mary had a small, specially cultivated crop of herbs, both for cooking and for medicinal purposes. She realized that their stocks of stored vitamins and medicines would eventually run out or go bad, so she had started the herb garden well before the Crunch. Her main references on herbs were *The Complete Medicinal Herbal* by Penelope Ody, *The Cure For All Diseases* by Hulda Clarke, and *Ten Essential Herbs* by Lalitha Thomas. Mary spent hours reading and rereading these books and making lists of seeds and cuttings that she wanted to find. She enlarged the herb garden each summer, expanding her plantings and adding a wider variety of herbs. One of the most important herbs in her plot were her echinacea flowers. Echinacea, also known as the purple coneflower, had a reputation as a potent natural antibiotic. Mary had a friend on the other side of town who raised dairy goats and recommended growing echinacea. Her friend had successfully used echinacea to treat her goats when they had udder and teat infections.

Two years before the onset of the Crunch, Todd had built a new and larger fence for the garden, measuring forty-by-one-hundred-and-thirty feet, served by three Merrill frost-free faucets at forty-two-foot intervals. As was Todd's usual habit, he "overengineered" the garden fence to make it deer proof. First, he bought treated six-by-eight-inch posts twelve feet long for the corners, and treated four-by-four-inch posts for the intermediate positions. The lower three feet of each post was buried in an oversized hole that was filled with concrete. Between the posts, Todd stapled up two panels of stiff "hog wire" mesh, one atop the other. Above this he stapled a strand of barbed wire. In all it created a nine-foot-high fence—more than high enough to stop deer from jumping over. As added protection against the ravages of smaller garden pests, Todd added a wrap of small mesh poultry wire to the lower portion of the fence.

Todd built a double gate for the garden out of four-by-fours. They typically used only one half of the nine-foot-wide gate to walk in and out. If necessary, however, both halves could be opened up to allow the tractor to drive in and out.

• • •

Most of the vegetable seeds came from the supplies of vacuum packed seed that many of the members had stored. Although it was several years old, most of this seed germinated satisfactorily, due to its packaging and storage in the cool basement. On Mary's advice, all of the group members were careful to select only non-hybrid seeds for their storage programs. The advantage of non-hybrid seed was that it "bred true" generation after generation. Although hybrid varieties often produced more, they could not be depended on for the use of their retained seeds for more than one or two generations. The other sources of seed were the seeds saved and dried from the previous year's crops. This seed also germinated well, so Mary made it a SOP for group members to save as much seed as possible from the vegetables produced each summer.

The garden, the corn patch, and apple trees outside of it became natural lures for deer. T.K. became the main meat supplier for the retreat. He usually set up to still-hunt early in the evening. In the summer, he'd sit just inside the edge of the corn patch. In the winter, he sat on a platform he built in a ponderosa pine near the east property line. Beneath this stand, he placed a salt block to attract deer. To conserve ammunition and keep things quiet, he hunted with his crossbow. He rarely missed his mark. The only detractor to hunting with a bow rather than a gun was that the deer did not die almost immediately as they usually did when hit by a rifle bullet. Unless T.K. got an incredibly lucky shot and hit a major artery or penetrated the deer's spine, the animal would run several hundred yards before succumbing to blood loss. This meant that they had to be packed back to the barn for butchering and cooling out. Dragging a full-grown deer, especially uphill or in foul weather, was a real chore.

Margie's extensive farming and gardening experience proved invaluable. It was Margie who taught the gardeners how to use the "double dug" method of cultivation, how to use companion planting techniques, and to plant marigolds around the perimeter of the garden. The marigolds, she said, discouraged a variety of harmful garden marauders.

One of the biggest problems for the garden was the ravage of birds. Because the Grays had not taken the precaution of laying in a supply of protective netting, valuable manpower had to be used to post a guard on the garden during the worst of the "bird season." Generally the guards were armed with either Todd's .177 caliber El Gamo air rifle or Mike's .22 caliber Feinwerkbau 124 air rifle. Both T.K. and Kevin preferred to use their Wrist Rocket slingshots. They quickly developed deadly accuracy with them. Never ones to waste anything, the larger birds taken in the defense of the garden were made part of the summer diet.

Each spring and early summer at the retreat were dominated by cultivation tasks, and the mid-summer with firewood cutting and hauling. The late summer was a time of frenetic activity at the retreat. In addition to the normal guard duty and chores, there were crops to harvest, and hundreds of jars to be canned. Fortunately, they had procured a large supply of Ball and Mason jars, lids, rings, and paraffin well before the Crunch. Most of the canning was done using the water bath method. This was the method preferred by Mary. In contrast, Margie preferred to do pressure canning. Complaining that it looked too dangerous, Mary shied away from the pressure canning operation.

The group had purchased large quantities of canning supplies, far in excess of their predicted needs. Mary had frequently pointed out that canning supplies would make excellent barter items in most survival scenarios. The greatest quantities purchased for this purpose were canning lids and paraffin.

In addition to canning, many foods were preserved by dehydrating. A few were preserved by pickling and salting. Because Todd and Mary had not gotten around to buying a dehydrator before the Crunch, they had to build their own. It was constructed by Lon and Dan, using a design from one of Mary's back issues of *The Mother Earth News*. It was a simple design that used an electric light bulb to provide low heat for a wooden box containing racks for a dozen large trays. The trays were made from old fruit packing boxes, and were covered with plastic mesh screen. Although less sophisticated than commercial dehydrators with thermostatic controls and exhaust fans, the new dehydrator worked well, albeit slowly.

Because electricity was at a premium at the retreat, Lon and Dan eventually built a solar dehydrator to supplement their electric model. This dehydrator took advantage of the fairly reliable hot days of the late summer in the Palouse. It consisted of a large wooden framework covered by window screen. It featured a pair of doors that swung open in the front, and racks for thirty trays.

One of the nice features of the Grays' farm was its large orchard of fruit and nut trees. Most of these trees were of mature size. A few of the apple trees were more than fifty years old, and still going strong. To hedge their bets, Todd and Mary started planting saplings soon after they moved in. These trees came from a nursery outside of Lewiston. The Grays resisted the urge to sprout seedlings from the fruit produced by their own trees, knowing that the chances of growing a productive tree from such stock were slim.

One of Todd and Mary's biggest regrets was that they never bought any livestock for their farm. With all of the activity required to get the retreat in shape, they never got to stocking the farm before the Crunch hit. The stock would have provided a valuable source of food, muscle power, transportation, and fertilizer for the garden. Livestock would have also eliminated the teasel weeds that were beginning to crop up in small patches all over the retreat. When Mary pointed this shortcoming out to Todd, he said, "Oh well, hindsight is twenty-twenty."

Bartering for livestock was put high on the list of priorities for a future time when a barter economy eventually developed. Mary made up a "livestock dream sheet" of the animals that she thought that the group would need and that their forty acres could support. She made up the list as a guide for future barter purchases. It included one Jersey cow, one donkey, and five saddle horses. Mary also wanted to buy a few rabbits, goats, ducks, and sheep, and breed them to eventually provide needed meat, milk, eggs, wool, feathers, down, and hides. She also would have included a pair of draft horses on the list, but she realized that such animals were scarce even before the Crunch. Although they would likely be bred in greater numbers in the future, the chances of the group obtaining a pair within the next ten years was remote.

The bucolic endeavors of that summer were disrupted on the fifteenth of September when Margie injured her forearm. It happened early one morning while she was splitting some kindling for the cook stove, in preparation for the day's canning operation. Working with a short-handled mine ax to split the kindling, she was momentarily distracted by the sound of the TA-1 field telephone clacking on the C.Q. desk. Taking her eyes off of her work for only an instant, Margie brought the ax down at an angle and it bounced off of the piece of wood that she was attempting to split. The ax blade struck the inside of her left forearm, making a deep, ugly gash. She let out a cry, but waited until it became clear that the call on the TA-1 was just a regular commo check. Then, applying direct pressure to the wound, she called for help.

The cut only bled a little at first, and Margie was not overly alarmed. By the time Mary was examining it a few minutes later, however, the capillary bleeding had begun to increase. To Mary's dismay, she also found that Margie had nearly severed two tendons.

Mary quickly applied a bandage to the wound and had Margie move to the kitchen. Mary put on one of her light green "scrub suit" uniforms and a surgical mask. Then she thoroughly washed her hands and forearms with Phisoderm and put on a pair of sterile surgical rubber gloves. Meanwhile, Rose washed down the kitchen table with rubbing alcohol. Throughout all this, Margie sat patiently at the table, with her arm raised above her head to help control the bleeding. By the time Mary was done scrubbing up, the bandage was soaked, and a thin rivulet of blood began to trickle down to Margie's armpit. "Please hurry, Mary dear," she said.

Mary was finally ready to begin after she had pulled a selection of surgical instruments from her bag and out of their sterile wrappers. She then paused to wash her hands yet again. "It's starting to really hurt. It's throbbing," Margie said with a groan.

Mary had Margie lay down and elevated her injured arm and her feet, to lessen the risk of going into shock. Soothingly, she said, "Don't worry. I'm going to give you something for the pain." Picking up a 20 c.c. hypodermic syringe, Mary quickly filled it with Lidocaine H.C.L. After tapping the sides of the syringe and briefly depressing its plunger to displace a few small air bubbles, Mary inserted the needle subcutaneously to three sites around the wound. She said soothingly, "The pain will start to subside within a few minutes. Just be patient, *my patient.*" Looking toward Rose, who was by now also wearing a surgical mask, she said, "I'll need more light. Bring the reading lamp from the living room, and put it here on the edge of the table. There's an outlet right over there." A minute later Rose returned with the lamp. Mary chided, "No, no, not so close, that thing's hardly sterile. Set it up farther down the table, but tip the shade so that I get the light over here. There, that's it."

Mary then picked up a pair of her black handled bandage scissors and cut away the now sodden bandage from the wound. Working with a blunt-tipped probe, she gauged the extent of the wound. For the benefit of Margie and Rose, who was looking over Mary's shoulder, she said, "The cut is ten or twelve millimeters deep, at its deepest point. There is considerable capillary bleeding and there are four small arterial bleeders. The bluish-looking one here is a vein, not an artery. It's a pretty big one, and luckily it still has its integrity. If it had gotten cut, there would already be a puddle of blood, so that's a piece of luck. The bad news is that we've got two tendons that have been nearly cut through, and another that's been nicked."

By now, four other militia members were hovering at the far end of the kitchen, whispering to themselves. Looking over her shoulder, she said to them, "You can make yourselves useful if one of you were to go out to the shop and get the electric soldering iron, the small one." Lon turned from the doorway of the kitchen and dashed in the direction of the shop. "What does she need a soldering iron for?" Della whispered to Doug, who was standing next to her.

Doug leaned over until his mouth was nearly touching Della's ear and whispered, "Cauterizing, I think. You don't have to stay and watch this unless you want to. It could get pretty gross."

Della whispered back, "No, I want to stay. I won't get grossed out. Besides, this is pretty interesting. I might have to do this someday." Doug nodded in agreement.

Mary continued on with her monologue. "I'm going to start by stitching up, or at least trying to stitch up, these four little arteries. I'm afraid to say that they are about the same size as the ones that I had trouble with when I worked on your gunshot wound, Rose. I'm going to use the smallest of my absorbable suture material. Anything larger, and I'd probably end up with an artery that was patched together, but that would leak like a sieve."

Just then, Lon returned with the soldering iron. Mary tossed her head to gesture toward the lamp. "Plug it in over there," she said.

"What about sterilizing it?" Lon asked.

"We don't have to concern ourselves with the tip, that will sterilize itself as it heats up. It's just the handle that I have to worry about. I'll just do all of the cautery at once, and then change gloves."

Mary spent the next twenty-five minutes suturing together the four small, severed arteries, muttering the occasional epithet. It was painstaking, frustrating work. To control the bleeding during this stage of the operation, she had Rose briefly put a sphygmomanometer cuff on Margie's upper arm, and slowly pump it up to pressure. Once the bleeding had slowed to the point where she could once again see her work, Mary told Rose to stop pumping. Mary had to suture one of the arteries closed because it was badly damaged. She managed to successfully rejoin the other three. After the suturing was done, Mary told Rose to release the pressure in the cuff, for fear of restricting Margie's blood flow for too long.

Throughout the operation, Margie remained calm. Mary occasionally asked her if she was feeling pain. She always answered no. Margie could not bear to watch the operation. She kept her head turned toward the wall throughout the procedure.

When full blood flow was restored, the patched together arteries showed no sign of leakage, but steady capillary bleeding resumed at both sides of the wound. Turning toward the kitchen doorway, Mary said, "Lon, Rose, I'm going to need your help." The two approached and looked at her expectantly. She said, "I need you to hold Margie's arm in place." After instructing them on how she wanted the arm held, Mary picked up the soldering iron. She said to Margie, "Now this might hurt, despite the Lidocaine, so try to hold still."

Mary rolled the tip of the soldering iron across spots of the flesh that had shown the worst of the capillary bleeding. The soldering iron made a hissing noise throughout this process. Margie said that she couldn't feel a thing, but that she didn't like the smell. "It smells like a barbecue," she said.

After she was done cauterizing, Mary donned a fresh set of gloves and took another look at the damaged tendons. She said, "I wouldn't know how to begin to work on these tendons, so we're going to have to hope that they heal them-selves. The best we can do is immobilize your hand, wrist, and lower arm for two months to allow them a chance to heal themselves." Mary then began the slow process of closing the wound with nonabsorbable three-zero silk sutures.

When she was finally done, Mary daubed the area of the wound with Betadine solution. Then she lightly wrapped Margie's lower arm in two-inch wide sterile gauze and pulled down her mask. A few minutes of consultation with Lon yielded a plan for making a splint. Lon returned from the shop five minutes later with a pair of heavy pliers and an eight-foot length of one-eighth-inch diameter steel fencing wire. Laying the wire directly against his wife's arm, Lon eyeballed a measurement for the splint. Then, with the help of the pliers, he began bending the stiff wire. After taking a few more measurements, he had the splint bent into shape within a few minutes. By the time he was done, Lon was sweating profusely from the exertion.

The finished splint lay on both sides of Margie's arm. It bent 90 degrees at the elbow, and had looped cross braces at both ends. To pad the splint, Mary used some heavy wadding from an enormous civil defense surplus bandage. After the padding was held in place on the framework of the splint by white bandage tape, Mary gingerly lowered Margie's arm into the confines of the splint. Next, she used almost an entire roll of three-inch wide gauze, securing the arm within the confines of the splint.

When she had completed the job, she asked Margie if the bandaging felt too tight in any spot. She replied, "I can't tell, yet. My arm is still pretty numb."

"Okay, Margie. Just let me know right away if you feel any discomfort. Now here's the fun part. You are going to have to keep that arm elevated for most of the day for the next two weeks. Also, you are going to have to constantly remind yourself not to flex your wrist or fingers. I know that will be tough, but if those tendons are going to heal properly, you have got to avoid putting any stress on them, okay?"

"Okay," Margie answered. After looking down at her heavily padded arm, she said, "Oh fiddlesticks! Why did this have to happen at a time like this? We were planning on putting up sixty jars of applesauce today."

Later in the day, Mary tested her supply of tetracycline. She used the standard WHO-approved "titers" test of dissolving a capsule into clear water. She knew a cloudy solution or precipitates would indicate that the capsules weren't safe and should be discarded. She was happy to see that the test resulted in a clear solution. Due to the age of the tetracycline, she gave Margie a considerably higher than normal dosage. In another year or two, Mary realized, she would have to begin titrating all of the retreat's supplies of medicines and vitamins.

CHAPTER 14
The Northwest Militia

"... arms ... discourage and keep the invader and plunderer in awe,
and preserve order in the world as well as property....
Horrid mischief would ensue were (the law-abiding) deprived the use of them."

—*Thomas Paine*

In June of the second year, a regular long-range reconnaissance patrol (LRRP) from the retreat met a farmer who seemed nervous and distressed. He said, "I'm sure glad to see you. I haven't been sleeping well for four days now. I don't have a CB, and I was afraid to leave my wife and babies to go ask for help. There's a bunch of bikers that took over Princeton. That's less than a mile north of here. I'm afraid that once they strip those houses clean, they might come down here. What they've been doin' is just terrible. They killed most of the men, and they've been raping the women that are still left alive. I also heard that they've been torturing the little kids. A couple houses got torched. They're a wicked bunch."

The man looked imploringly at Carlton and asked, "You've got those military lookin' guns and the organization, can't you do something about it?"

Doug Carlton, who was leading the patrol asked, "Do you know how many of them there are, and how they're armed?"

"I heard that there's at least twenty, maybe thirty, of that trash. Rumor has it that they got a machinegun."

"What kind of machinegun?"

"A big one, you know, with one of them ammo belts, on tripod legs." A few more minutes of questioning revealed little else, as all of the man's information was secondhand.

Heeding the training that he had received in his ROTC courses, Carlton took the initiative to deal decisively with the situation. After moving the patrol four hundred yards away from the farm into a dense grove of trees, Carlton consulted with the other patrol members. "Okay, here's the deal. We obviously don't have the necessary combat power in a seven-member patrol to handle this problem. What I'm going to do is split the patrol in half. Three members of the patrol will go on an extended recon of Princeton, while the other four will return to the retreat. The recon patrol will consist of Jeff, Lisa, and Kevin. The rest of us will get back to the retreat A.S.A.P and report on what we've heard."

Looking directly at Trasel, Doug ordered, "Jeff, I'm putting you in charge of the recon patrol because you have a lot more experience at reconnaissance than I do. Plan to be back to the retreat no later than dawn on the day after tomorrow. Your job is to observe and report. Period. Do your absolute best to avoid being detected, but try to get close enough to observe the details of what is going on. In particular, we need to know their total numbers, how well they are armed, what building or buildings they are occupying, and if they have any security out. If you spot anyone on security, it's critical to know where their posts are, or if they're using roving guards, and the routes they take. Also, we need to know if they change guards at regular times. Take complete notes. Get some accurate sketches of the layout. That's all. Have any questions?"

Jeff thought for a moment. "No questions, but I'd like to take both sets of binoculars and one of the five-watt walkie-talkies on the recon. I'd also like all the food out of your packs since you are heading right back and we will be out for an extra twenty-four hours."

Doug gave him a thumbs-up and replied, "Okay. Good luck."

After redistributing the loads in their rucksacks, Carlton, along with Rose, Lon, and Dan Fong headed back to the retreat. Still in a whisper, Jeff began to brief Lisa and Kevin on how he wanted to conduct the recon.

As soon as they had returned to the Grays' farmhouse, Mike and Todd debriefed the first increment of the patrol. Referring to the map board, Todd then gave a description of the area around Princeton. "It is a small town about sixteen miles west and slightly north of Bovill. As I recall, there are only about twenty houses in the town, strung out along this road, which runs east-west. There's a sawmill on the edge of town, and a gas station in the middle of town. Other than that, Princeton has all residential buildings. Most of the area around town is fairly well timbered. If there are indeed twenty-plus bad guys there, we could have a heckuva time taking them out." After a pause, Margie raised her still bandaged arm and asked, "Well ... aren't they likely to move on soon? Couldn't we just scare them off or just wait until they leave, and then go in to treat the injured and help to resupply the residents and rebuild whatever has been destroyed?"

Gesturing with his hand, Todd said, "Look, I realize that an operation like this is extremely dangerous. But as long as we let vermin continue to operate freely, they are going to be a thorn in our side. I'll never forget one thing that Jeff Cooper once wrote: 'Scaring hostiles away is never very satisfactory, be they mosquitoes, crocodiles, or people, because they will be back later, with friends.'

In my opinion there is only one way to deal with this sort of situation. We have to go in and wipe the brigands out. If we let them slip away, they'll just keep right on going with their mayhem somewhere else, maybe even here. We also have to remember that we've been making promises to provide security to the area, and we are honor-bound to follow through on those promises."

"I agree," Mike declared.

Todd continued, "Because there are so many of them, we'll no doubt need the help of the Templars on this operation. Assuming that we are going to go through with this, I plan to call Roger Dunlap right after this meeting. Could I have a show of hands of all of those in favor of my plan?" Margie was the only dissenter.

Todd's conversation with Dunlap over the CB was brief. After going through the prearranged change to an upper sideband frequency, Todd spoke into the handset, "Roger, a security matter of extreme importance and sensitivity has come up, and I'd like to meet with you to discuss it at the usual spot at 11 a.m. on the day after tomorrow."

Dunlap replied, "Wilco, out."

After he had radioed his message to Dunlap, Todd asked Mike if he could talk with him privately. They stepped outside the front door. Although it was dark, it was still pleasantly warm. Shona padded up to Todd and put her muzzle under his hand, imploring him to pet her. Todd obliged. "Mike, I need your advice. Even with the help of the Templars, are we going to be able to overcome that many people?" Without giving Mike a chance to reply, Todd said, "I mean, I can remember reading military tactics manuals where they say that the normal ratio of attackers to defenders is something like three-to-one. We won't even be meeting them one-to-one."

Mike looked in Todd's direction, unable to make out the features of his face in the darkness. "The figure you cite is correct, but that applies only to military units engaging other military units that are dug in and expecting an attack. I think that as long as we maintain surprise, we can pull it off. Hopefully, we might even do it without taking any casualties. The main problem will be coordination. Obviously, we can't mix our forces together with the Templars. That would be a nightmare from a command and control standpoint. We haven't trained together. Probably the best thing to do is use them for a support team, while we assault the buildings, or vice versa."

Todd threw in, "I was thinking the same thing." After a long interval he added, "Let's say, just for the sake of argument, that we *do* run an assault op on Princeton. We're talking about a whole bunch of buildings. What's to stop most of the bikers from slipping away while we are clearing the area house to house?"

"The Templars," Mike answered.

"You've seen Princeton recently, haven't you, Mike? Most of the houses are strung out for about three or four hundred yards. The Templars would have to be spread out at pretty wide intervals. If all the bikers poured out of town at one spot, they could just overrun the one or two guys who had line-of-sight to them. You know the old hammer and anvil technique that Jeff always talks about. If we are going to be the hammer, we're going to have to have a big anvil. Do you see what I mean?"

After a few moments' consideration, Mike replied, "Yes, I see exactly what you mean. What you are telling me is that it would take fifty or sixty men to properly secure the possible escape routes out of town. Orrrrrr, how about making ten people fight like sixty—give them the same combat power."

Todd tilted his head to the side and asked, "How, pray tell, does one do that?"

Mike joked, "The same way that one guy can catch more fish than ten guys combined, if he carries the right fishing tackle."

"I ... I still don't get your drift," Todd breathed, sounding bewildered.

"I'm talking about my favorite kind of fishing, and my favorite fishing lure—'The Dupont Spinner.'"

"Oh ho! Now I get it. Dynamite fishing, right?"

Mike laughed and said in a descending pitch, "Riiiiight. I think we can fab-up some improvised Claymore mines that should do the trick."

Todd slapped Mike on the shoulder and commanded, "'Make it so,' Mike. You're welcome to every stray body you can scarf up to help you out. Even if these bikers get away before we can pull this off, some homemade Claymores could always come in handy."

The next day was spent anxiously waiting. Other than two very brief radio checks, there was no contact with the recon patrol. Most of the militia members spent the day cleaning their guns, sharpening their knives and bayonets, and reloading each of their gun's magazines, carefully examining each cartridge. Most seemed deep in thought and prayer, and there was not much talking or the usual banter and joking.

For much of the day Mike used the services of Doug, Rose, Dan, Lon, and Marguerite in making the Claymore mines. Mike shanghaied Lon and Margie away from their plans to make a large pot of stew. He tapped Lon on the shoulder and ordered, "You two come with me. I've got a high-priority project for you to help me with. Todd said I could commandeer anybody I thought that I might need."

Margie asked, "But what about the stew?"

"We've got some bread to bake instead. Come with me out to the garage."

First, in consultation with Doug, Mike built a prototype. The others watched this process with curiosity. Next, Mike directed his crew as they set up the Claymore and an array of paper targets near the east property line. Mike yelled "Test Fire!" three times. They wore both earplugs and muffs. Taking cover behind a large deadfall log forty feet behind the prototype, they detonated it using a nine-volt transistor radio battery. It worked wonderfully. Each man-sized target set up at distances between five and twenty yards was pierced by at least five pellets. Mike decided it was time to set up their assembly line.

"Okay, here's the deal," Mike told his crew. "The shell for each Claymore will be a standard bread baking pan. We've got stacks of them on hand because Mary thought that they'd make a great barter item. They'll be even handier for our purposes." He then turned to look at Lon Porter. "Lon, you're in charge of the first step of the process. Your job is to tack weld four eight-inch timber spikes onto the corners of one side of each pan. The pan, of course, will be lying on its side once it is set up, with its mouth facing toward the bad guys. The spikes will act as legs to hold up the mine. To use them, all we'll have to do is point the mine in the proper direction, and press the legs into the ground. Then we press down on the front or rear legs to adjust the angle of the pan. Simple."

"The next step in the process will be handled by me. I'll drill two holes for blasting caps in each pan. Next, Rose will measure out and mold three quarters of a pound of C4 plastique into the back of each pan. She hands them to Doug, who measures out and pours one pound of number-four buckshot over the top, and scrunches it into place. Next, Margie, since your arm is not yet fully back in shape, I'm giving you an easy task. Your job is to cut the cardboard filler pieces and lids for each pan, and tape them on with duct tape."

"Once we get all twenty mines done to this stage, we'll finish them piece-by-piece. All that will remain to be done is covering them with a piece of this black ten-mil sheet plastic and taping it in place with this brown pressure-sensitive packing tape. That will semi-waterproof them. Next, they get a blast of olive drab spray paint to camouflage them. Voila, instant Claymores! To use them, all we'll have to do is poke holes in the C4 through the holes that I drilled in the pans and insert a blasting cap or a loop of det cord, as needed. For safety's sake, however, priming will wait until they're set up wherever we plan to use them. Okay, let's get to work."

Just before three a.m. the next morning, the patrol was spotted coming back into the perimeter by Dan, who was at the LP/OP. By SOP, the patrol crossed into the perimeter just to the south of and below the LP/OP. When they were fifty feet away, Dan challenged, "Halt, who is there?"

Jeff responded, "Jeff Trasel and two other militia members."

Dan whispered, "Advance to be recognized." Jeff walked up to within ten feet of the LP/OP bunker. Now in a whisper, Dan queried, "Fence post."

Also in a whisper, Jeff replied, "Chevrolet."

"Password for the day is correct. You may proceed. Positively identify the faces of the two other members of your patrol as they pass my post." The patrol was again identified by challenge and password at the front door by Della, who was serving C.Q. duty. She unbolted the door and let them in. After rebolting the door, she went to wake everyone up for the debriefing.

Everyone except Dan, who was still manning the LP/OP, quickly gathered for the debriefing. The three members of the patrol looked dirty and fatigued. All three still wore heavy coats of loam and green camouflage paint on their faces and the backs of their hands. "Start with the beginning," Mike said.

Jeff pulled his notepad out of one of the cargo pockets on his DPMs, and set it on the table. "As soon as Doug split the patrol, I issued my op. order to Lisa and Kevin, and established the new chain of command. After freshening our camouflage paint and checking to ensure that our loads were still quiet by jumping up and down, we moved out. Our first stop was back at the farm we had just been at, to refill our canteens. I wanted us to have plenty of water. Also, like I've always said, full canteens are quieter than half-empty ones.

"We made it to within binocular range of the south side of Princeton by four that afternoon. We went prone there and traded off positions once an hour—one observing and taking notes, one on security, and one resting. We stayed in that position until it was fully dark, then backed off, circled around to the east, and approached the town again from the north side. This time, because it was pitch dark, we were able to get within about fifty yards of one of the houses.

"We could hear voices, but couldn't make out what they were saying, except for the occasional obscenities and profanities that they shouted. We stayed in this spot until just before dawn, and then backed off about two hundred yards into the trees to observe for the day. I don't think any of us slept at all during that first night, but we certainly did the next day. We were really starting to get wiped out. As soon as it was my turn to rest, I was out like a light. After the sun went down yesterday evening, we backed off another couple of hundred meters and followed an azimuth back to the base of Mica Mountain; from there, dead reckoning it back to the retreat. There was no sign we had been detected at any time during the patrol."

Picking up the notebook, he read, "Strength: Total number of people observed was twenty-four. All, but two of this number, were positively identified as part of the biker gang. Of these twenty-two individuals, eighteen were men and four were women. We also saw two children running from house to house on one occasion, but could not be sure if they were local residents, or if they came with the gang. Four bodies were seen lying in the street throughout the period that we observed.

"Vehicles: We counted eighteen motorcycles parked in various places. Most of them were chopped Harleys. Five of them were equipped with scabbards for long guns. We also spotted a Ford van, which was accessed three or more times during the day by the bikers. This appeared to be their support vehicle. They may have other support vehicles, but it was hard to tell, as there were several other vehicles in the area. Some of these vehicles were obviously out of commission, but others looked operational, and might belong to the bikers.

"Weapons: Set up on top of a wooden crate in front of what used to be a gas station was a tripod mounted M60 machinegun, with one belt of ammunition loaded. We could not get close enough to see if there was additional ammo on hand. The bikers carried a wide assortment of weapons. At least six men carried handguns in hip holsters. One of the females once took off her jacket, revealing a revolver in a shoulder holster. Two of the men carried machetes in scabbards. Seven men seemed to carry long guns wherever they went. These consisted of: three M1 or M2 carbines, a pump action riotgun, a Ruger Mini-14, a scoped bolt action of some sort, and a sawed-off double-barreled shotgun. All of the men had beards. Most of the gang members wore black leather jackets or denim jackets. One wore an olive drab field jacket. No identifying gang markings could be seen on any of their jackets. Just like the old time pirates—only the amateurs flew flags.

"Guard shifts: One roving guard and one man on the machinegun at all times. Guards were observed trading off at 6 p.m., midnight, 6 a.m., noon, and again at 6 p.m. the next day. Relief guards arrived promptly at these hours. The roving guards' route started at the gas station and then went two blocks west, across the street, four blocks east, back across the street, and then back to the machinegun. The guards appeared to be relatively alert. For example, at just before 1 a.m., the roving guard reacted to the sound of a barking dog. He changed the direction that he was walking 180 degrees and went fifty yards off of his normal route to check out the noise. Once he was satisfied that there was no danger, he resumed his rounds. Although we did not observe additional guards, it is possible that another guard was on duty, most likely at some good vantage point.

"Significant activity: At 11:20 p.m. the first night, two shots in rapid succession were heard inside one of the houses. The reason for the shooting was never identified by the patrol.

"At 10:17 a.m. on the second day, two bikers began using one of the dead bodies lying in the street as a target for pistol practice. They fired about twenty to twenty-five rounds. Both were armed with what appeared to be .45 automatics. They turned the corpse into a rag doll.

"At just after 2 p.m., a naked woman of about fifty years of age was seen running out of one of the houses. She was followed closely behind by a half-clothed man, carrying an M1 Carbine. As soon as he got out the front door, he fired four times, hitting the woman in the back at least twice. He then walked up and shot the woman three times in the head. He was heard yelling, 'The bitch bit me! The bitch bit me!' At that point we had to restrain ourselves from opening fire at him." The heretofore professional tone of Jeff's voice changed noticeably as he muttered, "I never thought that I'd ever have the gut-level urge to kill anyone, but let me tell you, this guy was an inspiration."

After clearing his throat, Trasel continued with his report. "At 3:42 p.m., two of the bikers began working on one of the motorcycles, apparently adjusting its carburetor. They returned to the house that they had come from, just after 4 p.m." Jeff then laid the notebook down, and pulled three sketches out of another pocket. He walked over to the chalkboard and spent the next five minutes comparing the three sketches and combining them into a top-down view of the buildings in Princeton. Next, he traced in the route of the bikers' roving guard, and marked the position of the vehicles and the machinegun. After making a few more brief comments about the relative distances between buildings and approximate fields of fire, he asked for questions.

There was silence in the room for a few moments. Mike exclaimed, "That was a well-written patrol report. Everyone should take note of this. That's how a recon report should be prepared and given. Very professional, Jeff. It covered all of the key elements. It leaves me with a few questions, however."

"Shoot," Jeff said.

"First, what was your overall impression of the security that they had posted?"

"Their guards seemed pretty alert. They seemed to have blinders on, though."

Mike gave Trasel a quizzical look, and asked, "What do you mean by that?"

"I mean the center of their interest seemed to be the road that leads through town. It was as if they only expected an attack to come from either direction down the road, or possibly from one of the houses that face the street. They paid very little attention to the rest of their perimeter. Granted, there's a huge perimeter, but they didn't seem to make any effort at actively observing it or patrolling it. That's why I mentioned that they might have a guard posted in the second story of one of the houses, scanning their perimeter."

Mike asked, "Did you see any evidence of guards changing at any of the houses?"

"No, we didn't. But if I was trying to secure that little town, I wouldn't be focusing my security inward."

"That's because you have a Marine Corps mentality rather than a biker mentality. With their mind-set, the threats are from law enforcement, or possibly other gangs. In either case they'd come in by road. Under the current circumstances that security mentality is outdated. The threats now are from people like us, on foot, playing 'Batman in the Boondocks.' They just haven't realized it yet." Mike continued with his questioning. "What was your impression about their skill at arms?"

"From what I could observe, and I think Lisa and Kevin would agree, they don't seem to be particularly well-trained or disciplined. They do have enough discipline, however, to mount a regular guard shift. I guess if I had to sum it up, I'd say that what they lacked in skills and organization, they make up for by being vicious. These guys, and their women for that matter, are some of the most ruthless thugs I've ever heard of. I saw a lot, and heard a lot, when I was in the Corps, but I have never heard of anybody taking target practice at dead bodies. These guys are utterly Godless and obviously don't have a single moral or scruple left to guide them. I think they'd use force in a heartbeat."

After a considerable pause, Mike asked, "Okay, my key question is, do you think that with the help of the Templars, that we can take these hombres on—with a reasonable chance of success?"

"Dang straight we can, but we got to hit 'em hard and make them play by our ground rules."

Mike asked, "What do you suggest we do if we lose the element of surprise?"

"There would be only one good option, and that would be for everyone to beat feet out of there and link up later at a good defendable rally point a couple of clicks out of town. If we were to make a frontal assault with them prepared and expecting us, we wouldn't have a chance in hell. If, however, we catch them with their pants down, we'll wax most of them before they even realize what's happening."

Mike nodded his head. "Okay. Those were the only questions that I had. Anyone else?" Not one raised their hands.

Todd, who had been listening quietly to the debriefing, clucked his tongue and said, "Jeff, I'd like to congratulate you on leading such a professional and lucrative recon. I'd like you and Mike to come with me when I have my meeting with Roger Dunlap later this morning. At this point, I'd like to open the floor to suggestions on how we might go about cleaning house in Princeton."

Immediately, Dan Fong suggested that an ambush be set up outside of town. That idea was shot down for two reasons: First, the gang didn't show any signs of leaving anytime soon. Second, they could leave in two different directions.

Mary suggested that two teams be used to conduct an assault. The first team, or "support" team, would set up ambushes on the road in each direction out of town, as well as any other likely avenues of escape. The second team would sweep through the town, cleaning the looters out house to house. If any of the gang managed to escape, they could be shot or captured at the ambush sites. If the assault team had to withdraw from the town, the support team would provide covering fire.

It was Mary's plan that got the most votes. This set of tactics was later generically called a "stealth blitz with support."

Dan suggested that they bring along the six hand grenades captured from the pair of looters that were killed by T.K. Kennedy liked this suggestion, saying, "I think that it's only fitting that we utilize weapons that we captured from one bunch of looters in eradicating another. Sort of '*Dulce et decorum est*,' don't you think?"

"Pardon?" Lon asked.

T.K. replied, "That's Latin for 'It is sweet and fitting.'"

A unanimous vote approved Dan's suggestion on the grenades.

Next, Todd had Mike brief Jeff, Lisa, and Kevin on the recent construction of the "bread pan Claymores." Jeff broke into a devilish grin as he heard Mike describe his new toys. He chuckled, "Those sound ideal for ambushes by a support team."

Later that morning Todd, Mike, and Jeff drove to their meeting with Roger Dunlap. Jeff slept most of the way there. With them they took an example of each of their grenades and homemade Claymore mines. Dunlap, along with his "Com 2," was waiting in a camouflage painted Jeep CJ-5 at the cemetery when they arrived.

After hearing a repeat of Jeff's briefing and a suggested plan of attack from Todd, Dunlap answered, "Well, it sounds like you're giving the Templars the less difficult and dangerous task. Under the circumstances, and given the terms of our treaty, I cannot refuse. In fact, I'm sort of excited about the prospect." The five men spent the next two hours working out the details.

When everyone was satisfied that they understood what was expected of them, Todd commented, "Now all we have to do is get our ducks in a row and do it."

Dunlap asked Mike if he could return with him to the Templars' retreat to give a class on how to safely set up and detonate the Claymore mines. Mike agreed instantly.

Dunlap then suggested to Todd, "After his class, we'll bring Mister Nelson back to Bovill in one of our vehicles."

"Great. Sounds good, Roger. Bring along whoever is going to be leading your part of the operation. By then we'll have a complete operations order written, and provide them a briefing and a copy of the op. order. At that time we will also issue you your Claymores, wire, batteries, and blasting caps. As it stands now, it looks like we'll be able to move out tonight, and have everybody in position and ready to make the assault at dawn tomorrow."

At six in the evening, Dunlap, three other Templars, and Mike pulled up to the front gate. Mike gave an exaggerated wave as he stepped out to unlock the front gate. As he did so, he pronounced, "I want our people to get a good look at me. The last time some unidentified vehicles came roaring in here, the gal at our observation post shot first and asked questions later. As it turned out, she did the right thing. Wouldn't want a repeat performance tonight, now would we?"

Working out the details of the plan for the raid took nearly two hours. Dunlap and Ted Wallach took copious notes. When they were finished, Dunlap collected the Claymores and accessories. Taking no chances, Dunlap wired the small padded box of blasting caps to the front bumper of his Jeep to keep them well away from the mines and passengers while in transit. The militia members waved as Dunlap and Wallach drove away.

Todd turned to Mary and declared grimly, "I sure hope this works."

CHAPTER 15
The Raid

"You have never lived,
'till you have almost died.
And for those who fight for it,
life has a flavor that the protected will never know."

—*Anonymous quote penned on a sign
at a command post at Khe Sanh, RVN*

After prayers and yet another briefing, the militia conducted their final inspections and rehearsals. With their web gear and camouflage face paint on, the
militia looked fearsome. Mike, Lisa, Todd, T.K., and Rose wore bulletproof
vests and helmets. Mike walked up and down the line of raiders, shooting
questions. "What is the running password? What would a red star cluster flare
or six short whistle blasts indicate? What is your en route panic azimuth? On
which CB channel will we coordinate with the Templars? What is the alternate channel? What is our call sign? What is their call sign? Can you list the
chain of command?"

Next he had each member of the patrol jump up and down to check for
items that might be excessively noisy. The last item of business was a final
check of each patrol member's personal camouflage. Finally satisfied, Mike
ordered, "Aw-right pilgrims, let's saddle up. Lock and load." With a few hoots
and hollers, they filed out the door to two waiting pickups.

Margie, Mary, Shona, and baby Jacob were left to "hold the fort." As they
watched the two trucks drive away, both women started to cry.

The drive north was relatively quiet. They parked the trucks on a logging
road three miles south of Princeton. From there, they traveled on foot in
"Ranger file." The raiders were in position three hundred yards outside town
by 3:30 a.m. There, they lay in the chill darkness, waiting. Radio silence was
broken only once, at 4 a.m. Dan Fong, who was using an earphone with his
CB heard the call, "Ready Freddie, over." He whispered the reply, "Ready
Mikey, out." He rolled over to tap Mike on the shoulder, gestured to the earphone, and gave an "okay" signal. Mike nodded and patted Dan on the back.

At 5:20 a.m., Mike walked up and down the line of prone raiders, kicking them in the boots. Not surprisingly, a few of them had fallen asleep. After the adrenaline rush of their initial movement, lying down for two hours was enough to lull some of them into slumber. Mike whispered to each of them, "Quietly and slowly, stretch out and if need be, relieve yourself."

At 5:30, standing in a skirmish line, Mike gave the arm signal for "forward." Spread out at ten-yard intervals, the patrol moved forward toward the dim outline of the buildings in the half-light of dawn.

The raiders were already within the confines of the town before anyone was spotted. It was Kevin who was first seen by the bikers' roving guard. Two quick shots from Lendel's riotgun dropped the guard before he even had a chance to unsling his carbine. Immediately after he saw that the man was no longer a threat, Kevin quickly refilled his gun's tubular magazine from the elastic nylon shell holder mounted on the gun's stock.

After the first shots were fired, the rest of the raiders picked up their pace to a trot, and moved in the direction of their assigned buildings.

Jeff Trasel had been given the assignment of suppressing the bikers' M60 machinegun position. Soon after he heard Kevin's shots, thirty yards to the west, he came in sight of the machinegun position. The machine gunner, obviously nervous, was pointing the weapon in the direction of the commotion caused by Lendel. Fortunately, Jeff was approaching at a 90-degree angle to the muzzle of the weapon. Dropping to one knee, he fired four rounds from his HK91 at the man behind the M60. Three of his four shots hit the man in the chest and head.

Taking the initiative, Jeff rushed the position. As he reached the machinegun, he lowered the muzzle of his rifle and fired two more rounds at the chest of the dying biker. Crouching down behind the gun, he reloaded his rifle from one of the magazine pouches on his web gear, and then cross-slung it across his back. By now, he could hear more firing coming from down the street in both directions.

Jeff whispered a gleeful "Oh yeah," as he picked up the M60. Lifting the gun's feed tray cover, he could see that its bolt was in the rearward position, ready to fire. He muttered to himself, "Now I get to see if you work!" He snapped the feed tray cover back down into its locked position. With a quick search of the machinegun position, Jeff found another hundred-round belt of ammunition lying loose in a wooden box. Trasel unhooked the last round of this belt, and linked it back to the first round in the belt, forming a continuous loop. This he slung across his shoulder, bandoleer fashion. Trasel then hefted the twenty-three-pound weapon, folded its bipod legs into their closed position, and flipped the trailing end of the ammunition belt across his left shoulder.

At the far end of town, Todd Gray was running into trouble. He, Lisa, and Lon were all concentrating their fire on a house that held at least two bikers. The gang members were firing steadily but randomly from the house's downstairs windows. Because of their positions, both the gang members and the raiders were having little effect. When he heard a pause in the fire coming from his side of the building, Gray made a zigzag dash across the street, firing as he ran, and flattened himself up against the side of the house. There, he quickly reloaded his HK.

Todd dropped prone and inched his way down the side of the building until he was directly below the window from which the shooting had resumed. The muzzle blast from the gun firing only two feet above his head was tremendous. Taking a grenade from his cargo pocket, Todd pulled its pin, letting the spoon fly away. Fortunately, the sound of the grenade's primer and the hiss of the fuse were muffled by the noise of the shooting, which by now was continuous. After a silent two count, Todd tossed the grenade into the window. Just after he again dropped flat, the grenade went off with a roar.

With his ears ringing, Todd scrambled through the smoking window. He fired three times at the inert form of a man wearing only a pair of blue jeans. He then moved slowly and cautiously from room to room. When he reached the front of the house, he was greeted by unaimed pistol shots coming from behind a half-wall partition. Gray aimed carefully at a spot three feet below where he had seen a gun hand occasionally pop over the partition. Centering on this spot, he fired a ten-shot burst in a horizontal spread. There was no more firing in reply from behind the partition.

To be certain that he had been successful, Todd lowered his muzzle to fire another horizontal burst just above the base of the partition. He did this assuming that anyone left alive there would by now be lying prone. His rifle now empty, Todd pulled his .45 automatic from his holster and thumbed down the safety. He took a peek around the corner to find the still form of a woman lying in a pool of blood. Her hand clutched an AMT long-slide stainless steel .45 automatic. Her gun was empty, its slide locked to the rear. Todd raised his own pistol and fired a one-round coup de grâce at the woman's head. Listening carefully, he could hear the sound of someone sobbing upstairs. Todd shouted out the shattered front window, "I cleared the downstairs, but there's still someone upstairs. I need some help in here."

Lon Porter let out a hoarse, "On the way!"

Lisa followed his words with, "I'll cover from out here."

After Lon was in the front door, Todd shook his head twice and announced, "My ears are ringing two pitches at once. For the moment, I'm practically deaf. You'd better lead off."

"Okey-dokey, Boss," Porter said with a twisted grin.

Before they moved upstairs, the two men took turns reloading their guns. "How are you doing for ammo?" Todd inquired.

"I put almost sixty rounds through the FAL, and I haven't fired my three-fifty-seven at all."

"Well, it looks like you might get your opportunity." Gesturing toward the stairway with the muzzle of his HK, he said, "I'll follow you."

Farther down the street, Jeff was trying out his new toy. He fired first in reply to muzzle flashes coming from a second story window of a frame house. Leaning up against a wall, Jeff fired four bursts of about ten rounds each at the window and at the wall below it. There was no more shooting from the window. After firing the M60, Jeff yelled at the top of his lungs, "This is Trasel! This is Trasel!"

Jeff then moved further down the street. His second "target of opportunity" was two men, armed with handguns, running out of town down a side street. Jeff dropped to the ground, swung out the gun's bipod legs, and lined up on his targets. By now, the two men were more than three hundred yards away. Five short bursts sent the men kicking in the dust. He again yelled, "This is Trasel!" because, as he was to explain later, he didn't want anyone thinking that the M60 was still in unfriendly hands.

At the east end of Princeton, four Harleys roared to life and sped out of town. Della fired half a dozen rounds at the retreating forms without success. Her targets, four hundred yards away, rounded a bend in the road, and were out of sight. Across the street, she heard Doug say, "Save your ammo, they're out of range. The Templars will take care of them." Seconds later, they heard an explosion and the ripple of gunfire down the road. Raising her hand, Della gave Doug an "okay" symbol. Just then, they heard the sound of a shotgun barking from a nearby brick house. In a singsong voice, Della yelled, the familiar saying from their countless training sessions, "Okay Joe, I'll fire, you move!"

Carlton sprinted from car to car, then toward the house, approaching it from around the corner from which the shots were coming. He chirped, "Okay Joe, I'll fire, you move." As Della got up, Carlton started firing his M1A at one-second to two-second intervals to keep the man with the shotgun pinned down. At the side of the building, Doug and Della held a quick consultation and reloaded their rifles. Della resumed firing at the window while Doug went around to enter the house from the front. The man with the shotgun returned her fire only occasionally, with unaimed shots.

Just as Della was firing the last rounds from her second thirty-round magazine, she heard a grenade explosion inside the house. She waited anxiously for a couple of minutes until her husband emerged again from the front of the house. As he padded up to her, Doug smiled and said, "End of story."

After finding his assigned house empty, T.K. made his way down the main street, and then back up the alley that ran parallel to it to the north. He came under fire twice. On the first occasion, a man firing a bolt-action rifle from the roof of a mobile home sent a round whizzing by his ear. T.K. turned toward the source of the shooting, and dropped into a crouch. He lined up his sights and fired two shots in rapid succession. The first of the sixty-two-grain Sierra match bullets hit the man in the neck and the second hit him in the left eye. The back of his skull disintegrated in a cloud of pink vapor.

As he moved farther down the street, Kennedy came under fire from behind by a man shooting an M1 carbine from the concealment of a porch. T.K. was struck in the back by two bullets, and sent tumbling to the ground. He was momentarily breathless. Once he realized that his bulletproof vest had stopped the rounds, he rolled over and returned fire with his AR-15 in four quick double taps. His assailant was stitched by half a dozen bullets and lay gurgling on the porch. T.K. stood up and moved on, unconsciously swapping magazines and searching for new targets.

Holding his Smith and Wesson revolver in a low ready position, Lon began his slow ascent of the stairway, hugging the left-hand wall. From below, Todd covered the doorway at the top of the stairs. Once he was at the landing at the top of the stairs, Lon gestured for Todd to follow him. Gray then advanced up the stairs and crouched at the landing while Lon searched the upstairs rooms. After he had entered the second bedroom, Todd heard Lon fire three times in rapid succession, and then after a pause, a fourth shot. Next, Gray heard the tinkle of empty pistol cartridges hitting the hardwood floor as Porter reloaded his 686 using a speed loader. The last room was unoccupied.

Walking back to the stairwell Lon reported, "There was a young woman in the middle bedroom. All she was wearing was a tank top. She was sitting there crying when I walked in. Then I noticed that she had the tattoo of a rose and a skull on her shoulder. She got up and started toward me fast with a big sheath knife. That's when I shot her. She was only a few feet away. I never want to have to do something like that again."

Mike, Dan, Kevin, and Rose did most of the house clearing. They linked together as an ad hoc team, kicking in doors and moving from room to room, eliminating resistance. It was usually Mike who led the way on these assaults. His bulletproof vest saved his life twice that morning.

In one of the building entries, Dan Fong was slightly wounded by a pistol shot that grazed his upper arm. Soon after he applied a Carlisle battle dressing, the wound stopped bleeding.

After twenty minutes of house-to-house and room-to-room fighting, the shooting died down and finally came to a stop. In plain view, Mike jogged up and down the street, checking on the raiders. Once it was clear that there was no more resistance, he walked to the doorway of the service bay of the gas station. He tooted long blasts on his whistle for thirty seconds and then gave the call, "Okay guys, rally on me! Rally on me!"

A few minutes later, ten of the raiders were clustered around him in the back of the gas station. Just inside the door to the garage, Tom Kennedy sat with his rifle at the ready, watching the street. Mike ordered, "Okay, now that we've cleared all of the houses, we're going to go back through again in buddy teams, just to make sure that we didn't miss anyone. I want every single room of each house thoroughly searched. I don't care how long it takes. Also, make sure that every one of these 'One Percenters' that we shot is one-hundred-percent dead. It's the ones that you think are dead that get up and shoot you."

The final clearing process went relatively smoothly. One biker was found hiding under a bed. After he was ordered out from his hiding place, he made a leap for a window. Kevin Lendel fired his riotgun three times, leaving him in a heap beneath the windowsill.

In the back of the former tractor shop, T.K. and Lisa found a ten-year-old boy trapped in a wall locker that had been secured with a twisted piece of coat hanger wire in its latch. He was the only surviving resident of the town. The boy's hands were wrapped in bloodstained rags. When Lisa removed the rags, she found that both of the boy's little fingers had been cut off. Lisa asked, "Who did this to you?"

The boy mumbled something unintelligible in reply.

Lisa repeated her question twice more.

Finally, the boy gave a trembling reply, "It was Greasy. He promised that he was going to cut off one finger a day until they were all gone."

"Why did he do this to you?"

"Because ... because I wouldn't do what he wanted me to do. Greasy wanted me to use my mouth to, to...." With that, the boy's voice trailed off and he began to cry.

Lisa moved to hug the boy, but he pushed her away with a grunt. "You poor dear. Do you want some water?" Lisa asked.

"Yes please, ma'am."

Lisa pulled her canteen out of its pouch and handed it to the boy. He drank nearly all of it with loud gulps.

The Templars had set up two three-man ambushes in both directions on the road through Princeton. Each of these ambushes employed two Claymores apiece. Seven other individuals set up one-man ambushes along likely paths of egress from town. Each of these ambushers set up a single Claymore mine.

Only three of the Templars' ambushes were sprung. The first was initiated by a Claymore mine and followed by rifle fire. This ambush killed the four gang members who attempted to flee on their motorcycles.

The second ambush was sprung by a fourteen-year-old girl. Two men, both armed and one of them naked, were running down the trail directly toward her. Once she saw that they were in the fan of effect of her Claymore, she ducked behind the cover of a downed tree, and touched the bare pair of WD-1 wires to the terminals of a nine-volt battery. To her inexperienced ears, the sound of the explosion was startling. When she popped up with her AR-180 carbine to shoot anything still moving, she found there wasn't anyone alive left to shoot.

The third Templar ambush was sprung by their communications expert, a seventy-four-year-old retired Navy signalman. Situated at an ambush at a trail junction, he spotted a man wearing a black leather jacket and armed with an inexpensive Maverick riot shotgun running toward him. Not wanting to waste his Claymore, he took careful aim with his M1A and shot the man twice at a range of sixty yards.

Two hours after the shooting stopped, the Templars began to file into town singly or in pairs. They gaped at the bodies lying in the street and at the bodies of the bikers that were being dragged into a growing heap by the Northwest Militia.

One of the Templar women recognized the boy who had been found in the wall locker. She identified him as the son of her hairdresser before the onset of the Crunch. She asked, "Where's your mommy and daddy, Timmy?"

The boy gave her a vacant stare. After a long pause, he uttered, "They shot my dad when they first came. My mom's dead, too. Greasy stabbed her. I saw him do it."

With tears in her eyes, the woman asked, "Would you like to come and live with us? We live near Troy. It's safe there. There are no bad men there."

Still sullen, the boy said, "Sure, I guess so, Molly. But first I want to see Greasy. I want to see him dead." After a few minutes of walking from corpse to corpse, Timmy pointed out the body of the biker called Greasy. He walked over to the corpse and spit on it. Then he walked back to stand under the arm of Molly.

Taking the boy by the arm and leading him away from the corpses, Molly said, "Don't worry, Timmy. It's over now." The boy looked up at her and gave her a painful look of disbelief.

After posting a perimeter of security, Todd, Mike, Roger Dunlap, and Ted Wallach sat down for a quick meeting in the back of the gas station. First, they compared notes on the number of gang members that they had killed. Todd brought out matter-of-factly, "We killed sixteen. Captured zero."

Dunlap nodded and said, "We got seven in our ambushes. That adds up to twenty-three, which squares nicely with the figure that your man Trasel gave in his recon report. At most, one or two might have slipped away."

With an edge on his voice, Todd said, "I hope that we got every single one of them. There's no way to be sure, though." The discussion then shifted to their options for dealing with the dead bodies and captured equipment.

Most of the afternoon was spent in an even more thorough search of the houses, including, basements, crawl spaces, and attics. Both the Northwest Militia and the Templars were used in this search. No more bikers or towns-people were found, except for one putrefying corpse in a basement. Todd ordered that anything usable, including fired brass, should be collected. During this time, both of the groups sent small patrols out to bring back their respective vehicles.

All captured equipment from the gang was piled by the side of the bikers' van. The van itself provided some of their best finds. There, they found over two thousand rounds of assorted ammunition, a pair of night vision goggles, four cases of liquor, and one-hundred-and-twenty gallons of gasoline. In the various buildings and in the saddlebags of the motorcycles, they found still more ammunition, road maps, marijuana, clothing, and a pair of binoculars. In searching the bodies of the bikers and their personal effects, they also found the keys to the van and all the motorcycles.

The only particularly curious find was a box of nearly a hundred caltrops. These devices, three-inches long and an inch-and-a-half wide, were pieces of sheet metal cut in the shape of bow ties. Each of them was twisted 90 degrees in the middle. This twist insured that one of the four points on the caltrop pointed upward, regardless of how it landed on the ground. Mike surmised that the bikers had made the caltrops either for vehicle ambushes or perhaps to seed on roads to evade pursuers.

When it came to divide up the captured equipment, all that Todd asked for was the M60, its ammo, and accessories. The rest, he said, could go to the Templars. Dunlap quickly agreed to this proposition. Todd also offered to let the Templars keep four of the unused Claymore mines. Dunlap considered this a tremendous windfall, and expressed his gratitude.

From the heap, Todd and Jeff extracted four belts of 7.62mm ball ammunition, a twenty-millimeter ammo can brim full of metal links for assembling additional belts, and a rubberized green nylon bag containing a spare barrel and cleaning kit for the M60.

Todd took Dunlap aside, and described how they had taken the gear captured previously from looters and set it aside for the use of deserving refugees or charity groups. Dunlap nodded his head and agreed that it was probably a good course of action. With this in mind, Dunlap selected six of the best, captured weapons to set aside for Timmy. These included a Mini-14, an M2 carbine, two Springfield Armory XD .45 automatics, a Mossberg riotgun, and a Smith and Wesson Model 629 .44 magnum revolver. He also set aside all of the ammunition in the calibers that would fit these guns.

Dunlap announced, "We'll clean these guns up and crate them up with the ammo in some sealed cans and call it Timmy's trust fund." He later said that he would save the rest of the gear and food for refugees or for locals who were particularly in need.

All of the dead bikers were dragged to an abandoned frame house at the north edge of town. The dead townsmen were dragged to another abandoned house across the street from it. Then flammable items from nearby houses, including stacks of newspapers, firewood, cans of waste oil, furniture, and the bikers' marijuana were piled on top of the two piles of corpses. Tom Kennedy then conducted a funeral service in front of the house containing the dead townsmen. No one asked for any prayers for the dead members of the biker gang, but Tom said one anyway.

When the funeral prayers were over, Tom Kennedy lit a road flare and set both houses afire. Within minutes, they were both totally engulfed in flames. After half an hour, it was clear that neither of the burning houses presented a fire risk to any of the other houses in town, so both groups proceeded to load their vehicles. After exchanging handshakes, the Templars drove off in their three jeeps and the captured van. They remarked that they would be back later in the day with their large flatbed pickup and a ramp to collect the motorcycles, including the four that had been caught in the Claymore mine blast.

Mike soon had all of the militia loaded into their two trucks and headed back to the retreat. In the cab of the trailing vehicle—Kevin's Ford pickup—sat Kevin, Lisa, and Todd. After they were a few miles down the road, Lisa turned to Todd and gave him a sour look. She complained, "I can see why you asked for the M60. Tactically, it's worth as much as everything else combined. But you should have asked to keep those night vision goggles, too. They would have been great to use at the LP/OP."

Todd answered, "The only problem with those goggles is that they were the PVS-5 model. As I recall, that model needs a high-current two-point-seven-five volt battery, and it's a battery that's been known to explode if you try to recharge it. I didn't see any spare batteries when I looked through that pile of captured gear, did you?"

After a few moments, Lisa said glumly, "No." After letting out an audible sigh, she gave in, "If that's the case, then you were right when you insisted that we invest our money in trip flares, parachute flares, and the tritium sights and scopes, rather than night vision equipment."

Todd brought out consolingly, "Now don't get me wrong. I'm not saying that starlight gear is no good. It's just worthless without the proper batteries, and most of them are exotic, can't be recharged, and have a limited shelf life.

There are a few of the later models made that use standard batteries like the double-A nickel metal hydride and standard nine-volt rechargables we use in some of our electronic equipment. Now any of those would have been a good investment. The only problem was that all starlight gear was so expensive, particularly the third-generation stuff. And as for the Russian gear ... It was so poorly made I didn't bother with it, either. The imaging quality is low, the weapon sights don't hold zero very well, and the intensifying tubes burn out pretty quickly. If only we'd had the money, I would have bought some good quality American-made gear...."

Kevin interrupted with the words, "If only we had the money we would have bought a *lot* of things, like one of those surplus PSR-1A seismic intrusion detection sets; or, how about an amateur radio transceiver. I don't know about you, but I get pretty frustrated sitting there just *listening* to the shortwave receiver. I hear those hams talking back and forth and wish that I could join in on the action. Just think of the intelligence that we could be gathering. We could quiz hams all over the western half of the country about local conditions." Todd cupped his palm under his chin and quoted, "Oh well, hindsight is twenty-twenty."

CHAPTER 16
For an Ounce of Gold

"The Almighty dollar, that great object of universal devotion throughout our land, seems to have no genuine devotees in these peculiar villages."

—*Washington Irving,* Creole Village

In early May of the third year, just as the transplants were ready to be moved from the greenhouse to the garden, the group had a pleasant surprise. One afternoon, a young man on horseback with a High Standard Model 10-B bullpup shotgun slung across his saddle horn stopped at the front gate. Kevin, who was on LP/OP duty, closely scrutinized him through his binoculars. He recognized the man as one of the Troy Templars. Up the hill, Shona let out three low barks. The man didn't wait for anyone to come down from the house to greet him. He just leaned out of his saddle and stapled a handbill to the power pole nearest the gate and rode away.

Kevin called a message in to the C.Q. concerning what he had seen. Mike soon dispatched Doug and Della to go check it out. They weren't back until ten minutes later, since they had moved cautiously, treating the short walk as a patrol. Della was clutching the flyer. She blurted, "Sounds like big doin's in Troy!" as she handed the ink-jet-printed flyer to Mike. It read:

Announcing the
Troy Barter Faire
Come One, Come All!
For three days, starting the 21st of May
(The next full moon for those of you who have lost track),
the town of Troy is sponsoring a barter faire.
Bring your trading goods, and come prepared for some serious dickering.
Secure camping areas will be available at Memorial Park.
A barn dance with a string band is scheduled for the evening of the 22nd.
Security to be provided by the Troy Templars.

"Well, well, well," Mike muttered. Just then, Todd, still wearing his slippers, sauntered up. Mike handed him the flyer, which he quickly scanned.

Todd pronounced, "Tell everyone we'll be having a meeting at noon."

After everyone had quieted down, Todd started the meeting. He began, "I'm surprised that someone else hasn't set up a trading event before this. I guess that until the looters got thinned out, folks were too frightened to travel. You can't blame them. There, of course, has been small-scale bartering going on ever since the Crunch started, but that has mainly been between contiguous neighbors. I'm glad to see some organized commerce getting reestablished." There were vigorous nods of agreement. "Personally, I have no objections to us going to the Faire. My main concerns are about securing the retreat while we are gone, so I'll give the floor to Mike."

Mike Nelson stood up and cleared his throat. "Okay, the way I see it, we can't all go. We'll need a minimum of four of us to stay back here and hold the fort. I suggest that we draw lots." Todd then spoke up, "Does that sound acceptable to everyone?" There were more nods of agreement.

The militia members drew lots from lengths of dowels, as was their custom for such proceedings. The unlucky losers who had to stay at home were Todd, Jeff, Rose, and Marguerite. Margie offered to babysit little Jacob.

The main topic of conversation for the next three weeks was the Faire. It was decided that they would take Todd's Power Wagon and Kevin's F250 pickup. Mike would head the expedition. To the relief of some members, Mike decided that they could wear "civilian" clothes if they wished. He didn't need to remind them that they all had to be armed. By now, they would have felt naked without carrying at least a handgun.

After much anticipation, the big day arrived. Della and Mary were by far the best-dressed and most civilized looking representatives of the retreat. They both wore dresses. It was the first time that either of them had worn dresses or shaved their legs in a long time. The heavy leather belt and holster rig for Mary's Colt looked incongruous, but she didn't care. She commented that it felt good to get out of trousers and feel like a woman again.

Della wore a knee-length turquoise dress that she borrowed from Mary, who was about the same size. She decided to carry only her CAR-15 with a duplexed pair of thirty-round magazines.

The two pickups from the retreat left an hour after sunrise on the twenty-first. Heading to Troy in the pickups, they passed dozens of people on foot, on horseback, and in wagons. Mike laughed when he saw one man was riding a moped with a cage containing three live chickens strapped to the back.

When they reached the edge of town they noticed that there were only a few Fairegoers that had driven motor vehicles. There were literally dozens of horses tied up. Most had their saddles slung over fences or laying next to them.

Because of the value of the gear in the trucks, Mike insisted that they take turns guarding them and monitoring the CB radio—two members per two-hour shift. There were also orders to check in with the retreat via the CB once an hour.

Before they left the trucks, Mike called a huddle and reminded them that their main priority was to barter for kerosene. He asked that they take note of the items that other Fairegoers were looking for, so that the next day's increment would bring the most appropriate trading goods. Mike also reminded everyone to be careful about their personal safety, and not to reveal anything about the militia or their retreat to anyone they engaged in conversation. He warned them, "Be real vague. Change the subject. For goodness sake, don't reveal the location of the retreat or give any indication of our strength or logistics base. The people that you are talking with might be nice enough, but interesting tidbits of information tend to travel far and fast. I think it's best we take the cautious approach."

The Barter Faire itself was spread out up and down the main street. It seemed like a veritable horde, since they hadn't seen large gatherings of people for nearly three years. In fact, though, there were less than four hundred people in Troy at the Faire's peak. As promised, the Troy Templars were there, mostly armed with M1As and parkerized Ithaca Model 87 eight-shot riotguns draped across their chests with extra-long slings. Dan noticed that their quick detachable sling swivels were mounted on the sides of the barrels in the front, and on the top of the stock in the back, so the guns didn't flop upside down. Two Templars were posted at each end of town, and two walked a roving patrol. Their security force really wasn't necessary, however. Nearly everyone, with the exception of young children, was armed. About half the people carried holstered handguns. The rest carried long guns slung across their backs. More than a few carried both. This latter category included most of the Templars and the Northwest Militia.

It was a simple affair. Anyone with a sizable quantity of goods to sell simply rolled out one or more blankets on the pavement, and spread out their goods. Direct barter of goods and services was the most common form of payment, although there were a considerable number of pre-1965 mint date silver coins changing hands. There were several people swapping big game and furbearer hides. One man was making custom belts and rifle slings to order, right on the spot. He was also taking orders for making holsters and rifle scabbards. These were paid-in-advance orders that would be delivered or picked up on a later date. He was also selling leather gloves, and moccasins and sandals that had pieces of car tire for soles. The latter sold out very quickly.

One enterprising gentleman who folks called "Mister Steam" was one of the busiest dealers at the faire. He offered freshly recharged twelve-volt car batteries in trade for fifty cents in silver coin and a discharged battery. Without a discharged battery in trade, the batteries were three dollars each. Mister Steam was a portly man with a graying bushy red beard. He wore overalls and a pinstriped railroader's hat. Mister Steam recounted to Mike how three years before the Crunch he had joined a small engine hobbyist group in eastern Washington. Most of the members had one-cylinder gas-powered engines, and a few had older steam-powered engines. He described the group as "a bunch of us old farts who played with steam, Stirling, and hit-and-miss engines."

Since steam locomotives were one of his long-time interests, he started looking for a steam-powered stationary engine or tractor. He eventually found one: a half-scale two-cylinder Avery steam tractor. It produced fifty horse-power. He spent a year restoring it. He recounted, "I bought it, basically on a lark. My wife thought I was nuts, spending that much money on a 'big toy.' Well, it's no toy now. It's going to make me a good living the next few years. I can do a lot with the power take-off. I'm trying to work a deal with a machin-ist to help me set up a small sawmill. With fifty horses, I can run a mill and the alternator at the same time. I'll tell you, that engine is the best investment I ever made!" Before he left, Mike looked at the signboard advertising his batteries and displaying pictures of his tractor. At the bottom was a note penned with a bold magic marker: "Needed: Lithium grease and clean 90 weight gear oil! I will pay in silver!"

A vendor doing a very brisk business was Mr. Jones, the soap maker. Another was selling grain alcohol that he had distilled. He had the alcohol in an odd assortment of plastic bottles, jars, and cans. His sign read: "Pure Grain Alcohol. 180-Proof. Burns fine in kerosene wick lamps and Zippo lighters. Fine for sipping, too! One quart: 25¢ in genuine (1964 or earlier) coin or like value in barter goods." When he spoke with Kevin Lendel, the man said that he had built his still several years before the Crunch. He said that because he had copper-flashed all of the internal parts, and had used lead-free solder, it made alcohol that was safe to drink.

A few curious features of the Barter Faire were immediately apparent. First, there were only a few guns on display, and only small quantities of ammunition or reloading components. Of the few guns for sale, most were chambered in uncommon cartridges such as .257 Roberts, .25-06, .25-20, .35 Remington, and sixteen-gauge. Only two handguns were seen for sale. One was a well-worn Ruger Single Six .22 long rifle single-action revolver. The other was a Smith and Wesson .41 magnum with three boxes of fired brass and just eight rounds of live ammunition. Exorbitant prices were being asked for both of these guns.

Another interesting phenomenon was the number of live animals for sale. There were a great number of ducks, chickens, and rabbits. There were a few goats, sheep, piglets, and dogs for sale, as well, but only two horses. To even an untrained eye, the horses clearly looked old and broken down.

Most of the Fairegoers had come from the Palouse Hills region. A few traveled even farther. Some came from as far north as Coeur D'Alene and as far south as Lewiston. One stout man with gray hair whom everyone called "the Bee Man" had come all the way from Orofino on horseback. He was selling jars of honey, bee pollen, and beeswax candles. Doug Carlton chatted with him about the enormous .44 AutoMag pistol that he carried in a cross-draw holster. It sported unusual cream-colored grips. When asked about them, the Bee Man chortled, "Those black plastic grips that it came with were too thin and they started cracking the first year I got this thing. So I carved these new ones out of elk antler. They're real sturdy." When Doug asked him about the availability of ammunition for the unusual pistol, the Bee Man replied, "That's no problem, son, I reload. I make the cases by cutting down .308 Winchester brass. The only problem is that I only have one magazine for the thing. I'd give my gold tooth for a spare, but I don't suppose I'll ever find one!"

Most of the merchandise for sale would have been considered nothing but junk before the Crunch, but now every item was carefully scrutinized and considered. There was a lot of clothing, but not many shoes or boots. There were plenty of pots and pans and cutlery for sale, but not many hand tools. Predictably, there was a profusion of electrical and electronic items like lamps, clocks, and radios offered, but few interested buyers.

There were many signs advertising cars and trucks for sale, but Todd didn't hear anyone discussing actually buying one. One sign seemed particularly pitiful to him. It read: "For trade: Corvette Stingray. Power everything. Excellent condition. Stored in garage. Less than 4,000 miles on odometer. Will trade for a good quality spin-cast rod and reel and 40 rounds of .300 Weatherby Magnum."

In addition to the "for sale" signs, there was a profusion of "wanted" signs. Mike made a list of these items in his notepad. The list included: web gear, strike-anywhere matches, Mason jar lids, fish hooks, bleach, rolls of candle wicking, mouse and rat traps, non-hybrid garden seeds, kerosene lamp wicks, Visqueen, salt, band-aids, razor blades, cans of pipe tobacco, aluminum foil, Aladdin lamp mantles, small game traps, coffee beans, dental floss, pepper, rechargeable batteries—D cell, AA, and 9 VDC, sugar, baking soda, ant spray, decks of playing cards, Zippo flints, children's Tylenol elixir, duct tape, toothbrushes, cloth diapers, boot laces, and penicillin. He filled up another column with just the reloading and ammunition wants. Reloading: Large rifle primers, de-capping pins, 3031 and 4831 smokeless powder, Bullseye pistol powder; Ammo: .308 Win., .30-06, 7.62 x 39 mm Russian, .45 ACP, .38 Special, .303 British, nine-mm, .30-30, .22 Long Rifle, .22 Magnum, .243 Winchester, .45

Colt, twelve-gauge number-four and number-seven bird shot, twenty-gauge number-seven bird shot, and .44 Special and/or Magnum.

By a prearranged schedule, everyone from Todd's group got back together at the trucks at 4 p.m. Once there, they found that they had achieved their main goal of bartering for kerosene. They had collected eleven gallons. Most had been exchanged for ammunition.

They all had something to say about the day's proceedings, even Kevin, who was normally reserved. He said, "I must have had a dozen guys ask me about my H and K or my Gold Cup. It really got aggravating. They kept saying things like, 'Are you sure you don't want to sell it?' and I'd have to say, 'Yes I'm sure, absolutely not. End of discussion.' I felt like I should have carried a sign that said 'Don't Bother Asking Me About Buying My Guns.'" Several others said that they had had similar experiences. T.K. then said, "The thing about the Faire that impressed me was the fact that it all seems so medieval. Perhaps it was seeing all those pelts that gave it that feel. It seems like a cross between a mountain man's rendezvous and Barter Town from *Mad Max III*." With that, everyone laughed.

Mary then added, "Maybe we ought to just pick up the phone and give Tina Turner a call. Tell her we need her to do a repeat performance as Aunty Entity and supervise this mess. I wonder if she still has her slinky chain-mail?" There was more laughter.

"Okay," Mike said, "Now down to serious business. Aside from the kerosene, just what did everyone get in trade?"

Mary spoke up first. "I got three Alpine dairy goats: two does and a dis-related young buck. I traded all three of them for a hundred rounds of .22 long rifle and ten rounds of .308 ball."

With this comment, Mike let out a whistle. "Not bad, Mrs. Honcho, not bad at all," he said.

With a note of pride in his voice, Lon Porter said, "I got a six-inch Unimat lathe with a complete set of accessories in exchange for four gallons of gasoline. I even got the guy to provide his own container for the gas. I also bought a pair of moccasins for ten rounds of .22."

Della raised her hand and then said, "I got a pair of moccasins for the same price at the same time Dad got his. I also got a pair of fence-mending pliers, two wool carding combs, a glass food canning funnel, and a dress. All together, those cost two dollars in 'junk' silver dimes that Doug gave me to spend at the Faire."

After Doug saw that Dell was finished, he said, "I ran into a Templar with an HK91. We both stood there staring at each other for a few seconds. I could see that he was eyeballing my M1A, so I knew that he was thinking the same thing that I was. As I'm sure you all know, the M1A is the group-standard rifle for the Templars, just like the H and K is with ours. After a few offers back and forth, we decided to be reasonable and trade straight across. I gave him my M1A and all eight of my magazines for his HK and nine twenty-rounders. We said that we'd get back together tomorrow and swap our spare parts for the guns. I figured that I'd be better off with a group-standard rifle, and the two guns are basically comparable in quality and function. My gun was National Match grade though, so I suppose that Thomas—the Templar guy—got the better end of the deal.

"The only thing that I don't like about the Heckler and Koch is that it doesn't lock open after you fire the last round in a magazine, like M1As and AR-15s do. I guess I can make up for that little shortcoming by loading tracers as the last two or three rounds in each magazine. It's an old Army trick. When you see a red light, you change magazines. That was my only major purchase, or trade rather, of the day. I also bought two monstrous bags of jerky—one of elk and one of bear—for a pre-'65 quarter. I figure the jerky will be great for patrols and picket duty. Oh yeah, almost forgot. I also got three big fat Seattle phone books. They will be great for toilet paper."

Obviously anxious to speak, Lisa was next. "I got four little lambs. They are Targhee crosses. Three ewes and a ram. They are soooo cute. They're already in the back of Kevin's pickup munching on some grass hay. I traded two salt lick blocks for them. I also got a copy of *Raising Sheep the Modern Way*, some spare underwear, a hairbrush, and five pounds of homemade saltwater taffy from a really sweet Nez Perce Indian woman. All together, that cost ten rounds of West German seven-point-sixty-two ball. Later in the afternoon, I got four half-grown Khaki Campbell ducks in exchange for sixty sets of wide-mouth Mason jar lids and rings. This particular breed of duck is supposed to be good both for laying and for eating."

Dan then said, "I traded my Walther P-38, three extra magazines, and two hundred rounds of nine-mil ammo to some dude for a complete fishing outfit, a Bausch and Lomb spotting scope, a *Merck Veterinary Manual*, a big Craftsman socket set, and a leather working tool kit. The leather working set is pretty cool. It's a standard Tandy kit, plus some extras. It has a mallet, about twenty of those miscellaneous patterning tools, a swivel cutting tool, a couple of tubes of Barge cement, a rotary hole punch, a snap-and-riveting kit, and a whole bunch of other items. He also threw in a whole tanned cowhide. It was strange, though, the guy actually seemed more excited about the ammo than the pistol."

Next, Kevin reported on his transactions. "I got an entire buffalo hide in really good shape for ten rounds of .30-06. I figure that it'll help keep us warm up at the LP/OP next winter. Another guy traded me a small Bearcat scanner—one of the portable ones the size of a walkie-talkie—for twenty rounds of .45 ACP. It runs off of batteries, and we have plenty of ni-cads, so I thought, 'why not?' Not many people have any source of power nowadays. I figure that's the only reason the guy was willing to sell it so cheap. I also got a pair of Belgian white rabbits—a buck and a doe, for twenty rounds of .22 long rifle. My mother would be proud. She'd say that I got 'Such a deal!' The cage for the rabbits cost a lot more, though. For it, I had to give up a whole fifty rounds of .22 and three pre-'65 silver quarters. I think it's amazing what a few silver dimes or quarters will buy."

After a pause, Kevin said, "I feel sorry for all those people I knew who bought one-ounce gold coins as a 'survival hedge.' I can see now that a full-ounce gold coin is too compact a form of currency, and it isn't easily divisible. I suppose that people who bought the gold coins minted in the one-tenth-of-an-ounce weights are more fortunate. What would a full ounce of gold buy? That Corvette that we saw advertised? A half a dozen cows? Maybe. It certainly wouldn't do much good for someone trying to buy day-to-day necessities. It's pretty apparent that our stock of .22-rimfire ammo is a lot more useful as a store of value and as a means of exchange."

Mike was the last to give his report. "Okay, get this. I ran into a major coup. I bought a horse. It's not one of those nags you probably saw people trying to sell, either. It's a real nice Morgan saddle horse. Three-year-old mare, very gentle. I took the approach of looking at the horses that were tied up along the fence. I looked for groups of two or more horses, all carrying the same brand. Then I picked out the good-looking ones from those, one at a time, and inquired after their owners. It took most of the day to get anyone to talk a serious deal, though. Most people aren't in the position that they can spare a horse. This guy, who had four horses before the Crunch hit, and now has six, apparently could. When I first asked if he'd be interested in selling, he just said, 'Ah, I don't know, maaaaybe.' But when I told him that I had stabilized gas to barter, his eyes lit up. I got the horse for forty-five gallons of gas.

"The same guy also sold me a saddle, and a full set of tack, and grooming tools—you know, like a brush and a hoof pick and rasp—for another twelve gallons of gas. The saddle is quite nice, as well. It's an old original Ray Holes mountain rig, but the leather is still strong and in good shape. The guy, his name is Thebault, lives just west of Troy. I talked with Roger Dunlap about him, and he confirmed that the guy is trustworthy and circumspect, so I described to him how to find our retreat. He's going to ride over and swap the horse for the gas at the retreat in three days. I can hardly wait." With a grin that betrayed considerable pride, Mike said, "That was my one and only purchase for the day. Okay, does anyone else have anything important to report that can't wait until we get back to the hidey-hole? Okay, then."

After a pause, Mike continued. "Does anyone want to come back tomorrow?"

"Yeah!" they all yelled in a chorus.

"Yikes!" Mike roared. "You all sound like a bunch of cub scouts. I guess that makes me your den mother. When we get back home, we'll draw lots to see which four of us will have to pull security back at the retreat, so the others can come tomorrow." Putting on his oft-used John Wayne voice, he said, "Well, pilgrims, we'd better saddle up and head home before it gets dark."

The second day at the Barter Faire went much like the first. Constant watch was kept on the trucks. There were numerous requests of the members to consider trading their guns. A few of the militia members stayed for the barn dance. Della and Rose had so many men ask them to dance that they were exhausted by the time they bedded down near the trucks. The gathering, including the dance, was peaceful. Those who stayed for the dance got a ride home the next day when the third increment from the retreat arrived. In all, the Faire was a big success.

On the third day of the event, Todd ran into Roger Dunlap. They greeted each other warmly. Sitting near Roger's horse, the two discussed their hopes and fears about the future. They both commented that the Faire was encouraging evidence that civilization was returning to the region. Roger said that it was planned to be an annual event. Todd then said, "Hopefully, it won't be an annual event for very long. I'm sure that some enterprising individual is going to get up the gumption and a good-sized security force to set up a permanent trading post around here sometime soon. People are just aching for some sort of commerce. The number of folks who showed up here the last few days, and the distance that some of them traveled, shows that plainly enough."

Dunlap said, "Yes, I suppose you're right. Next there'll be a cobbler, and a blacksmith, and a barber, and so on. It's inevitable."

Todd chuckled and said, "There's one specialty that's bound to come soon after...."

"What's that?" Dunlap asked.

"A tax collector." Both men laughed.

Two days after the Faire ended, Thebault and two of his sons arrived on horseback with Mike's horse and tack in tow. They spent twenty minutes giving Mike and several other group members a lesson on hoof trimming. Thebault ended the lesson by saying, "If you have any problems with thrush, you can use Clorox, full strength. It doesn't work as good as Copper-Tox, so you'll have to use more of it, and dose it more often." Mike invited them to stay for lunch. The lunch consisted of venison stew, fresh baked bread, and spinach greens.

Several group members made it clear to Thebault that they too were interested in buying horses, and asked him to keep them in mind the next time he had a weaned foal available. Thebault seemed most interested in Dan Fong's mention that he might be persuaded to trade one of the guns from his collection for a good horse. In particular, Thebault said that he was looking for "a good quality pistol for shooting varmints."

Dan then described his T-C Contender single-shot pistol chambered in .223 Remington. He said, "I have plenty of ammunition for it, it's a very common caliber, and it would be a great gun for hunting varmints or animals up to the size of coyotes."

"No, no," Thebault said with a laugh, "What I'm looking for is a gun for shooting the other variety of varmints, the two-legged kind."

Dan laughed and then began to describe his Browning Hi-Power pistol with the tangent rear sight and detachable stock. Thebault asked if he could see the gun after lunch. Dan got his horse in less than a week, a four-year-old mare with saddle and tack. In exchange, Dan traded the pistol, its combination stock/holster, a cleaning kit, four spare magazines, a double magazine pouch, and seven boxes of 9 mm hollow-point ammunition.

CHAPTER 17
The Parting

"... But that same day
Must end that work that the ides of March begun;
And whether we shall meet again I know not.
Therefore our everlasting farewell take:
For ever, and for ever, farewell, Cassius!
If we do meet again, why, then we shall smile;
If not, why then, this parting was well made."

—William Shakespeare, Julius Caesar, Act V, Scene 1

On a warm June morning three weeks after the Barter Faire, a man on a Harley-Davidson motorcycle mounted with racks for two five-gallon gas cans pulled up to the gate at the county road. He got off of his motorcycle and stood waiting patiently. After being alerted by Lon, who was standing LP/OP duty, Todd, Mike, and Lisa walked at twenty-foot intervals down to the front gate to see what was going on. The stranger had short-cropped hair and was wearing an old olive drab army field jacket. He was carrying two Smith and Wesson 9 mm automatics, one in a shoulder holster and the other in a hip holster. He also carried a folding-stock Valmet Model 76 rifle in a leather scabbard mounted on the right-hand side of the motorcycle's frame.

From a distance of thirty feet, the man half-shouted, "Hello! Are you Mister Gray?"

"Yes, I am," Todd replied. "And who are you, sir?"

The stranger announced, "My name's Manny Olivera. I'm from Caldwell. I was given this letter by a guy who rode in to Caldwell on horseback from Idaho Falls. He got it in turn from a guy who drove in from northern Utah. When the fellow from Idaho Falls found out that I was headed north to Coeur D'Alene to join up with my cousin and his family, he asked me to drop this letter off to you." Gray approached the man warily as he held out the envelope.

Todd scanned what he had been handed. He let out a loud whoop, and exclaimed, "Mr. Olivera, you've just made me the happiest man in the world. Come up to the house for some lunch."

Without the caution normally shown to strangers, Manny Olivera's motorcycle was wheeled in the gate. "Aren't you going to ride up?" Lisa asked.

"No ma'am. Gas is precious stuff. I'd rather walk up. Will my bike be all right here?"

Lisa replied, "Sure it will. We've got security you haven't even seen yet. Those hills have eyes."

When the four reached the house, Todd called for everyone available to come to the living room. Todd held up the soiled envelope. "I've got a letter here that you'll all be interested in. Its return address reads, 'The Laytons. Care of Prines' Farm. 1585 County Road 20. Morgan City, Utah.'" A loud cheer went up and lasted for nearly half a minute. For the assembled group, Todd read the letter aloud. For the benefit of Lon Porter, who was up at the LP/OP, Todd wore his TRC-500 set to the VOX position. He began, "The letter is dated the twentieth of June of this year, pretty speedy, considering it came via pony express. Anyway, it reads:

Dear Todd, Mary, and Whoever Else Arrived;

Terry and I are writing to let you know that we are safe and living temporarily at a farm three miles north of Morgan City, Utah. (25 miles northeast of Salt Lake City, see enclosed strip map.) We walked most of the way here from Chicago. We had planned to stay here only a week to rest up and then press on to the retreat, but Terry took a bad spill off of a ladder, breaking her kneecap. That was nearly two months ago. I'm afraid that the break is not healing properly. I don't believe that there is any way that we will be able to continue on, at least not on foot.

We hope that all is well with you. This is the third letter that we couriered up your way. If you got either of the previous ones, I apologize for the redundancy. However, we figured that sending multiple letters by different couriers would be the best bet in getting our message through to you.

We are staying in a spare bedroom at the Prines' farm. They are wonderful people. Like most of their neighbors, they are Mormons, and thus were relatively well prepared for the collapse. To earn our keep I am being employed as a night security guard on the farm. I also help out with the heavy work during the day (mending fences, splitting wood, etc.). Terry is still confined to bed most of the time.

Because of Terry's injury, the Prines have agreed to let us stay on as long as we'd like, but we don't want to wear out our welcome and their stock of supplies. (Mrs. Prine's sister and brother-in-law and their two teenage boys moved in three weeks ago, and the stored food supply will soon be critical.) Is there any way that you could provide transportation to the retreat? I realize that this is asking a lot, and would involve considerable risk, so feel free to say no.

To avoid missing you, we promise that we will stay here until we either hear from you or somebody shows up. Please send word via courier or by radio, if you get a chance. Do you have the night-time CB voice message relay network set up, up there?

Well, that's all for now. Once again, we hope that all is well with you.

God Bless you all.

Ken and Terry.

Over lunch, Manny Olivera told of conditions in southern Idaho. He reported that some towns, including Caldwell, were left virtually untouched by the chaos. Others, including Idaho Falls and Boise, were devastated. He related, "Half of Boise burned down in a three-day period, just house after house. There were only two fire trucks available at the time because the money wasn't worth anything, and nearly all the city employees decided to stay home. The few firemen that did show up to try and fight the fire were kept pinned down by sporadic gunfire. My brother was there and saw it happen, and he told me all about it. It was pathetic."

Following lunch, Todd offered Manny some silver coins for delivering the letter. He refused the offer. Todd then asked, "Is there anything else that we can do for you aside from just feeding you lunch? It doesn't seem like much, considering that you came seventy-five miles out of your way to deliver this letter."

After a pause, Manny said, "I could use some gasoline, sir."

Without hesitating, Todd said, "Go start up your hog, and ride up to the back end of the garage. It's the Quonset hut building. We'll fill up your bike's tank and top off both jerry cans."

Olivera cocked his head and asked, "Is it good gas? A lot of people have had problems with their gas going bad in the last year or so."

"Don't worry. We added Sta-Bil stabilizer. It should be fine for at least two more years."

"I hear that they've started making ethanol—you know, corn gas—back in Iowa and Kansas. Won't work in all engines though."

Olivera soon filled his Harley's tank and two five-gallon cans. Dan Fong approached Manny and pressed a box of nine-millimeter hollow points into his hands. "Dude, I think that you're going to need these more than I will," Fong said earnestly.

Olivera smiled at Dan and replied, "*Muchas gracias.*" He stuffed the box of ammunition into one of the pockets of his field jacket and shook hands with everyone and thanked them once again. After T.K. ushered him through the gate and he rode off with a wave, Todd called for another meeting. Della replaced Lon at the LP/OP.

As the meeting progressed, it became clear that some of the members were enthusiastic for an expedition to go get Ken and Terry, while others, including Lon Porter and Lisa Nelson, urged caution. Lon was blunt. "We know pretty well what conditions are like in our immediate area, but anything over twenty miles away could just as well be the Antarctic for all that we know about it. There could be whole areas controlled by brigands. They could have road-blocks set up. Anyone traveling cross-country could run into people infected with diseases like cholera. I say that the risks outweigh the rewards."

After debate at length, it was decided that the group owed Ken and Terry enough that they had to make some effort at bringing them back to the retreat. It was T.K. who settled the issue. He said resoundingly, "I recall a quote from a man named Saganelian: 'Every risk has its compensation.' I'm willing to take nearly any risk to make us whole again. It's what we've pledged ourselves to from the very beginning. Granted, they're safe enough where they are, but they are taking advantage of the good graces of the Prines. The letter specifi- cally noted that the family is getting low on food. Further, I don't believe in saying 'tough luck,' and I don't believe in 'no-win scenarios.' We've simply got to undertake this mission. It should take three individuals, a four-wheel drive rig, and twelve or more cans of gas to do the job. Ideally, I think we should mainly consider the bachelors. That's why I'm nominating myself first."

Without a pause, Kevin, Dan, and Doug chimed in, "I'll go," almost simultaneously.

A moment later, Jeff Trasel declared, "Well, count me in, too."

Todd looked toward Carlton quizzically and asked, "What's your interest, Doug? You've never even *met* the Laytons."

Carlton replied, "Well, they're members, aren't they? We've been eating part of their stored food, haven't we? It was Ken that did the restoration on most of the rigs here. We wouldn't have reliable transportation if it weren't for him. It was Terry Layton that ram-rodded all the logistics. And she didn't overlook much, did she? We wouldn't have a deep larder if it weren't for her. The way I see it, I owe them plenty."

The debate over who should go centered on both the tactical skills of those who had volunteered, and how the militia could get along without them if they did not make it back. Unspoken, but doubtless in the minds of everyone present, was the aspect of marriage. In the end, T.K., Dan, and Kevin were selected from among the volunteers. To Todd, realizing that all three of them were bachelors, the words "they were expendable" came to mind. He knew that the three men didn't take offense though. Like so many decisions at the retreat, it reflected cold, hard logic. Husbands had the Christian duty to care for their wives. Bachelors were the logical choice for the risky mission.

The preparations for the trip took four days. First, T.K.'s Bronco was chosen as the vehicle to use. T.K. swapped batteries with Todd's Power Wagon. Because Todd's truck had been run more often, its battery had a better charge. The Bronco's gas tanks were drained into cans, and then refilled from the large storage tank behind the garage.

• • •

If Mary had her way, the Grays would have replaced their garage/shop building soon after they bought the retreat. Todd described it as "ugly as sin, but eminently practical." Mary referred to it as "just plain ugly." As best as Todd could tell, the building was an original World War II surplus galvanized steel Quonset hut. It sat on a concrete slab foundation, and had a pair of sliding doors at each end. Todd liked it because, like the house, it was essentially fire-proof. The only changes that Todd made to the building initially were welding bars over the side windows and adding lock hasps to the doors.

Because security of the garage was not considered as critical as that of the house, Todd did not overengineer the window bars. He made them out of standard concrete reinforcing bar stock, commonly called "rebar." Although the bars were made of mild steel, they would suffice in keeping out all but the most determined burglars. After mounting the hasps, Todd ordered a set of twelve "keyed-alike" one-and-three-quarters-inch Master brand padlocks from Grainger Supply. With keyed-alike locks, one key could open any pad-lock at the retreat, eliminating any confusion about keys. Todd eventually mounted hasps on the inside of the wood chute and each of the outbuildings. Another one of the keyed-alike locks was mounted on the front gate at the county road.

The garage was the site of what eventually turned out to be the most expensive of the Grays' "upgrades" before the Crunch—fuel storage. After requesting bids from several contractors, Todd and Mary selected a firm from Lewiston to build their underground fuel storage tanks. They opted for two tanks, each with a thousand-gallon capacity. One was for unleaded premium fuel while the other was for diesel for their tractor.

Luckily, the crew that installed the tanks didn't ask a lot of questions. The norm in the region was for aboveground tanks between three hundred and five-hundred gallon capacity. Todd mentioned to the work crew that the extra capacity would enable him to wait for fuel prices to drop to reasonable levels rather than having to buy fuel once a year at whatever the price happened to be. He also noted that he wanted underground tanks because he was "scared to death" of forest fires.

Todd and Mary hoped that their fuel tanks would not create suspicion. They felt that if they had bought tanks of any greater capacity, they would indeed set Bovill's "rumor control" network into motion.

Because the tanks were positioned on the far side of the garage/shop building, they were out of the line of sight from the house. This bothered Todd. He decided that the best way to confront this problem was to mount the ends of the filler pipes and the hand pumps for the tanks inside the garage.

This meant that Todd had to cut a three-foot-long trench through the concrete floor of the garage. Kevin helped him do the work. It took an entire afternoon and damaged one of Todd's picks, but the job was finally done.

Again with Kevin's help, Todd built a set of false wall cabinets out of plywood over the hand pumps. It too was fitted with a hasp and padlock. Because the pumps were hidden, there was no outward sign that the Grays even had fuel storage tanks. Kevin really liked the idea of the false cabinet. When Todd first mentioned it, Kevin grinned and said, "Neat trick, Todd."

• • •

The preparations for the trip continued for several days. Lon gave the Bronco a tune-up and idled the engine for an hour. He then did a complete inspection of the seals, belts, and hoses. Next, the Bronco's roof was unbolted and removed. Then the windshield was latched down to the hard point on the hood, and it was recovered with burlap secured by duct tape. Kennedy considered removing the doors, but decided that the ballistic protection that they provided, however slight, outweighed the advantage of being able to get out of the rig quickly.

Doug pointed out the fact that folding down the windshield to give them the ability to shoot on the move would also put them at risk. "All it would take is some joker with a roll of thin steel wire, and you might all end up looking like proverbial headless horsemen. I think we ought to install a cable cutter like I've seen on some Army jeeps."

Using Todd's welding rig, Lon and Dan soon fabricated a cable cutter on the front of the Bronco. It consisted of a vertical piece of steel bolted to the center of the front bumper that extended above the height of the roll cage. It had a notch cut at the spot where the vertical member angled outward near the top. The vertical piece was held by two cross braces that angled up from near the ends of the bumper. Todd didn't have enough steel stock of the correct dimension available with which to build the cable cutter, so they used steel fence T-posts, as they were about the right weight and length.

Over the next two days, the three men packed and repacked their gear, loaded extra magazines, and pored over road maps, considering every possible route, bivouac point, and rally point. All three were equipped with bulletproof vests to wear under their fatigues. Since there were only five such vests at the retreat (they belonged to the Grays, the Nelsons, and T.K.), they seemed like badges of honor. They also wore three of the six Kevlar "Fritz" helmets at the retreat. Next they test fired and confirmed the zero of their weapons. T.K. planned to carry his heavy barrel AR-15. Kevin opted to bring both his HK91 and his Remington 870. Dan decided to do likewise. All three also carried .45 automatics in Bianchi UM-series hip holsters.

They decided to also bring along Dan's monstrous McMillan sniper rifle and a hundred rounds of .50 Browning ammunition— a mixture of ball, tracer, incendiary and hand-loaded match-grade rounds. Fong also dug out his precious twenty rounds of special sabot ammunition. The sabot ammo, an exotic type of ammunition that had cost him twenty dollars per cartridge, fired the Winchester Saboted Light Armor Projectile (SLAP). The SLAP cartridges had a .30 caliber bullet encased in a sleeve of plastic. They were designed so that after the bullet exited the rifle's bore, the plastic sabot would peel back, sending the smaller bullet whizzing ahead with tremendous velocity. With such high velocity, the SLAP bullets were reportedly able to penetrate an inch-and-a-half of plate steel, or two-and-a-half inches of aluminum armor. When asked about the need for the rifle by Mike Nelson, Dan said in a singsong, "It's just in case we have to 'reach out, reach out and touch someone.'"

With a laugh, T.K. added, "'Long Distance, it's the next best thing to being there.'"

The Bronco was packed with twelve five-gallon gas cans, all freshly filled from the storage tank. Four of them went on the tire and gas can rack that T.K had mail-ordered from K-Bar-S in Las Vegas before the Crunch. It originally held just two cans, but using some loops of heavy gauge wire they doubled up the cans so the rack would hold four. They also stowed an ax, a shovel, two two-thousand-pound capacity "come along" ratchet cable hoists, two forty-eight-inch Hi-Lift "sheepherder's" jacks, a set of chains for all four wheels, Todd's pair of Woodings-Verona thirty-six-inch bolt cutters, a general mechanical and electrical tool kit, a can of ether-based starting fluid, spare hoses and belts, a spare fuel pump, a spare water pump and gasket, a spare thermostat, a spare starter, and a spare alternator. When packing these spares, Todd silently thanked Ken Layton for insisting on everyone buying vehicles with common parts.

The load also included four five-gallon plastic buckets containing wheat, rice, dried beans, and powdered milk, as a gift for the Prine family. On top of the roll cage, they strapped a rolled up Army "hex" camouflage net. Lon and Dan also welded on a mounting bracket for an extra tire on the side of the roll cage, giving them two spares. The extra spare was "liberated" from the spare carried on the Nelsons' Bronco. When the three mens' backpacks were added, it made an impressive load. T.K. asked, "Now where are Ken and Terry going to sit on the return trip?"

Dan replied, "Oh maaan. I hadn't thought about that. It looks like a Mister Prine of Morgan City, Utah, is going to get the gift of some five-gallon gas cans as well as the food we were planning to give them."

Tom, Kevin, and Dan spent the next day practicing three-man patrolling techniques, immediate action drills, and the like. Time after time, there were shouts of, "action left!" or "action front!" and the Bronco would either be violently maneuvered into turns, or back up suddenly, or come to a stop with the three men spilling out, guns at the ready. The three also shot up twenty-three rounds of .50 Browning. T.K. proved that the McMillan was an accurate long-range rifle. He scored regular hits on a man-sized target that was paced off at twelve hundred yards.

When T.K., Kevin, and Dan were ready to go, there were many prayers and a sad farewell, as everyone realized that the chances of their safe return were completely unknown. T.K. read the 54th Psalm. Mary and Lisa cried. As they roared out the front gate though, the three men were laughing and joking. To them it seemed a grand adventure. Dan, who was at the wheel, started singing his favorite song, "Bad Moon Rising" by Creedence Clearwater Revival. With his now longish hair blowing in the slipstream, he sang at the top of his lungs, "Hope you got your things together, Hope you are quite prepared to die, Looks like we're in for nasty weather, One eye is taken for an eye...."

CHAPTER 18
Chasseurs

"Ride with an idle whip,
Ride with an unused heel.
But once in a way,
there will come a day
When the colt must be taught to feel
The lash that falls,
and the curb that galls,
and the sting of the rowelled heel."

—Rudyard Kipling

The first eighty miles of the drive to Utah were uneventful. Life in the Clearwater River valley was obviously getting back to normal. There were cultivated fields and signs of regular commerce from Orofino through Kamiah and Kooskia. Grangeville was humming with activity. Large portions of the Camas Prairie were back under the plow. South of Grangeville, just below the White Bird hill, there was a large washout that had taken out all of one lane of the highway, and most of the other. Dan stopped the Bronco, got out, locked in the forward hubs, and shifted into four-wheel drive. It took an extra ten minutes to creep along what was left of the road, with Kevin guiding on foot. Two hours later they came upon three burned-out cars clustered together. This again forced them to slow down. Dan and T.K., who had encountered an ambush under similar circumstances, were both nervous until they were well clear of the cars. As they drove away from the wreck, Dan commented, "Oh maaaan, a little pucker factor there!"

Several of the small towns south of Grangeville were burned to the ground. Others appeared undamaged but abandoned. There was no rhyme or reason to the destruction. Scenes of total ruin were within line of sight of buildings that looked like they were transacting business as usual.

For their overnight layover, they selected a spot two miles off of Highway 95, just above New Meadows, near the Hell's Canyon National Recreation

Area. They parked the Bronco on a low-tree-shrouded knoll just off one of the gravel access roads to the Hell's Canyon Park. After parking the truck, they covered its headlights and windows with burlap and erected the camouflage net above it.

They made their camp some two hundred yards away, in a clump of even thicker trees. From this spot they could just barely discern the outline of the truck beneath the camouflage net. They positioned their sleeping bags like spokes of a wheel, with their feet almost touching. Because it was a relatively secure spot, they opted for one man guarding while the other two slept. They traded off this guard duty every three hours. Because of his night vision, Kevin got the midnight-to-3 a.m. shift.

After awakening at 6 a.m. and eating an MRE apiece for breakfast, they cautiously approached the truck, looking for any signs that it had been disturbed. They found none. Taking down and restowing the camouflage net took only a few minutes. Kevin and T.K. worked while Dan provided security. They were back on the road at 6:40 a.m.

Halfway between Wendell and Jerome, Idaho, they encountered a road-block. It consisted of a pair of pickup trucks parked bumper-to-bumper across a cut through a hill. Six men stood around the roadblock, armed with a variety of rifles and shotguns. They wore an odd mix of civilian clothes, digital ACUs, and BDUs. As soon as he saw the roadblock, Kevin hit the brakes, sending the Bronco skidding to a halt. A hundred yards away at the roadblock, a man with shoulder-length hair and holding an M1 carbine yelled, "You'll have to pay your toll before you can pass here!"

"This is a public highway, sir!" T.K. shouted in reply.

"Not anymore, it's not. You owe us half of the gas you are carrying."

Sounding emphatic, T.K. yelled in reply, "Oh no, we don't. We're not paying you any 'toll.'"

The man at the barricade answered with a quick shot from his carbine. The next few seconds brought a dizzying roar of sensations. Bullets fired by the ambushers whizzed by. A few were heard hitting the Bronco's roll cage. Dan Fong was struck by a bullet in his left shoulder, but it was stopped successfully by his Kevlar vest. T.K. and Dan fired rapidly in reply. Together, they fired more than forty rounds. They saw two of the bandits go down. Meanwhile, Kevin sent the Bronco roaring backward. The four surviving bandits ran out from behind the barricade, firing their weapons wildly. After he had backed up five hundred yards, Kevin again slammed on the brakes, and turned the Bronco around to continue their escape in a more conventional manner.

More than a half-mile away from the roadblock, the road followed the contour of a hundred-foot-high hill. After topping the hill, T.K. motioned to Kevin to pull over.

The truck came to a stop on the shoulder of the road, halfway down the reverse slope of the hill. After Kevin turned off the engine, T.K. avowed, "I think I can take them."

Dan asked, "What? From here?"

T.K. replied, "It's possible. 'Standoff' engagements are the best, you know." After taking a few deep breaths, he asked, "So Fong man, can I borrow your McMillan?"

"Suuuure," Dan answered. With that, he hopped out of the Bronco's back-seat and pulled out the McMillan's waterproof plastic Pelican carrying case. Opening the case, Fong lifted the rifle with an audible grunt, and inserted a six-round magazine of hand-loaded match ammunition, and handed the twenty-six-pound rifle to T.K.

Kennedy declared, "I *like* it!" as he chambered a loose round, leaving the magazine full, and clicked on the rifle's safety.

T. K. walked up the hill until he was near its crest. From there he inched along in high crawl position, with the rifle cradled in his arms. The weight and the bulk of the large rifle made this a slow process. Upon reaching the crest of the hill, he extended the rifle's bipod legs, flipped open the scope covers, and began to scan the area where they had been ambushed. As this was going on, Dan and Kevin crawled up until they too could just see over the ridge top. They each carried a spare loaded magazine for the McMillan.

Tossing a bit of dry grass in the air as he had done at countless high-power matches, T.K. judged the wind. He complained, "Darn, I wish I had a windage table for .50 Browning. I'll just have to guesstimate." Getting ready for his first shot seemed to take forever. First, he made several adjustments to the bipod. Then he squirmed around trying to get into a comfortable prone position. He tried placing his cheek on the stock several times before he found a position that was both comfortable and provided the full field of view through the rifle's ten-power Leupold scope. Next, he concentrated on getting himself relaxed and controlling his breathing. Then, and only then, did he pick his primary and secondary targets.

"I'll spot for you," Dan said, as he pulled out his binoculars. Dan lay propped up on his elbows, peering through the rubber-armored seven-by-fifty Steiner binoculars. "What do you make their range, about eight hundred?" Fong asked.

"More like nine-fifty," T.K. remarked coolly.

"Are you going to take out the guy with the scoped rifle first?" Dan asked.

"Yep." After a long pause, T.K fired.

Because they were traveling faster than the speed of sound, the bullets arrived before the sounds of the shots. The first bullet struck the ground behind the bandit's feet, kicking up a large puff of dust. "Three feet low, one foot left," Dan whispered. A few moments later, T.K. fired again. This bullet struck his intended target in the right side of his upper chest. To the other men looking at him, it looked as if he had been struck by some silent, magical force. The loud report of the bullet arrived nearly a second later.

The long-haired man carrying the M1 carbine turned to see where the shot had come from. Just a moment later, he was hit by a second bullet fired by Kennedy. The 750-grain full metal jacket bullet hit near his solar plexus, knocking him to the ground. Finally realizing what was happening, the two other men dropped to the ground.

"You've got their range now, dude," Dan said. T.K. fired twice more before he found his mark. The third man, who had still not yet determined where the shots were coming from, was hit in the head. The bullet entered just above his left eye socket and removed the top and back of his skull. T.K. changed magazines and resettled his cheek.

The last bandit, who was shaking uncontrollably, spotted a puff of dust kicked up by the McMillan's muzzle blast. He yelled out loud to his now dead companions, "I don't frippin' believe it. He's a *mile* away! Nobody can shoot that far!" The man began to crawl through the dust toward the barricade as quickly as possible. T.K. fired again, and missed. On his next shot, he hit the man in the lower abdomen, eviscerating him. "I'm hit! I'm hit!" he yelled, but there was no one alive to hear him. The man thrashed on the ground for twenty seconds, with his life ebbing out of his belly.

T.K. changed magazines again and cycled the bolt. He fired once more at each body to insure that they were dead. Now confident of the wind and range, he hit his targets with each shot. "They're deader 'n doornails now," T.K. delivered. He removed the partly empty magazine from the rifle and inserted a full one. Glancing down at the ground, he wondered about the large pieces of shiny brass that were scattered out to the right of the rifle. He abstractly wondered in a more extended tactical shooting situation, what would be more noticeable: the brass itself, or his movement in crawling to pick it up. He shrugged his shoulders and decided that it was by now an academic question.

Dan Fong lowered his Steiner binoculars and reached over to slap T.K. on the shoulder. "That's the most incredible shooting I've seen in my life."

"I guess those guys didn't know who they were messing with," Kevin muttered.

Fong smiled, and putting on an exaggerated accent said, "Old Chinese proverb: You may rob a man by the darkness of the new moon. But in the light of day, the payback is a bitch!"

After he had picked up his fired brass and walked down the hill, T.K. opened an ammunition can and reloaded the two depleted magazines for the McMillan. He warned, "Well, there's no use in going over there to check the damage. Besides, they might have a backup man hidden behind the barricade or in the rocks that we didn't see. Something like that could ruin your whole day."

Kevin stroked the stubble on his chin. "I agree. Let's get out of here. We'll let the buzzards handle the funeral, and let God sort 'em out." They spent a few minutes examining their road map for an alternate route around the ambush site. The detour would cost them nearly an hour and two extra gallons of gasoline.

Before departing, Dan Fong examined his Hardcorps vest and his flesh beneath it. "Stopped it cold. Looks like a little 110-grain soft nose slug from that M1 Carbine. Check out how you can see the weave of the Kevlar imprinted on the mushroomed out bullet. Cooool! I'm going to keep this as a souvenir."

"How's your shoulder, Fong man?" Kevin asked.

Holding the palm of his hand to a spot beneath his collarbone, Fong worked his arm in a circular motion. He proclaimed, "It'll probably be black and blue and sore as heck in the morning."

Putting on his Monty Python accent, T.K. said, "Classic blunt trauma." They all laughed, as Dan put his vest and DPM shirt back on.

As they drove away, Kevin started the three singing repeatedly in chorus, "Reach out, reach out and touch some one. Reach out, reach out and just say ... die."

They traveled without incident for the next five hours. Ten miles northwest of Portage, Utah, the trio encountered another ambush. The ambush was set up in a better location than the one that they had encountered earlier in the day. It was positioned just around a sharp bend in the road, so that Kevin had little time to react before reaching the obstruction. A stout barricade made of a double thickness of railroad ties blocked the entire road. It extended from the nearly vertical cut on the left side of the road to a steep dropoff of more than forty feet down to an old railroad bed to the right. With no other option, Kevin slammed on the brakes. They came to a full stop less than forty feet away from the ambushers.

Behind the barricade, nine men with rifles opened fire without warning. As quickly as possible, Kevin put the Bronco in reverse and hit the gas. Meanwhile, Dan and T.K. were firing rapidly at the bandits manning the ambush. T.K. was shooting his AR-15 in rapid double taps, with his forearms leaning up against the black padded dashboard. Dan was firing his HK91 from the backseat in a low staccato. The rifle's muzzle was almost directly between the heads of the two in the front seats. The sound of the muzzle blast in their ears was deafening. Dan saw three of the men behind the barricade get hit and go down.

After they had backed up fifty feet, Dan saw T.K.'s head snap backward violently. Soon after, he slumped forward over his rifle, with a tremendous gout of blood pouring from his face and beneath the back of his helmet. Just then, Dan felt a heavy blow to his own chest.

Once the Bronco had backed up behind the bend and out of sight of the ambush, Kevin again hit the brakes, and turned the rig around. He then drove at high speed for three miles before finding a spot on a side road that looked fairly secure where they could stop. By then, Dan had regained his composure. After feeling around under his fatigue shirt, he found that his vest had stopped a large caliber soft nosed rifle bullet. He leaned forward to check on Kennedy's condition. Checking for a pulse and finding none, Dan was sure he was dead. Examining T.K.'s body, they found that a bullet had hit him in the right eye, just below the lip of his helmet. The bullet passed all the way through Tom's head, exiting through a hole roughly two inches in diameter. They concluded that he had died almost instantly. Both men were still shaking as they checked for other damage. To their surprise, there wasn't much. The roll cage had been hit in three places and one bullet passed through the upper portion of the radiator. After it went through the radiator, it glanced off the top of the engine block, just to the right of the water pump, and then went almost vertically through the Bronco's hood, leaving an oblong jagged hole. Luckily, it did not penetrate the block.

With Fong on security, Kevin attempted to repair the pierced radiator. Rummaging through the tool kit, Kevin found a quarter-inch diameter carriage bolt that was four inches long. By cutting some rubber gaskets out of a piece of scrap truck tire inner-tube material, he was able to make a plug that passed completely through the radiator. He then applied a heavy coat of blue RTV silicone sealant to the gaskets and around the bolt. The inner-tube gaskets were positioned on both sides of the radiator, held in place by two large washers and a wing nut. Working rapidly, the repair took less than five minutes.

After waiting half an hour to let the silicone cure, with both men standing guard, Kevin refilled the radiator from one of their tan plastic five-gallon G.I. water containers. Lendel then replaced the radiator cap and started the engine. Kevin told Dan, "It still leaks about a drop every two or three seconds under full pressure, but that's negligible, considering the extra water we have on board. We'll just check every hour of driving. It should get us where we need to go. If the leak gets any worse, we can always loosen the radiator cap and run with the system unpressurized." Fong grunted in agreement.

After staring at each other for a few moments, Dan pulled out two ponchos from one of the backpacks. "Let's get his body wrapped up," he said sharply.

It was then that Dan noticed that Kevin's helmet had a large gash running along one side. "Dude. I think you'd better look at your helmet." Kevin took off his "Fritz" helmet to find that it had deflected a bullet that under other circumstances probably would have left him just as dead as T.K.

As he fingered the frayed yellow Kevlar material that blossomed through the helmet's woodland camouflage cloth cover, he asked, "What should we do, Dan, bypass the roadblock?"

After a moment's thought, Fong replied, "No way, Kev. Those S.O.B.s drew first blood. No warning or anything. They're looters, for sure. I say that we take them out."

Kevin nodded his head and delivered in a quiet, low voice, "Agreed. Let's go find a place where we can hide the Bronco and lay up until it's full dark."

As the sun set, Kevin and Dan applied a fresh coat of camouflage paint to each other's faces and the backs of their hands. Dan carried his HK-91. As was his habit, Kevin carried his riotgun. They walked slowly in single file for an hour until they got to the point where they had planned to separate. There, they once again compared their watches. Dan reached out to Kevin's hand.

Kevin grasped it firmly in response, but asked, "What's the handshake for, Fong man?"

"This might be goodbye, my friend."

Kevin shook his head. "Nonsense. As Jeff would say, we're going to 'kick tail and take names' like the Kolodney brothers and the Rugsuckers. Just think positive."

After a pause, Dan agreed. "Okaaay. Then let's do this one right the first time."

By 11 p.m., they were both in position. After approaching from the east, Kevin sat crouched sixty yards away from the bandits' camp, which lay just across the railroad bed, below the road barricade. Dan Fong was lying prone just back from the edge of the road cut, sixty feet north and twenty feet above the campsite.

Kevin pressed the red "push to talk" button on his TRC-500 twice. He then heard Dan break squelch twice in reply. At the camp, both men could plainly see six sleeping bags clustered around a small fire. A man holding a riot shotgun walked around the perimeter of the camp. The man could see little as he looked out into the darkness, as the light of the fire constantly ruined his night vision.

Both Dan and Kevin waited, watching the half moon's slow track across the sky and occasionally consulting their watches. Just before midnight, the guard walked up to one of the sleeping men and kicked him in the feet. "Hey, your turn, asshole," he yelled at the recumbent form. Shortly after, the second man sat up, extracted himself from his sleeping bag, and put on a pair of boots. Just after midnight, he stood up and took the shotgun from the guard he was replacing, who rolled out his own sleeping bag, and was soon asleep.

Shortly after the new guard took over, he began walking almost directly toward Kevin. Kevin held his breath. He could hear blood pounding in his ears. When the guard was thirty feet outside the camp, he stopped, dropped his pants, and squatted to relieve himself. Two minutes later, the guard resumed his normal route around the perimeter of the camp. It took ten minutes for Kevin's pulse to settle down.

A few seconds before 2:15 a.m., shortly after the moon had set, Kevin stood up and stretched silently, using a fencer's stretch. He then quietly padded toward the camp with his shotgun held to his shoulder. As he entered the dull light of the fire, he could plainly see the man on guard, who was facing away obliquely. Kevin judged the distance to his target at ten to twelve yards. To be sure that he hit his mark, he lowered himself onto one knee. As he lined up the glowing green tritium sights on his shotgun, he saw the guard's head jerk around to face his direction. Just then, Kevin squeezed the trigger.

The guard fell to the ground with Kevin's first shot. Kevin fired once more at the prone form. Then he deftly shoved two fresh rounds from the buttstock holder into the Remington's magazine. He stood and advanced toward the center of the camp, at a 90-degree angle to Dan's line of fire. As he walked forward, Kevin could hear Dan firing from the top of the road cut. Kevin began to fire steadily as he walked, tromboning the pump action with the gun still held to his shoulder. Meanwhile, Dan was firing two rounds at each of the men in their sleeping bags. As Kevin reached the fire, he heard a click when he pulled the trigger. The gun's seven-shot magazine was empty. He then quickly set the shotgun on the ground and pulled his Special Combat Government .45 automatic from his hip holster and brought it to bear, firing at any movement or any sleeping bag that still looked intact. None of the five bandits made it out of their sleeping bags before they were killed.

After emptying his .45, Kevin ejected its magazine, slapped in a fresh one from his magazine pouch, and thumbed down the gun's slide release, chambering a fresh cartridge. Dan's HK fell silent. Much more deliberately now, Kevin walked in a slow circle around the fire, putting one 185-grain hollow point into the head of each of the bandits, to make certain that they were no longer a threat. He walked back to the downed sentry and did the same. Speaking into the microphone of his TRC-500, Kevin reported, "They're history now."

Dan replied with a terse, "Roger that."

Kevin retrieved his shotgun from where it lay on the ground and then quickly reloaded both of his guns from the pouches on his LC-2 harness. Soon after, despite the ringing in his ears, he could hear the distinctive sounds of Dan reloading his rifle. Lendel began examining the camp in detail, while Dan continued to provide security from his over-watching position. Lendel found that all six men were quite dead. He also discovered three shallow graves at the west end of the camp. He assumed they were the bodies of the three other bandits that had been killed the previous day. He spent the next twenty minutes examining the mens' guns and packs.

The packs were the sort of inexpensive nylon packs with alloy frames he used to see at sporting goods stores for under forty dollars. They outwardly looked like real backpacking packs, but were imported from China. Not only were they of shoddy construction, but they were made with brightly colored nylon material. Even in the dim light of the fire, Kevin could see that they were sky blue and fluorescent orange. He snorted in contempt. One of the backpacks contained a large quantity of paper currency, which Kevin threw into the fire. Several others contained silver and gold coins, which Kevin set aside.

Aside from some ammunition, he found nothing else of value or usefulness in the packs; mainly clothes, canned food, and liquor bottles. Most of the guns were not worth bothering with. They consisted of two badly rusted Winchester .30-30s, a Universal M1 Carbine, a deeply pitted Rossi .38 Special revolver, a Mossberg Model 500 shotgun that had been crudely sawed off. Two caught Lendel's eye. They were a Remington Model 700 bolt-action .30-06 mounted with a Weaver K4 scope, and the riot shotgun—a well-made Benelli M/P.

Kevin decided to collect all of the guns. At first he was only going to take the Remington bolt action and the Benelli shotgun and burn the rest. Then he realized that the others, despite their poor condition, might still be shootable and have some barter value. If nothing else, the .30-30s and the Mossberg might have some usable parts that could be bartered.

Kevin tossed the looters' entire pile of firewood onto the fire and threw on the backpacks. Next, he filled a sleeping bag stuff sack with the coins and the ammunition. After looping the stuff sack through his belt and tying its drawstrings to one of his web gear straps, Kevin slung the captured rifle and shotgun across his back. Dan came down the hill and picked up the rest of the guns.

When they got back to the Bronco, their arms ached from carrying the load for the long distance. Kevin stowed the captured gear from the looters beneath the backseat. Next, they reloaded their empty magazines from the ammo in cans packed in the rig, and replaced them in the pouches of their web gear. After getting their packs out of the Bronco, they moved three hundred feet uphill to establish a camp. After all this, it was nearly 4 o'clock. Kevin told Dan that he was still too agitated to get to sleep. While he remained on guard, Dan pulled out his heavily patched down sleeping bag and laid it out on a poncho.

Just before he drifted off to sleep, he said to Kevin, "Good job, Kev."

Lendel shook his head, as he replied, "No congrats are necessary. It was like shooting fish in a barrel. We just gave them what they honestly deserved. Now go to sleep."

Dan awoke at 7:30 to find Kevin cleaning his Model 870. Kevin said to Fong, "I don't know how you could sleep like a rock after what went on last night."

Fong laughed quietly and said, "Au contraire! I'd only be sleeping light if those S.O.B.s were still *alive*."

While Dan put on his boots and stuffed his sleeping bag, Kevin finished cleaning his shotgun. After giving its barrel a final inspection, he slipped it back into place, slid the extra long magazine spring into position, and screwed on the extension magazine. He then reloaded the gun, carefully inspecting each number-four buckshot shell before loading it into the gun's magazine. He told Dan, "I already cleaned and reloaded your H and K."

"Thanks," Dan said.

Kevin snapped back, "No problemo."

After splitting an MRE and some dried apples, they cautiously moved back to the Bronco, took down the camouflage, and loaded their gear. While Kevin was warming up the engine and refilling the radiator, Dan consulted a road map to again familiarize himself with the day's route.

When they stopped to disassemble the roadblock at the ambush site, they decided to pile up some of the railroad ties and set them ablaze. They dragged each of the bodies—most still in their well-ventilated and blood-soaked sleeping bags—and heaved them onto the fire. They kneeled and said a brief prayer.

The remaining drive to the Prines' farm was peaceful. Because the entire region was dominated by well-prepared Mormons, there was far less disruption caused by the Crunch. Morgan City was easy to find, and appeared undisturbed. In fact, the only evidence of disruption was the town's inoperative traffic signals, and some dirty windshields and flat tires on parked cars and trucks.

As they slowly pulled up to the Prines' farmhouse, Ken recognized T.K.'s Bronco and ran out to greet them. He was wearing a huge grin. "What, only two of you came? I figured you'd have at least three or four guys."

Kevin sadly replied, "We were three, but we're just two now," jerking his thumb at the small pair of jungle boots protruding from the end of the rolled up ponchos.

"Who?" Ken asked with wide eyes.

After a few moments, Kevin blinked his eyes heavily and said, "It's T.K." The expression on Layton's face melted.

Ken walked back to the tailgate and stared down at the shrouded body. With his voice wavering, Layton said, "If I'd known something like this was going to happen, I'd have never sent word to the retreat. This ... this is all my fault."

Dan Fong shook his head and said, "It wasn't your fault, dude. It's rough wherever you go out there. We all knew the risks. But we're your friends. Some things are a lot more important than your personal safety. It was a matter of honor."

Ken stood looking into the back of the Bronco, still disbelieving that Tom Kennedy was dead. Kevin and Dan stood a polite distance away. After a few minutes, Ken turned back toward them, tears running down his cheeks, and shared a three-way hug. Just then, as Terry was hobbling out of the door on a pair of homemade crutches, Ken said, "I've never been so happy and so sad at the same time before in my life."

While refueling and packing up the Bronco early the next morning, Kevin Lendel gave the Prines the sealed plastic buckets of food that they had brought along, as well as four gasoline jerry cans, one of which was still partly full. After making their goodbyes, packing Ken and Terry's gear was relatively simple. All they had were their rifles, web gear, and Army surplus ALICE packs. None of the four could avoid occasionally looking at T.K.'s shrouded body. It served to subdue what otherwise would have been an animated conversation.

The trip home was uneventful. With the experience of the trip down, Dan and Kevin knew how to pick their return route to avoid trouble. More than halfway home, they made another "cold camp" about ten miles from where they had camped two nights before. They consciously avoided the opportunity that they had to camp in the same spot twice. The drive on the second day of the trip back was nearly as quiet as the first.

As the Bronco drove up the hill to the Grays' farmhouse, Shona barked repeatedly, but her wagging tail revealed that these barks were of the happy variety. Everyone at the retreat house ran outdoors for what turned out to be a painful reunion.

Soon after they arrived, Kevin gave the captured coins, weapons, and ammunition to Todd for safekeeping. Like the equipment captured previously, these items were secured in one of the wall lockers in the basement.

CHAPTER 19
Hello

"Pressure makes diamonds."

—Gen. George S. Patton

Todd set aside the entire afternoon for Ken and Terry's debriefing. Ken told most of their story, with Terry filling in the spots that Ken glossed over. Ken began, "As I'm sure you all figured out long ago, Terry and I waited too long to 'get out of Dodge.' We thought that once they suspended trading on the stock market that the government would do as it promised and take steps to put things back in order. I guess we violated Rule Number One: Never trust anything the government says. Anyway, we tried leaving town the night after Dan and T.K. bugged out. Unfortunately, as I'll explain, we didn't get very far.

"We spent most of the last day packing up the Bronco and the Mustang. The power was out, so I couldn't use my compressor to adjust the gas shocks on the Bronco for the heavier load. I ended up using a hand pump. We had everything loaded by about ten o'clock. Luckily we had pre-positioned most of our gear here at the retreat, so we didn't have any trouble fitting in what we had to take with us. As we were packing we had heard a few shots. I told Terry that I thought it was just a few guys taking advantage of the blackout to settle some old scores. Actually, I was just trying to make her feel less nervous. As I look back on it all now, I think I was more nervous than she was. Terry led off in the Mustang and I followed right behind her.

"We had planned to take the Eisenhower expressway, but we ended up not even bothering trying to get on the on-ramp. It looked like a parking lot. I could also hear more shooting going on and even see some muzzle flashes. So, I clicked on the TRC-500 and told Terry we'd try getting out through the West Side, using the surface streets. We went along fine for about ten blocks. The only problem was that it was dark. I mean D-A-R-K dark. No streetlights, no house lights, nothing. Occasionally you'd see dim candlelight in a window, but that was about it.

"As we were approaching one corner we had to make a sudden stop, because just as we got there, somebody rolled out a big Dumpster from one side, and one of those giant metal wire spools like the phone company uses from the other. We both had to slam on the brakes. All of a sudden, the whole world exploded. There was almost continuous shooting going on. They shot out all of the windows on the Bronco, and I felt the passenger-side tires get blown out. I flopped down toward the driver's side seat to get out of the line of fire, and in the process, I smacked my ribs against the Hurst floor shifter. It pretty well knocked the wind out of me.

"Just then, Wham!, the Mustang plowed into the front of the Bronk. Terry apparently didn't realize that my tires were shot out, and assumed that I had backed out of the problem. Just as I would have done, she didn't pop her head up to check first. From right there laying down on the seat, she just reached down to the selector lever of the automatic transmission, put it in reverse, and stomped on the gas. Too bad I was in the way. She probably would have made it.

"At this point, I yelled to her on the Trick Five Hundred, 'If you can ... bail!' Whoever it was, they were still shooting up our vehicles pretty well. Luckily, nearly all of the shooting was coming from the passenger's side of both vehicles, so we were able to snake out of the driver's sides without getting ventilated. We both just grabbed our weapons and our ALICE packs. We had neither the time nor the inclination to try and carry anything else. Besides, our feet were moving too fast.

"Terry here—who I've learned has a cooler head in real shooting situations than I do—came over the headset radio as I bailed out. She said, 'By bounds, follow me. I'll fire, you move.' I made my rush to the side of the street and squatted down behind a parked car.

"Then I radioed back to her, 'Okay, Joe, I'll fire, you move.' Then I started the old H-and-K to work. I shot anywhere from four to six rounds with each of her rushes. It was amazing. Trasel's training came right back. We just bounded down the street, back the way we had came, in three-to-five second rushes. Each time, I'd hear her say on the headset, 'Okay, Joe, I'll fire, you move.' Then I'd look for my next piece of cover and run like heck while she was popping away. We did that for about the first five rushes. We stopped shooting after that, once we realized that by then nobody was shooting back. I guess it was too dark for them to see us, aside from our muzzle flashes, so they didn't bother wasting ammo.

"We linked up at the end of the block, and checked each other over for bullet holes, more by feel than anything else. Miraculously, neither of us was wounded. As I mentioned before, I had gotten a good smack in the ribs. Aside from that, I was okay. Terry just had a few scratches on her right hand and right cheek from broken glass. We hunched down behind somebody's hedge at the end of the block for about three or four minutes. Like I say, we were checking each other for wounds.

"It was then, too, that we reloaded again. Only then did I realize that my second magazine was bone dry. I had gone through forty rounds and Terry had burned up about fifty. She had accidentally dropped the magazine that she had used up while she was running, but I still had my empty that I had stuffed into one of the cargo pockets on my trouser leg, so I had Terry stick it into one of the outside pockets of my pack.

"Just as we were about ready to take off again, I saw somebody down at the other end of the block set off a road flare. Within a few minutes, they set up a bonfire. By the way it took off, they must have started the thing with gasoline.

"They started pulling the contents out of the car and the Bronk almost right away. They must have realized that they hit a lucrative target, because they started yelling and screaming. They were whooping it up like Indians on the warpath. I heard Terry say, 'Those heathen bastards.' I said to her, 'What do you say we make 'em pay dearly for it?' She answered me, 'I don't know. Do you think it's right?' And I said, "It's as right as anything could be. They just tried to kill us, and they've taken almost everything in the world that's worth anything to us. I say we make 'em pay for it, with interest.' She just reached out and clenched my hand, real tight.

"We lay down side by side on the sidewalk to the right of that hedge, and got into good prone positions. Terry says to me, 'I've got the guys to the right of the bonfire, you take the ones on the left.' There was one guy who had what I think was my Remington riotgun and was holding it up at arm's length over his head. Even from the end of the block, I could hear him quite distinctly yelling, 'I got the power! I got the power!' He was silhouetted against the fire. I picked him for my first target. I waited till I could also see several other good targets, and then I whispered, 'One, Two, *Three!*' and then I cut loose.

"We both burned off a full magazine apiece. I saw the first guy I was aiming at go down for sure, and I think I at least wounded two others. Terry was able to do a bit better, because she has a tritium front sight on her CAR-15. As it was, I could barely see my sights. That's right, I didn't have the tritium front sight on my H and K. I'd replaced it with standard front sight post for a high-power match that T.K., Terry, and I went to a few months before. Unfortunately, I never got around to putting the night sight back on. Pretty stupid of me. The darned thing is still probably in my desk drawer back at our house in Chicago. Heck of a lot of good it's doing me there."

Terry interjected, "I squeezed off two rounds at each guy. I know for sure that I nailed three of them, and got some fairly decent shots at two others. I couldn't be sure. Even with their bonfire, it was pretty dark. I used up the rest of the magazine sort of randomly, shooting at places they might have taken cover."

Ken resumed telling the story. "After we both emptied our guns, we beat feet around the corner, reloading our guns as we ran. This may sound hard to believe but we were laughing. Neither of us had ever so much as been in a fist-fight before this. We had probably killed half a dozen men, and we were laughing about it. Amazing how quickly times—or people, for that matter—change. Anyway, we stopped halfway down that block for a brief confab. We decided that to get around the riffraff that ambushed us, we'd cut south two more blocks, then turn to resume our bearing back west.

"After we had covered about eight blocks in short buddy rushes we were pretty well stressed out and exhausted. It was practically pitch black and we could have gotten blown away by some nervous citizen on any given rush. I said to Terry, 'There's got to be a better way. We'll never get out of town by dawn doing it this way.' So we sat down in some big bushes next to a church, and draped a poncho over ourselves so that we could look at a street map with a subdued flashlight without turning ourselves into a target.

"From where we sat, we had at least ten miles to traverse before we'd be out of the thickest part of the city and the suburbs. We looked, but there were no parks that we could cut through or creek bottoms that we could follow. It was just continuous blocks of city streets.

"We sat there giving each other dumb looks for maybe twenty seconds, and then Terry said, 'Why not go underground, down in the storm drains, just like we talked about for nuke scenarios.' I whispered back, 'I love you!' Then she asked me, 'How are we going to get down there?' Then I reminded her about that thing in the book, *Life After Doomsday* by Bruce Clayton, where you take two hefty bolts and join them with a piece of wire, and then stick one down the pry hole on a manhole cover. In my pack I had some wire, but no bolts. I spent the next few minutes fishing through my pack looking for a reasonable substitute.

"What I came up with was my old Boy Scout knife-fork-spoon kit, you know the kind that all nest together? Anyway, I twisted the wire around the spoon and the knife. The knife ended up working just great, because it had a bottle-opening notch about halfway down it. That held the wire in place perfectly.

"I put my pack together again, and then spent the next few minutes groping around the street looking for a manhole cover. After a few embarrassing minutes, we found one. I handed my rifle to Terry, and I popped the knife down the hole. When I pulled up on the spoon connected by the wire, the knife toggled around nicely, just like a darned moly bolt. Next, I squatted down and put all my weight into lifting the manhole cover. Those things are heavy! After some grunting and groaning, I got the thing up, and slid it off to the side. I sent Terry down first, then handed down her carbine, then her pack, then my pack, then my rifle. I positioned myself on the rungs that were set in the concrete, and slid the lid back in place. I swear, it took a lot of strength. It closed with a thud that really reverberated down there.

"Once we got down in the storm drain, we decided to continue west in this storm drain that paralleled the street. Walking in a storm drain is a real bitch, especially with a backpack. The inside diameter is only about five feet. Terry was able to move along a lot faster and easier because she's shorter, and consequently didn't have to hunch over as far as me.

"One weird thing about the storm drains. The air down there was actually warmer than up on the street. Must have been the effect of the ambient ground temperature. Try as we might, we couldn't avoid walking in the rainwater in the bottom of the drainpipe. Our feet got soaking wet and ice cold pretty quickly. After a while, we didn't even bother keeping our feet straddled so that they'd be up out of the water. We just slogged along.

"We traveled west in the drain for several hours, keeping rough track of where we were by the number of gutter drains and manholes we passed under.

"At one point, we heard a lot of commotion and shooting above us. It was really eerie, hearing it reverberate around down there. As we passed under one gutter drain, I could hear a guy sobbing. He must have been lying right next to the grill in the gutter. I shined the light up for a second and could see that there was blood pouring down from the grill. There was a lot of it. Talk about blood in the streets!

"By four a.m., we were *exhausted*. About that time we came to one of those big four-way storm drain intersections. As chance would have it, this was the type with the catwalk made out of expanded metal running across the two levels. We got up on the catwalk, and found that there was just enough room for us to lie down lengthwise, positioned with our feet touching. We hung our packs and rifles on the ends of the ladders at either end. That's where we spent the next day. Stretched out on that catwalk. We just took off our boots and wrung out our socks and hung them up to dry. After only about half an hour we started getting chilly, so we broke out the sleeping bags.

"If anything, the chaos up above got worse all through the next day. The shooting was practically constant. There must have been a lot of buildings on fire because you could smell smoke, even down in the storm drains. Occasionally, we could hear the sirens of an emergency vehicle pass overhead. Surprisingly, we actually managed to get quite a bit of sleep. We must have been pretty well wiped out.

"At about five p.m., we got our boots and socks—they were still wet—back on and climbed back down to the east-west drain. We just kept going west most of that night. We stopped awhile to catch our breath and straighten-out our backs. I practically spaced out; a real troglodyte existence. All I could hear was the echoes of our breathing and the splashes of our footsteps. I thought it would never end. Then I saw dim light up ahead.

"We stepped out of the storm drain onto the banks of the Des Plaines River. It was about 6:00 in the morning. Just between nautical twilight and civil twilight, as Jeff would call it. Because the river bottom provided good concealment, we decided to stick to it. We followed the river bottom for about fifteen minutes before I found a good place to lay up for the day. It was a big clump of willows on the bank of the river. They were plenty thick, so I figured our chances of getting spotted there were about nil.

"By then, it was getting fairly light. We just rolled out our sleeping bags and took turns sleeping. About noon, we split an MRE. It was only then that I realized that we hadn't had anything to eat, and darned little to drink in nearly thirty hours. We just devoured that MRE. Next, one at a time, we cleaned our rifles. I'm glad that I checked on our .45s, too. Mine was soaking wet. I even had to unload the magazine and towel-dry each cartridge.

"About two in the afternoon, Terry woke me up with her hand held over my mouth. A group of about twenty people were walking right toward us, the same direction that we'd been traveling. We just held still and they passed by. They didn't have a clue that we were there. Most of them carried guns, but they carried them slung over their shoulders like they were out deer hunting or something. They were walking through all kinds of potential ambush zones, and they were at sling arms. Just plain stupid. They obviously chose the creek-bottom route to get out of Dodge just like we did. They had no tactical training, though. They were noisy. The idiots were talking out loud in a normal tone of voice. And they were walking in a clump, no interval whatsoever. No point man, either. They were just getting out of Dodge in a hurry, in broad daylight.

"Before sunset another group came through. This one only had about ten people; same *modus operandi*. Traveling in a gaggle like that, one grenade could have killed half of them. It was a pretty pitiful show. I doubt that they got very far in one piece, traveling like that.

"Just as it got dark, we powdered our feet, put on dry socks, packed up, and hit the trail. We followed the river west for two days, avoiding all contact, and laid up during daylight in clumps of brush or fields of harvested corn that had been left standing. By that point, the river was starting to curve around almost due south—not the direction that we wanted to go. About 8 o'clock the third evening on the river, we passed under a railroad trestle just north of Joliet. Voilà! The tracks ran east-west. We followed the tracks west for several nights without incident.

"Knowing we had a long way to go, we just split one MRE per day. We were constantly hungry. The only extra food that we got was an occasional sugar beet that we found on the railroad ballast. They were ones that had fallen out of hopper cars. We cut these up with Terry's Swiss Army knife. We also gleaned a few dried-up ears of corn at the edges of fields. We didn't turn up our noses, though. We gnawed on them like crazy. You hear people talk about being hungry, but let me tell you, missing a meal or two is nothing like being *truly* hungry. It's the only thing you can think about. It's about enough to drive you nuts. I figure that we were burning several thousand more calories a day than we were taking in. We both lost quite a bit of weight.

"At one point, we came across an abandoned railroad company high-railer pickup parked on a siding. I could have hot-wired it in a heartbeat, but unfortunately, someone had either siphoned all of the fuel out of it or run it dry. With that high railer, we could have been a few hundred miles closer to Idaho in just a day. Too bad. Anyway, we pressed on.

"As we approached each town of any appreciable size, we got off the tracks and cut around them. This took a lot of extra time, but I suppose it was worth the extra effort. We heard shooting and saw buildings on fire in some of the towns."

Terry interrupted Ken again at this point. "We had one scary incident near the town of Mendota. On the outskirts of town, we passed a sort of refugee or hobo or looter camp. They didn't have any fires lit, and most everyone must have been asleep. Anyway, it was dark and quiet, so we were practically in the midst of the camp before we realized it. Ken called me on the Trick and said, 'Act brave and keep walking.'

"Just then, some guy with a pistol on his hip who was drunk staggered toward the tracks and started to take a leak. He looked up at us—we were traveling at about a twenty-foot interval on opposites sides of the track and he asks, 'Who the hell are you?' to Ken. Ken told him, 'You don't want to know, mister. Just leave us alone, and we won't waste you.' We kept our guns trained on him, walking backward, and disappeared into the night. I was scared to death that he'd call the alarm and we'd be in the middle of a firefight. Either we scared him, or he didn't think we were worth hassling. Well, either way, he didn't go gunning for us. I guess we just lucked out. There were at least fifty people in that camp."

Ken picked up where Terry left off. "As we headed west, I realized that we were going to have to find some place to cross the 'Mighty Mississip.' The problem was that there were only a few bridges, and they were natural choke points—just about ideal for an ambush. The problem solved itself, however, when we got there. The night that we hit the banks of the Mississippi, it was in the middle of a heavy downpour. It was the first appreciable rain we had since we left Chicago. It was pitch dark, and pouring rain. Only some ex-Green Beret or LRRP would be lying in ambush on a night like that."

Jeff chimed in, "You left out Force Recon." Everyone laughed.

"We crossed on a long railroad trestle bridge just above East Moline. It was very scary. It was dark, the bridge was wet, and it wasn't designed for foot traffic. It seemed like it took hours, walking along in our ponchos, carefully stepping from one tie to the next to get across. Also, in the back of my mind, I couldn't help wondering if a train or high-railer might come barreling across. Of course, the chance of that was slim, but nonetheless, I couldn't get it out of my mind.

"Once we were on the west bank of the Mississippi, I breathed a sigh of relief. It was one of the few natural barriers that we had to cross, and it also marks a change in demographics. The population density is far lower west of the Mississippi. Fewer people, fewer encounters, fewer problems.

"Once we were into Iowa, the weather took a turn for the worse. We ended up spending three miserable weeks there on the reverse slope of a pile of grain at a big grain elevator about three miles out of a town called Durant. First it poured down rain steadily for four days. Then it turned to sleet. Then it turned to snow. It snowed off and on for two weeks. We mainly ate corn soaked in water. We spent most of our time huddled up in our bags, sleeping in shifts. Luckily, nobody came by during the entire three weeks.

"By now, it was late November, and we didn't see much of the sun. After the snow let up, we filled our backpacks with as much corn as we could carry. I left all of my paper money—about three hundred dollars—on top of the pile with a thank-you note to the owner of the elevator. It was there at the elevator that we realized that Terry had lost her TRC-500 somewhere along the way. Because one two-way radio is not much use, I salvaged the ni-cad out of mine, and left the radio there for the owner of the grain elevator. He probably thought it was pretty funny when he found the money, considering that by then it was damned near worthless. At least the TRC-500 would be worth something to him, at least for parts.

"We tried heading west again, but we didn't make much progress. On average, the temperature was twenty or thirty degrees colder than when we first left Chicago. When we first left, the days were clear and chilly and the nights were bearably cold. Out on the plains, we practically froze to death. We knew we had to find a place to spend the winter, but where?

"We ended up finding a place to stay in a little town called West Branch. Kind of ironic, it was the hometown of Herbert Hoover, the guy they blamed for the last depression. I guess in the long run, history will be kinder to Hoover, once people realize that the 1930s weren't all that bad. That so-called Great Depression was just a case of the sniffles compared to this one. Shoot, this one's double pneumonia."

Terry picked up the thread of the story. "We stayed at a farm just outside West Branch, which is about ten miles east of Iowa City. The farm was owned by a Quaker family called Perkins. They claimed that they were actually distant relatives of the Hoovers. I suppose they were telling the truth. There are probably hundreds of people in that area that are related. The Perkins were salt-of-the-earth country folk. They grew corn and soybeans mostly, on one-hundred-and-twenty acres. They had two small children. Because West Branch had had a lot of trouble with looters coming from Iowa City in recent weeks, we didn't have any trouble at all convincing them to hire us on for security in exchange for room and board. Mr. Perkins was pretty funny. He introduced us to his neighbors as his 'Night watchmen from Chicago with the space rifles.'

"The life there on the farm was pretty grueling. The weather was horrible, and the hours were lousy. We basically worked twelve-on, twelve-off shifts, rotating at 2 p.m. and 2 a.m. But we ate well. Mr. Perkins was incredibly hard working. He put in at least ten hours a day working on the farm. He'd often say, 'Work is life.'

"Early one morning in November, two vans pulled up to the front gate. I happened to be on duty, and Ken was asleep. I yelled down to Mr. Perkins, who was feeding hay to the cows, 'Do you recognize those vans?' He said, 'Nope.' So I screamed, 'Get back in the house, and wake up Ken and then your wife, right now!'

"I was standing in my usual spot, on the platform just inside the top door of the silo. Once I saw them stop, I sat down and put my elbows on my knees to get a good rest position to shoot. One guy got out of the first van with a pair of bolt cutters. Just after he cut off the padlock, but before he could swing the gate open, I fired my first shot. I missed. I fired a few more times, and finally hit the guy. By now, they were shooting back at me. I could hear bullets pinging off the silo like crazy.

"The next thing I heard was Ken opening up from the kitchen window with his H-and-K, 'Whump. Whump-whump. Whump-whump.' Between the two of us shooting, I guess they figured they had bit off more than they could chew. By the time they had backed away from the gate, we had shot out both of their windshields. They left the guy with the bolt cutters dead on the ground. A few hours later, when we were fairly sure that they weren't coming back, we went out to assess the damage. We had fired about seventy rounds between the two of us. All that we found was the dead guy, a cheap pair of Chinese-made twenty-four-inch bolt cutters, about fifty pieces of their fired brass, a lot of broken glass, and a lot of blood. Apparently, we hit more than one of them."

Ken carried on. "I apologized to Mr. Perkins for having shot right through the kitchen window. He just said, 'Shucks, that what they make that clear sheet plastic fer, ain't it?' We counted twenty-five holes in the silo, and ten in the house. No really serious damage though. Mr. Perkins said, 'Well, I guess I got my money's worth for the security force. Those space rifles sure are something. It sounded like World War Three.' We buried the dead marauder out in the garden. He's probably pushing up big healthy turnips by now.

"We made our goodbyes to the Perkinses in late April. We had our packs bulging with canned food, beef jerky, and pemmican. We also still had two MREs that we had saved. Traveling at night, mainly along railroad tracks and occasionally cross-country, we made it to western South Dakota that summer. In late September, realizing it was too late in the year to make it to Idaho, we started looking for a place to spend the winter.

"This time it took three weeks and a couple of run-ins with nervous ranchers with shotguns before we found someone who would take us in as 'security consultants' for room and board. We stayed outside a little town called Newell, in Butte County, with a family called Norwood. Real nice people. Cattle ranchers. We ate so much beef that winter, that we almost got sick of it. Both of us learned how to ride and care for horses that winter. We also learned the basics of horse shoeing.

"In all, it was a good winter. Because the Norwood's oldest boy, Graham, was also pulling security, we had the relative luxury of only eight-hour shifts. Graham carried an M1 Garand and an old Smith and Wesson Model 1917 revolver, chambered in .45 automatic. He was pretty good with both guns, and even better after we gave him a few pointers on combat shooting. The kid was incredibly fast at reloading the revolver using full moon clips. I swear, he could reload that gun faster than anyone I've ever seen reload a revolver using a speed loader.

"Fortunately, we didn't have any encounters with marauders that winter. We did hear that Belle Fourche, which was about twenty-five miles away, had got shot up pretty badly by a whole army of bikers before they were finally driven off.

"We left the Norwoods in late March. We rode out on horseback with Graham. He rode with us as far as Scottsbluff, Nebraska, where they had relatives. There, after delivering a few letters and renewing acquaintances, Graham had to head on back to the ranch.

"He, of course, took the two horses that we had borrowed, plus his own horse and the packhorse, back with him. We gave Graham a half a box of .45 automatic for his Model 1917 as a thank you and as a birthday present. He turned seventeen while we were on our ride to Scottsbluff.

"We stayed overnight at the Norwoods' relatives' place. It was there that we heard tremendous news. They had heard that their neighbor, named Cliff, was planning on taking a drive out to northern Utah. I was just dumbfounded. 'Taking a drive?' I asked. They said, 'Sure. We can go talk with him tomorrow.'

"The neighbor, Cliff, was indeed 'taking a drive' in a real live internal combustion engine automobile—a crew cab Ford pickup, no less—from Scottsbluff to Coalville, Utah. He was going there to visit relatives, and perhaps to stay. We couldn't believe it. This guy, Cliff, we never found out his last name, was a real lunatic. He had most of the back end of his truck filled with gas cans. He said that he hadn't heard from his cousins since before the stock-market meltdown, and wanted to look in on them to see if they were all right. He also said he had extra copies of a lot of genealogy and family history documents that he wanted to deliver to them. We didn't question his judgment, though, at least not to his face. He was happy to have someone well-armed along to 'ride shotgun.'

"I spent a day checking on the mechanical condition of Cliff's pickup, to be sure it would get us there in one piece. I replaced the fuel filter, replaced the lower radiator hose, adjusted the belt tensioner—it had one of the later type serpentine belts—and then I lubed the chassis, and changed the oil. Oh yeah, and I tracked down a spare belt for Cliff before we left, just in case it broke. If one of those serpentine belts breaks, you are totally out of luck, because that one belt drives just about everything under the hood.

"We left before dawn the next day. Most of the way, Terry sat in the back and I sat directly behind Cliff in the jockey seat of the cab. Compared to walking or riding horseback, as we'd been doing for the past two years, it seemed like we were flying in a spaceship. The landscape just roared by. Most of it was real lonely unpopulated basin and range country. Cliff played a Hank Williams Jr. tape—I think it was his only tape—over and over again. I don't know how many times we heard 'Tennessee Stud,' 'The Coalition to Ban Coalitions,' and 'A Country Boy Can Survive.' I was singing along with ol' Cliff after a while.

"Surprisingly, we didn't run into any trouble in all that distance. I suppose that the Good Lord was looking out after poor naive Cliff. The only signs of disorder that we saw were a few burned down houses and a lot of cars that looked like they'd been stripped to the bone.

"When we got to Coalville, we thanked Cliff dozens of times, and gave him twenty rounds of .223 ball to use in the folding stock Mini-14 Ranch Rifle that he carried in his pickup. He just yelled, 'Thanks for the amma-nishun pardner!' and roared off up the road. What a lunatic.

"Once we got to Coalville we were on foot again. We were just outside Morgan City when I developed a bad blister on my left foot. We decided to rest up for a couple of weeks, using our usual *modus operandi* as security guards. It was there that Terry fell off the ladder and broke her kneecap. It just didn't want to heal properly, so we had no choice but to ask to stay on. That's when we started sending you letters via any means possible. I guess that you know all the rest."

CHAPTER 20
Goodbye

"There were three friends that buried the fourth,
The mould in his mouth and the dust in his eyes;
And they went south, and east, and north,
The strong man fights but the sick man dies.
There were three friends that spoke of the dead,
The strong man fights but the sick man dies.
'And would he were he here with us now,' they said,
'The sun in our face and the wind in our eyes.'"

—Old Ballad

Digging T.K.'s grave began early the next morning. Todd picked the knoll above the LP/OP for the grave. He commented, "You can see half the county from up there. I think Kennedy would prefer this spot. It's a real 'reach out and touch someone' kinda spot." Nearly everyone wanted to help with the digging.

As they dug the grave, everyone shared their favorite stories about their experiences with T.K., and a lot of tears. At one point, Mary stopped digging to lean on her shovel. She said wistfully, "T.K. would have called this 'an excellent form of catharsis.'"

Mike was the first to get everyone into the storytelling mood. He recounted, "I remember one time just after he got out of college, T.K. and I were out for a drive in his 300-Z. He had just traded in his old car, and was really letting that car loose. I don't think he was trying to show off—that wasn't his style—he just wanted to see how the thing handled at high speed. We were zipping along about ninety.

"All of a sudden, he started to slow down because he had spotted a state trooper pulling onto the road. The trooper pulled us over a couple of minutes later. He walked up to the car and told T.K. that he had clocked him at eighty-two miles per hour in a sixty-five zone. He asked him to show his driver's license and car registration, so T.K. hands them both over, along with a 'Get Out of Jail Free' card from a Monopoly game. The trooper started laughing so hard I thought that he was going to bust a gut. I guess that we caught the trooper when he was in a good mood, because he didn't write Tom a ticket. He just gave him a warning to slow down."

After the laughter died down, Todd cleared his throat and chimed in. "One time just after T.K. graduated from college, he brought me along with him to a rifle match at a range outside of Palatine. As usual, T.K. kicked butt. He had the second highest score, and there were more than sixty people shooting that day. I ranked thirty-seventh. As I recall, T.K. tried to make me feel better about it by blaming it on my HK91, which is not quite as accurate as his glass bedded Garand with match sights. It was a nice gesture, but I knew that it was my shooting ability that was at fault, not my rifle. I never do as well in competition as I do when I'm just out at the range for fun. I get all nervous and even a bit shaky. Not T.K. though. He always had nerves of steel at high-power matches.

"After the match, we drove back to my apartment to clean our rifles and split a pizza and drink some root beer. As we were walking from the parking lot to my apartment, we ran into a guy who lived two apartments down, a real stoner type. Pointing to our Pelican rifle cases, he said, 'Hey Todd, you didn't tell me you were into music, man!' Apparently he thought that our rifle cases were guitar cases. Just as I was about to explain to him what was actually in the cases, T.K. interrupts and says, 'Oh yeah, man, we're with *The Group Standard*. We play gigs two or three nights a week.'

"My neighbor said, 'Cooool. I've heard about your band, man! A friend of mine heard you play once. I think it was at the U. of I. pub. He told me you were pretty awesome.' Then he pointed to T.K.'s case and asked, 'What instrument do you play, man?' Without cracking a smile, T.K. says, 'Bass staccato.' The guy just nodded his head pretending like he knew what T.K. was talking about. After we got inside my apartment and closed the door, we got into one of those hysterical laughing fits. I was practically crying.

"After I regained my composure, I asked T.K. what he thought he was doing brewing up a cock and bull story like that. He tells me, 'People like that steal people's guns to sell to support their drug habits. You're better off if you don't let people know that you own anything portable of great value. Besides, I couldn't resist. Didn't you love hearing him say that a friend had heard us play? What a liar!'

"I just had to call the kettle black. I said, 'Look who's talking, mister. You're lucky he didn't ask to see your 'bass staccato' guitar.'"

Jeff laughed with the others, and then handed his shovel to Todd, so that he could tell a tale of his own. Jeff began, "I've got the T.K. story to beat all T.K. stories. Some of you have probably heard this story, and I swear to God, I'm not bullshitting. It really happened. This was about nine years ago, back during the first time that I was in the group. About three months after Ken and I restored my Power Wagon, Kennedy volunteered to go out with me on a wood–cutting expedition. We got up early on a Saturday morning and drove up to my uncle's place outside of Valpariso, Indiana. We spent most of the day cutting down three oak trees and cutting them to stove length.

"I guess that our eyes were bigger than my pickup, because we had just plain cut too much wood. We stacked the back of the pickup sky high. We left all the wood that wouldn't fit in the pickup there for my uncle to use. There was so much wood that we used a full one-hundred-and-twenty-foot coil of green line rappelling rope tying it all down. Fortunately, with Ken's help, I had just installed overload springs, and had re-arched the rear springs and bought new shocks. Even still, the load was all green wood, so we had the springs pretty well squashed flat. It was a beautiful load of wood by anyone's standards.

"Anyway, on the way home from Valpariso, at about 9 o'clock in the evening, we stopped to refuel at a gas station on the South Side. While T.K. was pumping the gas, this brand-new white Camaro pulled up on the other side of the pump. This long-legged gal wearing a white nylon jumpsuit gets out, and she walks over to T.K. all swishy-like, and she says to him, 'I'm part of the underground economy, so I believe in barter transactions. How'd you like to trade some sex for some firewood?' Without missing a beat, T.K says back to her, 'How much firewood do you have to trade?'" They roared with laughter.

Even Rose, who had known T.K only briefly, had a story to tell. "I remember when T.K. was teaching me how to shoot. We were working on targets set up at two hundred yards, and I wasn't doing too well. He said to me, 'Relax! You're jerking the trigger. Remember, breathe in, then let half of it out. Then hold your breath, center your sight picture, and squeeeeze the trigger— like a nipple.' As soon as he said that, he got all embarrassed and his face turned red. 'Oh gosh! I'm sorry, I didn't mean to say that. Please, please forgive me.' All these years he had been teaching guys how to shoot, no doubt using the same spiel that he had heard when he first learned."

It was Todd and Jeff that placed T.K.'s body in the bottom of the grave. In his right hand, which was, by then, stiff with rigor mortis, Todd slid a round of .30-06 match ammunition. Before they got up out of the grave, they re-covered his body with the olive drab poncho, tucking under the edges.

An hour later everyone gathered at the grave again for a funeral service. In the interval, many of them gathered wildflowers and flowers from Mary's herb garden to place around the grave. Standing by the grave's edge, Todd said, "Our heavenly father. It's kind of ironic that it's T.K that we are burying today. I had always expected that if we lost any group members, it would be Tom who would have the proper words to say. Well, he's not standing here to do the honors, so I'll just have to do the best I can.

"Suffice it to say that we'll all miss Tom Kennedy very much. He was always the quiet, humble, and professional type. He never gave anyone any static, and he always pulled his share of the weight. I have never known a better man.

"We owe a lot to Tom. It was he who insisted that we go retrieve Ken and Terry from Utah, so I suppose that without him, we wouldn't have them back here with us. It was T.K. who taught so many of us rifle marksmanship lessons that have already saved some lives here, and probably will save a lot more lives in the future.

"In fact, it was T.K. that suggested that we form the Group in the first place. When I look back on that first night we discussed forming a retreat group, so many years ago, and think of what has transpired since then, all I can do is thank Tom yet some more. He handpicked most of the members of the group. He selected a congregation of outstanding and highly motivated and morally right individuals with a good balance of skills. So I guess we also owe T.K. our thanks for bringing us all together.

"I realize now that I'm going to miss T.K. a lot. It seems that you never really appreciate just how much someone means to you until they're gone. T.K. and I shared some great times together in college, and since then. Needless to say, he was the kind of friend that you could depend on in the best of times and the worst of times.

"T.K. was a true warrior, and very good at his craft. I'm sure his spirit will end up in some special corner of heaven where the good warriors go. Let us pray. Our heavenly father: We commend the soul of our Christian brother, Thomas Evan, to you. In the name of Our Lord and Savior, Christ, Jesus, Amen."

Todd led the recitation of a direct translation of the Lord's Prayer, which T.K. had preferred in recent years. Following handwritten notes, they recited each line in Aramaic, then in English:

aboon dabashmaya
Our father who is in heaven,

nethkadash shamak
Holy is his name,

tetha malkoothak
your Kingdom is coming,

newe tzevyanak
your will is being done

aykan dabashmaya af bara

on earth as it is in heaven,

hav lan lakma dsoonkanan yamanawashbook lan
give us our bread day by day

kavine aykana daf hanan shabookan lhayavine oolow talahn lanesyana
as we forgive those who trespass and sin against us

ela fatsan men beesha
deliver us from evil

Amen.

With his voice quavering, Todd enunciated, "Farewell, my friend." He picked up a handful of the dark Palouse soil, and let it trickle through his fingers into the grave. When he turned to walk away, everyone could see the tears trickling down his face.

After most of those who had gathered walked down the hill, Ken and Jeff remained to refill the grave. Just as they were finishing, Lon Porter walked up the hill, carrying a large cross that he had welded together from three-inch wide channel stock. With a raised bead of welding rod, he had made an inscription on its horizontal piece. It read:

Thomas Evan Kennedy
In God's Hands

The day after T.K.'s burial, Ken went down to the basement to take inventory of the supplies and equipment that they had pre-positioned. Because the keys to their wall lockers were long since lost, Todd opened the lockers with his "universal key"—his pair of red-handled bolt cutters.

Almost everything was just as they had left it. The only things that had been disturbed were some of the Laytons' bulk food containers. A few of the five-gallon plastic buckets containing wheat, rice, rolled oats, and powdered milk had been used. These items had been stored outside the locker. The Laytons did not object, as this represented less than 10 percent of their stored food. Ken told Todd that he had expected to find that their gear had already been divided up between the group members. Todd replied, "Are you kidding? We always knew that resourceful individuals like you both would make it here. It was just a matter of time."

Layton was overwhelmed by the sight of their stored gear and food. He was so excited that he asked Terry to come downstairs and see it all. She hobbled down on her homemade crutches. They spent ten minutes examining the contents of their two lockers, punctuated by "Ooohs" and "Ahhs." Nearly all of the Laytons' gear was still in excellent condition. One exception was a partially full bucket of wheat, which was full of weevils. It was set aside for the chickens. All of the rest of their buckets of wheat were fine, since Terry had used the dry-ice packing method years before. In this method, a five-gallon pail was poured nearly full of grain, and then a large chunk of dry ice was dropped in. Then she would wait while the dry ice sublimated, displacing the air in the container with heavier carbon dioxide. Once the dry ice was nearly gone—less than the size of a quarter—she would seal the lid. The other exception was their box of Cyalume chemical light sticks, which were past their expiration dates. After unsuccessfully testing five of the light sticks, Ken discarded the entire box.

Terry also had doubts about most of their supply of vitamins and medicines, which like the light sticks, were well past their expiration dates. She set them aside and commented, "Mary told me that most expiration dates are very conservative. Some pharmaceuticals do lose strength, but can still be used if dosages are increased. I'll ask Mary about titrating them. I remember her telling us about that at one of the group meetings way back when."

After having spent nearly three years living out of their backpacks, their cache of supplies seemed like a treasure trove. By relative standards, their wall lockers appeared to have everything that they could ever need or want. Pointing to the heap on the floor, Terry proclaimed, "Look at all this: *dozens* of pairs of clean socks, two pair of new combat boots apiece, six sets of DPMs, and all this ammo. We've got over nine *thousand* rounds; sheets and blankets; real toilet paper; eight cases of MREs; your spare riotgun and my little Remington 600 .308 bolt-action. Our reloading press and components. What are we going to *do* with all this stuff?"

Ken hugged Terry and affirmed, "Honey, we're going to start living the way that we should have lived for the past thirty-three months. I feel like we've come home."

Terry gazed into Ken's eyes and said, "We have come home, darling. We're home now, safe and sound."

The next day, Todd called for a meeting where new sleeping arrangements were discussed. It was decided that in deference to Terry's injured knee, Ken and Terry would get the Grays' bedroom temporarily. The basement would be reorganized, and yet another partition would be added to provide a sleeping area for Todd and Mary. To provide more privacy, the new partition was made out of wall lockers and half-inch plywood. At the same time, similar partitions were built replacing the blanket partitions that had been used by the Trasels and the Porters. Like the Porters, the Grays would sleep on folding cots. A few months later, after Terry was confident walking without crutches, Todd and

Mary got their old upstairs bedroom back, and the Laytons took their place in the basement.

Soon after the meeting, Lon reminded Mary about a sore tooth he had reported two days before. Lon said that the pain was getting worse. With the assistance of Margie, and referring to her copy of *Where There Is No Dentist*, Mary extracted the tooth. Mary had a good supply of Lidocaine, and had had the foresight to buy a set of dental tools before the Crunch, so the extraction was not painful. Mary was surprised, however, how much force it took to remove the molar. Thankfully, it came out in one piece, using her tooth-extracting pliers. The procedure turned out to be a valuable experience for Mary Gray. It was the first of nine teeth that she would pull in the next few years.

Three weeks after T.K. was buried, Todd and Lisa got together to decide how to dispose of T.K.'s gear. Because he hadn't written a will, they did not know how Tom would have wanted his possessions distributed. They came to the conclusion that most of it should go to the Carltons and the Porters, as they had arrived at the retreat with little more than the clothes on their backs. T.K.'s AR-15 and Anshutz bolt-action .22 target rifle went to Della. His M1 Garand rifle, stainless steel Colt Gold Cup .45 automatic, and Remington 870 were given to Lon Porter. His Colt Commander and Ruger 10/22 went to Rose. Because they were both almost the same size as Kennedy, Della and Rose split T.K.'s six remaining sets of DPM fatigues and two DPM smocks. Most of T.K.'s field gear was divided between the Porters and Doug Carlton. His New Lile fighting knife was given to Lon. His Bronco was given to the Laytons.

All of T.K.'s books went into the Grays' library shelves, which were long hence communally browsed. Kennedy's food and ammunition supplies were divided equally between the Porters and Carltons. Dan Fong asked if he could have T.K.'s TrinitY Fisherman utility knife, as something to remember him by. Todd filled his request immediately.

Kevin Lendel, who had practiced from time to time with T.K.'s Benedict crossbow, asked if he could have it. He too got his wish. This left only a few odds and ends, which Todd and Lisa divided almost at random amongst the militia members. The only things that Todd set aside were T.K.'s journal, photo album, Bible, and Catholic Missal. He hoped to return them to Kennedy's brothers someday, assuming that they were still alive.

CHAPTER 21
Federales

"Diplomacy is the art of saying, 'Nice Doggie,' while you're looking for a rock."

—*Will Rogers*

A farmer five miles west of the retreat radioed to say that she had spotted a twin-engine airplane at low altitude heading toward Moscow. Early the next morning, Roger Dunlap called in to say that they had heard from Moscow that the same plane had brought a representative of the provisional Federal government, and that a speech was planned for late in the afternoon at the Pullman-Moscow airport.

Most of the militia members at Todd's retreat wanted to go. They piled into the open back of Todd's Power Wagon, leaving behind the Porters and Nelsons to provide security in their absence.

On the drive into Moscow, they passed dozens of people on foot or on horseback heading toward town. As they wheeled up to the side of the Pullman-Moscow Air Terminal, they could see a gray painted U.S. Army Beechcraft C-12 parked on the taxiway. Doug pointed out the fact that the white painted tip tanks on the plane did not match the rest of the airplane. He commented out the corner of his mouth, "Those tanks probably came from a Beechcraft Super King Air. It's the commercial counterpart of the Army C-12." By the time that the address began, more than four hundred people had gathered in front of the airport terminal. The fall air was crisp.

The speech was given by the "Undersecretary of Information," Mr. Clarke, an overweight man with a florid face. He wore a polyester suit, and carried a chrome-plated Savage .32 automatic pistol in a hip holster. In comparison to his great bulk, the small pistol appeared almost laughable. Standing next to him was an Army warrant officer wearing a digital camouflage Nomex flight suit, and a green nylon mesh survival vest with bulging zippered pockets. He carried a standard Army-issue Beretta M9 pistol in a shoulder holster. Both men wore sky blue armbands with a white United Nations "wreathed Earth" logo. The two stood on the steps of the terminal, with the crowd forming a half-circle around them. Clarke opened a notebook and began reading a prepared speech printed on poor quality photocopy paper. He began, "This address was written by President pro-tem Hutchings of the Provisional Federal government. Here is his message:

'My fellow Americans. The United States is slowly recovering from the greatest tragedy in its history. I have recently been provided a detailed report on the extent of the catastrophe from the administration's chief scientist. Some of the report's findings are as follows: In the past three years, an estimated one hundred and sixty million of our citizens have died. Most died from starvation, exposure, and disease. Of the deaths by disease, more than sixty-five million were caused by the influenza pandemic that swept the eastern seaboard. Without antibiotics available, the disease simply ran rampant until there were no more hosts left to attack in the heavily populated regions.

'At least twenty-eight million are estimated to have been killed in lawless violence. In addition, more than five million have died of complications of pre-existing medical problems such as diabetes, heart disease, hemophilia, AIDS, and kidney disease. Hundreds of thousands more have died of complications of tonsillitis, appendicitis, and other ailments that were heretofore not life-threatening. The distribution of population losses ranged from in excess of 96 percent of the population in some northeastern metropolitan areas to less than 5 percent in a few areas in the High Plains, Rocky Mountains, the intermountain areas of the West, and the Inland Northwest. Order has been restored in only a few states, but we are making rapid progress.

'As you are no doubt aware, the economy is still in complete disarray. The formerly existing transportation and communications systems have been completely disrupted. In the coming months, our biggest priority will be on revitalizing the petroleum and refining industries of Oklahoma, Texas, and Louisiana. Next, we will strive to get electric power back on line in as many areas as possible. With bulk fuel, natural gas, and electrical power available, it is hoped that agriculture and the many industries critical to our nation's economic health will be reestablished.

'Here at Fort Knox, we have taken the lead in rebuilding a new United States. Already, with the help of security forces from other United Nations countries, we have pacified the states of Kentucky, Tennessee, Mississippi, and Alabama. But there is much more to be done. America must be put back on its feet again economically. Never again can we allow the economy to get so out of control. Strict economic policies will ensure that there will never be a repeat of the Crash. Wages and prices will, by necessity, be controlled by the central government. Many industries will have to be government-owned or government-controlled, at least in the foreseeable future. Reasonable limits on the press will stop the spread of unfounded rumors. Until order is completely restored, the Federal and state constitutions have been temporarily suspended, and nationwide martial law is in effect. The single legitimate seat of power is here at Fort Knox. It is only with central planning that things can be put back in order rapidly and efficiently.

'Kentucky, Tennessee, Mississippi, and Alabama are already under the control of nine United Nations sub-regional administrators. I will soon be dispatching UN regional and sub-regional administrators to the other areas that have independently reestablished order. These include Maine, New Hampshire, and Vermont, the southern portion of Georgia, most of Texas, part of Louisiana, most of Colorado, southwestern Oregon, all of Idaho, all of Utah, eastern Washington, all of Wyoming, and most of North and South Dakota.

'The UN Regional Administrators will oversee the many tasks required to accomplish a complete national recovery. For example, they will be setting up regional police forces, which will be under their direct control. They will oversee the issuance of the National ID Card. They will appoint judges that they deem properly qualified. Each Regional Administrator will bring with him on his staff a regional tax collector and a regional treasurer who will handle issuance of the new national currency. Rest assured that the new currency is fully backed by the gold reserves of the national depository.

'I hope that you, my fellow citizens, will do everything in your ability to assist your new Regional Administrators, the sub-regional Administrators, their staffs, and those that they appoint under them. Only with your cooperation will America be able to quickly restore itself to its former greatness. Given this day under my hand, Maynard L. Hutchings.' This document carries the official seal of the Provisional Federal government."

After looking up with a wide-faced grin, Clarke intoned, "I have some photocopies of the speech for those of you that would like them. I'll be happy to speak with any of you individually if you have any questions about how we will be handling things."

A gray-haired man wearing a Pendleton shirt and with a MAK-90 rifle slung across his back raised his hand and shouted, "Sir, I'd like to ask my questions now, and hear you answer them publicly." After pausing to look at some of the anxious faces around him, the man continued, "If I understand what you are saying, that this gentleman Maynard Hutchings is now the president of the United States."

"Actually his correct title is President *pro-tem*."

"I know what *pro tempore* means, Mr. Clarke. Can you tell me who elected this man Hutchings?"

"He was elected by a unanimous vote of the council of the provisional government."

"And who elected this council?"

Clarke's eyes dodged from left to right. Putting on an officious tone, he stated, "They were not actually elected. They were self-appointed during the darkest days of the crisis. They were men of great vision who saw the need to restore order, and took the great personal risk of doing something about it."

The gray-haired man with the assault rifle spoke up again. "Well … exactly who is on this council?"

"Fine upstanding men like yourself, sir. They come from all walks of life. There are two bankers, three lawyers, an IRS official, two businessmen, and an Army general."

"You mean to say that a bunch of cronies got together and decided that they were going to become the new federal government?"

"Now, as I said, President Hutchings was legally elected by a unanimous vote."

The gray-haired man pointed a finger at Clarke and again shouted, "Yes, he was *legally* elected all right, under the bylaws of this 'council,' which you have admitted was *self-appointed*. The term *legally* is not synonymous with *lawfully*." Clarke looked nervously from side to side.

After letting his words sink in, the gray-haired man asked, "What did this Hutchings fellow do before the Crunch? Was he with the federal government or the governor or deputy governor of Kentucky, or something of that nature?"

"President Hutchings was formerly the president of the Hardin County Board of Supervisors."

"You've got to be joking! Before the Crunch hit, I was the president of the University of Idaho, just ten miles from here, in Moscow. What's to say that I can't get together with some of my friends and declare myself the president of the United States?"

After a pause, Clarke replied indignantly, "Two things. One, you don't have more than fifteen thousand trained and equipped U.S. and UN troops under your control. Two, you do not control the sixty billion dollars in gold in the National Depository."

The former university president stroked his chin and asked, "When will elections be held?"

Clarke answered matter-of-factly, "None will be considered until well after the entire country is pacified and the economy has been revitalized. That may be several years. Now, if there are no further questions…."

He was again interrupted, this time by a man dressed in coveralls and wearing a baseball cap emblazoned "CAT Diesel Power" and carrying a holstered single-action revolver. He raised his hand and shouted, "You said something about a new currency. What's that all about?"

Clarke smiled again and replied, "Sir, I'm glad that you asked me that. The old federal currency has been declared obsolete, null and void, at least the paper money. The old coins are still considered legal tender, however. Distribution and acceptance of the new currency has already started in the Quad State area. In fact, I have an example of it here." Clarke then held up a small lime-green bill.

The man in coveralls asked, "Can I see that, mister?"

"Certainly," Clarke answered, and passed it into the crowd. It was passed hand-to-hand back to the questioner. After examining both sides of the five-dollar bill, he asked, "Is this new currency backed by the gold at Fort Knox?"

Clarke replied instantly, "Yes, indeed sir. Backed one hundred percent. We guarantee it."

"If it's backed in gold, then why doesn't it say 'Gold Certificate' or 'Pay the Bearer in Gold,' or something like that?"

Clarke looked at his pilot nervously. "Well ... uhh, due to the problems of transport under the ongoing crisis, the new currency will not be redeemable in gold, but it will still be lawful tender."

The man in coveralls shook his head vigorously. "That sounds like a bunch of horse hooey to me. In the Bible that's called 'diverse weights and measures.' That's an abomination. Either the currency is gold backed, or it isn't. If it's not redeemable in the gold or silver, then this might just as well be Monopoly money, far as I'm concerned." Murmurs began to sweep through the crowd.

Waving his arm, Clarke implored, "Sir, as I'm sure you recall, the old Federal Reserve currency wasn't redeemable in gold or silver, either. That didn't stop people from trusting the currency, now did it?"

The man again shook his head from side to side and retorted, "Well it darn sure should have! That was an abomination, too. I don't think this depression would have ever happened if we had *real* money. As far as I could tell, the thing that started the whole ball of string unraveling was when Uncle Sam fired up the printing presses round the clock." Throughout the crowd, there were shouts of agreement.

After a pause, the man in the coveralls crumpled the bill into a wad, and tossed it to the ground.

Clarke stammered, "You're oversimplifying a very complex chain of events. As the president pointed out in his statement, there will be vigorous controls on the economy to prevent another economic catastrophe. It's for the public good."

A heavyset middle-aged woman asked, "What was that bit your Mister Hutchings wrote about a National ID Card?"

Clarke replied nonchalantly, "Oh that's just one of the new Federal security measures. As you've probably heard, there were hundreds of thousands of Mexicans that crossed the border illegally following the economic collapse. The authorities have to be able to distinguish between residents and illegal aliens. Under the latest Federal proclamation, the new National ID card must be carried by everyone ten years old, or older, at all times. The latest version has a magnetic strip on the back that will make shopping very convenient. It works like a bank debit card. In the long term, the card will have to be presented to conduct any sales transaction. For now, at least, it will be required when crossing any of the new regional or sub-regional security checkpoints."

The murmuring in the crowd increased. Roger Dunlap raised his hand and in a firm voice asked, "What about our guns, what does your new government have to say about that issue?"

Clarke put on his saccharine smile again, and replied, "The Constitution guarantees the right of the people to keep and bear arms. President Hutchings is a strong believer in the Second Amendment. He has stated publicly that he believes that every resident can continue to enjoy the privilege of owning firearms for sporting purposes, even under this period of martial law. However, due to the exigencies of the current lawless situation, the president has seen fit to institute a system of national firearms registration. This is, of course, aimed at curbing the tide of lawlessness. The only way to stop the bands of vicious brigands roaming the countryside is to disarm them. As you know, there were many government weapons that disappeared in the early stages of the crisis. Dozens and dozens of National Guard armories were looted. All of those weapons must be rounded up. In addition, certain categories of weapons have been declared a threat to the public safety, under the executive order, in compliance with the United Nations Arms Control Harmonization Accord. That treaty was signed by the president last year."

Dunlap asked, "And what exactly are those categories?"

"Sir, I'll be happy to answer your more detailed questions later with you privately."

Dunlap raised his voice sharply. "No, Mr. Clarke! I want to know what categories of weapons have been outlawed, and I want to hear your answer right here and now. This is a matter that concerns all of us, and we deserve an honest answer, post haste!"

Again opening his notebook and leafing through poorly photocopied pages, Clarke cleared his throat and read, "'The categories of weapons banned by the United Nations Accord include:

All fully automatic weapons, regardless of prior registration under the National Firearms Act of 1934,
any rifle over thirty caliber,
any shotgun or weapon of any description over twelve gauge in diameter,
all semiautomatic rifles and shotguns,
all rifles and shotguns capable of accepting a detachable magazine,
any detachable magazine regardless of capacity,
any weapon with a fixed magazine that has a capacity of more than four cartridges,
all grenades and grenade launchers,

all explosives, detonating cord, and blasting caps,

all explosives precursor chemicals,

all firearms regardless of type that are chambered for military cartridges such as 7.62
  mm NATO, 5.56 mm NATO, .45 ACP, and nine-mm parabellum,

all silencers,

all night vision equipment including infrared, light amplification, or thermal,

all telescopic sights,

all laser aiming devices,

all handguns regardless of type or caliber' ... And..."

Clarke turned a page and went on. "The Accord further proscribes private possession of armored vehicles, bayonets, gas masks, helmets and bulletproof vests, encryption software or devices, and all radio transmitters—other than baby monitors, cordless phones, or cell phones.

"In addition: full metal jacket, tracer, incendiary, and armor piercing ammunition, all ammunition in military calibers, chemical agents of any sort including CS and CN tear gas, OC 'pepper spray,' and all military-type pyrotechnics and flare launchers."

"Now there will, of course, be exceptions for registering equipment used by properly trained law enforcement agencies that are under Federal or UN control."

Looking back up from his notebook, he recited with finality, "'Any firearm not meeting the new criteria and all other contraband listed herein must be turned in within the ten-day amnesty period after the UN Regional Administrator or sub-administrator, or their delegates arrive on site. Alternatively, if Federal or UN troops arrive within any state to pacify it, a thirty-day amnesty period will begin the day the first forces cross the state boundary. All other post-1898 production firearms of any description, air rifles, archery equipment, and edged weapons over six inches long must be registered during the same period. Anyone found with an unregistered weapon, or any weapon, accessory, or ammunition that has been declared contraband after the amnesty period ends will be summarily executed.' This may sound severe, but keep in mind that the new law was enacted to ensure public safety."

In the middle of the crowd, Dan Fong yelled, "Public safety my ass! Your so-called 'contraband' has saved my life several times in the past three years. Furthermore, do you think that looters are going to abide by your gun registration scheme? Only responsible and peaceable citizens would abide by it, and they are precisely the people who *don't* require any control, because they police themselves. You're nothing but a damnable fascist *tyrant*, that's what you are!" Holding his rifle above his head, he shouted, "You'll get my gun when you pry it out of my cold dead hands!" With that, the crowd burst into continuous loud applause and cheering.

In the midst of the tumult, Todd Gray worked his way through the crowd, and bounded up to the top step to stand in front of Clarke. When the cheering finally started to die down, Todd announced, "Ladies and gentlemen, my name is Todd Gray. Most of you have met me. I started the Northwest Militia. Most of you here have no doubt heard of us, and the Troy Templar organization. We are two local groups, composed of sovereign Idaho Citizens, that have been working together to restore a local Constitutionally-based government."

Todd turned 90 degrees so that he could see Clarke's face, and continued. "From what you have told us today, Mister Clarke, I don't think that there is much that your provisional government has to offer us that we cannot provide for ourselves. Restoring industry, utilities, transportation, and communications are indeed worthy goals. However, if doing so means surrendering our personal freedom, then our answer is an emphatic *no*. In fact, I find your concepts of 'necessity,' 'public safety,' and 'the public good' are completely out of line. And I believe that I speak for the vast majority of the Idaho and Washington Citizens assembled here."

Throughout the crowd there were cries of "Hear hear!" and "You tell 'em, Todd."

Todd looked directly at Clarke and commanded, "Without further ado, I'd like to invite you gentlemen to immediately get in your airplane and go find yourselves somebody more naive to swallow your globalist horse manure." As Todd spoke, Clarke stood stammering, and his already pink face turned noticeably red.

Before Clarke could reply, Gray went on. "Don't bother sending out your so-called 'Regional Administrator.' Whoever it is will either be sent packing or end up the recipient of a tall tree and a short rope." There were more cheers and applause.

Clarke looked at Gray and boomed, "I'm warning you! We represent the legitimate government of the United States and United Nations. You cannot defy us. To do so would be treasonous and seditious, and would be dealt with accordingly."

Gray lowered his right hand to rest on the butt of his .45. He cocked his head slightly to the side and shouted, "You do not represent *anything* legitimate, Mister Clarke. You represent a totalitarian globalist oligarchy instituted without the benefit of any semblance of democratic process, or incorporating a republican form of government." More shouts of agreement came from throughout the audience. Todd again looked Clarke directly in the eye and said, "You have ten seconds to get on that aircraft, and head back to Maynard-land."

Clarke stood his ground for a moment. Then, seeing his pilot make a dash for the plane, he followed close behind. Behind him, the crowd was taunting and jeering. From the door of the plane with the sound of the turbine engines winding up in the background, Clarke shook his fist and shouted in Todd's direction, "We'll be back!"

The crowd moved backward as the plane's propellers began to spin. Within seconds, the C-12 began its roll. Obviously in a hurry, the pilot did not bother taxiing the distance to the runway. He took off directly from the narrow taxi strip and turned to head southeast.

Still standing on the porch of the terminal with his hands on his hips, Todd watched the plane's progress until it was a dot on the horizon, and then disappeared. His hand still resting on the butt of his pistol, he muttered to himself, "Come back if you dare. And when you do, you'd better bring a lot of ammo, plenty of extra grub, and a good supply of body bags, because you're going to be in for a deuce of a gunfight."

• • •

In the months that followed the "visit" by the Provisional Federal government, a number of militias began to form spontaneously throughout the Palouse Hills region. The motivation was news of the Federals' ruthless and often bloody consolidation of power. Numerous stories of Federal atrocities were passed across shortwave and CB radio relay networks. If even half of them were true, it was clear that the Federals and their UN "partners for peace" were unmitigated tyrants.

Most of the new militias in the inland Northwest region were small, from two-man cells to squad size. A few were near company strength. Their organization, structure, logistics, training, and even their terminology varied greatly. Some had geographical names like the Moscow Maquis, the Weippe Wolverines, the Helmer Heilanders, and the Bovill Blue Blaze Irregulars. Others were named in memoriam, such as the Gordon Kahl Company, the 9/11 Company, and the Samuel Weaver Company. Many of the new militias were all male, some were mixed, and one—that started with a squad of former University of Idaho Sigma Epsilon sorority sisters—was all female.

As the best-known tactical organization in the area, the Northwest Militia was approached for advice by many of the leaders of these fledgling militias. They sought technical expertise and training on a variety of topics, and Todd and his militia did their utmost to comply. A few large-scale training exercises were held. Some of the group's excess logistics—mainly shelter half-tents and extra sets of web gear—were distributed on "long-term loan" to militias that had none.

The decision to again "give until it hurts" was based on the likely prospect of fighting a war of resistance in the near future. Unlike the resistance organizations that were formed in Europe during the Second World War, there would be no outside sources of finance or supply. Everything for the militias had to be provided from local resources. Todd reasoned that since he and his friends had been so richly blessed, it was their responsibility to help out as many others as possible in anticipation of an armed struggle that looked inevitable.

A few of the new militias asked to be directly incorporated into the Northwest Militia. In every instance, they were turned down. Todd was of the firm opinion that large militias would only make themselves lucrative targets. He advised all of the militia leaders to keep their organizations small—preferably three to twelve members. If they recruited any new members that brought them up over the twelve-man threshold, they should divide into separate and independent units.

There was a conscious decision to form what Kevin Lendel called "an organization without an organization." Most referred to this methodology as the "phantom cell" or "leaderless resistance" approach. All of the militias in the region, they decided, should share common goals, but should have wholly independent leadership.

Without central leadership, it would be impossible to decapitate the militia. Also, through strict "need to know" security measures, it would make it almost impossible to infiltrate more than one of the local militias. Everyone was warned not to give their names when conducting joint field exercises. They constantly stressed that given the disconnected cellular organization, if any member of any of the militias was eventually captured and tortured, that individual could at most expose the names of just a handful of members in their cell.

The other proviso that was constantly stressed was that virtually nothing was to be written down, aside from perhaps a few unit SOPs. There would be no written rosters, no description of assigned areas of operation, and no lists of frequencies or call signs. Further, no maps were to be marked with any notations whatsoever. They were even warned not to leave maps folded in such a way that they emphasized a particular operational area. Everything of potential intelligence value was to be committed to memory.

Coordination between the militias was actively discouraged, again for security reasons. Each militia picked out an area of operations, which they communicated by word of mouth to their neighboring militias. A few rallying points were agreed upon for eventual tactical coordination, but beyond that, everything was kept cellular. Aside from the assigned rally points, the local resistance cells were advised to operate wholly independently, using the leaderless resistance concept. They would use generalized principles and planning, but decentralized tactics and action.

One of the few militias that the Northwest Militia regularly trained with was the Moscow Maquis. The Maquis were led by a fifty-year-old man with piercing blue eyes named Lawrence Raselhoff. Raselhoff was both a dog breeder and gun dealer before the Crunch. Much of his gun inventory was handed out to unit members in the first few months after the Maquis was formed. Even though he was confined to a wheelchair, Raselhoff was an energetic leader. He often went to the field with his unit in a dogcart, on a dog sled, or on his white snowmobile. Both Todd and Mike had long conversations with Raselhoff, making contingency plans.

Many of the Northwest Militia meetings in the late fall of the third year concerned the possible invasion of the region by the Federals or their UN counterparts. It was decided that guerrilla warfare would be the most appropriate response. The threat of armored vehicles seemed the most obvious. Both Jeff and Doug had seen tanks and armored personnel carriers in action, and they could appreciate how well they could stop most conventional attacks. It was Doug Carlton who crystallized the approach that they would take in countering the armor threat when he said, "What we will really need are some anti-tank missiles—LAWs, Vipers, Dragons, or TOWs. Unfortunately, we have none available, and they are very difficult to improvise."

Lon asked, "What can we improvise? How about Molotov cocktails? Those are easy enough to make."

Carlton responded, "Molotov cocktails will work, but it takes a lot of them to stop a tank or APC. You also need to thicken the gas to make it stick. Otherwise it just pours off of any vehicle that the bottle breaks on. You can thicken it with laundry detergent. Styrofoam also works great. You want to get it thickened to the point where it has the consistency of heavy maple syrup."

He went on, "If you can get close enough to use them, what works even better than Molotov cocktails is a TH3 grenade—commonly called thermite in the civilian world. According to one of Todd's Kurt Saxon books that I read, thermite is really easy to make. It's a mixture of iron oxide—just rust—and powdered aluminum. It's a very powerful oxidizer that burns at something outrageous like five thousand degrees Fahrenheit. It's what chemists call an exothermic reaction. It will melt through two inches of steel tank iron like butter. I saw a TH3 grenade used at a firepower demonstration at Fort Knox. They laid a thick old car door sideways across a couple of sawhorses and set the TH3 grenade on top. They warned us several times not to look directly at the flames to avoid damaging our retinas, and then an NCO pulled the pin. The thing went completely through the door and dropped to the ground within a few seconds."

Rose exclaimed, "Wow, that would really do a number on a tank."

Doug warned, "Now keep in mind that employing either Molotovs or thermite grenades against armored vehicles or both would be very, very dangerous, particularly Bradley M2s or M3s. You've got to be right up close for Molotovs, and even closer for the thermite grenades."

A day later, Mike and Lisa Nelson started mass production of Molotov cocktails. Just the week before, they had been making goat's milk soap for the retreat, using lye that they had derived from ashes. But this week they were firebomb makers. For the Molotov project, they selected the most-untrustworthy gas stored at the retreat—that which was stored in small cans and the vehicles' fuel tanks. The gasoline was thickened with laundry detergent powder in an open fifty-five-gallon drum that was placed seventy yards away from the house. The noxious mixture was stirred with the handle of a broken rake. It was ladled into quart canning jars and sealed tight with Mason lids and rings.

An eighteen-inch long strip of rag was made for each jar for ignition. Lisa epoxied a one-inch square of "hook side" Velcro fastener to each lid. A corresponding one-inch square of "pile side" Velcro was sewn to the center of each of the rag strips. They soaked all these strips in diesel fuel and sealed them in individual Ziploc bags which were duct taped to the sides of each jar. To use a Molotov, the rag would be removed from the plastic bag, and attached to the jar with the Velcro. Then the rag would be lit with a match and then the jar could be thrown.

By separating the main fuel component from the ignition component, Lisa Nelson explained, it made the devices "about a thousand percent safer" to use or carry than the traditional rags-stuffed-into-wine-bottles method. When they did a demonstration of one of the prototypes, Lisa mentioned that they would have preferred to have developed some sort of friction igniter, but there weren't enough supplies of chemicals available. Instead, they opted for the method of packaging the diesel-soaked rags with each cocktail. Most of the cocktails were packed into the original cardboard cases that the canning jars came in, for ease and safety of transport. In all, they assembled two hundred and twenty of the firebombs. For safety's sake, the cases were stored in a dry corner of the barn.

Mike, Della, and Doug were named the ad hoc committee for thermite grenade construction. After a few days of inquiries, they discovered that there was a quantity of Creslite coarse brille aluminum powder in the hands of an owner of what had been a bronzing shop in Moscow. Before the Crunch, he had run a mail-order business bronzing items like baby's booties and judge's gavels. He was happy to part with his remaining sixty pounds of bronzing powder in exchange for one hundred rounds of .223 ball, and twenty rounds of .30-06 AP.

The iron oxide came from the owner of the paint store in Moscow. He still had two fifty-pound sacks of natural black iron oxide pigment in stock. Before the Crunch, he had mainly sold it to contractors who used it for tinting concrete. After some confusion, when he first tried to sell them some synthetic iron oxide powder, he came back from his large storeroom with two sacks of the chemically correct, "natural" item made by Pfizer, loaded on a dolly. He agreed to trade the two sacks for one hundred rounds of Federal .308 match grade ammunition. He was happy to get the ammo. They also found a fifty-foot reel of magnesium ribbon. It was in the hands of a former University of Idaho chemistry professor. He had taken home most of the chem lab's inventory for safekeeping. When he found out why they needed the ribbon, he refused any offer of payment. He declared, "Hey, it's for a good cause." The professor snipped off four feet of the ribbon from the reel to keep for himself, and handed Doug the rest.

The casings for the grenades were simply empty aluminum soda cans. The main igniting compound was road flare igniter, in conjunction with magnesium ribbon. A quiet call went out to the community, and road flares of all descriptions started arriving at the retreat in the next few days. A few had gotten wet at one time and were swollen. These were discarded. Mike was also disappointed to find that in response to the request for "flare igniter" a few neighbors were confused and sent the plastic caps and friction pads from road flares. What they needed instead was the black tar-like substance that protruded from the end of a flare. That was the actual igniter. It took some clarification before more of the correct material started to arrive. The flare igniter was moistened with alcohol to a putty-like consistency and molded around both the fuse and a two-inch long strip of magnesium ribbon. The tail end of the ribbon extended into the thermite mixture.

Mike, Della, and Doug used a hand crank concrete mixer from the Andersen's farm to combine the aluminum powder and iron oxide powder. They used a ratio of three parts aluminum powder to eight parts iron oxide powder. A blob of flare igniter, bisected by lengths of one-eighth-inch cannon fuse and the magnesium ribbon, was taped into the opening of each can on top of the thermite mixture.

The first of the finished products were declared "crude but effective." Only two of them were used for tests. When the first was lit, it worked as planned. The fuse ignited the flare igniter, which ignited the magnesium ribbon, which in turn ignited the thermite mixture. The large molten blob from the grenade burned through a piece of three-quarter-inch plate steel, then dropped a few inches and hit a half-inch plate. It went through that one too, and dropped again to hit another half-inch thick piece. It went nearly all the way through it too, before it finally burned out. Della Carlton was impressed. She shouted, "Wow! It reminds me of that scene in the movie *Alien*, where the acidic blood from the face hugger kept going through deck after deck of the ship!"

The second test was on a scrap piece of one-and-one-half-inch plate steel. It was set up at a slight angle. Despite the angle, the glob of furiously burning thermite went through with ease. All of the rest of the thermite grenades were saved for "operational tests." They had only nineteen pull-ring fuse igniters so most would have to be lit with a match or lighter.

Rose and Doug worked for part of several days, filling the soda cans with a small-mouthed kitchen funnel until they ran out of the thermite mixture. The cans were sealed shut with duct tape over the igniter plug. Then, while laying in neat rows on newspapers in the shop, the grenades were spray painted flat olive drab. There were seventy-seven of them.

CHAPTER 22
Infrastructure

"Put your trust in God, my boys, and keep your powder dry."

—Valentine Blacker, Oliver's Advice

Order was gradually restored throughout the inland Northwest region by the fifth year after the Crunch began. Lewiston, Moscow, and Grangeville established sheriff's offices. Each were staffed by men who were either police officers or sheriff's deputies before the Crunch. With the success of the trading post in Moscow, other trading centers were soon established at Troy, Potlatch, Juliaetta, Orofino, Kamiah, Kooskia, Grangeville, and Lewiston. In Moscow, additional businesses began to open up in proximity to the original trading post. These included a boot and saddle maker, a barbershop, a bakery called the "YREKABAKERY" (which read the same way from either end), and a competing trading post, called the Moscow Emporium. Moscow was the first town in the area to restore its civic water system. By the end of the year it even boasted a trash and manure hauling company.

The first county offices to reopen in Latah, Nez Perce, and Clearwater counties were tax assessor's offices. Staffed by volunteers, they straightened out the tangle of deeds for the numerous land transactions since the Crunch. Ironically, since there was no official currency, there was no taxation. The newly reestablished Latah County Board of Supervisors declared an indefinite tax moratorium, and a retroactive and universal amnesty on unpaid property taxes.

A three-man arbitrating panel was set up, deciding the disposition of abandoned lands—some of it now occupied by squatters—and land that was not held free and clear when the Crunch hit. In most cases, mortgage holders—if they could be located—settled for final payment in silver coin at the ratio of one dollar in silver coin for each thousand dollars in Federal Reserve Notes outstanding on their mortgages. In a few cases where less than half of the mortgage principal had been paid before the Crunch, mortgagees were evicted, and full title was returned to the note holders. In the summer of the fifth year, the Latah County Board passed a motion that allowed existing colorable "warranty" deeds to be transferred into true deeds of allodial title. Most other counties in northern Idaho and eastern Washington followed suit. Once the full implications of this change became known, the majority of landowners filed for allodial deeds. Allodial title-holders began referring to each other as "freeholders."

In May of the fourth year, word came from acquaintances, who lived near Bovill, that regular Sunday and Wednesday church services would be resuming at the town's Reformed church.

The first Sunday service brought a large turnout. Most of the militia members decided to go. Because it was only a few miles, they, of course, walked. Ken remarked that it seemed strange to be carrying rifles and pistols and walking at five-yard intervals while en route to a church service.

By then, with the help of daily physical therapy with Mary, Terry Layton's knee had healed and nearly her full strength and flexibility was regained. Terry had no problem with the weekly hike to church.

The Reformed church in Bovill was reestablished by Pastor David Karcherberg. Everyone called him "Pastor Dave." Many of his sermons stressed the need to work together to rebuild the community and the regional economy. Within days, the church was reestablished as the social hub for the community. The church building was soon put to use for other functions such as bazaars. It also doubled as the town's schoolhouse. Before the Crunch, the local schoolchildren went by bus to Troy each day for school. Since this was no longer possible, a new school was established at the church building.

Lon Porter, the militia's only agnostic, and Kevin, who was Jewish, volunteered to provide security back at the retreat during the church services. The day after they went to the second church service, Doug announced at dinner, "I've talked this over with Dell, and Jeff and Rose. We feel that our weddings were rather rushed and informal. Not to take away from the covenant over which T.K. officiated, but we are planning another service to recommit ourselves to each other and to Christ. It's going to be a double June wedding. Pastor Dave is doing the honors." There was applause around the dinner table.

Rose chimed in, "This'll be a great joy. But what are we going to wear?"

Mary answered, "Don't worry, I'm sure we can find something nice enough in my closet."

The re-weddings took place on the second Saturday in June. Just before the first ceremony began, Todd tapped Mary on the shoulder and pointed out the muzzles of the AR-15s and HK91s peeking over the tops of the church pews. He whispered, "I've heard of a shotgun wedding before, but this is the first battle rifle wedding that I've ever attended." Mary gave him a scolding frown and pinched Todd's side.

271

Lots were drawn to see whom the unlucky two people were who had to stay behind at the retreat to provide security during the wedding ceremonies. Mike and Kevin drew the short dowels. Although they missed the wedding ceremony itself, they were at least able to be at the reception, which was held back at the Grays' house. The only guests from outside the Northwest Militia who attended the wedding were Roger and Teresa Dunlap and five families from Bovill that they had met through the church.

There was a guard change scheduled for the middle of the reception. As Kevin walked into the back of the LP/OP to relieve Mike, he quipped, "Well Mikey, I never thought I'd ever pull a guard shift in a suit and tie." After Mike started back down the hill to the house, Kevin plopped down on the chair behind the M60. He quoted to himself, "'Things just get curiouser and curiouser.'"

Just for the occasion, the steel shutters over the windows were opened for the first time since the onset of the Crunch. After so many years of dim light, the full afternoon light streaming through the windows seemed brilliant. All sorts of sweets were made for the reception. Margie had made apple cider from the last of the past year's storage apples, and Della made cakes and candies. Todd also broke out two bottles of sparkling apple cider that he had squirreled away in one of the basement wall lockers. They played Rose's favorite John Michael Talbot and Enya CDs.

Toward the end of the reception, Rose got a wistful look in her eye, and then began to cry. Terry asked, "Are those happy tears, or sad tears?"

"B–both. I'm so very happy to be married again publicly, and this is a wonderful reception, but, but I just wish that my parents were here. I don't know whether they made it through it all."

Hugging Rose tightly, and with tears now welling in her own eyes, Terry moaned, "You're not alone, you're not alone. Most of us have family that we haven't heard from, either. All that we can do is trust in God for their safety. Hey, maybe there'll be a postal service getting started up soon, and you'll be able to write back to Aurora."

Before she left the reception, one of the ladies from church, who was wearing a taffeta dress and a Bianchi pistol belt, approached Mary. She praised, "I just love the way you have your house decorated, and those heavy shutters look just dandy. I'll bet you sleep well at night with those between you and the bad men." Mary just smiled and thanked the woman for her compliment. She didn't bother to mention the fact that the shutters were only the last line of the house's defense. She later remarked to Todd, "There are some aspects of our security precautions that the locals will probably never hear about. Wouldn't want to start any rumors, now would we?"

"That's true," Todd replied. "A defensive feature that becomes *known* is far less effective than one that's a surprise."

In July, shortly after one of the militia's security patrols visited the town of Potlatch, some twenty-five miles to the northwest, Dan Fong asked Todd if he could meet with him privately. Todd immediately answered, "Sure, let's go take a stroll." The two picked up their HKs from the "ready rack" by the front door, and walked side by side toward the wood lot. After walking for a while in silence, Todd asked, "What's on your mind, Dan?"

"After we went through Potlatch on our last patrol, I got to thinking. That town has been hit three times by brigands, and hit pretty hard. I was thinking that I might offer my services as a consultant to develop a real security set-up for the town, not just the on-again-off-again roadblock that they've been running. They've got the manpower for 360-degree round-the-clock security, but they've never really done anything about it. What they need is someone like me—someone with the proper tactical skills to get them squared away."

"All of those young widows we saw up in Potlatch don't have anything to do with your idea, do they?"

"Well, the thought of finding a wife did cross my mind. I've heard that five or six ladies up there might need a man around. You know, someone to 'console them in their time of need.'" Both men laughed.

Todd began twiddling his thumbs as they walked. "I suppose that with that many to choose from, you can find yourself a real cute gal."

"Physical attractiveness is not anywhere *near* the top of my criteria list, Boss. I'll be looking for a God-fearing Christian woman that can cook and sew and shoot straight. I don't want one of those frail 'Oh I can't lift it—it's toooo heavy' type women. I want to find a good sturdy and hard-working gal with some brains, and faith, and some common sense."

Todd chuckled and said, "Ah yes. 'Idaho: Where the men are men, and the women are too.'"

"I'm serious, Todd. It's time that I found a wife. I'm pushing forty years old. Besides, it's starting to feel a bit crowded here, especially with the baby starting to toddle around, and probably more on the way."

Todd stopped and looked Dan squarely in the face and said, "'Each man has to have the wisdom to find his own way.' If you feel that it is truly time to move on, you'll go with my blessing. I agree, things are getting too cozy here. And I suppose that now that there's less brigand activity, we won't need as many people that are combat ready here at the retreat."

Dan and Kevin took a horseback trip to Potlatch later that same week. They returned three days later. Todd soon called for a group meeting to hear about their trip.

Dan was visibly elated as he gave his report. "My mission was a complete success. The Potlatch 'Committee of Vigilance' as they call it, has agreed to hire me on at the rate of twenty dollars in silver coin per month. I'll also be given full allodial title to a vacant brick house on Main Street, if I agree to stay on for five years. I also got the freeholders to agree to supply me with all the firewood I need, as part of my compensation. They're giving me the title of 'sheriff.' I can select whomever I want for deputies. I'll have one full-time deputy on the payroll, and as many unpaid volunteers as I see fit. This is a real primo opportunity for me."

"Won't it be dangerous?" Rose asked.

"Sure, it'll be a little dangerous. But so was living in Chicago before the Crunch. And back then, a man couldn't carry a gun to defend himself without fear of getting arrested. Things are different now. I'll be the law in Potlatch." Just then, Mike Nelson whistled the main theme to the film *The Good, The Bad, and The Ugly*. It was followed by a chorus of "Wah-Wah-Waaah," by nearly everyone in the room.

"Oh maaan," Dan complained, "I can't get any respect. I've just been named a town sheriff, and you guys still razz me."

Mike retorted with, "You're just so razzable, Fong."

Todd threw out, "All teasing aside, we want to wish you good luck. I'm sure that you'll be very successful. You'll be in our daily prayers."

Kevin nudged Dan in the ribs and said, "I'll bet he'll be married inside of a month. The Fong man here was practically drooling over all those lovelies up there in Potlatch." The room was filled with howls of laughter and catcalls.

After the ruckus died down, Dan said, "Hey, I noticed that your eyes were pretty well locked on the ladies most of the time we were up there too, so lay off." With that, Kevin's face turned red and he sat down. The room was once again filled with laughter.

The next day, with the help of Ken Layton, Dan took on the task of reviving his long immobile Toyota four-wheel-drive pickup. This took several hours. They started early in the morning by wheeling the garden cart out to the wood lot. In it they carried a jack, a bottle of distilled water, a hydrometer, a five-gallon water can, a five-gallon gas can, five quarts of oil, an oil filter, a spray can of ether-based starting fluid, Mike's small tool kit, a pair of jumper cables, and the battery from Todd's Power Wagon.

Upon lifting the hood, they found that mice had built a nest on top of the engine block. After they had removed the mouse nest, replaced the oil in the crankcase, and added water to the battery and radiator, they found it was fairly easy to get the engine started. The only problem encountered came when Ken put the rig through an idling test. After ten minutes of idling, one of the heater hoses split, sending water cascading over the exhaust manifold and making clouds of steam. Replacing both heater hoses from Todd's reel of spare high-temperature three-quarter-inch hose took only fifteen minutes.

Both the top and bottom radiator hose were still flexible and showed no signs of cracks. This was fortunate, as Dan did not have a set of spare hoses. The stocks of spares on hand at the retreat would be no help—they were for late 60s-early 70s Fords and Dodge Power Wagons. As they were reinstalling the battery that they had borrowed from Todd's truck, Ken pointed out the incompatibility of the radiator hoses to Dan.

"I know, I know," he replied. "If only I'd bought a group-standard vehicle, I'd have a running rig for several more years. Don't remind me. I was an obstinate fool back then, and now I'm sorry for it."

Layton put his hand on Fong's shoulder and avowed, "I've got news for you Dan. You're still pretty obstinate, but at least you're not a fool. You never were a fool. If you had been, I wouldn't have associated with you."

Dan spent the next two days sorting through his gear and packing his truck. It soon became clear that he would not have room for all of his equipment and the remnants of his storage food. He packed the most important gear, and left the rest in a pile in the basement. He told the Grays that he would be back for the rest of it and his horse when he returned for the first of what he hoped would be regular visits.

There was no melodramatic farewell for Dan Fong. He simply made his goodbyes to each of the militia members and hopped in his truck. As he drove out the front gate, he was again singing along with his favorite Creedence Clearwater Revival tape.

Word came three months later that Dan had married a widow with two young children. They also heard that under Dan's direction, the Potlatch Vigilance Committee was setting up LP/OPs on three sides of town, and a roadblock on the fourth.

At one of Pastor Dave's first sermons, he mentioned that he would soon be setting up a charity to benefit refugees and others in great need. Immediately after the service, Todd and Mary approached the minister, and told him about their collection of coins and equipment captured from looters. Pastor Dave didn't hesitate about accepting the offer.

Later that day, when they began unloading the bed of Todd's pickup at the back door of the church building, the pastor could not believe his eyes. When Todd dumped out the sack containing the coins, watches, and jewelry, Pastor Dave remarked, "All this was from the looters? The Lord works in mysterious ways." Much of the captured equipment was sold at an auction to benefit the charity. Not surprisingly, some of the militia members bought some of the gear that they had secretly longed for.

Near the winter's solstice of the fourth year, Kevin asked Todd to call a special group meeting. He said that he wanted to make a proposal to the militia as a whole. When everyone was assembled, Kevin began, "I'd like to make a suggestion that we split the militia in half. We'd open up my house to shelter half of us there, while the rest would stay here. These are the reasons that I've considered. First, we really have too many people to live here comfortably. There just isn't the floor space. Second, having a second retreat would provide a fallback position, in case one or the other burns down or gets overrun in an attack. Third, the isolation created by splitting in two might help protect us if there is ever any sort of plague. Fourth, we are letting a lot of good talent go to waste that we've been seeing in some of these groups of refugees passing through. If we split into two retreats, then we will each be able to recruit a few more members."

After a pause to let his words sink in, Lendel added, "This will mean that we can bring in some people with needed skills like perhaps a doctor, a veterinarian, a plumber, a carpenter, or a blacksmith. Fifth, and finally, because my house is only a stroll down the road, we could have both radio and field telephone communications. That way, if either retreat came under siege, then the members of the other retreat could form a reaction team to outflank the attackers. What do you think?"

The discussion of Lendel's proposal went on through three additional meetings over the course of the next two days. Most of the debate concerned whether or not Kevin's house could be made into a defensible retreat. This matter was settled by Jeff, who suggested that a series of tunnels and bunkers could be dug under and around it. Waterproofing these bunkers could be accomplished using the Grays' four remaining rolls of heavy sheet plastic.

Jeff suggested that because there was not enough plate steel available, the windows of the house could not be properly protected. He suggested that ballistic protection for those behind the windows could be accomplished by constructing large wooden boxes to place just inside the windows. These boxes would be filled with rocks and packed soil. He mentioned the fact that sand would also work as filler for the boxes, but would be inferior because sand would pour out of the boxes, if they were hit repeatedly by bullets. The main detractor to the rock barricades, Jeff said, would be that they would block light. Kevin agreed, but added that on the positive side, they would also act as excellent heat sinks to absorb and slowly release heat gathered by the solar windows during daylight hours.

When it finally came to a vote, Kevin's plan passed overwhelmingly. It was decided that the split would be made the next spring. Mike would be the titular head of the new retreat, and Doug Carlton would be its tactical coordinator. Della Carlton would be in charge of gardening. Kevin, as the owner of the house, would become the logistics coordinator. Lon and Margie would also make the move to Kevin's. Meanwhile, back at the original retreat, Jeff would become the new tactical coordinator, and Rose would become the logistician.

CHAPTER 23
Vicissitude

"Necessity is the plea for every infringement of human freedom,
It is the argument of tyrants; it is the creed of slaves."

—William Pitt, before the House of Commons, November 18, 1783

Geographically distinct units were formed from the Northwest Militia, as planned, late in the April of the fifth year. To avoid confusion amongst the local citizenry that they protected, they designated those at the original retreat as "Todd Gray's Company" and those at Kevin Lendel's house as "Michael Nelson's Company." The responsibility for patrolling was divided along a line east-west between the retreats. Todd Gray's Company was to patrol the northern half of the sector, while Michael Nelson's Company patrolled the southern half. Separate CB channels were assigned to each company for locals to use to contact either company.

On the fifth of May, Mary was in the garden plot transplanting some young tomato plants that had been started in the greenhouse a few weeks earlier. As she was methodically digging holes for each of the plants, she heard a strange engine noise in the distance. Just moments after she first heard the noise, she was astonished to look up and see two light aircraft approaching from the south. She dropped her trowel, snatched up her AR-15, and ran to the house. By the time she was in the house, the Mallory Sonalerts were wailing, and everyone at the house was at their "stand-to" positions, scanning their assigned sectors of fire.

"Does anybody have any idea where those planes came from?" Mary asked. Sitting at the C.Q. desk, Jeff shrugged his shoulders, and reached over to turn off the "panic button," silencing the piercing alarm. The engine noise was clearly louder now. From the LP/OP, Terry called in on the TA-1, "They're pusher prop jobs, twin seat, tandem style. It's hard to tell, but it looks like there's just one pilot in each. They're definitely circling us. Everybody stay put." The planes circled the house a second time, just a hundred yards above the ground.

From the front of the house, Todd declared, "Hey, wait a minute, it looks like they're getting ready to land. Yep, they are landing down on the county road." The two planes landed in rapid succession on the straight stretch of county road below the house. Todd was surprised by how short a distance it took for the planes to land and come to a full stop. The planes looked identical, except for their color. One was painted dark green. The other was tan. He heard their engines roar up in tempo as the planes turned and taxied back to the front gate. The planes came to a stop at the front gate, and their engines shut down. Both pilots lifted their canopies and took off their headphones, almost in unison. Two figures, one tall and one short, hopped out of the planes, wearing digital pattern ACUs and tan boots.

Todd shouted loud enough for everyone at the house to hear, "They are painted drab, but those sure don't look military. Have any of you heard of anyone in the area that owns an ultralight?" There was no reply. Todd pondered for a moment. "Hey, you know, Dan told me that Ian Doyle was in an ultralight club. I sure wish Fong was still here. He's probably seen pictures of Ian's plane. He said that it was a zippy little thing, and I think he said that it was a two-seater."

"Who is this Ian fellow?" Rose asked.

Mary answered, "An old college buddy of Todd and Dan's. He has a wife and daughter. That might be him, or all of them, in those planes down on the road."

Ten minutes later, after a cautious squad-sized approach by the bounding-over watch method, Todd and Ian Doyle were sharing hugs. "Wow! Long time no see. What brings you here?"

"It's a long story, Todd. Suffice it to say that we left town in a hurry when a very large number of *muy malo hombres* took over. It was *muy peligroso* there. So we did some Van-dammage—just to whittle them down, you understand—and then we took off. It took a few inquiries in Bovill, but we found your place here easily enough."

Todd took a long look at the plane behind Doyle, staring at just below the wing root, where it was stenciled "EXPERIMENTAL." He said insistently, "You can tell me the whole story later. First tell me about these ultralights. They are really a sight to behold."

Ian turned to caress the fuselage of the flat forest green-painted plane behind him. "To begin with, technically, they *aren't* ultralights, although they use a lot of the same design features. Legally, these birds are classed as light experimentals. These birds are both Laron Star Streaks. I paid just under thirty thousand for mine, when I picked it up new from the factory in Borger, Texas, back in '98. We towed it home in its trailer behind our Suburban. The Star Streak comes with a lot of standard goodies like dual controls, an ICOM radio, electric start, electric brakes, three-position half-span flaps, electric trim, and a

278

pretty complete set of VFR instruments. I added a GPS navigation box and active noise reduction headphones to this one. It's essentially a poor man's general aviation plane, but legally it's a light 'experimental.' But it's too heavy to be classed as an 'ultralight' under FAA regs.

"With its enclosed canopy, it's one of the best light experimentals for long-range flying. In fact, one guy flew a similar model Laron from London to Beijing and wrote a book about it. As I'm sure you know, the main advantages of ultralights and light experimentals is that they are so thrifty on gas, and have a super short takeoff roll—usually under two hundred feet—and very low stall speeds. The Star Streak only weighs about four hundred pounds, empty. The other neat thing about our Larons and most similar light experimentals and ultralights is that they are not restricted to av-gas. In ours here, for example, you can burn any grade of gas down to about eighty-five octane. If I adjusted the carb jets, I suppose they would even burn ethanol or methanol. Luckily, I haven't had to try that yet."

Doyle turned to the trim woman with an olive complexion standing beside him. She appeared to be around thirty-five years old. "I'm sorry, I'm getting ahead of myself. This is my wife Blanca. I've written to you about her, but we haven't seen each other face to face since college, so you've never had a chance to meet."

The attractive woman in digital camo ACUs extended her hand, and Todd shook it firmly. Gray said quietly, "*Encantado.*" She replied in a soft accent, "A pleasure finally meeting you, Meester Gray."

"As you probably recall from my e-mail, I met Blanca when I was stationed down in Hondo," Doyle continued. "That was back in my 'Terry and the Pirates' days, when I was a lieutenant—not too long out of transition training. She was a civilian working in flight ops at Teguchigalpa. Blanca was already a qualified single engine pilot when I met her. Talk about love at first sight, *eh conchita*?" Blanca smiled and blushed, nodding her chin to her shoulder.

Gesturing to the other plane, Ian said, "We swapped for Blanca's Laron just after the stock market tanked. I got it from an old fart civilian who was in the Phoenix Metro ultralight club. He bought this one as a kit. He said that it took him almost two years to build it in his spare time. He finished building it in '99. It had very low hours clocked on the engine. His was stored in the same style enclosed trailer that we had for mine. I traded him my Sten gun, a suppressor with nomex cover, a whole bunch of magazines, and a thousand rounds of nine-millimeter ball for it. Fair enough swap, I suppose, since unregistered and suppressed submachineguns don't grow on trees. We could both see the hand-writing on the wall by then. He knew what I needed, and I knew what he needed: I needed some more transportation, and he needed some more fire-power. I asked him why he wasn't planning to bail out of Phoenix. He said that his wife refused to budge an inch. They had their whole life wrapped up in their house. Since he was stuck there, he didn't need the plane, but he certainly needed a serious self-defense gun."

Doyle stepped toward the back of the fuselage, deftly ducking under the wing, and went on. "The Star Streaks cruise at just over one-hundred-and-twenty miles an hour at eighty-percent power, which is pretty fast for a light experimental. Of course, that seems like crawling when you are used to wearing an F-16, but I like 'em. The cockpit layout is even similar to a Falcon. Not exactly fly-by-wire controls, though. This model uses an eighty-five-horse Hirth F-30 engine. It's a great little plant. It just hums along and sips gas—only about five gallons an hour at eighty-percent power. Both of these planes are identical except for the propellers. Mine uses a four-blade composite, but the prop on Blanca's is the older composite three-blade.

"The Hirth is a powerful little engine. It will make the Larons climb at twenty-five-hundred-feet per minute when it is in normal configuration with just one man on board, but of course a lot slower climb the way we have them loaded down right now. The planes have a rated useful load of five hundred pounds. I'm afraid that we exceeded that limit when we took off from Prescott. Between the heavy load and the high elevation of the airport, our takeoff distances were outrageously long—at least, that is, for a light experimental. But luckily, we had a long straight stretch of road to take off from."

Blanca looked around anxiously. "Ees there anywhere where we can put dese birds where they whon't get stolen?"

Mary answered, "We'll put them both in the Andersen's big hay barn, just down the road. It's a nice dry barn. The wings should hopefully fit through the front. It was left open on that side to let the big New Holland harvester in. It's a three-sided affair. The farm is deserted, and the barn is almost empty now. They gave us permission to use the place. Don't worry—when the planes are pushed to the back of the barn, no one will see them there. And, as further insurance, it's just within line of sight of our LP/OP, up on the hill."

"Ell-Pee-Oh-Pee?" Blanca asked, quizzically.

"Sorry, Blanca. I'm afraid that we are used to talking in 'acronese' around here, and not the Air Force acronym dialect you're probably used to. LP/OP is a ground pounder acronym for listening post/observation post." Pointing to the nearby hill, Mary explained, "Basically it's a glorified hole in the ground. If you look very closely, you can see it up on the hill there. It has a good view of the area. It's for observation in daylight, and for listening at night."

Moving the planes into the barn took only a few minutes. They were able to taxi the planes under power to within twenty feet of the barn. From there, they were pushed in by hand. Going in, the planes' thirty-feet long wingspans cleared the entrance with just a foot to spare on each side. As they were pushing the first plane in, Mary asked, "How many gas cans have you got in there and how far can you fly without refueling?"

Doyle pointed through the canopy at the rear seat area, and cited, "Originally, the Star Streaks only had a range of around three hundred and twenty miles at eighty-percent power. The main tank is fourteen-and-a-half gallons. But I added some big bladder tanks to both planes. They aren't connected directly to the primary fuel system. I cheated and installed a couple of little Black and Decker Jackrabbit hand pumps alongside the front seats, with extra long hoses. To transfer fuel from the bladder to the main tank, you just put the Jackrabbit in your lap and crank away. The bladder tanks extend our range to about four hundred and eighty miles without landing to refuel, when we are at max takeoff weight. If we were in a light configuration, they could maybe even go five hundred and fifty miles."

Ian's plane came to a rest with the tip of its nose less than a foot from the rear wall of the barn. He inched past the nose and walked around to the other side of the plane, talking as he walked. "They are both quite a bit lighter right now, since we have less gas and we had to barter some of our stuff for fuel." He tapped on the Plexiglas with his index finger and said, "I have these five-gallon gas cans strapped into the backseats of both birds, but they are nearly empty, too. Aside from some clothes, sleeping bags, tools, and aeronautical charts, most of the weight on board is fuel, oil, guns, ammo, water, and MREs. You know, just the essentials in life. At present we're down to less than eight gallons of fuel between the two planes...."

Mary interjected, "Don't worry about that. We still have over four hundred gallons of stabilized unleaded premium in the tank here. It will only be good for another year or two, so we might as well use it up. I think that it is nearly all ninety-two octane, but I'm not sure. I'll have to ask Terry—she's our logistics honcho. But she's up at the LP/OP right now."

After they had pushed the second plane in, Todd declared, "Don't worry about all your gear, we'll come down with the pickup truck later this afternoon and take it up to the house."

Before they left the planes, Doyle used a socket wrench to remove the nose wheels from both planes, and buried them under some loose hay near the front of the big barn. "They won't be going far without these," he said. As they walked out of the barn, Ian slung his suppressed MAC-10 over his shoulder. Blanca did likewise with a stainless steel folding-stock Mini-14 GB. Todd was disappointed to see that they didn't carry any extra magazines. He made a mental note to correct that glaring deficiency.

As they walked, Blanca was bemused at the way the militia members walked at five-yard intervals. "Why are you walking so far apart?" she asked with a laugh.

"Force of habit," Mary explained. "In case of an ambush, you are at much greater risk if you are bunched together."

They chatted amiably as they hiked back to the Grays' house. Once they were inside, Rose served up an early lunch of raw carrots, apple slices spread with reconstituted peanut butter, and freshly baked bread. It was over lunch that Ian and Blanca started to recount their story. Mary set a TRC-500 to the "Vox" setting, so that Terry Layton, who was still up at the LP/OP, didn't feel left out.

Munching on some bread, Ian began, "The 56th Fighter Wing had just started a rotation to Saudi. It was just two years before the Crash that we switched back from a tactical training wing to a tactical fighter wing. I came onboard just a few months into the transition. Anyway, when all the trouble started, since I was the wing maintenance officer, I was stuck back at Luke, catching up on paperwork. I was also taking an idiotic mandatory 'Diversity, Sensitivity, and Sexual Harassment' class. The frickin' class lasted a whole week. I had orders to catch up with the wing in late November.

"But then, when the riots got going in earnest, they planned an emergency redeployment of virtually all of the close air-support aircraft in the Air Force inventory back to the States. Some weenie at the White House must have dreamed that one up. Our wing was going to deploy to Hurlburt Field, down in Florida. Criminy! Could you imagine F-16s and A-10s versus rioters? Talk about overkill! I never heard what happened to our squadrons after that. I was too busy with problems of my own—like finding drinking water for Blanca and myself."

"And your daughter?" Mary asked.

Doyle's face clouded with emotion. Stiffening, he replied, "Linda didn't make it, ma'am. She died five years ago. She was in Detroit, doing her annual six-week-long 'Grandmom and Grandpop' visit with my folks. It was the first time that she was old enough to go on a commercial plane by herself. Blanca wanted to stay home to relax, do some pastels, and a bit of surfing the Internet. We were homeschooling her, so Linda wasn't on a normal school year schedule. Blanca and Linda liked to go up to Michigan in the fall. They get some nice fall colors up there."

Ian paused and looked at the ground. "By the time we realized the magnitude of the situation, most of the flights had been canceled, and the few that were still flying were booked solid. In retrospect, what I should have done was played the old 'you bet your bars' game and commandeered a D-model Falcon to zip up there to get her. Instead, I took the conservative route and just hoped that the riots wouldn't last long or spread outside the downtown area of Detroit. I also figured that if worse came to worse, my dad's gun collection could handle any rioters that came down their block. I was wrong. I got a call from one of their close neighbors who managed to make it out of Detroit alive. She said that looters got really pissed when my dad shot some of them. They torched my dad's house. Killed them all. I still feel like such a fool. I could have saved my folks and my daughter's life."

Blanca squeezed Ian's hand and said softly, "Don't do thees, E-an. We can no change history."

Mary's eyes were wet with tears. "I'm so sorry, Ian. I'm so sorry, Blanca."

Doyle shook his head from side to side and muttered, "Dwelling on it won't do any good. In times like these, you just have to suck it up and drive on."

Todd said a silent prayer. Then he looked up and asked, "So what happened to everybody at Luke?"

Doyle snapped out of his reverie and recounted, "To call it mass desertion would be to put it mildly. The mess halls only had limited food supplies, and we only had enough MREs onhand for short-term contingencies. I'm sure some of the overseas air bases had better stocks, but nobody ever expected a disruption of resupply of food *in CONUS*!

"When it became clear that the food wasn't going to last long, virtually everybody started to disappear. And when they went, they took a lot of equipment, fuel, and nearly every scrap of food on base with them. The Base Exchange, the commissary, and the mess halls were stripped clean. When I say everybody, I mean *everybody*. There wasn't a soul from 56th Log or 56th Medical left on base. Even the whole Support Group essentially vanished in about three days time. By the time I decided to pack it in, Luke was a ghost town. There were only seven pilots and about twenty ground crew guys left on the post. Most of them were young bachelors. By that point, I was the senior ranking officer on the base, so I could do pretty much anything I wanted. I was the *de facto* base commander. I just called a formation and released the remaining personnel on base on 'indefinite leave.'

"Unfortunately, my options were pretty limited. You see, there wasn't a single aircraft left on the ramp, or a single military vehicle left on post. By then, there were just a few POVs. Even the fuel trucks had disappeared. Now you've got to understand that they had two hundred and seventeen birds on the property books, mainly F-16 Cs and D models. Of those, they were all either out on the Saudi Arabia rotation, or off on 'emergency' flights that all mysteriously ended up being one-way missions. At least three F-16s, and the general staff Lear were out-and-out stolen. No flight plans were filed. The guys who took them just figured that they could get away with it. They just taxied out at O-dark-early and took off. And there was nobody left in the tower to say 'boo' about it. Those four had been the last airworthy planes on the base. The few planes that were left were just some stripped hangar queens.

"After that 'gentlemen, you are released' speech, I spent the rest of that day looking for fuel containers. Every gas can available had already walked off base.

The only good-sized containers I could find were some hydraulic fluid drums. But I was afraid that the fluid left in them would contaminate the gas. So I ended up scrounging a bunch of empty two-liter pop bottles from dumpsters around the BX. I drove home that evening with almost one hundred and forty gallons of av-gas in the back of the Suburban. I never went back to Luke after that.

"We were living off base in a rental flat top in Buckeye. It's basically a retirement community. When I got home, I talked things over with Blanca. We decided to hang tight for a few days. We packed up, but packed light. It was like one of those lifeboat games—'Now if you could only take five items, which five would they be?' The end result was that Blanca and I had to leave a lot behind. We spent a lot of that time listening to the radio for reports on the rioting. Only a couple of AM stations were on the air by then, and the news they were handing out was pretty sketchy. None of it sounded good. They spent half the time repeating the same FEMA 'Stay calm, remain in your homes, order will be restored shortly' tape. What a pile of bull. The tape even recommended calling 911 if we saw any looting in progress. I laughed and said, 'Oh yes sir, will do.' The phones had all been dead for *several* days.

"Our next-door neighbors had a police scanner. That was the best thing for monitoring where there was trouble happening. This was at the time when Phoenix and Tucson were burning down. Major chaos, let me tell ya. Once the looting started spreading out into the suburbs, we agreed that it would be *de mal aspecto* to stay in the Phoenix area much longer. Bright and early on a Tuesday morning, we wheeled the Larons out of their trailers, and bolted on the wings and tails, right there on our front lawn. It only took about fifteen minutes each to assemble and pre-flight them, since we'd had plenty of practice before, putting my bird together for weekend jaunts.

"While we were loading our gear, most of the neighbors just stood there and gawked. A few helped out with the fueling process. We handed our next-door neighbors the keys and title to our Suburban, and the keys to the house. I told them that anything inside was free for the taking. By then, we knew that we weren't ever coming back. Then we taxied off the lawn, down the driveway, and out the court. We hung a left, throttled up, and took off from Hastings Avenue. Some of the neighbors stood at the ends to block car traffic for us. Must have been *quite a sight* for the retirees. We flew from there straight to Prescott—that's in northern Arizona. We planned to stay at my cousin's place.

"My cousin Alex was a senior salesman with J&G Sales, a big gun distributor up in Prescott. With that job, I figured that he would be pretty well squared away, at least in terms of guns and ammo to barter for anything he could possibly want. Prescott is partly a resort community, and kind of a haven for gun nuts. J&G was there, Ruger had a factory there, and there were lots of custom gun makers, barrel makers, and stock makers. One little outfit made elephant guns on custom magnum Mauser actions before the Crash. Big .416 Rigbys and that sort of thing. The last I saw of them, they were still producing some smaller caliber long-range guns in H-S Precision Kevlar-Graphite stocks. They sold them on a barter basis. Real tack drivers.

"Prescott is not a big town, but it took us a while to locate Alex, since the phones were out there by that time, too. I hitched a ride from the airport, while Blanca stayed behind to guard the planes. From talking with Alex's neighbors, we discovered that he had hired out as a security man for some Tucson banking fat cats. They had a pretty elaborate hidey-hole set up just north of Prescott. There were four families living at the compound. At first they didn't want to take us in. Then they saw the firepower that we had with us, and they changed their minds. Officially, we were "security," just like my cousin. We had it pretty soft there, compared to most folks. We had plenty of water, and enough food to get by. We were in no hurry to leave.

"Things were pretty quiet there for four full years. A little local trouble, but nothing worth mentioning. Then we started hearing about this gang of escaped convicts and assorted riffraff that was slowly working its way up from New Mexico. Refugees told us that it was originally two gangs that combined into one big super gang. They would hit a town, linger a week or two, strip it clean, and then move on to the next one. They were like a swarm of locusts. There were over three hundred of them by the time they made it up to the Prescott area. Rumor had it that at least one of the two gangs had been doing this town-to-town hopping all the way from south Texas. By then they were getting pretty good at it.

"I took a recon flight in my Star Streak down to Wickenburg when they hit there, and it wasn't a pretty sight. They just swept through the town in one big mass of vehicles. Many of the houses were abandoned, 'cause folks had heard they were coming and didn't want to be around when they did. Basically, they burned down any house that anyone was shooting from. Then they went from house to house, taking anything of value. Even from the air, I could see them dragging some women out of houses and raping them on the sidewalks. We're talking total scum of the Earth. It made me wish I was flying a fully armed Fighting Falcon instead of my little Laron. I could have really kicked some tail. These guys were absolute savages, Todd." Doyle stopped for a few moments, and then added, "I got shot at some when I was on that flight, but I didn't find any bullet holes in my bird when I got back."

"Just three weeks ago, the gang was making their way up the Agua Fria, and hit the little town of Mayer. About eighty of us from town, mainly men, went on a little preemptive strike when we heard that the gang had moved into the town of Humboldt. Blanca, Alex, and I were all on the raiding party. We knew that Prescott would be next, because we were just twelve miles up the road. A Navajo kid about thirteen years old, who escaped from Humboldt just after they arrived, gave us the layout. He even volunteered to go back into town to scout which buildings the looters were in. That was a real help in planning the operation.

"Our little raid didn't have much in the way of military precision, but we sure did some damage. We knew that we couldn't kill them all, so we decided that the thing to do was to concentrate on their vehicles, especially their armored cars and APCs. We hit them at just after three in the morning. Since we were all on foot or horseback the last two miles in, they didn't know we were coming until we were already in their midst. They had the buildings that they were occupying lit up like Christmas trees. Our little Navajo scout had told us in advance which buildings they'd be in. We were only fully engaged for about five minutes. It was fast and furious, but like I said before, we did some serious Van-dammage.

"In the first couple of minutes, we had the advantage, because most of the looters were asleep. They made me the point man, since I had the only suppressed weapon in the raiding party. When I shoot Winchester Q-Loads—those are special low-velocity subsonic rounds—this thing doesn't make much more noise than a nail gun." Doyle held up the stubby Ingram M10 for a brief display, unscrewing the nomex-covered suppressor. "The term 'silencer' is really a misnomer. A 'can' like this is really just an elaborate sound muffler. Again, you can still hear the shot—sounds like a loud handclap. The normal sound is reduced so much that you can even hear the clack of the bolt going forward with each shot."

Doyle screwed the suppressor back on the M10 and set it down on the window seat. "Sorry, I digress. Getting back to what happened in Humboldt.... I got the chance to personally drop three of their sentries, shooting my MAC in the semiauto mode. I don't mind saying that it felt real good, after what I'd seen them do in Wickenburg. At first, we were the only ones shooting. Once the looters rolled out of bed and started shooting back, it was another story. They had a lot of fully automatic weapons, grenades, and rocket launchers of some sort. They really started hosing us down. Before they did though, we had torched more than forty vehicles with Molotov cocktails. Apparently, we got every one of their APCs and armored cars.

"Our retreat out of Humboldt was, let's say, 'less than organized.' Only twenty-nine of our original group made it back to Prescott alive by noon. Two more guys straggled in the next evening. Of the thirty-one that made it back, only three had been wounded, and those were all minor grazing wounds. Oddly enough, all five of the men and women who were on horseback were among those to make it back without a scratch. Not even any of the horses were hit. Either they were real lucky, or cavalry is making a comeback. My cousin Alex never made it back from the Humboldt raid." Ian skipped a beat, and then went on. "The looters didn't show up the next day or even the day after. Blanca and I waited at the compound, with the Larons loaded, fueled, and ready to go.

"Three days after our raid, they came into Prescott, and they must have been plenty pissed. The gang rolled in just after dawn. They didn't seem to care how many losses they were taking, and they immediately started to torch every building they got to. Blanca and I didn't wait until they made it to the north side of town. Everyone at the compound was by then either in town manning the barricades, or had headed for the hills. Most of the remaining stuff at the retreat went with two families that had a pair of diesel pusher motor homes. They were headed for Flagstaff or beyond.

"At that point, we realized that discretion was the better part of valor, so we took off, too. We used a nice long straight stretch of road that started a quarter-mile north of the compound. I had taken off and landed there many times before during the five years we were there. When we wheeled around after takeoff, we could see that almost half the buildings in the downtown area were on fire. We didn't stick around to see how things ended, but I'm afraid that the looters must have taken the town. Even though they didn't have any armored vehicles left, they had superior numbers and superior firepower.

"That day we flew to Cedar City, Utah. It was amazing, but they had almost two hundred gallons of av-gas still on hand at the airport. They said that they were going to get resupplied with fresh gas that was going to be trucked in from Oklahoma soon, so they were willing to sell it. We filled up every container we had. That batch of gas cost me twenty dollars in junk silver, my Olin flare gun, and a hundred rounds of nine-millimeter ball. Folks were fairly friendly there. Things are darned near normal there, compared to Arizona, but weird. They kept talking about the 'Federal Provisional Government,' the 'Regional Administrator,' and 'Local Autonomy.' It was like some freaky mantra they'd all been taught. It was creepy.

"The next day we flew from Cedar City to Brigham City, up in northern Utah. We had a letter of introduction from one family in Cedar City to their cousins, who had run the airport at Brigham City. They were talking about their new 'Local Autonomy' arrangement with the Federals there, too. We spent two days there. It took three separate transactions, but I managed to buy forty-one gallons of gas. In all, I swapped two hundred rounds of nine-millimeter hollow points, eleven dollars in junk silver, some hand tools, and a Fluke volt-ohm meter for the gas. A lot of it was low octane, and some of it hadn't been stabilized and was pretty pukey looking. It had those white streamers in it. I added a bottle of octane booster that I had been saving, plus half a bottle of alcohol to soak up any water in the gas, and said some 'Hail

Marys.' Luckily, the gas burned all right—just a few sputters—but it had me really worried.

"Next we flew to Grangeville, Idaho. That's real pretty country up there on that Camas Prairie. We made inquiries and scrounged up another twenty-three gallons of gas. That took our last ten dollars in junk silver, plus another hundred and twenty rounds of nine-mil. At the rate I was bartering off our ammunition and silver, I was praying hard that you folks would still be here in one piece. It was a big gamble, but we sure knew we didn't want to stay in Arizona, and we didn't have anywhere else to go. Our only other chance might have been to go to Show Low, Arizona, to join the Cooper militia—they call it the Continental militia—but we didn't personally know anybody there. We had heard they're good folks, but it is awkward just dropping in on complete strangers. Like I say, we prayed that you would still be here. In times like these, you just have to have total faith in the Lord.

"Yesterday morning, we flew from Grangeville up to Bovill. The folks were really nice to us there, too. From what they said, there wasn't hardly a drop of gas in town. They showed us on road maps and Forest Service maps how to find your place. We took off again immediately. Once we got here, and started circling, I recognized the layout from the way Dan Fong had described it to me. Speaking of whom, is Fong still alive?"

"He's alive, all right. He's got a job as sheriff, up in Potlatch. It's a small town about twenty-five miles northwest of here."

Blanca sang out, "We'll have to go vee-zeet him, someday soon."

Todd and Mary then spent a full hour describing their experiences at the retreat in the past five years. Todd ended this by detailing how half of the retreat members had recently relocated to Kevin Lendel's property. After listening to others, Rose Trasel told her story, including an account of her shooting incident and surgery.

It was after dinner that Ian Doyle approached Todd and asked, "Would you mind if Blanca and I stayed here? We could even help you out with your reconnaissance patrolling, using the Larons. What do you say?"

They were voted into the Northwest Militia the next evening, and their tactical training started the following day.

CHAPTER 24

Incursion

"Government is not reason; it is not eloquence; it is force!
Like fire, it is a dangerous servant and a fearful master."

—*George Washington*

Some bad news came over the CB only two weeks after Ian and Blanca arrived. Todd immediately relayed what he had heard to Kevin's house, via field telephone. A meeting of both companies was scheduled for 7 a.m. the next day, in Todd's barn.

The members of the two nascent companies sat in a semicircle in the hay that was scattered on the floor of the barn. Most had their rifles or shotguns lying across their laps or propped up against the wall of the barn within arm's reach. Everyone was there, except for Lon, who was on LP/OP duty just up the hill, and Lisa Nelson, who was handling the same duty back at the other retreat. Lisa had her baby girl, Rachel, with her at the LP/OP. Little Jacob, who was now three years old, sat in Mary's lap during the meeting. The boy sat patiently and politely, saying nothing. Rose had her baby daughter in her arms. She quietly nursed her during the meeting.

Goats wandered in and milled around during the briefing. Chickens scratched the dirt at the open doorway. Gray began, "Thanks, Mike, for getting your folks up here so promptly. You've by now all heard bits and pieces of this, but just so there is no confusion, let me start at the beginning. Here is what we know, based on what we've heard from ham radio operators and Radio Free America on shortwave, from what has come over the CB relay net, and—taken with a grain of salt—what the Federals are putting out on the shortwave. They've taken over WRNO and WWCR, and some of the fifty-thousand-watt eastern AM stations and turned them into their exclusive propaganda tools. We get the other side of the story from Radio Free America, in Maine and The Intelligence Report, in Michigan.

"The provisional Federal government now has partial or full control of nineteen states east of the Rockies. They've brought in a lot of foreign troops,

Belgians and Germans mostly, under some bravo sierra 'Presidential Decision Directive.' Our national sovereignty went out the window when the UN troops came in. Since we are so far removed, we can't tell exactly who is actually running the show back there at Fort Knox. But whether it's President-for-life Maynard Hutchings and his crowd, or the Europeans, or some supra-national world government, it doesn't make any difference. Martial law is martial law. A moose turd pie still tastes like a moose turd, no matter how much sugar you put on it." There were titters of laughter.

"The bottom line, in my estimation, is that since the U.S. is bankrupt, and our creditors—the international bankers, that is—have sent their bully boys to collect on the debt. They consider every square inch of real estate, every capital asset, and even your labor and the future labor of your children to be surety for that debt. It's sort of like when people buy cars on credit and then stop making the payments. The bank sends a repo man to tow the car away. If you can picture that on a global scale, what is going on is 'kingdom towing.' The Federals may think that they are still in control, but in reality they are just errand boys for the banksters—the Rothschilds and Bilderberg Group fat cats of the world.

"There are some folks—like Kevin Lendel—who have researched this more than I have. They go so far as to claim that we've actually been forestalling this situation since 1933, when Roosevelt first declared the nation bankrupt. Perhaps they're right. Perhaps what we are seeing is just a delayed reaction from something that started way back then. Think about it. We took out the loan in 1933. We let the debt get totally out of hand in the 1980s and 1990s. We stopped making the payments all together after the stock market crash, and then the banksters sent the 'tow truck' two years into the Crunch. If that is indeed what happened, it would explain a lot of things. It would explain, for example, how our courts began mixing law and equity in the 1930s, and started treating us all as 14th Amendment "persons" rather than as full state Citizens. It could explain why the courts haven't overturned laws like the National Firearms Act, and the 1994 Crime Bill, the 1996 Immigration Bill, and the USA PATRIOT Act, even though they are clearly unconstitutional. It could also explain where this make-believe animal called 'statutory jurisdiction' came from, effectively replacing the Common Law. Oh well, these are all issues that won't get clarified for several years. For now though, we've got to worry about a more immediate problem. It's coming at us like a Mack truck."

Todd continued, "The Federals are on the march, expanding their territory. They are handing out favors to any Quislings that go along with them, and whomping on anybody that doesn't play along. In at least five states, they've executed the governors on the spot and put their puppet governors in place. Instead of talking in terms of states, the UN likes to talk in terms of 'regions' as an overlay to the existing governmental structure. There are still state governors in the pacified states, but they are essentially subordinate to the regional administrators. And here's the kicker: The regional administrators report to, and get their direction from, the *UN headquarters* in New York, not the so-called Federal government at Fort Knox."

Todd waited for his words to sink in, and then went on. "The Feds have big detention camps set up in several states, at least one in each of the old FEMA regions. They are supposedly 'refugee camps' or 'relocation camps,' but everyone living around them knows the real story. The camps are to house any malcontents that they think they can 'reform through labor,' and for any high-profile types that they are afraid could be seen as martyrs if they wax them right on the spot. They just whisk folks away and shut them up behind concertina wire. The real hard cases are put in the old Federal prisons like El Reno. Lower security risks are put in the slave labor camps.

"Regardless of where they go, virtually all of the prisoners are poorly fed, beaten, and worked eleven hours a day. It is essentially a huge gulag system with a one-way door. The only way you come out is dead. In all, a lot like the *laogai* system in China.

"The Feds have made a few friends by getting the power grid restored in places. And, over a year ago, they conquered Texas and Oklahoma, where a few oil fields and refineries were already back in operation. So now they have plenty of fuel, oil, and lubricants for their campaign of conquest.

"Now, not everything is rosy for the Feds back east. They still haven't taken Vermont, New Hampshire, or Maine. They tried that for three summers in a row, and decided to let those states wait for a while. Ditto for most of Michigan. Talk about a hornet's nest for the Federales! Folks call it '*Militiagan*' now. The Federals are also having serious problems in the southeast, primarily the coastal states from Virginia south to Florida. Parts of those states have been officially 'pacified,' but in actuality there are still large-scale guerrilla movements there, even in the so-called 'pacified' areas.

"Starting this summer, they've been pushing for control of the western states in a big way. They have apparently decided to leave California and Arizona alone—at least for the time being—until they deal with the intermountain states. If and when they do get into California, they will face some tough resistance, especially in the northern half of the state, from the Harry Wu militia. They rightly predicted that the inland northwest would be a real burr under their saddle blanket. From what we've heard from the ham operators, things are nip and tuck over in Wyoming and Montana right now. The UN and Federal troops arrived there just about a month ago.

"Meanwhile, Colorado is only partly under their control. The Federals have been there since early last summer. It is kind of stalemate there. The

Federals control the big cities, while the militias control most of the small towns and the countryside. In the daytime the Federals control the highways too, but at night they belong to the militias. It's not much different than the situation that the Russians had in Afghanistan back in the '80s. Officially, the UN has declared Colorado 'pacified,' and they've declared 'victory' over the Colorado National Guard and the militias. But in reality, virtually all of the state, aside from the big cities and the open plains in the eastern part of the state, are still contested territory. I'm not sure how things will settle out in Wyoming and Montana, but my guess is that at least in the short term, it won't be too different than in Colorado.

"Now we have word that the Federals have started a sweep up through Utah and the banana belt in southern Idaho. A bunch of Quislings down there cut a deal with the Federals and UN 'peacekeepers' in exchange for what they are calling 'local autonomy.' They turned out to be a bunch of cooperative little slaves down there, all ready to roll over and play dead. How did Samuel Adams put it? 'I hope their chains rest lightly upon them when they bow down to lick the hand that feeds them.'" Todd paused for a moment and then went on. "On the advice of the Mormon church hierarchy in Salt Lake City, most of the LDS wards in Utah and southern Idaho have signed on with the Federales' local autonomy scheme. Just a few are resisting. In essence, though, there isn't a lot of organized resistance down there. Now by this please don't think that I'm denigrating the LDS church. I'm not. It's just their *current leadership* that has caved in.

"At last report, the Federals have two main forces in the west. They are calling them 'Corps' but they are actually more like divisional size. The First Corps is bogged down playing cat and mouse with the militias in Wyoming and Montana. Parenthetically, I should mention that we've heard that the Federals basically bypassed the Dakotas in their push west. They figured there wasn't enough population or resources worth bothering with, at least for now. They probably plan to double back and scarf them up after they secure the west coast.

"The Second Corps is the one heading our way. They have a huge convoy that is pushing north through Idaho, up Highway 95. From what I've heard, they've been hitting more and more resistance as they get farther and farther north. They just crawled up the White Bird Hill onto the Camas Prairie yesterday morning. They hit some highly organized resistance at Grangeville, and as of last night they were doing a blitzkrieg on Grangeville and surrounding small towns and farms. Parts of Grangeville burned down, from the latest reports." Those assembled murmured in dismay.

After waiting for the whispering to subside, Todd added, "What I was hearing on the CB relay net about their exact numbers and order of battle was garbled and even a bit contradictory, but that is the nature of raw intelligence

292

information. As near as we can tell, the Second Corps has got something like seven thousand men and nearly one thousand vehicles heading north on Highway 95." With that, Jeff Trasel let out a low "Wow!"

Gray continued, "Most of it is ground equipment, a mixture of U.S.-made, western European, and eastern European. Both Corps are composite, with a mixture of U.S. and UN units. Less than a year ago, the original Second Corps was divided into three parts. Two of those fractions went to form the nuclei of the Fourth and Fifth Corps, back east. Many of the Second Corps units have either been recently activated and filled with recruits, or are foreign units that are getting their first taste of fighting here in the states. The bottom line is that only about one-third of the Corps has much combat experience. We can probably use that to our advantage.

"The mix in the Second Corps is roughly 75 percent foreign, and 25 percent American. Oh yes, I should also mention, there are UN 'advisers' in each of the Federal units. The Second Corps only has a few helicopters, mainly for command and control. There are supposedly quite a few more helicopters presently with the First Corps over in Montana. They detached most of the Second Corps air wing to assist the First Corps. Yesterday I heard from a man who had binoculars on the convoy as it topped White Bird Hill, that for some reason they've got all their tracked vehicles loaded on some huge semi-truck Lo-Boy trailers...."

Doug Carlton, who was obviously getting agitated and itching to say something, raised his arm and said, "Sir, if you don't mind me interrupting, I know why." Todd turned his outstretched palm upward and toward Doug and replied, "By all means, go ahead, Doug. Please tell us anything you know that might help us—either strategically or tactically."

Todd took a step backward, and Carlton stood up and leaned on the barrel of his HK91. He drew a breath and said, "I was at Fort Knox, Kentucky, for ROTC Basic Camp. We had lots of briefings from each of the Army branches there. We had a chance to do some hands-on with some of their equipment, too. As I've told many of you before, my favorite day was field artillery day. We got a chance to actually prepare and fire some eighty-one-millimeter mortars and pull the lanyard on a 105 howitzer. They also put on a 'Mad Minute' firepower demonstration. That was a rush, let me tell ya. I'm sorry, for digressing. Anyway, the day we got our Armor branch briefing, they told us that operationally they put the tracked vehicles on either railroad flat cars or Lo-Boy trailers until they get close to the actual fighting. That reduces wear and tear on their tracks and suspension. By tracked vehicles, I'm referring to the M1A1 Abrams tanks, the track-mounted artillery, the M2 Bradley Infantry Fighting Vehicles, or 'IFVs,' the M3 Cavalry Fighting Vehicles, and the older M113 APCs."

"Eh–Pee–See?" Blanca Doyle asked quizzically.

Carlton turned to explain, "That stands for Armored Personnel Carrier. The M113 is on caterpillar tracks and carries a small squad of men. There is usually a Browning .50 machinegun on top, and optionally a couple of extra M60s. These older APCs have an inch and a half of aluminum armor. That'll stop most small arms. The newer Bradley IFVs carry a twin TOW missile pod, a twenty-five-millimeter chain gun, and a 7.62 coaxial machinegun. They have thicker armor with extra reactive armor panels on the sides to stop RPGs. The older APCs were basically a battlefield taxi. It rolls the infantry up to the front lines, the back door swings open, and they pour out. The Bradley is much more sophisticated, faster, and better armed. It weighs something like fifty thousand pounds. The M113, by comparison, only weighs a little over half of that. That twenty-five-millimeter cannon is nothing to mess with. Also, since most of the six infantrymen inside should have an individual 5.56 millimeter firing port weapon, they can fight either mounted or dismounted."

Doug hesitated for a moment and then said, "Well, strategically speaking, the Camas Prairie and Palouse Hills are mainly open and grassy, with just a few small stands of timber, mainly in the draws. Those are all real *tanker* country. They can cruise around wherever they want without any regard to staying on roads, at least in the summer months, when the fields and pastures are fairly dry. Up on those prairies, they've got line of sight to forever. It would be almost impossible to try to fight them there. It's not until you start getting into the heavy timber here in the eastern Palouse—east of Moscow, or in the upper reaches of the Clearwater River valley, that the tanks would start having mobility problems. When you get into thick timber and/or really steep terrain, virtually all the vehicles are forced to staying on established roads. That tends to funnel them into a few restricted avenues of approach."

Carlton stopped and scanned the semicircle of faces around him. "In fact, if we had known about their advance earlier, we could have organized and hit them down in the canyon lands, south of Riggins, before they came up onto the Camas. It's really steep and narrow down there and we could have bottled them up and really kicked some butt. Too late for that now. Like I say, between us and where they are right now, they're in tanker country. The only other place to conceivably stop them would be the Lewiston grade, before they come up out of the river confluence and onto the Palouse. But even if we had the time to gather a force—which we don't—that probably wouldn't work because there is no concealment on that grade for an ambush. They'd be able to spot us, stand off, and pound us with 'arty.'

"In terms of the route they will take as they continue northward, I would bet that they keep right on going up Highway 95. The other option, of course, is for them to take an axis to drop down into the Clearwater River valley on

Highway 13, and then go west on Highway 12 to Lewiston. From there, they could resume their original avenue of approach. A diversion into the eastern Clearwater River Valley could be very costly and time-consuming for them. It is restrictive terrain and therefore ready-made for ambushes and roadblocks. From what I've heard, Kamiah and Kooskia were big-time survivalist country before the Crunch. They have quite a large local militia structure developed down there these days."

Carlton shifted his feet, and went on. "A few moments ago, Todd was telling you about some folks down in the southern part of the state that have sold out to the Federals. The covenant communities up here in northern Idaho are mainly Mormon too, but there is no way that they are going to go along with any 'regional autonomy' scheme. They are dedicated patriots and will fight to the last man for their freedom. The Feds could get bogged down for weeks in that country, even if they do have seven thousand men in that division. So again, in my estimation, if the Feds have even halfway decent intel, they will consciously skip going through the upper Clearwater area—at least until they have the rest of Idaho under their thumb.

"The other thing that I want to mention is the risk of radio interception and radio direction finding. From here on out, we've got to assume that our CB transmissions are going to be monitored. They might even have some PRD-12 portable direction finders with them. If they have two direction finding sites operational in the area, and they coordinate with each other to get lines of bearing on us, they could pinpoint our transmitters in a matter of minutes. They call this direction finding 'DFing' for short. I saw a demonstration that an Army Reserve military intelligence company put on. That was at my ROTC Advanced Camp. They were calling in simulated artillery strikes within a couple of minutes after somebody keyed a microphone. I strongly suggest that we use strict radio silence unless in actual engagement from here on out. Using couriers is slower, but it sure beats getting DFed and having an artillery or MLRS barrage land on you. It can ruin your whole day.

"Any questions, or anything else you'd like my perspective on?" Doug asked.

"Yeah. If they do come straight up 95, how long 'til they get here?" Mary asked.

Carlton shrugged his shoulders, and answered, "That's not my bailiwick. Perhaps Todd or Mike could answer that."

Todd stepped forward and answered, "That is hard to say, Mary. I've talked this over quite a bit with Jeff, Doug, and Mike. Let me first digress to mention that, unfortunately, I made the mistake of giving our family name and mentioning the Northwest Militia and the Templars by name when I gave my little rebuttal speech a couple of years ago at the Moscow airport. I'm sure that that bastard Clarke made notes, and that they'll come looking for us. In retrospect, I don't regret speaking up, but I shouldn't have mentioned any names. Pretty stupid of me. I apologize. Oh well, hindsight is twenty-twenty. I suppose that I should have remembered the old Japanese proverb: 'The nail that sticks up gets hammered down.' It's hard to get a low profile back, once you've given yourself a high one. Once again, folks, I'm *very* sorry for shooting my mouth off."

Gray hesitated for a few moments, and kicked the hay at his feet. He blinked twice, looked up, and carried on. "Now getting back to your question … Mike and I concluded that the feces the Federals are presently in—down in Grangeville—will definitely slow their advance. Then they'll face some fighting in Lewiston, and then maybe even more in Moscow. From what we've heard, they are nice and friendly when there is no resistance. They just drop off their Administrators, tax collectors, and some garrison troops. They give the old 'We're with the government, and we're here to help' line. What a crock of bravo sierra. But when there *is* resistance in a town, the UN boys feel they have the green light to rape, plunder, and burn.

"When they end up looting a town," Gray added, "it can take a couple of days or more. Sometimes it's even three or four days before they can get the soldiers sobered-up, their pants zipped, and back on the road. Now assuming that they don't bypass us and keep going straight on up to Coeur d'Alene, I'd say that we have somewhere between four days and ten days before they get here. And, if by chance they do divert to make a sweep down the Clearwater, we could have three weeks or more to prepare. I agree with Doug, though. I don't think that the Feds will do that, so we aren't going to have the luxury of that extra time.

Gray then asked in a serious tone, "The next question, which I'd like to present to you all for a vote, is this: 'Do we melt back into the hills, fight them guerrilla-style, or just completely beat feet and disappear?' Let's see a show of hands. How many of you vote for the latter—for opting out and disappearing?"

Only Margie Porter raised her hand.

Gray then asked, "So, do we fight?" Everyone but Margie raised either their hands or their rifles with a mighty shout. He turned to face Mrs. Porter. "I can appreciate your reluctance, Margie, but consider this. If we did take off, where would we go? Unless they are stopped, the Feds will eventually conquer the lower forty-eight states. Then it will just be a matter of time before they consolidate their gains. Canada? I don't think so. Canada is part of the problem, not the solution. It was firmly in the socialist-slash-globalist camp even before the Crunch. We've heard that they've got UN 'peacekeepers' up there, too. Sooner or later, even Alaska will be on their list. Once they consolidate power, they'd eventually just track us down and exterminate us, no matter where we went. To them, we represent the old America—free, sovereign, and independent. The UN can't stomach having people like us around. What they don't realize is that we represent the quiet *majority* of the citizenry.

"Eventually people in the conquered states will rise up and put an end to the Hutchings puppet government, and kick out the UN. It is just a matter of time. As for me, I'm not willing to live as a slave and wait for that to happen. I'd rather start to make it happen myself." Doug Carlton shouted, "Oo-rah!" Gray continued. "The bottom line is that I'd rather die fighting on my own terms with a rifle in my hands, than to die whimpering and begging for mercy in some ditch with my hands tied behind my back." The men and women around him clapped and cheered. "Even if I die trying, my little boy there will grow up knowing that I at least *tried* to regain his freedom. I owe him that much." The metal walls of the barn reverberated with more applause, whistles, and shouts.

"Okay, then, here is my basic plan, at least off the top of my head, but as always, I'm open to suggestions. I propose that we evacuate both retreats and regroup temporarily at a place that Mike picked out a few miles from here, up in the National Forest. He found it when he was leading a security patrol last April. From what he's told me it's a good defensible location, well away from any roads, and it's in heavy timber for concealment. There is a good-sized level opening where we should be able to land the Doyles' Star Streaks." Nelson gave a thumbs-up in agreement.

Todd nodded back to Nelson and continued, "We'll use that valley as our initial base of operations. Within a few days, though, we will probably want to split back into two separate organizations and locate and operate independently. We wouldn't want to put all of our eggs in one basket. There is the chance that the Feds will have aircraft with FLIR pods, so I want to keep our signature small. Ten-man squads at most. If we pick up any recruits, we should start breaking up into smaller independent cells to stay under that ten-man threshold. Luckily, the hills are crawling with deer and elk, so there will be lots of false thermal targets to confuse them. If and when the Federals do get here, they will no doubt want to absolutely level our house and barn, and probably Kevin's too, just as 'examples.' I don't want to be in their sights when that happens. These Federals have no compunctions about throwing their weight around."

Ian Doyle chimed in. "I first heard about these goons when I was in Arizona. And I heard some more about them when we were in Utah, on our way up here. As far as I'm concerned, these Federals are no better than looters. They're just better armed and organized. They wear the cloak of legitimacy, but there's nothing legitimate about them. They're just another band of thugs, flying that Tidy-Bowl blue UN flag."

He continued, "Our two planes are available for recon, of course. And, I've also got some other goodies down in the basement." He thrust up a forefinger and blurted out, "Wait! I'll be right back." He left the barn abruptly leaving most of those gathered wondering what could be so important that he had to miss part of the meeting. While he was gone, the militia members started chattering among themselves about contingency plans and G.O.O.D. kits.

Doyle returned to the briefing after just a few minutes. Laying a bulky olive drab nylon duffel bag on the floor of the barn, he proclaimed, "Well, here they are. There are five of them. Well, originally I had seven, but therein lies a long story all in itself. I'll just make it simple and say that I've got five left. They are all, the later 'A2' model. I broke them down into halves so they'd fit here in the duffel." Doyle started to unwrap the front assemblies and rear assemblies of what at first glance looked like later-model Colt Sporters, padded by his extra sets of ACUs and BDUs.

As he continued to talk, he laid out the halves in pairs on the floor of the barn, and then began assembling them, snapping their pivot pins into place. "I got these gems from the AP's arms room, along with three Beretta M9 pistols. They were the last guns still in there. Unfortunately, there was no small arms ammo left on base. They only kept a small quantity onhand for base security, and that had been cleaned out when the APs left. The nearest ammo supply point was way the heck down at Fort Huachuca. Luckily, I had a few hundred rounds of commercial .223 at home, plus three .50 caliber ammo cans full of nine-millimeter ball, tracer, and soft nose." He added with a smile, "In case you are wondering, I did indeed sign Uncle Sugar a hand receipt for these guns. Heck, if I hadn't put them in safekeeping, who knows whose hands they'd be in by now."

Doyle went on, "The reason I ran to go get these was because I just had the idea of mounting these in a rack in the front of one of the Larons with some sort of remote firing mechanism. With five of them firing simultaneously, I could do some major Van-dammage. Oh yeah! My Star Streak will be C-A-S capable."

"What's C-A-S?" Lon asked.

Doyle turned toward him and replied, "C-A-S stands for Close Air Support."

Lon Porter eyed the M16s and stroked his chin and said forthrightly, "No sweat, I can probably fab that up for you in a day or two."

Mike Nelson added, "What about our M60? Could we build a mounting bracket for it on the other Star Streak?"

"Why not?" Doyle laughed. "We can have two armed birds in the air at the same time that way. Mounting the M60 should be even easier than mounting these sixteens. It'll be just like the old days, Todd. We'll just cut to size, file to fit, and paint to match!"

CHAPTER 25
Egress

"Stand your ground.
Don't fire unless fired upon;
But if they mean to have a war,
Let it begin here!"

—*Captain John Parker, Lexington Minute Company, April 19, 1775*

Just after the morning meeting, Mike Nelson and Ian hiked up to reconnoiter the new base of operations. They scouted a small valley four miles to the east that Mike had picked out months before. Ian said that the meadow in the center of the valley looked fine for landings. They walked the length and width of the meadow several times, looking for landing gear obstructions. They found none. The pair hiked back to the retreat, had a hurried lunch, and pre-flighted Ian's Laron. The flight to the valley took only a few minutes. They both wanted to see what the site would look like from the air. Ian made a test landing in the meadow. Before they took off again, Mike left his HK91 wrapped in a poncho, with his web gear harness lying beside it, in a thick clump of trees just beyond the east edge of the meadow. It was the first of what would soon become a small mountain of equipment. The site would soon be known as the militia's tactical command post or "TAC-CP." As they walked back to the plane, Nelson remarked, "I think we'll call this place Valley Forge."

The remainder of the two companies spent the day and evening in feverish preparation. The first order of business was for every individual at both retreats to repack their "G.O.O.D." backpacks. Lon Porter, Mike Nelson, and the Doyles consumed their next two days mounting the five M16s on Ian's Laron, and the M60 on Blanca's. There was no way to mount the guns in the cramped noses, and mounting them on the planes' fragile wings looked very difficult. The solution was simply to remove the planes' canopies and mount the guns in the front seat area, with their muzzles protruding over the front lips of the cockpits. A large narrow bin was constructed of sheet metal to hold the ammunition belt for the M60. When belts of ammo were linked together continuously and loaded into the bin, it was found that it would accommodate one thousand and sixty rounds.

In the case of the M60, the firing mechanism was made with a bicycle cable and the gearshift lever from Mary's ten-speed. The bike was in disuse, since its tires had partly rotted out and replacements were unavailable. For the five M16s, the fire control mechanism took five separate triggering rods, all linked together on a common axis bar. It in turn was linked by a "traveling arm" to a firing lever mounted on the front of the left armrest of the rear seat. Using scrap metal and more parts from the rack on Mary's bicycle, Lon built this mechanism in less than three hours. The sights were a home-brew affair, made out of six-inch-long sections of Schedule 40 one-and-one-half-inch white plastic water pipe, with crosshairs made out of stiff wire at the front of each. These tubes were attached to the gun mountings using bolts and fender washers. Stacks of washers were gradually built up until the point of aim in the crosshairs matched the bore-sight view. Test firing confirmed the point of impact.

Lon completed the mountings by fabricating brass catchers out of scrap sheet metal. He primarily used the front panel of Kevin Lendel's disused electric dishwasher, and license plates that had been taken off of the various cars and trucks at the retreat. The catchers would serve to both save the fired brass and links for reloading, and to prevent fired brass from causing any damage to the planes, or getting underfoot inside the planes.

Since the Larons had dual controls, it was simple enough to fly them from the rear seat. This required repositioning the throttles. It was a long reach to hit the starter switches, since there were no equivalents in the rear seats, and the visibility from the rear seats was not as good as from the front. The instruments were largely out of view as well, particularly on the green Laron with the wide M16 mounting rack. However, Doyle expected that the upcoming flights would be all "seat of the pants" flying anyway. Without the canopy, the slipstream would be tremendous at full throttle, but manageable in slow flight. The Doyles were given two pairs of the Grays' army surplus "Goggle: Sun, Wind, and Dust" to compensate for the lack of canopies.

The gun mounts themselves were a marvel of quickly improvised tube bending, machining, and welding. The mount for the M16s bolted directly onto the rifle's receiver extension tubes. It was found that in order to save space, the buttstocks and pistol grips would have to be removed. The removal of the buttstocks left the threaded buttstock hole available at the back end of each receiver extension. An eighth-inch-thick plate of two-inch-wide steel was drilled for these bolt holes. The missing pistol grips meant that there was nothing to hold the selector switch springs and detents in place. Rather than fabricate something special, it was expedient just to tape the selector switches in the "Burst" position. This kept them from falling out of the receivers.

The forward mounting point for each of the M16s was their forward pivot-pin hole. These pins (along with their springs and detents) were removed, and long carriage bolts were put in their place. These same bolts bisected a piece of tubular steel. It in turn tied into the main framework. Once assembled, the entire mount could be removed with the guns intact by simply unclamping four bolts. This, Lon predicted, would simplify cleaning the guns. The brass catching bins were assembled and mounted separately. They, too, could be removed easily if need be. They also had clever sliding metal doors at the bottom that allowed the fired brass to be shoveled out into a sack. The hand-guards of the five M16s were removed to provide better airflow for cooling.

Almost as an afterthought, Lon mounted Video 8 camcorders that belonged to the Grays and Kevin Lendel on each of the planes, using one-quarter-twenty bolts. It was Kevin Lendel who made the effort to mount the cameras. He explained, "The only way to counter the Federals' propaganda is with the truth, and what better truth to show than some exciting gun camera footage?" A third camera, from Pastor Dave's house, was borrowed to document any upcoming ground engagements. Charging the two sets of batteries for each camera took two days.

For the test firing, the M16s were fired in their semiauto mode, and the M60 was fired in a few brief bursts, in order to conserve ammo. Operationally, the M16s would be used in their "burst" mode. To those assembled for the test firing, Doyle explained, "The M16A2 has a three-position selector, just like the older A1s, but the third position produces a three-shot burst setting instead of traditional full auto. Instead of teaching troops proper fire discipline, the military decided to solve the 'spray and pray' problem by making a mechanical change to the rifle. The A2 selector mechanism has a little ratchet that clocks up to three and then stops the burst. You get subsequent bursts by releasing the trigger and pulling it over again. Pretty nifty technology, but a sad statement on the caliber of Army, Navy, and Air Force volunteers. It's sad, in my opinion, that they needed three-shot burst control technology to begin with. It should have been a training issue." He shook his head in dismay, and then went on. "Anyway, we will be using the burst setting. With thirty-round magazines, that will give us ten bursts of three shots each on each sortie. With five guns on line, that's fifteen rounds per burst. Should do the trick, eh?"

Lon asked Doyle, "You don't expect those M16s to stop tanks and APCs, do you?"

Ian shook his head and replied, "No, these M16s and the M60 are for antipersonnel use, and perhaps against unarmored vehicles. You'll need to figure out something else to stop tanks and APCs."

Doug Carlton smiled. "Don't worry, Ian. We have a goodly supply of thermite grenades and Molotov cocktails for that. We assembled them a year and a half ago."

The Doyles spent three full days ferrying supplies to Valley Forge in both of the Star Streaks. It required twenty-five round-trip flights. Landing at the meadow on the first ferrying trip, Ian and Blanca unbolted the guns from their planes to make room for cargo. On the subsequent flights, they carried fuel and oil—a total of fourteen five-gallon cans of unleaded premium and a case of forty-weight motor oil. Next was ammunition. They took all of the M60 belt links and more than half of the remaining .308 and .223 ammunition still available at both retreat houses. This totaled almost twenty-four thousand rounds. The last ferry trips carried, food, tents, sleeping bags, and cold weather gear. After that, the canopies were removed again and the guns were remounted and reloaded.

While the work on the planes went on, large quantities of gear were hauled to Valley Forge on pack boards, with garden carts, or on the Porters' sturdy mountain bikes. The bikes proved particularly useful. They were better at negotiating the rough terrain than the garden carts, and could haul nearly as much. Most of the loads were slung in stuff sacks on both sides of the center of the bike frames and on the panniers. It was impossible to ride the bikes when they were so loaded down, but walking alongside them was easy enough. The bikes could each carry two hundred pounds or more per trip.

In all, it took more than fifty round-trips to haul the supplies to Valley Forge. The militia members were careful to take numerous routes so that they wouldn't leave a distinguishable trail. After making several trips, Mary commented that it would have been prudent to establish a cache many months before. She remarked to Margie, "Just imagine if we didn't have a few days' warning like this? We'd be S.O.L.! And what if we had to beat feet in the dead of winter, even *if* we had some warning? There would be no way to move this much gear in just a few days. We should have pre-positioned half of our food, fuel, and ammunition at an off-site cache a long time ago. That way we wouldn't have to rush to move it all at once. We're very lucky that we got away with putting all our eggs in one basket for so long."

As the heaps of supplies grew under the trees at Valley Forge, they were covered by camouflage nets. Fortunately, the Grays and other group members had the foresight to buy dozens of waterproof containers before the Crunch. They were essential for keeping the weapons, ammunition, food, and field gear dry outdoors. The ammunition and links were stored in Army surplus ammo cans, mainly .30 and .50 caliber size. Much of the clothing and field gear was stored in light green "Bill's Bags" and Paragon Portage Packs. These were whitewater rafting "dry bags"—waterproof rubberized duffel bags—that Todd and Mary had purchased before the Crunch from Northwest River Supplies in Moscow. Some of the heavier items were carried in forest green Rubbermaid plastic storage bins.

Most prized for hauling and storage were the watertight "York Pack" hard portage packs that belonged to the Nelsons and Trasels. These were roughly the size of the Rubbermaid containers but completely watertight, and equipped with detachable shoulder straps. They were perfect for moving equipment to the new field site and ensuring that it would be protected from the elements. Everyone who saw the York packs wished that they owned a few, too. Firearms were stored in either hard Pelican cases or soft "Gun Boat" cases. Both were waterproof.

There would be just enough room for everyone to sleep in the low-profile two-man tents that were widely scattered under the trees. All of them were at least partially concealed under suspended camouflage nets. Most of the tents were either the Moss Stardome II or Little Dipper models. In the years before the Crunch, Moss was known as the country's finest manufacturer of expedition-quality four-season tents. Unfortunately, the standard colors for the Moss tents were light tan and red. In 1995, however, at the behest of one distributor, Moss began making up the tents in custom colors. They did several short production runs with dark tan material instead of red, and with forest green "rain flys" instead of tan. It was from these batches that Todd's group equipped themselves. The tents were so far superior to their existing tents that everyone bought the Moss Stardome IIs and Little Dippers. Most of their older tents were retained for spares.

The goats and sheep at the retreat were herded to Valley Forge. Their senior doe goat, their buck, their senior ewe, and their ram were tethered individually near the creek. The rest of the small goatherd and sheep flock stayed close to them.

Within hours after word of the approaching Federals began to circulate, the dozens of small militias in the region activated. In just a two-day period, nine of the militias were given an enormous quantity of food and equipment by the Northwest Militia. Most of this issue was termed a "long-term loan" with no firm expectation that it would ever be returned. Including previous distributions to the militias, by Todd's accounting, they handed out 21 guns with cleaning kits, 118,500 rounds of ammunition, more than 100 magazines of various types and capacities, 12 improvised Claymore mines, 46 improvised thermite grenades, 157 Molotov cocktails, 11 first aid kits, 3 backpacks, 12 duffel bags, 4 sleeping bags, 8 ponchos, 6 army shelter half-tents, and 23 sets of web gear. Mike's Morgan mare and saddle were loaned to a member of the Bovill Blue Blaze Irregulars, because they operated mainly on horseback, but were short two horses.

Mike allowed that they could make better use of the horse than he could.

In addition to logistics, the local militias (or "maquis" as some of them called themselves) were given updated detailed information on rally points.

They were told to strike any Federal or UN targets of opportunity within their areas of operations, at will. They were warned to keep their radio transmissions to an absolute minimum, or better yet, to leave their radios turned off altogether. They were also reminded not to write down any of the information or mark any maps with the information they were given. It was, as always, all to be committed to memory. This way, if any of them were captured or killed, it would deny the Federals any useful intelligence.

Six days after their initial warning, Terry got word over the CB that the Federals had arrived in Moscow. It was on that same day that some of the bulky equipment that couldn't be easily moved from the retreats such as the dehydrator, PV panels, radio equipment, deep cycle batteries, gardening tools, Lon's lathe, and the bicycle/generator were placed in the LP/OP fortifications at each retreat. Many of the Grays' personal mementos such as photo albums were stored there, as well. This gear was tightly packed and filled the LP/OPs up to the ceiling. Then the LP/OPs were carefully waterproofed with Visqueen, and their gun ports and entrances were buried. Finally, the fresh earth was camouflaged with sod that was cut more than a hundred yards away from each of the bunkers. This process turned the LP/OPs into oversized caches.

Realizing that their house and property would probably be singled out for the wrath of the Federals, the Grays' tractor was driven to the Andersen's barn for safety. All of the other vehicles, except Mary's VW, were gassed up and dispersed on logging roads within a few miles of the retreats. They were left empty, aside for some spare full gasoline cans. Mike reminded everyone to use their field SOP for hiding the ignition keys: The key was placed on the ground in front of the left front tire. Then the clutch pedal was punched in briefly, allowing the wheel to roll over the key to conceal it. In this way, if anyone from the Northwest Militia needed to use any of the vehicles, they would immediately know where to find its key.

Before making their final evacuation, Todd asked Lon, Mike, and Lisa to stay back at his house to help him with some final preparations. Everyone else left, carrying their final backpack loads to Valley Forge. Shona went with this increment. The bitch had gone on security patrols many times, so she was trained to stay close and stay quiet. The Doyles flew their planes to the valley with their last loads. These loads included the TA-1 field telephones, a meat saw, gambrels, a gutbucket, cookware, and eating utensils. Many of these items had been overlooked before. Once there, Ian and Blanca dismounted their planes' wings and tails, and wheeled the fuselages into the trees and concealed all their parts under camouflage nets.

The final work at the Grays' house took a full day. When they were done, Todd stopped to give his helpers each a hug, and he read the 91st Psalm aloud. In the distance, they could hear the crump of mortar shells landing. Mike commented, "Sounds like they are well off to the west, out beyond Bovill. Troy, maybe."

Todd grasped Mike's hand and shook it firmly. "Good luck, Mike. If things go as I predict, I should see you at Valley Forge in two to four days. If I get there and find you've beat feet, I will go with the assumption that you are heading toward rally point blue, below Mica Mountain. And then if you aren't there either, I'll come looking for you or a message in the 'dead drop' at rally point green."

Todd looked Nelson in the eye and implored, "Now just on the outside chance that I don't make it, promise me that you will help care for Mary and my little boy."

Mike replied somberly, "You have my solemn word, boss. I'll make sure that they are safe and sound. If you don't make it back, I'll provide for them." With that, Mike, Rose, and Lisa turned and headed east, in ranger file.

Todd shouldered his pack, and picked up his HK. He paused to turn in a slow full circle, looking at his farm. "To lose all this. What a crying shame," he said aloud. Then he headed for the point on the ridgeline he had selected and prepared, seven-hundred-and-fifty yards to the southwest.

· · ·

Roger Dunlap had bulled ahead with his decision for everyone to stay at the Templar retreat. Despite vociferous arguments from others in his group, Dunlap decided that the odds were that the Federals would head straight north from Moscow, and bypass Troy and Bovill. As Dunlap saw it, there was no way that they could evacuate if they wanted to, anyway. Their cars and trucks weren't working. They had several horses, but some of the group members were in no condition to walk or even ride. Three of their members were sick in bed, ill with a particularly virulent stomach flu. Another was pregnant, and a week past her due date.

When they first got word of the Federals in Grangeville, Dunlap had ordered slit trenches to be dug on three sides of the ranch house. When they got to Lewiston, he agreed to set up a cache of supplies a mile south of the ranch house. When the Federals arrived in Moscow, he agreed to let one young couple from the group, Tony and Teesha Washington, go to "babysit" the cache. Everyone else agreed to stay, most of them convinced—or at least hoping—that they would be bypassed. They hoped that they would be overlooked long enough for their ill to recover, and for their expecting mom to deliver.

A cavalry motorcycle scout zoomed down the county road near 2 p.m. He slowed when he came to the Dunlaps' gate, and then sped up again. The Templars' gate guard, hidden in an LP/OP near the county road, radioed in a report. Everyone who was able immediately went to their assigned trenches. The sick, elderly, and children stayed in the house. They waited.

Just after 4 p.m., they could hear many vehicles maneuvering down the county road, and on the logging roads to the south and west. They weren't in line of sight to the house or the gate guard. Then the sound of the engines stopped.

Wes, the retired signalman, scampered down the connecting trench line to Dunlap. He pointed a finger in Dunlap's face and said, "You're a fool, Roger! I told you that we should have built a travois or two! We could have had everybody up at the cache two days ago!"

Dunlap was momentarily speechless. He stared at Wes, and finally blurted out, "I'm so sorry."

Moments later, they heard the distinctive thuds of mortars being launched, far off in the timber.

"See, I told you so," Wes said sourly. Along with the others, Wes instinctively curled up in the bottom of his trench.

It took a long time for the first mortar shells to land. With their high parabolic flight, it took almost twenty seconds from the time they hit the bottom of the tubes until they landed. To the Templars, the long delay seemed like an eternity.

The first rounds fell long, on the north side of the house. The eighty-one-millimeter shells went off with a roar and threw up huge clouds of dust. They had all been set to "HE Quick," so they went off immediately after impact. They missed the trenches on the north side of the house by just a few yards.

On a hill seven hundred yards to the south, a young sergeant E-5 named Valentine from a fire support team was talking on a battered old PRC-77 field radio, and peering through a pair of cheap Simmons binoculars. With practiced precision, he intoned, "Drop one hundred."

The voice on the radio rejoined, "Shot, over."

Valentine tersely replied, "Shot, out."

There was a pause, and then the second barrage came. The rounds fell between twenty and sixty feet short of the trenches on the south side of the house. Dunlap's men and women covered their heads and got as low in their trenches as possible. Rocks and dirt showered down on them. Some of them started to scream.

Sergeant Valentine watched the impacting rounds, and keyed the microphone. "Add fifty. Fire for effect."

The next barrage continued for a full minute. Round after round landed in and around the ranch house.

Valentine surveyed the impacts, and again keyed the microphone. Still looking through the binoculars, he again keyed the handset. "Reee-peat."

Another minute-long barrage started. Fire broke out in the house. Soon there was a fire in the barn, too. Some of the rounds fell directly into the trenches.

The young NCO called in another laconic "Reee-peat."

The south wall of the house collapsed. The house and barn were now engulfed in flames.

The mortars fell silent, and the last of the rounds whistled in. Sergeant Valentine picked up the handset and commanded, "Cease fire. Tell your section well done. Good shooting, fellas." Then he reached into his ALICE pack and pulled out a silver tube with a white paper label. It was one-and-a-half inches in diameter, and a foot long. He pulled off its metal cap, and slipped it back onto the other end of the tube. Then, turning his head, he slapped the bottom of the tube on the ground. With a loud whoosh, a signal rocket roared out of the launcher. A moment later a green star cluster burst in the sky. In the distance, far off in the timber, he could hear two signal whistles blowing.

Two survivors crawled up from the trenches and ran. Only one of them had his rifle with him.

Alpha Company of the 519th Infantry Battalion began to move by bounds toward the objective. The platoons deployed on line and started to make their sweep. The two men who had run from the trenches were cut down by three bursts from an M249 squad automatic weapon.

When the troops were in the open areas south of the burning remains of the ranch house, Ted Wallach popped his head out of his trench. He began to fire an M1A rifle. He hit two of the infantrymen from the first platoon in rapid succession at a range of two hundred yards. Then Wallach was in turn hit in the head by a hail of return rifle fire.

After a sweep across the objective, in which the bottoms of the trenches were sprayed with fully automatic fire, the squads set up a defensive perimeter. Weapons that were recovered from the trenches were laid out in the circular drive. Beside them were the bodies of the two Federal soldiers that were killed, shrouded in body bags. A second more thorough search revealed the LP/OP. The bunker was hit by three grenades fired by an M203. The third one went through the door, killing the single sentry in it. The Templars that had died outside the house were left where they lay.

Captain Brian Tompkins, the Alpha company commander, looked tired. He sat down in the dirt next to the outhouse—the only structure left standing at the Templar retreat—and consulted his map. He jotted down a note in a small memo pad, laid a clear plastic protractor over the map, and jotted down another note. Then he waggled his forefinger at his radioman in a come-hither motion. The radioman got up from his prone position immediately. Out of habit, he handed Tompkins the dog-eared Communications-Electronics Operating Instructions (CEOI) notebook that he kept on a lanyard around his neck beneath his ACUs. The CEOI had not been changed in nearly six months. Brian Tompkins leafed through the CEOI, skipping past the frequencies and call signs. The CEOI had been unchanged for so long that he had them memorized. He turned to the TAC code section, looked up the three letter code for administrative pickup, and made another quick notation in his memo pad. Then, he reached for the radio handset and called in a brief report: "Kilo one seven, this is Bravo fife niner, over."

The battalion's duty radio operator replied, "Bravo fife niner, this is Kilo one seven. Go ahead."

Tompkins spoke slowly and clearly. "Prepare to copy...Objective Oak taken. Estimate one-niner enemy KIAs. Zero captured. Two friendly KIAs. S-1 report to follow. Send Hotel Yankee Mike to grid golf oscar fife niner eight three two fife one one. I say again, Grid golf oscar fife niner eight three two fife one one, to recover two-four captured weapons, three property booked weapons, and two bagged friendly KIAs. No intel sources available. Continuing to bivouac point Crimson. ETA four zero mikes."

"Please say again all after: 'S-1 report to follow.'"

Tompkins rolled his eyes at the radioman, who smiled and shook his head. Then Tompkins repeated the missed part of his report, even more slowly. "I say again: Send Hotel Yankee Mike team to grid golf oscar fife niner eight three two fife one one, for administrative recovery of two-four captured weapons, three property booked weapons, and two body-bagged friendly KIAs. No intelligence sources available. Continuing to bivouac point Crimson. ETA four zero mikes."

"Roger that."

The company commander keyed the handset again and blurted, "Bravo fife niner, out."

The battalion radioman echoed back, "Kilo one seven, out."

Tompkins passed the handset to his radioman. He said wearily, "You know, Specialist, this whole thing stinks. What the heck are we doing out here in Idaho shooting at more civilians? How many women and children do we have to kill before we're done? And how many of us are gonna die? We just lost two more good men, and for what?"

The radioman didn't answer. He was wearing a thousand-mile stare.

After a few moments, Captain Tompkins waved his arm in a "forward" motion to his platoon leaders.

They in turn motioned their platoon sergeants forward, and within moments the entire company was on its feet and moving east, in a traveling overwatch formation.

As they started forward, Tompkins muttered to himself, "Curse the New World Order, and the pale horse it rode in on. I pray to God that this ends soon."

• • •

Todd Gray devoted the next morning to deep meditative prayer. He spent much of his time reading Psalms from his pocket-sized King James Bible. Not long after noon, a mechanized infantry company approached his land. Two motorcycle scouts paused at the gate at the bottom of the hill. One of them shot off the padlock on the gate with an Uzi. Then they roared up the hill and dismounted behind the barn. Looking through his binoculars, Todd could see that they were both armed with Uzis. They were wearing uniforms in a flecked camouflage pattern that Todd didn't recognize. As they crouched behind the barn, one of them pulled a walkie-talkie from his belt and gave a report.

The armored personnel carriers arrived few minutes later. They were Russian built BTR-70s that had previously been part of the former East German National People's Army (NVA) inventory. Todd had expected German soldiers to be driving Marders or Luchs APCs. Then he realized that what he was looking at was a ragtag force that was put together in the wake of the Crunch in Europe. They were equipped with whatever was available at the time. The aging eight-wheeled machines had originally been painted gray-green by the NVA, then white by the UN, and were more recently repainted a flat olive drab green to make them more tactical. They were prominently marked "UNPROFOR" in black paint on the sides, and "UN" on the back. The latest coat of paint was starting to peel and wear off. Some of the white paint beneath was beginning to show, mainly on the high points and inside the wheel wells.

Most of the APCs stopped at wide intervals on the county road. Two continued through the gate to the Grays' circular driveway. They quickly disgorged one eight-man squad each. These squads searched the barn and shop, and then, hesitantly, tried to search the house. The lock on the chain-link fence around the house was not a big obstacle. One burst from an HK G36 shattered the lock and chain. The locked front door would be more difficult, as would the heavy steel window shutters. Todd chuckled when he saw the soldiers try to kick the door down. He whispered, "Knock yourselves out, guys."

The rear doors of all of the APCs at the county road opened up and squad after squad of infantry ambled up the hill. They were dressed in a motley assortment of German *Flecktarn* camouflage, Woodland BDUs, and the later-issue ACU digital camouflage pattern U.S. Army uniforms. Some of the soldiers, Todd noticed, had their HK rifles and various SMGs slung across their backs. Some were even smoking cigarettes. Todd clucked his tongue and whispered, "Ah, yes, just another casual day of looting for the Bundeswehr." One soldier unbolted a pick from the assortment of pioneer tools on the side of one of the waiting APCs and began to assail the door. Even from the long distance, Todd could hear the banging of the pick, and cursed shouts.

As the door was being attacked by one squad of soldiers, the others began to lose patience. One trooper hosed the Winco windmill with long bursts from an HK-21 light machinegun. Another shot out the tires of Mary's VW with a HK G36 5.56 mm rifle, and then started shooting chickens that scuttled around the barn. The dwindling flock ran around the barn twice before the soldier finally tired of the game and let the rest go.

After several minutes, the German soldiers gave up with the pick. Next, they tried opening the door with a Russian-made disposable RPG-18 rocket propelled grenade launcher. The rocket went through the middle of the door, leaving a neat hole two inches in diameter, but to the surprise of the soldiers, the door still didn't budge. A second RPG was carried over from the BTR and was aimed at the right side of the doorframe. It took the door completely off its hinges. The Germans spent the next few minutes putting out a small fire that the RPGs had started inside the house. After the smoke started to clear, a steady stream of soldiers went into the house, looking for loot.

Closely watching the house with his Steiner binoculars, Todd counted thirty-two soldiers entering the house. Even at this distance, he could tell by their arm gestures that two of the men who went into the house were either senior NCOs or officers. Despite the large quantity of logistics that had been evacuated, there was still plenty in the house to interest the soldiers.

Todd waited until he saw the first soldier come back out the door. Then Gray whispered, "Okay you goons, you want my house and everything in it? Well then, it's all yours!" Then he pressed a button on the panel in front of him. The house erupted in flames with a tremendous roar. Six sticks of dynamite hidden in separate parts of the house detonated simultaneously. Each of the six was taped to the seam on a five-gallon can of gasoline. Two of the cans were hidden at the ends of the attic, one beneath the kitchen range, one beneath the hide-a-bed, and two in the basement. The combined explosion was so powerful that it sent several of the heavy metal window shutters flying more than thirty feet outwards. The roof of the house split into two halves, and landed on either side of the house, engulfed in flames. A huge ball of fire rose from the house, billowing upward in a mushroom cloud. It gradually turned to black, then to gray as it rose higher in the sky. Todd smiled in satisfaction.

Knowing in advance that the vast majority of the gasoline wouldn't be fully vaporized, Todd hadn't expected such a dramatic explosion. Todd recalled from a college chemistry course that one gallon of gasoline could have the explosive force of fourteen sticks of dynamite, under optimal conditions. He had expected at best a one-percent yield of the potential explosive force of the six gallons of gas in the house. He knew that most of the gas would simply burn, and that only a fraction would become a true fuel-air explosive. The result, however, was far better than he expected.

A dozen of the troops that had been loitering away from the house when the explosion occurred ran into the shop to escape falling debris. Todd pressed another button on the Mr. Destructo panel. This time, three more cans of gasoline as well as the small remaining quantity of gas in the underground gasoline tank under the shop were detonated. The corrugated roof of the barn flipped over to land back on its base. "That's good riddance to bad rubbish," Todd cursed. The fireball from the shop immediately set the barn on fire, too. Fueled by the hay piled up inside, it was soon a mass of flames.

Around the house, the remaining German soldiers were in a panic. Most ran back toward the APCs at the county road. Three of them dived for cover behind a downed tree. Todd gave a thin-lipped smile and consulted his revised sector sketch. He hit another button, firing the fougasse that covered the area behind the fallen tree. It went off with a roar, shredding the three soldiers.

The pair of BTR-70s that were parked in the barnyard started their engines in rapid succession. The few surviving troops near the shop and barn piled into each of them. As they started toward the road, the 14.5 mm machine-gunner in one of the APCs fired his weapon in angry long bursts. Todd estimated that he fired more than a hundred rounds at the nearby hilltops. Two gunners in BTRs on the county road picked up the cue and began pouring fire into the Anderson's house and barn across the road.

As the first of the two BTR-70s neared the county road, Todd watched carefully through his binoculars. When he thought their position looked right, he triggered the vertical fougasse. At first Todd thought that he had hit the button too early, since the explosion went off under the BTR's front wheels. The twenty-two-thousand-pound vehicle didn't move perceptibly upward with the blast. The APC continued to roll forward briefly, then stopped. Smoke began billowing out of it. Some of the German soldiers ran toward the BTR. Two of them opened one of the back doors, hoping to help any survivors get out. They were greeted only by deep red flames and clouds of thick black smoke.

The fire in the APC grew more intense. By now, twenty German soldiers were milling around the back of the burning BTR-70. The BTR's rubber wheels caught fire, and then the 14.5 mm rounds and grenades inside the APC began to cook off. Fearing the explosions, the gaggle of soldiers instinctively backpedaled up the Grays' driveway. Todd couldn't believe his luck. He reached down and punched the button for the first of the fougasses that Mike had built. Chunks of scrap metal, short lengths of chain, and broken glass ripped through the cluster of soldiers, cutting down nine of them at once, like a huge invisible *djinn* hand. The survivors from this blast ran to the remaining intact BTRs, dragging two wounded soldiers with them.

All along the road, the drivers of the BTR-70s fired up their engines. Most of the 14.5 mm gunners rotated their turrets, firing in long wild bursts at the tree lines, mainly to the east. The AGS-17 gunners joined in, firing their thirty-millimeter automatic grenade launchers in seemingly random fusillades. The firing went on for several minutes. Todd smiled and laughed out loud, over-whelmed by the enormity of the expenditure of ammunition that was going on at the road below. Todd could also see fully-automatic small-arms fire coming from the firing ports on several of the BTRs.

The grenades and 14.5 mm tracers were igniting sporadic grass and brush fires. He realized that any moment one of the grenades might land next to him, but still he laughed. To his surprise, none of the rounds came within fifty yards of his position. Scanning with his binoculars, Todd could see the APCs remained parked during the firing. The Andersen's house and barn, he saw, were now fully engulfed in flames. In the midst of the roar of gunfire Todd susserated, "Go ahead. Burn up your ammo. Knock yourselves out. You're as green as grass. Sound and fury, hitting nothing. Burn it up! Burn it up boys. As for me, I think I'll save my ammo for precisely aimed fire at distinct targets, thank you very much."

After a while, the tempo of firing noticeably slackened and then nearly stopped. Todd fired off the remaining fougasses in rapid succession, even though there were no targets in front of them. Todd laughed and mockingly whispered to himself, "Vee are surrounded!" The gunners on the BTRs started shooting wildly again, and there was even more intense small-arms fire from the gun ports. Finally, the rate of fire slacked off again, and the column of BTR-70s started up the road, leaving the burning BTR behind. A few of the gunners still fired off unaimed bursts to either side of the road. Todd watched through his Steiners as they continued up the road until they were out of sight. "Run away! Run away!" Todd mouthed soundlessly. Todd heard their engines gradually receding in the distance. Then, all that he could hear was the crackle and occasional pop of the fires. Dozens of small brush fires were blazing in a thousand-yard semicircle around the remains of Todd's house.

Todd waited and watched. Most of the brush fires burned out quickly. A few on the drier southern-facing hillsides continued to burn longer. These too burned out when they reached the ridge tops. Luckily, none of them had been immediately below his position. The valley was still largely shrouded in smoke. As sunset approached, the fires at his house and at the Andersen's house were nearly out. They were still smoking heavily, but there were just a few spots of open flames.

• • •

Two hours after it was dark, Todd quietly disconnected the WD-1 wires from the Mr. Destructo panel, and wrapped it in his poncho.

He shouldered his pack and picked up the panel and his rifle. The smell of smoke was heavy in the air. Todd snorted quietly to clear his nostrils. He realized that the Germans might have left a "stay behind," so he didn't dare try to approach the house site to look for abandoned weapons. That could wait for another day. Todd silently and methodically started to hike in a circuitous route toward Valley Forge.

As he strode on, he quietly hummed the tune of one of his favorite songs, an old Shaker hymn, "How Can I Keep From Singing?" popularized by Enya. As he walked, the tune and the lyrics rolled over and over in his mind, in cadence with his steps:

My life goes on in endless song
above Earth's lamentations,
I hear the real, though far-off hymn
that hails a new creation.

Through all the tumult and the strife
I hear its music ringing,
It sounds an echo in my soul.
How can I keep from singing?

While though the tempest loudly roars,
I hear the truth, it liveth.
And though the darkness round me close,
Songs in the night it giveth.

No storm can shake my inmost calm,
while to that rock I'm clinging.
Since love is Lord of heav'n and earth
How can I keep from singing?

When tyrants tremble in their fear
And hear their death knell ringing,
When friends rejoice both far and near
How can I keep from singing?

In prison cell and dungeon vile
our thoughts to them are winging,
when friends by shame are undefiled
how can I keep from singing?

CHAPTER 26
Dan's War

"Unus quisque sua noverit ire via."

—*Properitus*

Dan Fong heard about the approaching troops while he was having his break-fast. The next-door neighbor's teenage girl burst into the kitchen and ex-claimed, "They say on the CB that there are Federal and UN tanks in Moscow and they are shooting at anything that moves, and searching house to house." Stepping outside, he could hear what sounded like artillery or perhaps tank main guns firing occasionally, far in the distance. Dan kissed his wife, snatched up his HK91, and dashed out the door. He was heading for the Town Hall.

The freeholders' council had an impromptu meeting. It took only forty minutes to decide what to do, but not until after a lot of arguing. It wasn't until it was made clear that there were seven thousand troops headed north and that they were burning everything in their path that the voices of dissent were silenced. The town council decided that Potlatch would be evacuated immedi-ately. It was agreed that to stay put would invite attention and inevitably the wrath of the Federals. The wilderness to the east of town was vast and thickly wooded. The entire population of Potlatch, roughly four hundred people, could simply walk a few miles into woods and escape notice.

Dan spent the rest of the day helping to coordinate the evacuation. He assigned his deputy the responsibility of policing the evacuees and making sure that every house was evacuated by noon the following day. He sent almost all of his storage food and the majority of his guns and ammo with his wife and adopted children, who planned to follow on horseback behind her father's flatbed diesel truck. It was one of only three trucks in town that was still running. All of the others that were running were diesels too. The lack of reliable gasoline and the lack of spare parts had resigned the rest of the vehicles in town to the category of scrap.

Dan spent some time making plans with his wife and saying his goodbyes. With the children out of earshot, he quietly confided to his wife that he had less than a fifty-fifty chance of living through the next few days. As sheriff, he said, he was charged with upholding the law and protecting both lives and free-held property in Potlatch. Dan had decided that he would stay to carry on with his job. Cindy didn't argue with her husband. She kissed him, and implored sweetly, "I love you, Dan. Do your best to live through this. Don't make me a widow all over again. I'll leave word where you can find me and the kids." With that, she slung Dan's well-worn HK91 across her back, and mounted their Morgan mare, Babe. She added, "Don't worry, I'm in good company. I've got Mister Heckler and Mister Koch to protect me."

Dan laughed. It was a favorite joke of theirs. He asked, "And Colonel Colt?" Cindy smiled and replied, "Yes, indeed, and Mister Sykes and Mister Fairbairn, for good measure. Keep your powder dry, Dan. I love you." Cindy Fong turned to wave several times as she rode away.

Dan now had very few of his household belongings left in Potlatch. His Toyota pickup truck had broken down nearly a year before, and was sitting immobile behind a neighbor's barn. The truck needed a new water pump, and despite his searching for many months, he could not locate one.

By nightfall, aside from Fong, the town was deserted. Based on what he heard on the CB, Dan calculated that he would probably have one day, or perhaps even two, to prepare.

Fong picked the military crest of a hill eighteen hundred yards southeast of the center of Potlatch. It had a commanding view of the valley below. Carrying his two most prized long guns and the rest of his gear took three exhausting trips. Fong spent twenty-five minutes disassembling, cleaning, oiling, reassembling, and reloading the two guns that he'd brought with him. The last step in the process was cleaning their optics with lens paper and a camelhair brush. He had test fired and re-zeroed both guns just a month before.

The first was the fiberglass bedded McMillan .50 caliber bolt-action repeater. There were still eighty-six rounds of ammunition left for it. The other rifle was his green composite stocked Steyr SSG .308 Winchester. It was a standard 1980s vintage SSG with double set triggers. Two years before the Crunch, Dan had mounted it with a three-to-nine-power Trijicon scope with a 56-mm objective lens. This scope used special crosshairs that were lit by vials of radioactive tritium gas. By turning a selector ring, it could be quickly switched to a green, red, or amber crosshair. In daylight, there were also settings for a standard black crosshair, or a magenta crosshair that was lit by a daylight-gathering dome on top of the rear portion of the scope. Dan often praised the Trijicon as "the next best thing to a Starlight scope for night shooting."

The only modification that Dan made to the SSG was the addition of a DTA brand three-prong flash hider. Long before the Crunch, he sent the barreled action of the rifle off to Holland's of Oregon for the gunsmithing.

Holland's cut one-half-by-twenty-eight threads on the muzzle, and installed one of their patented muzzle brakes. Dan was not so much interested in recoil reduction as he was the ability to mount a flash hider. He thought that a flash hider might attract suspicion in "peacetime," so he normally kept the less controversial muzzle brake installed. He always kept the DTA flash hider handy in the SSG's case before the Crunch, "just in case."

He completed the cleaning tasks just as it was getting dark. He rolled out his sleeping bag and immediately fell into a deep sleep. He spent half of the next day digging a small fighting position for himself, and camouflaging it with half of an army surplus "diamond" camouflage net. Then he went halfway down the back side of the ridge and dug a trench that was five feet long, ten inches wide, and twenty inches deep. He left his Austrian-made SSG rifle beside the hole in the McMillan's Pelican case with just one latch closed. Then he picked out a secondary fighting position three-fourths of the way up the next ridge. He was nearly exhausted by the time he finished digging the second foxhole. Luckily, as with the two previous holes, he encountered only a few hand-sized rocks. He finished camouflaging this last hole just before it got dark. For it, he used the other half of the diamond net for camouflage. Dan left his pack in the bottom of the hole, and quietly walked back to his primary position in the darkness. There, he curled up in his poncho and poncho liner and soon fell asleep.

When he awoke just after dawn, his first task was to systematically observe the area with his binoculars. He couldn't see any movement in or near town. He could, however, hear what sounded like cannon or mortar fire, far to the southwest. Dan kneeled to pray silently. He quietly recited the Lord's Prayer. He scanned Potlatch and the county road through his binoculars. He prayed some more. Fong stood up and nodded to himself. He knew what he had to do.

He was confident that the McMillan was still zeroed, since he had moved it only in its heavily padded Pelican case. He was more concerned about the zero of his SSG, since he had carried it on a sling from his house to the hilltop. He'd been careful to not knock into the scope while moving it, but he would have been more comfortable if he'd had the opportunity to confirm point of impact. With the hostiles so close, he didn't want to make any noise that could betray his presence.

He pulled out his favorite knife, the TrinitY Fisherman that he had inherited from T.K. He stared for a while at the fish symbol inlaid in brass in the knife's handle. The knife meant more to him than most of his other possessions. He began to peel a raw turnip to start his breakfast. He peered through his binoculars for a while, nibbling on turnip slices as he watched. Then he ate half of a small round loaf of wheat bread. He looked through his binoculars for a while longer, and then ate two sticks of elk jerky. Fong picked up his binoculars again. To the west, he could see Army scouts on dull painted motorcycles approaching town. He studied their movements carefully. He took a few swigs from his canteen. A few minutes later, he could see dismounted infantry approaching, walking on the shoulders of the state highway that traversed Potlatch. He wiped the TrinitY knife clean on his trouser leg and tucked it back into the brown leather sheath that was stamped "Matthew 4:19."

As they got closer, Fong "doped" the wind. His moistened finger revealed no discernible surface wind. Fong smiled and nodded. Looking at the trees spread out across the valley, and the dust kicked up by the vehicles, there were no telltale signs of wind in the distance, either. "This is going to be quite a nice shooting day," he murmured to himself, as he put in his earplugs. When he thought that the approaching troops and vehicles were just outside his maximum effective range, Fong emptied two canteens on the ground in the area beneath the muzzle of the rifle, to prevent dust from rising and giving away his position. He settled in behind the big rifle, popped open the scope covers, and picked out the most lucrative targets. There was an odd assortment of vehicles: American-made Humvees—some of them still in desert camouflage paint jobs from Iraq, ancient two-and-a-half-ton trucks—also American, and what looked like Russian BTR-70 wheeled armored personnel carriers.

He fired his first shot when the closest infantrymen were thirteen hundred meters away, and the nearest vehicles were nearly two thousand meters out. He alternated his fire between the closest of the infantrymen and the vehicles that were farther back. With the long travel time of the bullet—just over a second on the close shots, and much longer on the more distant shots—he was able to ride the recoil and get his optics back on target before each bullet hit. He kept up steady fire for twenty minutes, stopping occasionally to rest and reload his magazines. After he fired more than thirty rounds with uncertain results, he saw his first sure kill. It was a radioman at just over twelve hundred yards.

He declared, "That's one for sure. I won't count the 'maybes' or try to figure how many I get inside the trucks and APCs," keeping tally for a nonexistent audience.

His second sure hit was on an out-riding motorcycle scout. The rider went over backwards, and the dirt bike went down in a cloud of dust. There was still no breeze evident. "That's two," Fong said, as he worked the big bolt handle on the McMillan.

He paused to switch magazines. Fong switched back to firing at the dismounted infantry. Some of them were now within nine hundred yards, a distance that Fong considered uncomfortably close. Confident of their range, he hit each man with a single shot.

"That's three, four, and five."

He put a fresh magazine in the rifle, and then noticed that he now had far more empty magazines than loaded ones. He paused for a few minutes to refill his magazines. The sound of the growing pile of fired .50-caliber brass in the bottom of the foxhole made Dan smile. After taking a few deep breaths and working his shoulder in a small circle to relax his muscles, Dan brought the scope back up to his eye and resumed his work.

Fong placed the Trijicon's center dot on the chest of another soldier who was carrying what looked like a flame-thrower. The McMillan barked again. "That's six."

Fong noticed a point man only six hundred and fifty yards out, an easy range for the big .50 caliber. "That's seven." Clearly smarting from the casualties they were taking, the infantrymen were slowing down and now moving by bounds. With the infantry now in the open and fairly close—at least by the standards of his McMillan—they made fine targets.

He rapidly expended three full magazines for the McMillan. The troops still had no idea where Fong was, other than somewhere to the south. They could hear the supersonic crack of his shots, but couldn't see exactly where they were coming from. Most of Fong's body was in the foxhole, and the little that protruded was well camouflaged.

As he again reloaded magazines, Dan murmured to himself, "That's eight more kills for sure, which makes it fifteen."

He had saved his four magazines of precious SLAP cartridges for the APCs, which were maneuvering some nine hundred yards away. He went through all four of these magazines in less than ten minutes. Only one of the APCs stopped moving, but he was sure that he had made good hits on the sides and backs of at least three of the BTR-70 APCs. The APCs fired back blindly, spraying the hillsides with 14.5 mm and 7.62 mm rounds. A few rounds came within fifty yards, slapping into rocks with a loud clatter. The close hits made Dan nervous.

He reloaded two of his empty magazines with loose AP cartridges, and fired again, firing them rapidly at the two closest up-armored Humvees. Both of them came to sudden stops.

The brass in the foxhole was up above his ankles now. He looked down to his magazines and ammo boxes at the lip of the foxhole, and was astonished to find that he only had two loaded rounds of .50-caliber ammunition left. He fired these last two rounds single shot through the McMillan at the cab of a deuce-and-a-half truck that was nine hundred yards distant. With his second and last shot, the truck careened into a ditch on the side of the road and rolled over onto its side. Fong smiled in satisfaction.

The dismounted infantrymen were close enough now that he could hear them shouting. A few small arms bullets kicked up dust and ricocheted off rocks on the hillside above and below him. He guessed the distance to the closest of them was less than five hundred yards. He glanced at his watch. It was just after 10 a.m. Fong realized that he had to move quickly to keep any distance between himself and the enemy.

He folded the rifle's bipod and set it down beside the foxhole. Then he deliberately pulled back the camouflage net. He knew any sudden movements might be spotted by the approaching infantry. Dan cradled the big rifle in his arms and deliberately walked up and over the hilltop, using the brush for concealment. Once he was over the top of the hill, and out of sight to the valley below, he put his head down and began to run.

Halfway down the reverse slope of the hill, Dan stopped and carefully laid the McMillan next to the hole in the ground that he had prepared the day before. He pressed down the release button and pulled out the big rifle's bolt assembly and stowed it in his butt pack. Then he pulled the SSG out of the Pelican case and put the McMillan in its place. He snapped the heavy closure catches into place and ensured that the pressure relief vent knob was cranked closed. The entire case went into the hole. Then, with an audible grunt, rolled a log that he had prepared the day before over the hole to conceal it. "Don't worry, baby, I'll come back for you in a few days. You're just too big to carry, and I'm out of .50 ammo." He picked up the SSG and resumed his run down the hill.

He was out of breath when he stopped again, three quarters of the way up the next hill, roughly nine hundred yards from his first firing position. This was the secondary position he had picked out and prepared the day before. His backpack and two full canteens of water were waiting for him there. Only a few moments after he got down into a low prone position behind the Scharf Shuetzen Gewehr, the infantry crested the first hill that he had been on.

Dan paused a minute to regain his breath and to pick out the most important targets. He felt fine, other than a slightly sore shoulder from firing the .50. His first was a man that was gesturing in a forward arc with his arm. He went down thrashing and clutching at his chest. "That's sixteen. I'm a fisher of men."

He methodically reloaded the rifle's chamber with a loose cartridge to bring it back up to a full six cartridges. When he had time, Fong preferred the "shoot one, load one" method that kept the full magazine capacity in reserve.

Dan had two hundred rounds of Federal match-grade .308 Winchester ammunition, in cardboard boxes, for the Steyr in his pack. In the pouches of his web gear, he had seven of the five-round capacity rotary magazines loaded with Federal match-grade 168-grain ammunition for the SSG. He normally kept only two magazines loaded, to prevent their springs from taking a set, but for the occasion, he had all seven fully loaded. He also had just one ten-round box magazine, which was loaded with AP ammunition. Despite their larger capacity,

Dan actually disliked the ten-round Steyr magazines. He had owned two others previously. Both were replaced in succession by the factory, due to internal mechanical problems. He'd heard similar stories from other SSG owners, including the famous gun guru, Colonel Jeff Cooper. If they were that unreliable, he reasoned, he should stick mainly to the more robust five-round design.

He spotted an officer's shining silver hat insignia, and cut him down. Dan muttered, "What an idiot! Wearing garrison insignia in the field. Serves him right. That brings the count to seventeen."

He picked out two other soldiers that were signaling the others, trying to coordinate the advance. "That's eighteen and nineteen." Dan put a fresh rotary magazine in the rifle.

Across the canyon, the approaching infantrymen paused, and then turned to hurriedly run back over the hilltop. One of them dropped his rifle as he ran. Dan got just one of them as they retreated—a straggling machine-gunner. The man rolled on the ground, hemorrhaging. He shot him a second time, this time in the head, to put him out of his misery. "That's twenty."

Once the sounds of the retreat convinced him that they wouldn't be advancing again soon, Dan reloaded all of his magazines from the boxes in his pack. He shouldered his pack and clicked on the rifle's safety. Quietly, he moved six hundred yards to the northeast, selecting a good vantage point on the brushy military crest of a circular hill. He set up his small camouflage net and settled in. He spent a few minutes estimating distances to various points within his line of sight. Then he quietly ran patches through the bore of his rifle, nibbled at an MRE, and sipped from one of his canteens. The day wore on. He did a second and more thorough cleaning of his rifle, and inspected its optics. As the sun began to set, Dan whispered to himself, "How long is it going to take these guys to friggin' regroup?"

The enemy approached again, this time more cautiously, and this time from the north. The angle from which they approached was unfortunate for Dan. They didn't come into his line of sight until they were only four-hundred-and-fifty yards away. "*Much* too close," Dan whispered to himself. He could see them clearly now through the Trijicon. They were wearing the German *Flecktarn* pattern camouflage fatigues and carrying AK-74 variants of some sort, equipped with fat muzzle brakes. He fired as soon as several of them were in view. He saw many of them go down in the heavy brush—possibly killed or wounded, or possibly just too scared to move. The enemy fired back sporadically. Most of them expended magazine after magazine in long bursts, spraying the hillsides. They couldn't spot Dan. Fong turned the selector ring on his scope from black to green. It was dark enough now that he could see the dull green glow of the Trijicon's reticle bars and dot. The tempo of the infantry's fire increased. Dan could hear bullets hitting nearby.

Now at just under three-hundred-and-fifty yards, the enemy was getting uncomfortably close. Fong realized that if he didn't move soon, he would be outmaneuvered. He reloaded his SSG, this time with his one and only ten-round magazine. Dan put on his pack and stood up. Just as he started to run, he was struck by a bullet, knocking him back to the ground. It struck his right buttock and carried through to smash his pelvis. Through a gaping exit wound just below his belt, Dan could see part of his hipbone protruding. As he writhed on the ground in shock from the hit, a second bullet struck him, deeply slicing into his belly, sending his intact intestines sliding out to land at his side. "Oh crud," he exclaimed.

He breathed deeply a few times, partly regaining his composure, and then rolled back over to a prone position and retrieved his rifle. With considerable effort, Fong pulled the two quick release tabs on his ALICE backpack's shoulder straps, and twisted his upper body, sending the pack to the ground. He backed up slightly and got down behind his pack and rested the SSG's forearm on it. Fong looked down again in horror at his intestines and then his wounded hip. The hip wound was starting to spurt bright red blood. Fong reached for the first aid pouch on his web gear and pulled out a Carlisle bandage. He tore off its plastic cover and stuffed it into the exit wound below his belt. Strangely, the slit across his belly hardly bled at all. There was a lot of blood on his hands. It made the rifle feel slippery. Bullets continued to thump into the rocks around him. Three hit the backpack beneath his rifle in rapid succession.

Two platoons continued their advance, firing wildly into the gathering darkness. Where they were now, there was hardly any brush or rocks for concealment. Dan picked out two figures that were gesturing "forward" with their arms. Perhaps they were squad leaders. He shot them each once in the chest. Then he shot two soldiers that were at the lead, less than two hundred yards down the hill. "That's four more, to make twenty-four." His next target was a man who was waving and shouting orders—surely an NCO. He hit him low in the abdomen, sending him to the ground. The NCO was screaming something German. "That's twenty-five."

Their will broken, the lead platoon turned and started a disorganized retreat, pell-mell back down the hill. Some were shouting "*Ruckzug!*" Dan surmised that it was German for "retreat!" The second platoon soon followed. All of the shooting stopped.

As they ran, Dan shot three of the soldiers in the back, sending them tumbling to the ground. The remnants of the two platoons disappeared into the trees below before he had a chance for another shot. He gasped out loud, haltingly, "That's three more, for twenty-eight." The fallen NCO quit screaming. After so much shooting, the night was strangely quiet.

He rolled to his side and reloaded the SSG, using the last of his loaded five-round Steyr magazines. He wondered how he would be able to reload the empty magazines with his hands so wet and sticky. Dan looked down at his pile of intestines on the ground. Dirt and twigs were sticking to them. He shook his head and said, "Oh what a mess I am. Gut shot. Give me strength, Lord." The bleeding from the hip wound had slowed. It was then that he realized that only a small artery had been hit. There was plenty of blood, but the bullet had missed his femoral artery. If that had been hit, he reasoned, he'd be dead.

Fong peered through his scope at the tree line below, looking for targets. None dared show themselves. More blood, some of it half-clotted, gushed from the exit wound on his hip. Dan repositioned the bandage. Without the accustomed support of his lower abdomen, Fong's diaphragm went into spasm. He hiccupped, repeatedly. He shook his head and laughed out loud. In a falsetto child's voice, he joked, "Was your daddy in Civil War Two? Yes, but he died of the hiccups."

Dan spent another minute scanning the trees below, hoping to see another target of opportunity. His diaphragm was still in spasm. Then his hands started to shake uncontrollably. His entire body was taken in a long convulsive shiver. He rolled over onto his back, clutching his SSG in both hands. He muttered to himself, "The party's over."

With his strength failing, Fong lapsed into a disconnected semi-delirious speech to himself. "Not a bad life ... not a bad ratio. Twenty-eight-to-one. Hah! I made 'em pay dearly for Potlatch ... I hope I did the right thing, Lord...." He lapsed into unconsciousness for a minute, then roused briefly to sing quietly, "Hope you got your things together. Hope you are quite prepared to die. Looks like we're in for nasty weather. One eye is taken for an eye...."

A few moments later he spoke his last. "God Bless the Republic, death to the New World Order. We shall prevail. *Freedom*...." A broad smile spread across his face as he lost consciousness.

At civil twilight the next morning, the enemy resumed their advance. Some of the troops at first balked at moving forward. They complained that to advance was suicidal because they were outnumbered. It took several shouted orders and threats from a replacement Wehrmacht master sergeant to get them moving. The lead elements found Fong's body an hour later.

In the wake of the UN troopers, a German infantry major hiked up the hill. The major spent fifteen minutes walking around, closely examining the hilltop. When he had completed his inspection, he returned to sit on a boulder just up the hill from Fong's body. An out-of-breath corporal came trotting up to the officer and rapidly reported, "*Herr Major, die heckenschuetzen*...." The major flashed his palm and sternly corrected him. "We speak English, always English. Now start over."

The corporal frowned and then began again, haltingly, "Sir. The resistance men are gone. We could find no other bodies, sir. The rest of them must have escaped und taken their wounded with them, sir." The major shook his head in contradiction. He knew better. He asked the corporal, "What others? There were no other fighting positions, no other blood stains, no other empty cartridge cases, aside from those from our own Kalashnikovs. These Americans don't have any rifles that fire our 5.45-millimeter cartridge. That's the only sort of fired cases that I've seen scattered around. Hundreds of them. And as for bodies ... all we've found was this one Oriental. There was perhaps one other man, who got away with the larger caliber rifle. That was the one that was fired at us from the far side of the next ridge."

The corporal looked dumbfounded. He implored, "But sir, between here und the valley below, we have suffered some forty-six—how do you say—casualties, killed and wounded. Everyone says there must have been at least a unit of company size in these hills. There must have been." The major shook his head again from side to side. He somberly gazed at the eviscerated body for a few moments. He said with reverence, "He was quite a warrior, this one."

The corporal bent down to search Fong's body, which was still partially stiff with rigor mortis. It took considerable effort to pry the rifle from his cold, dead hands.

CHAPTER 27
Abrams

"The time to guard against corruption and tyranny is before they shall have gotten
hold of us. It is better to keep the wolf out of the fold than to trust to drawing his teeth
and talons after he shall have entered."

—*Thomas Jefferson,* Notes on the State of Virginia

All the members had been briefed on the Abrams tank. Months before, Jeff
Trasel gave the Northwest Militia and some of the other local militias a series
of briefings on armored vehicles, using his *Jane's* books and Army field manuals
such as FM 17-15 *Tank Platoon,* for reference. Seeing some of the tanks up
close was another matter. To Todd, they looked ominous and frightening.

• • •

Jeff began his M1 briefing, "The M1A1 Abrams tank was the principal tank of
the United States Army and Marine Corps before the Crunch. The M1A1
weighs sixty-seven-and-a-half tons. It is just over thirty-two feet long, twelve
feet wide, and nine-feet-six-inches high. It can travel at forty-two miles an
hour with the governor on, and even faster if the governor is disabled, as some
tankers are known to do. I don't know how things are now, but doing that
before the Crunch was grounds for an Article 15 disciplinary action. The M1
tank can climb a vertical obstacle forty-nine inches high.

"When the first Abrams tanks were fielded in 1983, as the 'M1,' they were
equipped with a 105-mm main gun. Variants produced since 1986 (the M1A1)
were fitted with a M256 120-mm main gun. The bigger gun was an
outgrowth of the escalating armor add-on cold war between the NATO
countries and the former Soviet Union. As each side added more and more
armor to their tanks, they saw the need for progressively bigger main guns to
punch through all that armor. The normal ammo load is forty rounds for the
main gun, and over twelve thousand rounds of ammunition for the machineguns, mainly 7.62-mm NATO for the coax."

"The armor on the Abrams is impressive. 'Chobham' layered armor panels are installed on the glacis and turret. In addition to the main belt of armor, there are also armored bulkheads between turret and engine, and special 'blow out' panels over the main gun ammunition compartment. M1s built after 1988 also have depleted uranium armor beneath the Chobham panels. Those are M1A2s. I suppose they weigh even more than the M1A1 model, but I couldn't find a spec on that.

"The M1 series tanks are powered by Avco-Lycoming AGT-1500 turbine engines. This fifteen-hundred-horsepower turbine gives the tank its distinctive quiet whining noise that can be heard above the sound of the treads when the wind is right. One interesting point is that it uses the same amount of fuel when idling or running fifty miles an hour cross-country. With a turbine, it always burns roughly the same amount of fuel. Needless to say, depots are often easier targets, if available. So when you have the chance, the best way to stop a platoon of M1 tanks is to take away their refueling infrastructure.

"There are several high technology goodies on an M1A2. They include GPS navigation systems, which could be working, assuming that the GPS satellites have been in stable orbits for the past four years. They also have a digital inter-vehicular information system, commonly referred to by its acronym, IVIS. With maintenance likely degraded, the IVIS systems probably won't be working, but their FM radios probably will. The laser range finders may or may not be working at this point. Also, of greater concern are the gunners' thermal imaging sight and a commander's Independent Thermal Viewer. Both of these can literally see heat. They are optimized for detecting the heat of vehicle engines, but they *can* see human body heat. I strongly suspect, however, that the thermal sights won't be working, due to the limited useful life and fragility of their sensor heads.

"In addition to the main gun, the Abrams carries a coaxially mounted 7.62-mm machinegun, a Browning M2 .50-caliber machinegun for the commander, and another 7.62-mm machinegun—the M240—for the loader. In all, the tank normally carries a crew of four.

"Tankers seldom operate alone. A single tank is very vulnerable to getting enveloped by infantry, particularly in limiting terrain. The tank platoon is the smallest maneuver element within a tank company. Organized to fight as a unified element, the platoon consists of four main battle tanks organized into two sections, with two tanks in each section. Tanks are normally accompanied by infantry for local security. On the march, they talk back and forth on SINCGARS VHF radios. The SINCGARS are frequency-hopping radios, but under the current circumstances, I'll bet that they are operating on fixed frequencies, and possibly without encryption.

"When they are in laager, they use field telephones, especially if they've stopped for more than a few hours. Count on it. The tanks have telephone boxes on the back for communicating with infantrymen. The infantry have digital field phones—sort of like ours—for when they are dismounted, and telephones boxes like the tankers' on their APCs like the M113s, M2s, and M3s. For some reason, when the Army designed the M1 tank, unlike the older M60 tank, they forgot to run cabling from the main commo panel inside, called an AM-1780, to the phone box, so their crews have to run WD-1 wire through the loader's hatch or one of the vision blocks and attach it to a field phone on the back of the tank.

"The M1 tank has vulnerabilities just like any other tank. When they are getting pinged with a lot of small-arms fire, they button up and pull in the thermal viewers so they don't get their optics shot up. That limits their visibility. That's when they have greater difficulty acquiring targets, maneuvering on rough terrain, or spotting approaching infantry. One other thing to consider is that although they carry a huge supply of ammo, they don't have an unlimited supply of vision ports. They carry spares, but if you keep shooting out the ports, or obscuring them by spray painting them, for example, eventually they'll be blind.

"Inside, tankers carry full-length M16s for crew protection from crunchies." Jeff detected a few puzzled looks and clarified, "Tankers call anyone dismounted 'crunchies.' That's tanker humor. Since M16s are ungainly to shoot out of a tank hatch, they don't have much more than the tank commander's Beretta nine-mil pistol for a 'get off my tank' weapon—hardly an ideal tool for the job. A stubby submachinegun or a perhaps a compact riotgun would work far better. In case a tank gets enveloped by infantry, the crew usually depends on co-ax machinegun fire from other tanks in the platoon to hose the crunchies off. It's a mutual support function.

"Oh yes, one other design flaw of the M1 that I should mention is that it doesn't have a bottom escape hatch like its predecessors, the M48 and the M60. Despite its shortcomings, however, the M1 Abrams is a very tough nut to crack."

Mary asked, "If their armor is so tough, how do we stop them?"

Jeff replied, "Well, like Mike Carney used to say on the shortwave, 'They've got to get out and pee, sometime.' The best time to destroy a tank is when it is parked somewhere in a garrison or *kasserne* setting, unoccupied. The only other halfway decent time would be when a tank is in the field, but parked. Then you might have a chance to take out the sentries and do a thermite number on it. If tanks are in motion, traveling in mutual support, and carrying live rounds, you can pretty well forget it unless you want to take a tremendous number of casualties.

"The five most susceptible targets on M1s are, number one: the ammo storage blow-out panels. These are on the back of the turret. They are often covered with strapped-down bags of camouflage nets and other gear. This works to your advantage. You can get on the back deck and shove a thermite grenade between and under the bags. If they are strapped down well, they'll interrupt the operation of the blow-out panels causing blow back into the turret. Very nasty.

"Number two: The fuel cells. You can see the two rear covers on either fender. Pull the pins, open the caps, drop the grenade in one of the strainers, jump, and run like crazy. Leave both caps open for propagation. The right tank is the one I would choose since if the fire doesn't get the whole tank, it will get the battery box and electronics routing box, which are right next to the right fuel tank.

"Number three: The loader's hatch, which is on left side of the turret. It is the thinnest bit of armor on the whole tank.

"Number four: The Tank Commander's hatch. The TC's hatch is relatively thin, just like the loader's, and has a conveniently provided lip to keep the grenade from rolling off if the hatch is battened down. If by chance it *isn't* battened down, throw in a frag grenade and follow it with gunfire! If the crew has the hatch in the open position but aren't sitting up in it, they are too stupid to live a full life anyway.

"And five: The engine cover, in the center of the back deck. It's a big, thinly armored target. Again, a thermite grenade will go right through it.

"Now remember boys and girls, if you are destroying a parked or otherwise unoccupied M1, don't forget to reach over and switch the M2 .50 cal to safe, and then you can pull the two pins on the left side and take it home as a souvenir! Of course, the back plate on the tank model is different than the standard ground model. There are no spade grips, and the charging system is on the left. But we have friends in the Moscow Maquis that happen to have a couple of spare standard M2 back plate assemblies, and at least one spare tripod with pintle. That'll be fun. And naturally you'll want to take as much ammo as you can before you burn up the tank. Ditto for any other stored gear, if tactical conditions allow you time to haul it.

"Another hint: If the commander has his hatch in the 'open-protected' position and the loader's M240 is mounted and has ammo, take the M240, shove the muzzle through the opening under the edge of the TC's hatch, and spray away. The bullets will bounce around very nicely inside that spam can and make Swiss cheese out of most of the crew. You can even use your personal weapon if necessary, but the Provisional government provides a machinegun and in most cases a long belt of ammo for just such purposes, so why not use it?

"Oh yes, I should also mention that there are also two small lifting holes, one on each side of the tank commander's weapons station—the demi-turret—which go all the way through. You can fire into these holes if the TC is buttoned up.

"Most of the techniques that I've just described involve climbing onto the tank. This should be done only if the beast is stationary. Never try to climb on a moving M1 series! Likewise, never try playing Tarzan and dropping or jumping onto it from a tree, overhang, overpass, or nearby bank. We will discuss some standoff techniques next time. Any other questions?"

• • •

In the dim moonlight on that July evening, Todd looked at the four Abrams tanks parked on the other side of the rise, and remembered Jeff's question. He belatedly asked himself in a whisper, "Yeah, Jeff, how do I get close to these monsters without getting myself killed?" He crept back down the reverse side of the hill and consulted with the others, quietly.

At just before 2 a.m., Todd reconnoitered the area around the tanks. Moving slowly and stealthily, the reconnaissance took nearly an hour. Curiously, he found no nearby infantry, and no sentries posted. He went back to brief the others and attach longer fuses to the grenades.

The crews inside the tanks were asleep. The tankers had become lackadaisical in their campaign across the western states. They had long since decided that the biggest threat that they would face was a high-powered rifle, perhaps something like a .375 H&H Magnum. A few .50 calibers were rumored to be floating around, but even those bullets bounced off an M1. The worst a .50 BMG could reportedly do was, by luck, jam a tank's turret ring with a well-placed shot.

The tankers didn't bother posting a guard, even though it was a violation of their official SOP. They had a saying, "There's a time for SOPs, and then there's real world operations." Except in extremely hot weather, the tankers slept "buttoned up" with their ballistic doors closed. Feeling virtually invulnerable under the current circumstances, some of them had also lost the habit of collocating with infantry at night. The infantry was noisy, frequently begged for extra food and smokes, and always woke the tankers up before dawn for "stand to." The general consensus among the tankers was that the infantry could take a flying leap. More and more, the tankers laagered by themselves.

At precisely 3:10 a.m., Todd, Mary, and Jeff lit the fuses of eight thermite grenades, on cue. There was one over a blow-out panel, and one on the engine cover of each tank. They taped them down with long strips of duct tape that they had cut in advance and wrapped around their pant legs. The tape ensured that once the thermite reaction started, the grenades would not roll off the tanks from the force of the venting molten metal. They walked away quietly at first, and then they ran. After they crested the top the hill and had starting down the reverse side, Todd whispered to Mary, "I feel like I'm playing ding-dong ditch-it."

Mary replied with a low laugh, "Ding-dong, thermite calling." After they had jogged on a few more yards, she added, "I'm glad we had that extra cannon fuse with us, so we could extend the fuses. I want to be a long, long way off when they go off." They didn't stop running until they were more than nine hundred yards away, on a ridge in heavy brush.

The automatic Halon fire suppression systems were turned off in three of the four tanks. They had been disabled by the crew because they had a tendency to go off unexpectedly. Even if they had all been working, the fire suppression systems wouldn't have helped much. The iron oxide in thermite provides all the oxygen required for the reaction. Thermite will even burn underwater.

Watching the tanks burn was gratifying. After a few minutes, they heard the deafening explosions of 120-mm shells cooking off. The four fires were still burning intensely as they turned and headed toward the rally point.

• • •

The green Laron Star Streak touched down in the meadow and taxied slowly toward the tree line, bouncing slightly on the uneven ground. Ian shut down the engine, pulled up his goggles and shouted, "I need a reload and about three gallons of gas!" He put the "safing" pin in the firing lever for the M16s and crawled out, over the receiver extension tubes. Doyle hopped out of the plane, and even before the others emerged from the trees, he started punching the release buttons and pulling out the empty magazines. Then he loosened the wing nut for the brass catcher door and shoveled the empty 5.56-mm brass and the empty magazines into a nylon sleeping bag stuff sack. Mary ran up, carrying five loaded thirty-round magazines, and breathed, "These are mixed one-in-three, just like the last ones."

Doyle popped each of the fresh magazines into place, and tugged on each to ensure they were firmly latched. He pronounced, "What I want you to do now, please, is go and get me another five spare loaded magazines. That way I can pick out an empty stretch of road somewhere to land and do my next reload by myself, without having to come all the way back here." Mary quickly did as she was told.

While she was gone, Doyle pulled back the charging handles of each of the five M16s, and let them fly forward, chambering rounds. Then he reached underneath each rifle and firmly tapped the forward assist buttons with the heel of his hand to ensure that each of the bolts was fully engaged.

As she poured gas into the main tank at the rear of the fuselage, Margie asked, "How did it go, Ian?"

"I caught some infantry in the open, and I shot up a couple of slick Bell Hueys on the ground. I made three passes at them from different directions. That was about ten or twelve miles southwest of here. Then I ran out of ammo. I think I got at least twenty guys, and probably made the helicopters unusable. It wasn't exactly like making a 'guns run' in a Falcon, but it *works*! I got the whole thing on video. I turned the camera on just before I made my first pass, and left it on for the next two passes. I was so pumped that I almost forgot to turn the camera off after I ran out of ammo and started heading back."

Mary returned with the extra magazines. As she handed them to Doyle, she said breathlessly, "These have the last of our .223 tracers. They are mixed one-in-five in this batch. Any reloads after these, and you'll be shooting straight ball."

He snapped back, "That's okay, Mary. I'm getting used to how these guns shoot. I'll have it down to a science after this sortie. If I open up from two hundred meters at a fifty-mile-an-hour ground speed, I can see the tracers hitting right where I want them. I won't need the tracers to help me with my aim much longer." He ran his hands over the wings, tail, and fuselage, searching for new bullet holes. He found none. Doyle handed the sack that held the fired brass and the five empty magazines to Mary, and then stowed the extra magazines in the canvas tool bag at his feet. He smiled and joked, "Well, I gotta go. I've got important people to kill!" Less than a minute later, he was airborne, headed west.

At the same moment, Blanca's Star Streak was turning sharply, with its left wing pointed straight down at the treetops. Blanca leveled the plane out and began her third strafing run. It was a mixed convoy of Humvees, two-and-a-half-ton, and five-ton trucks, five miles east of Moscow. By now, they were nearly all off to the sides of the road, and their drivers were taking advantage of the scant cover wherever they could find it. With great concentration, she lined up the improvised gun sight and flipped the shift lever, starting the M60 to work.

She estimated that she had expended at least two hundred rounds each on the two previous runs, so she had about five hundred rounds left. With a ground speed of only forty-miles-per-hour, she had a very stable platform and plenty of time to "paint" all of the trucks in the convoy. She stabbed at the rudder pedals, to keep the nose lined up on each of the trucks as they came in turn before her gun sight. She smiled, finally understanding Ian's professed love of CAS missions. It was a thrill.

Her first pass had stitched right up the middle of the convoy from behind, taking it completely by surprise. Her second pass, from west to east, had concentrated on the trucks on the north side of the road. She narrowly missed the telephone pole that lined the north side of the road. On this third pass, perhaps too predictably, she traversed the trucks in the ditch on the south side of the road, flying from east to west. Blanca began to hear bullets pinging into the plane, and she could see numerous tears in the fabric in the wing above her. Despite the hits, she decided to finish the run. The trail of bullets from the M60 passed the last of the vehicles, and Blanca quickly pulled back on the fire control lever to conserve ammo. Curiously, she noticed, the lead Humvee had two tall antennas instead of just the one she saw on the others. She wondered if this meant that it was the convoy commander's vehicle. She would have to ask one of the "ground pounders" when she got back.

Blanca banked the Laron sharply, and shoved the throttle forward. The surge of power palpably pushed her back into her seat. It was time, as her husband so colorfully put it, "to de-ass the A.O." With the large number of hits her plane had taken on the third pass, Blanca knew that she didn't dare attempt a fourth. As she turned back north, a .30-caliber bullet went through both walls of the rear cockpit. On its way, it went through the tops of both of Blanca's thighs. The wounds were not very painful at first, but the sight of them badly frightened Blanca. They bled heavily from the start. The slipstream splattered blood all over the rear cockpit. She thought that she had to land soon, or she would bleed to death. After a half-minute of sheer panic, Blanca gained altitude, got her bearings, and turned the plane toward Valley Forge. The throttle was still wide open, and despite the low altitude and the extra drag of the missing canopy, the plane was up to a ground speed of eighty miles an hour.

Blanca wrapped a long scarf that her mother-in-law had knitted for her around her thighs. It might slow the bleeding down a little, she reasoned. If nothing else, it was reducing the splatters of blood that were gradually painting her uniform and goggles. She looked up at her left wing, and then her right, and was horrified to see that many of the bullet holes had transformed themselves into long rips in the fabric. A flap of fabric eighteen-inches square was flapping frantically on the bottom of the right wing. Realizing her peril, Blanca pulled the throttle halfway back, slowing the plane to less than fifty miles an hour. As she continued toward the valley, the tears in the fabric continued to worsen, and the rudder controls started to feel mushy. Despite her reduced airspeed, large patches of fabric kept tearing away, albeit at a slower rate. Blanca looked back up at the wings and muttered to herself, *"Ay, ay, ay, ay, ay."*

She could see the meadow opening in the distance. She tightened both sides of her seat harness, and crossed herself. She repeated "Hail Mary" in Spanish three times. Blanca dipped the plane's nose down, and tried to turn left toward the valley. The rudder did not respond. In desperation, she pushed the left rudder pedal down until it stopped, and tipped the control stick to the left, gradually dropping the left wing tip. Ever so slowly, the nose started to walk around to the left. Once she was lined up on the meadow properly, Blanca throttled back even farther, spilling off airspeed, and she leveled the wings. The plane's stick felt unfamiliar. Just as the plane cleared the near edge of the meadow, it started to stall.

Luckily, Larons are forgiving aircraft, and the stall was not fully catastrophic. Blanca realized that she was losing altitude too quickly, and throttled up again, but it was almost too late. Minus nearly a quarter of its wing area, the Laron had insufficient lift and was descending at thirty feet a second, just coming out of the stall. By the time she hit the ground, the prop had spooled up and her rate of descent was slower, but the impact was still well beyond the rated stress that the landing gear was designed to absorb. To make matters worse, unknown to Blanca, the Laron's right tire had been punctured by a bullet.

The Laron hit the grass and bounced once. Blanca chopped the throttle completely. On the second bounce, the right side of the landing gear collapsed. The right wing tip edged into the ground, and the Star Streak went into a ground loop. The fuselage tore into the sod, sending chunks of dirt up through the skin of the plane. The right wing tip was torn off completely. Blanca instinctively pulled her knees up. The plane was still going fifteen miles an hour when it flipped over. After sliding upside down in a semicircle, the Laron finally came to a stop.

When the others arrived, they thought that Blanca was dead. The sight of her hanging upside down in the cockpit, unconscious and bathed in blood, was almost too much for Margie. Mary had the presence of mind to pick up her medic bag before she started to run toward the plane. Lon and Todd supported Blanca's weight while Mary snipped through the harness material with her black-handled EMT shears. Having seen gasoline pouring out of a puncture in the gas tank, there was no hesitation. They quickly carried her in a "fireman's carry" sixty yards across the meadow toward the TAC-CP. Mary checked her pulse at her carotid artery and examined her pupils. Then she deftly cut the ACU material back from each of the wounds on her legs. Mary could see that they were roughly an inch deep. To her surprise, the bleeding was slow. Large clots had formed at both the entrance and exit sides. "Looks like the major arteries are intact," Mary reported. Mary wrapped four pressure dressings on her legs, one each over the entrance and exit sides of the wounds.

Mary decided that it would be unwise and unnecessary to move her any further, at least for the present. She sent Margie for her surgical kit and some water. After another few minutes, Blanca regained consciousness. She looked up at Mary and asked, "*Que, que...?*"

Mary held her fingers to her lips and smiled at Blanca. "You did good, Blanca, *muy bueno*. Now rest."

Blanca lowered her head and smiled. She turned her head to see the crumpled tan Laron. She laughed and said, "*Ay, ay, ay, ay, ay.* I wasn't thinking straight. I should have recka-nized that I was going to stall. I theenk my bird is verry broken, no?"

Mary quickly replied, "Yes, but the Lord brought you back to us. You're going to be just fine. God is the great physician. Be still and rest."

Mary noted that the bleeding had nearly stopped, and asked Todd and Lon to fabricate a stretcher. They nodded to each other and jogged off. They returned ten minutes later. They were carrying a stretcher that they had improvised from two ponchos lashed onto a pair of pine saplings. Very gently, they lifted Blanca up and placed her on the stretcher. She was slowly carried to the shade of the trees near the TAC-CP.

Mary checked Blanca's blood pressure, declaring it "just a hair low." Her pulse was rapid at 125. She gave her some cayenne pepper powder mixed in water to slow the bleeding. Blanca said that the cayenne tasted terrible, but she drank it down. The bleeding nearly stopped. She had Margie help her remove Blanca's blood-sodden ACU pants. She prepped Blanca's arm and started a colloid I.V. drip. The hanger for the I.V. bottle was nailed to a close-by ponderosa pine tree. Mary explained that because she didn't know how much blood Blanca had lost, it was important to "expand" her blood. Blanca was asleep by the time the I.V. was flowing. Mary scrubbed her hands with a disposable Betadine-soaked double-sided square brush. Then she donned a pair of gloves and swabbed the wounds with Betadine. Blanca was lifted by Todd and Lon and a new poncho was spread on the ground beneath her.

Mary regularly checked respiration, pulse, and pupils. After doing some probing, she decided to leave the wounds open for drainage. She commented, "They clotted so well by themselves, the suturing isn't necessary unless she has to move her legs. We'll watch her real closely for any new bleeding, and cauterize if necessary. For now, I'll just do some light packing with saline-soaked bandages on the exit sides. It is best to provide drainage for several days. Based on my experience with Rose's gunshot wound, I'd say it'll be at least three or four days before we'll stitch her up."

Blanca was fully conscious as Mary bandaged her. A mosquito bar was set up to keep flies away from the wounds. Mary stayed by her side for three more hours, regularly reaching under the mosquito netting to check her pulse, respiration, and blood pressure. After three full units of the I.V. fluid were drained, the Heparin lock was disconnected. Mary started a chart on Blanca's vital signs in her notebook, and then went to her tent to rest. Margie took up the vigil. She was told to check her "vitals" and for new bleeding every fifteen minutes, to chart them, and to call Mary if Blanca awakened or if there was any additional bleeding.

The late afternoon was devoted to recovering useful items from the wrecked Laron. The most important item was the M60. Luckily, aside from a badly scratched flash hider and a bent front sight, it was undamaged. It was unbolted from the framework and carried back to the TAC-CP. Blanca's Mini-14 GB was safely secured by Velcro strap, so it too escaped any damage beyond some scratches to the black plastic pistol grip.

The video camera on the plane was still functional. The camera had been left running from the time Blanca started her first pass. As they discovered when they played back the tape three days later, it recorded the strafing runs on Blanca's four previous sorties, as well as the last one. The latest portion of the tape differed from the scenes of the earlier sorties in that it also showed Blanca's flight back, and the crash itself. It even included an inverted view of Mary, Todd, and Lon running up to the crashed plane. They watched the tape several times, using the camera's small viewfinder monitor. When she saw it, Mary said, "It's too bad that the TV show 'Real Life Video' is no longer in production. They'd certainly buy a tape like this!"

The small ICOM VHF radio had its antenna and headset connectors ripped off, but looked basically intact. Surprisingly, a static rush could be heard when Todd disconnected the plugs and turned the unit on and the squelch knob down. "Built to take a licking!" Todd said with a laugh. Everything of value was removed from the wreckage—even the fired brass and links, and the remaining fuel in the tank.

After unbolting the remains of the right wing, and the largely intact left wing, Todd and Lon were able to flip the plane upright by themselves. Both were amazed just how light the Laron was. Next, with help from Jeff Trasel, they unbolted the shredded tail and carried it into the tree line to the south. The two wings quickly followed. Moving the fuselage was easier than Todd had anticipated. Lon held the right side up by the mangled stub of the landing gear and Todd pushed from behind. They wheeled it ten yards into the trees. A half hour later, two camouflage nets were in place over the wreckage. Then they went to clean the M60 and swap out the barrel with the bent front sight. Using the intact barrel for reference, Lon used a brass hammer and a pair of channel locks to straighten the front sight. Then, it too was methodically cleaned.

Just before sunset, Ian landed his Laron and taxied it toward its normal hiding place. Lon ran over to help him push it back into the trees and camouflage it. Ian was shocked when he heard about the crash and Blanca's condition. He was relieved when he saw her. She was by then asleep. Doyle said quietly, "Thank you so much, Margie." She replied, "I'm just taking notes here. It was Mary who stitched her up. She says that barring any complications, she'll be fine in a few weeks." Ian sat down next to his wife, on edge of a Lamilite ground pad. He commented, "What a day, what a day. Thank you, Father God, for your protection." Margie joined him when he read the 34th Psalm aloud.

Blanca awoke that evening, in pain. Mary gave her some Tylenol and a cup of strong tea made with comfrey leaves, sweetened with honey. Blanca's pain began to subside a half hour later. Mary gave Blanca a strong dose of titrated tetracycline. It was supplemented with a supply of herbal ointment that she had prepared a month before. It was made with marigold, comfrey, and aloe vera. Mary also made Blanca another tea—this one made of echinacea and chamomile.

• • •

Life at Valley Forge gradually worked into a routine. Every three or four days a patrol would go out to conduct a reconnaissance, liaison, sabotage, or ambush. They were only back for a day or two between patrols. Small cooking fires were burned only during the day. Every evening either Todd or Mary would cuddle with little Jacob and lead him in prayers when his bedtime arrived. Jacob's prayers always ended the same way. He would follow along and say, "I pray that everyone that we know and love is happy and healthy, warm, dry, well fed, safe and free, and have their salvation, amen."

CHAPTER 28

Tenacity

"If ye love wealth better than liberty, the tranquillity of servitude better than the animating contest of freedom, go home from us in peace. We ask not your counsel nor your arms. Crouch down and lick the hands which feed you. May your chains set lightly upon you, and may posterity forget that you were our countrymen."

—*Samuel Adams, 1776*

Throughout the fall, the Second Corps (Composite) of the Democratic Army of the Provisional Federal Government was having serious trouble in northern Idaho. Resistance forces struck unpredictably and with surprising success. Convoys could only travel in daylight, and only with accompanying armor. There were seemingly no "rear" or secure areas for the Federal and UN troops. In one much talked-about incident, an eighty-two-year-old grandmother walked up to three Belgian lieutenants that were loitering at a city park in Lewiston, with their weapons slung. She said in a sweet, quavering voice, "I have something for you," and from a picnic basket pulled a hundred-and-ten-year old Merwin Hulbert .44-40 revolver. She shot and killed one of them, and critically wounded the second before the third soldier cut her down with two bursts from a PDW-80.

The guerrillas were almost impossible to locate. The vast areas of National Forest, much of it roadless, were ideal hiding places. The townsmen were sullen. Only a few cooperated with the authorities. Most of them clearly favored the militias and did their best to feed them with supplies and current intelligence. There were countless acts of sabotage against parked vehicles. They ranged from punctured tires and sand poured in fuel tanks to immolation with Molotov cocktails.

There had been some poisoning incidents, so many soldiers distrusted any fresh food that had been out of their sight. Despite a strictly enforced two-man rule, sentries disappeared or "woke up dead" with alarming regularity. Many deserted. Others were stabbed, clubbed, or shot. Nearly all of those killed had their weapons, web gear, and boots taken. Sometimes their bodies were found

336

with even their uniforms missing. The garrisoned soldiers didn't feel safe anywhere. Nor did the new Regional Administrator and his staff. They all had large complements of heavily armed bodyguards and traveled only in APCs.

The local militias had sufficient supplies of weapons and ammunition for an extended campaign. Increasingly, they were using captured weapons. Stories about the resistance, some of them apocryphal, were circulated by word of mouth and in a variety of mimeographed and photocopied broadsheets with names like "The Maquisard," "Resist!," "The Free American," and "Say No To The NWO."

These broadsheets carried a mix of resistance pep talks, interviews, and technical advice on ambushes and sabotage. One of them printed instructions for producing and purifying a powerful toxin called ricin, derived from castor beans. They advised mixing it in the solvent DMSO, so it could be absorbed directly through the victim's skin. Another broadsheet showed how to extract colchicine from fall crocus flowers.

A regularly recurring rumor was of the militias issuing "butter knife" guns to young teenagers who joined resistance cells. As the story went, they would send them out with older, less useful guns in odd calibers to shoot sentries or to ambush off-duty garrison soldiers. They were told that they could keep any weapons that they captured, and then pass the "butter knife" along to the next young volunteer. The resistance leaders called it "using a butter knife instead of wasting a steak knife." The practice was part of the new members' initiation for some cells.

The Federal government's shortwave stations and satellite TV broadcasts announced that they had "secured" Moscow, Lewiston, and Coeur d'Alene only a week after the arrival of the Second Corps. On the first of September, they declared "victory" in Idaho. The propagandists said "residual banditry" in Idaho was "contained and limited to a few small pockets" and that the state was officially "pacified."

The news of guerrilla successes spread rapidly. A resistance cell that called itself the Bombardiers carried out a flawless thermite and Molotov raid on a row of five parked helicopters during a heavy rainstorm. A guard and an avionics technician were shot and killed. Two pilots were badly wounded. All five helicopters, plus a twelve-hundred-gallon fuel bladder of JP-4 and a "Federally requisitioned" Ford pickup truck, were destroyed. The Bombardiers only suffered one minor injury in the raid. There was considerable pride in mentioning the fact that the oldest member of the cell was only sixteen. The youngest of them had just turned twelve.

Ironically, the destruction of the helicopters caused a great increase in Federal and UN air activity in the following weeks. To compensate for the loss of the aircraft, the Federals redeployed ten more helicopters from the First

Corps in Montana. They were all older models—mostly UH-1 Huey "slicks," Bell Jet Rangers and Kiowas, and two Huey Cobras. Two of the Jet Rangers still had multicolor civilian paint jobs. The expected newer model AH-64 Apache and UH-60 Blackhawk models never appeared. "Rumor control" in the resistance had it that the reason that the older helicopters were still flying and that the newer models weren't was because the latter used more exotic hydraulic fluids and had more recent generation avionics that were more prone to failure.

By the time the extra helicopters arrived in Idaho, the Northwest Militia had long since split back into two distinct companies. Todd Gray's company remained at Valley Forge. Meanwhile, Michael Nelson's company had displaced to a heavily wooded area five miles northeast, taking half of the logistic supplies with them.

• • •

Blanca Doyle gradually recovered from her wounds. In addition to the wounds to her thighs, it was found that she had broken her left wrist in the crash. Just twenty-five days after her surgery, she was hobbling around on crutches. By October, she had graduated to a cane, and her wrist was nearly healed. On November fifth, she announced that she was pregnant. Since she was immobile, first due to her injuries, and later because of her pregnancy, Blanca became the camp cook at Valley Forge. Meanwhile, Rose Trasel became the cook and full-time C.Q. at the other company's camp. She had her infant son to care for, so she could not go out on patrols. Thomas Kenneth, Trasel was eleven months old, and just learning to walk.

By the time winter settled in, all of their sheep and two goats had been slaughtered and butchered. They needed the meat. The decision to gradually butcher the animals wasn't difficult. They realized that there would be very little feed available in the valley for the winter, so they didn't dare keep more than their three best milking does. Further, the animals were a security threat. Their distinctive "maa" and "baa" sounds could be heard from a considerable distance. Some of the meat from each of the animals that they butchered was eaten within a few days, and the rest jerked. Once the really cold weather arrived in November, the quarters were hung high in trees in deer bags. As long as they stayed in the shade, they kept well. In early November an adult brown bear sow was attracted to the smell of two hanging sheep quarters. The next day they had four bear quarters hanging, too.

• • •

The Federals became famous for planting antipersonnel mines. They emplaced them without any regard to injuring or killing innocent civilians. Their favorite spots to lay them were on the shoulders of side roads in areas that were largely guerrilla controlled.

In mid-November, Margie Porter took a solo, unarmed reconnaissance trip to Bovill. As the recon was planned, for most of her route Margie would be shadowed by a friendly patrol to protect her. Her objectives were to see which buildings in Bovill were occupied by Federal troops, where they parked their vehicles, where they posted their sentries, and hopefully what time those sentries changed. She was still within sight of the patrol when she stepped on a large land mine, on the shoulder of the county road, just east of town. She died almost instantly. They carried her body back to Valley Forge, wrapped in ponchos. They buried her there. It was a very sad day for everyone. Little Jacob wailed. He didn't stop crying for his "Aunt Margie" until he fell asleep that evening.

Lon and Della were grief stricken. After a few days they got on with the struggle. If anything, the loss made them even more fearless and determined. It was also a major turning point in Lon's life. Realizing his mortality, he accepted Christ as his savior. He became a tireless fighter on patrols. For the first time, he actively asked to be the point man. He didn't fear death, for he knew that when he died, he would join his wife in heaven. And she had meant more to him than anything else.

• • •

There were three of them, each bound hand and foot, two NCOs and a private. They were in a sitting position, lashed to three trees in a row, with their hands tied between their backs and their feet tied together. They refused to answer questions, or even give their names. One of the two NCOs spoke distinctly to the others, "Still, still! Sprechen Sie nicht!"

Lon Porter's questions were met with silence. He was getting frustrated. He warned them, "If you don't cooperate, you will be shot. It is that simple."

The sergeant directly in front of him—the one who had been warning the others to be quiet—half-shouted, "That would be a violation of the Geneva Accords."

Lon replied mockingly, "Let me tell you something, Hans, or Dieter, or Heinrich, or whatever your name is. At this point I don't give a flying fig about the Geneva Convention, or the Hague Convention, or any other convention, for that matter. If I were in the U.S. Army, fighting in some other country, I'd play by those rules. But not here, not now. I'm not in the Army, and I'm not bound by the 'laws of land warfare.' All that I care about now is getting my country back. You're the guys that marched in here and took it from me. I grew up in a Constitutional Republic, and now I'm living in a police state. Now start answering questions, or you're fertilizer. How is it that you say that in German? *Dungmittel,* I think. I had only two years of German in high school and I spent some time in Switzerland, but it's coming back to me. *Dungmittel.* Yeah, that's it. *Du Arsch Gieger! Sprechen mach schnell, oder du wirst Blei essen! Sprechen Sie, oder Sie werden Dungmittel sein.*" He gestured with his captured Browning Hi-Power for emphasis.

The sergeant spat contemptuously, "You are bluffink."

Porter thumbed down the safety of the Browning, put the muzzle between the sergeant's eyes, and asked in a low tone, "You think I'm bluffing? I have *nothing to lose*, Dieter. Two weeks ago, my wife stepped on one of your land mines. She's dead! You've taken our land, looted our house and our neighbors' houses. Everywhere you've gone, you have raped, pillaged, and plundered. Virtually all that I own in the world now fits in just one duffel bag and a backpack. Put yourself in *my* position, Dieter. I can assure you that I am definitely *not* bluffing."

The sergeant hesitated a few seconds longer, staring at Porter's eyes. Then he started talking, all in a rush. Lon got all of his questions answered immediately, in English. He was amused when he found out that the other NCO was named Dieter. He said with a laugh, "Wasn't a bad guess. I just had the wrong guy."

As he headed back to their latest temporary CP, Mike asked Lon, "You weren't actually going to shoot him, were you?"

Porter waited a long time before replying, "Well, the thought did enter my mind, but to answer your question, no, I wouldn't have. I guess I'm too civilized for that. Technically, my bluff could be considered a form of torture by some people. I don't know exactly how I would categorize it. All that I know is that it worked."

"What do you plan to do with this bunch?" Lon asked.

Nelson answered, "Well, we'll just pump them for as much information as we can, and then brand them, take their boots, and turn them loose like the others, just before we get ready to displace."

The resistance had no facilities and insufficient logistics to keep prisoners. There were only two acceptable options. The first, death, was normally reserved for Quislings—fellow citizens who had actively collaborated. The other, branding and release, was the preferred method for both UN and Federal soldiers. Because it was obvious that many of the soldiers were drafted and didn't want to be in the service of the UN, it was rarely deemed appropriate to kill them. There were a few exceptions made for known war criminals. Most, however, got the standard "I" or "T" brands with a hot iron. The "I" brand was for "Invader." The "T" signified "Traitor." Some militias, such as Todd Gray's Company and Michael Nelson's Company, branded their prisoners' forearms. Other militias branded their prisoners' foreheads or cheeks. All released prisoners were warned that if they were ever recaptured while bearing arms on behalf of the UN or the Federals, they would be summarily executed.

• • •

On a reconnaissance patrol late in November, Jeff, Ken, and Terry encountered a pair of individuals who were armed, but didn't look like Federal soldiers. From a distance, Jeff could see that they were both black. They were wearing unadorned BDUs and woodland pattern boonie hats. The one in the lead, a man, was armed with a Thompson submachinegun with a horizontal foregrip. Following ten yards behind him was a tall woman, armed with an M249 SAW. Lying prone in high Latah orchard grass, Jeff and the Laytons watched as the pair approached. When they were ten yards away, Jeff recognized the man's face. It took just a moment longer for him to connect the face with a name. Then Jeff came out in a clear voice, "Tony! Get over here!"

Tony and Teesha Washington instinctively dropped to the ground when they heard the voice, obscuring themselves in the grass. Tony half-whispered, "Who is there?"

Trasel replied, "Jeff Trasel, Northwest Militia." The Washingtons slowly got up and walked toward Trasel. They dropped down again, slowly this time, just a few feet in front of Trasel.

Tony said, "I remember you. You were on the Princeton raid—you're the guy that commandeered the M60—right? Trasel nodded. "We got introduced with all the handshaking that was going on after the raid." Washington checked the safety on the Thompson, as he did out of habit dozens of times each day, and then went on. "This is my wife, Teesha. I'm not sure if you've ever met her."

Trasel shifted his gaze to Teesha. At five-feet-eleven, she was nearly as a tall as her husband.

She handled the SAW like she knew how to use it. Trasel replied, "I've seen her at a distance, at one of the Barter Faires, but we were never introduced. A pleasure, ma'am." Teesha nodded and smiled in recognition.

"My compadres here are the Laytons, Ken and Terry. Do you know them?" Seven yards on either side of Trasel, Ken and Terry gave small waves to the Washingtons.

Tony replied, "We only know of them by reputation. They're the ones that E&E'd all the way from Chicago, aren't they? That was a heckuva hike."

Jeff replied, "Yep, that's them all right, and 'escape and evasion' is their middle name." Jeff set his HK down. Jeff frowned. "I heard that your retreat got wiped out, and that everybody was killed. But you're here breathing. What happened?"

"We are the only ones that survived. Teesha and I were guarding a cache off-site when the Feds came. The ranch house got mortared, big time. They killed everybody there—thirty-two men, women, and children. We snuck back to the ranch early the next morning. We spent an hour looking at the ruins of the house and barn through the scopes on our M1As, from about two hundred yards. We didn't dare go too close at first. We were afraid that the Federals might have left an ambush. Just as we were debating on whether or not to go down there, an army diesel CUCV Blazer pulled in the driveway. Two Specialist E-4s got out, all nonchalant, and started loading up all the guns, backpacks, and web gear from the trenches. Then they picked up the first of two body bags and loaded it in the truck. When they were each holding an end of the second body bag and carrying it toward the tailgate, we nailed them. We shot those muthas twice each with our M1As."

"So what happened next?" Jeff asked.

"We figured that the way they were acting, there wasn't an ambush set up after all, so we gave them ten minutes to bleed out and hiked down the hill. They had already gathered up everything of value in the CUCV. So we just threw in our packs and rifles, and rolled the first body bag back off the end of the tailgate. We stripped off those clowns' web gear, threw it in the back, fired up the Blazer, and took off." Gesturing to Teesha's SAW light machinegun, Tony went on, "That's where the missus here got her Minimi. They had it in the cab of the CUCV. We ditched the CUCV about four miles to the east, way up a skid road in a bunch of yew trees. It took us three nights to carry all the weapons back to our cache point. That was a mile off the road. With just the two of us, it took a whole bunch of trips. We went back to the ranch in the middle of the night two weeks later. The bodies of the Federals were gone."

Washington gulped, and continued, "We spent most of that night burying our dead in the trenches and praying for them."

"We've been playing cat and mouse with Federals, since then. Between the two of us, we got seventeen UN troops, torched seven vehicles, and captured fourteen more guns. Whenever we've bumped into other resistance cells, we've doled guns out liberally, along with a lot of food and medical gear. The CUCV and the VRC-46 radio that was in it went to the Blue Blaze Irregulars. Right now, we're down to just six guns—the M249 Minimi, our two M1As, two .45 automatics, and my Tommy gun."

Jeff eyed the submachinegun. It had a Cutts compensator, and was missing a lot of bluing. He asked with an air of disbelief, "You didn't get that from the Federals, did you?"

"No, I inherited this puppy from my grandfather. He was in the Navy, back in World War II. He was a cook stationed on Midway Island. After the Japs attacked there, they got very serious about security, and this Model '28 became his constant companion. At the end of the war, he couldn't bear to part with it, so he disassembled it and brought it home with him. He put the barreled receiver in the bottom of one sea bag, and its stock and a bunch of magazines in the other. He just walked off the ship, bold as brass. Grandpa said a lot of his buddies brought home guns that way. Mainly they brought Colt .45s and captured Jap stuff like Nambus and samurai swords."

Washington looked admiringly at the Thompson, and recounted, "He kept it under his bed for years. He never shot it—just oiled it up once in a while. When he died of a heart attack, my dad and I went over to the house to help grandma move to the retirement home. When she pulled it out from underneath the bed, I nearly fainted. It was made at the Colt factory. My dad had seen it before, lots of times, but I had never even been told about it. It was a family secret. Grandma said to me, 'Your grandfather said that after he jumped off this mortal coil that he wanted you to have this.' You see, my grandpa and grandma knew that I was really into guns. My uncle and I had just started shooting sporting clays the summer before, and I had really started getting into it."

Jeff nodded his head, smiled, and asked, "When was this?"

Washington replied, "I had just turned nineteen. I was in junior college. That was back in '97. I didn't get a chance to shoot this thing until after I got up here. I'm pretty good with it, now. It runs like a champ."

"How did you first get involved with the Templars?"

"I was born and raised in Andover, Kansas—it's a suburb of Wichita. So was Teesha, here. Shortly after I got out of high school, a friend showed me a video called *America in Peril*. That really got me thinking. I had an Internet account at the J.C., so I started searching the web, using Google, looking for everything I could find on topics like survival, guns, food storage, wilderness medicine, and militias. Those web pages brought me up to speed very quickly. I started posting to a 'Survival and Preparedness' forum at The Claire Files. Roger Dunlap noticed one of my posts there, and we started corresponding by e-mail. Pretty soon he got me set up with PGP—that's a crypto program—so we could write back and forth without anyone snooping on us.

"The Dunlaps invited Teesha and me out to Troy for a two-week visit the summer before the Crash. It was an extension of our honeymoon trip to Yellowstone. It was kind of funny when we got there to Roger's ranch. You see, we had never met face-to-face, or even spoken on the phone—everything was by e-mail, you see—so none of the Templars realized that we were black folks. Roger just said, 'Hey, cyberspace is color blind, and so am I. Welcome!' That's the kind of guy he was. We liked the Templars a lot, and they liked us. I told the Dunlaps that I was going to try to find a job in Idaho after I got my degree.

"Officially we weren't Templar members when the Schumer hit the fan, but we figured that they were our best bet. We couldn't get through to them before we left because all the long distance lines were down, and our local Internet port server was hosed. My dad lent me his mini-Winnebago, and Teesha and I crammed as much as we could into it. Dad said that he was going to stick it out with his neighbors in the suburbs. We arrived here not long after the riots started, and we got immediately assigned to the ranch security and hunting detail."

Jeff drummed his fingertips on the stock of his HK, considering what he had heard. Finally, he intoned, "You know, we've bumped into a lot of the local militias in the last few months. We've done our best to help them out too, just like you. Up until now, we haven't invited any of them to join us. Either they were too inexperienced, or they had more people in their units than we wanted to add to ours. We like to keep our signature small. In your case, however, I think that the *Commandante* will make an exception. Are you interested?"

Teesha gave a toothy smile and nodded enthusiastically to her husband. Tony reached out to shake Trasel's hand and declared, "Sure, Jeff. We'll join if you'll take us."

CHAPTER 29
Tolvajärvi

"Ever so often, the tree of liberty must be watered
with the blood of patriots and tyrants."

—*Thomas Jefferson*

It was bitter cold. The snow had been coming down steadily for several days. As the patrol worked its way toward Potlatch in the dim twilight, they could hear the shrieks of a Katushya rocket barrage, followed by the distant rumbling of the impacts, far in the distance. All five of the patrol members were wearing hooded snow camouflage ponchos that Kevin and Della had sewn from white bedsheets. They were cut extra long to accommodate backpacks. All of them were wearing small, improvised snowshoes made from willow boughs laced with parachute cord and rawhide. They halted on a wooded knoll that was just out of line of sight to the town. This was both their bivouac site and objective rally point (ORP).

It was nearly daylight by the time they had set up their pair of tents and rolled out their sleeping bags. They changed trousers, hanging their wet ones up inside of the tents to dry. Then they prayed and shared a breakfast of venison pemmican, dried apples, and dried biscuits, washed down with water. They had kept their canteens under their coats to keep them from freezing. Mike and Lisa Nelson snuggled in their Wiggy's FTRSS bags, gradually getting warm after a numbing all-night march. Mike rubbed his hands together vigorously. They took turns rubbing each other's feet, trying to restore circulation. The air temperature outside the tent hovered around 5 degrees Fahrenheit. It would peak at just 10 degrees that afternoon. Just before he drifted off to sleep, Mike told Lisa, "Tonight will be one to remember. I wish Dan Fong was here to be in on it." Outside, Kevin stood the first day watch.

Contact with a local rancher in January in the sixth year of the Crunch had provided Michael Nelson's company with a valuable piece of intelligence: Potlatch was recently re-garrisoned by a company of the Belgian Chemical Corps, and their security was lax. The five-member raiding party consisted of the Nelsons, Kevin Lendel, and the Carltons. The snow had stopped for the present, but Kevin's pocket barometer was falling, telling them that more was on the way. There would be a half moon rising that evening, but it would be obscured by clouds.

At 7 p.m., Mike left alone to conduct a patrol leader's recon of Potlatch. He picked out a hillock two-hundred-and-fifty yards south of the nearest house. There, he spread out his poncho, rolled out his FTRSS bag, and set up his Bushnell spotting scope on its stubby tripod. Through the scope, Mike saw the Belgians change guards at 9 p.m. and midnight, right on schedule. At twelve-fifteen, Nelson headed back to the ORP. The raiding party struck their tents and reloaded their gear in their packs. At twelve-thirty Mike gave his revised op order. Then they did a final inspection. Two noisy canteens were silenced by combining their contents. When the cold weather had set in, in November, they had delubricated their guns and lightly relubricated them with Moly Coat—powdered molybdenum disulfide. Nonetheless, they manually tested their actions to ensure that they weren't frozen shut. Then they set off in a widely spaced single file, with their rifles and shotguns at port arms beneath their ponchos.

As they approached the town, the whine of a generator grew steadily louder. Mike had been told by the rancher that he should expect it. The Belgians had brought with them a trailer-mounted fifteen-kilowatt generator to power their lights, radios, and some small space heaters. On a listening halt, Mike smiled and whispered to Lisa, "This will be great. Not only will their night vision be ruined by the lights, but the noise of the generator will cover the noise of our approach." Mike had been told by the rancher that there were no civilians left living in town. There would be no confusing the bad guys and friendlies. They had also been told that the guard changed every three hours. The Belgians in the garrison company had originally been trained and equipped for chemical warfare decontamination. Here in America, their primary duty was to act as garrison soldiers. Most of their duty hours were spent guarding various facilities and manning roadblocks. Only occasionally did they get to use their cylinders to eliminate resistance fighters that the infantry had found hiding in bunkers. Their field SOP was to suit up and gas the bunkers and then leave for three days. Then they would return, again wearing their Mission Oriented Protective Posture (MOPP) suits and protective masks with green ring filters, in case any residual gas remained. Then they would drag out the bodies and gear. They liked the duty. The occasional gassing gave them the chance to gather plenty of booty. Because they were almost the only unit in the region with full MOPP suits, nobody else could handle their loot. If an officer from another unit made a fuss, they would offer them the doubled black plastic trash bags with the jocular warning, "Here, go ahead, take these! But, of course, remember that they are contaminated with VX, so be careful." Then the officers would make a quick and polite exit, leaving the bags behind. Incidents like those made the Belgians laugh.

Most of their time was spent in town garrisons, getting drunk. Occasionally some hashish would come in the mail pouch from friends in Belgium. Then they'd have their big parties. Sometimes they could even catch a local teenage girl to gang rape. The Belgians would have otherwise liked being posted to Potlatch, but there were no residents left in town. It wasn't as much fun without a few rapes.

Despite the Corps-wide "two-man rule," there was only one sentry on duty when Mike's raid patrol arrived. He was slightly drunk. His name was Per Boeynts, a Flemish-speaking Walloon private from the countryside northeast of Brussels. He hated being posted to UN peacekeeping duty in America. In the last year he had developed into a chronic alcoholic. At one-ten a.m., he stood just inside the doorway of what had been the sheriff's office, trying to stay warm. His coat collar was turned up, and he was wearing his long underwear, a set of cold weather fatigues with cold weather liners, a sweater, and his heavy wool greatcoat. Still, he felt cold. The thermometer read 3 degrees Fahrenheit. Per wondered what that equated to on the Celsius scale. He could hardly wait the hour and a half until his relief was due. Then he could get back to bed.

Per had left a pair of Dutch-made night vision goggles on the chair by the orderly's desk. By SOP they were supposed to be hanging on a cord around his neck. He hadn't bothered to put them on, because the lights in the buildings would cause them to shut off automatically, anyway. The night sentries often cursed 1st Sergeant Van Duyn for making them carry the stupid things. But it was SOP, he said, so they were ordered to carry them whenever on night guard duty.

Like the other pickets, he had been ordered to walk in a circuit outside. But Per decided that tonight it was too cold, and the snow was above his boots. When he walked in it, he got his lower trouser legs wet, and that made it feel even colder. Just inside the open door was good enough for him. After all, 1st Sergeant Van Duyn was asleep, so he wouldn't ever know the difference. He turned toward the desk to get another cigarette. As he flicked the lighter, he was struck at the base of his skull with a heavy ball-peen hammer. He fell on the desk and then rolled and landed on the floor. The hammer came down twice more, now on his temple.

After he was sure that the soldier was dead, Mike tucked the hammer back into his belt. It had become his favorite sentry removal tool in recent months. The private's rifle—a bullpup Steyr AUG with a forty-two-round magazine— was leaning up against the door molding. A thorough search of the office revealed the night vision goggles, a gray-green duffel bag, some local maps, a duty log book, rosters, and a jumble of papers and faxes written in four different languages—French, German, English, and what Mike surmised was Flemish. He also found six spare loaded thirty-round AUG magazines in an engineer's pouch, an M17A2 gas mask, an angle-head flashlight, two spare odd looking screw-in batteries that he assumed were for the night vision goggles, a brown cardboard box of ten olive drab U.S.-made batteries that looked like D cells marked "BA-3030," four sealed MREs, a walkie-talkie radio of a sort that he didn't recognize, four automatic atropine injectors, a jar of Belgian instant coffee, a German-English/English-German dictionary, and half a carton of Cuban cigarettes.

Mike removed the magazine from the AUG and cleared its chamber. Then he flipped the rifle's barrel release button and removed the barrel assembly. It was much more compact in two pieces. Mike stuffed everything but the gas mask in the duffel bag to be sorted out later.

He strapped on the duffel bag, underneath his poncho. He picked up his gun—a Remington 870 with tritium sights— waiting just outside the door along with his gloves. As he stepped outside, he could see Kevin approaching, carrying a plastic ammo can in each hand. Kevin whispered, "They are all billeted in the church building next door, all right. Their trucks are an absolute gold mine! Lisa found some cylinders marked with the skull and crossbones and 'VX.' That's nerve gas, isn't it?"

"It sure is nerve gas! Non-persistent type," Mike replied enthusiastically. "I read about it in one of Todd's Army manuals. It just takes a few parts per million and everyone it touches is dead in thirty seconds. A couple of tiny droplets the size of a pinhead will do the job. We certainly want to take all of those. I'm setting that as our new top priority."

All of them but Doug left fifteen minutes later, heading southeast, carrying the gear that they had removed from the trucks. They had with them three twenty-pound VX cylinders that felt like they were filled. Their valves were secured with safety wires. Doug Carlton followed their trail in the snow and caught up a quarter hour later. They slogged on through the deep snow in silence. As they topped a high hill, they turned to look back to the north. In the distance they could see the flames of the vehicles, generator, and billets building burning.

The patrol covered nearly six miles before dawn. It started to snow again heavily, and the wind came up stronger, still from the south, drifting the snow. It quickly obscured their tracks. As the morning light gathered, they made an abrupt turn in their direction of travel and moved a quarter mile into a dense stand of timber. They set up a new bivouac site with the tents widely spaced.

Once they were out of view of the others, Della kissed Doug, and declared, "I'm so glad that you're alive. That was one gutsy maneuver!"

Doug replied, "Well, somebody had to do it, and there was no reason to risk more than one of us. Besides, I'm the one with the most experience in a M17 series mask."

"Tell me how you did it," Della implored.

Doug paused from his work erecting the Moss Little Dipper tent and answered, "Well, first I scouted out the billets. They had everything closed up tight except for one door. They had a heater of some sort running in there. I could feel the heat coming out the door, and hear its fan roaring. It made great cover noise. The door was left cracked open because they had a fat power cable from the generator leading in. I stepped well away from the building and tested the wind. It was slow and steady from the south. I cut five six-minute fuses for the grenades. One for the generator, one for each of their trucks, and one for just outside the door. The generator was in a rectangular cabinet with a flat top—how convenient for a thermite grenade." He grinned.

He pulled the green rain fly out of the stuff sack, and continued, "As for the trucks, I opened their hoods and put the thermite grenades on top of the engine blocks, just in front of the air cleaners. Luckily, the Belgians' rigs don't have hood padlocks like most U.S. Army vehicles. I put the VX cylinder you set aside for me—the one that felt half-full—with its butt end poking in the door. I taped the thermite grenade in the notch between the valve stem and the body of the cylinder, so the thermite glob would be sure to cut the end of the casing off. From what I've heard from Lon about compressed welding cylinders and dive tanks, it probably took off like a rocket into the building once it began to vent.

"I checked the wind again, just 'cause I'm paranoid, then I lit the fuse for the grenade on the VX cylinder. I dashed over and lit the ones on the trucks, and then the one on the generator, and I beat feet out of there. After a couple of minutes, I watched my Bulova as I ran. Just before the first of the grenades was going to start its burn, I stopped, masked, and cleared. Then I started out after you again. It's a good thing that you folks left a clear trail in the snow. The visibility in one of those masks is the pits, especially in low light. And, I could hardly breathe with the mask on, so I had to slow down my pace. I took it off just before I caught up with you folks. Those things feel *very* claustrophobic. I was really happy to take it off. For VX, I really should have been wearing a full MOPP suit, since you can absorb that stuff right through your skin. But we didn't have one. Oh well, at least the mask would have given me a bit of protection if the wind had shifted." Doug finished clipping on the rain fly and delivered, "It was no big deal, Dell. It was all really quite easy." Della kissed him again.

Major Udo Kuntzler never went anywhere without his bodyguards. He had selected an American E-5 and two E-4s for the job. All three were recently Ranger school qualified. All three carried flattop M4 carbines with Trijicon ACOG scopes and MELIOS infrared laser sights. They also were each issued Beretta M9 pistols and AN/PVS-5 night vision goggles. He made sure that they were provided plenty of ammo to practice with. Kuntzler's personal weapon was a Heckler und Koch MP-5K PDW. He never went anywhere without it, either. He jokingly referred to his bodyguards as his "praetorians." He called the HK PDW his "American Express Card." He often jested, "I don't leave home without it."

Kuntzler was the UN adviser to the 3/2 Cavalry Brigade. He had been chosen for the job because he had both a strong grasp of tactics and good command of both spoken and written English. As the UN adviser, he was expected to go wherever the brigade went. He usually traveled in HHC-01—the headquarters company's M3 Bradley CFV. Once in a while, he would go out to oversee individual line companies.

On February twelfth, Kuntzler and his bodyguards were driving up Highway 95 in a Humvee to "liase" with the company commander of Bravo Company of the 3/2. He had to brief him about an upcoming search and destroy mission. Kuntzler worked on his op-order notes as they drove north. As usual, they were written in English. He wanted to do everything that he could to fit in, and to seem less foreign. Soon after they passed through Moscow, the Humvee struck a mine. It was a small "toe popper," but enough to blow out the left front tire. On the icy road, this event was more than sufficient to skid the Humvee into a deep ditch on the west side of the road. The left wheels were deep in slush, and the Humvee had nearly flipped over. The driver tried driving out, but despite four-wheel drive, the wheels spun helplessly. Even if they could get it out of the ditch, they would have to change the tire to get going again.

There were no other vehicles in sight. Kuntzler weighed his alternatives. There was no radio in the Humvee. Due to lack of maintenance facilities, radios were a scarce item reserved for command posts and maneuver units. Rather than wait where they were until help arrived, and perhaps risk contact with a resistance patrol, he decided that they would hike back to the security checkpoint at the outskirts of Moscow. It was just two kilometers away.

His guards put on their gloves and then their woodland pattern Gore-Tex over their M65 field jackets. The Gore-Tex coats had brown "bear suit" cold weather liners. Kuntzler was wearing just his fleck pattern field coat. He wished that his coat had a liner, and a hood like the Gore-Tex. Since today was to be a liaison visit rather than a field operation, he was wearing his sky blue UN beret. His ears started getting cold soon after he stepped out of the Humvee.

They had walked slowly, carefully eyeing the ground for evidence of mines. They had already spread out to a safe interval. Just as Kuntzler passed a telephone pole, there was an explosion. His sensations were overwhelmed. There was a roar of gunfire. A horrible burning sensation stung his face, his eyes, his mouth. For a few moments, he couldn't breathe. He fell to the ground gasping. His eyes were full of tears, and he couldn't see. He heard shouts and loud footsteps. He was kicked hard once in the testicles. The MP-5 submachinegun was simultaneously ripped from his hands. Then he was quickly handcuffed, searched, and blindfolded. His eyes were tearing uncontrollably and his sinuses were dripping heavily. Kuntzler heard more men shouting, and barking dogs. Within minutes, he was bound hand and foot and strapped onto a dogsled. He heard a man yell, "*Vive la Maquisards!*" as the sled pulled away. Kuntzler had no idea which direction the sled was traveling.

The ambush had been set up forty-five minutes before. The ambushers hid in the clumps of grass and snowdrifts, sixty yards back from the road. They had placed five toe poppers in the northbound lane of the road. They were staggered slightly, so at least one of them would be run over by a tire. Next, they buried a plastic baggie filled with a half-pound of CS powder that they had extracted from a Smith and Wesson riot control grenade. The baggie was buried just beneath the snow on the west side of the road. A one-third stick of dynamite with a blasting cap was wired directly below it.

The ambush went almost exactly as planned. The Humvee arrived ten minutes after their intelligence source said it would. They had hoped that after hitting the mine it would roll completely over, but lying at a 35-degree angle in the ditch was good enough. It wasn't going anywhere. Within a few minutes, the soldiers were out of the stranded Humvee and approached the kill zone on foot. Two of the soldiers carried M4 carbines. Using a locking cable release, Jeff switched on the tripod-mounted video camera to record the action. He waited until his intended target—the man with the different style uniform and the briefcase—was a pace in front of the CS mine. Then Jeff Trasel command-detonated it with a Claymore clacker. Tony, Teesha, Ian, and Mary hosed down the three guards. Their target was overwhelmed by the cloud of CS powder and was easily subdued. Lawrence Raselhoff and his Moscow Maquis came out of the tree line just as planned, just after the shooting stopped. One dogsled headed straight to the ambush site. The other carried a Maquisard to search the Humvee.

At first, they were all elated by the fact that they had captured so many fine weapons and night vision devices. They didn't realize it until later, but they had also just captured some very important documents and the man who would become the most valuable intelligence asset in the Pacific Northwest theatre of operations.

• • •

The UN Regional Administrator was angry. Reginald Snodgrass had a reputation for having a bad temper. On two occasions he had carried out summary executions right in his office, with a revolver. When he was mad, he didn't care if he made a mess. Someone else always cleaned it up. His staff tried to find things to keep themselves busy and away from the building on his "bad hair days." In this instance, he was angry because he didn't like having to leave his warm office in the dead of winter. He much preferred having people come to his office in Lewiston for meetings, where he felt secure.

This particular meeting was to be held at the abandoned town of De Smet, nineteen miles north of Moscow. Granted, it was a convenient central location for the commanders of the garrison forces and the civilian authorities from Coeur d'Alene, Lewiston, Moscow, Pullman, Kellogg, Sandpoint, and Saint Maries to meet. But Reggie didn't like the meeting spot. One of his advisers had been ambushed within earshot of Moscow, just five days before. Anything outside the city limits of Moscow was bandit country, in his book.

Despite his reservations, Snodgrass realized that he had to be at the meeting. Word had it that heads would roll. Not only was he expected to be there but he wanted to see the fun when they started pointing fingers. Since he was a civilian UN Administrator, and the problem at hand was strictly one of military security, he knew the fingers wouldn't be pointed at him. As a ten-year veteran of British civil service before he joined the UN, Reggie Snodgrass knew how those games were played. He grumbled to his aides about the weather as they all loaded up. At least they had the privilege of traveling to the meeting in a well-heated APC.

The meeting itself was held in the front parlor of the old De Smet mission building. It was situated on a hill, with a broad circular driveway. When Snodgrass and his staff arrived, ten minutes before the scheduled start time, there was already a roaring fire going in the fireplace. Coffee, brandy, and finger foods were served before the meeting got started. These niceties and the inevitable ensuing chatter delayed the start of the briefings for twenty minutes.

The meeting was a big event, just as Snodgrass expected. Even the Second Corps commander and his staff were there. It was what the Yank soldiers called "a big dog and pony show" or "a real goat rope." Reggie loved American colloquial terms. Outside, there were two tanks and more than thirty APCs— an assortment of BTRs, BMPs, Marders, and Bradleys—in a semicircle around the mission grounds. Most of the large security detachment was ordered to stand outside their vehicles so that there would be no chance of infiltrators escaping their gaze and slipping through the perimeter. There were also road-blocks set up on all four approaches to town. The security arrangements had been planned more than a week in advance. Realizing that a gathering of commanders would be a tempting target, nothing was left to chance. Engineer Corps personnel spent three chilly days searching the building and grounds for bombs, using both bomb-sniffing dogs and metal detectors.

The first briefing was a general situation overview. It was given by Colonel Horst Blucher, G2 of the UNPROFOR Second Corps. Other, more detailed briefings were scheduled for later in the morning. Blucher was a tall angular man with a booming voice. Standing before an acetate-covered map board and holding a retractable pointer, he read from prepared notes. "Zuh security situation in western Montana, northern Idaho, and eastern Washington is very much worsening. In northern Idaho, our Second Corps has, to date, killed 295 terrorists, and captured 17. These latters, of course, have all been thoroughly interrogated and dispatched. An additional 172 troublesome civilians, all deemed potential security risks and/or politically unreliable and/or possible resistance sympathizers, have been transported to zuh work and rehabilitation camp at Gowen Field.

"Since arriving in this region, we have suffered 918 casualties, killed and wounded. Another 97 of our soldiers, mainly American nationals, are missing—and presumed either dead or deserted. 126 of our vehicles and 11 aircraft have been destroyed, mainly by arson. An additional three trucks and one APC have been stolen and not yet recovered.

"Over 400 weapons of all descriptions are missing, and presumably now in zuh hands of these terrorists. Of those, most were lost in ambushes. A surprisingly large number were taken by deserters. Another 312 weapons, mainly vehicular mounted, have been written off our property books as 'destroyed.'

"Zuh strength of zuh terrorist bands in northern Idaho was originally estimated at around 150. Now, despite heavy losses that we have inflicted, their strength is estimated at over 700, and growing. They are actively recruiting in the towns and on ranches. Their recruits are mainly young, healthy, and already proficient with firearms. In this region almost every adult male, and many females, are skilled hunters and scharf shooters. This dreadful winter weather has decreased zuh number of attacks, but at zuh same time reduced our own effectiveness in our counterinsurgency campaign. These terrorists are using zuh inclement weather to their advantage, to conduct training of their new recruitments at remote camps within zuh National Forests...." Just then, a loud bang was heard in front of the building. It rattled the windows. Colonel Blucher stopped abruptly. There were anxious murmurs in the room. A few officers pulled pistols from their holsters.

The Bundeswehr major who was in charge of interior security for the meeting ran to the door to see what had happened. A blast of cold air spilled in as he stood at the main door. He shouted back to those assembled, "Nothing to worry about, just a small time-delayed bomb underneath one of the Unimog trucks from Moscow. It wasn't close to the building at all, and it didn't even set the truck's fuel tank on fire. These constant little acts of sabotage are so inept and pathetic."

Colonel Blucher laughed, and looked down at his notes, preparing to resume his briefing. He felt strangely dizzy. He couldn't focus on the papers, and the light in the room seemed to dim. His hands started to tremble. He looked up and saw that most of the men in the room were either doubled-over in their chairs or prostrate on the floor, twitching. Blucher's knees buckled and he fell on the floor with a gasp. He heard a lieutenant in the back of the room yell "Gas!" Just before he died, Blucher felt himself wet his pants, and his bowels sloughing.

• • •

The turning point for many Americans came in May of the sixth year since the Crunch, when the Federals announced that, due to widespread forgery of the National ID Card, they had begun a pilot program implanting a magnetic biochip in the right hand of newborn babies. The biochips held 1,332 lines of data. Passing the hand over a scanner would show a dossier of the individual, and their account balances. By May of the next year, the announcement said, every U.S. resident, regardless of age, would be required to have either a National ID Card or the new Mark IV biochip. And, as of the following May, the biochip would completely replace the National ID Card, and all paper currency would be null and void. After that, without the Mark IV, residents wouldn't be able to function day to day. They couldn't transact business at any store, enroll in a school, pay their property taxes, or transfer the title of an automobile or land. Resistance was popping up throughout the country, even in previously "safe" areas, soon after the National ID Card announcement. News of the Chicago Blindings a month later was an even stronger catalyst for resistance. A boisterous anti-government demonstration in downtown Chicago was dispersed with the aid of a Dazer alexandrite laser. The handheld Dazer system had been developed by the U.S. Army CECOM in the early 1990s. It was designed to destroy enemy electro-optic systems such as FLIRs, starlight scopes, and thermal sights. Given its power and 750-nanometer wavelength, it was far from "eye safe." It could destroy a human retina instantly. In the Chicago incident, a French infantry NCO "painted" the front ranks of the crowd with a Dazer for just a few seconds. More than eighty people were permanently blinded. The Chicago Blindings went down in the history as an infamous act that rivaled the Boston Massacre and Pearl Harbor.

No troops from east of the Mississippi could be spared for the western campaigns. The new Second Corps commander was instructed to "hold until relieved" and specifically not to detach any forces to attempt to re-pacify southern Idaho. No move was to be made into southern Idaho until the situation in the north was more favorable. He reconsolidated and reorganized his available units, and waited. The Federals were at a full standstill and in a defensive posture throughout the Second Corps area.

In a surprise move on the fourth of July, in the sixth year after the market crash, the Idaho legislature declared secession from the union. Oregon, Washington, California, North and South Dakota, and Alaska followed suit in the next two weeks. Within days, the lightly manned garrisons in southern Idaho fell to the rebels. Most surrendered, without a serious fight. The Second Corps was bogged down in northern Idaho, fully engaged against the resistance forces. The newly assigned Second Corps commander sent countless faxes to the UN headquarters, begging for reinforcements and replacements. The answer was always the same: "None available."

Still more disheartening news for the Second Corps came on July tenth. Two line companies, Bravo Company of the 114th Armor Battalion and Alpha Company of the 519th Infantry Battalion, had turned coats en masse. Their commanders had parlayed directly with the resistance and then enthusiastically put their entire units under the operational control of the Northwest Militia. When they went over the hill, they took all their equipment with them. Even more importantly, they supplied the resistance with current maps, plans, op orders, CEOIs, and cryptographic equipment.

CHAPTER 30
Radio Ranch

"The people of the United States are the rightful masters
of both Congress and the Courts, not to overthrow the Constitution,
but to overthrow the men who pervert the Constitution."

—*Abraham Lincoln*

Edgar Rhodes had just turned seventy-two when the Crunch hit. He had lost his wife two years earlier, to cancer. His only son, an electrical engineer, had moved his family to Brazil a decade earlier. Edgar was alone at the ranch. The sign by the front door read "Radio Ranch," and the place certainly lived up to its moniker. He had selected the property forty years earlier, specifically because of its favorable ridge top siting. The ranch parcel was thirty-five land-locked acres. His road transited deeded right-of-ways through two neighboring properties to get out to the county road. Edgar liked the privacy. The ranch had plentiful water—a big spring near the bottom of the property—but not much else. There were no trees and there was not much topsoil. Rocks poked through the surface of the soil throughout the property. But Edgar liked his ridge top. He said that it gave him "line of sight to the world." Eventually, five antenna masts were scattered around the house. The largest was his "moon bounce," perched atop a sixty-foot tower. There were also dipole and sloper antennas stretched as far as eighty-eight yards from the house, in several directions.

Edgar used a pair of hydraulic rams to lift the water to the house. They were very inefficient, but reliable. The twenty-five gallons a minute at the spring yielded only five gallons a minute at the house.

• • •

Thirteen months after the Federals invaded the Palouse Hills region, Edgar was the recipient of a package that he hadn't expected. A knock on his door at 11 p.m. woke him from a sound sleep. Edgar put on his robe and slippers and picked up his Belgian Browning twelve-gauge shotgun. He was about to snap on the 24 VDC porch light, when he heard a muffled but familiar voice through the door, "Edgar, it's me, Vern. Leave the light off! I need to ask you a favor! You've got to hide this package." Edgar drew back the heavy bars that he had built for the top, middle, and bottom of the door. He opened the door warily, and asked, "What's so important you have to come here in the middle of the night?" He could see his neighbor in the dim moonlight. There was a woman with him. They were silent. Edgar motioned inward with his hand, and said, "Well, come on in."

Vern and the woman crept in, groping in the dark front hall. After Edgar had rebolted the door, he lit a big "triple wick" candle and carried it to the kitchen. Vern and the unfamiliar woman followed him. They sat around the table, with the candle between them, lighting their faces.

It was then that Edgar could see that the woman was emaciated. She appeared to be around sixty year old, with graying hair. Her eyes were sunken, and the skin around her jaw seemed taut. She also looked frightened. She kept glancing at Vern. Vern spoke in a jumble. "I've just gotta ask your help. This is Maggie. She escaped from the Federal camp down at Gowen Field, three weeks ago. Folks have been shuttlin' her north, here into rebel-controlled land. I can't keep her. I can barely feed my own family. I figured that since you were alone, and that because you eat good, that, well, you know...."

Edgar raised his hand to signal Vern to stop his chatter, and then asked, "Can you cook, Maggie?"

She nodded.

"Can you mend clothes?"

She nodded again.

"Do you know how to shoot?"

She nodded again.

"Can you speak, Maggie?"

She laughed, and answered, "Of course I can speak!"

"How old are you?"

"Fifty."

"How is your strength? You look something terrible thin."

"I've lost a lot of weight, but I still have my strength. Will you hide me here?"

Without a pause, Edgar answered assuredly, "Certainly, ma'am. Nobody bothers me here. The Federals have never noticed me. Even if they did, they'd think I was an eccentric old hermit. Come to think of it, I *am* an eccentric old hermit. I suppose some day they'll come looking, to confiscate my radios. But in the meantime, since I'm so far off the county road, nobody is going to notice that there's somebody else living here." Maggie beamed and said quietly, "God bless you."

Vern stood up and made his goodbyes, thanking Edgar Rhodes repeatedly, and giving Maggie a hug. As Edgar shook his hand, Vern said, "Now you take good care of this little gal, Edgar." He turned and disappeared into the darkness.

Edgar made Maggie a batch of scrambled eggs before bed. He apologized for not having any coffee or tea. As he walked her down the hall to the guest bedroom, he said, "You can tell me all about your adventures in the morning."

The next morning, Edgar went looking on the front porch, where he expected to find Maggie's luggage. There was none. She had only the clothes on her back. They consisted of a long and tattered gray dress, a pair of filthy tennis shoes with no socks, and an oversized man's forest green trench coat.

Over a breakfast of eggs, flat bread and honey, and slices of cheese, Maggie told her story. "We lived in Payette. My husband had died five years before the stock market crash, so I went to live with my daughter and her family. Three weeks after the troops and the UN administrators arrived, they came for our whole family: my daughter, my son-in-law, their two children, and me. Both my daughter Julie and my son-in-law Mark were with the resistance. They were trying to organize groups in the neighborhood for sabotage. One of our neighbors must have informed on us.

"They surrounded the house at 6 o'clock in the morning. Must have been forty of them. They said that they'd burn us out if we didn't come out with our hands up. They dragged Julie and Mark away in handcuffs. They took Mark's guns and CB radio as 'evidence.' They gave me, and the children, just five minutes to pack a few clothes, while they stood there with Kalashnikovs pointed at us. Then they searched me again, and they took everything that I had packed in the suitcases and the duffel bag and scattered it across the yard, looking for 'contraband.' They laughed and kicked me while I was picking it all back up and trying to repack it.

"When Mark shouted at them, the soldiers threatened to kill him. Finally, after I had most of the clothes picked up, they threw the bags up into the back of a big canvas-topped Army truck, and handcuffed me next to Julie and Mark. They even handcuffed the kids. We were all connected to a big heavy chain—it looked like a big boat anchor chain, running lengthwise down the middle of the truck bed. It was welded down at both ends.

"They stopped and picked up another family later the same day, the Weinsteins. By the time they had them loaded in the truck, Mrs. Weinstein was having a nervous breakdown. To her, it was the Holocaust all over again. They had lost great grandparents and several great aunts and great uncles in the Nazi years in Germany. Seeing it happen all over again was just too much for her.

"We were nearly fifteen hours in that truck, without a drop of water. They only stopped once to let us relieve ourselves, and we had to do that in full view of everyone. They did what they called 'double locking' the handcuffs, so that they wouldn't tighten up, but even still they left horrible red marks. Poor Mark lost some of the circulation in his left hand, but the guards wouldn't do anything about it. When they finally took the cuffs off of him, his hand was all puffed up. He must have had permanent nerve damage in that hand.

"Gowen was a horrible place. We were put in a barracks with eleven other families. There were fifty-nine of us in that barracks, at first. We had one large pot, and we had to do all of our cooking in that, as best we could. There was a weekly ration of spuds. And once in a while, there would be some beans, or bread, or wheat. But there was never enough. Once in a blue moon we'd get some rotten lettuce or cabbage.

"We never got a trial. There was never even any mention of it. And when we asked about appealing our confinement, or asked when we would be released, they just laughed at us. Most of the adults were expected to work. Some of it was just make-work. Others worked in the sweatshops. At Gowen, the big industry was boots. Julie was one of the boot makers. She worked eleven hours a day, with fifteen minutes for lunch. If she didn't do her quota of stitching, she was beaten.

"They came most every day, to take away one or two people for interrogation. It was usually the men. They came back, usually a day or two later, looking ghastly. Sometimes they couldn't walk. They were usually bleeding. Sometimes they were bleeding out of the rectum from being kicked so much. They often talked about the torture: beatings, whippings, electric cattle prods. Oh, and the bruises, so many bruises! I thank the Lord that I never got picked up for interrogation. I don't think that I could have survived it.

"After three weeks, they came for Mark. He fought them. He hit one of the Belgian soldiers square in the nose, and I think he broke it. His nose bled like a headless chicken. They started beating Mark even before they drove off with him. They never brought Mark back. We were sure they must have killed him.

"They let some of us older women go out to gather firewood, between the inner and outer fence. The inner fence was new, and had that dreadful razor wire. The outer fence was old. I found a gap where the chain link had parted at the base of a post. I pulled it up and squeezed through. I knew that if they spotted me outside the second fence that they'd shoot me down. But by then, I didn't care. I just wanted out of there. Julie had often told me, 'Mom, if you ever have the chance to go, then *go!*' She said that I shouldn't worry about her and the kids. So I went without regrets.

"I walked for three days, drinking out of stock ponds before somebody found me. Seven families helped hide me and move me along, by car, by wagon, and on horseback. All those families were a wonderful blessing. And now I'm here."

Edgar asked, "Do you have any family, other than your daughter and her kids?"

"No."

"Then you are welcome to stay here, indefinitely."

A week after she arrived, Edgar took Maggie as his common-law wife.

Five weeks after Maggie's arrival, Edgar unknowingly brought a bug back with him when shopping at the monthly Moscow barter market. He soon got over it, but when Maggie got the flu, she quickly grew dehydrated and weak. She died while Edgar was sleeping.

Edgar was convinced that if it were not for her malnourishment at the Gowen camp that Maggie would have recovered from the flu. Cancer had robbed him of his first wife, and now the Federals had robbed him of his second. He never forgave the Federals for that. Before he met Maggie, he had no desire to join the resistance. He sided with them, but did nothing to actively help. But when Maggie unexpectedly came into his life and then so unexpectedly left, it changed him. The day after he buried Maggie, Edgar started packing.

• • •

Soon after joining the resistance, Edgar was put in charge of the fledgling Signals Intelligence Section. He had had communications intelligence (Comint) experience many years before with the Naval Security Group. He had been stationed at Skaggs Island, at the north end of the San Francisco Bay. He soon put that experience to good use. Their well-camouflaged intercept site tents were generally set up on low hills, usually within twenty miles of Moscow. They had already been operating for nearly a year, on a makeshift basis, using just a couple of Uniden multi-band scanners. When he joined, Edgar brought with him a wealth of Comint knowledge, organizational skills, and lots of additional equipment. This included Drake and Icom shortwave receivers, two additional scanners, a pair of "Gunnplexer" microwave transceivers, a spectrum analyzer, three cassette tape recorders, and several custom-made antennas. Edgar transformed the amateurish section into a professional unit of Comint specialists.

Edgar was a half-century older than most of the men and women in his section. They treated him like their adoptive grandfather. He was a self-professed "crotchety old man," and they loved it. During some quiet times, he entertained them with old ditties that he played on his ukulele. He sang 1940's pop songs like "They Got an Awful Lot of Coffee in Brazil" and "Three Little Fishies." The young resistance fighters loved them.

The section got their most prized piece of equipment from the Keane Team, the winter after Edgar took over. It was a Watkins-Johnson AN/PRD-11 VHF man-portable intercept and direction finding set. It had been captured from the Federals, complete with an H-Adcock antenna array. Using microprocessor-generated time-of-arrival calculations with the H-Adcock antenna, the PRD-11 could provide lines of bearing on VHF signals, on a three-digit display. The "W-J" could also do intercept (without DF) of HF signals. With the single W-J, they could only produce individual lines of bearing, but even this was valuable for building an intelligence picture of the battlefield.

The original sealed batteries for the PRD-11 were soon expended, but the resourceful crew at the intercept site provided the correct voltage for the system using car batteries. All of the other equipment at the site was similarly powered by car batteries, all of which were laboriously carried to the site, and back down to town for recharging.

Eventually, there were six men and two women on the intercept team. They manned three round-the-clock intercept-shifts, with two intercept operators per eight-hour shift or "trick." The "day trick" also had two extra staff members. The first was a Battlefield Integrator/Briefer who plotted "best estimate" enemy unit locations on an acetate-covered map board. The other was a Traffic Analyst or "TA," who reconstructed the enemy networks by analyzing the pattern of traffic. The TA's most important time of the day came during the network roll calls that were conducted by the Federal and UN units each morning. Assisting the operational team were a full-time cook, three security men, two teenage message runners, and five "sherpas" who hauled food, water, and batteries to the site.

Most of the sherpas used captured ALICE pack frames with cargo shelves, a few had less comfortable 1950s-vintage army pack boards. All but one sherpa spent their nights with their families in town.

They moved the intercept site roughly six times a year. Each time, this required the temporary requisition of an extra thirty sherpas or a dozen pack mules. Edgar and his team were careful not to operate any radio transmitters from the site—only receivers. Knowing the Federals' direction-finding capability, the last thing that they wanted to do was key a microphone. All of their messages and intelligence reports were sent out in handwritten notes, carried by couriers.

In addition to generating intelligence reports, Edgar's team was also in charge of giving communications security (ComSec) training to the leaders of all the militias in the region. Edgar tailored his ComSec lectures to match the expertise of each militia. One afternoon he gave a lecture to Frank Scheimer, the executive officer (XO) of the Blue Blaze Irregulars. Edgar had heard that this militia had a number of captured radios, but that they weren't savvy in their use.

Edgar sat Scheimer down before him, and waited while the XO readied his pen and notebook. Once he had his attention, Edgar began, "I won't bore you with an explanation on the theory of radio wave propagation. That would take too long, and besides, it is redundant to a handout that I will give you when

I'm done. Take the time to study it in detail, and ask me for clarification if you have any questions, before you head back to your operational area tomorrow. It is essential that you know the difference between ground wave and sky wave, the difference between AM and FM broadcast modulation, skip zone versus skip distance, the various frequency bands, and to know the ways that signals in those bands propagate through the atmosphere. The handout also includes basic instructions on how to use the phonetic alphabet, CEOIs, and so forth.

"So study that handout well, and then teach it to both your CO and your subordinates.

"My goal today is to first let you know what sort of equipment is out there—friendly, enemy, and captured enemy, and to teach you ComSec in a nutshell, so you won't get yourself killed or give the enemy valuable intelligence. The key acronym that I want you to remember is LPI: Low Probability of Intercept.

"First let me give you a general rundown on the equipment out there. Most of the long-range traffic you hear is in the High Frequency or 'HF' range. Beyond about twenty miles, most of the HF you hear propagates by multiple bounces off the various layers of the ionosphere that are described in your handout. How well HF propagates depends on the sunspot cycle. Right now, we are just coming down off of an eleven-year peak in the cycle, so HF is coming in remarkably well. The important thing to know about sky wave HF is that for all intents and purposes it is invulnerable to most tactical DFing equipment. This is because it comes in at 'near vertical incidence'—straight down from the ionosphere. With all the currently fielded tactical DFing equipment, you can't get a useful line of bearing—or 'LOB'—from that. But remember, ground wave HF *can* be DFed, but again, that is only at relatively short range.

"You've probably heard the shortwave 'pirate' stations like Radio Free America and The Intelligence Report that run at around 6955 and 7415 KHz at night, and higher freqs during the day. And, you've probably wondered why the Feds haven't shut them down. It's because the Federals can't DF them, so they don't have a *clue* where they are located. You see, those signals are coming from deep inside rebel-held territory, and the Feds are intercepting them via *sky wave*. It must be driving the Feds nuts. I guess that's why they try to jam them so much.

"Back before the Crash, the NSA had some pretty sophisticated HF-DF equipment back at Fort Meade, and the Army had a one-of-a-kind system called Track Wolf. It was made by a company called TCI down in Fremont, California. They used chirp sounders to judge the conditions of the ionosphere, and some pretty sophisticated algorithms to make sense of near vertical incidence sky waves. Track Wolf, for example, depended on two out-stations along a *thousand-mile long* baseline to generate useful cuts for HF-DF. Pretty sophisticated stuff. But, to the best of my knowledge, those systems aren't operating today. If they were, the Feds would have already used what's left of their ragtag air force to fly into rebel territory and bomb those transmitter sites.

"Most of the two-way equipment out there is Very High Frequency—VHF. VHF operates almost strictly ground wave—or line of sight—and is *very* vulnerable to DF."

The XO jotted down on his notepad:

HF Sky wave - No DF

HF Ground wave - Can be DFed!

VHF (All ground wave) - Can be DFed!

"There are lots of civilian two-meter hand-talkies. Of course, the old networks of two-meter repeater stations are long since gone, but those radios still work great in line of sight. Some of the hand-talkies and a lot of the old in-dash rigs are *frequency agile*."

The XO cocked his head and blinked, so Edgar explained, "When they came from the factory, the two-meter radios could receive all the way from 118 to 170 megahertz but because of FCC regulations, they could transmit from just 144 to 148 megahertz. However, before the Crash, a lot of hams not so legally modified their hand-talkies to transmit all the way from 140 to 170 megahertz! This was an almost standard job, done with the snip of a diode and reprogramming the EPROM, using the radio's keypad.

"The frequency agility mod can be done on ICOMs, Yaesus, Kenwoods, Alincos, and Azdens, for example, but *not* the later Radio Shack models. Those darn 'Rat Shack' hand-talkies made from the early '90s onward are not frequency-agile with just the snip of a diode. They intentionally designed them so the frequencies couldn't be opened up. Oh well. The bottom line is that probably *more than half* of the two-meter rigs out there before the Crash were frequency agile, and even more now that there is no FCC to worry about.

"You can do a similar mod to some CBs. I have a Cobra 148 that I modified to 26.815 megahertz to 28.085 megahertz. Most of the later CBs have surface mount components and therefore they can't be modified, but the older ones can be modified fairly easily. When you operate out of band, you can run into antenna length and tuning problems. Antennas are, of course, optimized for certain wavelengths. When you go too high or too low in frequency, you can get a standing wave ratio that is too high—sometimes over one-point-three-to-one. That's exacerbated when you are operating mobile—from a vehicle—because you are probably already running quarter wave or less. Even with the bad Standing Wave Radio (SWR), things will work, but just not efficiently; one important proviso. If you're going to operate out of band, never use a linear amplifier. With a wacky SWR, you are liable to burn up your linear amp. But that's probably neither here nor there for anyone in our current situation. The whole idea is to keep your electronic signature small. Try to operate with the minimum effective radiated power. Running power is suicide, these days. Keep your radiated power low.

"Speaking of CBs, you should try and locate a Uniden President HR 2510. This is a ham radio that you can modify to transmit and receive in the citizen's band range. You can open this model up all the way from 26 to 30 megs. It has a frequency counter that you can finetune down to 10 kilohertz. The CB band is a curious animal, you see. There are a few dead business channels such as 27.195 megahertz—between channel 19 and channel 20—that your average CB can't receive. Nor can they receive the out-of-band freqs that are just above and just below the forty regular CB channels. This makes for some interesting possibilities if you have the right equipment. There's one drawback, though. Uniden stopped making the HR 2510 back around 1992. If you looked around a bit before the Crash, you could find brand new ones or slightly used ones at CB shops. Back then they cost any where from $250 to $450, so they weren't for the budget-minded. Lord knows where you'd find one now, but keep your eyes peeled, you might get lucky. When peaked tuned, a HR 2510 can pump out thirty-five watts AM, and forty-two watts single sideband. But again, what you want these days is minimum ERP."

Scheimer scribbled notes down furiously.

"By the way, the common cellular telephones can be modified to talk unit-to-unit on fixed frequencies within their normal 800 megahertz band."

"You can even have fun with unmodified hand-talkies. Just operate a pair at offset frequencies. For example, radio number one is set to transmit at 144.9725 and receive at 148.025. Radio number two is set for the reverse. Thus, the average listener gets only half of the conversation. The downside is, of course, that only two radios, or teams, can actively use a radio this way, and a team can't communicate among itself this way, since their radios are only set to contact the other team. This is even more fun in a modified dual-bander. For example, a Kenwood TH-79A, once modified, runs essentially 136-to-174 megahertz and 410-to-470 megahertz. The factory original transmit specs are 144-to-148 and 438-to-450 megs. So if you play the cross band offset game, the two halves of the conversation can be separated by nearly 300 megahertz. Not too much risk of somebody hearing both sides of *that* conversation.

"Another trick is to operate AM on frequencies where FM is the norm. Anyone listening in the FM mode will only hear garbage and noise. However, AM radios can be off-tuned to an FM signal, allowing the AM detector to 'slope-tune' the FM transmissions. That enables reasonable listening clarity.

"So much for civilian hardware. Most of the enemy tactical gear you'll run across is VHF, which means it operates line of sight, and it is frequency modulated. There are a lot of frequency-hoppers, but from what we've determined, they are all being operated at fixed frequency. There is also a lot of encryption gear, but it is not being utilized. It appears that the expertise on how to do things, like precise time synchronization from a net control station, or remote injection of encryption keys from a net control station, no longer exists in most units. They've formed a lot of these units from scratch, so the collective memory, at least on the more arcane and high-tech topics, was lost.

"They also are very slow to replace their CEOIs, and in some cases they use simple letter-for-letter transposition ciphers. I guess they feel invulnerable to decryption because they have *Green Hornet* decoder rings. Any schoolboy can crack a transposition cipher. We've been using all of these amateur factors to our advantage. Because they use their radios so much more than we do, we actually have a better Comint-derived intelligence picture of what is going on than the Federals.

"Now, let me tell you a way you can do your own encryption that is simple but virtually indecipherable. It's called a 'book code.' Get yourself two copies of the same book. A big fat novel works best. It has to be the same book, from the same publisher, and the *same edition*. Don't use a Bible or a dictionary, because that is too obvious, and because in a dictionary each word only appears once. To encode, you look through the book and first find the words you want to encode. You write down groups of numbers, starting with page number, then paragraph number, then line number, and the number of words into the sentence where your word sits. If you can't find the complete word, then you spell it out a letter at a time, using the first letters of words you select. You write it all down in groups of three numbers. Between each group, you say 'break.' So a transmission would sound like: '202, 003, 015, 003 Break. 187, 015, 006, 018 Break,' and so on. As you use each word, you scratch it out, so you never use the same code groups twice.

"The only risks with book codes come when a radio operator, or a copy of the book, or even just the title of the book are compromised. For that reason, you should change books frequently. You should also institute a list of 'telltale' operating procedures that an operator can use to discretely let everyone on the net know that he has been captured and is being forced to transmit under duress. Back before the Crunch, there was also the risk of a book code being decrypted. Conceivably, the NSA could have set one of their Cray super computers to work and break the code by brute force, or perhaps by determining which book was being used, by working from databases of known texts. Under those circumstances, I'd recommend using pairs of obscure novels— either long out of print or published by a small 'vanity' publisher, for your codebooks. But under the current circumstances, I'd say that book codes are relatively secure, so long as you don't *ever* reuse code groups." After a pause, Edgar added, "And needless to say, regardless of the encipherment system you are using, the party is over once the code book falls into enemy hands. They'll be reading *all* your traffic, past, present, or future.

"If he is spelling out letters, rather than giving the position of complete words, the guy transmitting says 'Lima' before the applicable groups. After every five groups, you change frequencies, using a large preset frequency table. You make the switch short and sweet. Just say something like 'Zap 22,' to change to a frequency from the table, like 146.3 megs. That way, they aren't likely to transcribe the entire encrypted message, and they are much less likely to be able to coordinate with other out-stations to get a cut or fix on your location. The guy transmitting waits a ten count to allow the guy at the receiving end time to retune his receiver; then he continues with the next five groups. There is no need for the fellow at the receiving end to key his microphone unless he needs you to repeat some groups. For example, he'd just say, 'Please say again, last five groups, Zap 14,' and retunes. Once he has the full message down, he just says 'Roger out,' and then he decodes it using his companion book, off-line. *Simple*.

"Book codes are similar to what the military and spooks call 'one-time pads.' One-time pads are computer generated, and naturally working computers are few and far between these days, so a simple book code is your best bet. I suppose that if we still had PCs and Macs, we could be running Nautilus or PGP Fone, and really get those Federal boys scratching their heads.

"The Federals and their UN counterparts have far more elaborate intercept systems than ours, some of which are road-mobile. We've even spotted some of the old mobile FCC intercept vans. Their *modus operandi* is to watch the spectrum on a spectrum analyzer—a box that looks like an oscilloscope. When a signal's 'spike' appears on the screen, they tune to that frequency and listen briefly, to distinguish whether it's a Federal or UN signal or something from a resistance unit, or civilian traffic. If the signal looks significant, a message is passed by intercom to someone 'sitting pos' at one of the DF consoles. That operator tunes to the same frequency and takes a line of bearing. Then they radio to another intercept site several miles away, and get a comparison line of bearing (LOB). This two-LOB 'cut' is plotted on an acetate-covered map. Three or more LOBs constitute a 'fix.' After comparing the map to known Federal/UN unit locations, the shift commander can authorize an artillery fire mission, or can dispatch a foot patrol to investigate. When things work right, the Federals can get 'steel on target' less than five minutes after a transmission is made, even if the transmission lasts less than a minute.

"A three-LOB fix generates a circular error probability or CEP of around half a kilometer across. And that circle—well, actually it's an ellipse—is good enough for artillery work. Especially when they use a serious area effect weapon like their rocket thingy—what do they call that, M-S-L-R?"

The XO corrected him. "MLRS. It stands for Multiple Launch Rocket System. They also have some old Russian 122-mil rocket launching trucks. They call those Katushyas. I'm not sure if you've ever heard a rocket battery do its thing from anywhere nearby. It sounds like the gates of hell opening up. You just pray that you aren't the intended target. The Federals call the rockets their 'grid square eliminators.'"

Edgar resumed. "And again, the CEP plots that the Federals can do are *within* a one-kilometer map grid square. You put the DF capability together with the rockets, and you're talking serious trouble for any of the militias that aren't using their radios properly. That's why ComSec is *so* important."

The XO jotted on his notepad:

Intercept = DF = MLRS = Death

The lecture went on for another hour, followed by a long series of questions and answers. Most of Scheimer's questions were about the pieces of radio and cryptographic equipment that his Blue Blaze Irregulars had captured. Eventually, Scheimer added to his notes:

Use short transmissions, only!
Use lowest power possible to get the message across.
Lower power means LPI.
Change frequencies and callsigns daily!
Don't mention frequencies or CB channels, even if encrypted. Instead, use brevity
    codes, such as "Zap 1" for 147.235 MHz, and "Zap 2" for 142.370 MHz.
Build an extensive frequency change table, and change it regularly.
Use offset transmit and receive frequencies.
Use encryption as much as possible!
Narrow-band vs. wide-band frequencies.
Use variable speed tape recorders to create "burst" transmissions.
Use directional antennas vs. whips, where practical, to increase range with same
    power, and lower probability of interception.
Bounce transmissions off of steel grain elevators to confuse enemy DF.
Don't transmit from a bivouac site!
Use excess captured radios and 60-minute tape recordings of nonsense code groups,
    at fixed frequency, to make enemy waste field arty ammunition. ;-)
Move at least one kilometer after each five minutes of transmission.
Don't use the same bivouac site twice.

Assume that "everything you say can and will be used against you" by Comint
collectors.

A better antenna beats more power, since you get:

1) Less power usage, hence LPI, and

2) Better reception and transmission.

• • •

The two Northwest Militia base camps kept in contact with the pair of microwave transmitters that had been donated to the resistance by Edgar Rhodes. The
Gunnplexer microwave transmitters used ten-gigahertz Gunn oscillators and
weatherproofed eighteen-inch diameter aluminum parabolic dish antennas.

The pair of systems had been built five years before the Crunch, by Edgar.
Rhodes borrowed design ideas from Richardson's *Gunnplexer Cookbook*.
Because the Gunnplexers transmitted in a tight beam, and were at an unusually
high frequency, they had a very low probability of interception.

When he first delivered and set up one half of the Gunnplexer system at
Todd Gray's camp, he explained, "I used a crystal-controlled solid state oscilla-
tor's harmonic at ten gigahertz to phase lock the Gunnplexer's frequency
output. Without it, the Gunnplexer has a very unstable frequency output. But
with the phase lock, it holds to plus or minus ten cycles.

"Back before the Crash, my cousin and I used this setup for two-way
communications at ranges of up to two hundred miles. My cousin lived on the
north side of Moscow Mountain up until the Crash. That was sixty-five miles
as the crow flies from my place. We had line of sight, so the microwave link was
just about ideal. It gave us just crystal-clear comms."

CHAPTER 31
Keane Team

"Is life so dear or peace so sweet as to be purchased at the price of chains and slavery? Forbid it, Almighty God! I know not what course others may take, but as for me, give me liberty, or give me death."

—*Patrick Henry, Virginia Convention Speech, March 23, 1775*

Greetings and "war stories" went on for half the morning. They had met at a rally point four miles northeast of Troy, in a dense stand of fir. Most of those attending used maps and captured GPS receivers to navigate to the obscure rally point. Coordinating the meeting took two weeks, with messages sent by the well-experienced network of resistance horseback and mountain-bike couriers. It was the first time that so many resistance leaders in the region had gathered together in one place since before the Federal/UN invasion. Lawrence Raselhoff, Mike Nelson, and Todd Gray already knew each other. The only relative newcomer was Matt Keane. He was known by both Tony and Teesha Washington, but none of the others had met him.

When Mike Nelson shook Matt's hand, he said, "*The* Matt Keane. Wow. I've heard about you and your 'Keane Team.' Your reputation precedes you, sir. You're a living legend. They talk about you on the shortwave all the time. That kayak raid your unit did on the Italian encampment at St. Maries—that was brilliant! And rumor has it that you were the ones that dynamited the UNPROFOR headquarters in Spokane last summer. Was that really you?"

"Yeah, that was us," Matt replied in a soft drawl. After four years back in the Pacific Northwest, he still spoke with a trace of his acquired southern accent. He added, "But some of the things they say on the shortwave are outrageous exaggerations. For instance, they say that on a provisioning raid I once killed six sentries in less than ten minutes with a bayonet. That's not right. It was only four. My sister Eileen got the other two. And we used axes. One thing that they *did* get right was that we're the ones that did the demo job on the UNPROFOR building."

369

"How did you ever sneak that large a quantity of explosives in there?"

Keane looped his thumbs into his ghillie cape netting, and answered, "We knew we couldn't get close on the street. They had a stand-off perimeter with anti-vehicular barricades a block in all directions. So we decided to do an old-fashioned sapping job. For almost a year we had been saving up the unexploded bombs and mines that we had defused. We had quite a pile of them. We went in through the city storm drains, and dug a tunnel into the HQ's basement boiler room. We had to tunnel only about fifteen feet. The tough part was the concrete walls of the storm drain and the brick basement wall. We did a blitz job with a couple of short miner's picks on that last wall, the night before we touched it off.

"We had word in advance that they were going to have a party up at the old convention center, so there were only two guards inside the headquarters building. They were the only ones there, aside from the gate and perimeter guards. Even the radio operator skipped out to go to the party. One of the interior guards was on our side. He made sure that the duty roster was adjusted so that he had duty that night. He also conveniently got the other interior guard so drunk that he passed out. So we didn't have to worry about the noise from our picks and the falling bricks. My little-big brother designed a special trolley for hauling the explosives in the round cross-section storm drains. We calculated that we hauled in around 1,950 pounds. We laid it all up against the center load-bearing wall and tamped it with the gunnysacks full of dirt that we had saved from digging the connecting tunnel.

"The charges went off at 9 a.m. sharp. Our inside man had told us that they had a 8:45 a.m. staff meeting scheduled up on the third floor. All four floors and the basement compacted down to a rubble pile less than twenty feet high. There was just one of the sidewalls left standing, and it was only the height of the first story. A couple of weeks later someone wrote 'MENE, MENE TEKEL' in letters six-feet high on that wall, just like from the book of Daniel. For some reason the UN people never painted that graffiti over—from what I've been told, it's still there. Maybe they didn't realize what it meant. Or maybe they did, and deep down they realized it was true. Their days *are* numbered and they *have* been weighed and found wanting.

"Our inside man took a video of the charges going off from six blocks away, and then he immediately headed for the hills. The UN press release said that twenty-three of their people were 'killed by a freak gas explosion,' but that was pure hokum. We got word later from a mortician in a resistance cell that the actual count was one hundred and twelve."

Mike nodded his head and offered, "It was a beautiful demo job. I don't think *any* of the Tidy Bowl men got out of there alive. Horrific, but that's war."

"Reminds me of a verse eight from the 35th Psalm: 'Let destruction come upon him at unawares; and let his net that he hath hid catch himself: into that very destruction let him fall.'"

Mike added, "They caught themselves in their own net all right. Blown up with their own land mines! As my dear departed friend Tom Kennedy used to say, '*Dulce et decorum est.*'"

Matt nodded his head and said, "'Sweet and appropriate,' indeed."

"You've studied Latin?"

"Of course. I was homeschooled. We studied hard, eleven months a year. We didn't get the same slack that the public school kids did. By the time my brother Chase was twelve, and I was fifteen, our parents had to hire tutors for some subjects. They hired Dr. Cecil, a Jesuit fellow from Gonzaga University, to teach us Latin on weekday afternoons and alternating Saturdays. I still have dreams about all the conjugations we memorized. It's something that you never get out of your head.

"Neither of my parents got past geometry, so they also hired a neighbor down the street, to teach us trig and calculus. Mister Critchfield had just retired from teaching higher math, also at Gonzaga. My dad bartered the labor for a bathroom remodeling for the six months of trigonometry, and a kitchen remodeling for the eight months of calculus."

Mike cocked his head and asked, "Where are your folks now?"

"My dad stepped on a mine last summer. He lived for a couple of days. Chase and Eileen and I had the chance to pray with him before he died." Matt exhaled loudly, and went on. "My mom got killed by willy-peter bomb, just six weeks ago. I guess you've heard that the Feds have started burning every remote cabin they can spot, whether it looks occupied or not, just on general principle. It fits into their 'denial operations' strategy: Deny us any food sources, and deny us shelter."

Mike nodded.

Keane continued. "My mom had been crippled up with arthritis and was staying by herself at the cabin, while we were out playing maquisards. We heard from neighbors who lived in the mine tunnel on the adjoining claim that there wasn't anything left of my dad's cabin."

"I'm sorry to hear that."

"Don't misunderstand me. I envy my parents. We'll be with them in heaven someday. If I keep that in mind, I can fight fearlessly. I fear only the righteous wrath of God. Like Paul said, when he was in chains in a Roman jail cell: 'Not that I speak in respect of want: for I have learned, in whatsoever state I am, therewith to be content. I know both how to be abased, and I know how to abound: everywhere and in all things I am instructed both to be full and to be hungry, both to abound and to suffer need. I can do all things through Christ which strengtheneth me.' That's Phillipians 4-11 through 13. Those verses are a great comfort to me. I fear *no* man, and *no* circumstance."

Keane gestured with his forefinger, and continued, "Getting back to the 'denial operations' concept, just consider this: I had a friend who was a reserve Army intelligence officer before the Crash. He often told me that the three essential abilities on the battlefield are 'to shoot, move, and communicate.' Without all three you are ineffective in any conflict. If you look at how the Federals are operating, they are doing everything they can to deny us all three. They've declared our guns contraband. They're restricting travel with their checkpoints and internal passports, and they've banned private possession of radio transceivers. Very systematic. But we are beginning to do the same to them, and they can't stop us because they can't often locate and engage us. We are denying them ammunition and other key combat logistics by burning their depots and arsenals, we are impeding their ability to maneuver tactically and to move their logistics with our ambushes and sabotaging their vehicles. And, we are taking down the power grid and phone system faster than they can put it up, so they can't communicate long distance or spread their propaganda. We're going to win in the long run. It's simple mathematics. There are *a lot* more of us than there are of them. It may cost us a lot of lives ... but in the long term? They're doomed."

Mike asked quietly, "I heard Tony Washington mention that you used to be a racist, but now you are not. What's up with that?"

"I wouldn't say that I was a racist, *per se*. I equate racism with supremacism. If anything, I was a separatist, not a supremacist. And yes, frankly, I *was* reluctant to work with blacks. I had always kept my distance. But fighting alongside the Washingtons certainly reformed me. They were with us on the St. Maries kayak raid. Tony saved my life two different times that day. I owed him. And I owed him an apology."

Mike cocked his head and asked, "So you've sworn off racism? You don't have *any* animosity toward blacks?"

"Absolutely none. They're fighting and bleeding along with the rest of us. I'd be happy to have anyone of Tony's caliber join the Keane Team regardless of race. I don't care if they are white, black, or *green*." Matt grinned and added, "We're *equal opportunity* destroyers."

Mike shook Keane's hand, and looking him in the eye, declared, "You're a good man."

Planning the big raid took a day and a half. There were extensive discussions, and detailed analysis of maps, photographs, and floor plans. This was followed by sand-table exercises and a briefing by a reliable "turned" Federal supply sergeant who had formerly lived at the barracks. Coordinating an operation this large was difficult. It included diverse units with distinct command structures, organizations, and standard operating procedures. The planners also had to be diplomatic in dealing with the leaders of less experienced militias. Some of them were amateurish, and several had overgrown egos.

• • •

Rather than traditional squads and platoons, the Keane Team was organized into something they called "Thomas Triads." These were mini-squads of three guerrillas each. The philosophy behind the triads was that three men was the minimum number that could be combat effective.

A three-member guerrilla team did not present a signature that was easily spotted, except in the most open terrain. A single triad was used for reconnaissance or sabotage patrols. Two to four triads could be combined to conduct an ambush. Three to twelve triads could be combined for a raid.

In a defensive mode, or "in laager," one member of the triad was on "guard" while the second was on "sleep," and the third was on "support"—tending to cooking, fetching water, and/or gathering edibles. Every eight hours the roles rotated. Thus, each triad provided for its own security, and, depending on circumstances, its own sustenance.

The rule of thumb was: if more than five triads had to be combined for an operation, it was verging on conventional warfare, and that immediately following the operation, it was time to displace, disperse, and go back to low-echelon guerrilla tactics. The guerrillas spoke with dread about "going conventional." Meeting the better-armed Federals toe-to-toe was rightly recognized as foolhardy.

The origin of Thomas Triad organization was forgotten. Keane explained, "It's just what we were taught by another group. I don't know who the 'Mr. Thomas' who dreamed this up was, but it works. Some guy in California, that's all I heard. Maybe he's in that Harry Wu outfit. Results are what counts, and the triads produce results, so that's the structure we use."

• • •

A week before the planned Moscow barracks raid, the thirty-member Keane Team and the forty-eight-member Moscow Maquis rendezvoused at a hilltop north of Troy for final coordination and to conduct rehearsals. Since their two units were the intended spearhead for the upcoming raid, rehearsals were critical. They had arranged the rendezvous with two short radio transmissions. The transmissions were under thirty seconds each, consisting of a few four-letter code groups read aloud.

At 4 a.m. the morning after they made their rendezvous, a call on a 500-milliwatt Maxon headset radio came in from the western picket triad. "We have movement. Definitely men on foot. Stand to. Will advise."

The "stand to arms" order was quietly and rapidly passed around the defensive doughnut. Within a minute, a second call came in, "I can see them clearly through my NVGs. Most are carrying M16s. They're all wearing Kevlars and digital pattern camos. Definitely looks like Federals, at least a platoon strength unit. With as much noise as they're making, probably a lot bigger."

The night watch officer radioed back to the picket, "Execute night-defense plan Alpha." His platoon sergeant heard the command, and echoed it in whispers to the triads on either side of the command bunker. Each triad in succession passed it down the line in both directions, verbally. The watch officer muttered to himself. "Federals? Man! This is going to get ugly. Why couldn't it be the French or Italians? The Federals must have DFed us."

Hearing the radio command, the picket teams from the south and north immediately pulled into the main defensive doughnut, which stretched eighty-five yards along a ridge. The east picket triad stayed in place, as did the one to the west. The west pickets were not spotted as the Federals passed by their well-camouflaged foxhole, which sat under a clump of hawthorn bushes. Under the Alpha plan, the pickets were not to fire unless fired upon. Their job was to wait until contact with the main doughnut occurred, and then to fire on the attackers from the rear, to produce confusion. The pickets generally called this role a "DIP" (Die in Place). Few expected an isolated triad to ever survive a night raid by a large enemy force.

The Federals continued their advance, directly toward the Keane Team's doughnut. The radio man at the west picket called out the distance from the doughnut: "500 meters ... 450 ... 400 meters ... they're moving fast ... 300 meters." The watch officer switched frequencies on his Maxon and radioed, "Hit the west strobes, now!" A twelve-year-old girl in one of the western-most foxholes of the main doughnut sounded a warning blast with a boater's air horn, gave a silent two count, closed her eyes, and pulsed the strobe lights three times, at five-second intervals. The six commercial photography strobe lights were wired to the limbs of trees two-hundred-and-fifty meters forward of the doughnut, and twenty meters apart. They were set up to flash in unison. The first flash caused the image intensifier tubes on the Federals' starlight scopes and NVGs to shut down. The series of flashes also ruined the approaching Federal troops' night vision for several minutes. Some stumbled and fell. There were numerous curses and shouts of surprise.

With their recent training, the defenders recognized the air horn signal, and waited with their eyes shut during the three flashes, counting aloud. Then, with well-rehearsed precision, the Keane Team launched a counterattack, while the less practiced Moscow Maquis members held their places. The Keane Team ran down the hill directly at the Federals, in triad formation.

The air horn sounded again. The charging guerrillas knew that this second blast was a ruse to get the Federals to close their eyes for another fifteen seconds. During this time, the six triads of guerrillas continued down the hill directly into the lead Federal platoon, firing with discriminate care. They fired two shots at each soldier, mowing down most of the lead platoon like a hay cutter. The few survivors turned and ran. Overestimating the size of the counterattack, the middle company of Federals also panicked and ran. They ran headlong into the trail formation.

Thinking that these were guerrillas who were counterattacking, the trailing companies fired in long bursts, killing twelve members of the retreating platoons, and wounding fourteen others. The remnants of the retreating company did not stop. They continued past the rear company, shouting incoherently. Seeing their panicked flight, hearing their shouts of "retreat," and seeing the muzzle flashes of the approaching guerrillas, the middle company caught bug-out fever, and also bolted. All but a few members of the remaining company on the north-flanking hill, stood fast. They began to concentrate their fire on the guerrillas, stopping the charge. Three of the guerrillas—from two different triads—were killed.

Before they retreated, Matt and Eileen Keane threw tear gas grenades at the Federals' hillside positions. The wind was favorable, so the grenades had good effect. The triads retreated back up the hill in good order, giving mutually supporting fire, moving by bounds.

Without waiting for the Federals to counterattack, the guerrillas counted heads and got ready to displace. Triads were quickly reorganized to make up for those that had been killed. They quietly helped each other with their packs and headed east, toward their widely scattered prepared hide positions.

As part of the prearranged plan, a triad of teenagers stayed back and set up the trip wires for four Claymore mines. Since they had practiced setting up the wires in the dark several times, it took just a hundred seconds. Less than two minutes after they left, they heard the gratifying sound of three of the four Claymores detonating in rapid succession.

• • •

The Federal attack on the Keane Team/Maquis position did not delay the Moscow raid. It was decided that operational security had not been breached. Their mistake, they realized, was in using a 5-watt transceiver from a camp location, and being DFed. That mistake would not be repeated. The Keane Team and the Moscow Maquisards made new SOPs that any transmissions over 500-milliwatt strength would only be made after displacing the transmitter at least two kilometers from any encampment.

For their operations, the Keane Team normally wore field expedient ghillie capes patterned after Matt Keane's. They had been made by cutting up captured Federal vehicular hexagonal or diamond shaped camouflage nets, and adding additional frayed burlap garnish. But since there were several militias involved, it was prearranged that for this raid only, every raider would wear a standard camouflage uniform with a special identifying four-inch wide blue sash around the waist. They were meant to reduce the risk of friendly fire incidents. For OpSec reasons, use of the sashes was kept secret until just before the raid. The sash material was distributed during the final inspections and rehearsals in the hills northeast of Moscow. There were 188 members in the combined raid team.

A twelve-year-old militia "drummer boy" videotaped the raid from a concealed position two hundred yards south of the barracks' main gate.

The Moscow barracks were a pair of dormitories on the old U of I campus. Three buildings near the dormitories had been flattened "for security reasons." A fifteen-foot high double fence wrapped around the buildings. The wide area between the dorms was used as a motor pool.

The Moscow raid started with a "Trojan horse" ruse, utilizing a BTR-70 wheeled APC that had been captured from the Federals more than a year earlier. The resistance had kept it deep in the Clearwater National Forest, hidden under camouflage nets at the end of a disused logging road. They had kept it ready for a "special project" all this time. Fresh fuel and extra ammo for its 14.5-mm gun had been laboriously carried to it, and special efforts were made to keep its batteries charged. The resistance even dispatched a mechanic to ensure the APC's road-worthiness.

The APC drove up to the Moscow barracks' main gate at BMCT ("Before Morning Civil Twilight"). The gate guards dutifully opened the pair of gates and waved it through. As one of the gate guards was logging the APC's bumper number on his clipboard, he looked up in surprise to see the muzzle of a sawed-off double barrel shotgun. The man holding the shotgun held his forefinger to his lips and whistled, "Ssshhhh." The guard didn't make a sound. He was visibly shaking.

The four gate guards were quickly herded into the guard shack and bound and gagged. A hidden "panic button" that was presaged by the turned Federal in the Moscow Maquis was disabled with snips from a pair of wire cutters. One of the raiders stayed behind to guard the prisoners. He was holding an M16 with bayonet fixed.

The APC wheeled into the well-lit motor pool. The solitary guard at the motor pool shouted at the APC, "Will you get on your radio and tell those idiots at the front gate that they forgot to close the ga..." He was killed with eight head shots, fired through one of the APC's gun ports with a silenced Ruger Mark II .22 pistol. After the guard went down, a resistance soldier popped out and jogged to the motors' shack. He returned carrying a sheet of plywood festooned with keys, each labeled with a vehicle's bumper number. He walked up and down the double row of vehicles, occasionally tossing sets of keys wrapped in white handkerchiefs in front of an APC or tank. When he threw the key rack board itself to the ground near the fence, the militia APC disgorged sixteen troopers, all wearing tanker CVC helmets. They ran in pairs to six BTR APCs and two M60 tanks. In less than a minute, they had unlocked the vehicles' hatches and loosened the locks and chains on their controls. A whistle sounded and they nearly all started up simultaneously. Two of the APCs didn't start because they had dead batteries.

The horizon was getting noticeably lighter. Upon hearing the captured vehicles starting up, the rest of the raid team went into action. A detonating cord explosion neatly cut gaps in the back fences. A steady rain of LAW rocket and RPGs began to impact both barracks buildings. They were fired from the roof of the nearby five-story library building. At the same time, seven well-experienced snipers began to fire on any targets that presented themselves in or around the dormitories.

The captured APCs and tanks lumbered out of the motor pool and split up. They began a heavy barrage of fire from the 12.7-mm and 14.5-mm guns on the APCs. There was also sporadic fire from the main guns of the M60 tanks. Both dorms were hosed down liberally. Most of the fire was concentrated at the ends of the buildings, which housed the arms rooms. After a minute of continuous fire, a white parachute flare went up from the "Trojan horse" APC. A heavily reinforced company of sixty-five resistance fighters, all wearing blue sashes, rushed out of a classroom building across the street and through the open front gates. At the same time, another sixty, also wearing sashes, charged through the breaches in the back fences. The firing from the tanks and APCs stopped. The resistance infantry poured into the barracks, first securing the arms rooms and the C.Q. offices. There was little organized resistance. The Federal soldiers had been completely surprised by the raid. Most were sleeping when the shooting started.

Although most of the Federals kept their loaded small arms at the ends of their bunks, all of their rocket launchers and crew-served weapons were out of reach in the locked arms rooms. The shouting resistance fighters systematically herded the Federals into the cafeterias. Only a few Federals fired at the militia as they cleared the halls. Those that did were quickly cut down. Just three militiamen were killed and five wounded in taking the dorms.

All told, they captured 442 Federal soldiers. The Federals suffered 53 injuries, many of them critical. The militia also captured included the Corps commander and his entire staff. More than 80 Federals were killed in the raid, mostly in the opening "prep" fire. The fighting was over and the fires extinguished by the time the sun crept over the hills in the east.

The original op order called for an occupation of the barracks not to exceed one hour. During this time, they systematically searched for useful logistics and for maps and papers that might have intelligence value. A procession of two-and-a-half and five-ton trucks were backed up to the dorms to load up the captured supplies. As the militias were getting ready to leave and "melt into the hills," nearby Federal unit commanders started to call in, one after another, through the field telephone switchboard, to ask for their terms of surrender.

Matt Keane at first thought that the calls were a trick. "They want to know how *they* can surrender? But they outnumber us. This is crazy! They should be pounding us with arty right now."

Mike Nelson shook his head, and said, "No. Just think about it, Matt. Their headquarters is gone, and their commander is no longer commanding. The snake has been *decapitated*. For the subordinate units, this is their chance to surrender gracefully. They've probably been waiting for an opportunity, and this is the best one that we could have given them."

Once the first two maneuver units in the Corps surrendered, nearly all the rest—as far north as Coeur d'Alene in the north and Grangeville in the south—capitulated in rapid succession. One field artillery battalion made some trouble. They shelled the downtown and campus areas of Moscow on the afternoon of the raid. Dozens of civilians were killed. But since the battalion's battery locations were known, a heavy counter-battery MLRS barrage soon silenced them. Then, like most of the other units before them, they capitulated via radio or field telephone. Militia teams were sent out to each unit in APCs and trucks to formalize the surrender and disarming process.

At sunset, Todd Gray was given the honor of lowering the UN flag at the Moscow barracks, and raising the Idaho flag. Once he had raised the flag, he kneeled down and prayed his thanks. Seeing this, the ranks of armed militiamen and disarmed Federals on parade did likewise. It was a solemn and emotional moment.

CHAPTER 32
The Amendments

"Food is power. We use it to change behavior.
Some may call that bribery. We do not apologize."

—*Catherine Bertini, UN World Food Program Executive Director, 1997*

Continental Region 6—the former United States, Mexico, and Canada—was gradually falling into the hands of guerrillas. Even formerly pacified areas saw increasing resistance, both passive and active. Guerrilla bands were operational as far south as the Yucatan peninsula, and as far north as upper Newfoundland. The UN was steadily losing its grip on the region, and could do nothing about it.

A particularly embarrassing incident for the UN came the day that President Hutchings was to give one of his biannual "State of the Continent" speeches. When Hutchings and his entourage arrived at the Fort Knox TV studio in their APCs, they found the studio staff and several MPs attacking two of the building's steel doors with crowbars and a sledgehammer. An empty tube of "Krazy Glue" cyanoacrylate epoxy was found near one of the doors and bagged as evidence. The lock cylinders of every door were frozen in place. After resorting to using a cutting torch, they finally got into the building twenty minutes before Hutchings was scheduled to go on the air.

Once inside, the studio staff found some of the inner door locks similarly jammed, but they were less of an obstacle. A couple of quick blows from a sledgehammer opened each door. The staff fumbled with flashlights, trying to determine why the lights weren't working. They soon found that the saboteur had removed all of the circuit breakers from the main breaker box. The floor cameras had their lenses smashed, but a spare handheld camera from the mobile van was brought in and set up on a tripod. Maynard Hutchings finally went on the air twenty-five minutes late, "due to technical difficulties" and without his usual makeup. In his speech, he glowed about the "outstanding cooperation" shown by the UN Partners for Peace, recent victories over bandits in Michigan and Colorado, and the "rapidly decreasing rates of terrorist acts." He promised regional elections "real soon."

The following week, a firing squad from the Fort Knox Provost Marshall's office executed the TV studio saboteur. He was the thirteen-year old son of an Ordnance Corps major who was stationed at the Fort and lived in nearby Radcliffe, Kentucky. The major and his wife were executed by another firing squad two days later. President Hutchings was quoted as saying, "Parents should be held accountable for their children's actions."

Throughout the North American continent, a pattern was clearly evident. Resistance was the strongest, the best organized, and the most successful in rural areas. Unable to wipe out the elusive guerrillas, the UN administration and their Quislings began to concentrate on eliminating the guerrillas' food supplies.

In areas where resistance was rampant, "temporary detainment facilities" were constructed to house anyone thought to be politically unreliable. Special emphasis was placed on rounding up suspect farmers or ranchers, or anyone remotely connected with food distribution businesses. When farmers were put into custody, their crops were either confiscated, plowed under, or burned. Bulk food stocks were carefully monitored by the authorities. Despite these efforts, the guerrillas rapidly gained in numbers.

As the war went on, resistance gradually increased beyond the UN's ability to match it. Every new detainment camp spawned the formation of new resistance cells. Every reprisal or atrocity by the UN or Federal forces pushed more citizens and even Federal unit commanders into active support for the guerrillas. Increasing numbers of commanders decided to "do the right thing," and support *The Document* (The Constitution) rather than the Provisional government's power elite at Fort Knox. Units as large as brigade size were parlaying with the guerrillas and turning over their equipment. In many instances the majority of their troops joined the resistance. County after county, and eventually state after state, was controlled by the resistance.

The remaining loyal Federal and UN units gradually retreated into Kentucky, Tennessee, and southern Illinois. Most held out there until the early summer of the war's fourth year. Militias and their allied "realigned" Federal units relentlessly closed in on the remaining Federal territory from all directions.

When word came that Hutchings, his cabinet, and most of the senior UN administrators had flown to Europe on the night of July first, the UN and Federal forces capitulated en masse. There was no final battle. The war ended with a whimper rather than a bang. The resistance army units rolled into Fort Knox on July fourth, unchallenged. They lowered the UN flag and raised Old Glory without much fanfare. Resistance soldiers cut up the UN banner into small swatches for souvenirs.

The capitulated armies were soon disarmed and demobilized. Apart from a few soldiers that were put on trial for war crimes, the rest of the U.S.-born soldiers were allowed to return to their home states by the end of August. The

UN's own barbed wire internment camps made a convenient place to put the UN soldiers while they were waiting to go home. It took more than a year to send the UN forces back to Europe by ship and airplane.

The Europeans chafed at being billed for the demobilization and troop transport. The "return bounty" reparation was fifty ounces of gold per enlisted soldier, two hundred ounces per officer, and five hundred ounces per civilian administrator, payable before delivery. The new interim Restoration of the Constitution Government (RCG) made it clear that if the bounty payments stopped, the demob flights would stop.

Maynard Hutchings committed suicide before his extradition process was completed. Most of his staff and a few divisional and brigade commanders were eventually extradited from Europe, given trials, and shot. Hundreds of lower-ranking military officers and local Quislings were arrested and similarly put on trial. Sentences included head shavings and brandings. In a few rare cases, there were death sentences. Only a few UN troops who professed fear of retribution if they were returned to their home countries were granted asylum. Each of these individuals was given separate hearings by the RCG. Most of them eventually bought citizenship.

The first elections since before the Crunch were held in all fifty states in the November following the Federal surrender at Fort Knox. The Constitution Party and Libertarian Party candidates won in a landslide. A former Wyoming governor—a Libertarian—was elected president. Based on rough population estimates, the new House of Representatives had just ninety seats.

• • •

In the three years following the elections, nine constitutional amendments were ratified by the state legislatures in rapid succession. *The Document* went through some major changes.

The 27th Amendment granted blanket immunity from prosecution for any crimes committed before or during the Second Civil War to anyone who actively fought for the resistance.

The 28th Amendment repealed the 14th and 26th Amendments. It also made full state Citizenship a right of birth, only applicable to native-born Citizens who were the children of Citizens. It allowed immigrants to buy state citizenship. It clarified "United States citizenship" as only having effect when state Citizens traveled outside the nation's borders, and outlawed titles of nobility such as "esquire."

The 29th Amendment banned welfare and foreign aid, removed the United States from the UN and most foreign treaties, capped Federal spending at 2 percent of the GDP, capped the combined number of foreign troops in the fifty states and on Federal territory at one thousand men, and limited the active duty Federal military to a hundred thousand men, except in time of declared war.

The 30th Amendment amplified the 2nd Amendment, confirming it as both an unalienable individual right and as a state right, repealed the existing Federal gun-control laws, preempted any present or future state gun-control laws, and reinstituted a decentralized militia system.

The 31st Amendment repealed the 16th Amendment, and severely limited the ability of the Federal government to collect any taxes within the fifty states. Henceforth, the Federal government's budget could be funded only by tariffs, import duties, and bonds.

The 32nd Amendment outlawed deficit spending, put the new United States currency back on a bimetallic gold and silver standard, and made all currency "redeemable on demand."

The 33rd Amendment froze salaries at six thousand dollars a year for House members and ten thousand for Senators, limited campaign spending for any federal office to five thousand per term, and repealed the 17th Amendment, returning Senators to election by their state legislatures.

The 34th Amendment restored the pre-*Erie Railroad v. Tompkins* system of Common Law, invalidated most Federal court decisions since 1932, and clarified the inapplicability of most Federal statutes on state Citizens in several states.

The 35th Amendment reinstated the allodial land-title system. Under a renewed Federal Land Patent system the amendment mandated the return of 92 percent of the Federal lands to private ownership through public sales at one dollar in silver coin per acre.

The nation's economy was slowly restored. But with the nine new amendments, the scope of government—both state and Federal—was greatly reduced from its pre-Crunch proportions. Small government was almost universally seen as good government. For the first time since before the First Civil War, it became the norm to again refer to the nation plurally as *these* United States, rather than singularly as The United States. The change was subtle, but profound.

• • •

Two years after the Fort Knox surrender, NET produced a three-hour documentary entitled *CW II: The Resistance War*. The documentary included extensive on-camera interviews with resistance fighters. The pro-militia bias of the producers was evident, but they in no way tried to portray the resistance as angelic. Notably, one of the many video clips included was of a raid on a Federal supply depot near Baltimore. In this footage, a group of five unarmed Federal soldiers could be seen slowly walking out of a warehouse with their hands raised, only to be shot down by resistance fighters.

The vast majority of the atrocities documented in the film was committed by the Federals and various UN military units. An amateur video shot by an Austrian UN soldier showed a protest at a relocation camp in Tennessee being quelled by copious RPK machinegun fire. Some of the most damning footage was filmed by the Federals themselves—including the notorious Chicago Blindings, and graphic scenes of reprisal executions in Florida, Texas, Illinois, and Ohio. The footage from Florida showed more than a hundred bound and gagged men, women, and children being shot and pushed into a waiting mass grave with a bulldozer. Interviews with "turned" UN soldiers revealed that local unit commanders had filmed the mass executions to gain favor with their higher-ups. As one former British airborne regiment Captain put it, "These videotapes of the executions were a way of earning Brownie Points. 'Look what a good boy I've been! Look how I achieved such a high reprisal body count.' It was sickening, but that was the norm."

Todd and Mary Gray watched the film at Kevin Lendel's ranch house, using a newly purchased DSS satellite dish. Kevin taped it with a VCR that he had bought for a dollar-fifty in silver coin just two weeks before the grid-power came back on line. The Grays were surprised and proud to see how much of the resistance video in the documentary came from action in their own region. It included gun camera footage from the Doyles' Laron ultralights, the snowy ambush and capture of Major Kuntzler, the implosion of the Spokane UNPROFOR headquarters, and the final assault on the UN barracks in Moscow.

As Todd tried to get to sleep that evening, memories of the recent war came flooding back. Mary sat curled beside him on the bed, under a small twelve-volt DC halogen reading light—her usual evening habit. She was rereading one of her favorite novels, *The Red and The Black,* and nibbling on dried apple slices. Noticing that Todd wasn't asleep, she asked, "What's the matter, hon?"

"It was that film we saw today. It made me think of all the friends that we've lost since the Crunch. I really and truly miss them. It was quite a price to pay for our freedom. All over the country folks lost family in the Crunch, and then more in the war. And across the Atlantic Ocean, there are thousands more that lost sons in the war. The Europeans will hate our guts for at least a generation, maybe a lot longer."

Mary closed her book with a loud thump and set it aside. "Let 'em hate us! If the 'You're-a-peons' can't stomach a sovereign and freedom-loving nation, then that's their problem. I think that deep down they must *envy* us. We looked tyranny in the eye and said, 'No way. Your day is done, Mr. Tyrant. *Adios.*' There's nothing *wrong* with that, Todd! And we can be proud of our militia's record. There are no skeletons lurking in the closet. We didn't shoot anybody that was trying to surrender. And today, as a nation, we can be proud that we liberated

Canada and are supporting and supplying the resistance movements in Switzerland, and Finland, and Spain. We can do that with a clear conscience."

Todd nodded his head, but the expression on his face showed that he was still concerned. Mary ran her fingers through Todd's graying hair and said consolingly, "Our son Jacob is growing up in a free and God-fearing country. That's the bottom line." A moment later she added, "And as for what happened during the war, we can't change that. It's fodder for the history books, and will be neatly analyzed by 'Monday Morning Quarterbacks' in more documentaries like the one we saw today. We can count on it."

Todd sighed. "You're *right*. I can't go back in time and fix any of my mistakes. But I wonder if Jacob or our grandchildren will ever have to go through the same thing?"

Mary didn't answer Todd for a full minute. The only sound in the room was the ticking of a clock on the bedside table. Finally, she said, "It's in our fallen, sinful nature for tyrants to rise up in every nation. And unfortunately, it's also in our nature that the vast majority in every nation is either too stupid or too apathetic to do anything about it until the tyrants have put up their barbed wire and spilled a lot of blood.

"Grandpa Krause liked to quote a stand-up comedian from back in the '80s who said, 'There are three kinds of people in this world: Those who *make* things happen; those who *watch* things happen; and those who just wonder *what the heck happened?*'"

Todd nodded and chuckled at Mary's quote. He had heard her recite it before, but under different circumstances.

Mary continued, in a more serious tone, "While most people were still wondering what the heck happened, we *made* something happen, Todd."

Todd breathed, "Yes, we made it happen. And you're right. Tyranny is a product of our sinful nature. Hopefully films like we saw today will be reminders that will keep people vigilant, so tyrants don't spring up so often. Thank God for our Constitution. It kept us from having to confront tyranny on our own soil for a lot longer than the average European. And hopefully now that it has been restored, we'll have another two or three centuries of uninterrupted freedom. From now on, the Federal government is not going to be allowed to corner the market on coercive force. Far more force is being retained by the states, and by the people. That's why we keep that APC out in the barn. And there are thousands of *other* APCs and tanks in private hands scattered all over the country. There may be more rough times ahead, but we're ready for whatever might come. And when we go to God, we'll go knowing that our children are prepared, too." Todd stroked his hand across Mary's belly, and smiled. It was beginning to swell with their second child. "We'll raise them up solid. Just like us, they'll have the faith; they'll have the friends; they'll have the skills; and they'll have the tools they need to pull through."

Mary smiled and kissed Todd. She reached up and switched off her reading light. She whispered, "I love you darling."

"I love you too. With all my heart." He was soon asleep. And he slept well.

CHAPTER 33
Semper Paratus

"No free man shall ever be debarred the use of arms."

—*Thomas Jefferson, Proposal for Virginia Constitution*

Twenty-seven years after the Crunch, and five years after the liberation of Europe, Kevin Lendel's middle son had just started his freshman year at Boston College. At the end of the first week of the fall semester, Solomon Michael Lendel stood near the front of a lecture hall before his physics class started, chatting about the Olympic games. One of his classmates bragged of traveling to see the games in England, and was recounting his experiences. They were the first Olympic games since before the Crunch, and were still a big topic of conversation. Sol had watched part of the games on television.

A buzzer announced the start of class, and the Tektronix MPEG-3 teleconferencing monitors automatically switched on. On a row of monitors, students at three remote classrooms could be seen and heard, via the fiber-optic system. As Sol took his seat in the front row, his coat flapped open briefly. One of the students standing near him went pale when she noticed that he was carrying a pistol in a shoulder holster. She shouted, "He's got a gun! He's carrying a concealed weapon! That's not allowed on campus!"

The professor gave a stern look. He said, "Son, take off your coat." Sol flushed and stood up again. He did as he was told, revealing a well-worn XD .45 pistol and a counter-balancing pair of spare loaded magazines in a hand-crafted shoulder holster. The leather rig was tooled in a floral Heiser renaissance pattern.

There was an anxious pause while everyone in the classroom stared silently, wondering what would happen next.

The professor cleared his throat. "Young lady, this gentleman is not carrying a concealed weapon. I can see it as *plain as day*." There were roars of laughter.

"But..." she protested weakly.

The professor motioned with his hand, enunciating, "Take your seat, son." Sol tossed his sheepskin coat across the back of his chair, sat down, and opened his notebook.

The professor interlaced his fingers and rested his hands on the podium. He continued, "There is no University policy on the carrying of firearms, whether concealed or not. Nor should there be. Granted, open carry of guns has gradually gone out of style in the big cities these last few years. There isn't much crime in the streets these days. However, this young gentleman's choice to carry a gun—for whatever reason he chooses—is his own. He is a Sovereign Citizen and *sui juris*. The state has no say in the matter. It is strictly an individual choice, and a God-given right. The right to keep and bear arms is an absolute, secured by the Bill of Rights. I should also remind you that it is one of the main reasons we spent four horrendous years fighting the Second Civil War. How quickly we forget. Now let's get on with class, shall we?"

Glossary

10/22 A semiautomatic .22–rimfire rifle made by Ruger.

1911 See M1911.

9/11 The terrorist attacks of 9/11/2001, which took three thousand American lives.

AAA American Automobile Association

ACP Automatic Colt Pistol

ACU Army Combat Uniform. The U.S. Army's new "digital" pattern camouflage uniform that replaced the BDU.

AK *Avtomat Kalashnikov.* The gas–operated weapons family invented by Mikhail Timofeyevitch Kalashnikov, a Red Army sergeant. AKs are known for their robustness and were made in huge numbers, so that they are ubiquitous in much of Asia and the Third World. The best of the Kalashnikov variants are the Valmets that were made in Finland, the Galils that were made in Israel, and the R4s that are made in South Africa.

AK–47 The early generation AK carbine that shoots the intermediate 7.62 x 39-mm cartridge.

AK–74 The later generation AK carbine that shoots the 5.45 x 39-mm cartridge.

AM Amplitude Modulation

A.O. Area of Operations

AP Armor Piercing

APC Armored Personnel Carrier

Apgar A scoring system used to evaluate the health of newborn babies, typically taken at one minute and five minutes after delivery.

AR Automatic Rifle. This is the generic term for semiauto variants of the Armalite family of rifles designed by Eugene Stoner (AR-10, AR-15, AR-180, et cetera).

AR-7 The .22 LR semiautomatic survival rifle designed by Eugene Stoner. It weighs just two pounds, and when disassembled, all of the parts fit in the buttstock. The stock is foam filled, so the rifle floats.

AR-10 The 7.62-mm NATO predecessor of the M16 rifle, designed by Eugene Stoner. Early AR-10s (mainly Portuguese, Sudanese, and Cuban contract, from the late 1950s and early 1960s) are not to be confused with the present-day semiauto only "AR-10" rifles that are more closely interchangeable with parts from the smaller caliber AR-15.

AR-15 Semiauto civilian variants of the U.S. Army M16 rifle.

AR-180 A low cost gas piston–operated .223 made primarily from stamped steel. Designed by Eugene Stoner. Early AR-180s (made in the U.S. and Japan) use a proprietary magazine, some of which do not interchange with AR-15 magazines, because their narrow magazine catch notches wee on the opposite side of the magazine. These are not to be confused with the present-day AR-180B rifles that can use standard AR-15 or M16 magazines.

ASAP As Soon As Possible

ATF See BATFE.

AUG See Steyr AUG.

BATFE Bureau of Alcohol, Tobacco, Firearms, and Explosives (a U.S. Federal government taxing agency)

BBC British Broadcasting Corporation

BDU Battle Dress Uniform. Also called "camouflage utilities" by the USMC

BLM Bureau of Land Management (a U.S. Federal government agency that administers public lands)

BMG Browning machinegun. Usually refers to .50 BMG, the U.S. military's standard heavy machinegun cartridge since the early twentieth century. This cartridge is now often used for long-range precision counter-sniper rifles.

BP Blood Pressure.

C-4 Composition 4, a plastic explosive.

CAR-15 See M4.

CAS Close Air Support

CB Citizen's Band Radio. A VHF broadcasting band. No license is required for operation in the United States. Some desirable CB transceivers are capable of SSB operation. Originally twenty-three channels, the Citizen's Band was later expanded to forty channels during the golden age of CB, in the 1970s.

CLP Cleaner, Lubricant, Protectant. A MIL-Spec lubricant, sold under the trade name "Break Free CLP."

C.Q.   Charge of Quarters

CUCV   Commercial Utility Cargo Vehicle (1980's vintage U.S. Army versions of diesel Chevy Blazers and Pickups, currently being sold off as surplus).

DF   Direction Finding.

D.I.A.S.   Drop-in Auto-sear

DMV   Department of Motor Vehicles

DPM   Disruptive Pattern, Marine. The camouflage cloth pattern developed for the U.K. Royal Marines.

FAL   See FN/FAL

FEMA   Federal Emergency Management Agency (a U.S. Federal government agency). The acronym is also jokingly defined as "Foolishly Expecting Meaningful Aid."

FFL   Federal Firearms License

FN/FAL   A 7.62-mm NATO battle rifle made by the Belgian Company Fabrique Nationale (FN).

Fougasse   An improvised mine constructed by filling a pipe this with explosives (originally, black powder) and projectiles.

Frag   Short for fragmentation.

GCA   The Gun Control Act of 1968. The law that first created FFLs and banned interstate transfers of post-1898 firearms, except "to or through" FFL holders.

Glock   The popular polymer-framed pistol design by Gaston Glock of Austria. Also derisively known as "Combat Tupperware" by their detractors, because they were the first maker to ship their pistols in a plastic box with a snap lid. Glocks are a favorite of gun writer Boston T. Party.

Gold Cup   The target version of Colt's M1911; has fully adjustable target sights, a tapered barrel, and a tighter barrel bushing than standard M1911s.

G.O.O.D.   Get Out of Dodge

GPS   Global Positioning System

GRFD   Guaranteed Reserve Forces Duty

HK or H and K   Heckler und Koch, the German gun maker.

HK91: Heckler und Koch Model 91   The civilian (semiauto-only) variant of the 7.62-mm NATO G3 rifle.

IFV   Infantry Fighting Vehicle

IV   Intravenous

Kevlar   The material used in most body army and ballistic helmets. "Kevlar" is also the nickname for the standard U.S. Army helmet.

KJV   King James Version of The Bible

LAW   Light Anti–Tank Weapon

LC–1   Load Carrying, Type 1. (U.S. Army Load Bearing Equipment, circa 1970s to 1990s.)

LDS   The Latter Day Saints, commonly called The Mormons. (Flawed doctrine, great preparedness.)

LP   Liquid Propane

LP/OP   Listening Post/Observation Post.

LRRP   Long-Range Reconnaissance Patrol

M1 Abrams tank   The United State's current main battle tank, with a 120-mm cannon.

M1 Carbine   The U.S. Army semiauto carbine issued during WWII and the Korean conflict. Mainly issued to officers and second-echelon troops such as artillerymen, for self-defense. Uses '.30 U.S Carbine,' an intermediate (pistol class) .30-caliber cartridge. More than six million were manufactured.

M1 Garand   The U.S. Army's primary battle rifle of WWII and the Korean conflict. It is semiautomatic, chambered in .30-06, and uses a top-loading, eight-round en bloc clip that ejects after the last round is fired. This rifle is commonly called the Garand. (After the name of its inventor.) Not to be confused with the U.S. M1 Carbine, another semiauto of the same era, which shoots a far less powerful pistol-class cartridge.

M1A   The civilian (semiauto only) version of the U.S. Army M14 7.62-mm NATO rifle.

M1911   The Model 1911 Colt semiauto pistol (and clones thereof), usually chambered in .45 ACP.

M2 Bradley   The U.S. Army's current tracked APC.

M4   U.S. Army-issue 5.56-mm NATO selective fire carbine. (A shorter version of the M16, with a 14.5" barrel and collapsing stock.) Earlier issue M16 carbine variants had designations such as XM177E2 and CAR-15. Civilian semiauto only variants often have the same designations, or are called "M4geries."

M9   The U.S. Army-issue version of the Beretta M92 semiauto 9-mm pistol.

M14   The U.S. Army-issue 7.62-mm NATO selective-fire battle rifle. These are still issued in small numbers, primarily to designated marksmen.

M16 The U.S. Army-issue 5.56-mm NATO selective-fire battle rifle. The current standard variant is the M16A2 that has improved sight and three-shot burst control.

M60 The semi-obsolete U.S. Army-issue 7.62-mm NATO belt fed light machinegun that utilized some design elements of the German MG-42.

M240 The current U.S. Army-issue 7.62-mm NATO belt fed light machinegun.

MAC Military Armament Corporation

MELIOS Mini Eye-Safe Laser Infrared Observation Set (AN/PVS-6)

Mini-14 A 5.56-mm NATO semiauto carbine made by Ruger.

MOPP Mission Oriented Protective Posture

MRE Meal, Ready to Eat (U.S. Army field rations)

NATO North Atlantic Treaty Organization

NCO Non-Commissioned Officer

NFA The National Firearms Act of 1934. The law that first imposed a transfer tax on machineguns, suppressors (commonly called "silencers"), and short-barreled rifles and shotguns.

Ni-Cad Nickel Cadmium (rechargeable battery).

Ni-MH Nickel Metal Hydride (rechargeable battery) improvement of Ni-Cad. Does not develop a "memory," shortening battery life due to recharging unexhausted batteries.

NRVC Non-Resident Violator Compact, an agreement signed by more than thirty states, to share records of motor vehicle registrations and driving privilege suspensions in a computer database.

NWO New World Order

PDW Personal Defense Weapon

PETN Pentaerythritol Tetranitrate; a stable, flexible high-order explosive. The filler used in primacord (detonating cord).

Pre-1899 Guns made before 1899—not classified as "firearms" under Federal law.

Pre-1965 1964 or earlier mint date circulated U.S. silver coins with little or no numismatic value. These coins have a silver content of 90 percent.

PV Photovoltaic (solar power conversion array). Used to convert solar power to DC electricity, typically for battery charging.

PVC Poly-Vinyl Chloride (white plastic water pipe)

ROTC   Reserve Officer Training Corps

RPG   Rocket Propelled Grenade

RTV   Room Temperature Vulcanizing

SAW   Squad Automatic Weapon

SINCGARS   Single-Channel Ground and Airborne Radio System. The U.S. military's current issue frequency-hopping VHF radio transceiver.

SIGINT   Signals Intelligence

SLAP   Saboted Light Armor Projectile

SOP   Standard Operating Procedure(s)

SSB: Single Sideband (an operating mode for CB and amateur radio gear).

Steyr AUG   The Austrian army's 5.56-mm "bullpup" infantry carbine. Also issued by the Australian Army, as their replacement for the L1A1.

S&W   Smith and Wesson

SWAT   Special Weapons and Tactics. (SWAT originally stood for Special Weapons Assault Team until that was deemed politically incorrect.)

TA-1 & TA-312   U.S. military hard wire field telephones.

Thermite   A mixture of aluminum powder and iron rust, that when ignited, causes a vigorous exothermic reaction. Used primarily for welding. Also used by military units as an incendiary for destroying equipment.

T.K.   Tom Kennedy

TRC-500   A 500-milliwatt VHF FM transceiver formerly marketed by Radio Shack.

USC   University of Southern Colorado

VDC   Volts, Direct Current

VHF   Very High Frequency

VOX   Voice Activated

VW   Volkswagen

WD-1   U.S. military-issue two conductor insulated field telephone wire.

WWCR   World Wide Christian Radio, an international shortwave broadcast radio station.

Y2K   Year 2000 (Coined by David Eddy). The scare associated with the millennial ("Year 2000") date change that took place at 0001/01/01/2000

Index

Note: In general, this index covers neither the events nor the characters of this book—for that story, get reading! Instead, here you'll find major references to tactics, techniques, and technologies.

About the Author

James Wesley, Rawles is a former Army Intelligence officer. He writes and edits SurvivalBlog.com, the Internet's most popular daily blog on survival and preparedness topics. Rawles is a frequent lecturer and talk radio guest on survival topics such as food storage, wilderness medicine, communications, off-grid power, and retreat security.